Praise for THE IMMORTALS:

'Edge Chronicles, the intricately wrought fantasy series that brings Paul Stewart's elegant, tight prose into fruitful fusion with Chris Riddell's stylish illustrations, reaches an epic climax in *The Immortals*.'
The Bookseller

'It's a huge adventure-packed novel, filled with delights for the series' many, many fans, not least that extraordinary world and its creatures captured in Chris Riddell's endlessly beautiful, bizarre and marvellously detailed line illustrations. A real summer treat.'
Daniel Hahn, *New Review* (supplement to the *Independent on Sunday*)

'Innovative, moving and totally compelling, it's bound to be a runaway.'
Annie Everall, *Bookseller, Children's Buyer's Guide*

'I have read many fantasy novels, but what makes this stand out is the sense of adventure and the wonders of travel.' *Newsacademic.com*

[10-star review] 'This is an innovative and vibrant book. The astonishing imagination and outstanding illustrations make this one of the most original and dramatic fantasy series available today. This is fantasy for the 21st century . . . prepare yourself for the experience of a lifetime.'
www.fantasybookreview.co.uk

'The world that has been created for this series is so well imagined . . . For new readers, it really is a good introduction – it's a great stand-alone read, but also hints at past events, at a level just right to encourage you to go back and explore past stories.' *www.play.com*

'This has to be one of the best books in The Edge Chronicles! The characters are brilliant. The dialogue is excellent. There is so much action it's hard to contain the excitement . . . I think this book is amazing!'
www.ciao.co.uk

'This is the final tale in The Edge Chronicles sequence and it's a fabulous climax to the most original and dramatic fantasy series being written today . . . it's a must-have for all fans of The Edge and will bring legions of new fans to the series.' *www.bcfreviews.wordpress.com*

'Amazing.' *Sky Kids Magazine*

'Better than *Lord of the Rings*!' Joel Morris, *The Simon Mayo Show*

Praise for THE EDGE CHRONICLES:

'The Edge Chronicles are the best books I have read so far in my life.
My favourite book out of all the trilogies is *The Last of the Sky Pirates*.'
Aranga, Macclesfield

'I really enjoy your books The Edge Chronicles – they are the best
books that I have ever read, and trust me that's a lot. My favourite
book is either *Stormchaser* or *The Last of the Sky Pirates*. I think that
you guys are a perfect team!' *Tommy Legge, website*

'I think the simplest thing to say is that your books ROCK!!!'
Robbie, Dublin

'. . . your books are a real gift to literature. The illustrations are beautiful
and the stories are exceptional. I love how the books fit together like
a jigsaw and how everything falls into place. When I read them I feel
happy, excited, sad and moved all at once. I was constantly amazed
and surprised. Thank you for creating The Edge Chronicles. They have
touched my heart and I'm sure they've done the same for many others.'
Katie, Oxon

'I love the combination between the detail of writing and
pictures as it sort of pulls you into the book as if you are
encountering what the characters are.' *Jamie, email*

'I enjoy your vast imagination on the series Edge Chronicles.
Your books grip me into turning each page with thrilling
adventure and murderous betrayals.' *Jonathan, Vancouver*

'I wanted you to know how much The Edge Chronicles have
meant to my children – you have encouraged them to enjoy reading.'
Diana, Brighton

'*The Winter Knights* is another great installation to the series.
What I love about this book and the rest in the series is that each
book could easily stand on its own or be read in any order, but when
you put them all together, details from one or another book come out,
showing the in-depth connection of everything that happens in life.'
Mike Bram, website review

TWILL
A TREE GOBLIN

'From the time that I was a young sapling, I worked in the docks of Hive, loading and unloading the phraxships that ply their trade between the great cities of the Edge. But not any more. Times have changed, and Hive ain't the place that I once knew.

'Kulltuft Warhammer and his High Town cronies now run the show, and the opinions of the likes of me and my mate Gorlan don't count for much. As the sergeant says, we're just phraxcannon fodder, paid to march and fight in the Hive militia. Careless talk can get you dragged away and thrown down the Hive Falls in a barrel, and with a wife and six nestlings to support, I can't afford to be outspoken.

'Gorlan, by the way, is a grey trog from the caves of Hive, and he and me were pressganged at the same time. He's a fine and loyal friend, and I couldn't have chosen a better comrade to watch my back in the fight they say is coming any day now. It's all Kulltuft Warhammer's fault, in my opinion, but like I said, careless talk can get you killed . . .'

THE EDGE CHRONICLES:

JOIN THE FREE ONLINE FAN CLUB AT
www.edgechronicles.co.uk

BARNABY GRIMES:

www.barnabygrimes.co.uk

For younger readers:

FAR-FLUNG ADVENTURES:

www.farflungadventures.co.uk

THE EDGE CHRONICLES

THE IMMORTALS

PAUL
STEWART & CHRIS
RIDDELL

CORGI BOOKS

THE IMMORTALS
A CORGI BOOK 978 0 552 55128 1

First published in Great Britain by Doubleday,
an imprint of Random House Children's Books
A Random House Group Company

Doubleday edition published 2009
Corgi edition published 2010

1 3 5 7 9 10 8 6 4 2

The Random House Group Limited supports the Forest Stewardship Council
(FSC), the leading international forest certification organization. All our titles
that are printed on Greenpeace-approved FSC-certified paper carry
the FSC logo. Our paper procurement policy can be found at
www.rbooks.co.uk/environment.

Set in Palatino

Corgi Books are published by Random House Children's Books,
61–63 Uxbridge Road, London W5 5SA

www.kidsatrandomhouse.co.uk
www.rbooks.co.uk

Addresses for companies within The Random House Group Limited can be
found at: www.randomhouse.co.uk/offices.htm

THE RANDOM HOUSE GROUP Limited Reg. No. 954009

A CIP catalogue record for this book is available from the British Library.

Printed and bound in Great Britain by
CPI Bookmarque, Croydon, CR0 4TD

This book is dedicated to

Joseph and William, our sons, who have shared
our journey through the Edgelands, sustaining us
with their enthusiasm, advice and countless
conversations for nearly two decades.

THE
EDGE
IN
THE THIRD AGE OF FLIGHT

THE FARROW
RIDGES

NEW H

DEE

HIVE

THE MIDWOOD
DECKS

GREAT GLADE

THE EASTERN
WOODS

THE
GORGES

· PART ONE ·

GREAT GLADE

i. THE LAKE LANDING ACADEMY
ii. WAIF GLEN
iii. THE HALL OF WHISPERS
iv. GREMLOP & DREW'S PHRAXCHAMBER WORKS
v. THE COPPERWOOD CREEK BRIDGE
vi. AMBRISTOWN PROWLGRIN ROOST-STABLES
vii. GALSTON PRADE'S MANSION
viii. THE THOUSANDSTICKS STADIUM
ix. THE LULLABEE ARCH
x. SQUALL RAZORTOOTH'S PIT HOUSE.

SO...

COPPERWOOD

EAST GLADE

NEW UNDERTOW

THE SILVER PASTURES

OLD FOREST

NEW LAKE

NORTHERN OUTER CITY

THE CITY
OF
GREAT GLADE

THE
PRADE
MINE STOCKADE

DOCKING GANTRY

THE KEEP

WHEEL HOUSE

MINERS CABINS

vii.

ix.

viii.

A

C

K

B

D

F

E

G

H

THE WELL

i.

ii.

Wheel House
A. PHRAX RUBBLE
B. PHRAXENGINE
C. WHEEL
D. LIGHT FUNNEL
E. WASTE SPOUTS
F. SIFTING PLATES
G. SLAG HEAP
H. PHRAXCRYSTALS

DEW POND

PRADE

iii.

iv.

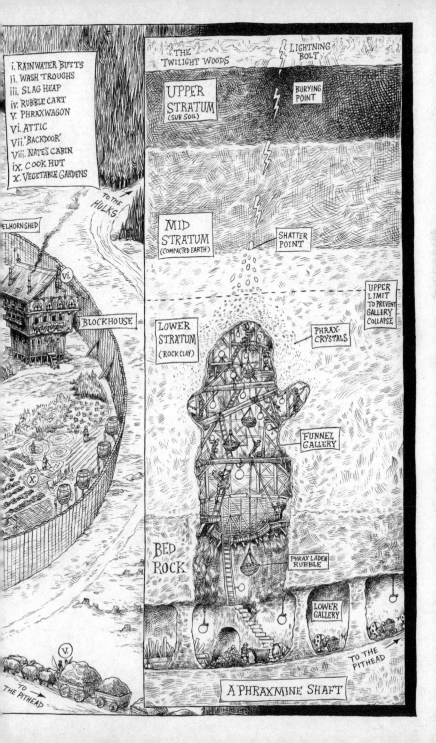

i. RAINWATER BUTTS
ii. WASH TROUGHS
iii. SLAG HEAP
iv. RUBBLE CART
v. PHRAXWAGON
vi. ATTIC
vii. "BACKDOOR"
viii. NATE'S CABIN
ix. COOK HUT
x. VEGETABLE GARDENS

THE TWILIGHT WOODS

LIGHTNING BOLT

UPPER STRATUM (SUB SOIL)

BURYING POINT

MID STRATUM (COMPACTED EARTH)

SHATTER POINT

UPPER LIMIT TO PREVENT GALLERY COLLAPSE

LOWER STRATUM (ROCK CLAY)

PHRAX-CRYSTALS

...ELHORN SHED

TO THE HULKS

vi.

BLOCKHOUSE

FUNNEL GALLERY

x.

BED ROCK

PHRAX LADEN RUBBLE

LOWER GALLERY

v.

TO THE PITHEAD

TO THE PITHEAD

A PHRAXMINE SHAFT

· CHAPTER ONE ·

The eerie, booming call of the steam klaxon reverberated through the cabin, wrenching the dozen snoring phraxminers from their sleep. Some sat up immediately and looked round, bleary-eyed. Some slid from their floating sumpwood bunks and, still half-asleep, trudged off to the communal wash troughs. A couple of them simply rolled over and dragged the tilderfleece covers over their heads.

The klaxon sounded a second time, like some great forlorn creature calling for its mate. A groan went round the cabin. Someone cursed.

Nate Quarter sat up with a start – and cracked his head on the wooden slats of the bunk above. He slumped back onto the grimy pillow and rubbed his forehead ruefully. It was the same every morning when the dawn klaxon sounded. One moment he would be having a pleasant dream about winning a hand of splinters at a gaming table on a skytavern, and the next he'd be seeing stars and clutching his bruised forehead.

From the bunk above him came a deep rumbling laugh. 'Should sleep in your helmet, young'un.'

'Thanks for the advice, Rudd,' Nate replied as the smiling face of a young cloddertrog appeared. 'But if you were really concerned for my welfare, you'd swap bunks with me.'

'Sorry, Nate, just can't do it.' Rudd shrugged as he climbed down from the top bunk. 'Cutters get the top bunks, with you glowworms down below. I'll race you to the troughs.'

Outside, the klaxon boomed a third time.

Sitting up slowly this time, Nate swung his legs round and dropped down from the sumpwood bunk to the wooden floor. Dust flew up as Nate's feet touched the ground, and the dried mud on the

7

bare boards got between his toes. With a sigh, Nate wiped the bits from the bottom of first one foot, then the other, before pulling on his boots. He crunched across the floor to the low, circular doorway through which his friend had just disappeared, leaving a cloud of dust in his wake.

There was no getting away from it in a mining stockade, thought Nate irritably. The mud.

It got everywhere; in your hair, under your nails, in the folds of your clothes. And no matter how many times the cabin was swept, there always seemed to be more left. Food tasted of it. Every surface was coated with it. Even the air was filled with a hazy mist of muddy dust. It made his scalp gritty and his skin grimy – and it left a nasty taste in his mouth.

Nate crossed the wide expanse of compacted earth outside – fringed on three sides by the sleeping cabins – to the line of huge wooden troughs that jutted out from the log wall of the stockade. Already, the troughs were bustling with phraxminers, busy washing the grime of nightdust from their faces, and Nate had to jostle to claim a place beside his cloddertrog friend.

The two of them made an odd couple. Rudd, like all of his kind, was broad-shouldered and barrel-chested. Powerful muscles rippled beneath the mottled skin of his large arms and squat legs. Born cave-dwellers, the cloddertrogs made natural miners, their prodigious strength invaluable when it came to wielding a pickaxe at the pitface. Nate, on the other hand, was lean and lightly muscled, tall for his fourteen years, but fresh-faced beneath his closely cropped hair. A fourthling whose family had originally come from Great Glade,

8

Nate Quarter was a skilled lamplighter, his job taking him all over the mine workings far below ground.

Rudd eyed Nate humorously, before plunging his huge head back into the trough of swirling water and cleaning out his ears with his fingers. Nate joined him, plunging his own head down into the cold water.

It felt so good. He rubbed his neck and shoulders, then under his arms. He ran his fingers over his head, prodded around his ears, his eyes, and took in a mouthful of water. His head popped up, beads of water clinging to his cropped hair as he swirled the clean-tasting water around his mouth and spat it back into the trough.

Before him, the small globe embedded in the bottom of the trough purified the water instantly with its grain of sepia phraxdust. All around, the brackish green rainwater which had collected in the stockade water butts above poured down through wooden spouts, turning crystal-clear as it hit the line of wash troughs beneath.

Nate shook his head and wiped a hand over his face. It felt good to be clean. But it wouldn't last, he knew. It never did.

'The scars are fading,' said Rudd.

Nate craned his neck and looked back over his shoulder. The angry red welts did look better, and when he reached round gingerly with his fingertips they were less hot to the touch. Yet the injustice of the beating would take far longer to fade from his memory.

Nate was proud of his skill as a lamplighter, and justifiably so. It was one of the most important jobs in the mine. Without lamplighters, it would have been impossible to mine for stormphrax.

Stormphrax!

The most extraordinary, the most beautiful, the most sought-after substance in all the Edgelands. Ground to dust, a single speck could endlessly purify even the foulest water, whilst a shard of crystal, when harnessed, had enough explosive energy to arm weapons, fuel engines and power mighty skyships.

Stormphrax. Lightning from the mighty storms that collected over the Twilight Woods. Discharged from the boiling storm clouds, the lightning bolts solidified in the twilight glow as they zigzagged down to earth.

Once, long ago, heroic knights from the lost city of Sanctaphrax had set out on quests for the precious lightning bolts that had landed in the perilous woods. In twilight, stormphrax weighed no more than sumpwood – but in darkness, a single shard weighed more than a thousand ironwood trees. With its tip embedded in the dark earth, it took only moments for a lightning bolt to bury itself out of reach of even the most intrepid knight.

Now however, many centuries later, humble phraxminers searched for these elusive lightning bolts, tunnelling deep below the woods in mines lit by lamps that filled them with a twilight glow. Maintaining these lamps was Nate's job.

A week earlier, a lamp had gone out in number three chamber on Nate's watch. When mining for stormphrax, it was vital for the twilight glow to be maintained at all times if the exposed crystals were not suddenly to become immeasurably heavy. Thankfully, the consequences had not been too severe. Some scaffolding had collapsed and a pit prowlgrin had suffered a crushed leg when a single crystal dislodged itself from the pitface in the sudden blackness and crashed down through the chamber. Certainly, it could have been a lot worse.

Not that the mine sergeant, Grint Grayle, had seen it that way. The thin, gimlet-eyed Grayle, his face crisscrossed with scars that testified to countless knife fights and worse, had relished this chance to pick on the young lamplighter. He'd given Nate an ultimatum. Accept the loss of a shift's wages for negligence, or take a flogging.

A burly hammerhead mine guard had stepped forward with a copperwillow cane in his fist. Nate had no choice. A flogging – however unjust – was nothing compared with losing a whole shift's wages. Particularly with the five cartloads of phrax-laden rubble they'd just mined on that shift.

Nate took his punishment as the grinning mine sergeant looked on. He knew that he'd filled the lamp in number three chamber with darkelm oil. If it was empty, then someone had deliberately emptied it.

'Wouldn't have happened if your father was still alive,' said Rudd. 'He was the best mine sergeant in the Eastern Woods.'

Nate looked at his friend and smiled.

He and Rudd had found themselves in the same digging team three years earlier. Nate had just lost his father and the hulking cloddertrog – the strongest and best cutter in the mine – had taken him under his wing. A mining stockade was no place to be orphaned and friendless, and Rudd had watched Nate's back. He was a true friend.

'He certainly was, Rudd,' Nate agreed, stepping back from the trough and taking the grubby square of towel the cloddertrog handed him.

His father would never have allowed flogging in the mine in his time. In fact, his father had built a reputation throughout the mining stockades of the Eastern Woods for fairness and safety in the mines he ran. How ironic, then, that he should have died in a freak accident, to be replaced by Grint Grayle, an ambitious sergeant with a reputation for brutality.

If indeed, Nate had thought to himself often over the past three years, it had been an accident . . .

· CHAPTER TWO ·

Drying himself as he went, Nate returned to the cabin. He took his clothes from the hook at the bottom end of the floating bunk and put them on. Thick trousers with a belt and braces; an undershirt, a woollen waistcoat and heavy leather topcoat. He buckled the ironwood shoulder guards into place and secured the strap of his mine helmet under his chin. Then, crouching down, he unlocked the small chest suspended beneath his bunk and lifted the lid.

Inside was everything he owned in the world. It wasn't much.

His birth parchment, his silver naming spoon, the letters NQ engraved on the handle, and two mine sergeant's epaulettes – embroidered red chevrons – which his father, Abe Quarter, had worn for so short a time. With Rudd's words fresh in his mind, Nate stroked the epaulettes, tears springing to his eyes . . .

'Wouldn't have happened if your father was still alive.'

Just beside the other items in the chest was a small leather pouch. Nate picked it up, untied the drawstring and slid the small medallion it contained into his hand. He turned it over. It was a tiny painting – faded paint on cracked wood – set into a frame of ornate gold and threaded onto a thin length of yellowed cord.

It was the only thing he had that had belonged to his mother, handed down through the family for generations. And when she had died and his father had taken his infant son with him to seek their fortunes in the Eastern Woods, it had come too.

'Always remember,' his father had told him, 'that you come from one of the old families of Great Glade. This portrait proves it. I gave it to your mother on our marriage day, and now I give it to you, son.'

Nate stared at it, a smile tugging at the corners of his mouth as he dried his eyes. He'd always liked the miniature painting. It was a portrait of a young lad with deep indigo eyes and a smile on his face, wearing an oversized suit of gleaming armour. Behind him, picked out in muted colours, were the fabulous towers and spires of an ancient city. Most likely, it was no more than a coincidence, yet there was something about the ancient face in the tiny portrait that reminded him of his father.

'Get a move on, Nate,' said Rudd. 'Else we'll be late.'

'Sorry, Rudd,' he said, slipping the medallion back into its pouch and shutting the box of memories. 'Just thinking about my father . . .' He locked the ironwood chest, tugged the pulley chain to raise the sleeping bunk up to the ceiling and hurried across the cabin to the door. 'Wait for me,' he called.

Outside, the air was colder, but no fresher. Despite recent rain, a pall of dust, rank with the odour of burnt woodalmonds, hung in the air above the mine stockade. As he followed Rudd across the muddy yard, Nate glanced up over the roofs of the cabins at the wheelhouse beyond. Its jutting chimney belched clouds of steam into the air, while beneath, a steady stream of rubble and dust poured out from the waste spouts of the light funnel onto a great slag heap. This was the reason for the all-pervasive mud, and Nate knew there was no escaping it.

It was all part of the phraxsifting process. A phraxengine turned a huge wheel which, in turn, drove the funnel – a long, revolving tube which was split into three sections, each one separated by a plate studded with graded holes. Making use of the fact that stormphrax becomes heavier in darkness, the light funnel sorted out the worthless rock from the priceless crystals embedded in the phraxrubble from the mines.

The valuable crystals were collected and stored in the phraxkeep under armed guard, while the rubble – collected by gnokgoblins with shovels and hammelhorndrawn carts – was dumped outside the walls of the stockade. Each week, a phraxbarge visited the mining stockade to collect the precious stormphrax and ship it back to Great Glade.

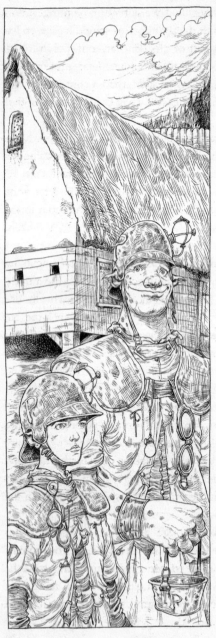

Nate adjusted his helmet strap and caught up with Rudd. The pair of them joined the phraxminers pouring out of the other cabins. They formed a long line, slotting in one behind the other, and shuffled slowly and silently towards an open-sided hut where two red-faced mobgnomes were dishing out breakfast. The first was ladling a thick grey slop into a shallow bowl, the other added vegetables.

'No tripweed for me,' said Nate cheerfully. 'Can't bear the stuff.'

The mobgnome shrug-ged.

'I'll have his,' said Rudd with a smile.

'You'll get what you are given,' snapped the mobgnome, forking out a single portion into his bowl. He looked past the expectant cloddertrog. 'Next.'

Rudd and Nate took their food to the trestle tables, where baskets of barleybread and pitchers

14

of woodale had been laid out, and were about to squeeze into a narrow space between two underbiter goblins who'd budged up to make room, when someone shoved Nate hard in the small of his back, sending him tottering forward. He clutched the slopping bowl to his chest, for there would be no seconds if any got spilled.

'Well, well, well, if it ain't the little lamplighter,' came a gruff voice.

Nate turned to see a brawny figure standing before him. It was the hammerhead mine guard who'd given him the flogging the previous week. There was a taunting smile on his brutal face as his great fist closed round the handle of the copperwillow cane at his belt. Nate turned away. He didn't want any trouble. The mine guard, however, had other ideas. He grabbed Nate by the shoulder and pulled him roughly round.

'Don't turn your back on me, lamplighter,' he said. 'Daddy's not here to look after his precious little boy any more – remember?'

'I remember,' muttered Nate, his eyes blazing.

Beside him, the underbiters hurriedly finished their breakfast and, climbing from the bench, made themselves scarce. Rudd placed his bowl down on the table and, stepping calmly forward, took Nate's from his trembling fingers and placed it down alongside his own.

'Maybe not, Thuggbutt,' said Rudd coolly. 'But *I* am.'

The mine guard turned his brutal face towards Nate's friend. 'This is nothing to do with you, Rudd,' he growled.

'Well, I say it is!' snarled Rudd, his face reddening with sudden anger. He shoved the guard hard in the chest, sending him sprawling to the ground, the stew and tripweed splashing down his face and chest. Rudd stood above him, his clenched fists raised. 'Fancy trying your luck with me, eh?' he demanded.

The hammerhead glowered, but did not take up the challenge.

'Thought as much,' said Rudd. He clapped his arm round his friend's shoulder. 'Come on, Nate. Tuck in before it gets cold.'

Behind them, as they took their places, the hammerhead guard scrambled to his feet and looked down at his fouled uniform. 'You're

15

going to regret this, Rudd,' he spat. 'There's a new mine sergeant now. Times have changed.' He turned and stomped off heavily to the wash troughs.

Rudd snorted. 'But you still need us to get the phrax out of the ground!' he called after him.

Nate sighed. His friend had got him out of more scrapes than he could remember, but he feared that one day that temper of his was going to get him into trouble. He picked up his spoon and began poking at the stodgy broth. It was mainly trockbeans, boiled to a mush and flavoured with tiny morsels of meat – though it didn't do to enquire too closely what animal it might have come from. Although the mine owners promised bed and board to their workers, they spared every expense they could.

'A banquet fit for a mine owner!' Rudd announced seemingly seconds later. His spoon clattered into the empty bowl. He drained his mug of woodale and patted his stomach. 'Just what I needed. Though next time, Nate, take the tripweed and I'll have it.'

Nate chuckled. The food and drink were vile, but most phraxminers didn't care. Not when there were fortunes to be made deep below the Twilight Woods. Soon his own bowl and mug were empty, and the pair of them climbed to their feet. All around them, the rest of the phraxminers were doing the same. Together, they tramped off across the camp. Past the wheelhouse they went, the air filled with the hiss and hum of the phraxengine and clatter of hammelhorndrawn rubble carts; between the stagnant dewpond, thick with vicious woodmidges, and the creaking light funnel; and on through the heavy gates that were set into the stockade's great perimeter wall. Before them lay a two-mile hike.

They'd barely covered a hundred strides when Rudd started grumbling. 'Still don't see why they couldn't have built the camp nearer the mine.'

Nate laughed and punched his friend on the arm. 'You know it's too dangerous to live too close to the Twilight Woods,' he said, 'even for a great thick-skulled trog like you, Rudd. The golden glow would tempt you in, and before you knew it, the woods would have robbed you of your senses. You'd be lost for ever, unable to die, the flesh rotting from your bones as you stumbled blindly on . . .'

'Yes, yes,' said Rudd irritably. 'Don't go on. All I mean is, two miles between the stockade and the pithead! Isn't that being just too cautious?'

Nate didn't reply. His attention was fixed on the forest around them.

For him, walking through the Eastern Woods was the best part of every day. He stepped from the boarded walkway onto the forest floor, savouring the loamy smell that rose up as he tramped through the lush vegetation. Around him, the beams of sunlight flickered through the leaves and, as the bustle and mud of the mine stockade was left far behind, Nate listened out for the calls and cries of the forest creatures.

There was the hooting of a distant giant fromp; and another, answering its cry. A moment later, from far above his head, he heard the chattering of a flock of emerald green skullpeckers . . .

Slowly, as they drew closer to the mine, a different sound filled the air. It was low and indistinct, a muffled rumbling interspersed with a loud jarring clatter; the sound of phraxrubble-laden mine wagons being hauled up from the depths of the mine and emptied at the pithead in a great mound. The night shift was delivering the fruits of its labours and waiting, no doubt, to be paid a 'rubble price' by the mine sergeant.

Ahead, the golden light of the Twilight Woods glowed between the trees – beautiful, yet treacherous. The sickly odour of scorched woodalmonds returned, stronger than ever.

There was something about that unchanging golden light that beguiled any who strayed into the Woods. They became dis-orientated, slowly losing their memories, their senses, their sanity. Their very bodies decomposed. Yet they could not die, for the golden light granted them a terrible immortality; a living death that Nate could barely comprehend.

'Anyway, there's your answer,' he said to Rudd, nodding to his left.

The pair of them looked across at an ancient abandoned stockade which had been built on the very edge of the woods. Numerous stakes, the size of tree trunks, had fallen, leaving the perimeter wall looking like a gappy grin. Inside, the wheelhouse and cabins were little more than heaps of wood, while the light funnel had been removed completely.

Rudd shrugged. 'I sometimes wonder whether twilight madness wouldn't be better than the lives we phraxminers live,' he said. He sighed wearily. 'At least you wouldn't know when the mine sergeant's cheated you on your rubble price.'

Nate said nothing. Occasionally, some poor wretch who had lost themselves in the Twilight Woods would stumble out of them again and be rescued. 'Death cheaters', they were called, and Nate had seen a few – gibbering drooling and half-crazed living skeletons for the most part, robbed of everything but their lives by the treacherous Woods. He would walk *ten* miles if it meant avoiding that fate. And so, he knew, would Rudd. But then the cloddertrog was never at his best when a long shift was about to begin.

Up ahead, the pithead came into view. It was a low broad timber-lined cutting, sloping down into the earth. At the far end, flaming torches illuminated the entrance to the mineshaft – a narrow doorway, above which a pair of jagged tilder antlers had been nailed. In a clearing beside the pithead, there stood a rough-hewn log cabin which housed the mine guards, and next to that was the rubble heap onto which mine wagons, pushed by prowlgrins, were emptying their contents in a cloud of dust. A little way off, a scrawny shryke peered out of a high-sided stockade on wheels – the tally wagon – and made a careful note of each load.

'Come on, move it, you twilight-touched oafs!' bellowed a horribly familiar voice just up ahead, 'or I'll fine every one of you half a shift's rubble price.'

Rudd and Nate exchanged glances.

At the pithead, they joined the group of phraxminers, who were milling about waiting for the last of the night shift miners to leave. They shuffled past in a straggly line, their heads down and shoulders slumped. They looked exhausted, and were covered with grime, from the tops of their helmets to the soles of their boots. As they went by, a few of the older miners wheezed and coughed the distinctive dry phraxcough, wisps of water vapour curling up from their mouths.

Nate shivered. It came to all phraxminers who stayed too long in the mines, as the purifying phraxdust embedded itself in the lungs and slowly turned the blood to water. 'Phraxlung', it was called. Joints swelled, limbs withered, and the unfortunate victim eventually drowned. The only cure was to make your fortune and get out of the mines as soon as you could.

Nate's father had known this, and didn't allow any miner to serve longer than five years at the phraxface without a six-month break. But he wasn't thanked for it. In fact, that was about the time the first whispers of discontent began – discontent that some were quick to exploit for their own ends.

Nate looked across at the entrance to the mineshaft. Mine sergeant Grint Grayle, the brutal scars on his thin face contrasting with his elaborately braided side-whiskers and expensive high-collared topcoat, tapped his cane impatiently. The object of his irritation – two emaciated lop-eared goblins who were struggling at either end of a stretcher – stumbled forwards.

'Another accident,' said Rudd, nodding towards the blanket-covered mound in the centre of the stretcher.

Nate nodded gloomily.

'Come *on*!' bellowed Grint, the cane prodding the shoulder of the lop-ear at the back. 'Get that out of the way. You're holding up the day shift.' He glanced across at the waiting miners. His gaze met Nate's and held it defiantly. Then he winked. Nate felt his cheeks colour and his ears burn. He turned away.

'Don't rise to it,' Rudd advised his friend. 'Grint's just looking for an excuse to dock our wages.'

'I know,' said Nate, his voice hushed but hard. 'I need this job. It's all I have. I'm not going to throw everything away by picking a fight with a mine sergeant, however crooked he might be . . .'

'Right, you lot,' the mine sergeant shouted across. 'Get down there. A new seam's been unearthed, and I expect a wagonful of phraxrubble from each of you by the end of the shift at the very least.' He tapped his cane and smirked. 'Well? What are you waiting for?'

· CHAPTER THREE ·

The miners shambled forwards, lighting the side lamps on their helmets as they approached the entrance to the mine. Grint Grayle ticked their names off his list as they passed him. Nate stepped up to the pit entrance, his gaze fixed on the tunnel beyond. As he walked past, the mine sergeant stuck out his cane. Nate tripped and stumbled forwards, landing heavily on the ground. He looked round to see Grint's thin face sneering down at him.

'Better watch your step, Quarter,' he smiled. 'And keep those lamps lit.'

'I shall, mine sergeant,' said Nate through gritted teeth as Rudd helped him back to his feet.

The pair entered the mineshaft, Rudd in front, Nate following close behind. Their footsteps echoed eerily down the narrow tunnel. With the sides and ceiling of the rapidly descending shaft shored up with timber scaffolding of every size and description, the miners referred to it and others like it as 'the Sanctaphrax Forest' – for reasons lost in the mists of time.

'Bullying swindler,' Nate muttered.

Soon, the early-morning sunlight spilling into the tunnel behind them was replaced with the golden glow cast by lamps fixed to the vertical stanchions and cross buttresses. Maintaining that steady twilight glow in the mine was essential if the crystals of stormphrax were not to become too heavy to move. And it was the lamplighter's responsibility to maintain it.

'You know, I wouldn't be surprised if Grint himself wasn't siphoning off the lamp oil,' Nate whispered to his friend.

Rudd turned. 'But why?' he said.

'I don't know,' said Nate. 'But I'm telling you, Rudd, he's got it in for me.'

Rudd shook his head. 'You're imagining it, Nate,' he said. He ran his finger down the faded scar on the side of his face. 'Grint hates everyone.'

As they got close to the bottom of the shaft, the low rumble of approaching mine wagons reverberated through the tunnel. A moment later, a team of pit prowlgrins came into view, each one gripping the rear handle of the laden wagon it pushed with bony forepaws. Overworked and underfed, the creatures were pitifully scrawny, with scars – old and new – showing through their dull, mangy fur. Behind the line of wagons came a tall shryke, urging the prowlgrins on with savage blows from her ironwood flail.

'Poor things,' Nate murmured, his jaw set with impotent rage.

Rudd nodded. As most miners had learned to their cost, it was useless to expect the shryke drivers to treat their charges well. Grint had lost no time in recruiting the vicious bird-creatures after the death of Nate's father, and the prowlgrins had paid the price ever since.

As they reached the bottom of the sloping shaft, the tunnel levelled out and entered a larger chamber. Five other tunnels led off it, like the spokes of a cartwheel. Two of the tunnels were in darkness. Their funnel galleries had already been fully excavated, the lights extinguished and the shafts closed. The three other tunnels were golden with a twilight glow, and from them came the sounds of scraping and hammering. Some of the day shift were already at work.

To their left, set into the soft rock, were the stores; a series of racks, shelves and hooks where the phraxmining equipment was kept. Rudd armed himself with his tools – a handspike, a sickle, a rasp and a pair of long-handled pincers – and slid the various handles into the leather loops which hung from his thick belt. Then he picked up the heavy double-headed pick and swung it over his shoulder.

'I'll see you at the phraxface, Nate,' he said.

Nate was crouching down beside a huge barrel, filling his long-spouted oilcan from a spigot. He looked up at his friend. 'Yeah, be there after my rounds,' he said.

It had been Abe Quarter's idea to give his son a specialist skill. That was why he'd taught him everything there was to know about lamplighting. He'd shown him how to trim the wicks, how to bleed the air ducts, how to synchronize the valves and, most important of all, he'd drilled him in the most accurate way of calibrating the degrees of light, until Nate could gauge twilight at a glance. As a lamplighter, it was Nate's job to keep the mineshaft and galleries lit to exactly the right degree. Too dark, and phraxcrystals would rain down like leadwood bullets; too bright, and any miner striking a crystal with a pick would cause a massive explosion. Only twilight would do.

With the heavy oilcan making his gait lopsided, Nate Quarter set off on his rounds. He headed along the tunnel and stopped at the first lamp, where he unscrewed the cap to the oil reservoir, inserted the spout into the hole and carefully poured in oil until the red bar inside the lamp gauge rose to the top. Then, having screwed the cap back into place, Nate snipped off the charred strands of the wick and adjusted its height. When he had satisfied himself that the drip feed and valves were working as they should, he moved onto the second lamp in the tunnel.

As he made his way slowly towards the funnel gallery at the end of the tunnel, the noise grew louder – scraping, rasping, thudding, and the echoing clatter of the chunks of phrax-rich rubble as they tumbled down the spiralling phraxchutes and into the carts at the bottom. He entered the bottom of the first of the working funnel galleries he came to, and adjusting his goggles, looked up to see the dozen or so phraxminers clinging to the scaffolding or slung out on hanging harnesses, hard at work.

Seeing to the lamps at each level as he went, Nate slowly climbed the rickety ladders until he was high up in the vaulted shaft. Dust and larger pieces of rock fell down through the air, tapping against his helmet and tumbling harmlessly away. This was an old shaft. The massive bolt of solid lightning that, thousands of years earlier, had plunged down through the mid-stratum of compressed earth and shattered into countless million pieces, was all but gone. Yet it was up here, where the miners now were – at the point where the forks of that lightning came together and the bolt was at its thickest – that the largest crystals of stormphrax were to be found. It made the accurate calibration of the light all the more vital.

'All right, Nate?' came a voice from just above him, shouting above the sound of the digging.

Nate looked up and smiled. 'Morning, Killim,' he said.

The tusked goblin had been a good friend of his father's. He grinned back toothlessly.

'Getting bigger every day, Nate, so you are,' he said. 'Bigger and uglier . . .' he added, and began to laugh – a dry, wheezing laugh that turned almost at once to a raw, hacking cough. He blew out a cloud of vapour, then clutched hold of a timber strut as, doubled over, he struggled to catch his breath. Slowly, he recovered. The colour returned to his cheeks. He looked up, pulled a filthy rag from his back pocket and dabbed at his streaming blue eyes. 'That's better,' he gasped. The old-timer smiled at Nate. 'Best get back to work before the mine sergeant docks my rubble price.'

Nate carefully checked the twilight calibration of the lamp overhead while Killim returned his attention to the phraxface. He watched as the old goblin painstakingly scraped away at the rock around a sparkling crystal of stormphrax with his handspike. Even in the twilight glow, a misplaced blow striking the crystal itself risked causing an explosion violent enough to destroy the entire mine. The old tusked goblin was a master of his trade, able to dislodge and clean a crystal in a fraction of the time it took most of the other miners. Long years of experience had given him the dexterity to work safely and fast.

Unlike the rubble, which was crudely sieved of its tiny shards of crystal, cutting out an intact shard of stormphrax was a skilled art. Killim finished the cut and held the gleaming shard of pure lightning up to the light before placing it carefully in the lightbox at his side. The mine sergeant would pay him handsomely for it up top. Shard

24

price was twenty times rubble price, and every miner knew it.

As the morning passed, Nate tended to the rest of the lamps. The second funnel gallery was not as high as the first, the seam only half-excavated. Apart from one faulty feed valve, which he replaced, all the lamps were in good working order. Up one side of the long sloping entrance tunnel and down the other, Nate continued his work. The oilcan grew lighter. By the time he had finished seeing to the lamps in the newer, smaller, third chamber, it was approaching noon – not that the time of day meant much in the constant twilight glow.

He went back to the stores, returning the empty oilcan and lamp tools to the rack and selected a handspike and pair of pincers. Then, humming tunelessly, he readjusted his ironwood helmet and set off for the new funnel gallery.

'How's it going, Rudd?' Nate called out above the noise of chipping and scratching that echoed all round him.

Rudd turned from the phraxface and wiped his brow. The dust and sweat had mixed to form a thick muddy paste which he smeared down the side of his face. He grinned.

'She's a beauty,' he said. He pointed to the crystal he'd been working on. 'A stave, by the looks of things, and nicely cracked.'

The miners had names for all the different types of lightning bolts. A splint, a stagger, a rake; a ragged sleeve, a nest of worms . . . It all depended on how the lightning bolt had solidified when it struck the Twilight Woods.

Some split into two prongs, some into several, and some into countless tiny filaments, impossible to mine. A stave was a single, zigzag-shaped shaft. As a young'un, Nate had always added lightning bolts just like them to his pictures of battling skyships. He thought that was the way *all* lightning looked. Now he worked down in the phraxmine, he knew just how rare they actually were. Every miner longed to work on a stave, yet many would spend an entire lifetime down at the phraxface without ever seeing one.

Standing next to Rudd on the narrow platform as his friend returned to the crystal he was cutting around, Nate lifted his handspike, and began scraping and scratching at the porous rock above his head. Drips of water fell as he did so, splashing onto his goggles and trickling down inside the collar of his jacket. Little by little, he chipped delicately away at the rock. Tiny particles dropped down beneath him.

'Look at that,' said Rudd, clasping the glittering crystal – the size of his fist – to his chest. 'Beautiful.' He placed it carefully in his lightbox. 'And large,' he grunted. 'Should get a good shard price.'

Nate returned to the phraxface. As he prodded at the rock with the tip of the handspike, he heard the sudden change in tone that all miners listened out for. Most of the time, the porous rock made a dull rasping noise when scraped, but when a concealed crystal was near, the sound took on a silvery bell-like quality. Rudd noticed it too.

'Looks like you've found a shard yourself, Nate,' he said. 'Careful now.'

Nate didn't need reminding. Frowning with concentration, he scratched at the surface of the rock. Fine dust sprinkled down through the air. He worked at a small section of the rock, picking away patiently until, with a soft *crunch*, a larger piece of rock fell away to reveal the glinting tip of the jagged crystal above.

'Magnificent!' said Nate delightedly as he set to work digging out the embedded crystal from the surrounding rock. Finally, with a soft grating sound, the glittering shard came free. Nate placed it in his own lightbox. 'Absolutely magnificent!'

· CHAPTER FOUR ·

For the rest of the shift, they worked nonstop on the seam; Nate, Rudd and the other dozen miners who had been assigned to the fifth funnel gallery that morning, cutting slabs of phrax-rich rubble but not finding any more shards. Compared with Rudd, Nate was slow, stopping increasingly often to catch his breath and rub his aching shoulders. The hefty cloddertrog never seemed to tire. By the time the siren went, signalling the end of the day's work, the mine crew had all but filled three of the wagons with rubble.

'Most we've ever done in a single shift,' said Rudd as he gathered up his tools and headed down the ladder. 'And two shards between us! Grint will have to give us a good price.'

Nate followed him close behind. 'I wouldn't count on it,' he muttered.

At the bottom of the shaft, the scuttlers – the lowest and most menial workers in the mine – were already busy sweeping and shovelling away the debris ready for the next shift. As he jumped down to the ground, Nate's ankle went over on a piece of rock, and he stumbled against one of the squat goblins, knocking his broom from his bony hands.

'Sorry, sorry,' said Nate, retrieving the broom and handing it back. 'Oh, it's you, Slip.'

The scuttler – a bandy-legged grey goblin with a look of permanent terror in his eyes – nodded.

'Yes, it's me, Slip,' he said, his voice husky and halting. 'Grey goblin, from the nether reaches, nineteen years of age and in his twelfth year of service . . .'

Nate listened patiently. Scuttlers lived most of their lives down in the mines, always there to keep the oil drums full and the

28

tunnels free of vermin. Although they were far below the Twilight Woods, the forest's pernicious influence permeated the underground tunnels, seeping through with every droplet of water and breathed in with each particle of phraxdust. The miners, with their shift work and distant living quarters, were in little danger, but for the scuttlers it was simply a matter of time before they ended up completely deranged. That was why, at any opportunity, they would repeat details of their lives, in a vain effort to keep their minds from slipping away for ever.

'Bad infestation, Slip uncovered. Piebald rats. Last night,' he said, his husky voice stopping and starting as he concentrated hard. 'Battered nine of them, did Slip. One, two, three, four, five, six . . .' He counted off the number slowly and deliberately. 'Seven, eight, nine. All dead. And Slip laid traps, for the rest . . .'

'Come on, Nate.' Rudd's voice floated back along the tunnel.

Nate smiled at the scuttler. 'I'd best be going,' he said.

'Yes, best be going,' said Slip. 'Best be off. But afore you do,' he said, his voice lowering to an intimate gravelly rasp. 'Afore you leave, there's something Slip wants to tell you.' He reached out and grasped the sleeve of Nate's jacket. 'A warning, Nate, 'coz your father, good he was to us scuttlers. Gave us time up top . . .'

'A warning?' said Nate softly.

'The mine sergeant,' said Slip, nodding vigorously. 'Grayle Grint. I mean, Grint Grayle. Slip heard him say that flogging wasn't enough – that next time, he'd fix you for good, Nate Quarter. So, watch out for yourself.'

'Fix me for good? But how?'

'He didn't say,' said Slip. 'Not exactly. But Grint knew your father didn't trust him, Nate. And then he had that accident. Now Grint's suspicious of you. And we don't want no more accidents, do we, Nate? No more accidents.'

'No,' said Nate thoughtfully. 'No, we don't. You see anything suspicious, you come and tell me, Slip.'

The grey goblin nodded, his piercing blue eyes wide. 'Slip'll tell

you, Nate. Don't you fear. Old Slip'll keep a watch out . . .'

Clapping the scuttler gratefully on the shoulder, Nate set off after Rudd. He found him leaning against the timber-lined wall at the bottom of the sloping tunnel of 'the Sanctaphrax Forest'. All round them, like a herd of tilder moving through the trees, the other miners were passing in between the wooden props which jutted up at all angles from floor to ceiling as they made their way to the surface.

'What kept you?' asked Rudd.

'Slip,' said Nate.

'What, that little scuttler?'

Nate nodded. 'Confirmed my suspicions,' he said, 'that Grint Grayle *does* have it in for me. Slip overheard him—'

'Been underground too long, that one,' Rudd interrupted. 'You can't trust the word of a twilight-touched scuttler.'

'Yes, but—' Nate began.

'I swear, Nate, you're too friendly for your own good,' said Rudd. 'You get the weirdest little creatures latching onto you . . .'

'Like you, you mean?' said Nate, laughing, and it was Rudd's turn to punch *him* on the arm.

They emerged from the fake twilight of the tunnels into the genuine dusk of the forest, the low orange sun sinking down towards the horizon. Nate and Rudd exchanged greetings with the miners on the night shift, just arriving to begin work. Then they stopped at the tally wagon and gave in their lightboxes, and had their shift earnings calculated.

'Day shift, ain't yer,' clucked the scrawny shryke in the wagon and checked her list. 'A shard. Good size . . .' She placed it on the scales and added small ironwood weights until the two trays balanced. 'Will get you . . . fifty gladers. And then your rubble price . . . Three wagons full at five gladers . . . Minus deductions . . .'

'Deductions?' said Nate, staring hard into the shryke's yellow eyes.

'Mine sergeant's upped the stockade tax,' she said. The bird-creature's cold eyes narrowed. 'You don't like it, you can sleep out in the woods.'

She cackled as she peeled off promissory notes from a bundle in her taloned fist.

'Thirty-five gladers. Don't spend them all at once!'

Nate bristled, his fists clenched. But Rudd lay a calming hand on his shoulder.

'Take it,' he urged. 'Thirty-five gladers ain't bad for a single shift, Nate, and we don't need the trouble . . .'

Reluctantly, Nate took the notes and placed them in the inside pocket of his tunic. Minutes later, Rudd did the same.

'It's not right,' Nate muttered as they left the tally wagon and its escort of brawny mine guards behind at the mine entrance.

Along with the other miners, the pair of them headed back towards the camp. His hunger and his tiredness seemed to melt away as Nate pounded over the creaking boards, replaced instead by burning resentment at the mine sergeant and his cronies. The other miners, though, like Rudd, seemed content that their shift was over

31

and they were back at last above ground – and with money in their pockets.

They marched on noisily through the increasingly shadow-filled forest. The sun set and darkness swept in across the sky, high above the canopy, pitching the forest below into the impenetrable gloom of night. By the time they came to the fork in the track, the rowdy miners had already relit their helmet lamps, and the yellow beams of light were bouncing from tree trunk to tree trunk.

'You look like you need cheering up, Nate,' said Rudd, glancing round at his friend. He stopped. 'So what's it to be? More slop at the stockade?' He nodded up the left-hand fork, the lamplight shining along the track which led to the stockade. He swung round, till the same beam of light danced along the track to their right. 'Or an evening at the Hulks?'

'Hard call,' grinned Nate – and set off after the others along the well-trodden path which would take them to the miners' tavern.

'Good choice,' said Rudd, clapping his friend on the shoulders.

The pair of them fell into step with a group of returning miners. As they neared their destination, the atmosphere grew rowdier and rowdier.

There were a dozen mining stockades in the area, each one run by a different mine owner and housing anything up to two hundred miners each. Mining was thirsty work and Mother Hinnyplume – an enterprising shryke matron who, some twenty years earlier, had passed that way quite by chance – had immediately spotted a gaping hole in the market. Six months later, the Hulks – two ancient wrecked sky galleons, lodged in a massive lufwood tree, which had been shored up and turned into a tavern for the nearby stockades – was up and running.

At first, the mine owners had tried to shut the place down. They feared that the woodale, winesap and woodgrog on sale in the tavern would lower productivity in the mines. But they were wrong. The miners worked harder than ever, knowing that at the end of their long day's work, they were to be rewarded with a night of carousing. What was more, the cut of the shryke matron's profits which the mine

owners took ensured that half the wages they paid out to the miners went straight back into their own pockets.

A cheer went up when the glittering lights of the Hulks came into view at last. Nate smiled as he heard the pounding music and looked up to see the great timbered sides of the old skyships, peppered with gantries and walkways and illuminated with strings of lamps. The two mighty vessels had crashed centuries before, and were skewered by the branches of the great tree that now grew around them. Mother Hinnyplume had built onto the original hulks until the former shapes of the great vessels were all but buried beneath cabins, gantries and viewing platforms.

The first of the miners marched up the wooden walkway that wound round the tree, shoved the swing doors open and strode inside. Nate and Rudd were jostled from both sides and behind as the eager crowd funnelled through the narrow opening, laughing and shouting as they spilled into the cavernous hall beyond. Originally the aft hold of the old skyship, it was now open from keel to the captain's cabin, several storeys above. Huge ale vats, embedded in the walls, disgorged a steady stream of frothing woodale into drinking troughs below.

Rudd and Nate drew up a bench and sat down. They weren't the first. The tavern was already half full of workers from the other stockades, loud with deep, hearty voices and gales of laughter.

Rudd leaned across to a passing tavern maid – a young gabtroll with a funnel-shaped cap and a filthy apron over her threadbare dress – and took two empty tankards from her upraised tray.

'Stick 'em on the slate, Gelba,' he said. He handed Nate one of the tankards and dipped his own in the nearest trough. All round him, the cluster of fellow miners did the same. Rudd raised his tankard high. 'To Gallery Five!' he roared.

'Gallery Five!' The bellowing cry echoed round the hot dark tavern as the twenty-strong team lifted their glasses and quaffed the woodale to the dregs in one fluid movement.

Two more gabtroll tavern maids brought broad platters of snowbird wings and highly spiced tilder sausages. They laid them in front of the hungry miners, who tucked in with relish.

34

'It's not so bad, is it?' said Rudd, turning to Nate. 'This life.'

Nate shrugged. His father had hoped for better things for him.

'Food. Place to sleep. Constant work . . . Y'know, I've been hearing all kinds of stuff from Hive. That new pink-eye recruit was saying . . . 'Parently, there's no work to be found. All sorts are living on the streets. Begging.' His face grimaced indignantly. '*Begging!* Can you believe it, Nate, eh?'

Nate shook his head. Distant Hive, like Great Glade – the city of Nate's birth – was fabled for its wealth and opulence. Could such rumours really be believed?

Rudd was beginning to slur his words. 'And, of course,' he said, stumbling to his feet and sweeping his arm around expansively. 'Best of all. We've got all this . . .'

A puzzled frown passed across his face as his arm struck something solid. He glanced round blearily and found himself staring into the furious gaze of a massive hammerhead goblin. The hammerhead looked down slowly at the woodale dripping down the front of his ornately embroidered topcoat, then back into the cloddertrog's reddening face.

'A . . . apologies . . . Thuggbutt,' Rudd muttered, recognizing the hammerhead before him. He pulled a rag from his back pocket and began dabbing uselessly at the wet patch.

The hammerhead knocked his hand away viciously. Two more hammerheads, even taller and broader than the first, loomed at his shoulders. They had phraxpistols holstered at their sides.

'It . . . it was an accident,' Nate said, climbing to his feet.

The first hammerhead thrust his brutal face into Nate's. 'You again,' he snarled. 'Nate Quarter, the lamplighter I gave a flogging to just last week – and who, only this morning, was so . . . disrespectful.'

Nate held his ground. He too had recognized Thuggbutt and the others at once. They belonged to Grint Grayle, the mine sergeant, and were leading members of the mine guard. They didn't often come to the Hulks, preferring the relative comfort of the mine sergeants' mess – but when they did, it invariably spelled trouble.

'We're not looking for any trouble,' Nate persisted. 'And I'll make good any damage . . .'

Thuggbutt laughed unpleasantly. 'Let's see how you make good *this* bit of damage,' he said, suddenly pulling a heavy ironwood cudgel from inside his topcoat and striking Nate hard across the side of his head.

Nate spun round and tumbled heavily to the floor. For a moment, everything went black. The next minute, there were legs all around him and arms reaching down towards him. The tavern waif was peering at him through huge black eyes, his ears twitching as he searched Nate's thoughts to find out what he would do next, while Mother Hinnyplume herself – her gaudy red and purple feathered cape flapping – carved a path through the gawping crowd, a flail cracking menacingly in her claws.

'I'll have no fighting in my tavern,' she screeched.

'There will be no fighting, Mother Hinnyplume,' came a gruff, slightly nasal voice. '*I* shall see to that.'

Grint Grayle stepped forward from the shadows. He pulled a phraxpistol from his belt and raised it. Nate stared in horror, unable to move. The barrel of the weapon was pointing directly at his chest. Their eyes met. The mine sergeant's jaw clenched, his upper lip curled – and at that instant, Nate Quarter knew with absolute certainty that the death of his father had been no accident. Now, he too was about to be disposed of, in what later would be passed off as an unfortunate drunken brawl.

'No!' howled a loud voice.

It was Rudd. Elbowing the closest hammerhead hard in his gut, he threw himself through the air. The phraxpistol went off, filling the great hall with a blinding flash, the tang of woodalmonds and a *crack* so loud that, for a moment, the pounding music seemed to fall silent. Nate looked down, to see his friend slumping to the ground at his feet, a hole the size of a woodsap in the back of his skull.

The triumphant expression on Grint Grayle's vicious scarred face turned to one of fury. Nate spun on his heels.

'Don't let him get away!' the mine sergeant's voice roared as he reloaded his weapon.

Head down, Nate shoved his way between the scrum of bodies lurching this way and that as they struggled to find cover. Behind him, he could hear the mine sergeant bellowing for the guards to 'Stop him!' The hammerheads came after him, cursing and swearing as they barged into miner after panicking phraxminer in their path. Without looking back, Nate reached the door and plunged into the cool night air outside.

He could scarcely take it in.

Rudd, his friend, was dead. Decent loyal Rudd, who'd watched his back and done his best to protect him in the rough, lawless mining camp ever since his father's death. Rudd, who had toiled tirelessly at the phraxface and asked nothing more of life than a pitcher of woodale and good companions to share it with. Rudd had saved Nate's life – at the cost of his own.

The mine sergeant had finally shown his true colours. He wanted Nate Quarter out of the way, and he no longer cared who knew it. Nate knew that if he valued his life, then he had no choice but to leave the phraxmines of the Eastern Woods.

But first there was something he had to do . . .

· CHAPTER FIVE ·

Nate hurtled down the spiral walkway and out into the clearing beneath the massive lufwood trees. The full moon shone down over the jagged outline of the Hulks and, as he made a run for the safety of the forest, Nate heard the thud of heavy footsteps pounding down the stairs behind him. Skidding over muddy ruts where delivery wagons had churned up the soft earth, he dodged between mounds of rubbish waiting to be burned, and stacks of empty woodale vats. Woodmice and piebald rats scurried for cover.

Gliding across the night sky, a solitary razorflit spied the movement, widened its gimlet eyes and dived. It sliced through the night sky at an angle, before twisting its wings back and sinking its claws into the back of a squealing rat. For a moment, as the razorflit wobbled in the air, it seemed as though it had taken on prey too heavy for its slender build – but then, with a flap of its wings, it righted itself and soared off towards the surrounding trees, where it would perch on a branch and eat its supper at leisure.

Far below in the moonlit clearing, Nate urged himself forward over those seemingly endless last few strides of exposed bare ground, and into the obscurity of closely packed tree trunks and matted undergrowth beyond. He kept going, panting hard, his heart pounding in his ears.

'After him!' the mine sergeant's thin, braying voice sounded from the open door of the tavern high above. 'And bring him back alive for a flogging he'll never forget!'

Fern fronds and tree vines slapped and slashed at him as Nate zigzagged through the forest, his breath puffs of cloud in the cold moist air. Bushes, thick with curved thorns, scratched his raised hands and lowered head. And as he ploughed on, they snagged on his clothes, the brittle thorns cracking and splintering as he wrenched himself free.

From behind him came the guttural calls of Grint Grayle's hammerhead guards as they pursued him like some wounded tilder they'd let slip on a hunting party and were now running to ground. Nate blundered into a fallen log, soft with decay, that fell to sponge-like pieces as he crushed it underfoot, then stumbled over a broken branch, before tripping on a gnarled tree root.

It was no good, he realized with mounting panic.

Here in the dense undergrowth, the one asset he had over his hulking pursuers – his speed – was of no use. Already, he could hear the snarls and grunts of the hammerheads getting closer on either side of him. If they got in front, they'd cut him off, and then he'd be finished. Nate knew that his only chance of escape lay in the deep forest away from the mining settlements. There, the undergrowth was less dense and the trees were taller – but stray *too* far from the sounds of mines and the wheelhouses and he risked losing his bearings and getting lost for ever.

As he ran, Nate tore off his heavy jacket and hurled it back over his shoulder into the shadows to distract his pursuers, before veering to the west, away from the track, towards the stockade. The forest deepened and the canopy far over his head became denser. Far below, deprived of the nourishing sun, the undergrowth began to thin out. Nate speeded up, darting between tree trunks that became more and more enormous the further he ran. Knobbly-barked scentwoods rubbed branches with majestic lufwoods. Ironwood pines grew in wild stands, the soft mattress of needles sweet and aromatic as Nate raced across them.

Behind him, but more distant now, he could still hear the chilling screeches and roars of the three hammerhead goblins as they called to each other through the trees. Nate realized he couldn't go much further without risking being out of earshot of the stockade. It was time to go to ground – or rather, Nate thought, looking round, to take to the trees . . .

Not far off, to his right, was a lullabee. The strange turquoise light given off by lullabee groves was, around this solitary specimen, but the faintest glow, yet Nate spotted the tree instantly.

Lullabees – with their huge gnarled trunks and tree knots, ideal for handholds and footholds – had been his favourite trees to climb as a young'un. With the agility of a lemkin, he would scamper up their bottle-shaped trunks to a perch high in the spreading branches and sit there for hours. Now, he would have to do the same.

Nate dashed to the tree and grasped one of the low jutting knots, capped with curled twists of parchment-like bark, and heaved himself onto it. He reached up, clamped his hands round two smaller whorls and pushed off with his left foot. Then, without pausing, he pulled himself up to a higher tree knot and continued, hand over hand, leg after leg. Despite the darkness of the forest, the tree's faint glow helped him, illuminating his path up the colossal trunk until he came to the first of the enormous spreading branches.

Higher, Nate climbed, branch after branch. A soft breeze set the long, fluted leaves rustling around him. All at once, he saw what he had been hoping to find – a drinking trough.

The lullabee tree had no blossom and bore no fruit. To seed itself, it needed heat: intense heat – the type of heat that came only from the direct strike of one of the lightning bolts that, in the midst of a thunderstorm, would hurtle down from the turbulent clouds above. When the tip of a bolt hit one of the great bulbous growths, the parchment bark would turn to ash, the sap inside would boil and froth until, with a loud hiss, the swelling would abruptly split open. As it did so, countless million bean-shaped seeds would be propelled up into the air, to be carried off by the wind on papery wings. What was left – bowl-shaped depressions in the branches – were known by many denizens of the Deepwoods as 'drinking troughs', because of the rainwater that collected in them after storms.

Clearly, it hadn't rained heavily for some time, for this particular trough was dry, Nate noted as he slipped into the shallow depression and sat back to wait . . .

'Came this way,' said a gruff voice from below him moments later, and Nate's heart missed a beat as he realized just how close behind

him the hammerheads had been.

'Almost had him, we did. Then you stops for his jacket!'

'Slippery little runt, and no mistake!'

There was a soft crack and a sudden flash as one of the hammerheads lit a copperwood torch. Then another. A flickering light danced over the silky fluted leaves above Nate's head.

'Face it,' a gruff voice grumbled. 'We've lost him.'

'Or he's lost hisself out there!' said another, 'in these here woods.'

'Then good riddance to him,' said the third, and spat. 'He can starve out here or get flogged to death when we catches him sneaking back into town. Same difference.'

For a moment, there was silence. Nate leaned forward and peered down cautiously. Below him, he saw the three hammerheads from the Hulks standing in a triangle, their backs turned to one another as they peered round the forest, thrusting their blazing torches into the shadows.

Nate trembled, yet couldn't take his eyes off them. They were wild, hard, barbaric hammerheads that Grint Grayle had working for him. Their bodies were covered with tattoos; intricate black bars and swirls that curled round their arms, legs, shoulders and over their heads – tattoos that had been common on the bodies of goblin warriors centuries earlier in the First Age of Flight, but were seldom seen any more amongst the civilized tribes.

Looking down at those fierce, ink-stained faces lit up by flaming torchlight, Nate felt as if he'd gone back in time to the days before stone sickness had struck, when the majestic sky galleons, buoyed up by massive flight rocks, sailed the skies over the savage Deepwoods on epic voyages of exploration and adventure.

'Could have killed him nice and neatly in the Hulks if that mate of his hadn't got in the way,' growled the shorter, most powerfully built hammerhead, and Nate realized that it was Thuggbutt speaking.

'Certainly did the little runt a favour – even if the cloddertrog did pay for it with his life.'

'Not the only one looking out for him, neither,' said one of the others. 'That little scuttler down the shaft. I spotted him whispering to Quarter on the last shift. The little piece of vermin must have tipped him the wink.'

Nate sat back in the trough, head spinning and hardly daring to breathe. Far below him, the hammerheads' angry voices grew fainter as they tramped back the way they'd come.

'Well, I'll tell you something for nothing,' a voice floated back.

'What's that, then?'

'That scuttler's going the same way as the cloddertrog when I catches up with him.'

'Too right – but it'll keep till day shift.' Thuggbutt laughed unpleasantly. 'That little scuttler's not going anywhere . . .'

The voices faded away. Nate sat up. He caught sight of the glittering flames disappearing into the shadows. Then they, too, were gone.

· CHAPTER SIX ·

Nate climbed quickly down the tree and leaped to the forest floor, then paused. Far in the distance he could hear the sound of the steam klaxon in the stockade calling a shift to the wheelhouse. To the east, at the other end of the path, lay the pithead. He started running.

He was tired, but there was no time for rest. As he loped over the springy forest floor, Nate's head cleared and a plan began to form. It wasn't long before he caught sight of the walkway up ahead, the silvery boards glowing in moonlight for a moment, before being plunged back into shadow.

Nate skidded round to the left and headed east, keeping the path in sight as he ran parallel to it. The forest began to thin. All round him the chorus of night creatures filled the air. Fromps coughing and quarms hooting and squealing, and nattertoads croaking their alarm as his heavy footsteps hammered past.

Nate noticed none of them. He was concentrating on ordering his thoughts, working out a way through the nightmare that was threatening to envelop him. He remembered how, when he was a child, his father would carefully adjust the lamp beside his bed, setting it to just the right glow to keep the shadows in the corners of the room at bay. Now, Nate knew, he would have to adjust the lamp for himself – or risk not seeing the dawn of another day . . .

By the time the pithead loomed into view, its angled roof silhouetted against the golden glow of the Twilight Woods beyond, a plan had formed and Nate knew what he had to do. He also knew that it would not be easy.

Checking all around, he emerged from the trees and sprinted across the bare earth to the entrance to the mineshaft. He crouched down and caught his breath. There was no one about. The night shift was seldom as well patrolled as the day shift. With the mine sergeant asleep in his barracks back at the stockade, the guards usually sloped off behind the tally wagon to play a few hands of splinters. Nate glanced back over his shoulder, then darted inside and, keeping to the side wall so that he could slip behind a wooden strut or stanchion at a moment's notice, he hurried down 'the Sanctaphrax Forest'.

At the bottom – where the tunnel opened out into the store gallery – he paused to take a lamp from a hook and light it. The scraping and hammering sounds of mining echoed back along the tunnels from the galleries. Nate frowned. Slip should be asleep by now. It meant that Nate needed to head for one of the empty funnel galleries, for it was there – in the tall, dark, stormphrax-stripped chambers – that the scuttlers had their quarters.

Glancing round over his shoulder once more as he reached the entrance to gallery number one, Nate slipped inside. Hanging from the crossbeams of the abandoned scaffolding overhead were dozens of small hammocks, each one containing a sleeping scuttler. Crudely fashioned from tilderhides – with ropes tied to the boned legs and the fur still in place – the hammocks resembled nightbats, sleeping upside down in a cave.

Lowest of the low in the pecking order of the phraxmine, scuttlers were recruited by the mine sergeants to keep the shafts clear of rubble and vermin. The wages were poor, the conditions terrible and the risk of twilight madness a constant threat. Despite this, there were always fresh recruits willing to take their chances. For all scuttlers dreamed that one day they themselves would become miners and have the opportunity to make their fortunes before the mine destroyed their minds.

Nate stepped gingerly forwards, trying to avoid the pools of brackish water, thick with slime. The stench was overpowering. He climbed a section of the scaffolding – making sure with each step that the rotting timbers would support his weight – and shone the lamp down into each of the hammocks in turn. There were groans, whimpers and the occasional barely audible curse as Nate patiently worked his way along the line of sleeping scuttlers until he found his friend.

'Slip,' Nate whispered and, leaning down, prodded the sleeping goblin.

Slip muttered and rolled over onto his side. Moments later, a rasping snore echoed round the gallery.

'Slip,' Nate hissed a second time.

This time, the small creature sat up on his elbows, his eyes wide with terror. He raised his arms protectively.

'Slip didn't meant to oversleep,' he said, his husky voice high and tremulous. 'Slip's a good worker, he is. He'll get up now. Get to work at once . . .'

Nate leaned forwards and touched Slip reassuringly on the shoulder. The goblin flinched and let out a little cry of alarm.

'Listen, Slip . . .' he began.

'Yes, Slip. That's what they call me. Grey goblin, nineteen years of age and in his twelfth year of service. And never, not in all that time, has Slip overslept. Not once. Not never . . .'

'Slip, it's all right,' said Nate. He shone the lamp into his own face. 'It's me, Nate. Remember?'

'Nate?' said Slip. 'Nate.' He nodded vigorously. 'Nate Quarter. Son of Abe Quarter. Yes, Slip can see that now . . .'

'Slip,' said Nate, breaking across the wide-eyed goblin's babbling. 'Slip, we've got to get out of here.'

The scuttler fell abruptly still. His wide eyes grew, if possible, wider still.

'We were overheard. You and me,' Nate explained, speaking slowly and clearly. 'A mine guard heard you warning me about the mine sergeant, and now he wants us both dead. They've already killed Rudd. We've got to get out of here.'

Slip took a sharp intake of breath. 'Killed Rudd?' he repeated, his words barely audible. 'Your friend, the cloddertrog? But that's terrible. He was a good'un. Always treated Slip kindly, did Rudd . . .'

'He saved my life,' said Nate, his eyes misting over. 'Now we've got to get out of the phraxmine.'

The scuttler reached out and seized Nate's arm. 'Slip can't,' he said. 'He can't get out of here. This is where he works. In the phraxmine. His job, his home . . .'

'But if you don't, you'll die,' said Nate. 'You don't want to die, do you, Slip?'

The scuttler lowered his head. He scratched his ear. When he looked up again, he was shaking his head.

'Slip knows about dying,' he said. 'Slip's brother died. A phraxcrystal crushed him in his sleep. He went still and silent. And cold. Icy cold. Slip doesn't want to be icy cold. Slip doesn't want to die.'

'Then come with me,' said Nate.

Without another word, the scuttler picked up the small leather bag he'd been using as a headrest and slung it over his shoulders. He climbed from his hammock and descended the scaffolding. Nate followed him down. Side by side, they left the darkness of the abandoned funnel gallery behind them.

With the night shift still in full swing, the main tunnel was comparatively empty, most of the miners hard at work at the phraxface. A couple of lamplighters on their rounds nodded to Nate. A blank-eyed scuttler carrying canteens of water elbowed his way past them, and a convoy of pit prowlgrins trundled across their path. But as they reached the store gallery, Nate stopped and put his arm out, bringing Slip to a halt.

He put out his lamp and looked more closely. One of Grint Grayle's hammerhead guards was seated on a low stool, a phraxmusket resting on his lap, guarding the entrance to 'the Sanctaphrax Forest'. What was more, Nate recognized him. It was Thuggbutt.

'Trapped,' murmured Nate bitterly. There was no way past the great hulking brute.

'Fined three months' wages,' the hammerhead was growling to his companion, a mangy mobgnome with a jutting lower jaw. 'Three months!' He shook his great tattooed head in disbelief. 'And stuck down here on guard duty! And for what? It ain't my fault the lamplighter got away, is it? But high-and-mighty Mine Sergeant

Grint won't listen. Oh, no, not him . . .' He picked up the phraxmusket and passed it from one huge hand to the other, and back again. 'I tell you, just as soon as the shift's over and those scuttlers come out to play, there's one of them that's going to get a nasty shock, and no mistake . . .'

Nate turned to Slip, expecting that he'd have to comfort the terrified little goblin. Instead, he was surprised to see a broad smile on his face.

'Don't look so worried, Nate Quarter,' said Slip, patting him on the shoulder. 'We're going up top. Slip will show you how.'

'You will?' said Nate, astonished.

'Of course. Slip does it all the time. Ever since your father died and they stopped scuttlers going up top, Slip's been going anyway . . .'

'Show me,' said Nate.

The scuttler took his arm and led him back into the main tunnel, where he stopped and whistled softly. For a moment he stood, silent and still, his big eyes peering through the twilight glow, before his face broke into a delighted grin.

A pit prowlgrin came bounding towards them, pushing a wagon before it. Slip greeted the creature by blowing into its flared nostrils, and then motioned for Nate to climb into the wagon. Nate did as he was told, and was joined by Slip, who pulled a dusty tarpaulin over them both.

The wagon jolted into movement, and Nate felt them being transported through the tunnel, past the hammerhead guard and his companion, and up the sloping tunnel towards the pithead. It was a journey of a few minutes and yet, with each shudder and jolt, Nate knew he was one stride closer to leaving the mine and his old life for ever; one stride closer to escape . . .

Suddenly, they juddered to a halt and, throwing off the tarpaulin, Slip jumped out of the wagon. They were at the pithead, with not a guard in sight. Slip reached into his bag and drew out a dead rat, which he fed to the prowlgrin, before sending it back down the shaft with a pat on its haunches.

'Did Slip do well?' the scuttler asked, turning to the lamplighter.

'Very well!' said Nate delightedly. 'Very well indeed!'

· CHAPTER SEVEN ·

The pair of them picked their way back through the forest, keeping some ten strides or so away from the path. Clouds had gathered overhead, blocking out the moon and turning the forest pitch black. Nate couldn't see a thing, but the goblin – his wide eyes accustomed to the darkness of his underground gallery – steered them both through the undergrowth.

'Fallen log,' he would whisper back to Nate. 'Thorn branch. Muddy hole . . .'

When they came into view, the lights of the stockade seemed especially bright. Slip held back at the edge of the clearing and crouched down behind a dense combbush. Nate stopped beside him and took in the scene. Over the stockade wall was the cluster of sleeping cabins beneath the towering wheelhouse, the hammelhorns of the night shift taking the rubble carts out to the slag heaps beyond the stockade as the phraxrubble rumbled down the light funnel. High above the smoke and dust, the spindly silhouette of the docking gantry stood out against the slowly brightening sky.

'That's where our escape lies,' said Nate, pointing to the gantry. 'Not back in the woods, but up there,' he whispered, 'in the sky.'

Slip followed Nate's gaze, his eyes wider than ever.

'But first, there are things to do,' said Nate. 'And we're running out of time. Come on, we'll go in by the back door.'

Avoiding the pools of light that spilled from the tall perimeter lamps inside the stockade, the two small figures scuttled round the fringes of the forest. Then, at a narrow gap in the perimeter wall – where a hungry weezit had been digging for barkgrubs in the rotten timber – they squeezed through and ducked down behind a pile of freshly-sawn scaffolding timber. Nate peered out.

'Just as I thought,' he groaned.

One of the tattooed hammerheads was standing guard outside his cabin. He turned to Slip.

'I need you to climb onto the roof of that cabin over there and get in through the thatch as quietly as possible – as if you were trapping a rat. Can you do that?'

Slip nodded.

'Under the third bunk, there's a small ironwood chest. I want you to bring it to me. That, and the small leather knapsack you'll find hanging on my hook. I'll be waiting for you up there.' Nate pointed above the steaming wheelhouse to the docking gantry beyond. 'Up there is escape. Understand, Slip? Escape.'

The goblin nodded earnestly. 'Escape,' he repeated, eyes wide.

Nate watched the bandy-legged grey goblin scurry away. 'Earth and Sky be with you,' he whispered as Slip climbed, swiftly and silently, up the side wall of the cabin and onto the roof, before disappearing headfirst through the thatch. He picked himself up and hurried off. '*And* with me!'

He crossed the sleeping mining camp, keeping to the shadows between the cabins, then circled round behind the wheelhouse and the fortified phraxkeep beside it, where all the stormphrax produced by the mine was carefully stored, awaiting weekly shipment to Great Glade. In the shadow of the phraxkeep was a solid-looking three-storey cabin, its upper floors decorated with ornately carved balconies and elaborate gargoyles.

It was the mine barracks – the blockhouse – home to the mine sergeant and the guards. While the rest of the camp lay quiet as exhausted miners caught up on much-needed sleep, the lights in the ground floor of the blockhouse blazed.

Head down, Nate dashed across to one of the lower windows. He grabbed hold of the sill, pulled himself up and peered inside. For the first time since his father had brought him to the camp – and how long ago that now seemed – he found himself looking into the notorious mine sergeants' mess.

Even though it was the middle of the night, the place was

heaving. Visiting mine sergeants and pit drivers, ministered to by a shuffling gaggle of gabtrolls, were shouting their demands for food and drinks over loud thumping music. Grint Grayle was standing by a roaring fire, leaning back against the fireplace with one arm on the ironwood mantelpiece, a semi-circle of cronies before him. His dark eyes were glaring; his face was flushed.

'If that little barkslug of a lamplighter shows up in the stockade,' he sneered, 'I'll have him tied to the docking gantry and flogged to death in front of the whole camp. You all saw how he tried to kill me last night in the Hulks, didn't you? You're all my witnesses!'

The cronies nodded in agreement.

Nate didn't stay to hear more. Lowering himself to the ground, he went to the corner of the cabin and climbed up. At the second storey, clinging onto the rough bark with his fingers, he eased himself along the horizontal logs to a jutting balcony. He climbed over the balustrade and paused. The din from downstairs continued without let up.

The balcony shutters were unlocked. Nate opened them, stepped inside the room – and gasped.

Grint Grayle had been up to something, that much was clear. His father had known it. He knew it. What neither of them had realized was just how successful the mine sergeant had been.

The huge room was stacked from floor to ceiling with crates, boxes, baskets and sacks which, as Nate went through them, revealed every commodity, luxury or medicine from the three cities. There were silks, wall hangings and fine fashions from Great Glade, crates of the very best vintage wines from the caves of Hive, not to mention ointments, salves and priceless elixirs from distant Riverrise. Nate could hardly believe his eyes. So much wealth – and in the Eastern Woods, wealth meant power. It was no wonder that, with such riches at his disposal, Grint Grayle's mess was full of cronies prepared to do his every bidding.

But how had a mine sergeant in a stockade out in the Eastern Woods been able to amass this treasure house of luxury? Nate had a pretty good idea, and he wasn't going to leave the mining camp until he'd uncovered Grint's dirty little secret. He owed that to himself and to his father.

Nate made his way through the extraordinary warehouse to Grint's private chamber beyond. A comfortable sumpwood bed hovered in one corner, a large double washstand in the other, with an ornate full-length mirror in a blackwood frame against one wall. He was turning to go, when something caught his eye.

There was a greasy smudge on the right of the otherwise spotlessly gleaming mirror. Nate took a closer look. It was a handprint: spatula-fingers, large and splayed. Nate raised his own hand and laid it over the mark. His fingers were longer but thinner than the ones on the glass. Pressing firmly, he leaned forwards. There was a muffled *click* and a low *swoosh* as the concealed door swung back to reveal a secret staircase behind.

'So, this is it,' Nate murmured.

He stepped through the narrow doorway and climbed the creaky wooden stairs. The stairwell was dark and dirty. Thick nightspider webs, heavy with dust, dangled from the corners. None, though, touched Nate's face. Clearly someone had been this way before him – and recently.

He found himself in a low flat-ceilinged loft. There was a small unglazed window to his right, slatted shutters bolted securely across it. Ribbons of light from the perimeter lamps of the mining camp poured in through the gaps in the wood. To his left were a couple of broken picture frames, a statue of a leaping tilder fawn – its head and one leg missing – and some rusty lamps that had leaked their oil across the dusty boards . . .

At the centre of the attic sat a large wooden chest. Nate frowned. He'd seen plenty like it stored in the phraxkeep, their wax seals stamped with the mine owner's crest, awaiting shipment to Great Glade. Stooping down, he noticed at once that the seal on this chest was broken. With trembling fingers, he reached forward and lifted the lid. As he did so, the gloomy attic was flooded with light.

'Sky above!' Nate exclaimed.

The chest contained two exquisite shards of pure stormphrax

and more than a dozen gauze bags of refined phrax-crystals. Nate was gripped by a cold rage. The gleaming fragments of lightning represented endless hours of backbreaking toil carried out by countless miners – many bone-thin and ravaged by phraxlung – only for the mine sergeant to steal them for himself. For every ten lightchests sealed and shipped to Great Glade, Grint Grayle must have been taking and hiding one for himself. This was just the latest.

Nate reached inside the chest, the golden glow of the phraxlamp set into the lid staining his fingers, and picked up one of the crystal shards. He frowned, turned it over in his hand, then shook his head. There was no doubt about it. This was the very crystal that he had mined on his last shift. He looked back into the chest. And, yes, the other was Rudd's phraxcrystal. He remembered the hook-like twist at its end. Fifty gladers they'd been worth. With the right buyer, Grint Grayle would stand to make fifty thousand. Sky alone knew how much the whole chestful was worth. The mine sergeant was rich enough to buy all the luxuries the three cities could offer, and bribe anyone he couldn't bully – except, that is, for Abe Quarter. Nate was more convinced than ever that Grint Grayle had been behind his father's 'accident'.

'This one's for my father,' he said as he unfastened his lightbox and slipped his crystal into the twilight glow inside. 'And this one's for Rudd,' he added, sliding the second crystal in beside the first.

Now, there was one final thing to do, he thought, returning his attention to the phraxlamp inside the wooden lightchest.

Just then, from the room below, there came sounds of movement. Nate froze. Had Grint Grayle returned? Had he pulled the mirror door shut behind him . . . ?

· CHAPTER EIGHT ·

'Stop thief!' The anguished bellow, like the howl of a wounded tilder, echoed up the staircase and filled the attic.

Nate looked round. Apart from the stairs, the only way out was the window with the shutters. He leaned forward and grasped the lid of the lightchest. Then, in one smooth movement, he turned the oilflow pin of the phraxlamp half a turn to the right and realigned the feed valve. He quickly closed the lid. The bellowing grew louder.

It was Grint Grayle.

He was already on the bottom stair and heading up. Nate could hear him cursing under his breath. Turning on his heels, he dashed across to the window. He slipped the bolts, pulled the shutters open and crawled out onto the ledge.

Jutting out into the air beyond was a stout wooden beam, at the end of which was a rope and pulley. Arms outstretched, Nate walked along the great beam, trying hard not to look down. He crouched and reached for the rope. It had a hook on one end and, far below, a counterweight at the other. This must be how the lightchests were lifted from the ground up to the attic, Nate realized. Now it was his means of escape.

'Whoever you are, you're making a big mistake! Nobody robs Grint Grayle and gets away with it . . .'

Nate grasped the hook and swung down. For a moment he hung there. Then, with a rusty squeak from the pulley, he began to descend. Above him, he heard the mine sergeant stomping across the attic floor. A moment later, looking up, he saw Grint Grayle's furious face appear at the window. His eyes were blazing, his bony cheeks bloodless with rage, his whole face contorted as he bellowed down at the fleeing lamplighter.

'Nate Quarter! I might have known!' He cupped his hands to his mouth. 'Guards! *Guards!*'

Nate glanced down, half expecting to see the hammerheads waiting to grasp him the moment he set foot upon the ground. But there was no one there. No one in the sergeants' mess had heard Grint Grayle above the din they were making.

'*Guards! Guards!*' he screeched again, his voice high-pitched and cracking with frustration. '*Don't let him get away!*'

Nate looked up. The mine sergeant had his knife out but, though he had dared to climb out onto the jutting wooden beam, he didn't seem to have the nerve to continue to the end. The counterweight passed Nate as he descended to the ground.

He looked up again. Grint Grayle shook a furious fist at him from the window, before disappearing abruptly back inside. Nate let go of the hook as his feet touched the ground and ran full-pelt towards the wheelhouse, and on to the zigzag staircase that led up to the docking gantry.

Taking the stairs three at a time, Nate clambered up. Higher than the shuddering light funnel disgorging clouds of dust he went; higher than its rubble-laden wheel, and up above the wheelhouse, its chimney belching steam. He reached the docking gantry with his lungs about to explode and dawn breaking in the sky overhead, and paused. Slip was there, waiting for him.

'Did you get it?' Nate panted.

Slip nodded and climbed to his feet. Nate looked at what the grey goblin had been sitting on. His ironwood box of memories. Beside it was the empty knapsack and Slip's bedroll.

'Oh, thank you, Slip!' he said, clapping the former scuttler warmly on his shoulder. 'Well done!' He patted the lightbox hanging from his shoulder. '*I've* got something useful for our travels too,' he said.

'Travels,' Slip repeated.

Nate slipped both the box of memories and his lightbox inside the scuffed leather knapsack and looked up. There, right on time, was the early-morning phraxbarge on its weekly visit to the mining stockade to collect the stormphrax they'd mined for shipment back to Great Glade. The sleepy guards, who'd been up all night waiting for the barge, loaded it with three sealed lightchests, then traipsed past the lamplighter and his companion, oblivious to the wildly gesticulating mine sergeant far below. As the guards disappeared down the staircase, Nate hurried across the gantry and pressed ten crisp gladers into the bargemaster's hand.

The bargemaster looked at the money, then looked at Nate. 'Welcome aboard,' he smiled.

Just then, with a distant crash, the great doors of the blockhouse burst open and a dozen hammerhead goblins raced out, each one armed with a phraxpistol or musket. Behind them, the mine sergeant was bellowing loudly and flapping his arms, urging them on.

The hammerheads stormed down the wooden stairs of the blockhouse, only to trip and go flying head over heels. A phraxpistol went off with a bang and a flash of light. Then another. And another. There were screams and anguished cries as more of the goblins tumbled out of the blockhouse and down the steps on top of the others.

At the top of the docking gantry, the grey goblin chuckled. 'Slip did that,' he said quietly.

'You?' said Nate.

'Slip uses wire to make rat snares down in the mine galleries,' he said. 'Same stuff makes excellent tripwire, it does.'

'Slip!' Nate burst out laughing. 'You're full of surprises. Come on, we'd better get aboard.'

Ahead of them, the great spherical phraxchamber mounted at the top of the small upper deck hissed and creaked as the phraxbarge prepared to depart. Steam billowed from the high funnel and a metallic clanking sound filled the air as the anchor chain was raised.

Nate seized the bow of the phraxship and swung his knapsack across onto the deck. Slip did the same, and the two of them jumped on board. At the same moment, the sky pink with the dawn light, the steam klaxons went off, booming loudly all around the stockade as they woke the day shift miners sleeping in their cabins.

Nate and Slip stood at the starboard bow, hands resting on the balustrade as they looked back down. Far below them, the scene on the steps of the blockhouse was one of chaos. It was like, Nate thought, the panic of woodtermites whose nest mound had been breached. Some of the hammerheads, tiny from up above, were scurrying about. Others lay stunned in the dust. In amongst them, the head of the colony – Grint Grayle – was leaping up and down.

'*Get them!*' he shouted. '*They're on the phrax—*'

The klaxon sounded again, drowning out his braying commands. The vessel slipped anchor and rose steadily into the pink-tinged air. Grint bellowed all the louder, waving at the phraxship, trying desperately to get the bargemaster's attention – only to groan with a mixture of frustration and rage as, oblivious to the meaning of the commotion, the bargemaster waved back at him.

And from the deck below, as the phraxbarge gathered speed, Slip the goblin scuttler and Nate Quarter did the same.

When the third klaxon call had faded away, Slip turned to Nate. 'We've escaped,' he said.

Nate didn't answer. He was staring intently at the blockhouse.

Below them, Grint was pointing up at the departing vessel and shouting at the hammerheads. They, in turn, aimed their phraxmuskets at the ship's phraxchamber. Grint Grayle did the same. Nate swallowed. He knew well enough that if a leadwood bullet struck the centre of one of the curved panels, it might penetrate the outer shell of the chamber. And if *that* happened, the explosion would reduce the phraxship to splinters and dust in the blink of an eye.

The mine sergeant, Nate realized, was even prepared to destroy the barge if it meant killing him . . .

But the order to fire never came. Instead, Grint Grayle, the hammerheads, the drunken visiting mine sergeants and pit drivers who had staggered from the mess, and bleary-eyed miners stumbling to the wash troughs, all looked round at the blockhouse. There was a mixture of expressions on their faces. Horror, bewilderment, bemusement . . .

Slip turned to Nate. 'What's happening?' he said.

'You'll see,' said Nate, a grin tugging at the corners of his mouth.

As they watched, the blockhouse began to tremble. The sound of splintering and creaking filled the air. The trembling became a shaking, which grew more and more violent. Pieces of guttering, gargoyles and all, tumbled down through the air; a balcony crashed to the ground.

The crowd of onlookers shuffled backwards, then stood stock-still again, gawping, their heads craning upwards. Only Grint Grayle – looking smaller by the second as the phraxbarge flew higher and further away – was moving. Dashing this way and that, he was flapping his arms about wildly; at the blockhouse, at the phraxbarge . . .

All at once, there was a series of almighty crashes as the floors of the mine barracks buckled and gave way, one after the other, as an unimaginable weight fell through them. The walls crumpled and collapsed, sending huge logs thudding down to the ground and a dense cloud of clogging, choking dust billowing up into the air.

As the dust settled, all that remained of the packed storerooms that Grint Grayle had created inside the blockhouse was a pile of splintered timber, broken boxes and shattered crates. Slip turned to Nate, his eyes glistening with amazement.

'Slip doesn't understand,' he said softly. 'What happened?'

Nate grinned back at him. 'Just an accident with a phraxlamp,' he said.

· CHAPTER NINE ·

'Professor Lentis,' whispered the dean of the School of Edge Cliff Studies. 'Just the fellow I was hoping to meet.' His brow furrowed with concern. 'Any news?'

Quove Lentis, High Professor of Flight pursed his lips. 'Yes, Lodestone. Yes, there is news . . .' He smiled wryly as the dean's usual lugubrious expression brightened optimistically. 'Which would you like first?' he said in a low voice. 'The good news or the bad?'

The dean's face slumped. 'The good,' he said. 'No, no, the bad . . . No, wait a moment . . .'

It had been touch and go whether he would catch the High Professor of Flight at all. Now the dean was beginning to wonder whether it had been worth the effort.

He had sat through a particularly long Founder's Day debate. It had been noon when proceedings had got underway, but the view through the huge round windows of the debating chamber of the Great Glade Academy had turned from bright sunlight to a twilight glow, and then darkened to the star-studded blanket of night as the speeches had continued. Seated up amongst the other academics on the second of the three huge floating benches, Dean Lodestone's mind had wandered often and far away. It was only the sound of thunderous knocking that had roused him from his reveries.

Looking about him, he saw that his neighbours, and all the other assembled academics on the floating benches, had risen to their feet and were pounding their seat cushions on the bench backs in front of them in ritual applause. At the floating lectern in the centre of the chamber, the Most High Academe of the Great Glade Academy, Malleus Durvilix, bowed low, his jewel-encrusted mitre of office wobbling precariously on his shaven head. The applause grew louder.

Cassix Lodestone, dean of the School of Edge Cliff Studies, sighed and stroked his neck beard thoughtfully. He was a small fourthling with a long pointed nose and bright deep-set eyes that twinkled from beneath bushy eyebrows, giving him the air of an inquisitive quarm in search of a thousandfoot grub.

Unlike the other 'cushion-holders' on the benches around him, Cassix Lodestone took no interest in the long complicated speeches – speeches designed to impress the other academics and enhance the speakers' reputations. No, the only reason he had taken his seat on the cushion reserved for him on the great floating benches that afternoon was to get a better view of the wide tiled floor far below.

Not for nothing was the debating chamber of the Great Glade Academy known as 'the Hall of Whispers'. While the academics made windy speeches in the air, beneath them the high professors of the academy moved from tile to tile on the floor below, making deals, giving out favours and confirming appointments – all in hushed whispers.

Like an intricate board game, the tiled floor of the Hall of Whispers had its rules. Only two academics could occupy the same tile at once, and an academic hoping to approach a high professor could do so only by walking over unoccupied tiles.

Cassix Lodestone's bushy eyebrows quivered as he scanned the floor and saw his quarry. There wasn't a moment to lose. Gathering his papers together and hitching up his grey robes, Cassix barged his way unceremoniously past his fellow academics and down the central aisle that ran between the rows of benches.

From below, there came the sound of creaking ropes and grinding gears as the bench-tenders reeled in the three great benches. Standing at the gate of the second bench, at the front of a lengthening queue of jostling academics, Cassix waited tensely.

'Come on, come on,' he muttered impatiently. The benches seemed to be taking an age to descend to the tiled floor.

Inches from the bottom, Cassix threw open the gate and jumped

down. To the right and left of him, the two other benches reached the ground and their occupants spilled out across the tiles. The dean of the School of Edge Cliff Studies surveyed the hall with a cool eye. He was an old hand at this game.

The high professors stood in the distance, each on their chosen tile, as eager academics approached at the prescribed slow walk, for it was forbidden to run, on pain of expulsion from the debating chamber. Cassix checked over his shoulder and stepped onto a tile, cutting off three academics from the School of Twilight Studies. With a thin smile, he set off at a diagonal, past a red-faced under-professor in green robes, then back round three tiles.

'Almost there . . .' he muttered as he neared the unmistakeable figure of the High Professor of Flight pacing back and forth on his chosen tile. Tall, stooped and with that curious forward stabbing motion of his head, he looked like one of the pied herons that would stride across the shallows of the Great Glade lake.

'Professor Lentis!' Cassix Lodestone whispered as loudly as he dared, and broke into a rather undignified shuffle, just in time to step onto the tile ahead of the red-faced under-professor. 'Any news?'

The High Professor of Flight had not seemed overjoyed to see him, Cassix had to admit. His eyes narrowed and his small, thin-lipped mouth became even smaller and thinner-lipped. And when he spoke, his voice made it clear that he had better things to do than waste his time with a dean from one of the minor schools.

'Well? What's it to be, Lodestone?' Lentis snapped. 'The good news? Or the bad news?'

Cassix shrugged. 'The good news,' he decided.

'Very well,' said Lentis, nodding. 'The good news is the *Archemax* has returned . . .'

'Sky be praised!' Cassix said, his drooping features suddenly perking up. 'When did it arrive?'

'Last night,' said Lentis, plucking a piece of lint from the front of his robes and letting it float to the floor. 'She docked in the workshops down at the Ledges some time after midnight – and is still there. Apparently, she sustained structural damage over the Mire. Struck full on by a blowhole.' He shook his head. 'That wretched captain had her flying too low, by all accounts . . .'

'And the bad news?' said Cassix, hardly daring to breathe.

'I'm afraid that neither Ifflix Hentadile nor any of his party were on board.'

'None of them?' said Cassix. He looked down at the floor, crestfallen, his slack jowls trembling as he shook his head back and forth. 'Was there any sign of . . . ?'

'None,' said Quove Lentis. 'Not a trace. The phraxship moored at the Edgewater waterfall as agreed, and waited almost two months for the expedition's return.' He paused. 'In vain.'

'But . . . but couldn't they have waited a little longer?' asked Cassix.

'Just how long is "a little longer", eh, Lodestone?' asked Lentis, his voice querulous as he tilted his head back and stared down his thin aquiline nose at the agitated dean of the School of Edge Cliff Studies. 'Another month? Six? A year?'

'I don't know, but—'

'It was difficult enough persuading the Great Glade council to lend us the *Archemax* for that amount of time. Trade doesn't stop just because your little expedition seems to have disappeared.' He laughed humourlessly. 'And what with the current difficulties with Hive, I don't have to remind you, Lodestone, the council has more important matters to consider . . .'

'I know, I know,' said Cassix Lodestone hurriedly. 'And I'm grateful for your support, High Professor.' He shuffled through his papers, before unfolding a creased chart, covered in annotations. 'But as you can see, we have made great progress in the field of cliff studies, and this expedition showed every sign of making an extraordinary breakthrough . . .'

Lentis casually reached out an arm and dusted his sleeve. Then the other. 'Yes, so you said before,' he muttered, 'which is why I secured a phraxship for your expedition – and at great personal cost to my own reputation, I might add. Unfortunately, it seems this gamble of yours hasn't paid off . . .'

'But *all* exploration is a gamble!' Cassix blustered. 'Our scholarship depends on our understanding of the world – and that understanding is growing the whole time. Why, up until recently, it was believed that anyone falling off the Edge would fall for ever. Yet, if our theories are correct, we may well be able to prove that this is not the case; that the Edge cliff does in fact come to an end somewhere down there, far beneath the clouds.' His dark eyes glittered with excitement. 'And it is the descenders, Lentis, those brave explorers, venturing where no one has dared venture before, who are testing these theories . . .'

'You and your theories,' sniffed the Professor of Flight. 'Unlike you and your colleagues in the School of Edge Cliff Studies, we in the School of Flight pride ourselves on dealing in facts, not fantasies. Chamber design, valve pressure, phraxthrust – in short, the determining factors that have enabled the glorious Third Age of Flight . . .'

Cassix held up the chart imploringly to the high professor. 'Last time, the descenders reached the beginning of the great fluted decline. Here . . .' He stabbed at the parchment with a long bony finger. 'And this time, they were to follow the central column further into the lower depths, deeper than anyone has ever descended before. Who knows what this expedition might have discovered? If there is any chance at all of their survival, we must send a phraxship back to the Edge!' Cassix's eyes, beneath his bushy eyebrows, twinkled brightly. 'Why, with the knowledge we'd recover, next time we could—'

'Next time!' The High Professor of Flight's head jabbed forward like a pied heron spearing an oozefish. 'Why, my dear Dean, that's just what I've been trying to tell you . . . There won't *be* a next time!'

CHAPTER TEN

'Spare a hive-talent or two, sir,'

Togtuft the archivist glanced down at the creature crouching on the grimy scrap of cloth spread out on the cobblestones that marked his begging patch. He was an emaciated black-eared goblin, toothless and sunken-eyed, his ragged clothes clinging to his body with the help of countless lengths of knotted string and rope. Beside him lay an upturned cap. A filthy bandage was wrapped around his left foot, which jutted out before him.

Togtuft hesitated. Life in the great city of Hive was becoming harsher by the day.

The beggar looked up, a glimmer of hope in his eyes. 'I can't work, sir. Blackrot,' he added, nodding to the bandaged foot. 'I've got nowhere to live and I 'ent eaten for a week. Just a hiver or two would make all the difference . . .' He rattled off the words he'd said a thousand times before, his voice frayed and whiny.

'Come on,' Togtuft's colleague, Klug, told him gruffly. 'This thing's heavy.'

But Togtuft ignored him. The smell around the beggar was making the old archivist's eyes water. A swarm of blackbottles and tilderflies buzzed round the injured foot, crawling in and out of the folds of the filthy gauze. Togtuft looked at it closely. He'd heard a lot about the beggars – that none of them were genuine; that they all had mansions in Hightown; that they were lazy feckless individuals who simply refused to work, even faking injuries to elicit sympathy and loose change from their betters. Why, only the night before, in the bridge refectory, he'd heard a rumour that beggars would bandage a scrap of rotting tildermeat or oozefish to their feet to trick passers-by into thinking they had blackrot . . .

'Togtuft,' said Klug impatiently. 'Come *on*.'

Togtuft sighed. Even if it was a deception, he thought, how desperate would someone have to be before they started strapping rotten fish to their feet for the sake of a couple of hive-talents? He reached into his pocket, pulled out a few coins and tossed them into the empty cap.

'Thank you, sir,' said the black-ear, grinning toothlessly. 'Earth and Sky be with you.'

Togtuft felt his ears redden with embarrassment. He smiled awkwardly, and turned away. Klug had walked on, and Togtuft quickened his pace to catch up with him.

Klug Junkers was a mottled goblin, tall, rangy and loose-limbed, from a prosperous family in Back Ridge, one of the oldest parts of Hive. Togtuft Hegg, in contrast, was a long-hair from Hightown whose family, despite appearances, had always had to watch every talent. The pair of them had first met when they'd joined the Sumpwood Bridge Academy as archivists – and had been firm friends ever since.

'You're too soft,' Klug grunted, glancing round as his friend drew level. His mottled face was bright red and taut with exertion as he struggled on, the heavy blackwood box clamped to his chest.

'Here, let me take it for a bit,' said Togtuft.

Klug stopped and passed the box over. Togtuft gripped it tightly, and the pair of them continued down the greasy cobbled street.

They had just emerged from a workshop on the outskirts of Low Town, Hive's bustling hub of industry and commerce, where foundries and breweries rubbed shoulders with shops of every description, from ironmongers to herbalists, and the narrow streets thronged with artisans, tradesfolk and factory workers.

Maggrin's glass-grinding workshop was a thin timber-framed building, sandwiched between a glue factory and an abattoir, and shored up at the front with stout girders of roughly hewn ironwood. The sign – *Maggrin: Master Glass-Grinder* – was rusting and chipped. Yet every Sumpwood Bridge academic worth his salt knew that behind the dilapidated exterior lay a workshop run by

the most gifted craftsman in all of Hive. Maggrin's eyeglasses, it was said, were so good that he could make a cavern mole see. That was why, when the ancient light magnifier had finally proved unusable, Klug and Togtuft had pooled their meagre savings to have Maggrin repair it.

Raising enough money hadn't been easy. After all, an archivist's stipend was barely enough to keep body and spirit together. Their robes were threadbare, their funnel hats battered and crushed – and many was the time that, by the end of the month and with not a single talent between them, the pair had gone hungry. But when it had come to having the light magnifier repaired, neither Togtuft nor Klug had given it a second thought. They'd given paid lessons, they'd sold all but the most vital rock-callipers in their small laboratory, they'd cut down on their already spartan meals . . .

But it had been worth it.

Now, at last, they would be able to examine properly the sliver of cliff rock they'd received from their friend – a mottled goblin in the School of Edge Cliff Studies in the far-off city of Great Glade. Of course, if the High Archivist ever got to hear of it, Klug and Togtuft would be in deep trouble. The old underbiter, like many Hive academics, had no time for Edge Cliff Studies.

'Construction! Invention! Restoration!' his croaky voice would boom out across the refectory. 'Just as the mighty achievements of the great Vox Verlix have taught us!'

And it was true, the Sumpwood Bridge Academy had trained generations of architects, engineers and inventors who had transformed the city of Hive from a collection of tree ridge villages into the second of the three great cities of the Edge. But such practical disciplines held no interest for Klug and Togtuft. No, what excited them were the tales they heard from their friend in the Great Glade – tales of the intrepid descenders and their expeditions, deep down into the abyss below the Edge.

'So, how much did you give him?' Klug asked, glancing back at the beggar.

'Couple of hivers,' said Togtuft, his voice straining with the effort of holding onto the heavy blackwood box. 'Not much.'

'Enough to keep us in barleybread for a week.'

Togtuft sighed. 'At the end of the day, I've got more than him,' he said.

Klug laughed. 'Not now you haven't. I'm telling you, Togtuft, you're too soft.' He clapped his friend on the shoulder – and immediately wished he hadn't. '*Whoa* there!' he cried, lunging for the box as the long-hair stumbled forward on the uneven cobbles.

'Careful,' said Togtuft, righting himself. 'After what we paid Maggrin to mend this, I don't want to go dropping it on the journey home!'

They turned a corner, and headed down a steep narrow alley lined with ramshackle stalls. A stiff breeze, wet with fine rain, blew into their faces. It set the rows of pots and cauldrons hanging from hooks to their left clanking and jangling, and wafted the juicy aromas of frying hammelhorn sausages and glimmer onions from the braziers at the far end of the alley. A one-armed hammerhead, squatting on a fetid cushion between a lamp seller and a spice merchant, clamoured for loose change as they passed.

Togtuft sighed. 'It's getting worse,' he said.

'Yes, and it's going to get even worse before it gets better,' said Klug, nodding grimly. 'Especially with the long-hair clans of Hightown calling the shots . . .' He smiled at his long-hair friend. 'No offence intended, Togtuft.'

'None taken,' he said. Togtuft was all too aware that it was members of his own clan who were responsible for the deteriorating situation in Hive.

'They've used up Hive's stormphrax in weapons and left the phraxfleet to gather dust,' said Klug, shaking his head. 'Little wonder trade is suffering and the streets are full of beggars . . .'

'War is all long-hairs understand,' said Togtuft ruefully. He shook his head. 'I can understand why Great Glade's cut off stormphrax supplies to the city. It might be treason to say so, but I reckon I'd do the same if I was a Great Glade phraxmerchant who wasn't getting paid . . .'

Klug laughed. 'There's about as much chance of you being a phraxmerchant as there is of me being the general of the "Battleaxe Legion"!'

They turned the corner into a crowded alley.

'Spare a bit of change to help a wounded battle veteran . . .'

'Couple of hivers for a slice of scuttle pie and a mug of bristleweed tea . . .'

'Eight hungry mouths to feed . . .'

As they reached the end of the alley, there were more and more of the beggars. Klug and Togtuft had to pass between dozens of them lining the narrow street, each one, it seemed, more miserable and bedraggled than the last.

'For the love of Earth and Sky,' came the cracked voice of a toothless cloddertrog matron, her one arm reaching out pleadingly. 'Spare me something, kind sirs – *anything* . . .'

Togtuft stumbled past her, the heavy blackwood box clutched to his chest. This time it was Klug who paused. He reached into his pocket.

'Open Sky protect your spirit till the very last day,' she muttered a moment later, tucking the coins away beneath the folds of her tattered shawl.

Togtuft glanced round at his friend, a single eyebrow raised. Klug scowled.

'All right! All right!' he said. 'So I won't eat tomorrow.'

They emerged onto a wide road which ran alongside the river. The massive Sumpwood Bridge, with its elegant, gravity defying arch of struts and girders straddling the mighty gorge, stood to their left. Klug took back the blackwood box, and the pair of them headed towards it.

As they left Low Town behind them, the beggars thinned in number. Anyone caught asking for change in the bridge district risked a savage beating by the legion guards. Yet those who were out and about – barefoot, heads lowered, dressed in patched jerkins and worn breeches, frayed skirts, tattered shawls and threadbare topcoats – looked no better off.

'Worse and worse,' Togtuft breathed.

Marching towards them was a contingent of guards from the Battleaxe Legion, thirty in all, gleaming phraxmuskets on their shoulders. They were resplendent in burnished helmets, heavy topcoats, bleached double-buttoned waistcoats and white breeches. As they passed, their long-hair corporal suspiciously eyed the two archivists and the box they carried from beneath the rim of his polished copperwood helmet.

'Just keep walking,' whispered Togtuft to his friend out of the corner of his mouth. 'And don't look at him.'

The guards passed by, their leathery feet slapping rhythmically on the cobbles.

'Good riddance!' muttered Klug, looking over his shoulder after them.

They turned right at a market stall where a lugtroll matron was selling sapjuice, pastries and small wooden trinkets, passed between the gatehouse towers and onto the Sumpwood Bridge itself. Their footsteps sounded bell-like and hollow on the buoyant wood, and a soft keening whistle filled their ears as the breeze passed through the crisscross of carved girders and bracebeams. After the hard cobblestones beneath their feet, it was suddenly as though they were walking on air.

Arched like a vast rainbow, the Sumpwood Bridge was a mighty feat of engineering. Many claimed that it was second only to the ancient Great Mire Road, built by the legendary Vox Verlix during the Second Age of Flight. The bridge had been constructed almost two hundred years earlier when fourthling archivists – stumbling across designs for an immense blackwood bridge that once spanned the sewer library of Old Undertown – had decided to use that same design for a bridge that would cross the gorge and link the two main city ridges, east and west.

With its ornate 'rolling' balustrades and elegant towers, the Sumpwood Bridge was the most impressive construction in all of Hive – and one that, in happier times, passengers on board the visiting skytaverns had flocked to see. Lining the bridge on both sides were artfully designed long galleries, raised on stilts and jutting out over the river below. These housed the schools belonging to the Sumpwood Bridge Academy, the centre of learning in Hive. Dedicated to the pursuit of knowledge and the improvement of their city, each one bustled with architects, engineers and inventors.

Though dwarfed by the size of the Great Glade colleges and academies, the Hive schools had had successes of their own. It was a Hive scholar who first perfected the double rudder that prevented single-pilot phraxcraft from turning turvey. And another who invented a device for detecting the presence of phraxdust in the air.

'Who's that?' said Togtuft.

The pair of them paused and looked at the figure standing on the steps of the School of Restoration. At first glance, with his torn muddy clothes and hangdog expression, he could have been another beggar. But there was something about his upright bearing that singled him out as someone who had not yet given up hope.

Klug frowned. 'Isn't that a Great Glade topcoat he's wearing?'

Togtuft shrugged. They walked across to him.

'Can we help you?' asked Togtuft.

'Depends,' came the gruff reply. 'I'm looking for Togtuft Hegg and Klug Junkers, two archivists of the School of Restoration.'

'And you are?' said Klug, easing the heavy box down onto the bottom step.

'I,' he said, pulling himself up to his full height, 'am Cirrus Gladehawk – until recently, captain of the phraxship, *Archemax*.'

· CHAPTER ELEVEN ·

'*The city lights of my beloved Riverrise look beautiful tonight. The air is perfumed with darkelm oil,*' Golderayce One-Eye thought.

Who are these descenders that take it upon themselves to violate the eternal night beneath the Edge cliff?

He climbed from his hanging sumpwood chair and crossed the chamber to the far window, his lampstick tapping lightly on the floor as he went. The tiny flitterwaif gripping onto his arm flapped his wings for balance, and settled back to sleep.

'*A night breeze blows softly. The great city of Riverrise hums gently in the lamp glow,*' he thought. *I must be vigilant. On my guard. Darkness is friend to waifkind and we must protect it.*

The copperwaif opened the shutters of the window of the keep, high above the city. Once, the waifs of the Nightwoods had openly sent their thoughts out into the never-ending darkness and listened intently for the distant replies. Now, in the great city that had grown up beneath the Riverrise spring, the waifs guarded their true thoughts with a mask of outer thoughts. After all, you could never be sure who was listening.

He breathed in deeply. The tangy scent of the burning darkelm oil lamps that blazed constantly from the top of every building, every bridge, every viaduct and road filled his nostrils. It reminded him, as it always did, of everything he had achieved. After all, who would have thought that he – a humble copperwaif, Golderayce One-Eye – might have brought light to the darkness? Yet, that was what he'd done. Literally. He had founded Riverrise, and now he ruled over it with an iron fist.

But he had to watch his back constantly, for there were many of his own kind who would use any perceived weakness to try and depose him. After all, it had happened before. The nagging pains in his left shoulder and right knee, where waif darts had struck him, bore testimony to the fact that he was never safe. And as for his eye!

He pulled a silk handkerchief from his pocket and dabbed it at the sightless left eye. That, though, was another story . . .

He prodded the flitterwaif, who promptly woke up and stretched its wings. Its glowing red eyes scanned the darkness, before it leaped from his wrist and flapped out of the window into the night. Golderayce waited. His old bones ached, his back hurt and he felt so very, very tired.

'Beautiful night. Twinkling lamps. Peaceful city,' he mused. *What do you expect? You're more than three hundred years old. Of course you're tired, you stupid old creature . . .* Golderayce thought bitterly to himself.

His copper-tinged ears twitched as he heard the

flutter of tiny wings. The flitterwaif was returning. He held out a gnarled fist as the tiny creature reappeared from the darkness, a large white moth in its mouth, and landed on his arm.

'*All clear!*' the flitterwaif's whispered thought sounded in its master's head. '*The keep is safe, Master. No assassins . . .*' It broke off to eat the dusty moth, devouring first one papery wing, then the other, before cramming the plump body into its mouth.

Reassured, Golderayce stuck his head out of the window. To his right, he saw two of the custodians on guard duty at the gates of the keep, their long phraxpipes at the ready to prevent anyone reaching the sacred waters of the Riverrise lake, guarding the path to the Garden of Life – for the life-giving waters were his and his alone.

The keep and the custodians ensured that only Golderayce, the Custodian General of the Riverrise spring, had access to it. Those in the city below knew that any who trespassed would meet a swift and certain death at the hands of the mindreading guards. This was the source of Golderayce's power, and had been ever since he'd blocked Kobold's Steps with the imposing keep.

Below him, the roof lamps of the city shone like stars against the backdrop of darkness, separate constellations twinkling down in the warehouse district, across the viaduct and in the crowded alleys of Kobold's Mount. He opened his mind to the babble of the city – the sounds of the countless thousand voices that, as a rule, he would keep at bay – and sighed. Everything was as it should be, and yet . . .

He looked up. His face creased with concern. Like closing a curtain to cut out the light, he shut out the thoughts rising up from below.

'*The mighty spring flows well.*' **A storm is coming. I can feel it in the ancient marrow of my bones**, he thought, staring at the water of the Riverrise spring gleaming in the lamplight as it tumbled down from the pinnacle of rock, far above, beyond the clouds. **Yet this is no ordinary storm. There is something strange about it . . .**

Golderayce swallowed hard. Storms were tricky to handle at

the best of times in Riverrise. The custodians who tended to the Riverrise spring above the clouds needed also to control the thirsty residents of the city far below.

'*The health-giving waters bless us all,*' he thought. **We don't want any more water riots at the viaduct. This time, I shall show no mercy . . .**

Just then, there was a soft knocking at the door. The waif shut the window and listened.

'*Enter!*' His command sounded in the heads of those outside.

The door opened and a couple of gabtrolls bustled into the room, one carrying a tray, the other a small silver goblet.

'*Ah, Gilmora, Gomber,*' thought Golderayce, '*is it that time already?*' **Get on with it, you stalk-eyed imbeciles!**

'Indeed, Custodian General,' the gabtrolls chorused as one, slurping as their tongues flicked over their eyeballs, and immediately began fussing about the room, plumping up cushions, filling the oil lamps, setting a place for the waif's evening meal . . .

The gabtrolls were conscientious servants, if a little awkward and clumsy, and skilled with poultices, tonics and soothing elixirs. Gilmora was dressed in her heavy jacket, every pocket bulging. She wore a pointed bonnet and had so many talismans and charms around her neck it was a wonder she could stand. Gomber, with his eyestalks sticking out of two holes in his funnel hat, waved his lampstick about, directing his wife self-importantly.

'I'll put your . . . *slurp* . . . supper down over here,' said Gilmora, showing him the simple tray with a single dish on it. 'A nice piece of raw fromp heart. Your favourite, Custodian General.'

'Your goblet, Custodian General,' said Gomber, placing the empty silver cup next to the dish on the tray. His eyes bounced around on the end of their stalks. 'I've polished it . . . *slurp slurp* . . . specially.'

Golderayce nodded. '*Thank you, you're too kind.*' **Stop fussing and get out, why can't you?**

He closed the shutters and turned to see Gilmora and Gomber scraping and bowing as they backed awkwardly away.

'Was there anything else?' asked Gilmora, her slurping voice breaking into his thoughts.

'*No, that will be all.*' **Get out! Get out!**

The gabtrolls scuttled towards the door and left. The catch clicked softly into place. Golderayce crossed to the buoyant tray hovering in front of the sumpwood chair and lifted the cover from the platter. The smell of the raw fromp heart filled the room, sweet and musty. Golderayce's eyes widened as he looked down at the glistening offal.

'*Delicious! My favourite,*' he thought. **I'm not hungry at all. The very sight of it turns my stomach. I know what I need . . .**

Picking up the goblet, he crossed the chamber to a vast cabinet in the corner of the room. He pulled a small key on a chain from around his neck and pushed it into the lock. He turned the key, opened the doors and reached inside.

The cabinet was full of priceless objects – vases, carvings, statuettes and figurines; tiny boxes inlaid with blackwood and clam nacre and huge pieces of jewellery encrusted with black diamonds, marsh gems and mire pearls. There was a gilded telescope, a tasselled scarf of finely embroidered silk, a crystal looking-glass, a pendulum clock – all of them gifts from the various dignitaries and leaders of Great Glade and Hive who had come and gone over the centuries.

Golderayce was interested in none of them. So far as the waif was concerned, their only use was that they made the most valuable object of all look so insignificant. His gnarled fingers closed round the battered ironwood flask. He pulled it out and, having removed the stopper with his teeth, tipped it up above his goblet.

Carefully, he allowed a trickle of the sparkling, crystal-clear liquid splash down into the bottom of the goblet, before stoppering the flask and placing it back in the cabinet.

'*A simple drink,*' he thought. **The water of life, direct from the source!**

The ancient waif raised the goblet to his lips and drained its contents. He crossed the room and slumped down into the sumpwood chair. His eyes closed, his huge ears quivered, the barbels at the corners of his wrinkled mouth writhed and curled as a contented smile spread across his ancient face.

Golderayce opened his eyes and looked down at the quivering fromp heart before him.

'Delicious!' he thought. ***Delicious!***

· CHAPTER TWELVE ·

'Your name?'

The soft, gentle voice sounded in his ear, making the dusty, battered figure in the bedraggled tilderfur jacket and intricate harness stir and raise his head from the ground. He lifted a gauntleted hand to shield his eyes from the bright glare.

It had been so long since he'd glimpsed daylight. He'd feared he might never see it again.

'Your name?' the voice asked again.

He sat up slowly, his bulky backpack tugging at his shoulders, the phraxglobes mounted onto it gently steaming in the warm air. On either side of him stood rows of buildings. Wonderful buildings! A broad winged academy with minarets and a vast circular window; a crenellated college with a mirrored dome; clock towers and belfries, pillars and porticos, and countless gleaming statues.

'Your name?'

The figure looking down at him was dressed in long robes, pointed shoes and an elaborate four-pronged headpiece – the clothes of an academic from the First Age of Flight.

'My name,' the bedraggled figure answered, climbing unsteadily to his feet, 'is Ifflix Hentadile of the School of Edge Cliff Studies.'

· CHAPTER THIRTEEN ·

At the sound of the low mournful boom of the steam klaxon, Nate looked up. Down in the ever-bustling windowless Depths, it was impossible to tell what time it was. With the klaxon call, he knew that night was fast approaching.

Outside, the booming cry sent the roosting snowbirds scattering. Great flocks of the graceful, white birds swirled across the evening sky like a winter snow flurry, their honking calls filling the air. The klaxon boomed a second time as the silhouette of a mighty vessel, dark against the golden sunset, loomed on the horizon.

High above the jagged spear points of the forest canopy, the huge ship sailed out across the sky. From its great snub-nosed prow to the high rudder stanchion at its stern, the skyship was over two ironwood pines long, and deep-bellied, both fore and aft. Its great timbered aft hull was lined with row after row of shuttered cabin holes, from the ornately carved windows of its upper level, down to the simple openings in the depths, five decks below.

At its middle, the vessel was girded in forged iron, a great wheelhouse with jutting gantries and ladders rising up from the deck. Above that, supported by a metal scaffold of girders and crossbeams, sat a huge metal chamber, its circular surface consisting of moving metal plates attached to levers and gears. From deep within the chamber came a low rumble, like the sound of muffled thunder, while at the plates on its outer surface, the brittle, snapping sound of icicles breaking could be heard. A jet of bright white light, like a blowtorch, hissed from the chamber's propulsion duct. Above – from a low broad funnel – great clouds of ice-cold steam billowed up into the evening sky.

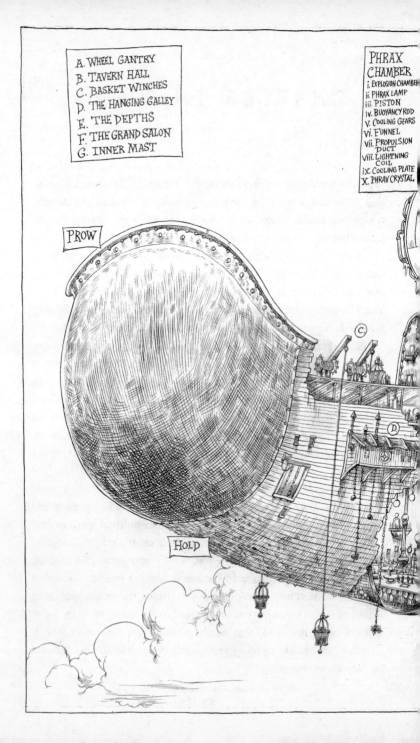

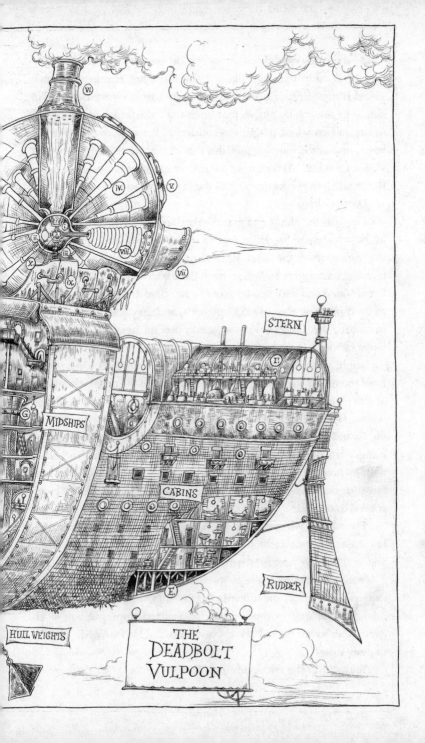

STERN

MIDSHIPS

CABINS

RUDDER

HULL WEIGHTS

THE
DEADBOLT
VULPOON

As darkness spread out across the Deepwoods, the lamps of the mighty skyship twinkled like a thousand stars, turning the dark vessel into a glittering jewel. They blazed from every part of the ship – in the crystal globes that lined the balustrades of the upper decks and crowned the jutting rudder; at the windows and cabin holes, and at the hanging gantries that clung like sky limpets to the sides of the hull. At the prow, a string of glowing lamps picked out the ornate letters hammered into the armour plating.

Deadbolt Vulpoon.

This was the oldest and grandest of the great skytaverns, and one of the wonders of the Third Age of Flight. Named after a legendary sky pirate from the First Age, the mighty phraxship had been ferrying passengers and cargo from the Eastern Woods to the city of Great Glade and back again for over a hundred and fifty years. Now, as the moon rose above the Deepwoods, and the snowbirds wheeled overhead, the *Deadbolt Vulpoon* continued on her way, bound for Great Glade.

Bright against the dark night, a solitary snowbird – separated from the rest of the flock – landed beside one of the galley chimneys at the stern of the ship, then fluttered down to a window ledge below. Head tilted, it looked in through the circular windows at the Grand Salon, at the dancing revellers, and at the tables full of hungry travellers in the dining cabins. It tapped against the glass with its pointed yellow beak for a moment, before flying down to a lower deck, where it perched on the rail of the balustrade, its head cocked to one side.

'Snowbird,' whispered an elegant young fourthling in the very latest Great Glade fashion as she stopped her evening deck stroll and grabbed her partner's arm.

'Well, whatever Papa says,' he said, ignoring her and waving an expensive-looking cane towards the forest behind, 'I, for one, don't intend to set foot in those rough uncivilized mining towns ever again. Can't wait to get back to New Lake . . .' He frowned. 'What's that my dear?'

'Snowbird,' she said, pointing. 'There.'

Her companion nodded as he spotted the white bird. 'Make a fine trophy,' he said.

'Oh, darling!' she said. 'How could you? They're such beautiful creatures . . .'

'Look perfect stuffed and mounted in a glass case on the dining-hall mantelpiece.' He chuckled. 'If only I had my phraxpistol on me . . .'

'Well, I'm glad you haven't. Don't you know it's bad luck to kill a snowbird?'

The pair of them turned their backs on the white bird, linked arms and continued their promenade. As they retreated, the bird hopped down onto the deck and began pecking at the wooden boards hopefully. Just then, a noisy family of pink-eye young'uns, each one clutching a stick, came careering along the deck in pursuit of a rolling hoop. The bird flapped up into the air, over the copperwood rail and down the steep side of the port bow. It came to rest on a jutting sill beside a half-open cabin hole.

From the other side of the small grimy window, a gnokgoblin matron grinned toothlessly. She slipped out of her hammock and hobbled towards the window.

'What have we here?' she croaked as she watched the snowbird looking back at her, its head cocked to one side. 'Ain't you a bold one, and no mistake!'

She paused and gripped the charms which hung at her neck.

'A safe voyage and a cosy fireside at the end of it,' she whispered. 'That's all I ask . . .'

'Who's there, Gramma Pleat?' came a small voice from behind her.

The gnokgoblin turned and smiled down at her little grandson. She leaned forward, let him wrap his arms around her neck, then stood up straight and folded her own arms beneath his legs. She turned back to the window.

'See?' she showed him. 'It's a snowbird. That's good luck, that is.'

'Good luck?' repeated the young'un, his voice light with curiosity.

'Oh, yes, Tag,' came the reply. 'It's good luck just *seeing* a snowbird, but to have one landing on the window just next to your hammock, well, that's just about the luckiest thing of all.' She stroked her grandson's hair softly. 'The Eastern Woods are behind us now. We're going to find somewhere lovely to live in Great Glade, you and I,' she said. 'We'll have warm water and soft sheets, and food upon the table three times a day. You'll see . . .'

'And will Momma and Papa and the rest of the family join us there?' he asked.

The words sent dark shivers through the gnokgoblin's old bones. She remembered the morning, several weeks earlier, when she and Tag had returned from picking mushrooms in the forest to find their small village deserted. The stockade gates had been left open and the huts inside were all empty. There were bowls of broth, half-eaten, on the tables; there were cauldrons of bristleweed tea still bubbling over the fires. As for the villagers that dwelled there, not a trace. It was as though they had all simply vanished into thin air . . .

'Sky willing, Tag,' she cooed, and squeezed him warmly. 'Sky willing.'

The snowbird flapped its wings and flew off. The young'un peered after it.

'Gone,' he said.

'Gone,' said Gramma Pleat.

The snowbird wheeled up high over the great skyship, past the rumbling phraxchamber, coated in tinkling icicles, round the huge funnel belching out ice-cold steam, then down in a graceful diving arc as its bright yellow eyes spotted a tempting morsel far below. Down it swooped, beneath the hull, its feet spread wide to catch the tasty-looking translucent barkgrub seemingly hanging in mid air. The snowbird gave out a honking call of triumph as its talons closed on the prize – only to give a squawk of dismay moments later when it discovered that this particular tempting morsel was in fact a glue-coated logfloat attached to a silken line, and that its feet were stuck fast.

The next instant, the line jerked and the startled snowbird found itself upended and being hauled towards a hanging gantry jutting out from the ship's fore hull. A trapdoor opened and, with another squawk of alarm, the snowbird disappeared inside.

Down in the depths of the *Deadbolt Vulpoon* – below the decks with airy cabin holes, where there were no cabins, just ship's beams with hammocks strung between them – Nate Quarter turned up his lamp. In front of him, in the narrow hammock, was his knapsack, his lightbox and his open ironwood chest. He turned the gilt-framed medallion over in his hand.

The tiny portrait of the ancient character, so like his father in appearance, stared up at him. There was something vulnerable about the expression on his face – the half-smile, the slightly raised left eyebrow . . . Whoever he was, he looked like someone young trying to be older than his years; more experienced, more confident . . . The impression was confirmed by the armour he wore. It was like a costume, the over sized breastplate with its pipes and dials exaggerating the slight build of its wearer.

'Showing the world a brave face,' Nate whispered, staring at the medallion in the lamplight, 'when inside, you don't feel brave at all.' He smiled. 'Just like me . . .'

· CHAPTER FOURTEEN ·

Two days earlier, Nate and Slip the scuttler had left the mining camp at dawn on board the phraxbarge, to the sound of the blockhouse crashing to the ground and taking the mine sergeant's ill-gotten gains with it. The exhilaration of that moment hadn't lasted long. As the phraxbarge rose higher into the early-morning cloudbanks, the feeling had disappeared, to be replaced by a dull, gnawing anxiety.

Beside him, on the deck of the small barge, Nate was painfully aware of Slip looking up into his face, seeking reassurance. Yet what should he say? His father was dead, his best friend had been murdered and now, with mine sergeant Grint Grayle and his henchmen after him, he had been forced to leave the only place he had ever known as home. The pair of them were adrift in a dangerous bewildering world, and Nate felt as small and frightened as Slip obviously was.

Nate forced himself to smile. 'We're at the start of an adventure,' he said to the scuttler by his side, trying to sound convincing. 'A wonderful adventure!'

As the morning passed, thick cloud had swept in from the west. Nate reached out across the balustrade to the twisting swirls of mist that wrapped themselves round his arm but evaded his grip. He breathed in the clean moist air, juicy with the tang of the dripping foliage that rose up from the canopy beneath. Suddenly, out of the greyness, there came a loud booming call from up ahead. The phraxbarge replied, its own whistle high-pitched and reedy as it soared upwards. A moment later, looming out of the cloud, Nate and Slip saw the dark outline of the imposing skytavern hovering before them.

The phraxbarge flew higher, closer. The cloud thinned. The vast skytavern sounded her steam klaxon again.

Every week, the *Deadbolt Vulpoon* would come to the same spot in the Deepwoods – at a point the ship's engineer deemed more or less the same distance from all the mining stockades. The great vessel would hover motionless, high above the forest canopy for half a day, waiting for the phraxbarges to arrive so that the precious crates of stormphrax could be transferred.

As the skybarge emerged from the last scraps of cloud, Nate saw that they were not the first to arrive. Half a dozen phraxbarges from the other mines had already tied up, with gangplanks from the skytavern jutting out along the length of her bow, each plank bouncing up and down as teams of luggers and loaders – their backs bowed – transferred the precious cargo from the phraxbarges to the skytavern.

Their phraxbarge slowed, the barge hands running forward to tie up under the supervision of the bargemaster. As they came alongside, a gangplank was lowered from the skytavern down to the barge and secured. Nate and Slip stepped aside as the crew hurried past towards the rear of their vessel.

The first of the heavy crates of stormphrax – knotted ropes holding it steady as it was hoisted from the lamplit hold – was shifted to the skytavern. With the creak of winches and a loud cry from the neighbouring vessel, the crate emerged from below deck and swung in the air. Reaching hands brought the crate gently down onto the deck of the barge, where it was untied and then carried by the luggers and loaders across the gangplank to the armoured hold at the prow of the skytavern. Nate gripped the knapsack containing both his lightbox and his box of memories.

'Come on, Slip,' he said. 'Time we were leaving too.'

The pair of them gathered up their belongings and took the stairs to the upper deck. Nate thanked the bargemaster for a safe passage – but the old tusked goblin was supervising the shifting of the cargo and was far too engrossed to notice the young crop-haired youth and his bandy-legged companion as they followed the luggers and

loaders across the swaying gangplank and onto the skytavern. Nate concentrated on keeping his balance – and not looking down.

'Welcome aboard the *Deadbolt Vulpoon*,' came a soft, slightly sibilant voice.

As he stepped from the precarious plank onto the vast deck, Nate found a tall foppish individual barring his way. Slip stopped beside him. The rangy goblin – a hammerhead, by the look of him, but without either the distinctive tattoos or gold ear and neck rings that had once defined this warrior clan – looked at them loftily, one after the other. He pulled back a braided cuff and cleared his throat.

'I take it you're travellers,' he said, 'not luggers or loaders?'

'That's right,' said Nate. 'We need a berth for Great Glade. How much is it?'

'Depends,' said the hammerhead with a sniff. 'A grand cabin, complete with sumpwood bed, bathing cauldron and day and night attendance would be a thousand gladers.'

'A thousand,' repeated Nate, feeling the glader notes in his pocket.

'Each,' said the hammerhead. 'But then, sadly, they're all occupied.'

'Shame,' said Nate with a relieved sigh.

'Other cabins vary, depending on the level of comfort required – bed or sleeping ledge; size of cabin hole . . . That sort of thing. Prices range from fifty to five hundred gladers.'

'Each,' said Nate.

'Each,' the hammerhead confirmed with a curt nod of his head.

Nate flicked the corners of the notes. He glanced round at Slip, who was waiting patiently by his side. He realized his cheeks were reddening under the dismissive gaze of the hammerhead. 'Anything cheaper?' he said.

'Cheaper than an inside lower deck cabin?' said the hammerhead. He sucked in air through his sharpened teeth. It was clear he wasn't going to make much of a percentage out of these two. 'There's the depths,' he said, the words short and hissed. 'But I can't really advise it. All you get is a hammock – and they're a rough crowd down there.'

'Sounds fine,' said Nate cheerfully. 'What do you think, Slip?'

'A hammock? For Slip the scuttler?' he said, and chuckled. 'Home from home, that's what Slip thinks.'

'It's settled then,' Nate told the hammerhead. 'Two for the depths.'

'Ten gladers, then,' said the hammerhead. He scowled. 'All together.'

Nate pulled the bundle of money from his pocket and peeled off the promissory notes. He handed them to the hammerhead and slipped the rest – a paltry twelve gladers – back into his pocket. The hammerhead took the money without acknowledgement and handed over two lufwood tokens in exchange.

Nate examined them. On one side, carved into the tablets of

polished wood, were the words *Deadbolt Vulpoon*; on the other, a crude cross section of the ship, with a hole punched through the very bottom of the hull at the stern.

'Phraxweapons?' The hammerhead nodded towards Slip's bedroll and Nate's knapsack. 'Phraxweapons are not permitted on board any skyship for safety reasons.'

They both shook their heads and opened their belongings to show him.

'No phraxweapons,' the hammerhead confirmed with a cursory glance, before waving them aside. 'The depths are that way . . .' He pointed down at his feet and turned away.

The hammerhead was no longer interested in the lowly miners with their five-glader passes. Instead, he had his eyes on the young fourthling couple who had just come aboard from a privately chartered phraxbarge. He'd noticed the fine cut of their clothes, their fashionable funnel hats and carved blackwood canes, as well as the expensive and extensive luggage that accompanied them, carried by a pair of hefty lugtroll servants in matching topcoats.

With an ingratiating smile, the hammerhead leaned forward, his soft fingertips pressed together. 'Welcome,' he said, voice oily and head tilted to one side. 'Welcome aboard the *Deadbolt Vulpoon*.'

Clutching their passes, Nate and Slip went through the arched doorway behind the hammerhead – and stopped. Their eyes widened. Before them lay a vast polished deck, with brightly lit corridors and stairways radiating off it, leading to every part of the massive skytavern. Each doorway and window frame, every beam and stanchion, had been carved into an intricate tracery of entwined leaves. It was as though the very timber was turning back to the trees from which it had once been hewn. Ornate lanterns hung from gilded hooks at the end of every crossbeam, while gleaming in the light below them were sumpwood chairs, laden with plush cushions, bobbing at the end of delicate chains.

Some of them were occupied. A portly tufted goblin was deep in conversation with three giggling gnokgoblin matrons. An elderly fourthling with a plaited white beard and side-whiskers sipped at a

woodlily-shaped goblet, his eyes closed. A little further off, a long-legged mobgnome, a parchment cascading over his knees, ran a bony finger slowly down a long list of figures . . .

'The stateroom and apartments are located at the top of the main stairs, sir, madam,' the hammerhead's obsequious voice rang out.

Nate and Slip turned to see the fourthling couple strolling towards them, arm in arm. Scuttling after them, weighed down with luggage – skychests, hat boxes, caskets and trunks – came the two lugtrolls. They all passed Nate and Slip without so much as a sideways glance, and continued towards the sweeping staircase to their right, with its deep-red carpet and gold stair rods.

Nate and Slip took the staircase to the left – and the one after that, and the one after *that* . . . Down flight after flight they went, going deeper and deeper into the cavernous hull of the great skyship. With each cabin deck they passed, their surroundings grew darker and more cramped. The single lamp that flickered at the centre of the lowest deck was barely enough to see by.

Nate paused and peered in through one of the open cabin doors. Inside were three stacks of bunk beds, each one filled with a goblin or troll and their belongings. There was a babble of voices and the air was rank with the smell of tilder tallow and unwashed bodies.

'Wha' you gawping at?' a rasping voice demanded, and a wizened mottled goblin reached out a filthy hand and slammed the door shut.

Nate and Slip kept on down the stairs, which creaked with every step they took. Given the state of the cabins, Nate was beginning to wonder what in Sky's name a five-glader hammock was going to be like? As he emerged at the bottom of the stairs, he paused.

He turned to Slip. 'Remind you of anywhere?' he asked.

The scuttler beamed delightedly. 'Just like the Sanctaphrax Forest!' he exclaimed. 'Only not as steep!'

Like a low horizontal mineshaft, the depths of the *Deadbolt Vulpoon* stretched off into the gloom, with no cabin holes to let light – or much air, for that matter – in on the scene. Instead, there was a forest of crossbeams and upright struts from which row after row of hammocks had been strung. The majority seemed to be occupied by the most bedraggled and disreputable collection of individuals Nate had ever seen. Old miners, blue-eyed and phraxtouched; tattooed goblin trappers covered in animal pelts; cloddertrog knife grinders and sly, shifty-looking individuals in greasy topcoats and battered hats.

'What about those?' said Slip.

Nate turned to see the grey goblin pointing at a couple of hammocks slung between a strut and the outer hull, through which a tiny chink of light appeared – together with some much-needed air.

'Perfect, Slip,' he said, and clapped the grey goblin on his shoulders. 'Well done.'

Settled at last, Nate lay back in the hammock. All around him, the beams and struts rumbled and trembled as the cloudpilots – far, far above their heads at the bulging phraxchamber – readjusted the buoyancy rods and cooling plates, and shoved the huge flight lever from 'hover' to 'forward'. With a gentle rocking and a sharp lurch, the mighty skytavern thrust ahead.

They were off. At last . . .

· CHAPTER FIFTEEN ·

That had been two days ago. As the great ship steadily steamed over the vast tracts of the Deepwoods, Nate and Slip kept themselves to themselves in their small corner of the depths. The wraith-like figures of their fellow passengers came and went as they visited other parts of the great ship, scavenging and turning their hands to menial tasks – for no one travelling in the depths had any money to speak of, not once they'd paid their passage. Nate's own twelve gladers nestled in the depths of his jacket pocket.

Twelve gladers. It was all they had between them until they got to Great Glade. They would have to make it last.

In the darkness, Nate turned to his friend. 'Slip? Slip? Are you awake?' he whispered.

Slip's big worried-looking eyes stared up at him through the gloom.

'Slip's awake, Master Nate. Slip's just lying here thinking . . .'

Nate heard the grey goblin's belly rumble noisily. His own stomach gurgled in sympathy.

'What were you thinking about?' Nate asked.

'About what Slip and Master Nate are going to do in that great big city so far from the mines . . .'

Nate lay back and stared at the crossbeam above his head.

'First, we'll go and see my uncle, Quove Lentis, High Professor of Flight,' Nate said, in a voice he hoped sounded more confident than he felt. 'I've never met him. He was my mother's brother, and he and my father had a big falling out before I was born . . . But I'm sure he'll be able to help.'

Below him in the darkness, Slip didn't reply. But Nate could feel his eyes staring up at him.

'Then we'll visit the rich phraxmerchant who owns our mine, Slip. His name is Galston Prade, and he has a big mansion in New Lake. I haven't met him either, but I found his name in my father's papers. When he hears about what that mine sergeant of his is up to, he's bound to give us a big reward and then . . .'

'Then?' said Slip, sitting up. He was hanging on Nate's every word.

Nate wanted to talk to Slip about the two phraxcrystals that nestled in the lightbox and how, if they ever needed to, they could sell them for a good price. But down here in the depths, surrounded by the ragged flotsam of the Eastern Woods, it was wiser to keep quiet.

'Let's just say I've got a plan,' he said. 'We'll be all right. You and me, together.'

'You and me,' Slip echoed in the darkness. 'Together.'

His stomach rumbled again, noisily.

'But now,' said Nate, placing the lightbox next to the ironwood chest in his knapsack and strapping it shut, 'it's high time I found us something to eat!' He swung down from the hammock and handed the knapsack to the grey goblin. 'Here, Slip, guard this with your life,' he said. 'I'll be back as soon as I can.'

'Slip'll guard it,' said the goblin, hugging it tight to his puny chest with surprisingly powerful arms. 'Don't you worry.'

As Nate left the depths and climbed the zigzag flights, one after the other, he felt faint with hunger. The higher he went, the smarter and better cared for the corridors became, and as he passed the entrance he'd first taken and continued up the stairs, the flickering lamps gave way to elegant globes, and the stained boards to thick patterned carpets. And it became much quieter. On the deck above the most opulent cabins of all, Nate came to two heavy doors.

He crept closer. The panels, top and bottom, were carved with intricate pictures of hunting scenes. Standing on his tiptoes, Nate peered in through one of the circular windows . . .

His jaw dropped. On the other side of the glass was a vast dining hall. Even though the doors cut out the sound, he could see that the place was thronging with animated groups of goblins and trogs, trolls and fourthlings, who were seated at great round tables and clustered inside floating booths. Nate stared longingly at the platters of food they were being served, his mouth watering. To his left, a well-dressed family of cloddertrogs were tucking into steaming slices of salted hammelhorn and spiced tilder; to his right, a hammerhead in a gaudy topcoat was using a large knife to carve succulent pieces from a glistening spitroast woodhog.

Nate's stomach gurgled loudly, half in protest, half in expectation . . .

Before him, a tall thin, impossibly elegant tufted goblin matron, her greying hair plaited and coiled up on top of her head, was delicately eating a huge bowl of delberries with a pair of tiny silver tongs. Nate loved delberries. As he stared through the glass, he could almost taste that sudden explosion of syrupy juice as her teeth broke through the berry's smooth skin . . .

Nate gripped the door handle and pushed hard. As the door swung open he was struck by a wave of moist warmth and deafening clamour and the most delicious mixture of smells. In front of him, far above his head on a jutting balcony, was the source of all those wonderful aromas.

For there, he could see a row of huge ovens, trays of roasting meats and racks of baking pies and loaves of bread being pushed in and pulled out of them on long flat spatulas. There were bubbling vats and steaming cauldrons being stirred and seasoned on the flaming hobs. There were heavily laden spits being slowly turned over low flames – everything tended to by scurrying cooks in starched coats and conical hats with pleated brims. They battered and basted, never still for a moment; they made their way through mounds of woodbeet, lake cabbage, tripweed and earthapples; dicing, slicing, peeling and paring . . .

Nate was momentarily overcome by the wealth of sights and smells, his stomach grumbling and his head fuzzy . . .

'Out of my way, young master,' a voice sounded in his ear.

Nate turned to see a lugtroll in a lopsided bonnet and a spattered apron veering round him, the laden trays balanced on each of her hands swaying precariously.

'Sorry, I . . .' he said, and stepped to one side – only to be shoved in the back by a huge flathead, a barrel of sapwine strapped to his back.

He turned on Nate. 'Excuse me, young master,' he growled menacingly. 'Got thirsty customers to see to . . .'

He turned and lurched away. Nate watched him for a moment as he lumbered from table to table, turning the key at the top of the jutting spigot, and filling the goblets of those who wanted it.

'Are you going to stand around . . . *slurp* . . . blocking the aisles up all evening?' said a gabtroll, bustling past, a large pail of ice hanging from the crook of her arm and a bowl of steaming vegetables balanced on her head.

'No. Sorry, I . . .'

The gabtroll looked him up and down from both directions with her stalk-like eyes.

'I don't think the young master belongs here in the Grand Salon,' she said kindly, taking him by the arm and guiding him towards the door. 'Do better to try the hanging galleys on the fore hull, that's a good young sir.'

Light-headed, Nate stumbled out of the door, and the gabtroll turned smartly on her heels, straight into the path of the flathead wine butler. There was a loud crash of breaking platters and shattering goblets as the tray clattered heavily to the floor, followed by a derisory cheer – which was snuffed out a moment later as the door shut behind him.

Nate hurried along a broad corridor. The walls were lined with portraits of former captains of the *Deadbolt Vulpoon*, the older the painting, the simpler their clothes, with ruffs, frills and embroidered jackets giving way to modest leather jerkins and bicorn hats. Coming to the midships, he took a long spiral staircase up, emerging – red-faced and panting – on a jutting viewing gantry. All round him was velvet darkness; above, the towering phraxchamber, silhouetted against the sky.

High at its top, coils of steam billowed from the funnel in lamp-stained twisting plumes that trailed behind the ship, before dissolving into the night. At the back of the chamber, the air shimmered like liquid in the blast of the white light that roared from the phraxchamber's propulsion duct and thrust the mighty skytavern forward. Above the throb and hum of the vast chamber, Nate heard another sound – a sharp tapping, like the chinking of glass, as the metal plates of the outer casing moved over its surface, dislodging the long heavy icicles that had gathered there.

'Come on,' Nate muttered, tearing himself away from the extraordinary sight. 'Got to get to the hanging galleys!'

Promising himself that he would return to this fascinating spot, he hurried round to the other side of the platform and took a second set of stairs back down into the ship. Past the wheel gantry he went, where a uniformed lugtroll stood at the ship's wheel; past the captain's quarters, large and opulent-looking, its shutters drawn. At the next landing, he paused at a small window and peered out at the basket winches for a moment. These were used to lower passengers down to the forest canopy on sightseeing trips to the thrillingly dark and savage Deepwoods below.

Nate hurried on. Once again he smelled frying food and, following his nose, scurried along a narrow bare board passage-way to his right. The sound of voices grew louder and, turning a corner, he found himself at the end of a long line of hungry passengers shuffling forwards to the open doors of what must be a hanging galley, judging from the delicious smells wafting from it.

As he drew closer and stepped inside, the smells grew stronger. Nate's mouth began to water. The galley was poorly lit and filled with wreaths of smoke and billowing steam. At its centre stood the cook, a sweaty-looking cloddertrog in a filthy apron and filthier headscarf, who was standing at a huge cauldron of bubbling oil. He was working his way along a line of strange-looking creatures which hung from translucent threads, unhooking them, dunking them in a vat of fragrant spiced batter and dropping them into the cauldron of boiling oil, where they hissed and spat. Beside him, a short, plump gnokgoblin matron wielded a long-handled spatula, turning the frying pieces and plucking them from the oil when they'd turned a golden brown.

Nate smiled. Unlike the impossibly expensive delicacies served up in the ornate Grand Salon, the food in this galley, which was clamped to the side of the skytavern's fore-hull, was freshly caught, simply cooked and, best of all, Nate thought, cheap.

Skyfare, it was called – the collection of airborne creatures that would cling to the logbaits hung from the sides of the phraxship. Mist barnacles and sky lobsters, the baits attracted; cloudfish and windsnappers, and long gelatinous worms that gathered in clumps – and made for excellent eating. For centuries, captains of the old league ships and sky pirate ships had simply had these parasites skyfired off into Open Sky. Today, on board the mighty skytaverns, they were food.

Nate felt once again for the curled-up gladers in his pocket as he shuffled forwards. A thin, pasty-faced pink-eyed goblin in a shapeless hat and grubby topcoat barged straight into him.

'A thousand pardons, my dear young fellow!' the pink-eye exclaimed in an oily voice, seizing Nate's coat by the lapels with one hand and making an elaborate show of brushing imaginary dust off Nate's shoulders with the other.

'That's all right,' said Nate, smiling at the shabby individual's exaggerated concern and good manners. 'No harm done.'

'So very gracious of you to say so, young sir,' the pink-eye smiled, doffing his shapeless hat before pushing past and out of the galley.

Three shuffling steps later and Nate found himself at the front of the line, the great cauldron bubbling enticingly before him.

'Two pieces,' he said.

He watched as the gnokgoblin matron expertly scooped two delicious-looking pieces of golden fried skyfare from the cauldron and placed them carefully on crisp barkpaper. She folded them into two neat parcels and presented them to Nate.

'That'll be five gladers each,' she said.

Ten gladers! Nate thought. Nearly all he'd got left – but then

the skyfare looked, and smelled, so delicious. He reached into his jacket pocket and frowned. The pocket was inside out. And his shirt was untucked. He remembered the thin, pasty-faced pink-eye barging into him . . .

'Ten gladers?' the gnokgoblin matron repeated.

'I know, I . . .' Nate made a show of going through his pockets, one by one, his ears burning with embarrassment. 'I . . . I can't seem to . . .'

'Then, young master, I'm afraid I can't serve you,' said the gnokgoblin. 'Pity, cause this is the house special.'

'It is?' said Nate, his stomach gurgling more noisily than ever.

'Yes,' said the gnokgoblin, handing Nate's parcels to the next customer. 'Fried snowbird, caught only this morning.'

· CHAPTER SIXTEEN ·

Nate slipped away. He'd failed. Twelve gladers he'd had. Not much, but enough for a delicious meal. Now he had nothing, and both Slip and he would have to go hungry. With his head down, he retraced his steps, past the line of waiting passengers, out of the galley and back to the central stairs.

The staircase ran alongside the huge mast, which extended from the base of the phraxchamber down to the reinforced mid hull, where the heavy lode weights swung. It was formed of six mighty ironwood trees that had been clamped together. The outer bark had been stripped, the wood polished and varnished, to create a magnificent hexagonal column which formed the backbone of the *Deadbolt Vulpoon*.

Nate headed down the stairs, scarcely noticing the salons and crew cabins he passed. He'd fallen victim to a pickpocket. He could have kicked himself for his stupidity! And what was he going to tell Slip? Poor trusting Slip, down in the depths, defending their belongings, while he, Nate, got tricked and robbed like some Eastern Woods yokel.

Lost in his thoughts, Nate was only dimly aware of the growing hum of laughter and chatter the lower he went until, stopping at the top of a flight of wooden steps, he looked down and saw a carved sign above the heavy copperwood door below.

Tavern Hall.

This was the very heart of the great phraxship, Nate knew, where many of the passengers spent most of their time, drinking, carousing and spending money at the gaming tables. It was no place for a penniless young lamplighter down on his luck.

Nate was just about to trudge wearily back up the way he'd come when something on the top stair beside his foot caught his eye. He stooped down for a closer look. It was a coin. A halfglader. With a wry smile, he picked it up and slipped it into his pocket, before continuing down to the bottom of the flight.

'Not quite penniless,' he smiled to himself, before straightening his clothes, taking a deep breath and pushing open the heavy copperwood doors.

He wasn't sure what he'd been expecting, but the sight that met his eyes as he stepped into the great tavern hall of the *Deadbolt Vulpoon* overwhelmed Nate.

'Perhaps I *am* just an Eastern Woods yokel after all,' he muttered to himself as he took in the scene before him.

He was standing on a gantry just below the densely carved ceiling beams of a cavernous hall, five times the size of the Hulks back in his small corner of the Eastern Woods. A circular stairway led down into the heart of the tavern hall, which was dominated by a great curved woodale bar.

This bar, constructed from the finest buoyant sumpwood, was built around a cluster of four huge casks. From these gigantic barrels, gleaming metal pipes snaked out in all directions like a Deepwoods tarry vine, twisting and curling their way over the polished wood of the floating woodale bar to large taps, over fifty in all, each with an attendant in an ale-flecked apron. Round all of them, waving their empty flagons, thirsty drinkers jostled good-naturedly and waited their turn.

Away from the seething mass gathered round the sumpwood bar, Nate could make out clusters of individuals hunched over gaming tables. Tall lamps of elaborate design, set into the tables, glowed dimly from all corners of the huge tavern and from the luxurious private balconies that lined its walls. The figures Nate could see in these balconies were, judging by their elegant clothes, the richest passengers on board, kept safely apart from the unwashed masses at the lamp tables below.

A glance across the wide expanse of the tavern floor was enough to tell Nate that many of these passengers shared the depths of the phraxship with him. Just like him, their main concern seemed to be money, for they clustered round the lamplit gaming tables like woodwolves round a kill, eyeing every move made by those seated at them, eager to wager their own forlorn coins in the hope of striking lucky.

Clutching his solitary halfglader in his fist, Nate Quarter set off down the staircase to join them. He made his way past the throng around the sumpwood bar at the centre of the tavern hall, and entered the bewildering display of dimly glowing lamps, each one shedding a golden glow onto the game unfolding below it. As he approached the first table, he recognized what was being played.

With their eye-shields and feathered quills, there was no doubt in Nate's mind that the circle of gamblers were playing shuttle. They all stared unblinking at a spinning disc in the middle of an elaborate board of inlaid tilder ivory, waiting to see on which tree symbol it would fall. As soon as it did, they would take their quills and note their scores on the barkpaper in front of them, with cries of delight or groans of dismay.

A party of noisy cloddertrogs were playing shove-glader at the next table, which was long and narrow and covered in chalk markings, while a particularly raucous bunch of flatheads and hammerheads were engrossed in a round of hench just beyond. From the level of noise, the game was clearly reaching the point when one of them would win the copper pot full of carefully arranged glader coins, which stood at the centre of the great round table.

Nate moved on. Rumblestakes. Two-Bit Drop. Carrillon. Some games he knew, but had never played. Some he could play, but not well. Some, he didn't recognize at all. It was only when he approached a low circular table surrounded by high-backed chairs that he realized the circle of gamblers occupying them were playing a game he both recognized and was reasonably good at.

Splinters.

It was a game of strategy and skill that Nate had learned at his father's knee during long cold winter nights in the mining stockade. The thin slivers of buoyant wood, pointed at both ends, were plain on

one side and elaborately decorated on the other. Nate knew them all off by heart. They included the 'Knight Academic', the 'Most High Academe' and the gruesome 'Grinning Gloamglozer', along with the 'cloud' splinters – over twenty in all – sixty 'tree' splinters and, most significant of all, the 'Hatching Caterbird'.

Each player in the high-backed chairs was dealt ten splinters, which they kept close to their chest, discarding those they didn't want by letting them float out over the table, to be plucked from the air by an opponent, who discarded their own splinter in turn. This floating and catching could last for hours as each player calculated what splinters their opponents held and which floated above the table, waiting for the right moment to strike.

Nate stood at the back for a moment, watching the state of play and gauging the skill of the players.

They were good, all six of them.

Particularly skilful was a dour-looking fourthling. The others around the gaming table called him the Professor, though with his crushed funnel hat and topcoat, so short it barely reached his waist, he did not look like any academic Nate had ever heard of. He seemed to be building a useful hand of 'storm cloud' splinters, while letting the 'tree' splinters float past. Next to him, a sour-faced pink-eyed goblin in a shabby topcoat seemed out of his depth. He'd floated several 'Academic' splinters, and was having trouble catching anything to his liking. Two webfoot goblins squabbled quietly between themselves while, opposite them, a grumpy mobgnome matron with a head cold tutted loudly as she snatched another splinter from the air above the table. The black-eared goblin next to her, in a triple-buttoned embroidered waistcoat that was stretched taut across his enormous belly, smiled and grasped his splinters to his chest.

Clearly, Nate realized, he'd been just about to strike, but then had thought better of it.

The splinters above the table continued to circulate in the warm air from the huge lamp in the centre. It was tense; very tense. Suddenly, the mobgnome matron sneezed noisily and pushed back her chair.

'It's no good!' she croaked. 'The splinters are just not floating my way this evening. I'm out!'

Tossing her splinters into the air, she got to her feet and waddled off towards the crowds at the sumpwood bar. In the shadows around the table, the motley bunch of spectators seemed to shrink back. This game – with the handsome pile of gold gladers gleaming in the middle of the table – was just about wrapped up, and everybody knew it. It was a straight battle between the fourthling and the black-ear, and anyone joining the table now would just be throwing away their halfglader stake.

'What, nobody fancies joining the Professor and me?' smirked the black-eared goblin, his eyes wide with mock surprise. 'It'll only cost you a halfglader.'

Without a second thought, Nate slid into the vacant chair and tossed his halfglader onto the pile in the centre of the table.

'Well, well, well,' said the black-ear, squinting at Nate. 'A young phraxminer, I see. You do *know* how to play splinters, I take it.'

Nate smiled as he effortlessly plucked ten splinters from the air and fanned them out with a flick of his wrist. 'A little,' he said.

The dour-looking fourthling in the crushed funnel hat next to him smiled. 'And do you know the origin of this fine game of skill and strategy?' he asked. He plucked a 'Black Cloud' from the air and let a 'Weeping Willoak' float free.

'I know it's been played in the towns of the Eastern Woods for a long time,' Nate ventured, careful to keep his mind on the splinters floating past. Deftly, he plucked a 'Professor of Darkness' from under the black-eared goblin's nose without him noticing, and let go of an 'Ice Fog'.

'It originated over three hundred years ago at a place called the Armada of the Dead, far out in the Mire,' the fourthling said, his dark eyes never leaving the splinters floating above the table. 'It was where the sky pirates scuttled their ships when stone sickness first struck. In their isolation and boredom, they devised this game using splinters shaved off sumpwood planks.' He chuckled. 'They say old Deadbolt Vulpoon himself was one of the finest splinter players there's ever been . . .'

'Yes, all very interesting, "Professor",' the black-ear said scornfully, dithering over a 'Raintaster' before plucking it from the air and releasing a 'Lufwood Sprig'. 'But this is no time for your history lessons . . .'

Nate looked at the splinters in his hand. Apart from the 'Professor of Darkness', he had nothing to trouble the fourthling or the black-ear and, he realized, glancing at the two webfoots opposite who continued to squabble, nor did they. Time was running out. The fourthling had a strong 'Cloud' hand and the black-ear seemed to be holding an unbeatable 'Sanctaphrax' hand. He could strike at any moment.

Just then, Nate saw one of the webfoots let go of the 'Professor of Light' splinter, which floated up into the air above the table.

'So tell me, why do they call you the "Professor"?' said Nate casually, his eyes fixed on the 'Professor' splinter.

'Because he's always spouting on about history and other boring subjects,' jeered the black-ear unpleasantly. 'And the rich passengers in the baskets throw him halfgladers in return. Downright demeaning if you ask me . . .'

'Nobody *is* asking you,' said the fourthling quietly, throwing the goblin a dark look.

It was the moment Nate had been waiting for. He flicked out a hand and grasped the 'Professor of Light' splinter before either of them noticed. Casually, he let a 'Lullabee Grove' float free. On their own, the 'Professor' splinters weren't worth much, but together, the 'Professors of Light and Darkness' beat almost every other splinter hand there was.

Now, Nate thought, careful not to let the triumph register on his face, he had a real hand of splinters!

Whether the fourthling had allowed the goblin to goad him, or just wanted the game to end, Nate wasn't sure, but the Professor chose this moment to strike.

'Scuttle,' he said in his quiet expressionless voice.

When a player uttered this word, all at the gaming table had to reveal their hands by sticking the sharpened ends of their splinters into the tabletop. The webfoots broke off from their whispered squabbling to emit growls of disgust as they simply let their splinters float free. Their hands – like the one the dispirited pink-eye clutched to his chest – were, they knew, too weak to bother to declare.

Pity, thought Nate, because one of the webfoots, he noticed, had been holding the 'Hatching Caterbird', an excellent splinter, but almost useless without a 'Lullabee Grove' to go with it.

The Professor allowed himself a thin smile as he stabbed his splinters into the table. 'Grey Cloud, White Cloud, Flat Anvil, Ice Storm . . .' The wily fourthling had built up a strong 'Storm Cloud' hand that would be hard to beat.

Hands shaking, Nate pushed his splinters into the soft wood in front of him, pitted with tiny holes from countless previous games.

'Mist Bank, Deep Elm, Apprentice Fogtaster . . . So far, so ordinary.' The black-eared goblin snorted with contempt. 'That the best you can do, phraxminer?' he sneered.

'Not quite,' said Nate, stabbing his last two splinters into the table. 'Professor of Darkness and . . . Professor of Light!'

There was a gasp from behind the chairs from the spectators, and the Professor leaned forward and clapped Nate warmly on the shoulder.

'Didn't see that coming. Nicely played, young sir,' he said. 'The "Professor" beaten by the "Professors". I like it . . .'

'Not so fast,' hissed the black-eared goblin, his dark eyes boring into Nate's as he stabbed his splinters into the table. 'The Hatching Caterbird . . . *and* the Lullabee Grove!' he said. 'Beats the Two Professors. I win, I think!'

The goblin reached for the pile of gold gladers at the centre of the table.

'I don't understand . . .' Nate began. 'I let go of the Lullabee Grove, but the Hatching Caterbird was in the webfoot's hand . . .'

'Simple,' said the fourthling, climbing to his feet, a thin blade glinting in his hand. It flashed in the lamplight as, with a flick of his wrist, he slit the sleeve of the black-eared goblin's undercoat.

Three identical 'Hatching Caterbird' splinters floated up from the torn coat sleeve.

'We have a *cheat* at the table.'

This time his voice boomed above the noise and clatter of the surrounding tables, which seemed to fall silent at the sound of the word. *Cheat, cheat, cheat* . . . The word spread in whispers round the cavernous tavern hall, until all eyes were on the dispute at the splinters table.

'We settle this now,' said the fourthling, confronting the black-ear, who was on his feet, rubbing his wrist and eyeing his accuser with a look of pure hatred.

'Whatever you say, Professor.' He spat the words out into the silence.

Tables and chairs were pulled away all round them, leaving a wide expanse of floor between the two protagonists. Sitting rigid in his high-backed chair, Nate looked across the splinters table at the fourthling and the black-ear facing each other, legs apart, arms at their sides and fingers flexing. He had a ringside seat. He swallowed hard. The air seemed to crackle with intensity. Someone behind Nate stifled a cough; over at the sumpwood bar, a dropped flagon clattered to the floor.

The fourthling and the black-ear didn't take their eyes off each other for an instant. Suddenly, in the blink of an eye, there were two flashes of metal as the arms of both individuals shot out in front of them. A moment later, the black-ear let out a strangulated gurgling cry and crashed down to his knees, clutching his great belly.

There, at the centre of a growing crimson stain, was the fourthling's long-handled throwing knife, embedded up to the hilt.

The fourthling removed his crumpled funnel hat and pulled the black-ear's knife from it, before crossing the floor slowly to his defeated opponent and seizing his own knife by the handle.

'Close,' he told the black-ear, who was staring up at him with bulging eyes, 'but not close enough.'

He pulled out his knife, wiped it on his sleeve and stepped back. The black-eared goblin groaned and pitched forward, face first onto the tavern floor.

Nate sat, rooted to the spot, horrified by what he'd just witnessed. Behind him, one of the webfoots leaned forward and whispered in his ear.

'Your "Two Professors" win after all. The pot is yours.'

Nate looked up into the goblin's scaly face, trying to make sense of his words.

'Go on, take it!' The webfoot gestured to the pile of gladers at the centre of the table.

With trembling fingers, Nate scooped up the gold coins and promissory notes, filling the pockets in his jacket until they bulged on either side. There must have been over two hundred gladers in all! He paused for a moment at the sight of two tapkeepers in ale-stained aprons dragging the body of the black-ear from the tavern hall, feet first. Then, his head clearing, Nate found his voice.

'But you must take some of this, Professor,' he began, turning back to the table. 'After all, he cheated both of us. Professor? . . . Professor?'

Slipping the splinter of the Professor of Light into his top pocket, Nate looked around, but the fourthling in the crumpled funnel hat had gone.

· CHAPTER SEVENTEEN ·

From high above came the boom of the steam klaxon, just as it had each morning for the past two weeks. One, two, three times it sounded in the dawn stillness. Far below in the depths, Nate rolled over and opened his eyes.

'Great Glade,' he whispered and, gripping the side of the hammock, peered down. 'Slip, we're here. We've arrived, Slip . . . Slip?'

The hammock below was empty. Just then he felt a light tap on his left shoulder and, turning, found the bandy-legged grey goblin standing on the other side of his hammock, a small glass bottle in his outstretched hand.

'Darkelm oil,' Slip announced with a gap-toothed smile. 'Slip's been up since dawn, siphoning it off from them big globe lamps up where the rich folks live.'

Nate smiled in return, taking the bottle from his friend. 'You didn't need to do that, Slip. I've still got plenty left from my winnings to buy lamp oil . . .'

Slip shook his head determinedly, his big eyes wide with concern. 'No, friend Nate. That money's got to last us in the Big Steam . . .'

'Big Steam?' said Nate, stifling his urge to laugh. 'Is that what they call Great Glade up where the rich folks live?'

'Not exactly,' said Slip earnestly. 'It's what they calls it in the hanging galleys. Slip's heard them. The Big Steam – where the avenues are wide and the factories never sleep, and all are welcome, who aren't afraid of honest toil . . . That's right, isn't it, friend Nate?'

Nate laughed. 'Whatever you say, Slip. Whatever you say.'

He undid the strap of his knapsack and carefully removed the lightbox inside. Opening it up, Nate unscrewed the cap attached to the underside of the lid and, with the bottle unstoppered, ran a trickle of darkelm oil into the lamp's reservoir. The two glittering crystals of stormphrax glinted in the light. Satisfied with both the wick and the flow valve, Nate closed the lid with a click.

'It'll last for a couple of weeks now,' he said. 'By which time we should be nicely settled in Great Glade . . . sorry, the Big Steam – and have no need to siphon off oil from others' lamps.'

'Nicely settled,' echoed Slip, a faraway look in his eyes. 'Who'd have thought it? Slip the scuttler, nicely settled in the Big Steam . . .'

'Come on,' said Nate, swinging down from his hammock. 'Let's get up top and stake our place at the balustrades before the crush.'

Slip gathered his bedroll, while Nate secured his knapsack, and they headed up the flight of wooden stairs that led through the great phraxship. On the third landing, a huge family of gnokgoblins cut in ahead of them. Their leader was a dumpy, open-faced matron, who chivvied her young'uns along with a mixture of wheedling, pleading and sudden bursts of anger.

'Come on now, Glemp, we're nearly there. That's the way, Gala. And Gamp, try not to dawdle, there's a dear . . . *Gussock*, stop that at once!'

Stepping out of their way, Nate counted off the young'uns. There were thirteen in all, both small and large, as well as a tiny baby strapped to the matron's back. The young'uns all had bulging bags slung over their shoulders, while behind them came uncles, aunts and assorted old'uns, lugging crates and boxes, both on their own and in pairs.

'Come on, Slip,' said Nate. 'We'll cut through midships and come out on the fore deck. We'll get a better view from there.'

Slip followed as they took several turns down long corridors already bustling with passengers, gathering their belongings together and preparing to disembark. Five minutes later, Nate and Slip emerged on the fore deck, which was beginning to fill up. The two of them made their way through the growing crowds of passengers, all of them wrapped in topcoats, shawls and blankets against the crisp early-morning air and clustered round their piles of belongings. The excited babble of voices rose and fell as they crowded round the portside balustrade. Nate and Slip found a space beside half a dozen hefty cloddertrogs in heavy work clothes.

'Look, Slip,' Nate breathed.

Far below, the borders of Great Glade were coming into view. Although dawn had broken over the city, the lamplighters had not yet had the chance to extinguish the streetlamps, and all over the vast city, pockets of light glittered like moonlit pools.

Spread out far below them in the dawn light were the twelve districts that made up the magnificent city of Great Glade. In the far distance, the sparse lights and clearing fires of the Southern Outer City twinkled next to the fringes of the Deepwoods forest. To the east, smoke, steam and factory glow picked out the industrial districts of East Glade and Copperwood, while to the west, the academy domes and spires of the Cloud Quarter stood out against the pale yellow sky. Beneath them lay the pleasant parkland of the Silver Pastures, the bustling hive towers and woodhalls of New Undertown and the rich mansions and wide avenues of prosperous Ambristown.

Nearer – and getting closer with each passing minute – lay the southern districts of Old Forest, beautiful New Lake, with its fine houses and, to the west, the Ledges – the bustling harbour district which waited to greet the returning skytavern. Nate could smell the faint tang of woodsmoke rising from the Northern Outer City, just below them now as they came round in a sweeping arc, but his eyes were focused firmly on the glittering district at the very centre of the great city.

The Free Glades.

This, after all, was where it had all begun, centuries before. Now just one of the twelve districts, the Free Glades had once stood alone, a solitary beacon of freedom and hope in the vast darkness of the perilous Deepwoods. Nate searched for the legendary landmarks as they came into view.

The great jagged silhouette of the Ironwood Stands, once home to the renowned Freeglade Lancers. South Lake, with its ancient clams; the beautiful shimmering waters of the Central Lake, with its ancient library and academy; and North Lake, with Lullabee Island, home to the oakelf brotherhood. Nate's gaze took in all these places, steeped in history from the dawn of the First and Second Ages of Flight, but it lingered longest on one: the mysterious and mystical Waif Glen and its beautiful Garden of Thoughts.

His father had spoken of it often: the arbours and alcoves beside clear pools and waterfalls; the avenues of evergreens fringing lawns of fragrant herbs. How exotic and beautiful it had sounded to Nate, growing up in the dust and din of the mining camps. The glen was a place of tranquillity and healing, and his father had even taken Nate there once as a tiny child, no older than two or three, as he searched for a way through his grief at the death of his beautiful young wife. Nate couldn't remember it, but his father's words came to life in the dreams of his boyhood – beautiful dreams of that place of tranquillity and healing . . .

'Nate! Nate!' Slip was tugging his arm excitedly and pointing wildly into the near distance. 'We're coming into dock! Look!'

Nate leaned as far over the balustrade as he dared and craned his neck forward to see past the phraxship's great snub-nosed prow. Sure enough, the *Deadbolt Vulpoon* was approaching the Ledges – a series of high bluffs that rose up from the ragged forest fringes on the western approach to Great Glade.

A vast array of timber cradles and gantries sprouted from the cliffs in ordered tiers, or 'ledges', offering berths for the numerous phraxships plying their trade in this, the Third Age of Flight. Large twin-funnelled cargo carriers with side-mounted phraxchambers; heavy-beaked tugboats and lighters, fast and sleek, with their phraxchambers mounted below the hull; the high-funnelled vessels of the phraxguard and the brooding, low-set phraxrams, with their sinister phraxcannon berthed below them. These and a hundred more of varied size and design lay berthed, prow first, in the timber cradles, or tied up, sideways on, at the gantries.

All at once, from behind Nate in the midships, came the sound of cheering and calls of 'good luck' as the wealthier passengers from the staterooms and fine cabins of the aft hull stepped aboard the *Deadbolt Vulpoon*'s private phraxlaunches – small, elegant vessels with cushioned seats, fringed canopies and tall, thin funnels billowing ribbons of white steam behind them.

Having wined, dined and seen the wonderfully wild Deepwoods from the safety of the skytavern's hanging baskets, it was time for the mine owners and factory masters and their wives; the high professors, the fleet admirals and phraxmerchants, to return to their luxurious homes in the more fashionable districts of the great city.

Nate smiled as the wealthy young heir to a phrax fortune and his new bride, together with their smartly uniformed lugtroll servants, sailed past the port bow aboard their launch. Below them on the gantries of the Ledges, luggers and loaders, lightermen and crane marshals, well-wishers and ledge hawkers were gathered in an excited, jostling throng waiting for the skytavern to dock.

No crowded gangplank and seething mass of bodies to push past for that fine young couple, Nate thought, as the *Deadbolt Vulpoon*'s snub-nosed prow eased itself into the vast timber cradle jutting from the grey rockface just ahead.

With a loud *clang* and a judder that had the crowds at the ship's balustrades gripping the rail in front of them, the mighty phraxship entered the cradle, hit the dampening stanchions, and was held fast. The tinkling sound of thousands of tiny ice shards dislodged from the phraxchamber high above the midships mixed with the cheers of the crowd. In the distance, trailing a long ribbon of vapour, the phraxlaunch sailed off to the north and the beautiful district of New Lake with its privileged young passengers.

'Come on, Slip,' said Nate, shouldering his knapsack. 'Time to seek our fortune in the Big Steam.'

'Where the avenues are wide and the factories never sleep . . .' the goblin beamed back at him. 'Slip's ready, friend Nate.'

· CHAPTER EIGHTEEN ·

Half an hour later, and they'd shuffled down one of the half dozen broad swaying gangplanks in the midst of a dense, bustling crowd of disembarking passengers, and fought their way good-naturedly through the chaos of the crowded gantry platform – full of tearful reunions of long-separated gnokgoblin clans, excited dances of greeting between burly cloddertrogs, and heavy back punching and chest thumping as flatheads and hammerheads got reacquainted. By the time Nate and Slip had left the platform and descended in huge baskets down into the bustling alleys and narrow streets of the Ledges district, another hour had passed, and they were exhausted.

High above them, in its massive sky cradle, they could see the huge prow of the skytavern, still swarming with individuals as the important business of unloading its cargo holds got underway. It would take the rest of the day and into the night before the *Deadbolt Vulpoon* was ready to take on fresh supplies of goods and passengers and set off once again, in the early light of dawn, for the Eastern Woods.

That life, Nate realized more forcibly than ever, was behind him now. Ahead lay an uncertain future in this strange, overwhelming city that he'd heard so much about.

They stopped at a small stall run by a dumpy goblin matron and bought crusty fresh-baked loaves and a jar of sweet hyleflower honey, which they ate in a shady square, surrounded by the tall thin houses occupied by the dockworkers of the Ledges. Pausing only to fill their water pouches at a small fountain, Nate and Slip soon found themselves in the broader streets and leafy avenues of Ambristown – named after Ambris Metrax, one of the pioneers of phraxship design. The houses here were grander than those in the Ledges, and the families who lived in them boasted cloudpilots, phraxengineers and quartermasters amongst their number. Indeed, in Ambristown, any who didn't earn their living in the skies were referred to, somewhat dismissively, as 'groundlings'.

Footsore and weary, Nate and Slip turned a corner into a wide avenue. Opposite them, surrounded by a semi-circle of tall lufwood trees, was a round barn-like building with the distinctive tall conical 'hive' roof common in goblin architecture. From the trees came the barks and growls of roosting prowlgrins.

'Just the place!' said Nate excitedly. 'Follow me, Slip.'

The goblin looked uncertainly from the trees to his friend and back again, but did as Nate asked, following him inside.

'Greetings, strangers,' a cheery voice sounded from the roofbeams above as they entered. 'Eastern Woods by the look of you. Just out of the mines, I'll be bound.

Nate looked up to see an elderly tufted goblin in a tilderleather apron sitting on a sumpwood stool, which was tethered to a crossbeam high in the roof timbers. From hooks and pegs around the walls and beams, harnesses, bridles and saddles hung in a bewildering array.

'How can you tell?' asked Nate, impressed.

'When you've run a prowlgrin roost as long as I have, you get to see all manner of folks passing through,' the goblin chuckled, unhooking a double saddle and head harness from an overhead beam and winching his stool down to the floor. 'Forest Ridge fur trappers, resin traders from Four Lakes, Nightwoods herbalists. You name it . . .' He frowned. 'Just the one prowlgrin?'

'Er . . . yes. I mean, I think so . . .' Nate began.

The goblin looked them both up and down. 'Your mate – he's a little'un. Don't need a whole prowlgrin to himself.'

He stood up, handed the double saddle to Nate and walked outside. Nate and Slip followed. The goblin walked over to the nearest lufwood tree, his large tufted ears twitching, and gave a short sharp whistle. In answer, a large heavy-set prowlgrin with dark eyes and gleaming black fur, leaped from the branches and landed nimbly on

powerful widespread toes just in front of them.

'Meet Tallix,' said the goblin, tickling the prowlgrin round the nostrils. 'He'll cost you thirty gladers. Half refunded on return.'

'We'll take him!' said Nate, ignoring the look of wide-eyed alarm on Slip's face.

He counted out the money in coins and notes, and put the remaining gladers back in his pocket.

'. . . And four for the saddle and harness.'

Nate reached into his pocket and handed the goblin another four gladers.

'Much obliged, young sir,' the goblin smiled. 'I'll saddle him up. You'll find Tallix here dependable and hardworking, but please, no rooftop galloping – the constabulary don't like it, and it plays havoc with the prowlgrin's feet, trust me.'

Nate nodded, and watched as the goblin pulled the harness over Tallix's head, placed the double saddle on his back and tightened the strap round the creature's girth.

Five minutes later, Nate and Slip were travelling down the broad tree-lined central avenue of Ambristown on prowlgrinback. Beneath them, Tallix took long purposeful strides, sidestepping carts and wagons as they trundled across his path, and once even leaping several feet over a small group of cloddertrogs who were arguing over a load of spilled timber.

'Hey, not so tight!' Nate had to exclaim as, behind him in the double saddle, a terrified Slip clung on round his waist.

'Not like Slip's pit prowlgrins, this one!' protested the grey goblin. 'He's too big, too powerful. He's . . . *ooohhh!*'

Tallix took another leap, clearing a hay cart, before landing and resuming a slow steady climb up the rapidly steepening avenue. At the top of the road, as they passed beneath a tall arch of gleaming marble, the elegant towers and shining spires of the magnificent academies of the Cloud Quarter came into view. Slip sat forward in the saddle.

'Slip never saw nothing so beautiful before,' he murmured. 'The village Slip grew up in was made of mud and straw.'

Nate smiled. 'These buildings are constructed from the finest marble and polished cliff rock. Nothing but the best for the esteemed schools and colleges of the Great Academy,' he said. 'And the finest views in Great Glade, by the look of it.'

He scrutinized the ornate name plaques over the grand entrances all round them.

'That's the Institute of Phrax Studies there,' he said, pointing to an imposing building to the right.

Broad and squat, it had a tall tower at its centre and a series of flying buttresses on both sides, which gave the impression of a crouching nightspider, ready to pounce.

'And that large building,' he said, 'that's the famous School of Weather.' He nodded towards a vast yet elegant construction with ornate pilasters and a sweeping, latticed roof. 'Centuries ago in the ancient floating city of Sanctaphrax, there used to be a school or academy for every type of weather. Rain. Fog. Mist. Snow. Even drizzle!' he said. 'But these days, they all study under one roof.'

'It's a mighty *big* roof,' said Slip, wide-eyed, and they both laughed.

Tallix continued climbing the steep hill to a level square, then up to another, and another, until they were high above the rest of Great Glade and looking down at the spires and rooftops of the schools and academies below. In front of them, on the highest peak of the Cloud Quarter, was the finest building of them all – the Debating Chamber of the Great Glade Academy: the Hall of Whispers.

It had imposing silver doors beneath an arched porch, gleaming walls studded with lines of thin lancet openings, and a gabled roof set with huge round windows and crowned with five pointed turrets. Nate reined in Tallix and pointed to the turrets.

'Those are the towers of the high professors. Earth, Air, Light, Darkness . . .' He counted them off on the fingers of his hand. 'And Flight.'

He climbed down from the saddle and held out a hand to Slip.

'My father spoke of this place,' he said as the grey goblin got down unsteadily. Nate tied Tallix's reins to a tall lamppost. '*And* of my uncle, Quove Lentis, High Professor of Flight. He's my mother's brother . . .'

'And he'll be able to help us, friend Nate?' said Slip. 'Find us positions, maybe, in this magnificent place?'

Nate smiled. 'Well, there's no harm in asking,' he said.

· CHAPTER NINETEEN ·

The two of them climbed the steps of the arched porch to the silver doors, where two lancers on magnificent-looking prowlgrins stood guard. With the famous chequerboard collar to their topcoats and the distinctive red banderbear badges on their sleeves, they were unmistakeable.

'Freeglade Lancers,' breathed Nate, stopping in front of the smartly uniformed gnokgoblins.

'The very same,' smiled one of them, pushing back his polished funnel hat with its ironwoodpine sprig cockade. 'Corporal Hudder, First High Branch Troop, Silverbark Company, Third Old Forest Roost, at your service.'

'I'm looking for my uncle, the High Professor of Flight,' said Nate.

'Your uncle?' said the corporal, exchanging a look with his comrade. 'Well, at this hour you should be able to find him in his tower chambers – that is, if his private secretary lets you see him. Very important academic, your uncle.'

'Fourth door on your right, marked "Flight",' said the second lancer helpfully, rapping on one of the silver doors with his lance.

The doors slowly opened and, thanking the lancers, Nate and Slip stepped into the marble hallway beyond. Ahead of them were six doors. The largest one, fashioned from golden copperwood, opened into the Debating Chamber; the other five led to the turrets above. Nate found the one marked 'Flight', pushed it open and began a long climb up a narrow set of worn stone stairs.

By the time they reached the top, both Nate and Slip were blowing hard and had to pause in the small circular chamber with its narrow window slits for a few moments to catch their breath.

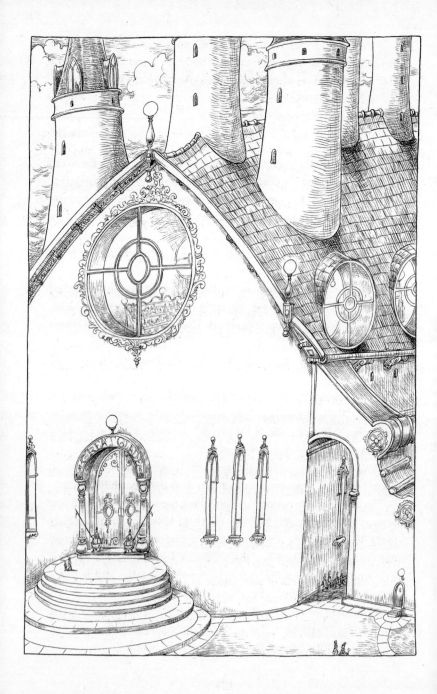

'What can I do for you, young sirs?' said a chubby round-faced low-bellied goblin in an embroidered belly sling and crushed hat of quarm felt, who was seated at a large lectern covered in barkscrolls.

'I'd like to see the High Professor, my uncle,' said Nate, wiping his forehead with the back of his sleeve.

'Your uncle?' said the low-belly, squinting at Nate humorously. 'Can't say as I can see much of a family resemblance. You, for instance, young sir, look quite good-tempered . . .'

'Squeeve! Who is it?' came a bad-tempered call from the next room. 'Whoever it is, tell them I'm busy, Sky curse it!'

The low-belly rolled his small twinkling eyes and mouthed the words 'Excuse me' to Nate and Slip, before getting up and disappearing behind the heavy embroidered drapes behind him.

'What . . . ? Who . . . ? By Earth and Sky . . . !'

The voice dropped, and Nate could hear only low murmuring through the curtains. Suddenly, they parted and the low-belly emerged to usher Nate through to the chamber beyond.

'The High Professor will see you now,' he said with a beaming smile. 'Perhaps I can offer your friend here some mosswort tea while he waits?'

Slip nodded uncertainly as Nate pushed the curtains back and stepped into a bright sunlit room with windows on all four sides and a high vaulted spire ceiling. In the centre of the chamber, surrounded by marble pedestals and open crates, stood the tall stooped figure of the High Professor of Flight, his long-tailed topcoat flecked with glittering dust. He held a claw-ended chisel in one hand and a lump of stone in the other.

'My nephew, you say?' he snapped, his small beady eyes narrowing to slits as he peered at Nate down his long aquiline nose. 'You're not one of my sister Quentia's lads. Phraxmerchants, all three. Why, by the look of you, you're a . . . a . . .'

'Phraxminer,' Nate said helpfully. 'Yes, Uncle . . .'

'Uncle? You call me uncle. But if you're not one of Quentia's sons, then . . .' Quove Lentis paused and his narrow eyes widened as the truth slowly dawned. 'You're not telling me that you're . . .'

'Yes,' said Nate, stepping forward and offering his uncle his hand in greeting. 'I'm your sister Hermia's son, Nate. Nate Quarter . . .'

The high professor took a step back, still clutching the chisel and lump of stone.

'So Hermia had a son,' he said softly as if talking to himself. 'With that damned upstart, Quarter . . .'

'My father was no upstart!' said Nate, feeling the blood rush to his cheeks. 'He was a mine sergeant – one of the best in the Eastern Woods!'

'Mine sergeant?' said Quove Lentis, turning away and placing the lump of stone on the pedestal. 'Eastern Woods.' He spoke with an icy disdain as if merely pronouncing the words left a bad taste in his mouth. 'Do you see this?' said the high professor. He pointed to the stone on the pedestal. 'This is the head of an ancient statue, dug from the ruins of Old Undertown. It was excavated and brought back to me by a recent expedition in grateful thanks for my support. And do you know why?'

Nate looked at the stone head. It was chipped and cracked, but the features were still distinct. The wide nose, the broad cheeks and heavy jowls . . . He shook his head.

'No, of course you don't,' said the high professor loftily. 'This is a likeness of my ancestor, none other than the legendary Most High Academe, Vox Verlix, the greatest architect of the Second Age of Flight. "Lentis" was the junior branch of the family, but nonetheless!' Quove Lentis's eyes blazed. 'This statue once adorned the great Palace of Statues in Old Undertown. And now *I* have it, all these centuries later, to remind me of my great family name . . .'

'But, Uncle, I—' Nate began, but the high professor silenced him with a wave of the chisel.

'A great family name,' he repeated, 'that my sister Hermia chose to drag through the Copperwood mud by marrying a common labourer. A common labourer, I might add, who had the audacity to criticize me – *me*, Quove Lentis, High Professor of Flight – for disowning her. He was probably just after her money. Well, I put a stop to his little game . . .'

The high professor trailed off. His beady eyes had a faraway look as he remembered the bitter words from so long ago. His thin lips twitched and he gripped the claw-ended chisel fiercely for a moment before opening his fist and allowing it to fall with a clatter to the floor.

'So, Nate Quarter, phraxminer from the Eastern Woods,' Quove Lentis said in a thin nasal voice, dripping with contempt. 'What *is* it, exactly, that I can do for you?'

Nate took a step towards the stooped professor until his face was close to his and their eyes level.

'Nothing,' he said defiantly. 'Nothing at all.' He turned on his heels. 'Come on, Slip, we're leaving,' he said a moment later as he pushed the curtains aside, strode past Quove Lentis's private secretary and marched down the turret stairs. Slip thanked the low-belly goblin for the mosswort tea and hurried after him.

'What happened, friend Nate?' he asked. 'What did your uncle say?'

But he got no answer until they were back in Tallix's saddle and heading down the hill towards the Free Glades district, far in the distance.

'I don't want to talk about it,' said Nate, his cheeks still burning from indignation and humiliation.

What had he been thinking, barging into that arrogant professor's chamber and expecting to be greeted with open arms? Hadn't his father told him how shabbily the high professor had treated his mother? He'd been such a fool, Nate thought bitterly. Why, he'd dishonoured his father's memory by even talking to that evil twisted academic with his stupid statue and proud family name. Tears of bitter shame sprang to his eyes, which he angrily wiped away with the back of his hand.

'We don't need the high professor, Slip,' Nate said quietly. 'Or any of those high-and-mighty academics . . .'

'We don't, friend Nate?' said Slip, from behind him in the saddle.

But Nate did not reply, lost as he was in thoughts of his father.

· CHAPTER TWENTY ·

They rode in silence for an hour or more. Descending the steep hills of the Cloud Quarter, they found themselves amongst clusters of fine timber mansions that fringed the south lake of the Free Glades district. Out on its shimmering surface, the long narrowboats of the clam tenders bobbed in the early evening sun, while groups of prosperous-looking webfoot goblins promenaded along the broad timbered boardwalk that ran the length of the western shore.

They paused to let their thirsty prowlgrin drink his fill from the clear waters of the lake, rolling his dark eyes and emitting a low growl of pleasure as he did so. Ahead of them to the north, the towering spikes of the Ironwood Stands stood out, black against the golden sky. Once home to the Freeglade Lancers, it was now a refuge for the rare giant tree fromps that, centuries earlier, had roamed the forests of the Deepwoods in their thousands.

'What shall we do now?' Slip asked, his large eyes full of concern.

Nate turned to him and smiled. 'Forgive me, Slip, I didn't mean to worry you. Tomorrow,' he said, patting Tallix on the side, 'we shall look for work in the Copperwood District. A skilled lamplighter and his apprentice shouldn't have any trouble finding employment . . .'

'Apprentice?' said Slip excitedly.

'Of course, Slip,' said Nate, with a laugh. 'The two of us together, remember?'

'Slip remembers,' said the grey goblin happily, climbing back into the saddle behind Nate.

'As for tonight,' said Nate as they set off again, 'tonight we're going to spend in a very special place . . .'

'Where?' asked Slip excitedly.

'You'll see,' said Nate with a smile.

They travelled along the western shore of South Lake, past the opulent city houses and characteristic tall mansions. Then, following the sun, they headed west round the high bluffs that skirted the magnificent Ironwood Stands. They came to more buildings; simpler wooden constructions where humbler artisans and traders lived. Two lop-ear young'uns were playing a game with small sticks and a handful of flat stones. Tossing the stones in the air, they would try to catch as many of them as possible on the back of their hand. Then, depending on how many they had caught, they would use the same number of sticks to make a line. The first one across the road, was the winner.

As Nate and Slip's prowlgrin approached, the young'uns hurriedly gathered together the dusty sticks and stones and scampered to the side of the road. Slip waved at them as Tallix ambled past.

As they approached the shore of the Great Lake, a flock of reed herons strutted across the dark, gleaming mud. In the distance, a small flotilla of fishing coracles floated in a circle near the middle of the lake, goblin fishermen balancing at the prows, their long cone-shaped nets poised. At Lake Landing, Nate spotted the famous academy jutting out into the lake from the far shore. This was still the headquarters of the Librarian Knights, although many of their number now lived and worked in the Institute of Phrax Studies, which their leading professors had established at the beginning of the Third Age of Flight.

They continued down the lake road until, with the lights of the New Undertown district twinkling in the middle distance, the dense circle of spikebriars and milkthorn thickets which enclosed Waif Glen came into view.

'This is the place,' said Nate excitedly, and he twitched Tallix's reins, making the great black prowlgrin increase his pace to a sort of lolloping, bounding gallop.

They arrived at the entrance to the glen – a small opening in the impenetrable wall of thorns – a couple of minutes later. A full moon had risen low in the sky. Climbing down, Nate and Slip led Tallix to a roost pillar beside the entrance and watched as the prowlgrin leaped a dozen strides into the air and landed on a jutting branch beside five other prowlgrins, all fast asleep and snoring contentedly. Then they turned and followed a narrow, winding path that led them through the dense thicket of milkthorns and spikebriars. As they passed by, the eyes of countless waifs – flitterwaifs, nightwaifs, ghostwaifs – glittered in the depths of thorns.

Emerging on the other side, Slip gasped and grabbed Nate's arm. 'This is even more beautiful than the Cloud Quarter,' he whispered. 'Slip's never seen anywhere as beautiful as this. Not ever . . .'

For a moment, the two of them stood at the foot of a long gravel path beneath the glittering silver moonlight, marvelling at the sight in front of them. Long avenues of darkglade trees for solitary contemplation led away on one side while on the other, groves of white-barked snowbeech trees for communal tranquillity shimmered in the moonlight. Ahead of them lay fragrant lawns of herbgrass and meadow hay for rest and healing, while at the very centre of the beautiful Gardens of Thought, ringed by deep pools and trickling waterfalls, towered the magnificent gladewillow.

Everywhere about them were the motionless forms of Great Gladers who had come to sleep in Waif Glen beneath the stars. In the distance, the curtain of gladewillow leaves parted and the waif, Thornesse, Keeper of the Garden of Thoughts, stepped out into the moonlight.

'*Greetings, friends,*' her soft voice sounded in both Nate and Slip's heads at the same time. '*Welcome to the tranquillity of the garden. May you find a restful night's sleep here with us.*'

'Thank you . . .' blurted out Slip.

Smiling, Nate put a finger to his lips. Here in the Garden of Thoughts, no speech was necessary.

Thornesse the waif disappeared back behind the gladewillow curtain. She was the seventh keeper to have tended the garden since its foundation in the First Age of Flight. More than three centuries had passed since the first keeper – a wise and deeply spiritual waif by the name of Cancaresse – had looked after the Garden of Thoughts. Finally becoming too frail for her duties, she had been escorted back to her place of birth in the distant Nightwoods by a commander of the Freeglade Lancers, who had never returned.

Halfway along the gravel path, Nate and Slip took a narrow track that led into a meadow of lush woodthyme, and lay down. In a few moments, as a cooling breeze wafted over them, they both fell into a deep, dreamless sleep.

· CHAPTER TWENTY-ONE ·

Felftis Brack, mine owner Galston Prade's chief clerk, eased himself into the cushioned cradle of his floating chair and reached for his favourite quill. Over two feet long and ending in an exquisitely sharpened nib, it was fashioned from a caterbird's tail feather, found many years before on Lullabee Island in the Free Glades district. The luxuriant black and white feather quivered over the chief clerk's hunched shoulder as he leaned forward and dipped the quill into the inkwell of his sumpwood lectern.

In the small dusty study, where row after row of locked drawers spanned the walls from varnished floor to high-arched ceiling, the tall thin fourthling cut a curious figure. He wore a long glistening topcoat of oiled snailskin leather, the tails of which trailed down from the floating stool to the floorboards, two strides below. Beneath this extravagant garment, which creaked with every flourish of the quill, Felftis Brack wore a velvet undercoat, festooned with bunches of carefully labelled keys, each corresponding to one of the hundreds of locked drawers that lined the study walls.

His long legs were clothed in thin drainpipe trousers that ended just above the ankle, revealing two large, lightly webbed feet. These, together with the chief clerk's greenish complexion, suggested a strong strain of webfoot goblin blood in Felftis Brack's ancestry, something emphasized by the tall spike of hair that rose from his forehead. Carefully combed and oiled, it resembled the magnificent crests that topped the heads of his forebears.

The caterbird quill hovered over the ledger which lay open on the chief clerk's lectern as Felftis Brack scrutinized the accounts from his master's phraxmine. He smiled, a look of sly pleasure passing over his pallid face as he licked his lips greedily.

'Excellent work, Grayle. Excellent . . .' Felftis chuckled to himself, the feathered tip of his quill quivering over his shoulder as he made an entry in the ledger in his precise copperplate script.

Just then, there came a sharp rap at the study door. With his quill poised, Felftis Brack looked up from the ledger. His brow furrowed with irritation.

'What is it?' he called out in a clipped voice.

The door opened and a stooped gnokgoblin wearing a topcoat of the Prade family livery – black and yellow cuffs and crushed green velvet – entered the study.

'Humble apologies for the interruption, sir,' he said softly, 'but there are a couple of phraxminers outside asking to see the master.'

'Phraxminers, you say?' Felftis Brack's eyes narrowed suspiciously. 'Well, there's no point in disturbing the master. I'd better see them, Hink. Show them in.'

'Very good, sir,' said the gnokgoblin, leaving the study.

Felftis Brack laid his quill to one side and sat back in his floating chair, his hands behind his head. It seemed the accounts would have to wait. The door opened a second time, and a young phraxminer with cropped hair entered the room, followed by a wiry grey goblin, his huge dark eyes darting nervously round the drawer-lined chamber. The chief clerk released the weights beneath his floating chair and descended slowly to the floor.

'I am Galston Prade's chief clerk, Felftis Brack. What can I do for you?' he asked, getting to his feet, his snailskin topcoat creaking.

He noticed with satisfaction how both young miners' eyes paused momentarily on the elegant double-barrelled phraxpistol at his belt. It was just as well, Felftis thought, to show these Eastern Woods types that he wasn't to be trifled with.

'My name is Nate Quarter,' the taller of the two began. 'Son of Abe Quarter, former sergeant of the Prade phraxmine . . .'

'So, you're mine sergeant Quarter's son?' said Felftis, taking a closer look at the lad.

He was young, his clothes were worn and scruffy and, by the evidence of the blades of woodthyme and meadowsage sticking out of his collar, he had been sleeping rough in a ditch somewhere. But the lad did have the same look of defiant confidence his father had had, Felftis noted.

It was a look he remembered only too well on the face of Abe Quarter, all those years ago, when the young miner had joined the Prade phraxmine. Felftis had been a junior clerk on the way up, but even back then, he had been struck by Abe Quarter's honesty and integrity. Felftis had followed his career as he rose to be mine sergeant – just as he, Felftis, had risen to the heights of chief clerk. Now, here was his son, with some grey goblin scuttler, standing in front of him in his study with that same look on his face . . .

'I was sorry to learn of your father's accident,' the chief clerk said, an expression of deep sorrow crumpling his pale features. 'Most unfortunate . . .'

'I believe Grint Grayle, the new mine sergeant, was responsible,' said the young phraxminer, his eyes blazing. 'But I can't prove it. What I can say with certainty though – because I've seen it with my own eyes – is that the mine sergeant is stealing . . .'

Felftis gasped, his face a picture of astonishment. 'Stealing?' he said.

'Stealing from the mine,' said Nate. 'For every ten chests of stormphrax shipped back to Great Glade, Grint Grayle keeps one for himself.'

'But the chests are sealed,' said Felftis. 'Sealed and stamped with Galston Prade's own personal crest, and kept in the keep until shipment.'

'As mine sergeant, Grint Grayle is in charge of the keep,' Nate explained. 'He breaks the seals on the lightchests, steals the best shards for himself and ships the rest back to you.' He frowned. 'The Prade mine produces far more than you can be aware of. I thought Galston Prade ought to know . . .'

'Upon my word!' the chief clerk exclaimed. 'But this is outrageous.' He shook his head, his spike of oiled hair waving like a lufwood tree in a gale. 'On behalf of my master, Galston Prade, I can't thank you enough for this information, Nate Quarter,' said Felftis, his hand outstretched. 'I could tell the moment I saw you that you had your father's honesty and integrity.' He shook hands warmly with Nate and Slip in turn. 'Rest assured, this matter shall be dealt with.' He paused. 'And as for you, Nate Quarter . . . Do you intend to return to the Prade phraxmine?'

The young phraxminer shook his head. 'Those days are behind us now, aren't they, Slip?'

The goblin scuttler nodded his head.

'No, Slip and I intend to find honest employment in Copperwood,' said Nate.

'Excellent, excellent,' smiled the chief clerk. 'Well, thank you again.'

With his arms open wide at his side, he ushered them to the door. Nate and Slip stumbled backwards awkwardly. Striding round them, his large webbed feet slapping on the varnished boards, Felftis Brack seized the door handle.

'And good luck for the future,' he said. 'Of course, I need hardly add,' he continued in a low voice as he pulled the door open, 'until this matter is resolved, you must speak of it to no one else.'

The two phraxminers nodded as they stepped out of the study and Felftis closed the door firmly behind them.

· CHAPTER TWENTY-TWO ·

Outside the chief clerk's study, Nate and Slip stood for a moment at the top of the broad marble staircase with its ornately carved stanchions and curved mouldings, looking down the long sweep of the stairs. Nate rested his hand on Slip's shoulder.

'We've done what we can,' he said. 'Now the rest is up to Galston Prade.'

'That clerk in the strange topcoat believed us, didn't he, friend Nate?' said Slip.

'I'm sure of it,' said Nate. 'And I'll tell you what, Slip, I certainly wouldn't like to be in Grint Grayle's shoes when Galston Prade gets to hear about what he's been up to.'

The grey goblin nodded seriously. 'Serves him right for mistreating pit prowlgrins, that's what Slip says.'

They descended the grand staircase, crossed the large hallway, lined with statues, and went out through the arched doorway into the spacious gardens beyond. The sun was high, coming and going from behind clumps of cloud that passed slowly across the sky like herds of migrating hammelhorns. Nate glanced up.

'If we set off now,' he said, 'we should make it to Copperwood before dark. What do you say, Slip?'

'*Say*, friend Nate?' he said. 'Slip says he can't wait to start a new life in Copperwood.'

'Yes, me too,' said Nate.

The pair of them headed down the gravel path towards the prowlgrin roosts, where visitors to the mansion tethered their prowlgrins. As they rounded a dense silverbeech hedge, they stopped and looked up at the roost pillar in front of them. Three prowlgrins were tethered in its branches. Two were deep orange; the third, a skewbald. Each was eating from the metal troughs that were secured by iron brackets to its branch, a splattering of bloody giblets and offal staining the dusty earth below.

'Where's Tallix?' asked Slip, staring at the empty branch above their heads.

'There now, isn't that nice?' a voice sounded nearby, followed by a deep rumbling purr of satisfaction.

Nate and Slip turned to see Tallix perched on a low wall a little way off, at the edge of a herb garden that had been laid out in a complicated geometric pattern of squares and circles. The shapes bisected each other, creating spaces in between which were filled with loamy earth and overflowing with aromatic herbs. Woodthyme and meadowsage; sweet lavender and orange nibblick; featherdill, scallions, blackanis and waterchives . . . Each one offered up a scent that together – warmed by the sun and stirred by the soft breeze – formed an intoxicating perfume that rose up into the air as Nate and Slip approached.

'Oh, hello,' said a girl, peering round the flanks of the prowlgrin. She had long fair hair the colour of golden gladewheat, tied up at the back with elaborate braids. 'Is this magnificent creature yours?' she asked.

'He is,' said Nate, frowning. 'We tied him up at the roost pillar . . .'

'What's his name?' she asked with a smile.

'Tallix,' said Nate, 'but . . .'

'A noble name for a noble creature. Isn't that right, Tallix?' she said, ruffling the prowlgrin's beard and tickling him under his chin till his purring growl became louder than ever. 'I've always loved black prowlgrins,' she said. 'They're so loyal . . . So dependable . . .'

Tallix looked up at her through dreamy eyes and purred contentedly.

'He seems to like you,' said Nate, smiling as the tall willowy girl emerged from behind Tallix and stood facing him, hands on her hips.

She was wearing an old topcoat with numerous pockets containing

trowels, shears and small digging forks. At her feet, Nate noticed, was a wicker basket overflowing with bunches of freshly cut herbs, gathered for use in the mansion kitchens.

'Oh, it isn't me,' she smiled, and tossed a strand of long fair hair out of her eyes. 'It's the woodsalvia.'

She held up her hand and revealed a clump of dark succulent leaves, some of them bruised and secreting a pale juice that smelled a little like bristleweed tea and had stained the girl's fingers a delicate shade of purple. She rubbed a finger and thumb together slowly.

'Woodsalvia balm,' she said, and stroked the soft fur below Tallix's quivering nostrils. 'It's perfect for saddle rash, isn't it, Tallix boy?'

Nate frowned. 'Saddle rash?' he said.

'He's used to a single saddle,' she said, nodding. 'This double saddle is bigger. It's been chafing . . .' With one hand holding up the edge of the heavy lufwood and tilderleather saddle, she used the other to rub the fragrant oil into Tallix's back. The purring became louder still. Then, satisfied she hadn't missed anything, she re-tightened the prowlgrin's saddle straps and patted him warmly on the flanks. 'He should be fine now,' she said.

'Thank you,' said Nate, impressed.

He wondered if the elderly gnokgoblin butler approaching from the other side of the gardens knew that his kitchen maid would make an equally skilful prowlgrin groom. As Nate watched, she picked up the basket and slipped it onto her arm, her clear green eyes gleaming in the morning sunlight. Then, after wiping her hands on her topcoat, she reached into the basket.

'Here,' she said, seizing a bunch of the succulent leafed woodsalvia and thrusting it into Nate's hands. 'Take this. Just in case . . .'

And with that, she turned on her heels and, her feet crunching on the gravel, walked briskly off towards the kitchens, the basket swinging to and fro on her arm. Nate hesitated for a moment, then, plucking up courage, was just about to call after her to ask her name, when she reached the mansion, pulled the door open – and was gone.

Nate smiled wistfully. 'Come on, then,' he said to Slip. 'Let's get to Copperwood.'

The pair of them climbed up into the double saddle, Slip at the front this time, with Nate looping the reins over the grey goblin's shoulders. They were about to set off when the gnokgoblin butler shuffled past, clutching a pair of shears and an empty basket.

'If it's herbs you're after,' Nate called to the butler, leaning across in the saddle, 'your beautiful kitchen maid has already gathered a basketful . . .'

The gnokgoblin frowned and scratched his head. 'Kitchen maid?' he said. 'Beautiful?' He chuckled throatily. 'Been a long time since old Wandle's been paid a compliment on her beauty, I reckon,' he said, his eyes twinkling.

'She was here a moment ago,' said Nate, puzzled. 'Green eyes. Long fair hair that shone like—'

The gnokgoblin butler laughed all the louder. 'That bain't the kitchen maid,' he said.

'No?' said Nate.'

'No,' said the gnokgoblin. He wiped his eyes on the back of his sleeve. 'That's the master's daughter,' he said. 'Eudoxia Prade.'

· CHAPTER TWENTY-THREE ·

'Whoa, there boy,' said Nate, trying his best to rein in the skittish prowlgrin. '*Whoa!*'

The warm westerly breeze had swung round to the north, becoming colder and stiffening to a near gale. The fluffy clouds overhead had turned to dark brooding banks. A storm seemed likely, and Tallix – like his wild ancestors – was being gripped by an urge to go galloping off through the streets of Great Glade to greet the howling wind and driving rain.

'Slip doesn't like it, friend Nate,' the grey goblin said, his voice trembling as the prowlgrin trampled about, tossing his head and emitting curious whinnying barks of excitement.

'We'll be fine,' said Nate. His knuckles were white as he gripped the straining reins. 'Though I think, rather than going back through busy New Undertown, it might be safer to take the northern route to Copperwood . . .'

He gave the prowlgrin a little more rein. Tallix immediately lurched forwards and cantered off down the road, his thick black fur blown about like gladebarley in the wind.

'Sli-i-i-p sti-i-ll do-oe-oe-sn't li-i-ike i-i-t,' Slip said, his voice juddering as he bounced up and down at the front of the saddle.

'Just grip on with your legs,' Nate told him, wishing he felt as confident as he sounded.

They skirted round the choppy lake at a pace, the glowering sky above turning it a dark, forbidding grey. Reed herons stood huddled in clusters on the banks, their backs to the wind; windswifts flitted over the surface of the water, feeding on the clouds of woodmidges that had begun to swarm. Turning left up a broad tree-lined avenue that led away from the lake, they headed north east. Soon, the opulent mansions and luxurious lakeside residences of New Lake were behind them, replaced by rows of double-storey hive houses with tall conical roofs. The traffic on the road increased, not that Tallix was deterred. Bounding along with great arcing leaps, he jumped over every obstacle he came to – once coming down on the back of a wagonload of heavy logs before leaping back into the air again.

'Oi, you wanna learn to ride that thing!' the cloddertrog wagon driver bellowed after them, shaking his fist.

Nate's apologies were lost to the wind as Tallix galloped on. Ahead of them the mighty trees of the Old Forest district, the last remaining area of original Deepwoods still standing in Great Glade, were silhouetted against the sky; pale green on deepest, darkest grey. With a whinny of delight, Tallix bounded towards them and, holding on grimly, Nate and Slip had no choice but to go with him.

'Trust your prowlgrin.' Abe Quarter's words of advice to his son came back to Nate as the trees loomed closer.

All very well in theory, thought Nate, but Tallix seemed to be charging straight for a vast lufwood tree at the end of the avenue. A family of woodhogs, squealing with indignation, scuttled out of their way. The prowlgrin gathered speed.

'Friend Nate!' Slip gasped. 'Friend . . . *whoooah!*'

Beneath them, Tallix gave an excited yelp as, with his powerful back legs kicking off, he soared up high into the air. Nate and Slip felt their stomachs sink to their boots. A moment later, and with a resounding *thud*, Tallix landed on a broad lower branch, clinging on with his stubby forepaws, gathering his hindquarters, before kicking off again. Up, up, higher and higher the prowlgrin jumped, before crashing through the forest canopy. The great empty expanse of low sky opened up before them.

Nate gripped on tightly as they bounded on over the treetops. Before him, the grey goblin was rigid. Nate leaned forward. 'Are you all right, Slip?' he asked.

Slip looked round slowly, and Nate was surprised to see a huge grin plastered across the grey goblin's face.

'All right?' he said. 'Slip's better than all right! Slip's never had such an exciting ride – now he knows to grip on with his legs.'

He turned back and resumed his statue-like rigidity. Nate smiled to himself as they galloped on across the treetops of Old Forest, the bustling streets of Great Glade left suddenly behind. All around, the treetops dipped and swayed, their pale leaves opening up to reveal darker depths below. Suddenly, something caught Nate's eye. It was a bright light, turquoise blue, glowing to his right. The canopy closed up and the light disappeared, only to reappear a moment later, brighter than before.

Whatever's that? Nate wondered.

He tugged at the reins, trying to slow Tallix down so that he could get a better look. Above, there was a flash of lightning and a distant roll of thunder, followed by heavy drops of rain. As it grew heavier, drumming on the leaves around them, the excited prowlgrin's intense frenzy seemed suddenly to have been spent, and Tallix eased up. They came to a stop at the top of a towering ironwood pine and peered down through a break in the canopy at the curious greeny-blue glow, now just ahead.

'Let's take a closer look,' said Nate.

Tallix headed down through the forest, the wind hissing and howling all round them. As they came lower, Nate and Slip realized that the turquoise light was coming from two immense lullabee trees that – through intricate cultivation and over hundreds of years – had been plaited together, twig by twig and branch by branch, to form a colossal archway. The arch was at the centre of a vast clearing, with barracks, guard rooms and munitions stores both on the ground and fixed high up in the surrounding trees. On the far side of the lullabee arch was the drill field which, as Tallix approached, Nate saw was filling up with battalions of guards.

'Whoa, boy,' said Nate, and tugged at the reins.

Tallix came to a halt. They were standing at the end of a stout jutting willoak branch that afforded a perfect view of the activity below, and protection from the falling rain.

'My father told me about this,' said Nate, nodding knowingly. 'It happens every day, at three hours.'

'What does?' asked Slip.

'You'll see,' said Nate.

A regiment of Great Glade guards, six abreast, was marching across the field from left to right, their phraxmuskets resting on their left shoulders and the sprigs of forest foliage at the top of their funnel hats fluttering in the wind and rain. From the opposite direction, a company of Freeglade Lancers – traditional thornwood lances now supplemented by twin phraxpistols at their sides – trotted in from early patrol beneath the arch and joined them. All round the clearing, sliding down long poles from the tree barracks, came cohort after cohort of guards, who gathered in rows before being marched across the drill field to the barked commands of their sergeants.

Soon a vast phalanx of troops had formed on the ground beneath them, a patchwork of colours as the various groupings of the Great Glade Guard – from the chequerboard-collared Freeglade Lancers and blue-uniformed Cloddertrog Constabulary to the distinctive grey and orange jackets of the Waif Guild and Outer City Scouts – ordered themselves in ranks. A Freeglade Lancer corporal on prowlgrinback stepped forward and raised a hammelhorn bugle to his lips. He blew hard.

The two note clarion call heralded the arrival of a mighty cannon, thirty strides long and cast in solid brass. Drawn by a dozen hammelhorns in tandem harness, the cannon emerged through the glowing lullabee arch and rumbled over the hard ground, attendant guards marching along on both sides.

'It's the *Thunderer*,' breathed Nate. 'The most powerful phrax-weapon ever built . . .'

Positioned next to a flagpole at the head of the great gathering of soldiers and guards, the phraxcannon's massive barrel was cranked upwards till it was pointing over the top of the nearest trees. The hammelhorns were led away. From the left, on a jutting platform, the guard general – a powerfully built tufted goblin, the braids of battle honours and ribbons of victories fluttering from his jacket as his tall funnel hat swayed on his head – stepped forward. He addressed the troops in a deep, booming voice that was whipped away on the wind.

Neither Nate nor Slip made out a single word – but the troops must have . . .

As one, they marched on the spot, they sloped arms and hoisted their heavy phraxmuskets from one shoulder to the other; turned about face, then marched to a halt and stood crisply at ease. A silence fell. Two individuals broke ranks. One raised the Great Glade flag; a red banderbear against a white ground, the pennant flapping in the cold wind. The second stopped at the base of the phraxcannon, where he reached forward, seized the flashpin and tugged hard.

There was a *crack* and a *hiss*. Nate clamped his hands over his ears, nudging Slip to follow his example. The next instant, in an explosion of billowing white cloud, a heavy phraxshell burst from the end of the barrel and, with a rushing *whoosh*, shot high up into the air. It soared over the treetops, a gleaming ball

149

of light that flew past the outlying Northern Outer City and on to the Deepwoods where, with a booming *crack!* and a dazzling flash, it exploded high above the forest.

'Great Glade!' bellowed the massed ranks of its loyal guards, sworn to protect the great city till their last breath.

With the daily ceremony over, the phalanx broke up. Nate looked down at the emptying drill field wistfully as it returned to the normal routine of barracks life. He would have liked to look over the phraxcannon for himself; to stand on the edge of the drill field and maybe even to walk through the great lullabee arch, where – or so the stories went – the famous caterbird who watched over his friend, the great 'Twig' Verginix, had hatched more than five centuries earlier, when the whole area had been a vast lullabee glade. But the rain was falling steadily now and they would be hard pressed to reach Copperwood by nightfall if they didn't push on.

· CHAPTER TWENTY-FOUR ·

Flicking Tallix's reins sharply, they set off once more, driving through the forest at mid branch level. They didn't stop again until Old Forest was behind them and, leaping from the broad branch of a lufwood tree, they landed in the rolling parkland and flower gardens of the Silver Pastures district.

After the dense foliage of Old Forest, the Silver Pastures felt airy and spacious, its expansive parkland dotted with rustic buildings – cottages, barns, byres and granaries. Down to a trot now, they picked their way along winding paths and past great swathes of original grassland, the long blade-like leaves swaying in the wind like a mighty lake. Once, the Silver Pastures had been ten times as large – a great oasis in the middle of the inhospitable Deepwoods, where vast migrating herds of wild tilder and hammelhorn would gather to eat their fill of sweet gladegrass. Now, much of the land had been ploughed up or built on, and what was left was fenced in to contain the smaller herds of domesticated hammelhorn and tilder.

As they rounded a small copse of sallowdrops fringing a dewpond, they disturbed a flock of vulpoons that flapped up screeching into the air, their shaggy feathers fluttering in the wind. Tallix slowed and sniffed. His nostrils quivered and, with a growl that started in the depths of his stomach, he howled loudly and galloped off in their direction.

'Tallix! Tallix!' Nate cried out, and tugged as hard as he could at the reins.

But nothing would stop the prowlgrin. Gathering speed with every stride he took, he sprinted towards the far side of the dewpond, and as he drew close, Nate saw the body of a dead hammelhorn lying on its side by the water's edge. The vulpoons were beginning to land once more, and hopped about it, stabbing at the carcass with their razor-sharp beaks.

Tallix stopped of his own accord, and began pawing at the ground and snorting.

'All right, boy,' said Nate softly.

He dismounted. Slip jumped down beside him. Nate unbuckled the saddle and the two of them stood by as their prowlgrin hurtled off, bellowing loudly. The vulpoons screeched with frustration as the prowlgrin brushed them aside, pounced on the carcass and began to feed.

Slip watched, transfixed. He had often fed the pit prowlgrins in the phraxmine, labouring back and forth with buckets of rancid offal. How those poor half-starved creatures would have relished the feast that Tallix was enjoying, Slip thought. Beside him, Nate turned away and tried to drown out the sounds coming from the dewpond by putting his hands over his ears and whistling tunelessly. By the time Tallix came trotting back, there was nothing left of the hammelhorn but its two curling horns and the needle-like pelt.

'Better now?' said Slip.

As if in reply, Tallix rolled around in the grass before him, cleaning the blood from his fur. He was purring loudly as he climbed to his feet. Nate refastened the double saddle, buckling it tightly around the prowlgrin's now swollen girth, and he and Slip climbed back into the saddle. Nate twitched the reins, and the three of them trotted off once more. Glancing over his shoulder, Nate had to admit that the prowlgrin had done a very effective job at cleaning up the dewpond.

It was early evening when, ahead of them, they saw the curious gold-tinged steam above Copperwood. The rain had cleared and the wind had dropped and, pumped out constantly from the phrax-driven workshops and factories and illuminated by the globe lamps, the steam hung over the industrial district like a vast halo. Tallix trotted along the road, seemingly none the worse for wear after the long journey. They approached a low arched bridge spanning a

small river which marked
the northern border of the
district and clip-clopped
over its wooden boards.
As they reached the far
side, Nate glanced down
to find a face staring back
up at him.

'Greetings, stranger.'

Nate tugged at the
reins and brought Tallix to
a halt. 'Greetings,' he said
in reply.

It was a gnarled
slaughterer who had
spoken, his face creased
and his spiky hair as white
as snow. He was sitting
on the bank below the
bridge, a wicker creel by
his side and a hook and
line dangling down into
the swift current from the
end of his fishing rod.

'One more, and I'm
done,' said the slaughterer,
nodding towards the
basket which, as Nate
looked, trembled with
movement as the fish
inside it wriggled and
flopped about.

'Good fishing, is it?'
asked Nate.

'Best in the twelve

districts,' said the old slaughterer, and grinned toothlessly. 'These be steam fish. They grow fast and fat on the cloud dew from the stiltshops.'

Nate was surprised. Back in the Eastern Woods, the slagheaps and waste middens leached into the streams, turning them muddy brown and killing off the fish that once had teemed in their waters. He looked across at the rows of tall stilted workshops, swathed in mist as each one billowed thick steam from the tops of their towering chimneys.

'Tell me, friend,' said Nate, 'do you know of any work to be had here in Copperwood?'

'Work, you say?' said the slaughterer. He shoved the end of his fishing rod into the mud, the shaft resting on a crutch-shaped branch, and climbed to his feet. 'Ay, there's work enough to be had in Copperwood.'

Smoothing down his bulging pocket-filled jacket, he clambered up the riverbank and approached the prowlgrin. Nate dismounted.

'Best thing you can do to find work is go to the hiring posts,' the slaughterer told him. 'That's where the factory owners and stiltshop overseers put all their vacancies and requirements.' He clamped one hand on Nate's shoulder and pointed with the other. 'You want to go along that road there, till you comes to a small square. You can't miss it. There's a statue in the middle of Mangobey Cartshank – founder of our fair Copperwood . . . Anyway, turn left, and you'll find the hiring posts along a ways, on your right.'

Thanking the slaughterer, Nate seized the reins and led Tallix, with Slip still in the saddle, away from the babbling river and into the industrial district. On either side of the broad paved road were the stilted workshops – or stiltshops, as the slaughterer had called them – each one of a slightly different design, depending on what they produced. One was tall and thin and studded with small windows; another was squat and L-shaped, with a tall three-sided chimney; while a third was comprised of three pitch-roofed buildings joined one to the other by tiled walkways. The only feature they all had in common was the tall scaffold of stilts they stood upon, which elevated the buildings high above the ground to allow easy access for the phraxbarges that delivered raw materials and collected the finished products.

'This way,' said Nate, glancing up at Mangobey Cartshank's thick beard and glaring eyes. He turned left onto a narrower road lined with shops and stores which, like all the other buildings in the district, were raised up high above the thoroughfare and hummed and steamed with activity.

The hiring posts came into view – eight tall poles with lengths of diamond-shaped trellis linking them, sandwiched between two stilthouses. Countless pieces of waxed parchment had been nailed to the crossboards and fluttered in the breeze. Nate helped Slip down from the saddle. Tallix jumped up onto a roost post, settled down comfortably and immediately fell asleep.

'*Hammelhornskin rilker required,*' '*Experienced wood turner needed,*' '*Hardworking metalworker to start immediately . . .*' Nate read off the words on the squares of parchment as he scoured the hiring posts for something suitable. His gaze fell upon a note that looked newly posted. He read it quickly through, and grinned. 'Sounds just right for us, Slip,' he said. 'Listen to this.'

Slip turned from the parchment he had been struggling to read and listened.

'*Experienced lamptender and mate wanted in busy phraxchamber works,*' Nate read out. '*Apply Clemp Sprake, foreman, Glemlop and Drews's stiltshop, Steamhammer Yard.*' Nate smiled. 'Perfect for a qualified lamplighter and his apprentice I'd have thought . . .'

'Do you think there'll be anyone there this late?' asked Slip, his large eyes looking up and down the lamplit street.

'In the city that never sleeps?' said Nate, clapping his hand on the grey goblin's shoulder. 'Of course there will, Slip.'

· CHAPTER TWENTY-FIVE ·

Glemlop and Drew's stiltshop was situated on a gently rising hill just to the south of Copperwood's central square, surrounded by numerous other factories. It was a vast construction, formed of two wedge-shaped buildings which mirrored each other, and were joined together with a covered bridge high above the ground, teams of gnokgoblins with laden barrows scurrying from one to the other. Nate was relieved to see the windows still blazing with light and the twin chimneys pumping thick steam into the air.

He and Slip approached the tall factory gates, *Glemlop and Drew* picked out in ornate ironwork letters arching over their thick bars. Nate reached out to tug the bell pull that hung from an iron chain suspended from the left-hand gatepost – but before he had a chance to pull it, the gates swung open. A hulking great figure, twice the size of even the heftiest cloddertrog miner Nate had ever seen, and dressed in a heavy cloak and hood, stepped out of the shadows. With little more than a low grunt, he motioned for them to enter.

Once inside, the gatekeeper pushed the heavy gates shut with an effortless sweep of a gloved hand, before ushering them over to the baskets that hung from the towering stiltshop. Nate and Slip stepped into a large wickerwork construction, big enough to accommodate ten workers at a time, and grasped the handrail. The gatekeeper shuffled over to a thick rope and began to pull on it, hand over hand. Creaking, the basket rose swiftly in the air and ascended to the stiltshop high above.

As he peered down over the edge of the basket at the great hooded figure tugging on the rope, Nate caught the fragrant smell of freshly mown gladegrass. Perhaps, he mused, the gatekeeper had slept under the stars at Waif Glen, just like he and Slip had.

The basket reached the stiltshop and passed through a trapdoor into the cavernous heart of the factory itself. Stepping out, Nate and Slip found themselves staring up at five vast metal chambers suspended by chains from the roofbeams, each one in various stages of completion. On the scaffolding around them, an army of cloaked and hooded workers hammered, riveted and soldered curved sheets of metal, like the scales of a fish, into place. Beside them, on sumpwood workbenches, engineers and gear fitters worked on the intricate mechanisms that would connect the outer scales of the chamber to one another, while below, on vast anvils on the stiltshop floor, phrax-powered hammers beat out metal sheets, ready to be cut and shaped.

It was to these huge contraptions with their glowing lamps that Nate's gaze was instinctively drawn. Powered by phraxcrystals, the lamps of the machines needed to be calibrated and tended to at all times.

Two figures turned from the first of the three great hammers and motioned for Nate and Slip to approach. Overhead, the cacophony of hammering and hissing made it impossible to speak or be heard. The two figures – like all the workers – wore heavy hoods and cloaks. They took Nate and Slip by the arm and led them up a spiral staircase at the centre of the stiltshop and into a large glazed latticework chamber high in the roof rafters.

Nate and Slip looked around them as they entered, and the second of the two figures pulled the circular glass door shut behind him with a *clang*. Instantly, the din of the stiltshop was silenced, though Nate's ears still rang for several moments afterwards. The two figures pulled off their hoods and cloaks. One was a heavy-set flathead goblin with one dark brown eye and one of piercing blue. The other was a tall thin fourthling with braided side-whiskers and an aquiline nose.

'I'm looking for Clemp Sprake,' said Nate.

'You've found him,' said the flathead goblin, sitting down at a floating lectern on which the pieces of a lamp lay in a disordered heap. 'I suppose you've come about the lamptending job.'

Nate nodded. Ignoring the rest of them, the fourthling turned away and began examining a sheaf of blueprints which hung from a cord in the centre of the chamber. Clemp Sprake looked closely at Nate, then at Slip, his eyes narrowing suspiciously.

'Have you any experience of working in a stiltshop?' he said, his voice gruff and abrupt.

'Not exactly,' said Nate. 'But I'm hardworking, diligent, and a very quick learner. And my apprentice here is—'

'We at Glemlop and Drew's require an experienced lamptender,' Clemp Sprake said, cutting him short. 'If you don't have experience of stiltshops, you're no use to me.'

'But I do have experience of—' Nate began.

'I said, you're no use to me,' said the foreman irritably.

Nate looked at Slip and shrugged, and the pair of them were about to leave when the tall figure of the fourthling turned from the blueprints.

'What exactly *do* you have experience of?' he asked. He pushed back the folds of his short-sleeved topcoat and thrust his hands deep into the pockets of his triple-fronted waistcoat. 'Well?' he said.

'I'm a lamplighter,' said Nate, 'and this here is my apprentice, Slip. Back in the phraxmine in the Eastern Woods, it was my job to keep the lamps burning at precisely the right degree of light to ensure that the phraxcrystals—'

'Lamplighter?' Clemp Sprake interrupted. He shoved the various bits and pieces of the dismantled lamp towards him. 'If you know about lamps, then fix this.'

Nate stepped forward. The lamp was a rear-feed sumplamp. Although too cumbersome for use in the phraxmines, he had seen one before. The trick, he knew, when adjusting the wick, was to ensure that the cotter screw was aligned with the bevel crank . . .

'My name is Friston Drew,' said the fourthling, his eyes watching the youth's nimble fingers. 'Before he died, my partner and I built up the finest phraxchamber works in Copperwood. We employ only the most skilled workers; the finest in their fields . . .'

'I was the best lamplighter in the Prade phraxmine, sir,' Nate

broke in, glancing up as he cocked the oil spigot and screwed the reservoir to the base. 'My father taught me everything he knew . . .'

Just then, the door burst open. A tall expensively dressed youth strode into the chamber, twirling a bone-handled cane. 'Evening, Father,' he said cheerily.

'Branxford,' the older fourthling said, peering over the top of his steel-rimmed spectacles. 'To what do we owe the pleasure?'

'Can't a son visit his father without there being a reason?' said Branxford. He smiled. 'Though since you're asking, there is a little matter I'd like to raise . . .'

Friston Drew shook his head wearily. 'Don't tell me,' he said. 'You need an advance on your allowance.'

'There's a phraxlaunch that's just come onto the market,' said Branxford, tapping the lectern with his cane. 'An absolute beauty, Father! Its phraxchamber is a work of art . . .'

The stilthouse owner snorted. 'And you expect me to pay for it?' he said. 'Just like that! Have you no pride, Branxford? Eh? Don't you think it's time you started working for a living?' He nodded across the room to Nate and Slip. 'You could learn something from these two.'

Slip handed Nate the cotter pin, and Nate buried his head in the lamp as he wound the wick through the complicated arrangement of tiny spigots and wheels. His ears burned bright red as he felt Branxford Drew's gaze boring into his back.

'Look at the skill this young lamplighter has at his fingertips,' said Friston Drew. 'The way he is able to re-calibrate this sumplamp in moments shows that he has spent years of patient study, which he is now passing on to an apprentice . . .'

Nate glanced round to see Branxford glaring back at him and Slip, a look of barely concealed loathing on his face. His nostrils were flared; an eyebrow was arched.

'Look like a couple of itinerant phraxminers to me,' he sneered, then turned back to his father. 'Come on, Father,' he said, his voice wheedling. 'If I don't come up with the cash, I'll lose the launch. And she really is a beauty . . .'

Shaking his head, Friston Drew pulled a wad of notes from his pocket. He peeled off half a dozen.

'Then there's the shipwright's commission,' said Branxford. 'And the small matter of the berthing costs . . .'

Drew pulled off a dozen more of the notes and thrust the whole lot into his son's outstretched hand.

'This is the last time, Branxford,' he said grimly. He nodded across to Nate. 'This young chap's father taught him everything he knows, whereas it seems that I—'

'Spare me the lecture,' said Branxford, slipping the folded notes into his waistcoat pocket. He turned on his heels and marched back across the room, his topcoat flapping. Dropping his shoulder, he brushed against Nate as he passed him, making the young phraxminer grip hold of the lamp protectively. The door slammed as Branxford disappeared from view down the spiral staircase. Nate placed the lamp down on the floating lectern, lit the wick and lowered the cowl. The chamber was filled with a bright yellow glow.

'There,' he said.

Friston Drew crossed the room towards him, his smiling face gleaming in the light. 'Very impressive,' he said. 'I think we can use your skills here at Glemlop and Drew's. How does sixty gladers a week and comfortable lodging sound?'

'Thank you, sir,' said Nate, noticing Slip's delighted gasp. 'We won't let you down.'

· CHAPTER TWENTY-SIX ·

Nate stepped out of the apothecary's shop into the busy main square of Copperwood. Around the statue of Mangobey Cartshank, the stalls of the market traders groaned beneath the weight of produce; huge violet-tinged glade cabbages, stacks of corncobs a stride long, and great steaming mountains of freshly pickled tripweed.

In the steam-nourished gardens and allotments that filled every available space beneath the cabin rows of Copperwood, vegetables grew fast and enormous and kept the stiltshop workers well fed. Between the shifts at the phraxchamber works, Nate's own allotment was lovingly tended by Slip, and was awash with magnificent blue pumpkins of fantastic size.

Had it really only been six months since they'd arrived in Copperwood? Nate could scarcely believe it. What with the ever-changing demands of the job, evenings in the town and excursions to Waif Glen and Old Forest, Nate felt he had lived all his life in Great Glade. And as if he didn't have enough to do, he'd even taken up the city's favourite sport, the exhilarating game of thousandsticks . . . Though, to be honest, he was now beginning to regret it.

Nate stretched, and then grimaced at the painful twinge in his back.

'Serves me right for getting in the way of a hill charge,' he muttered, patting the glass phial he'd just purchased, which nestled safely in his heavy work jacket.

He'd had a long and arduous day at work. The morning had been taken up with an emergency on the foundry deck, caused by a clumsy hammerhead who had accidently driven a stave through a lamp cowl, shattering the glass and snuffing out the light. The phraxhammer had threatened to go critical, and it was only Nate's quick thinking – improvising with one of the glassworker's blowtorches while he replaced the cowl – that had averted a full-scale catastrophe.

Then all afternoon it had been Nate's job to supervise the loading of finished phraxchambers on board the visiting phraxbarge. Twenty lamps he'd had to keep fuelled and perfectly calibrated, to prevent the intricately tooled chambers with their shards of stormphrax from losing buoyancy and crashing down to earth. It had been a perfect loading, and the foreman, Clemp Sprake, had thanked Nate and Slip personally and given them a ten-glader bonus.

Just as well, thought Nate, otherwise he could not have afforded the tiny phial of finest Riverrise water, which had come from the aqueduct of the far-off City of Night. A few drops of the crystal-clear liquid and his aching back would be no more than a distant memory.

Nate turned out of the square and made his way down a broad avenue lined with stiltshops, each one wreathed in clouds of steam. At the far end, he turned left and climbed onto a timbered walkway that snaked its way through luxuriantly sprouting garden plots until he reached the cabin rows. Built on low stilts, three cabins high and fifty long, with each tier connected by ladders and boasting a generous balcony, the cabin rows were where the workers of Copperwood made their homes. Like everywhere else in the district, they bustled with life – cloddertrog matrons hanging out their laundry; goblin and mobgnome young'uns playing skittles while their mothers boiled lake gourd and snowleaf stew in huge cauldrons on the balconies above.

Nate loved it, and so did Slip. Reaching the cabin row where they lodged, Nate glanced up to see his friend up on the second-tier balcony, reclining on a sumpwood cradle and hollowing out a blue pumpkin twice his size.

'Don't tell me,' Nate called up, 'pumpkin stew for supper. Or is it pumpkin pie?'

'Neither, friend Nate,' Slip laughed, waving a large ladle covered in seeds. 'It's pumpkin fritters. Old Ma Pantin from below-door showed Slip how . . .'

'I can't wait,' chuckled Nate as he climbed the ladder to the second-tier balcony. He'd just have time for a quick bite before thousandsticks practice – if he was quick, that is.

He stepped onto the polished copperwood of the balcony, with its rich smell of resin oil, and was about to make his way along to the tenth cabin, when a sound from above made him pause. It was a low rumbling groan – the sound of someone, or something, in pain. And it was coming from the third tier. Nate walked back to the ladder and began to climb.

The cabins on the third tier of the cabin row were mostly empty, a clan of gnokgoblins having moved out in the middle of

the night a month earlier without telling anyone they were leaving. There were a couple of hammerhead foundry workers at the far end, and the mysterious gatekeeper from Glemlop and Drew's, who had a cabin just above Nate and Slip. He kept himself to himself, and neither Nate nor Slip – nor anyone else for that matter – had ever seen him without his heavy cloak and hood.

Nate reached the third-tier balcony and heard the groan again. If it *was* the gatekeeper, he sounded in a bad way. He approached the tenth cabin and gently knocked on the door. A low growl, rising to a strangulated howl, sounded from inside the cabin.

'Are you all right?' Nate called. 'Do you need help?'

From the other side of the door there came a *thud*, followed by a scratching sound – then silence. Carefully, Nate tried the handle. The door was unlocked. Slowly, he pushed it open and stepped gingerly inside. The cabin was dark, but even in the gloom Nate was surprised to see that it was almost completely devoid of furniture. In one corner, the heavy cloak and hood hung from a hook; in the other . . .

Nate stopped stock-still and felt his heart hammering in his chest. There was a large circular nest of finely woven gladegrass, looking like a great cocoon, which filled the corner of the cabin. Within it, the huge figure of the gatekeeper, dressed in what at first glance seemed to Nate to be a heavy fur coat, lay slumped.

'Hello . . . ?' Nate approached the figure. 'Can I help?'

With another groan of pain, the gatekeeper rolled over and Nate found himself face to face with a huge and hairy mountain of a beast. When their eyes met, the creature threw back its head, bared its teeth and groaned at the ceiling.

'You're . . . you're . . .' Nate trembled, hardly daring to move. 'A banderbear!'

'Wuh,' the gatekeeper groaned softly, and raised a giant paw to its cheek. 'Wuu-uh?'

The creature was truly enormous – even down on its broad haunches it was taller than Nate – and built like a vast pyramid. It had great tree-trunk legs and long powerful arms. Every one of the four claws at the end of each limb were as long as Nate's forearms, while the two tusks that curved up from its jutting lower jaw were longer still. Only the creature's ears – delicate and fluttering – did not look as though they had been hewn from solid rock.

Nate had heard stories about these amazing creatures, looked at pictures of them in faded bark-scrolls, but he'd never before seen one in the flesh. These solitary giants had long ago abandoned the polluted forests of the Eastern Roosts and the busy trade routes around Great Glade. Even in far off Hive, their yodels were seldom heard these days. Who could have guessed then that beneath the heavy cloak and hood there was a banderbear living in the very heart of the city?

The creature fixed Nate with its sad eyes. 'Wuu-uh?' it groaned again.

Despite its size, the banderbear struck Nate as looking oddly vulnerable. He swallowed nervously.

'What's the matter?' he said.

The banderbear opened its mouth wide, grimacing with pain as it did so. It prodded around clumsily inside with a single claw.

'Uh-uuh!' it moaned.

Nate drew closer and found himself staring into the creature's cavernous mouth, over the rows of savage yellowed teeth and down the dark gaping tunnel of its throat . . . And then he saw it. At the back of the mouth, on the left, was an angry abscess, red raw and flecked with pus, deep in the gum.

'Looks nasty,' Nate muttered. 'No wonder you're in pain.'

'Wuh-wuh! Whu-uuuh!' the banderbear groaned, and a large tear rolled down its furry face from the corner of each eye.

Without thinking twice, Nate reached into the pocket of his work coat and pulled out the phial of expensive Riverrise water. He uncorked it.

'Here,' Nate whispered. 'I've got something that'll help.'

Gently, he poured the contents – all thirty gladers' worth – onto the red and swollen gum. The banderbear flinched but held its great head still.

The effect was almost instant, for Nate just had time to withdraw his hand from the creature's mouth before it was up on its feet, paws held out wide to its side. A moment later, the banderbear fell upon him, and Nate felt those great powerful arms wrap themselves warmly around his body. He breathed deep the sweet odour of dry gladegrass as he was crushed against the creature's belly in a delighted embrace . . .

'Wuh-wuh,' said the banderbear at last and released its grip. It pointed to the phial in Nate's hand and scratched its head questioningly.

'This?' said Nate. 'It's Riverrise water. I bought it from a gabtroll apothecaress for a knock I picked up at thousandsticks.' He smiled. 'But you needed it more than me.'

The banderbear shook its head in wonderment, its eyes twinkling.

It clearly understood just how expensive the medicine was. It raised a giant paw to its chest and tapped on it lightly.

'Weelum,' he said.

Nate held out his hand. 'Nate,' he replied. 'Pleased to meet you, Weelum.'

The banderbear's eyes twinkled and his tiny ears fluttered.

'Weelum, Nate,' he said, his voice a deep rumbling growl as he took Nate's hand and shook it solemnly. 'Fr-wuh-iends.'

· CHAPTER TWENTY-SEVEN ·

'The gatekeeper?' said Slip, his eyes wide with astonishment. 'A banderbear? And living up the ladder from Slip and friend Nate all this time? Why, who'd have thought it?' He shovelled another pumpkin fritter onto Nate's platter and joined him at the small cabin table. 'This city is full of wonders,' he said. 'A cosy cabin and a fine job. Great big vegetables springing out of the ground, just asking to be eaten. Bucketloads of fish in the streams, just waiting to be caught. And now . . . now, banderbears!'

Slip shook his head at these marvels, unheard of in the grim mining camps of the Eastern Woods.

'Not forgetting the best pumpkin fritters I've ever tasted!' said Nate, clearing the last morsel from his plate. 'Give my compliments to Ma Pantin, Slip. I'm off to thousandsticks practice.'

He climbed to his feet, only to wince with pain at the twinge in his back.

'Thousandsticks practice?' Slip queried, clearing the table and picking up a trowel and spade. 'Why doesn't friend Nate help Slip down at the allotment. Give his back a rest?'

'Thanks, but no thanks,' smiled Nate, crossing the cabin to the bunks in the far corner, where a jumble of equipment lay next to his box of memories. 'I'll take the thousandsticks hills any day over that pumpkin patch of yours, Slip.'

Bending down stiffly, Nate picked up heavy padded breast- and backplates and slipped them over his shoulders. Next, he strapped on the thick boots with their iron cleats, before pulling a wide spatula-like glove – his shoving glove – onto his left hand and picking up the long thousandstick, with its heavy club at one end and splayed wicker 'claw' at the other, from where it was propped against the wall. Scooping up the padded helmet next to it in his gloved hand, he made for the door and onto the copperwood balcony, the iron boot cleats clattering underfoot.

'Take care, friend Nate,' Slip called after him.

'I'll try,' Nate called back as he clambered down the ladders to the ground below, though even as he spoke, he knew it would be a tall order.

The citizens of Great Glade took their favourite sport seriously, and none more so than the team from Copperwood – especially now, with the annual Reckoning almost upon them. With only three months to go, the hundred-strong team from the Copperwood district was training ferociously.

In the Reckoning, they would be playing against teams from the eleven other districts on the Great Glade field out in the Silver Pastures. The field consisted of an outer track, which surrounded six low hills connected to each other by a series of paths or 'inner tracks', with a single high hill at the centre.

Having marched for a minute or so round the outer track, the *crack* of the phraxpistol would signal that the teams could enter the field. At this time, tactics took over, as each team tried to dominate the inner tracks, blocking opponents while giving their team mates a clear run at the 'high pine' – a tall pole atop the central hill.

The aim of the game was for a player to climb to the platform at the top of the pole and claim victory for his team. It sounded simple enough, yet a Reckoning match could take a long time. The previous year, six hours had passed before New Lake had finally won, by which time the total number of players on the field had dwindled to less than half.

Any player who fell, set foot, or was shoved, onto one of the gravel beds between the inner tracks was out of the match. Using their gloves and thousandsticks, players endeavoured to do just that to their opponents. Pushing, prodding and lifting were all allowed, with any number of players joining in what was termed a 'great shove'. Tripping, hitting or kicking, however, were *not* allowed – and nor, on pain of expulsion from the game, was the use of the thousandstick as a weapon. In the fever of a close match, rules were of course broken, but with six hill marshals on prowlgrinback and a seventh sky marshal hovering above in a phraxcraft, few got away with it.

Nate was running late after his encounter with the gatekeeper and, curiosity awoken, his head was still buzzing with thoughts of the banderbear living just overhead. Where had he come from? he wondered. Who had hired him at the phraxchamber works? And why did he wear the cloak and heavy hood whenever he went out?

Cramming his helmet onto his head, he clattered down the walkway and out onto the avenue which led to Mangobey Cartshank Square. It was probably this that saved him, for at that moment a two-seater phraxlaunch came hurtling round the corner, a jet of phraxflame blasting out behind it and thick clouds of ice-cold steam leaving a trail of frost on the roofs, windows and walls of the buildings it passed.

Nate didn't see it coming. With a sickening crunch, the jutting foil on the portside of the vessel struck him a glancing blow on the back of the head, spinning him round and sending him sprawling.

The pilot brought the sleek craft to an abrupt halt, then flew back round to hover above him. Nate's padded armour and helmet had saved him from injury, but his expensive thousandstick had been snapped in two. Getting slowly to his feet – the pain in his back more intense than ever – Nate looked up at the elegant phraxlaunch, its low funnel pumping out clouds of steam into the golden lamplit night as it hung in the air above him.

There was a low-slung burnished metal canopy over the padded seats, casting the two occupants into dark shadow. The figure at the wheel leaned forward and, as he stared down, his face twisted into a sneer of contempt.

'Oh, it's you,' he said.

Nate stared back at Branxford Drew evenly, aware that it might not be wise to argue with his boss's son. Ever since their first meeting, Nate had been aware that the pampered factory owner's son disliked him, and as Nate had grown more successful in the phraxchamber works, that dislike had turned to something bordering on hate.

'You really ought to watch where you're going, lamplighter,' he snarled. 'Could have been a nasty accident.'

Nate nodded. Branxford glanced down at the shattered thousandstick beside him and smiled unpleasantly. He reached into his elegant waistcoat and drew out a ten-glader note, which he let flutter down to the ground below. It came to rest at Nate's feet.

'Buy yourself a new stick, lamplighter,' Branxford sneered. 'When we New Lakers run into you at the Reckoning,' he snorted, 'you're going to need it!'

His lips curled into a scornful smile, and there was hatred in his eyes. But Nate ignored it. The factory owner's spoiled son no longer interested him, for he was staring into the eyes of the phraxlaunch's passenger, who had leaned forward and was gazing down at him – the clear green eyes of Eudoxia Prade.

· CHAPTER TWENTY-EIGHT ·

The low afternoon sun streamed in through the upper windows of the Long Gallery of Lake Landing. It made the polished floor gleam like liquid gold, and bathed the portraits and statues that hung from the walls and stood on pedestals in a warm glow that seemed almost to bring them to life.

'I'd forgotten how beautiful Lake Landing is,' the tall figure in the stylish, though slightly shabby, clothes of a skytavern gambler commented, his dour expression softening as he stared at the ancient lufwood panel painting before him.

'It's been a long time since you were last here, Ambris, old friend,' noted his companion, who was dressed in the flowing robes of an academic. He stroked his neck beard thoughtfully. '*Too* long – and with so many disappearing these days, I was beginning to fear that you too might have gone missing.'

'Not missing, just plying my trade, Cassix,' the tall figure replied, 'aboard countless skytaverns, from the *Blue Lemkin* out of the Northern Reaches to the *Deadbolt Vulpoon* from the Eastern Woods.'

Brow furrowed, he adjusted his wire-rimmed spectacles and, stooping forward, peered closely at the intricate brush strokes. The portrait was of a stout gnokgoblin with wise hooded eyes, a crumpled brow and wearing the robes and chains of high office.

'By the look of his clothes,' said the curator, adjusting the embroidered sleeves of his long dark robes, 'this is a portrait of a High Master of the Lake Landing Academy in the First Age of Flight . . .'

'Parsimmon, I think you'll find, old friend,' interrupted Ambris, pushing back the peak of his crushed funnel hat as he stood up straight.

The old curator turned to him, a single bushy eyebrow raised.

'Parsimmon?'

'The first High Master of Lake Landing was a gnokgoblin by the name of Parsimmon,' the tall figure explained, thrusting his hands deep into the pockets of his breeches. 'He started out as a lowly assistant librarian and worked his way up, serving as High Master for approaching seven decades.' He smiled, his thin lips stretching across his uneven teeth, and added, 'If I'm not very much mistaken, that is.'

The curator sighed and shook his head. 'The *Professor*, mistaken?' he said, his gnarled fingers interlaced. 'I don't think so.'

Ambris turned to him, a look of surprise on his face. 'How did you know they call me that on the skytaverns?' he said.

Curator Cassix Lodestone smiled. 'Oh, I keep one ear to the ground and the other to the sky, Ambris. Your skill at the gaming tables is the

175

talk of the Twelve Districts – equalled only by your encyclopaedic knowledge of the past. After all, you were always my most promising student.'

Ambris smiled in turn and shook his head ruefully. 'Ah, yes, the good old days,' he said. His face hardened. 'Before the Academy got cold feet . . .'

A decade had passed since the original Society of Descenders – a division of the School of Edge Cliff Studies – had been forced to close through lack of funds. Its laboratories and stone polishing chambers had been cleared; its staff and members told to disperse. Some had found posts in the other colleges and schools, but their dean, Professor Cassix Lodestone, had been so steeped in Cliff studies that no other institution would have taken him in, even had he chosen to seek a position with them. Six months or so ago, after years of struggling for support and the more recent controversy after the failed voyage of the *Archemax*, he had left the School and accepted the job of curator in the Long Gallery of the Lake Landing Academy, although his knowledge of painting and sculpture was limited, to say the least. As for his talented deputy, Ambris Hentadile, robbed of his academic apprenticeship when the Society was closed, he had left the Cloud Quarter for ever ten years earlier, using – some would say, misusing – his sharp intellect that had once singled him out for academic greatness, to prosper at the gaming tables of the skytaverns that crisscrossed the Edge skies.

'Now the School of Edge Cliff Studies itself is threatened,' Cassix Lodestone was saying, turning away and continuing along the gallery, his hands clasped behind his back. 'Their funding has been cut. Various academics have been lured away . . . I'm telling you, Ambris, now that Quove Lentis, High Professor of Flight, has withdrawn his support for Edge Cliff Studies, there'll be no more expeditions over the Edge . . .'

He fell still, aware that a grizzled woodtroll was standing within earshot. The old fellow was probably a gallery visitor, there to admire the paintings, but Cassix Lodestone knew that it was always as well to be careful. He waited until the woodtroll had crossed the gallery to the opposite wall before returning to his theme.

'It's all so short-sighted,' he said, shaking his head wearily. 'Who knows what fascinating – not to say, crucial – academic discoveries could be made?'

The Professor nodded as the pair of them made their way slowly along the row of portraits. He paused before a painting which represented the historic moment when New Undertown's Council of Three had become the famous Council of Eight, early in the Second Age of Flight. Cassix stopped beside him.

'Cancaresse – the Keeper of Waif Glen. Parsimmon, again,' said the Professor, pointing to the characters staring back at them from the painted wooden panel. 'And that low-belly was mayor of New Undertown more than five centuries ago. Hebb Lub-drub, his name, I believe. And beside them are Fenbrus Lodd and his daughter, Varis; the Professors of Light and Darkness and . . .'

Ambris Hentadile fell still. He stared at the figure on the left – an old individual with a clipped beard, simple homespun robes and an expression of absolute calm in his grey-green eyes. Like Ambris himself, his academic apprenticeship had been cut short, and he had subsequently been imprisoned for decades. Yet he had emerged from his stinking cell to take up a position on the Council of Eight, from which he guided the Free Glades through war, and on to years of peace and harmony.

'Cowlquape Pentephraxis,' Ambris breathed. 'The great scholar of Earth and Sky . . . He championed the pursuit of knowledge wherever it lay.'

'Indeed,' said the former dean sadly. 'But High Professor of Flight, Quove Lentis, is no Cowlquape Pentephraxis. Unfortunately, our dear Lentis has decided that an alliance with the waifs of Riverrise – securing, as rumour has it, his own personal supplies of water from the sacred Riverrise spring – is more important than the quest for knowledge. And we all know the waifs' views of Edge Cliff Studies. They consider it blasphemy of the worst kind.'

'Then it's true,' Ambris Hentadile broke in. 'There will be no attempt to rescue the last expedition. My brother . . .'

Cassix Lodestone took a sharp intake of breath and stared fixedly at the painting, ignoring his companion's searching gaze. 'Ifflix,' he said. 'Poor, dear Ifflix . . .'.

'Ifflix Hentadile,' said Ambris, nodding. 'My younger brother. He joined the School of Edge Cliff Studies because of me. He revived the Society of Descenders because of the stories I told him when he was a young'un. He led that expedition to make me proud. And now he has been shamefully abandoned . . .'

Cassix clasped his friend by the hands. 'Oh, Ambris, I'm so sorry.'

'Yes, well, I for one am not prepared to leave things as they are,' said Ambris grimly, his brow knitted with resolve. 'That's why I'm here in Great Glade. I'm going to put together an expedition to go in search of my brother, and I'm looking for trained descenders to go with me.'

'I'm afraid you won't find any in Great Glade who'd admit to being descenders, let alone join an expedition,' replied Cassix, shaking his head. 'Even talking of it is likely to land you in the constabulary cells.'

'But I've got to do something!' Ambris Hentadile's voice was raised, causing several visitors to the gallery to look in his direction and Cassix Lodestone to seize him by the arm.

'There is somewhere you could try,' he whispered urgently, his eyes darting round the gallery as he spoke. 'The Sumpwood Bridge Academy in Hive . . .'

'Hive?' Ambris said.

At that moment, a jumble of excited voices and a clatter of footsteps echoed around the high vaulted ceiling of the gallery. Cassix, his lips pursed and cheeks flexing and unflexing as he gritted his teeth, turned to the front entrance to see a dozen noisy young'uns scurrying into the hall and come sliding across the polished floor. They swept past the legs of the Professor and the old curator like water round lake reeds, heedless of the calls of the gabtroll matron with them to 'slow down'.

Cassix Lodestone turned on his heel, his bright deep-set eyes blazing. 'Be careful! Be careful!' he cried out as they clustered round a huge glass statue, gleaming in the sunlight that streamed in at the far end of the hall. 'No touching . . . I said, *no touching!*' He glanced back at the Professor. 'Excuse me one moment, Ambris, while I . . .'

He broke away and strode across the floor, the wooden soles of his clogs rapping against the varnished floorboards as he brushed past the other visitors to the gallery. His agitated voice floated back as he addressed the gabtroll.

'Madame you must keep the young'uns in your charge under control. Otherwise I shall have to ask you to leave . . . No *touching!*'

Ambris Hentadile smiled to himself. Cassix Lodestone, it seemed, was as protective of the paintings and sculptures in the Long Gallery as he had once been of his students. How excited he must have been when Ambris's younger brother had revived the Society of Descenders and gained support for an expedition. Now those hopes and dreams lay shattered. As Ambris watched, the old curator flapped protectively round the fragile statue of Tweezel the venerable spindlebug, companion of Mother Maris, founder of the Gardens of Light and inventor of the varnish that had made possible the Second Age of Flight.

Commissioned shortly after his death to commemorate his three hundred and fifty years of life, the statue was a work of art. It had been fashioned by teams of master glassworkers, who had spent long hours carefully blowing into the glowing balls of molten glass with long pipes to form its thorax, its abdomen and its curiously angular head, while others had teased out spindly legs and delicate feelers with their callipers, pincers and crimping knives. The statue of the glassy insect they had created was so life-like, it was as though the wise old creature was still there among them.

To live for three hundred and fifty years, Ambris Hentadile mused. How much the spindlebug must have seen in that time! Born in the untamed Deepwoods, educated in the streets of ancient Undertown, servant to Linius Pallitax, the greatest Most High Academe ever to have taken office in Old Sanctaphrax . . . Living through all three ages of flight!

While I . . . ?

Ambris Hentadile turned away. Suddenly, his own achievements seemed so very small – his brief academic career, brilliant but short lived; the years of idle gambling, bar fights and lectures delivered in baskets suspended over the Deepwoods to bored goblin matrons.

'Some "professor" I am,' he murmured ruefully. But it's all about to change, he told himself. There would be no more gambling. He would rescue Ifflix; he owed his little brother that much at least. And besides, the prospect of venturing over the Edge had begun to clear his head, drive away all the old bitterness, and give his life a new meaning. He liked the feeling.

Ambris turned from the picture and made his way down the hall in the direction of an increasingly flustered Cassix Lodestone. The curator's arms were flapping and his voice had become shrill. Other visitors to the Long Gallery were looking at him askance – or rather, *most* of them. One young fourthling, Ambris noticed, was standing in front of a large portrait of a Commander of the Freeglade Lancers mounted upon prowlgrinback, oblivious to the disturbance.

What was more, Ambris suddenly realized, he recognized him. He came closer, clearing his throat as he did so.

The youth didn't seem to notice. He was staring intently at a particular part of the painting, his attention gripped by a detail in the picture – a small medallion which hung from a leather cord round the commander's neck.

It was a portrait miniature on a small round lufwood panel. In ancient times, in the Knights Academy of Old Sanctaphrax, such self portraits were attached to the knights' swords in a special ceremony. That was in the First Age of Flight. This portrait, though, was from early in the Third Age of Flight, if the Professor wasn't mistaken.

It was of Commander Rook Barkwater of the Freeglade Lancers, hero of the war for the Free Glades and the countless skirmishes and raids in their defence afterwards. Later, he had travelled with the waif, Cancaresse, to Riverrise when that mysterious city was still half myth and little more than a rocky spire rising up from the

terrifying Nightwoods. Commander Barkwater had never returned.

'I wonder what ever became of him?' the Professor mused.

Realizing that someone was talking to him, the youth looked round. In a flash, the expression on his face changed from one of mild puzzlement to sudden recognition.

'Professor!' he exclaimed, and thrust out his hand. 'How good to see you!' He frowned. 'After the knife fight, I couldn't find you. I wanted to thank you. For protecting me in the skytavern.'

'You won that splinters game fair and square, lad,' said Ambris Hentadile with a shrug. 'Besides, I can't abide the powerful picking on the weak.' He nodded towards the portrait in front of them. 'Any more than Rook Barkwater could.'

'You know who he is?'

'Of course,' said the Professor, his face creasing up with amusement. 'And from the way you were staring at the painting, I thought you did too.'

The youth shook his head. 'No, I was just passing by when something in the painting caught my eye . . .'

'The medallion round his neck?' the Professor asked.

'Yes,' said the youth, blushing.

'It's a sword miniature by the look of it,' said the Professor knowledgeably, 'of an ancestor from the First Age of Flight. Probably a keepsake passed down the generations from—'

'Father to son?' whispered the youth, his eyes returning to the painting.

'Yes, quite possibly,' said the Professor with a smile. The lad would make an enthusiastic student of history. He paused. 'By the way,' he said, 'in all the excitement, we were never properly introduced. I'm Ambris Hentadile, otherwise known as the Professor. And you are?'

'Nate,' said the youth, his gaze still on the tiny portrait round the commander's neck. 'Nate Quarter.'

'*Quarter?*' said the Professor with a delighted smile. He pushed his spectacles up onto the bridge of his nose. 'By Earth and Sky, that's a coincidence.'

'Coincidence?' said Nate.

'Barkwater – Bar-*kwater*,' said the Professor, pronouncing the second half of the name carefully. 'Over the centuries, the Barkwater name became shortened to Quarter. It's a common enough occurrence with the old Free Glades names. "Pentephraxis" to "Rackis"; "Pompolnius" to "Pulnix" – and so on. Who knows, you might even be distantly related to the great Rook Barkwater himself, Nate Quarter!'

The Professor laughed, but stopped when he saw the look of wide-eyed wonder in the youth's eyes.

'Are you all right, Nate? You've gone as white as a spidersilk sail.'

'I'm fine, Professor . . . fine,' said Nate, his hand slipping inside his underjacket and closing round the medallion beneath.

His father had always told him that they were descended from one of the oldest families in Great Glade, and it now seemed that he was right. Nate felt a great wave of pride surge within him, mixed with a sharp pang of sorrow that his father wasn't here to see the portrait of their illustrious ancestor hanging here in this magnificent gallery. Standing next to the Professor, so knowledgeable and well informed, Nate felt suddenly shy. After all, no matter who he might be descended from, he was still just a humble lamplighter working in a stilthouse factory in Copperwood.

Just then, a cry of greeting echoed across the hall. The Professor turned to see a young fashionably dressed Great Glader striding towards them, her arms outstretched and a beautiful smile on her lips.

'*There* you are, Nate,' she said, tossing her hair away from her face. 'I've been looking all over.'

'Eudoxia,' said Nate, excited to see his friend. Over the last few weeks the pair of them had spent more and more time in each other's company – despite Branxford's mounting displeasure. 'You remember the Professor I told you about – the one who helped me on board the *Deadbolt Vulpoon*?'

'At the splinters table?' said Eudoxia, her head tilted to one side.

'That's it,' said Nate. 'Well, this is him.'

'Ambris Hentadile,' said the Professor, extending his hand. 'Pleased to meet you, Miss Eudoxia.'

'And I'm pleased to meet you, Professor,' said Eudoxia sweetly. 'Nate told me how disappointed he was that he couldn't thank you for your kindness at the time,' she added, a beguiling smile plucking at the corners of her mouth.

'If there is any way I can repay your kindness . . .' said Nate.

The Professor pushed his crushed funnel hat back on his head and scratched his temples. 'As a matter of fact, there *is* something,' he said. 'I'm looking for lodgings while I attend to a few matters here in Great Glade. I don't suppose you know of anywhere . . . ?'

'Lodgings!' said Nate, a broad grin spreading over his face. 'Well, that's easy. There are half a dozen rooms for the asking in the cabin row where I live.' He exchanged smiles with his companion. 'It's not fashionable like New Lake or steeped in history like the Free Glades district, but in my humble opinion Copperwood is the friendliest, most welcoming district in the Big Steam.'

Ambris Hentadile glanced round at Cassix Lodestone. The old curator had finally managed to move the excitable young'uns to a corner of the gallery where they could do no harm and was returning, the silver threads of his embroidered sleeves glinting in the deepening sunlight. Ambris leaned forward and patted Nate warmly on the arm.

'Thank you, Nate Quarter,' he said. 'It sounds perfect.'

· CHAPTER TWENTY-NINE ·

'What in all that is sacred is going on?' said Togtuft Hegg, Hive archivist of the Sumpwood Bridge, looking up from the light magnifier, where everything had suddenly blurred. 'I can't see a thing.'

'It's coming from outside,' his colleague – Klug Junkers – replied, jumping to his feet and striding to the door.

The whole chamber was shaking now, with books and papers slipping from the tabletops, apparatus clattering about on the shelves and dust rising up from every surface, filling the sun-shot air with a cloud of dancing specks. The rumbling grew louder. Togtuft put the valuable light magnifier carefully down on the floor, pulled off his heavy topcoat and placed it over the fragile instrument, then followed Klug outside.

'Make way! Make way!' a loud voice shouted from their left as a rotund gnokgoblin carrying a long tasselled spear strode across the bridge, waving his free arm about stiffly.

Behind him, clattering over the sumpwood boards, were eighteen orange prowlgrins, triple-harnessed and lined up in six rows. Their freshly brushed fur gleamed like burnished copper and, as they struggled forward, the sprays of ornamental feathers secured to their shoulder straps waved in the breeze. Despite their number, their eyes bulged and their legs shook with the effort of pulling the heavy load over the trembling boards of the swaying bridge.

'It's amazing they can move at all,' said Klug with a grin. 'Look at the *size* of her!'

Togtuft shook his head in wonder. Even among grossmothers, clan leader Meadowdew was huge. Vast rolls of fat hung from her face, obscuring her eyes and reducing her breathing to a series of snuffled snorts. Like molten wax, the fat flopped down, swallowing up her neck and resting on her heaving shoulders. As for her body, great folds of flesh sagged over the sides of her carriage, the woodrose-pink taffeta of her dress straining at the seams, threatening at any moment to give way to an undignified tear.

'There must be a High Council meeting,' said Togtuft.

Klug nodded. Why else would Grossmother Meadowdew have left the magnificent Gyle Palace on the summit of East Ridge, squeezed herself into her state carriage – a specially designed eight-wheel affair with a vast padded bench, ornate gold trim and a framework capable of supporting half a dozen ironwood trees – and endured the bumps and jolts of the steep cobbled streets of Hive as she made her way to the great Clan Hall high atop West Ridge?

'*Make way!*' bellowed the gnokgoblin, and jabbed his spear at a bevy of cloddertrog urchins, all wide-eyed with wonder at the sight before them and hoping to touch a fold of fat to bring them luck. 'Go on, clear out of it!'

As the entourage came closer, Klug and Togtuft saw attendants – gyle goblins with huge feathered fans – flitting round the vast carriage like iridescent damselbugs fluttering round a lake lily. They beat the downy fans up and down, trying in vain to keep their queen cool. But neither they, nor the silk carriage parasol that cast a shadow across her grotesque head, were enough to stop the sweat pouring down her bloated features and turning the woodrose-pink to deepest magenta.

Unable to raise her arms high enough, Grossmother Meadowdew depended on personal attendants to minister to her needs. One gyle goblin, sitting cross-legged on a ledge beside her headrest, would lean forward every few seconds and mop the folds of her dripping brow with a huge grey lake sponge. Two more attendants crouched on the footplates, each one massaging thick unguents into soft folds of skin, while a fourth knelt on a jutting platform behind the driver's seat, feeding the grossmother spoonfuls of thick pink honey that he ladled from a large urn into her lolling mouth.

'May gyle honey drip into our poor mouths!' chanted a

harassed-looking cloddertrog matron with eight bony young'uns in tow as she reached out and touched a wobbling fold of over-hanging flesh.

The carriage rumbled noisily on, setting the bridge creaking and swaying. Once – and then again, where the bridge narrowed – the great wheels became wedged between the side rails of the bridge. Then it was a matter of shoving the back of the carriage and whipping the prowlgrins until, with a loud squeal, the carriage moved forwards once more. The grossmother slurped and snorted all the while, seemingly unaware of the commotion she was causing.

'May the golden blessings of the colony flow down to us all,' called out a stooped flathead, his filthy bandages flapping as he hobbled towards the carriage, brandishing a crutch.

'Away with you!' roared the gnokgoblin, lunging towards him with the spear.

The gathering crowd jostled one another and reached out to grasp at this symbol of the good luck and prosperity that they all desperately wanted. The carriage trundled on, the gnokgoblin herald angrily batting the desperate clutching hands away with his long spear. But he was fighting a losing battle.

'Grossmother Meadowdew! Grossmother Meadowdew!' the crowd chanted in unison.

'Stand back! *Stand back!*' came gruff voices from the far side of the bridge, and Klug and Togtuft turned to see half a dozen guards of the Low Town division of the Hive Militia tramping towards them at a half run, the ornate *H* insignia on their tall stovepipe hats gleaming in the high sun. Their short topcoats were buttoned back to reveal waistcoats, chequered with bulging pockets and jangling with attachments – lamps, keys, hooks; sometimes medals. In their hands, raised and pointing forward, they carried phraxmuskets.

'All right, clear the road!' shouted their leader, a rangy White Lake webfoot warrior. His bare feet echoed on the wooden boards of the bridge as he strode this way and that, pointing the barrel of the phraxmusket into the faces of any he considered not to be moving briskly enough.

All round him, the others in the militia were doing the same, either driving the onlookers back along the bridge or forcing them to climb onto the balustrades on either side, so that the carriage might pass through unimpeded. Slowly – though no less noisily – the entourage of Grossmother Meadowdew made it to the far end of the bridge.

Klug chuckled. 'Now all those prowlgrins have got to do is haul her up to West Ridge. Think they'll make it?'

Togtuft shrugged. 'Poor creatures,' he muttered, and frowned. 'I wonder what's going on up there?'

'That's for them to know and us to wonder, I reckon,' said Klug. 'What you and I need to do is finish our experiment – now our world's stopped shaking,' he added, and laughed.

Up in the elegant Clan Hall at the top of West Ridge, Kulltuft Warhammer – the powerfully built leader of the long-hair goblins and High Clan Chief – scowled. He pressed his nose against the glass of first one of the tall windows, then another, scouring the road which wound its way down the hill beneath him for any trace of the absent clan leader. He banged his staff down heavily on the floor, the skull handle trembling as he did so.

'Where *is* she?' he muttered irritably. 'Noon, I said, and it's already . . . already . . . what *is* the time?'

'Ten off one hour,' said Firemane Clawhand, his chief guard, gruffly.

'Almost an hour late!' Kulltuft Warhammer snarled, the tips of his elaborately spiked hair quivering with irritation. 'Let's hope our beloved grossmother isn't stuck fast on the Sumpwood Bridge being tickled by beggars, or we'll be here till nightfall!'

Gathering his feathered cape around him, Kulltuft strutted across the clan hall, kicking impatiently at the snarling heads of the quarmskin rugs that littered the floor. In the centre of the hall was a large table with five sides, a different clan chair standing

at each one. He had called a council meeting to vote on whether or not to put Hive on a war footing against their enemies in Great Glade. It was to be the most momentous decision the council had ever taken, yet only three of the clan chairs were occupied.

To the right, on a tall-backed throne hewn from dark grey leadwood, sat Turgik, clan leader of the hammerheads, his legs sprawled and dark eyes glaring down furiously at his feet. Tall and muscular, the look of intense consternation on his face was typical of all furrow-browed goblins. Though leader of the hammerhead clan for little more than three months, Turgik had already developed a reputation both for his quick thinking and his even quicker temper.

To his right, Leegwelt the Mottled – clan leader of the lop-ears – moved slowly back and forward on a padded rocking chair, the ironwood runners rumbling on the floorboards beneath. Small, plump and with a face covered in round copper-coloured patches, Leegwelt had benefited from the open hostility between the other elders of his clan, playing one off against the other and growing fat on the bribes most of them paid him.

On the opposite side of the table sat Ragg Yellowtooth, clan leader of the tusked goblins, prodding at a piece of meat stuck between his two front teeth; both of them yellow, long and jutting – and the reason for his name. With his great paunch and lazy expression, Ragg Yellowtooth let the affairs of the Clan Council wash over him, and generally could be relied on to agree with anything the High Clan Chief said.

'Keeping us all waiting,' Kulltuft Warhammer muttered furiously through gritted teeth as he swept past them, his feathered cape flapping and skull-mounted staff hammering on the floor. He took his place between Ragg Yellowtooth and Leegwelt the Mottled, his hair spikes quivering as he cursed under his breath.

'She's on her way,' Firemane Clawhand announced from the far window. He tapped on the glass with the metal hook that glinted at the end of his left arm. 'Leastways, I can see a cloud of dust on the road. And it's coming closer.'

Kulltuft Warhammer sat back in his throne. Raised upon a mound of skulls, the high arch-backed chair with its carved curlicues and sweeping ball-ended arms, was higher than the rest. The gurning, yellowed skulls beneath it had been taken from every battle fought, stretching back far into the past. Many were older than Hive itself; some, older even than the Goblin Nations, while others – tufts of hair still clinging to the bony jaws and around the eye sockets – had only recently been added, when venerable elders had passed away, their spirits finding a home in Open Sky.

Kulltuft Warhammer's right foot rested on his favourite skull, worn flat at the apex where he rubbed his bare heel over the hard surface. Slowly, his breathing became more even and the quivering ceased. The contact with the skull gave him a great sense of well-being and, as his foot moved back and forward, he felt charged with the legendary power of its owner, Hemtuft Battleaxe, the greatest warrior chief of them all.

'She's here,' Firemane Clawhand announced – unnecessarily, for already the four assembled clan chiefs could hear the gasped huffing and puffing of Grossmother Meadowdew as she lurched towards the chamber doors. With a loud crash, the two ironwood doors flew back on their hinges, slamming into the walls behind, and the clan leader of the symbites loomed into the doorway.

''Scuse,' she mumbled, her voice sounding as though her words were bubbling through treacle. 'Held up.'

Ragg Yellowtusk raised an eyebrow lazily, but kept his thoughts to himself. Turgik the furrow-brow was less reticent.

'She certainly is,' he whispered behind his hand to his neighbour.

Leegwelt's mottled face broke into a smile, for as the grossmother advanced towards her chair it became apparent that she was surrounded by a circle of gyle goblins, each one propping her up with a crutch. She waddled slowly across the floor, looking for all the world as though she had been raised up on moving scaffolding. Gasping for breath by the time she reached her seat – a reinforced quilted sumpwood settle, almost five strides long – she sat down heavily. For an instant, the floating chair dipped down to the floor before rising slowly up again beneath its huge occupant.

As the last of the gyle goblin attendants scuttled from the chamber, Firemane Clawhand moved forward and placed the ceremonial cudgel – a polished blackwood club studded with ironwood bolts – at the centre of the table before them. Then, without meeting the gazes of any of the clan leaders, he took up his position at Kulltuft's left arm, standing with his legs apart and his eyes staring straight ahead.

'Let the Grand Council meeting begin,' he announced.

With a soft groan, Kulltuft Warhammer leaned forwards and picked up the cudgel. Bitter experience of meetings collapsing into rancorous bellowing, and even bloody fights, had led to its use. A clan chief might only address the council when the 'mace of Hive' was in his possession. Cradling it in his arms, Kulltuft looked round the table.

'We all know why we're here,' he said, his voice low and dark. 'I propose we go straight to a vote.'

Surprised, the other clan leaders looked round at one another. Eyebrows were raised. Grossmother Meadowdew muttered something unintelligible; Turgik the furrow-browed looked more worried than ever. Finally Leegwelt the Mottled raised a hand. With a grunt of irritation, Kulltuft passed him the cudgel.

'A matter of such importance must, I feel, be discussed by all present,' he said.

Kulltuft raised his hand.

'Otherwise, we run the risk of plunging headlong into a crisis from which there might be no escape,' Leegwelt continued, ignoring the seething long-hair goblin to his right and addressing his comments to the others, who nodded sagely at his words. 'I say we must consider *all* courses of action, not just the one that the High Clan Chief proposes . . .'

'Give me that here,' Kulltuft growled, seizing the cudgel and brandishing it in the air. 'The rich merchants and phraxmine owners of Great Glade have had things their own way for too long. They have grown wealthy on the trade with our great city, charging what they like for their stormphrax – more and more each season – until our clans grow thin and can take no more of it, and steal away from the hive huts in the dead of night.' He looked from one to the other of the clan chiefs, nodding as he spoke; inviting them to nod back in agreement. 'They want to humble us. Belittle us. They want to bring us to our knees. But we shall not be cowed. We shall stand up straight, our heads held high, look them in the eye and demand that they supply us with stormphrax at a fair price. And if they don't . . .'

Leegwelt and Grossmother Meadowdew exchanged glances across the table. The pair of them had heard it all before. After all, hadn't Kulltuft Warhammer come to power vowing to deal with Great Glade 'from a position of strength'? They could see, however, that young Turgik the furrow-browed was being swept away by the High Clan Chief's words. Suddenly, his face set in a snarl of hatred, Turgik brought his fist down heavily on the table.

'Death to the Great Glade robbers and thieves!' he roared.

Grossmother Meadowdew gurgled with disapproval and nodded towards the cudgel. Turgik should not speak without its being in his hand. The young furrow-brow reached forward, but lost out to Leegwelt, whose mottled fingers closed firmly around the handle.

'I acknowledge that the high price of stormphrax is causing hardship to our citizens,' he said, choosing his words carefully, 'but surely we must consider negotiations with Great Glade. *They* raise their prices, so *we* build up our militia – then *they* feel threatened and raise their prices again. Now we have phraxcannon and muskets and weaponry of all kinds, yet our merchants and traders are facing ruin . . .'

'I sometimes wonder whose side you're on, Leegwelt,' Kulltuft growled under his breath.

Turgik nodded; Ragg Yellowtusk shook his head.

'The choice is clear,' the old lop-ear continued. 'We halve the militia, break up the weapons and use the stormphrax they contain to power our factories and merchant vessels. Show the Great Gladers that we mean them no harm . . .'

'Or we take their stormphrax by force!' Kulltuft roared, tearing the cudgel from Leegwelt's grasp. 'It is time to vote.'

He looked round the table, from one clan chief to the other. Ragg Yellowtooth frowned slightly, but left it unclear what he thought, whereas Grossmother Meadowdew gurgled her assent as distinctly as she was able. Of Turgik, there was never any doubt, either as to whether he wanted to cast his vote, or where that vote would fall. Kulltuft nodded warmly at him before turning his gaze to Leegwelt. His cold dark eyes bore into the old lop-ear's mottled face.

'Well?' he said. His face broke into an unpleasant smirk. 'There is clearly a majority in favour. So . . .'

Leegwelt reached forward stiffly, his mottled face pained. He wrenched back the cudgel. 'As I have pointed out on so many occasions, the council no longer reflects the population of Hive,' he said, trying to remain calm though his heart was thumping in his chest. 'Half of its citizens are not represented at all. The cloddertrogs. The mobgnomes. The venerable shrykes. Why, even the fourthlings have no say – and I can tell you, *they* would not back these proposals . . .'

'The fourthlings?' Kulltuft said icily, his right cheek twitching violently. His voice rose. 'The fourthlings! Those filthy, lowdown, double-dealing parasites! Half of them have got relatives in Great Glade. Their loyalty lies with them, not with Hive. They are spies, traitors . . .'

Leegwelt raised the cudgel. '*I* am speaking,' he said.

But Kulltuft would not be still. He could not. Foot rubbing back and forward on the ancient skull, his face twisted up with rage.

'It is because of the treacherous fourthlings that our fair city has been brought to its knees. And you, *you* Leegwelt, propose that they are given *more* power!'

'I am speaking,' Leegwelt repeated evenly. 'I have the mace of Hive.'

'You have the mace of Hive,' said Kulltuft, his voice suddenly loaded with hushed menace. His foot fell still and the twitching stopped as the colour drained from his face. '*You* have the mace of

Hive,' he repeated, climbing to his feet and towering above Leegwelt the Mottled from the top of the heap of skulls. 'But *I* have the militia of Hive!'

In one smooth movement, he lunged forward, seized the heavy blackwood club from the startled lop-eared goblin's hand, swung it in a wide circle through the glittering air and brought it down in a crushing blow on Leegwelt's head. There was a dull thud and a splintering of bone. Kulltuft struck him again, and again, before tossing the blood-flecked cudgel onto the table below him.

The clan chief fell back in his seat, the slow rocking of the chair gradually coming to a halt. His head slumped to one side. Blood trickled down the side of his shattered skull.

Kulltuft sat back down on the high arched chair, his snatched breath coming in short jerks. Beside him, Firemane Clawhand, who had been ready to wield his axe in his master's defence should it prove necessary, crossed his arms. The twitch in Kulltuft's right cheek jerked more wildly than ever as he scanned the circle of faces seated at the five-sided table. Turgik's eyes were blazing; while only the tight whitened lips of Ragg Yellowtooth's mouth betrayed his innermost feelings. Grossmother Meadowdew swooned dizzily, soft slurping noises coming from her mouth.

'We are agreed then,' said Kulltuft Warhammer, his voice tight and clipped. 'Unless there are any more objections . . . ?' he added, and glowered fiercely at each of the other clan leaders in turn, his right foot tapping on the ancient skull as he did so. 'Good. Then my proposal is approved. The High Council has spoken.'

· CHAPTER THIRTY ·

'*Time for my afternoon constitutional*,' Golderayce One-Eye thought as he pulled himself out of his hanging sumpwood chair. *I must see to the sluice gates, and replenish my supply of the precious waters of life before my frail body gets too weak . . .*

The copperwaif gathered his lampstick and sunshade, and pushed the empty ironwood flask deep into his pocket. Then, tap-tapping wearily across the chamber in the keep, the sleeping flitterwaif gripping tightly to his forearm, he headed for the door. It opened with a low whisper and Golderayce stepped outside, to be assailed by the sound of a thousand voices babbling inside his head. He stepped to the balustrade and glanced once more down the sheer rocky drop to the city below him, bathed in its golden lamplight and churning with the sound of countless thoughts.

'*Truly, this is the city that never sleeps*,' he mused. *Chattering, chattering, every accursed hour of every accursed day.*

The flitterwaif stirred, opened its blood-red eyes and launched itself off into the darkness in search of food. Golderayce turned away. The creature would be waiting for him when he returned.

Supported by the lampstick he clutched in his frail hand, he shuffled along the terrace of the fortified keep and onto the path. He looked ahead with his one good eye. It was a long way to the top and, even though the path was mercifully clear of fallen rocks and boulders, an unpleasantly steep climb lay ahead.

But, of course, he had no choice. He'd already left it late to undertake the arduous trip. He could only hope it would not take too much out of him. Head down, the thick barbels at the corners of his mouth trembling as he breathed out, he set off.

Soon, with the brightly illuminated keep behind him, Golderayce was enveloped in a blanket of matt black as he made his way slowly upwards, his gait ponderous and uncertain. Only the dim glow of the lampstick punctured the intense darkness. Its small pool of light confirmed that he was still on the path, but illuminated nothing more – yet it was not the presence of night that disturbed the Custodian General and left him unsteady on his feet. After all, the Nightwoods were his home; he was used to the lack of light. No, what made the ancient waif's legs shake and his palsied hands tremble was the weight of years suddenly pressing down on his tired shoulders.

'*Soon be there,*' he thought to himself encouragingly, and he patted the bulge in the pocket of his robes. *The precious contents of the ironwood flask must never run dry.*

As he drove himself on, his breath coming in short wheezing gasps, the path gave way to a stairway cut into the rock itself. Dragging himself up, one step after the other, his ancient heart beat weakly inside his chest. Above his head, and coming closer with every step, was the dense covering of cloud that swirled, thick and viscous-looking, above the city.

It was the cloud, of course, that had kept the land below in perpetual darkness for all those thousands of years. And Golderayce was grateful to it for that. Without it, the Nightwoods – the eternally dark place of his birth – would have been a dazzling bright cacophony of noise, instead of a black silence punctured only by whispered thoughts. Until, that is, the establishment and growth of the great City of Night below. Now, even up in the keep with its walls of cliffstone ten feet thick, there was little respite from the accursed chattering.

It was his own fault, though. He had been responsible for founding the city all those years ago. But then again, he'd had no choice – not since the first of the immortals had arrived.

Golderayce and his waif kin had constructed the fortified keep first, to protect access to the sacred spring. Further below, they had built the city itself, to accommodate the outsiders who inevitably followed as news of Riverrise spread. And spread it did – throughout the First, Second and now the Third Age of Flight –

and he, Golderayce, had lived through them all, ensuring Riverrise remained in waif hands, whatever it took . . .

As the clouds gathered around his head, the tangy odour of the burning darkelm oil was replaced by the moist, almost metallic smell of thick cloud. There was a hint of toasted woodalmonds in the air too – confirmation that, as he already suspected, a huge storm was imminent.

The darkness seemed to thicken, then curdle, as he entered the cloud cover, and Golderayce's senses were snuffed out one after the other. This was the part of the long journey to the top of the jutting pinnacle of rock that he disliked the most, when he could neither see ahead nor hear his stumbling footfall. Even the chattering thoughts of the denizens of Riverrise fell still.

'*But then this too will pass,*' he thought to himself. '*Everything does.*' He sighed wearily. *Except for me . . .*

As he continued through the damp woolly cloud – a nagging pain slowing him down even more than usual – the ancient copperwaif found his mind wandering. Just as distant storm clouds were gathering, so were the whispers, carried across the Deepwoods from waif mind to waif mind in a great stream of thought. Whispers of strange disappearances . . .

And if the persistent reports coming in from Hive and Great Glade, as well as from settlements all over the Deepwoods, were to be believed, these disappearances were growing in number. It wasn't only individuals and families who were going missing, but entire villages.

Golderayce frowned and stooped down awkwardly to rub his twinging ankle. The odd thing was that of all those who had disappeared, none – not a single one – had ever been heard of again, not even by the most talented waif listeners in all the Edge. It was as though they had simply vanished into Open Sky.

The air grew slowly warmer; the clouds began to thin. And, as it always did, Golderayce's heart gave a little flutter – a mixture of pleasure and relief – as his one huge eye was once again able to make out his surroundings. What with his general weakened condition, not to mention the increasingly painful ankle, the walk had taken far longer than he'd hoped, and by the time he emerged above the clouds, the sun was already sinking in the sky.

But it was bright still and, as he knew to his cost, strong enough to blister his sensitive papery skin. He paused, turned off the light at the head of his lampstick, pushed up his parasol and raised it above his head, then – praying to Earth and Sky that he had energy enough to make it to his destination – struggled up those last remaining steps towards the very top of the rocky apex.

All at once, as he emerged from behind a tall jagged rock, the Garden of Life opened up before him. There were trees and bushes all around, and a circle of pointed pinnacles studding the outside like a mighty crown. Golderayce's senses were on fire now. His skin tingled with the warmth of the air as he walked down a winding path, each side lined with syrupy fruits and brightly coloured flowers which drenched the hissing air with sweet, succulent perfumes.

The copperwaif, though, had no interest in the fruits and flowers of Riverrise. All that concerned him were its life-preserving waters. His frail body tottered on, close to exhaustion, toward the turquoise lake, past delicate trees with lacy fronds and tall banks of silvery grass that fluttered in the warm scented breeze. And then he reached the spot that always caused a shiver to run down his tiny misshapen spine whenever he passed it: the grave marker, so out of keeping here in the Garden of Life.

Golderayce paused for a moment next to the tall, cowl-shaped rock, the raised parasol shadowing his face as he stared down.

Maugin, he read. *The Stone Pilot.* The edges of the letters carved into the slab of rock were picked out by shadow.

It was all so long ago, yet as fresh in his mind as the day it had happened. But then what choice had he had? He'd been young and impetuous. Ambitious. The sacred spring at Riverrise belonged to the waifs, not this strange outsider who had refused to leave . . .

Yet not a day went by that Golderayce didn't regret the blowpipe and the dart dipped in blackroot oil that had spelled instant death. How was he to know that, as the hooded figure crumpled to the ground, a dark silhouette on the horizon – growing closer by the second – heralded another arrival?

With a deep sigh, Golderayce completed those final steps to the lake. At the water's edge, he knelt down on the rock and leaned forwards, cupping his shaking hands and drawing up the crystal-clear liquid to his parched lips.

As the first drops coursed down his throat, the effect of the life-giving water was instantaneous. The waif's eyes cleared, his ears fluttered, while the barbels at the corners of his wrinkled mouth trembled and coiled as a smile spread across his ancient face. He had another tiny sip, then another, drinking until his body felt strong and invigorated once more, and his thoughts were razor-sharp.

Golderayce pulled the ironwood flask from his pocket and plunged it into the water, watching how the tiny bubbles rose to

the surface as it filled, before pushing it back inside his robes. He climbed to his feet and glanced across at the iron sluice gates.

Behind him, warming his back, was the setting sun, red and jelly-like as it slipped down below the distant horizon. In front of him lay the Edgelands to the east. His eyes narrowed. Far away, beyond the clouds and the forest and the sweeping grasslands, was the jutting Edge cliff itself, where those so called *descenders* lowered themselves into the abyss below, infecting the pristine darkness with their insidious impudent thoughts.

The waif shuddered, his fingers tingling and nostrils twitching. Something was approaching, of that he was certain. He could feel it with every reinvigorated fibre of his being. Something vast, something momentous; something from far beyond the Edge, that was getting closer with every passing minute . . .

The question is, thought the ancient waif to himself, *what?*

· CHAPTER THIRTY-ONE ·

'Gather round, my friends. Gather round, all of you, for I have wonderful news to tell.' The tall figure, with his shining white robes looked about him, his handsome face smiling benevolently.

Chopwood, a young'un in his seventh year, joined the others as the band of excited young woodtrolls skipped through the village. Alerted by their cries, woodtrolls of all ages had come rushing out to see what the noise was about. Matrons flung open the windows of their treetop lufwood cabins. Old'uns and young'uns alike emerged from the low arched doors and hurried down ropes and ladders to the village square below. Woodcutters abandoned their half-chopped logs, while hammelhorn and tilder herders left their animal pens and hurried after the rest.

Soon, they were all gathered around the tall lullabee tree at the centre of the village, where the white-robed stranger stood. As one, the crowd looked up at him expectantly, their breath held.

The handsome figure in his strange old-fashioned clothing had appeared out of the forest an hour earlier, and the woodtroll village had been buzzing with gossip and rumour ever since. Who was this unexpected visitor and what could he possibly want?

The stranger raised his hands. He smiled.

'My friends,' he said. 'I have travelled far to bring you the good news. I come from a place of astonishing beauty; a place that had been destroyed, but has now been renewed. It is a place that welcomes all who travel there. The poor. The downtrodden. The overlooked.' He smiled warmly. 'Good honest folk like yourselves, who break your backs each day just to put food on the table, will be greeted there and treated like the most exulted clan chief in Hive or the wealthiest Great Glade merchant.'

'But where *is* this place?' they all asked, the young'uns' eyes wide with wonder; the old'uns' leathery brows furrowed with confusion.

'Far, far away,' the stranger told them, his blue eyes flitting from one to the other of the upturned faces. He paused. 'Away from the paths . . .'

As one, the villagers took a sharp intake of breath. Away from the paths that linked one woodtroll village to the next; the paths that offered them security and protection, that from the moment of their birth every woodtroll was instructed *never* to leave . . . ?

Chopwood could barely believe his ears.

'Trust me,' the stranger told them, his voice soft and reassuring. 'For I shall lead you there. I shall be your guide.'

The woodtrolls gazed up at his shining face.

'Pack your things and I will lead you to a new and better life.'

It didn't take long for the villagers to pack up. After all, their belongings were few, and the guide had assured them that there were houses and possessions just waiting for them in this place of plenty, a new beacon of peace and prosperity.

With his most precious possession clutched in a clammy hand – a small carved hammelhorn that his uncle Barkham had made for him for his first birthday – Chopwood followed his mother, father and three sisters out of their cabin and down the ladder. They joined the other villagers, who were already milling about in the centre of the village. The sun would not rise for another couple of hours, but everyone was far too excited to sleep.

'Are we ready?' the guide called out.

'We are ready,' the villagers called back.

They had formed themselves into a long line, with families on foot at the front, followed by wagons and handcarts, and herds of livestock tethered together at the rear. Blazing torches were clasped in trembling hands. The guide looked back. Then, satisfied, with what he saw, he raised his staff high in the air.

'Then follow me!' he cried.

The small band of woodtrolls trundled forwards. Wheels clattered and boots thudded on the trampled-down mud of the path as they left the cabins behind them.

It was almost an hour later when they came to a steep curve in the path they had taken. If they kept to it, Chopwood knew that it would lead them eventually to the woodtroll village where his favourite cousin, Splinter, lived. But they didn't continue that way. As they reached the sharp corner, the guide – his staff raised in his left hand and a blazing torch in the other – continued walking into the forest beyond. Those at the front of the long line of woodtrolls followed him.

Chopwood swallowed anxiously, his heart thumping inside his chest. The edge of the path came closer. Half the village had already followed the strange figure in the white robes, venturing bravely into the forest. His father and sisters had gone . . . He glanced round at his mother, who nodded back at him reassuringly.

If everyone else is doing it, Chopwood thought, then surely it must be all right.

Squeezing the wooden hammelhorn tightly, the young woodtroll took a deep breath. His left foot stepped onto the dry leaves and needledrop of the forest floor. Moments later, he glanced back anxiously, to see the line of beaten earth disappearing off to his left.

He had left the path.

· CHAPTER THIRTY-TWO ·

The outer track of the thousandsticks field was rapidly filling up with teams representing the twelve districts of the great city. The academics of the Cloud Quarter led the procession round the track, followed by phraxship hands from Ambristown, dockers from the Ledges, clerks from New Undertown and heavy-set cloddertrogs from the Free Glades district. Behind them came the cadets from Old Forest, marching in stiff formation, herders from the Silver Pastures, trappers and hunters from the Southern and Northern Outer City districts and factory workers from East Glade.

Next, it was Nate's turn to step beneath the flag-furled archway and out onto the compacted mud of the outer track. Surrounded by his team mates from Copperwood, he marched past the huge crowd that filled the steep wooden stands surrounding the field, his head held high. It seemed to Nate as if the whole of Great Glade had turned out on this bright wintry afternoon to witness the biggest match of the year – the Reckoning.

His heavy padded helmet, burnished copperwood body armour and leather shoving glove no longer felt like the awkward encumbrances they once had. After six long months of weekly practices and thousandsticks matches they felt as natural as an old suit of clothes. As for his new thousandstick, it had become an extension of his right arm, with its plaited leather 'claw' at one end for scooping and sweeping opponents off their feet, and the heavy round 'club' at the other for prodding and pushing.

Nate ran through the practice drills in his head as the steady thud of boots on baked earth filled the air around him. The Overhead Claw, the Downward Club, the Brace, the Lift . . . His fist clenched the ironwood shaft of his thousandstick as he rehearsed them in his

1. PHALANX SHOVE
2. HILL ASSAULT
3. HILL DESCENT
4. BLOCKERS CLEAR SNAKE TRACK
5. RUNNERS RACE TO NARROW TRACK
6. ASCENT OF HIGH HILL
7. ASCENT OF HIGH PINE
8. HIGH PINE VICTORY

SKY MARSHAL

CLAW
THOUSANDSTICK
HELMET
SHOVING GLOVE
CLUB
FRONT & BACK ARMOUR
CLEATED BOOTS

fig i. THE OVERHEAD CLAW

fig ii. THE DOWNWARD CLUB

fig iii. THE BRACE

fig iv. THE PITCH FORK

mind. In the pit of his stomach, woodmoths had awoken and were busy fluttering their wings.

Suddenly, from all around, there came a mighty roar as the crowd acknowledged the last of the twelve teams entering the field. Nate turned his head. Behind Copperwood marched the team from New Lake. Unlike the forge hands, furnace tenders and lamplighters who had to find time to practise after their shifts in the factories of the Copperwood district, the New Lakers were professional thousandsticks players for the most part.

They had been recruited from far and wide and included, Nate knew, ex-miners from the Eastern Woods and brutal-looking hammerheads all the way from Hive. They played and practised every day of the year, and were paid handsomely by the rich phraxmerchants and factory owners of New Lake for their trouble. At their head, resplendent in white body armour and brandishing a blackwood thousandstick, marched the captain of the New Lake team, Branxford Drew.

Nate turned away, but not before he felt the full power of the hate in Branxford Drew's stare. It was a look he'd grown familiar with . . .

It must have been about three months ago, by Nate's reckoning. He'd recently made friends with Weelum the banderbear, and had taken to visiting the gatekeeper in his lodge by the factory gates after his shifts.

Sitting together round a pot-bellied stove, Weelum had slowly taught Nate the rudiments of his language. To the untrained ear, the language of these strange secretive denizens of the Deepwoods appeared deceptively simple. Just three guttural sounds in the back of the throat – 'wuh', 'waah' and a more aggressive exclamation, 'wurgh!'. But it hadn't taken Nate long to realize that there was much more to banderbear communication than that. Indeed it wasn't so much a language of sounds, as a language of movement.

A simple 'wuh', when combined with a twitch of an ear, the sweep of a claw or tilt of the head, could mean a thousand different things. Nate learned that the language of the banderbears was not as short and gruff as it first appeared. In fact, once he'd mastered a few of the basic movements and understood more of what Weelum said to him, Nate began to comprehend how poetic the language of these solitary creatures was.

'Morning' in banderbear, for instance, was *now the bringer of warmth has climbed the highest tree*, while 'night' was *time of the silence of the eyes*.

'Wuh-wuh,' Weelum would growl, tusks bared and one claw raised. 'Wuh,' his clenched fist touching the tip of the chin, and Nate would hear, *Watcher in the time of the silence of the eyes greets he who is the keeper of light.*

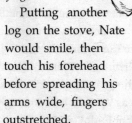

Putting another log on the stove, Nate would smile, then touch his forehead before spreading his arms wide, fingers outstretched.

'Wurgh!' he would exclaim. *The forest distances grow small with your friendship.*

One night, at the end of a long shift working on a series of replacement phraxchambers for the Great Glade fleet, Nate had left the factory and started across the yard towards the gatekeeper's lodge. He was walking beneath the stilts when he spotted a familiar figure hurrying towards the gates. It was the girl he'd met at the mansion in New Lake, the mine owner's daughter,

Eudoxia Prade. As he'd watched, Branxford Drew burst from the shadows in hot pursuit.

'Wait, Eudoxia! Wait!' His voice sounded both irritated and imploring. 'You don't understand . . .'

Eudoxia paused just inside the gates and turned, her beautiful green eyes blazing.

'Oh, I understand all right,' she declared as Branxford caught up with her. 'Where I come from, it's called stealing!'

'The old man can afford it, and besides, what he doesn't know about can't hurt him . . .' Branxford reached out and grabbed Eudoxia's wrist. 'And he won't find out,' he said, viciously twisting her arm, 'will he . . . ? I said, *will* he?'

Nate started forward, his fists clenched – only to stop moments later in the middle of the yard. Eudoxia had suddenly dropped her shoulder and, with a graceful flick of her leg, taken Branxford's legs out from under him. The oafish bully landed flat on his back in a puddle of clear water. As he struggled back to his feet, Nate was shocked to see a small silver phraxpistol in his hand.

'Wurgh!'

Weelum appeared out of the night behind Branxford, enveloped him in his cloak and clasped him in a suffocating bear hug. The phraxpistol clattered to the ground.

'Umph! Umph! Urrumph!' Branxford's muffled protestations sounded from beneath the banderbear's cloak. Only his legs were visible, kicking about, as Weelum held him tight.

Nate looked across at Eudoxia. 'Are you all right?' he asked.

'Fine!' said Eudoxia, her eyes still blazing with anger. She suddenly checked herself. 'I know you, don't I?'

'We've met,' said Nate, feeling a blush begin to spread up from his neck and across his cheek. 'At your father's house. I had the prowlgrin with saddlerash.'

Eudoxia's face softened. 'Of course. Nate, isn't it? How is the prowlgrin?'

'He's fine. That woodsalvia you gave me worked like a charm.'

'I'm glad to hear it,' said Eudoxia, turning to leave.

'Perhaps...' said Nate, painfully aware of his reddening face, 'we could go for a ride some time... That is, if you and Branxford...'

'There is no "me and Branxford",' said Eudoxia hotly. 'I don't go out with sons who steal from their fathers...' She paused, then smiled as she walked through the gates and over to the roosting post where her prowlgrin was sitting patiently. 'Yes, Nate, I'd like to go for a ride some time. I'd like that very much.'

Nate turned away. 'Wuh-wuh,' he said, touching his left elbow and then his shoulder.

Weelum nodded and let go of Branxford, who staggered forward, goggle-eyed and gasping for breath.

'Eudoxia?'

'Eudoxia has gone,' said Nate, handing the factory owner the silver phraxpistol.

'Miss Prade, to you, lamplighter,' rasped Branxford, snatching back the pistol and pocketing it. 'And in future, you and the gatekeeper had better mind your business or I'll throw both of you out on the streets!'

'We work for your father, not for you,' said Nate coolly.

Branxford stared at Nate for a moment, a look of loathing on his face. 'We'll see about that,' he muttered, before striding through the gates and hurrying off down the street.

'Wuh,' said Weelum to Nate as they watched him go. 'Wuh-wuh.'

The mighty Copperwood has sown a twisting sapling.

· CHAPTER THIRTY-THREE ·

Nate scanned the crowd as the thousandsticks teams continued to process round the outer track, waiting for the steam klaxon to announce the beginning of the Reckoning. There, in a box decked out in the dark ochre and white chequerboard colours of the Copperwood district, sat Eudoxia, next to Slip and Weelum the banderbear. The Professor was meant to be with them, but as Nate returned their waves, he was unable to spot him. Behind them was a seat reserved for Friston Drew, the factory owner, who, despite living in New Lake and having a son who led the New Lake team, always supported his workers from Copperwood when it came to thousandsticks. He didn't seem to be there either.

Strange, thought Nate. If they didn't hurry, they'd miss the start of the match.

Suddenly the steam klaxon boomed and, with a full-throated roar from the crowd, the twelve teams, more than a thousand strong, burst from the outer tracks onto the wooden boards of the inner tracks that connected the ring of low hills to each other, and to the central high hill.

'Form up, we're taking Hill Three!'

The word came back through the ranks as the Copperwood team, thousandsticks held at shoulder height, pounded along one of the boarded tracks. Peering over the helmets of his team mates, Nate could see the combined teams of New Undertown, the Free Glades and Ambristown coming towards them from the opposite side of the field.

'Brace!' came the command from the Copperwood captain, Gerrix Brove, a lathe turner for the Quentling Brothers' metalworks, and the team instantly responded.

The smallest slipped through to the front of the formation, while the biggest fell in directly behind. The rest, including Nate, their thousandsticks held horizontally across their chests just beneath their chins, provided ballast, packing in tightly at the rear.

'Ummph!' the crowd roared collectively as three hundred thousandsticks slammed into the Copperwood formation of one hundred.

Towards the back, Nate's helmeted head jerked back as the force of the impact rippled through the team. At the front, the rattling clatter of thousandsticks clashing filled the air as the front ranks attempted to get the upper hand.

'Shove!' roared Gerrix Brove and, head down, Nate pushed into the back of his team mates in front with all his might.

Sweat stung his eyes and he fought for breath as a player behind him shoved hard in the small of his back. Unable to make out much of what was happening in front, Nate poured all his concentration into placing one foot in front of the other to inch forward along the track.

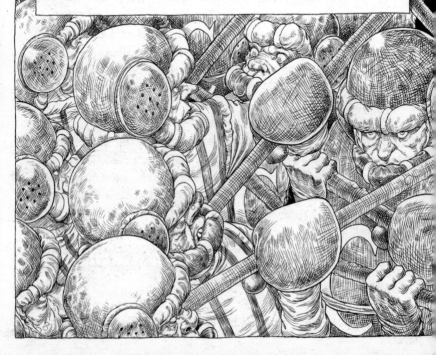

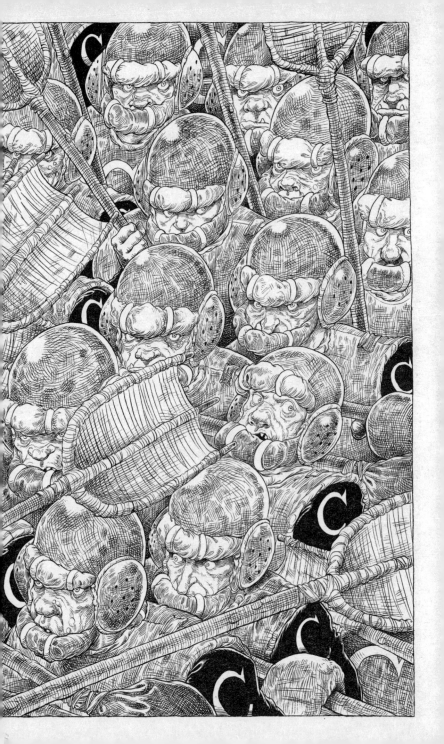

'*One*, two, *one*, two, *one*, two . . .'

Half groan, half grunt, it was the familiar chant of a thousandsticks team involved in a shove. Nate had practised it endlessly along with the rest of the team. Keep formation. Keep going forward, he repeated over and over to himself in his mind. The few beat the many if they shove as one . . .

'Ah! . . . Aah! . . . *Aaah!*' the crowd sounded, telling Nate that they were reaching the critical point, where one formation would have to break in the face of the other's power.

'Go on, boys! That's it, go on . . . Yes!' Brove urged the Copperwood team on.

A thunderous roar greeted the sudden surge that sent Nate stumbling forwards down the track. The New Undertown, Free Glade and Ambristown teams scattered as their formation buckled and broke, and the Copperwood formation shoved them off the inner track onto the gravel – and out of the game.

'Scramble!' shouted Brove, and Nate, as one of the fastest in the team, surged through the ranks of his team mates and up the low hill ahead.

As he, along with twenty others, reached the top of Hill Three, they looked across to see the other five hills bristling with thousandsticks, and the gravel beds between the inner tracks strewn with fallen and dejected players, who were picking themselves up and leaving the field. On Hill Five, Branxford Drew, surrounded by the broad-shouldered hammerhead goblins of the New Lake team, acknowledged the cheers of the crowd with a wave of his blackwood thousandstick.

The Reckoning was just beginning . . .

'The last of the hammerheads arrived over a month ago,' Eudoxia had told Nate, 'recruited for New Lake by my father personally in Hive. So why hasn't he come home yet?'

Nate couldn't answer her.

Since their encounter at the factory gates of Gremlop and Drew's, when Eudoxia had confronted Branxford about him taking money from his father's safe, Nate and she had become firm friends. They went on rides, they got together after work to walk through the Copperwood allotments; once they'd even met up at the Lake Landing Academy in the Free Glades district. It was where, quite by chance, Nate had run into his friend, the Professor, from the skytavern.

Strange, Nate had thought often since, how fate throws people together. It could, it seemed, also keep them apart.

He and Eudoxia were in the stables of her father's mansion on the shores of beautiful New Lake. They had just returned from an exhilarating treetop gallop through Old Forest, and Tallix and Majestix were perched on their roost branches, blowing hard but growling with contentment.

'Perhaps there's some other business keeping him in Hive?' Nate ventured.

He didn't like to see Eudoxia worried. Nate had come to appreciate how tough and resourceful this daughter of a rich mine owner actually was, so different from most of the pampered, richly clothed New Laker girls he'd seen. If she was worried, then it must be something worth worrying about, Nate knew. Yet he felt powerless to help.

'What does your father's chief clerk say?' asked Nate as they walked out into the gardens that led down to the lake.

'Felftis Brack?' Eudoxia said with distaste. 'He just keeps saying that I shouldn't worry my "pretty little head" about it, and do I need an increase in my dress allowance? I mean, honestly! My father has disappeared in Hive and his chief clerk is concerned that I don't have enough ball gowns!'

Nate smiled. Even in her topcoat and riding breeches, spattered in tree pollen and bark rust, his friend still managed to look stylish and elegant. Eudoxia caught him staring at her, and her green eyes flashed.

'Don't tell me you agree with that slimy snail, Nate!' she exclaimed.

'No, of course not,' protested Nate. 'Look, perhaps I could ask

the Professor to look into it. He might be a skytavern gambler, but he does seem to know an awful lot of important people . . .'

They had reached the jetty at the lake's edge, and Nate stared out across the broad, shimmering expanse of water, so beautiful and tranquil. The Reckoning was less than a month away, and despite the rumours about the strengthened New Lake team, Nate was feeling confident. After all, he and the rest of the factory hands in Copperwood had been training for months.

Suddenly he felt Eudoxia's hand on his arm. Looking up, he followed her gaze back towards the steps of the mansion.

There, emerging from the entrance hall, was Felftis Brack, his snailskin topcoat flapping at his scaly heels and his tufted quiff quivering. Beside him walked Branxford Drew, funnel hat in hand. Reaching into his expensive fur-lined topcoat, the factory owner's son handed the chief clerk a barkscroll. In return, Felftis handed Branxford a tightly bundled wad of gladers. They shook hands and Branxford left.

'Perhaps,' said Eudoxia, a frown clouding her face, 'you might ask that "Professor" of yours after all.'

· CHAPTER THIRTY-FOUR ·

With all six low hills on the thousandsticks field successfully occupied, the Reckoning now became a game of tactics rather than brute force. The cadets of Old Forest and the herders from the Silver Pastures held the hills on either side of the Copperwood team. Nate could see them in tight huddles discussing their next move. On the far side of the field, the Cloud Quarter team of academics had made an unlikely alliance with the rough factory hands of East Glade, and now crowded together on the top of Hill One. But the team with the upper hand, Nate saw in an instant, was New Lake, which now held two of the hills, the hulking hammerheads forming a phalanx on each of them and clashing their thousandsticks together in a rhythmic beat, much to the delight of the crowd.

It was now that the faster, more agile thousandsticks players like Nate came into their own. With the help of their larger and heftier team mates, or 'blockers', they had to get onto one of the two snaking inner tracks that led to the high hill at the centre of the field. And with six hundred players still in the Reckoning, it wouldn't be easy.

'Runners!' barked Brove. 'Find your blockers!'

Nate joined the eight blockers who would attempt to clear his way. The other Copperwood runners did the same. Already, Nate could see as he glanced over, Old Forest had organized themselves into a 'three-way wedge' and were flooding down onto the tracks, heading for the high hill. From Hill One, the Cloud Quarter and East Glade teams saw their chance and instantly made for the hill Old Forest had just left. As Nate watched, they came surging up onto Hill Two and then down the other side into the rear of Old Forest, who were caught off guard and scattered.

'Cadets,' Gerrix Brove said ruefully. 'Brave, but green as saplings!'

Below them, the three teams splintered into clusters of thousand-sticks duels, with the crowd roaring on the individual contests.

'This way!' ordered Gerrix Brove, and the Copperwood team fell in behind their captain and set off at a sprint.

On Hill Six, the Silver Pasture's team leaped into action to head them off, but Nate and the Copperwooders were too quick for them. By the time the herders had come down onto the tracks, the Copperwood blockers stood in their way. There was a huge collision of thousandsticks and a great surging melee, but the Copperwood team's tactic had worked. Nate and his fellow runners were off on the track towards the high hill.

Up ahead, leaping down from Hills Four and Five, came the New Lake hammerheads with strange guttural-sounding war chants.

'*Unkh! Aargh! Unkh! Aargh . . .*'

The wave of Copperwood runners ahead of Nate rebounded off the hulking hammerhead blockers in their path and tumbled into the gravel. Nate, without checking his run, swerved in, then out, round two of the blockers, then past a third. Sticking out his glove, he handed off a fourth, who went barrelling backwards into a cluster of his team mates, sending them all sprawling.

Around the field, the crowd were on their feet. 'Copperwood! Copperwood! Copperwood!' they roared.

Nate had reached the snaking path to the high hill and swerved down it. Not a single New Laker had laid a glove on him.

'Careful! Careful!' he told himself as his heart hammered away beneath his body armour.

The track to the high hill was narrow, hardly wide enough for one player and he knew that, up above in the phraxlighter, the sky marshal would be scrutinizing every step he took. A single foot in the gravel and Nate would be disqualified. Behind him, he could hear the curses of his hammerhead pursuers as they blundered off the narrow track.

'Out! Out!' Nate heard the sky marshal call overhead.

'Yes!' the collective roar of the crowd greeted him as he reached the high hill and began to scramble up.

Head down and jaw clenched, Nate gripped his thousandstick tightly.

'*Yes!*' the crowd roared again.

Someone else must have reached the hill down the other track. Looking up, Nate felt the woodmoths flutter into action once again in his stomach.

That someone else was Branxford Drew . . .

'You wanted to see me, sir?' said Nate.

'Yes, come in, my boy, and pull up a chair.' Friston Drew the factory owner ushered the lamplighter into his office and closed the door.

It was the night before the Reckoning and Nate was eager to get back home to the cabin and practise his thousandsticks moves one last time before the match. But Friston Drew had been looking so worried and careworn these past few weeks that, when he'd asked Nate to come to his office at the end of his shift, Nate had been loath to refuse.

Friston Drew sat down in his high-backed sumpwood chair with a heavy sigh and massaged his temples with his fingertips.

'This is something I should have done a very long time ago,' he said slowly, looking up at Nate with solemn dark-ringed eyes, 'but somehow, until now, I just couldn't bring myself to do it . . .'

'Do what?' said Nate.

'You've been an excellent worker, Nate Quarter. And true to your word, you've learned quickly and applied yourself to your tasks with enthusiasm and good humour. One day you'll make an excellent phraxengineer.'

'Thank you,' said Nate, his face colouring.

'Alas, the same cannot be said for my son, Branxford. He has proved a great disappointment to me. Not only has he shown no interest in the factory, but he has run up enormous debts and even taken to stealing from me. The last straw came when my neighbour in New Lake, Galston Prade, informed me that Branxford had offered to sign over Gremlop and Drew to him in the event of my death, in

222

return for a substantial payment in advance! Of course, Galston sent him packing, but it is the thought of it that I find so disappointing – attempting to sell his inheritance like that . . .'

Friston paused for a moment and looked down at the scattered documents and working drawings on his desk.

'Which is why,' he said, looking up and clearing his throat, 'I would like to make you, Nate, my junior partner – a junior partner who, one day, will inherit the business. After all, you have proved to be the son I always wished I'd had. How does "Gremlop, Drew and Quarter" sound to you, my boy?'

Nate swallowed hard. He didn't know what to say. Branxford already hated him with a passion. This would make things immeasurably worse.

'And don't worry about Branxford,' said Friston Drew, as if reading Nate's thoughts. 'You leave him to me. I've drawn up the necessary papers. All you have to do is sign. But there's no rush. Why don't you sleep on it? You can give me your answer tomorrow.'

'Tomorrow is the Reckoning,' said Nate.

From outside there came the sound of a muffled cough.

'So it is!' exclaimed Friston Drew. 'Branxford speaks of little else. Why, I've just received a bill for a set of white body armour and a carved blackwood thousandstick, would you believe? Well, never mind, things will keep till after the match, Nate. I hear our Copperwood team is not to be underestimated this year.'

'It certainly isn't,' said Nate with a smile.

The factory owner smiled back. 'Much like yourself, Nate Quarter.'

· CHAPTER THIRTY-FIVE ·

Clawing his way up the steep side of the high hill with his thousandstick, Nate struggled to the top – but not before Branxford Drew. As he got to his feet and looked up, Nate saw that Branxford was already half a dozen rungs up the towering high pine. He hadn't a moment to lose.

Around them, the crowd rose to a new crescendo of excitement. They'd already witnessed mighty shoves, ambushes, two hill captures and a breakaway pursuit. Now there was a double climb. It was proving to be the most exciting Reckoning for years.

In the distance came the rumble of thunder even though there wasn't a cloud in sight. But the crowd were too engrossed in the contest to pay it any heed.

Nate grasped the first rung and began to climb the tall, gently swaying pole. High above was the platform they were both making for. The first to haul himself onto it and raise his thousandstick would earn victory for his team. In his wildest dreams, Nate had never thought he'd get this close. But he wasn't there yet, and if he dropped his thousandstick now, then it would all be over.

'Concentrate!' he told himself fiercely.

Above him, Branxford was tiring, blowing hard and pausing between rungs to regain his breath. Nate pushed himself on, reaching up for rung after rung with his gloved hand and clutching the thousandstick with the other.

In the stands around the stadium, the crowd seemed in turmoil. People were leaving their seats, hurrying down the wooden steps, mingling with the players on the outer track, gesticulating wildly. Overhead, the sky marshal swooped low and steered his phraxlighter down towards a contingent of constables that had just galloped in on wild-eyed prowlgrins.

But the two climbers were oblivious to the commotion beneath them. Now almost face to face, on opposite sides of the high pine pole, they matched each other rung for rung.

'It's all over . . . lamp-lighter . . .' gasped Branxford Drew breathlessly 'Your . . . glittering . . . career . . .'

Nate ignored him. Reaching up, he pulled himself a rung clear and continued to climb. The platform was tantalizingly near.

'The factory . . . It's gone . . .' hissed Branxford. 'And . . . my . . . stupid . . . father . . . with it.'

Nate looked down into the hate-filled face of the factory owner's son. 'Gone?' he breathed. He grasped the platform above his head with his gloved hand.

In the stands around the field there came the sound of screams and wailing.

'The thunder . . . That

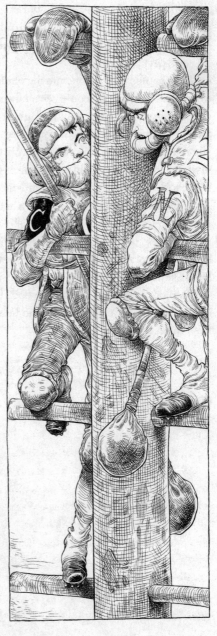

... was ... the sound ... of a phrax ... explosion ...' Branxford spat the words out as he climbed up in pursuit of Nate. 'Lamps ... set ... to go ... out ...' An evil sneer spread across his face. 'I ... suspect ... murder.'

Nate hauled himself up onto the platform and stood up. From the top of the high pine, he could see all the way to the distant stiltshops of Copperwood. Sure enough, a great white cloud was rising in the sky above it. The crowd could see it too. Many of them were streaming away from the field and off towards their homes in the district. Others were staring and pointing at the lone figure standing at the top of the high pine, thousandstick held limply at his side.

'You!' gasped Nate, looking down at Branxford, who was a single rung from the platform. 'You did this!'

'Who do you think they'll believe?' sneered Branxford. 'The grieving son of a factory owner – or a thieving lamplighter? Goodbye, Nate Quarter.'

Branxford swung his blackwood thousandstick viciously at Nate's legs. With a startled cry, the lamplighter toppled headlong from the platform ...

PART TWO

HIVE

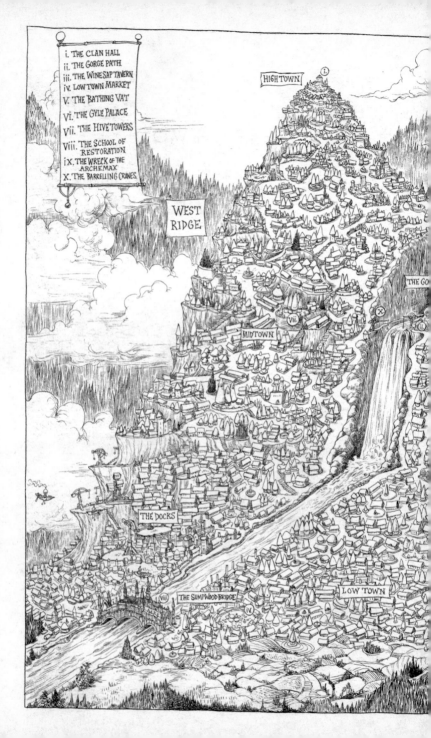

i. THE CLAN HALL
ii. THE GORGE PATH
iii. THE WINESAP TAVERN
iv. LOW TOWN MARKET
V. THE BATHING VAT
Vi. THE GYLE PALACE
Vii. THE HIVE TOWERS
Viii. THE SCHOOL OF RESTORATION
iX. THE WRECK OF THE ARCHEMAX
X. THE BARRELLING CRANES

WEST RIDGE

HIGH TOWN

THE GO

MIDTOWN

THE DOCKS

THE SUMPWOOD BRIDGE

LOW TOWN

THE PEAK

EAST
RIDGE

BACK
RIDGE

MID TOWN

THE CAVES

THE CITY
OF
HIVE

· CHAPTER THIRTY-SIX ·

Nate opened his eyes. His head hurt; a dull throbbing band of pain across his forehead which intensified when he tried to sit up. His right arm was tightly strapped and his chest felt decidedly tender. He was lying on a soft bed of fragrant gladegrass, carefully layered and woven with the expertise of a banderbear.

Overhead, low beams crisscrossed the ceiling, from which wooden trugs, barley sacks and tallowrope nets hung down, bursting with white steam celery and purple gladeonions, steamtubers and woodplantains. There were garden tools – rakes, forks, spades, trowels and shears – dangling from mounted hooks on the wall beside him, and a tall stack of pumpkin casks and bedding trays that looked ready to topple at any moment.

Nate felt a damp compress on his forehead, deliciously cool and soothing and, turning his head, found himself looking up into the clear green eyes of Eudoxia.

'You're awake,' she smiled, removing the compress and soaking it in the copperwood bowl by her side before placing it gently on Nate's forehead once again. 'That was a nasty fall you took. We were worried . . .'

'We?' Nate's throat felt tight and scratchy, and his voice was barely a whisper.

'Me, Weelum, Slip, and the Professor of course,' she replied. 'Here, drink this. Pure cold steam water, fresh from Slip's roof well.'

Eudoxia held a flask to Nate's lips and he drank gratefully.

'You've sprained your shoulder and cracked a few ribs. Nothing too serious. I've treated prowlgrins in far worse shape. What you need is rest, and plenty of it . . .'

'Wuh!' came a familiar voice from the far side of the bed. 'Wuh-wuh.'

Nate turned his head to see Weelum the banderbear tapping a tusk with the third claw of his right paw. *The keeper of light has escaped lightly from the heavy fall.*

Nate smiled ruefully. 'That's easy for you to say,' he told him. 'You're not the one who feels like they've been hit on the head by an unlit phraxshard.' He paused as the memory of the thousandsticks match came back to him. 'I remember standing at the top of the high pine and seeing a great cloud rising up over Copperwood . . . Then I was falling and . . .' He tried to sit up, only to be enveloped in pain once again. 'Where am I?' he gasped. 'And how did I get here?'

As if in answer, there came the sound of a hatch being lifted on rusty hinges, and Slip the scuttler's face appeared at Nate's bedside, his wide eyes clouded with concern.

'You're safe now, friend Nate.' The grey goblin set aside the huge blue pumpkin he was carrying and took Nate's left hand. 'Safe in Slip's stiltshed on the allotment,' he said, and added, 'You haven't ever seen Slip's stiltshed before, have you, friend Nate?'

Nate shook his head.

'Built by his own hands, nice and hidden and out of the way among the tuber stalks. Too busy practising thousandsticks – and look where *that's* got you . . .'

Slip's lower lip was trembling and his large eyes were filling with tears. Eudoxia put an arm around him.

'Don't worry, Slip,' she reassured the grey goblin as large teardrops trickled down his cheeks and dropped from his trembling chin onto Nate's blanket. 'Nate's had a nasty fall, but his thousandsticks armour saved him. What he needs now is peace and quiet and time to heal.'

'Peace and quiet,' Slip repeated, nodding slowly and trying to smile. 'And time to heal. Slip understands. Come on, Weelum. Let's leave friend Nate to sleep, and go and dig up some gladeonions.'

'Wuh,' replied the banderbear, shaking his head and making a juddering sweep of his right arm, his claws trailing for a moment along the floor. *Such pain in the back for such bitter fruit.*

Nate smiled and shut his eyes as the cool compress was refreshed and placed back on his feverish brow with gentle hands . . .

'Nate . . . Nate . . .'

He wasn't sure how long he'd slept, but when he opened his eyes, sunlight was streaming into the small wooden stiltshed from a circular skylight in the thatched roof. His head no longer hurt, and Nate was able to sit up with only a twinge of discomfort.

At the foot of the gladegrass bed was the Professor, sitting astride a sack of cloudturnips. His angular face looked drawn and tired, and his usually neatly combed sandy-coloured hair was dishevelled and windblown.

'How are you feeling?' the Professor asked, his cool blue eyes as penetrating as ever behind the silver-framed spectacles.

'Much better, thanks, Professor,' Nate said. 'A little stiff – and my chest is sore. But my headache has gone.'

'Good, I'm glad to hear it,' said the Professor with a thin smile. 'I suppose you're wondering what happened, and how you got here?'

Nate nodded.

'Well,' the Professor began, 'I'd better start by telling you about the disappearance of Eudoxia's father. You asked me to look into it, remember, a few weeks ago?'

'I remember,' said Nate. 'But what's Galston Prade got to do with all of this?'

'Eudoxia said he had gone to Hive to recruit hammerheads for the New Lake thousandsticks team,' the Professor continued in his dry, carefully modulated academic voice – a voice which Nate had never heard raised in anger. 'Well, that's as may be, but I've spoken to several blockers in the New Lake team who tell me that the hammerheads had been recruited and were bound for Great Glade before Galston had got even halfway to Hive. According to them, the chief clerk, Felftis Brack, had already arranged everything, and there was no need for Galston's journey. And that's not all . . .'

The Professor calmly removed his spectacles and polished each lens in turn with the lapel of his topcoat, before putting them on again.

'A junior clerk in Prade's office told me that Felftis Brack had instructed him to draw up a document after Galston left for Hive. An extremely interesting document, by all accounts. It was an agreement between Felftis and Branxford Drew, giving the chief clerk a controlling share in the phraxchamber works when Branxford inherits, in return for five thousand gladers paid immediately.'

'It's beginning to make sense . . .' murmured Nate. 'Galston turned Branxford down when he came to him with just such an offer. With Galston out of the city, Felftis felt free to make a deal himself. Eudoxia and I saw him hand the money over to Branxford . . .'

The Professor nodded. 'But it seems it went deeper than that. Branxford and

Felftis got impatient. They rigged a lamp to go out in the works directly beneath Friston Drew's office, blowing the old man sky high just as Branxford and you were climbing the high pine.'

'He admitted as much to me before he knocked me off!' Nate blurted out, his face flushed with indignation. 'But how could he do it? I mean, to his own father . . . ?'

He hesitated as he remembered his own conversation with the old factory owner. Of course! Branxford must have been eavesdropping and learned that Friston Drew was about to disinherit him and make Nate a partner in the works. He grasped a handful of blanket in the fist of his left hand and twisted it savagely.

'He murdered him!' he exclaimed. 'Branxford Drew murdered his father! I remember it all now, and he wants to blame it on me!'

The Professor sighed. 'I'm afraid you're right, Nate, my lad.' His dour expression grew harder. 'Sky above, I've seen my fair share of scoundrels in my time,' he said. 'Knifeticklers and snatchwallets, gamblers who would sell their own grandmother to secure a wager. But what Branxford did . . .' He shook his head. 'He and Felftis had it well planned. The phraxchamber works were deserted because of the big match, and they must have ambushed Friston in his office. I chased off a couple of Felftis's cronies who were planting stolen working drawings and forged accounts in your cabin just before the thousandsticks match. I was on my way to the field to warn you when the explosion happened, and arrived just in time to see you fall.'

Nate stared back at his friend, his eyes wide with outrage at the Professor's words.

'Branxford accused you of murdering his father, and of attempting to murder him too, right there on the field. Told the constabulary that you'd been cheating his father and had been found out, and that he had the evidence to prove it.'

Nate buried his face in the blanket.

'Things were turning ugly, so I grabbed the sky marshal's phraxlighter and got you out of there, right from under their noses, together with Slip, Weelum and Eudoxia. I'm afraid I had to play a little bit rough and it seems that, so far as the Great Glade Constabulary are concerned, we're all in this together. They're calling us . . .'

'The Copperwood Gang,' came Eudoxia's voice from the hatch as she climbed into the stiltshed and stood up, dusting off the sleeves of her topcoat. 'And I, Miss Eudoxia Prade, rich heiress from New Lake,' she continued, with a tinkling laugh, 'have been kidnapped by you and am being held to ransom. We're the talk of the city!'

Nate looked up and, despite himself, had to smile at the mixture of indignation and amusement on Eudoxia's face. The Professor, however, remained unsmiling and serious.

'Slip, Weelum and me, we're named as your accomplices, Nate. They've searched the Copperwood cabins, the phraxchamber works, and it's only a matter of time before they start on the allotments. Our descriptions have been posted on roost poles and tether posts all over the twelve districts, and there's a watch on all phraxships in and out of the Ledges – not to mention patrols in the outer city districts. They've got most of the Old Forest Militia out looking for us, together with guards from every factory owner and mining boss in New Lake.'

'We've got to get out of the city,' said Eudoxia, her green eyes flashing defiantly, 'and go to Hive. The Professor has friends there, and I have to find my father.'

'Yes, but how?' said Nate, painfully aware of his strapped arm and cracked ribs.

The Professor stood up and swept back the tails of his topcoat to reveal two silver phraxpistols holstered at his side.

'There might just be a way,' he said slowly.

· CHAPTER THIRTY-SEVEN ·

A pale moon hung low in the sky over the steam gardens and allotments of Copperwood. Bathed in silvery light, the huge vegetable forms – some as tall as the surrounding stilthouses – rose up from the rich steam-nourished earth and spread their extravagant leaves.

A cluster of crinkle-edged cabbages, each as big as a hammelhorn, nestled beneath the sturdy stands of white steam celery that sprouted six feet high. Red tubers, their feathery fronds fluttering in the wisps of steam, carpeted the ground beneath rows of half-submerged gladeonions and blue pumpkins, the size of prowlgrin carriages. Here and there, half-hidden by the thick vegetation, small sheds rose up on spindly timber stilts, lufwood ladders leading to hatches in their floors.

In a distant corner of the Copperwood allotments, a hatch opened and a tall individual in a tattered topcoat and crushed funnel hat stepped down onto the first rung of the ladder and began his descent. Pausing at the bottom to push aside the curling fronds of a gladeonion, the Professor scanned the balconies of the overlooking cabin rows, his spectacles glinting in the moonlight. Satisfied that he wasn't being observed, he set off through the allotments in the direction of the Copperwood bridge.

Several hours later, the Professor had left the cobbled streets and stilted workshops of Copperwood far behind and was striding along a compacted mud road rutted with wagon tracks and potholes. The weather had turned cold as he'd made his way through the sleeping city and his breath was coming now in thick clouds, while the streets were slippery with glittering frost.

He'd avoided the patrols of Great Glade guards in East Glade and Old Forest, but in New Lake he'd had to creep past a pair of fat low-belly goblin constables asleep beneath the statue in Barley Fields Square. The yellow glow from their crackling brazier fire flickered on the bronze statue of a charging banderbear, its tusks bared and claws splayed in a menacing lunge. It commemorated an ancient battle which had taken place on this spot back during the wars for the Free Glades in the Second Age of Flight. The Professor glanced over his shoulder at it as he went on his way. The statue looked tall and majestic – so different from the shambling mountain of fur that young Nate called his friend.

As the dawn broke, the Professor quickened his pace. On either side, the road was fringed with freshly hewn log cabins, mud-baked hive huts and newly dug ground pits; holes in the earth, roofed over with forest thatch, that were favoured by trogs. Over the rooftops, just beyond the recently cleared fields and pastures, and silhouetted against the pale sky, towered the Deepwoods forests themselves, as yet untouched by the expanding city.

This was the Northern Outer City, newest and poorest of the twelve districts. Here, hunters, trappers, small farmers and herders clung to the topcoat tails of Great Glade and made a living as best they could.

Up ahead, a prowlgrin's bark made the Professor shrink back once more into the shadows. He flattened himself against the wall of a gladeoak cabin, phraxpistols in hand.

Moments later, a patrol of eight Freeglade Lancers galloped past, the feet of their prowlgrins pattering softly on the hard earth. The Professor waited a few seconds, then, holstering his pistols, stepped back onto the road. A few dozen shacks later, he stopped outside a ramshackle pit house sunk into the ground, with a rough thatch of lufwood sprigs and barkmoss and a heavily braced door of ironwood. The Professor descended the mud steps which led down to the door. He knocked three times and waited. From inside came the sounds of bolts being drawn back and beams lifted. The heavy door opened an inch and a bloodshot eye peered out.

'Who is it?' a gruff voice snarled.

'Ambris Hentadile,' the Professor replied in a low whisper.

'Who?'

'The Professor,' he tried again. 'From the *Deadbolt Vulpoon*. You lost everything at the splinters table and I paid for your food and grog for the rest of the voyage, remember?'

'The Professor?' the voice murmured. 'The Professor! Why, of course!'

The door was flung open to reveal a brawny-looking individual in a grimy nightshirt, clutching a phraxmusket. His face was weather-beaten, the coppery skin covered in deep creases and fringed by short, close-cropped silver hair and elaborately braided side-whiskers. His deep-set eyes were the colour of dark mahogany and sparkled mischievously from beneath heavy black eyebrows.

'Good to see you, Captain Razortooth,' said the Professor with a slightly exaggerated bow of respect.

'Always the gentleman,' beamed Captain Razortooth, revealing a mouthful of matt gold and brown decay. He ushered him across the threshold. 'But please, call me Squall. I'll have no standing on ceremony in this Wilderness Lair!'

The Professor smiled as he stepped inside to find himself in a subterranean mud-walled room full of cluttered shelves and skychests, hanging telescopes and cloud gauges, and a vast array of animal pelts. In one corner there was a low-slung hammock; in the other, a battered-looking tavern table with two stools.

The original Wilderness Lair, as the Professor knew well, was the fabled bastion of the sky pirates in the First Age of Flight. Those swashbuckling adventurers had defied the tyrannical leagues of Old Undertown, engaging in mighty sky battles and hiding out in the eerie wastes of the Edgelands, where they moored their sky galleons at the precarious cliff face of Wilderness Lair.

What days those must have been, the Professor had often thought. Now, here he was, standing before one of the last of a dying breed – a sky pirate of the Third Age of Flight.

Instead of a magnificent sky galleon moored beneath the lip of the Edge cliff, this sky pirate ran an illegal phraxlighter which was chained up to a nearby Deepwoods tree. Instead of engaging in epic battles with leaguesmen, Captain Squall Razortooth had to content himself with dodging prowlgrin patrols and the militia of phraxmarines, who would confiscate any unauthorized phraxcraft piloted by unregistered engineers – and with good reason, as the Professor knew full well.

These home-made vessels, cobbled together from scavenged scraps, were notoriously unreliable, especially in the hands of self-taught or incompetent phraxpilots. After crashes, explosions and several appalling skytavern tragedies, the authorities of Great Glade had clamped down on these latterday 'sky pirates'. That had been more than two hundred years ago. Now, they were almost unheard of.

The few sky pirates that remained were, like Squall Razortooth, simple forest folk from distant Deepwoods settlements, who had journeyed to Great Glade to train in the flight academies, only to drop out or fail the rigorous examinations. Making use of what little they'd learned, they flouted the rules by taking to the sky in illegal phraxlighters and creating their own chances, ferrying renegades, contraband and desperate travellers who needed passage, no questions asked.

Few of these sky pirates or their vessels lasted long, usually crashing or exploding far out in the forest, never to be seen again. Squall Razortooth was the exception.

Thrown out of the flight academies after a drunken brawl, plain old Neb Sawtooth as he was then had already been well on the way to becoming an accomplished phraxpilot. Undaunted by his expulsion, he'd worked for years in the factories and workshops of East Glade, yet always harbouring the ambition of returning to the skies . . .

All this, the Professor had learned at the splinters table of the skytavern, *Deadbolt Vulpoon*, as a destitute Squall Razortooth poured his heart out to him. Finally, Squall had told him, he'd managed to pilfer enough tiny shards of stormphrax to begin the construction of a small phraxlighter of his own. This he'd done in utmost secrecy out in the Northern Outer City, where fewer questions were asked.

Then, in true sky pirate tradition, he had named himself Squall Razortooth – *Captain* Squall Razortooth – and he had taken to the skies in his phraxlighter, which he had called the *Gladedancer*.

With few rivals, Squall had made a good living and slowly amassed enough to buy a ticket on the *Deadbolt Vulpoon* to visit the settlement of his birth in the tree ridges of the far west. But, like many such tiny communities, Squall had found it ruined and deserted, and had returned to Great Glade aboard the skytavern, broken-hearted and drowning his sorrows. It hadn't taken long for the tavern gamblers to strip him of his hard-earned wealth. But the Professor had taken pity on the ruined sky pirate and been touched by his story.

That had been ten years ago. Now, the Professor needed his help.

Squall showed him to the table and drew up a stool. The Professor sat down and ran his fingers over the surface of the table. It was carved with the names of the sky pirates who had sat there long ago, when the table had graced a tavern.

Zephyr Razorflit. Thunderclap Tilderstag. Cloud Wolf . . .

'It's a beauty, isn't it?' smiled Squall, stroking the surface of the table lovingly. 'Traded it for twenty fromp pelts and a quart of woodgrog from an old shryke in New Undertown. She claimed it originally came from a tavern in Old Undertown – though you've got to take that with a grain of phraxdust . . .'

'Beautiful,' replied the Professor. 'I've always loved things from the past. Especially from the First Age of Flight – the age of the sky pirates . . .' He looked up from the table and into Squall Razortooth's dark mahogany eyes. 'Talking of which,' he said quietly, 'I find myself in need of a sky pirate. One of the old school; brave, daring and . . . loyal.'

The sky pirate smiled. 'I suppose you do, Professor,' he said, 'especially with the whole of the Old Forest Militia out looking for you and a thousand-glader reward on your head . . .'

'You've seen the wanted notices?' said the Professor.

'Could hardly miss them,' said Squall. 'They're posted all over the district.'

'I couldn't afford a thousand gladers, but—' began the Professor, only for Squall to hold up a hand to silence him.

'I won't take your money, Professor,' said the sky pirate. 'Not after the kindness you showed me back on the skytavern. She's a bit battered, and not quite the ship she used to be, but the *Gladedancer* will take you far enough out into the woods to get you clear of the Great Glade Militia.'

He reached up to a shelf and took down two glasses and a flask of fiery woodgrog. Pouring two measures, he handed one glass to the Professor and raised the other.

'To the sky pirates of old!'

CHAPTER THIRTY-EIGHT

'Your turn, Nate,' said Eudoxia with a mischievous grin. 'Must I?' sighed Nate.

'If you want to get out of Great Glade, you'll allow Miss Prade to do her work,' said the Professor solemnly, his mob cap pulled low over his face and the goblin matron's shawl tightly knotted round his shoulders.

'Go on then,' smiled Nate. 'Do your worst.'

Eudoxia selected a small charred ember from the selection she'd gathered from the ash bucket of the stiltshed's stove.

'Hold still,' she told him, reaching up and drawing two small vertical lines between Nate's eyebrows, and two more across his forehead. She blurred them with her thumb.

'What are you doing?' he asked.

'Ageing you,' she said simply. 'They're looking for a young lamplighter, not a portly old fourthling farmer.'

She returned to her work, drawing on thin lines like raven's feet, which fanned out from the corners of his eyes, and thicker marks which ran from the sides of his nostrils to the corners of his mouth. Then she rubbed white ash into his hair and placed the battered wide-brimmed hat of woven gladegrass on his head.

Stepping back, she admired her handiwork. 'Why, if I didn't know better, I'd swear you'd just finished ploughing a forest field in the outer city!' she laughed.

Nate examined himself in the small mirror Eudoxia held up. He certainly looked the part. With the mud-stained breeches and the three undershirts rolled up and stuffed inside his shabby embroidered waistcoat, he looked for all the world like an old plough hand.

Beside him, Slip was unrecognizable beneath the heavy hooded cloak of an oakelf, while Eudoxia herself was resplendent in wagoner's overalls, a peaked hat and a magnificent moustache that she had fashioned from clippings of Weelum's fur. Much to everyone else's amusement, the Professor was dressed in the gaudy dress, mob cap and decorated shawl of a goblin matron, while Weelum towered over him as his cloddertrog attendant, in a heavy rain hood, tightly wound neck scarf and full-length cape. In one gloved hand he clutched a parasol; in the other, Nate's knapsack. Over his shoulder were slung a second backpack and assorted bedrolls.

Nate knew that if they were indeed to get out of Great Glade undetected, then they all had Slip to thank for it. For it was the little grey goblin scuttler who'd used his skills to sneak back to the cabin row and retrieve a tilderleather backpack of cooking utensils, strikefires, bedding rolls and the like, as well as Nate's knapsack, with its precious lightbox and even more precious box of memories. Not only that, but night after night, as the ring of the Old Forest Militia had slowly closed in around them, Slip would disappear silently into the darkness. Then, just before dawn, the hatch to the stiltshed would creak open and Slip would appear, carrying his latest find from the washlines of Copperwood and East Glade – a cloak, a dress, or a cloddertrog rain hood.

Finally, the Professor decided, they were ready.

'They'll be expecting us to make our escape at night,' he told the others as they pulled on the assortment of pilfered clothes. 'So we'll walk out of here in broad daylight in an hour or so's time, when the streets fill up.' He looked them each up and down, before nodding with approval. 'Nate and Eudoxia go first, and Slip follow just behind. Nate, tell the banderbear to stay close behind me. And to keep quiet!'

'His name is Weelum,' Nate told the Professor.

'Wuh-waah!' growled Weelum, tapping the side of his rain hood with a gloved paw, then thumping his chest. *The glass eye's heart is cold towards Weelum.*

'What did it say?' asked the Professor.

'Weelum understands,' said Nate.

He knew that, unlike his friends Eudoxia and Slip, the Professor was unsure of the banderbear, and regarded him as an unpredictable wild creature who had no business living in a city like Great Glade. But whatever the Professor's views, Nate wasn't going to leave Weelum behind.

As midmorning approached, they climbed down from the stiltshed and slipped out of the allotments and into the busy streets of Copperwood. Nate and Eudoxia walked side by side, pretending to be lost in conversation, while a few paces behind, the hunched figure of Slip in his oakelf robes followed silently. A little way back, but within earshot, the Professor walked somewhat stiffly, his face all but obscured by the lace-edged mob cap, with the looming figure of

Weelum behind, trying not to step on the Professor's trailing skirt.

They approached a couple of hefty cloddertrog constables who were lounging next to a glowing brazier in the shadows beneath the statue of Mangobey Cartshank, phraxmuskets over their shoulders. One was warming his outstretched hands in the shimmering heat, the other was gripping a mug of steaming oaktea. There was a 'wanted' poster tied round the base of the statue, with the names of the four members of the 'Copperwood Gang' listed, and news of the thousand-glader reward in large black letters. Not that the guards noticed. Neither of them gave the disparate group so much as a glance as they walked past, and continued towards the bridge over Copperwood Creek.

As they passed by it, Nate recalled the first time he'd done so. He remembered the gnarled slaughterer with his fishing rod and creel, and the sound advice he had given about checking for vacancies on the hiring posts . . . How long ago that now seemed. Then he had been fresh-faced and full of hope, setting out on a new life in 'the Big Steam'. Now, he was on the run.

'It started at the thousandsticks match,' Eudoxia was saying, her low voice breaking into Nate's reveries, 'this feeling between the Professor and Weelum.'

It had been a week since Nate had seen anything but the inside of the stiltshed, and despite his aching ribs, sore shoulder and the fear of discovery, it felt good to be out in the fresh air of Copperwood.

'It was just after you fell,' Eudoxia went on. 'I looked down at the field and spotted the Professor running towards the sky marshal's phraxlighter. The sky marshal had landed and was having an argument with the constables. The Professor just jumped in, took off and headed straight for the high pine. He scooped you up, then turned, flew straight past Branxford – who was waving that black thousandstick of his and shouting – and came barrelling towards us in the Copperwood box.'

She reached up and pressed her fingers to the two halves of the moustache, making sure that neither of them had slipped.

'I think he was hoping to find Friston Drew in his seat,' she said, 'but all he found was Slip, Weelum and me. The constabulary was clattering up the steps towards us, and I could see you lying in the phraxlighter hurt, so I instinctively climbed aboard, and Slip followed. I could tell the Professor wasn't happy, but it all happened so quickly. He saw that I wasn't going to leave you, so he took off again – which was when Weelum reached up and grabbed the side of the phraxlighter, and wouldn't let go. He just wanted to come with us, you see. He was worried about you.'

Eudoxia glanced round at her companion and smiled, her eyes sparkling.

'Just like the rest of us . . .'

They were walking down a narrow alley, each side lined with market stalls. The high sun shone down on the burnished pots and kettles that hung from hooks, and on the displays of lace laid out on the trestle tables. Eudoxia hesitated for a moment, her fingers plucking at an embroidered prowlgrin blanket, before moving on.

'Mind you, the Professor was furious,' she said, turning back to Nate. 'Up we went, rolling and juddering, half turvey-turned by Weelum's weight, with the Professor cursing and swearing. I thought we were going to crash right there and then, but the Professor managed to bring the phraxlighter down in a hayrick on the edge of the Silver Pastures. Said we were lucky to be alive. The hull was split in two and the rudder smashed to pieces. But the phraxchamber was intact and didn't explode.'

'Thank Sky,' Nate said.

'Thank Sky indeed,' said Eudoxia. 'We made a run for it on foot, with Weelum carrying you on his back all the way to Slip's stiltshed. Not that that made any difference to the Professor. He just kept saying that now we'd all be on the run, and that it hadn't needed to be this way. He wouldn't even look at Weelum . . .'

'It wasn't Weelum's fault,' said Nate. 'The ones to blame are Felftis Brack and Branxford—'

He paused, a look of shock on his face. There, just ahead of them, was the phraxchamber works – or at least what was left of it. The stilthouse itself had toppled over on its side, the roof chimneys either twisted or shorn off at the base, and a great blast crater now lay in the centre of the yard, fringed with splintered and shattered stilts, pointing accusingly at the sky.

Already, though, repairs were underway. New stilts were being erected, the stilthouse had been bound and braced with chains and cables, and an army of workers was busy preparing to right it once more with steam cranes and levers.

At the gates, they'd been busy too, Nate noticed. The wrought ironwork lettering of *Gremlop and Drew* had been replaced with a painted lufwood sign that read *Brack's Phraxchamber Works*.

'What next?' muttered Nate. 'Brack's phraxmine?'

'Not if I've got anything to do with it,' replied Eudoxia fiercely.

· CHAPTER THIRTY-NINE ·

By late afternoon, they'd arrived in the Northern Outer City district without any major mishap. A party of oakelf brothers had passed them in New Undertown and been surprised when Slip didn't respond to their greeting, and the Professor had appeared to snub several goblin laundresses at a fountain in East Glade, but apart from that their disguises had held up very effectively. So effectively, in fact, that at first glance Squall Razortooth hadn't recognized the Professor when he knocked at his ground pit door.

'Come with me, Madam,' the old sky pirate had chuckled at last, when a red-faced Professor had pulled off the lacy mob cap before hastily returning it to his head, 'to the back of my Wilderness Lair!'

The five of them followed him round the side of the pit house and along a path through the fields behind, towards the towering treeline of the Deepwoods. As they entered the forest, Nate felt his pulse quicken, and behind him he heard Weelum give a low growl of excitement.

'Silence!' hissed the Professor over his shoulder in response.

They continued down the path, which wound through a grove of copperwoods, until they reached a tall ironwood pine. Squall stopped. Nate looked up, but saw nothing at first. As he squinted more closely into the dense foliage though, he caught sight of a vessel moored to a lower branch – a medium-sized phraxlighter with an underslung phraxchamber and twin side funnels. Above it, on a timber platform lashed to the tree trunk, was a workshop, complete with hanging furnace, bellows, forge bench, tool racks and phraxlanterns.

'She's not much,' beamed Captain Squall Razortooth proudly. 'But she's mine.'

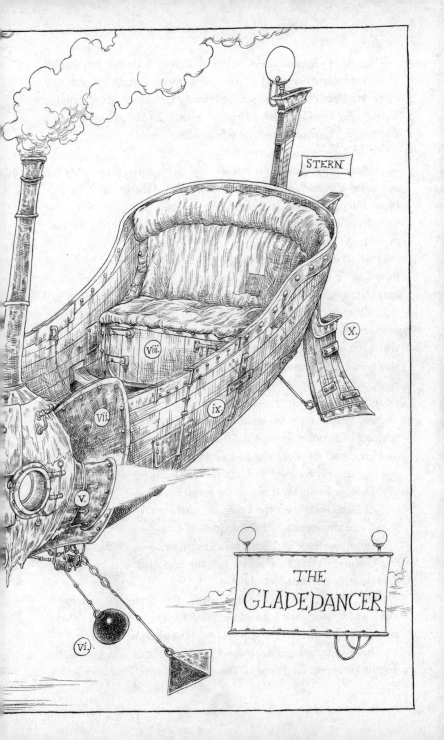

STERN

X.

viii.

 vii.

ix.

v.

vi.

THE
GLADEDANCER

The others looked up. Constructed from a timber frame, the phraxlighter had been clad with countless misshapen scraps of metal, each one riveted into position. It scarcely looked capable of flight. Up near the lopsided beak-like prow, a name had been painted onto the side of a burnished rectangle of bronze.

'*Gladedancer*,' Nate murmured.

Squall climbed up the ironwood pine with surprising agility for one of his age, and from the platform overhead there was the sound of scraping and tools, pots and benches being moved. When the captain emerged and stepped down into his phraxlighter, he had been transformed.

Instead of the grubby nightshirt and oil-stained breeches, Squall now wore a heavy topcoat of deep ochre, with embroidered collar and buttoned-up coat-tails. His waistcoat was of dark fromp fur with silver buttons, and his trousers were double-seamed green felt of the finest quality. On his head, setting off his freshly combed side-whiskers, was a crumple-brimmed funnel hat of oiled leather; at his side was a long-barrelled phraxpistol with a carved handle of tilder ivory, while strapped to his back was a pair of angular parawings, folded back and spring-loaded.

Seating himself at the controls, Squall shifted the chamber gears. A cloud of steam rose from the side funnels as he cast off from the platform, and the *Gladedancer* rose in the air. Immediately, Squall reached smartly forward and adjusted the hullweights, bringing the phraxlighter smoothly down to the forest floor.

'At last!' exclaimed the Professor, tearing off the lacy cap and shawl and clambering out of the dress.

The others followed suit, revealing their own clothes beneath the costumes. Weelum reached into the backpack and handed the Professor his crushed funnel hat.

'Er . . . thank you . . . Weelum,' said the Professor somewhat awkwardly, taking the hat and brushing it off with his hands. 'Now, perhaps you'd like to take your place in the phraxlighter?'

The banderbear nodded and, clutching the luggage in his mighty paws, climbed aboard. The others followed him, taking their places on the narrow benches behind the sky pirate.

'Eudoxia!' laughed Nate, moments later, as the *Gladedancer* wheezed into action, clouds of ice-cold steam billowing from the side funnels as the phraxlighter rose slowly from the ground.

'What?' said Eudoxia, gazing round at him through wide green eyes.

'Your moustache!'

Touching her upper lip, she giggled and peeled off the twin twists of banderbear hair and placed them in Nate's hand.

'A memento,' she said and smiled. 'For that memory box of yours.'

· CHAPTER FORTY ·

With great clouds of icy steam billowing from its side funnels, the phraxlighter rose into the air. At the prow, on a padded seat, sat Squall Razortooth in front of a seeming jumble of cogs, pulleys and flight levers. Behind him, Nate and Eudoxia perched on a low bench, arm in arm and each clutching the side of the vessel with their free hands to steady themselves. On the wide built-in seat at the stern, Weelum sat hunched over and trembling, his small feathery ears quivering with unease. On either side of the great banderbear, squashed and uncomfortable-looking, sat Slip the scuttler and the Professor.

As they rose above the forest canopy, the sweet smell of bruised leaves filled the air. A moment later, the evening sky opened up around them, ribbons of crimson cloud set against the pink and orange blush of dusk. They were some twenty or thirty strides above the rippling ocean of leaves when Squall leaned forward and, with expert fingers, began adjusting the levers and handles in front of him. The phraxlighter came to a halt and hovered unsteadily in the twilight air.

The controls appeared as cobbled together as everything else on the *Gladedancer* and yet, Nate could see, they were carefully engineered and intricately fashioned. Three pipes – one silver, one copper and one bronze, and each of different widths – emerged through a hole in the hull and ended in a riveted copperwood box in front of Squall's seat. Two stout levers stuck out at the top, the first connected to the rudder and the second set to raise and lower the pendulous hull weights. A steam gauge, with numbers and a black needle on its face, was mounted on a circular plate beside them. As for the row of flight levers on either side of the pilot's chair,

256

they had clearly been fashioned from anything that had come to hand – a length of pipe, a black stove poker, the polished barrel of a phraxmusket . . .

Squall Razortooth adjusted the hull weights and, glancing over his shoulder, noticed the look of intense concentration on Nate's face. The old sky pirate smiled, his leathery skin crinkling at the corners of his dark mahogany eyes.

'Hold on tight there, my fine young couple,' he chuckled, winking at Nate and Eudoxia. 'The old *Gladedancer* is going to do some fancy steaming!'

He pulled back on a flight lever. As he did so, two plumes of steam billowed out from the side funnels and jets of white phraxflame blazed from the propulsion ducts of the twin phraxchambers.

With a jolt, the *Gladedancer* leaped forwards at astonishing speed, forcing Nate to strengthen his hold on the side of the vessel. Next to him, he felt Eudoxia's grip tighten on his arm. The wind slammed into his face as, in front of him, Squall hunkered down low in his seat. On either side, the phraxchambers hummed and the funnels hissed, while the low whistle of the propulsion ducts rose steadily higher in pitch.

Looking round through narrowed eyes, Nate could see that the air was full of phraxships of all shapes and sizes. The vapour trails from their funnels crisscrossed the evening sky. Heavily laden merchant ships with low-slung phraxchambers, phraxtugs pulling lines of sumpwood barges, small phraxlighters in arrowhead convoy, and mighty skytaverns bound for distant settlements, were all busy plying their trade in the evening sky.

The high-pitched whistle of the propulsion ducts now changed to a hissing roar, and with it the timbers of the *Gladedancer* creaked and juddered, the plates of metal shifting about. Everything began to rattle as the phraxchamber sent tremors through the rickety vessel.

Behind Nate, Weelum was bent low, his head tucked into his chest and his mighty arms encompassing the Professor and Slip on either side of him. Below, the jagged treetops of the forest canopy sped past in a blur.

Squall turned in his seat, and Nate saw a look of concern pass across his weather-beaten features as he gazed back over his shoulder to the horizon far behind them. The sky pirate's eyes narrowed. A moment later, he pulled a telescope from the folds of his embroidered frock coat and looked through it. Nate turned and tried to see what he was looking at, but with the naked eye all he could make out was the dim glow of a distant phraxvessel, its night lanterns already blazing.

'What is it?' asked Eudoxia, pushing her hair back as she turned her head and the wind whipped it across her face.

'Trouble,' said Squall Razortooth through clenched teeth.

'Trouble?' Nate repeated.

Squall handed him the telescope. Nate put it to his eye and adjusted the focus. The phraxvessel revealed itself to be a sleek beak-prowed patrol vessel of the phraxmarine, with a low-slung phraxchamber and a long thin funnel billowing out an impressive trail of steam. As Nate watched, it turned in the sky until the heavy beak was pointing directly at them and began following the *Gladedancer*, like a vulpoon hunting a woodmouse.

Nate handed the telescope back to the sky pirate. 'They're heading towards us,' he told him.

'Aye, lad,' said Squall ruefully. 'Spotted our steam trails most likely – thin and sleek as spidersilk, not like the rest of these chuggers around us.' He indicated the merchant ships and timber barges in the distance with a wave of his hand. 'It's what the phraxpatrol is trained to do. But spotting's one thing,' he chuckled, winking at Nate and Eudoxia, before turning back to the controls. 'Catching's another!'

Squall reached forward and eased the copper pipe as far back as it would go. Immediately, there was a twin roar from the propulsion ducts of the phraxchambers and the jets of phraxfire doubled in length and thickness. As they did so, the *Gladedancer* seemed almost to screech in protest as the wind howled through the riveted joints and splintered cracks in the battered hull.

Nate looked down over the side of the vessel. They were

dropping lower in the sky and the rushing blur of the forest canopy was getting closer. Just in front of him, the sky pirate was hunched lower than ever in his seat, his hands fluttering over the flight levers. The *Gladedancer* swerved and shuddered as the tallest of the treetops seemed to rush up to meet them, only to vanish behind moments later, their branches whistling past Nate's ears and making him flinch. Beside him, Eudoxia trembled, her hand gripping his arm more tightly than ever. Weelum's deep growls of alarm from the stern competed with the whistling roar of the propulsion ducts, while the Professor's usually calm voice now rose to an excited bellow.

'They're falling behind! . . . We're losing them!'

Ducking, as a branch of an ironwood pine whirred overhead, Nate glanced back. Sure enough, the patrol ship was now a glowing spot in the orange sky, getting smaller by the moment.

'A few more strides and we'll be free and clear . . .'

As if in answer to the Professor's words, there was a sudden screeching sound of metal shearing from metal as the struts of the right-hand phraxchamber tore themselves from the *Gladedancer's* hull, sending both chamber and funnel spiralling down into the forest below. Moments later, there was a muffled thump and a cloud of sepia dust mushroomed up into the sky behind them.

Squall squirmed in his seat as he struggled with the controls, attempting to regain control of the *Gladedancer* as it bucked and listed dangerously to one side. Any moment now, Nate could see, as he clung to Eudoxia with one hand and the side of the vessel with the other, the phraxlighter risked slamming into one of the treetops ahead.

With a grunt of effort, Squall eased the left-hand phraxchamber down until the roar of the propulsion duct fell to a low hum and shards of ice began tumbling down into the forest below. At the same time, by realigning the hull weights, the old sky pirate managed to right the listing *Gladedancer* as its speed slowed. Behind them, the lamps of the patrol vessel grew brighter once more as it steadily gained on the stricken phraxlighter.

'We're going to have to act fast,' Squall said as he rose from his seat and turned to Nate and his companions. 'There are ropes with grappling hooks in the stern. Hand them round. You'll each need one. When I give the word, drop the hook down into the trees below, and when you feel it catch on a branch, swing down to the trees. You'll be able to climb down to the forest floor . . .'

Nate blanched. 'But Weelum,' he said, 'he can't climb trees.'

Behind him, the Professor was already pulling grappling hooks and coils of rope from beneath the bench at the stern of the phraxlighter. He separated the tangle of ropes with shaking hands and passed them out to Nate, Eudoxia and Slip, keeping one for himself.

'Can't climb trees, you say?' Squall repeated. 'Well, who'd have thought it?'

'No banderbears can climb trees,' said Nate.

'Wuh-wuh,' said Weelum, looking up, touching his shoulder and head lightly, then describing a circle in the air with a raised claw. *The moon climbs in the treetops, the banderbear walks beneath.*

'I'll use a grappling hook,' said Squall. 'Our friend here can try his luck with these.'

He shrugged the straps of the parawings off his shoulders and handed them to Nate. Between them, Nate and Eudoxia secured the parawings to the trembling banderbear, buckling the harness across his great chest.

'Wuh-wuh, wurgh,' Nate whispered in his friend's twitching ear, his left hand fluttering. *Jump, then pull on the cord, to float like a leaf on the wind.*

'Wuh,' muttered the banderbear uneasily, with a long sweep of an arm. 'Wuh.' *The ways of the pirates of the sky are strange indeed.* He looked down. And as he stared at the blur of green as the *Gladedancer* forged on over the treetops, Weelum's body trembled with fear.

'We don't have much time!' shouted Squall.

'Come on, Weelum,' urged Nate. 'I'll see you down in the forest.'

'*Waah!*' cried Weelum, and without glancing back, he gripped the cord in his trembling paw and stepped off the side.

The phraxlighter pitched wildly as the heavy creature tumbled

away into the darkening sky. Nate watched Weelum tug on the dangling rope. With a soft *click* and a loud *whoosh*, the great lufwood and tilderskin parawings sprung open, the rush of oncoming wind making them billow and flex, and the banderbear glided off through the air.

'Earth and Sky be with you,' Nate murmured as he reached down and wound the end of the grappling hook rope around his right hand.

'Now for the rest of us!' said Squall.

Exchanging glances, Nate, Eudoxia, Slip and the Professor stood up, rucksacks and bedrolls slung about their backs and shoulders. Gripping the bows with one hand, they dropped the grappling hooks down over the side of the phraxlighter. Squall adjusted the flight levers, slowing the *Gladedancer* still further, then pulled a locking bar down to hold the levers in place. He climbed to his feet.

Slip's grappling hook caught on a branch first. With a cry of surprise, he was jerked from the side of the phraxlighter and swooped down towards the forest canopy below. Eudoxia was next, with the Professor disappearing a moment after her. As Squall took his place next to him, Nate glanced down, wondering when his own grappling hook might snag a branch.

'Sky protect you, lad,' he heard Squall saying and was about to reply when, with a great tug – so strong it felt as though his arm was being wrenched from its socket – he was yanked from the stricken craft.

For an instant, Nate felt he could fly. His head spun and his stomach turned somersaults. Holding his breath, he swung down through the air, the green canopy rushing up to meet him. A moment later, he plunged through the dense foliage and ended up dangling from the rope, the three-pronged grappling hook lodged into the fork of an ironwood pine branch above his head and the shadowy forest floor far below.

'Nate, over here!'

He glanced round. The Professor was suspended from the upper branches of a lufwood tree some distance to his right. Close by, Eudoxia was climbing up her rope, hand over hand, to the lullabee branch above her head, with Slip, who was already standing on a jutting branch to her left, reaching out to help her. Seconds later, Nate heard a soft crunching noise and a grunt of expelled air as Squall's rope went suddenly taut, and the captain appeared beside him, hanging down from his own grappling hook.

Overhead, the *Gladedancer* was listing heavily to port as, unencumbered by passengers now, it zigzagged on across the Deepwoods. Behind, the beaked prow of the Great Glade patrol ship came into view, closing in for the kill.

'Farewell, old girl,' Squall Razortooth murmured sadly as the *Gladedancer* headed towards the looming silhouette of a huge copperwood tree.

As it struck, there was a blinding flash, followed a moment later by an almighty roaring *crash!* as the phraxvessel exploded. Dazzling flashes of molten metal sped off across the sky in broad arcs, before burning out or tumbling down into the forest below. A passing skein of snowbirds scattered in all directions, squawking with alarm. A moment later, all that remained of the *Gladedancer* was the faintest whiff of toasted almonds – and a moment after, that too was gone.

High in the darkening sky, the patrol vessel turned and headed back in the direction of Great Glade, a trail of steam pouring out behind it.

'That's that, then.' Squall Razortooth shook his head. 'My career is over. What use is a sky pirate without a skyship? I mean, who would want to employ me now?'

Nate reached out a hand to the old sky pirate. 'I would,' he said.

· CHAPTER FORTY-ONE ·

By the time Nate and the old sky pirate had unhooked themselves and climbed down to the forest floor, it was dark and the Deepwoods were alive with strange noises. There was chattering and screeching, howling and roaring; the snapping of twigs and the rustling of leaves. Fromps barked, quarms coughed and hooted, and a thousand other unseen creatures added their own clicks, chirrups and rasping calls to the night-time chorus.

Slip, Eudoxia and the Professor were waiting for them at the foot of the great lufwood tree. Their faces were drawn and anxious.

'What do you think we should do now, friend Nate?' Slip asked softly, his huge dark eyes flickering with concern.

Nate frowned.

'I've given countless lectures from the hanging baskets of skytaverns on all aspects of Deepwoods flora and fauna,' the Professor admitted, 'but I've never actually spent a night this far out, down on the ground.'

'And I've ridden through the forest canopy on prowlgrinback,' Eudoxia added. 'Though like you, Professor, I've never been this far from Great Glade.' She shuddered. 'In the dark . . .'

Slip nodded vigorously. 'Slip was born in the forest – but he can't remember much about it. What do you think we should do, friend Nate?' he repeated, his eyes wider than ever.

Squall Razortooth turned to Nate and clapped him on the back. 'I'm afraid this old sky pirate is a cloudlubber, lad. Not much use down here in the Deepwoods.'

Nate looked from one expectant face to the other. 'I've been out in the Eastern Woods,' he began, 'but they've been thinned out, and are pretty well-travelled these days. I'm afraid the Deepwoods themselves are every bit as strange to me as they are to the rest of you.'

Just then, in the distance, through the strange cacophony of the night-time forest, Nate heard a familiar sound. He turned slightly and cocked his head to one side. The others looked at him questioningly.

'What is it?' said Eudoxia.

'I thought I heard . . .' Nate began. 'Yes, there it is again. Can you hear it? There . . . Yodelling!'

Eudoxia nodded, a puzzled frown on her face. Nate screwed his eyes closed as he concentrated on the faint but unmistakeable sound.

Back in Coppertown, Weelum had told him how, despite the solitary nature of their lives, banderbears would maintain contact with one another by yodelling. Their booming voices would carry across the vast distances of the Deepwoods, passing on tales, one to the other, warning of danger and, on occasions, calling all of their number to assemble at one of their great convocations, when banderbears would come together from every corner of the forest.

'It's Weelum,' said Nate excitedly.

'It's certainly a banderbear,' said the Professor, 'but can we be sure it's our friend, Weelum?'

Nate raised his cupped hands to his mouth, filled his lungs with air and yodelled back as best he could, his long broken cry echoing off into the shadow-filled night. It was answered at once, the yodel coming in a long musical burst of greeting.

'It *is* him!' cried Nate. 'I'm sure of it!'

The yodelling came again, the long tremulous phrase rising at the end.

'He says to come now,' Nate said, turning to the others. 'To follow his calls . . .'

'But it sounds so far away,' said the Professor uncertainly. 'Might it not be wiser to wait until morning? After all, it is my understanding that the Deepwoods are at their most dangerous after dark . . .'

'If an old sky pirate might make so bold . . .' said Squall Razortooth, reaching into the depths of his frock coat and withdrawing his hands.

All at once the air around them was bathed in a bright yellow glow. Everyone turned, to see the sky pirate's grinning face illuminated by the light that was streaming up from his hands.

'Sky crystals?' said the Professor, wonder in his voice. 'I've heard of them, of course. But I've never seen any.'

'The very same, Professor,' said Squall. 'We all think we're so clever now in this Third Age of Flight, but those sky pirates of the First Age knew a trick or two worth remembering, like these sky crystals. Not only do they create light, but when struck together, they make sparks – and, since they work in the rain, they're better than any strikefire . . .'

Far in the distance, Weelum's yodelling cry sounded again.

'They'll light our way and ward off any unwelcome creatures lurking out there in the dark,' said Squall.

The Professor nodded. 'Very well,' he said.

They hastily gathered up their belongings, slipping rucksacks and bedrolls onto their shoulders. Then, with Squall at the front, the sky crystals in his hand glowing brightly and showing the way ahead, they set off. Eudoxia and Slip followed immediately behind the sky pirate, walking side by side, their hands clasped together. Nate and the Professor brought up the rear. All five of them were cocooned in the yellow ball of light that illuminated their immediate surroundings and, they hoped, might keep the Deepwoods creatures at bay.

They walked through the forest in silence for the most part, weaving their way between the huge tree trunks with their spreading roots corrugating the forest floor. Every so often, Weelum's yodel would confirm that they were still heading in the right direction. Down into deep dales, they trudged, stepping over flat-topped mushrooms and dew-drenched moss, as mist coiled round their ankles. Then up undulating slopes they climbed in single file, brushing past feathery white ferns and swaying sallowdrop trees, heavy with fruit. Around them, just outside the sky crystals' reassuring glow, the dark forms of forest creatures moved through the undergrowth.

'Don't you worry, Miss Eudoxia,' Slip whispered, his voice quavering. 'Slip's job down the mine was to get rid of nasty crawly things. Slip'll protect you.'

'You mustn't worry either, Slip,' Eudoxia replied, patting his arm. 'My father taught me to take care of myself. I'm a crack shot with a phraxpistol . . .'

'What's *that*?' breathed Squall Razortooth, suddenly stopping and squinting up into the branches high above their heads.

Nate listened. A soft whooshing sound filled the air, rising and falling like a huge pair of bellows tending an unseen forge.

'Well I never!' muttered the Professor delightedly. 'Look, there! It's a giant tree fromp, as I live and breathe!'

Nate screwed up his eyes and peered into the shadows. High in the branches of a mighty ironwood pine, hanging from a huge tail, was the shaggy white form of a gigantic animal. As Nate's eyes adjusted to the gloom, he could just make out the fromp's great fur-fringed ears and long prehensile trunk, which snaked down and swayed gently back and forth. The creature's chest rose and fell as it breathed in and out in soft hooting gulps. The fromp opened one deep blue eye and gazed down at them balefully.

'Amazing creatures,' the Professor whispered. 'Impressive-looking, but completely harmless I understand. They're perfectly adapted to life high up in the pines, eating the blackbark beetles and resin grubs that live there . . .' He shook his head in wonder. 'I've never actually seen one in the wild before . . .'

The yodel, louder now, sounded from over the next tree ridge.

'Come on,' said Nate. 'Not far now . . .'

They clambered up over the steep forest ridge and down through clumps of dew-covered ferns on the other side, until they came to a stand of ghostelms. Their white trunks rose up from the dark loamy forest floor, straight and smooth-barked.

'Wuh-wuh!' came the sound of a familiar voice, and the great shaggy form of Weelum the banderbear came lurching through the trees towards them. He interlaced his claws at his chest. 'Wuh-waah-wuh!' *Our songs have become one at last.*

'Weelum!' Eudoxia cried out, rushing up and embracing the banderbear. 'It's so good to see you,' she told him, and pulled away. 'We'd have been lost without you!'

Beside her, Slip the scuttler nodded enthusiastically.

'It's certainly good to see a friendly face,' the Professor added, smiling broadly.

Nate raised one hand to his forehead and held out the open palm of the other to Weelum. 'Wuh-wuh,' he said. *What path would you have us take?*

In answer, the banderbear motioned for them to follow, and set off between the white tree trunks. After some forty or fifty strides, the banderbear stopped and turned to Nate.

'Wuh-wurra-wuh,' he announced proudly.

'What did he say?' asked Squall Razortooth, the glow from the sky crystals revealing his weather-beaten face, flushed and glistening with exertion.

'He said that . . .' Nate began uncertainly, looking around at the thin white tree trunks all about them, '. . . that we should sleep *here* for the night.'

The sky pirate gazed up at the ghostelms, a look of confusion on his face.

'I thought you said these here banderbears couldn't climb trees,' he said. 'Mind you,' he added, noting just how high above their heads even the lowest branches were, 'by the look of this lot, I'm not sure *we* could either.'

Weelum shook his head, his tusks gleaming in the light of the sky crystals, and pointed. 'Wuh,' he said.

There, at the foot of the nearest elm, was a low mound, perfectly camouflaged against the dark forest floor. Nate knelt down. On closer inspection, the mound was a closely woven construction of sallowdrop leaves and fern fronds over a frame of ghostelm

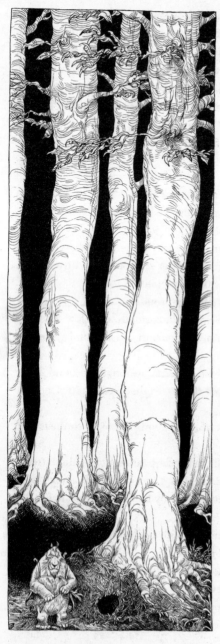

branches, which nestled in a carefully excavated hollow. Nate crawled inside through a small opening and found himself in a spacious den, lined with fragrant barkmoss.

The Professor's head appeared at the entrance behind him. 'Extraordinary!' he marvelled. 'Room for us all to sleep in comfort, yet almost completely undetectable from outside. Our friend Weelum really is a marvel.'

Moments later, Eudoxia, Slip and the old sky pirate joined them and began unpacking their bedding rolls, each exclaiming at the snugness and comfort of the banderbear nest. When they had settled, Weelum himself crawled inside, his arms full of succulent sallowdrop fruit, which he handed round.

'Wuh-waah,' he growled, handing Squall a sallowdrop with one paw and his parawings, neatly folded and strapped into place, with the other.

'Weelum owes pirate of

the sky his life,' Nate translated. 'Squall Razortooth is friend to the banderbears for ever.'

Looking up, Nate saw in the sky-crystal light that the old sky pirate's eyes were glistening with tears.

'Legend has it that the great sky pirate, Captain Twig, was friend to the banderbears,' Squall said, taking the parawings and shaking Weelum's great paw warmly. 'Tell him, Nate, that this old sky pirate is deeply honoured to be his friend.'

· CHAPTER FORTY-TWO ·

Nate woke and looked up at the intricately woven roof of the sleeping nest above his head; long thin fronds of oakwillow interlaced with thick glade fern and briargrass, and lined with rootmoss from nearby lufwood trees.

Five weeks they'd been travelling, and each night the banderbear had woven a new nest from the vegetation around them, each one perfectly camouflaged to blend in with their surroundings. Sometimes he used copperwood sticks and gladegrass; sometimes thatches of snagwood or clods of soft bark lichen, but always when preparing the nest site, the banderbear worked with amazing speed, skill and judgement.

Often, during those dark Deepwoods nights, Nate would stir from his sleep at the sound of footfalls and growls from outside the nest, only to drift back to sleep as one nocturnal prowler or another passed by, oblivious to their presence. It was the combination of materials that Weelum chose for the sleeping nest so carefully each night that both hid the travellers from sight and disguised their scent from the many predators in the endless Deepwoods. After five weeks of travel, Nate had become familiar with the different smells of the various sleeping nests, and had only to catch the fragrance of fresh gladegrass or newly picked barkmoss to feel both safe and drowsy.

Looking around, Nate realized that he was the only one still in the nest. Outside, he could hear the sound of his companions preparing breakfast.

Over the weeks, they'd developed a routine for life on the march through the forest. Slip the scuttler would rise at first light with Weelum, and set off with the waterflasks, and a blackwood bow which Squall had made for him during the first few days of their journey. While Weelum foraged for the fruits of the forest, Slip liked nothing better than to climb through the branches of the trees, gathering snowbird eggs, scooping up thousandfoots and barkgrubs, and bringing down a plump gladegoose or two with a well-aimed arrow.

By the time he returned, having filled the flasks with tree dew or from the lullabee 'drinking troughs', Eudoxia and the Professor would have built a hanging fire in the brazier pot that Squall had fashioned from a large ironwood pinecone, and be sitting in the branches of a tree, having one of those discussions of theirs. And, while they talked about the politics of Hive, the economy of the Eastern Woods, or the best hand to play at 'Dead Skull' splinters, the two of them would set to work, cooking the latest delicacy that Slip produced from his forage sack.

The smell of roast gladegoose or barkgrub sausages usually brought the old sky pirate out of the sleeping nest, yawning loudly and complaining good-naturedly about his aching bones. While the Professor helped him up into the tree and Eudoxia gave him a mug of steaming charlock tea, the sky pirate would reach into his frock coat – now looking a little ragged and the worse for wear – and produce his charts.

Originally their plan had been for Squall Razortooth to get them out of Great Glade aboard the *Gladedancer* and drop them at the settlement known as the Midwood Decks. From there, the Professor had told them, they would be able to buy passage on a phraxbarge to Hive. Somewhere in that great city, Eudoxia's father Galston Prade had disappeared, seemingly without a trace, and the Professor had contacts there who might be able to help in their search for him.

Eudoxia, Nate knew, was desperate to get to Hive as soon as possible. The journey from Great Glade to the Midwood Decks aboard the *Gladedancer* should have taken no longer than a couple of days. Unfortunately, it had not worked out that way. But with the loss of his beloved phraxlighter, Squall had taken his travelling companions to his heart – especially the banderbear – and was determined to chart their course as accurately as his skills permitted.

Which is where Nate came in . . .

Every night, several hours before dawn, Nate would leave the nest and climb the nearest tall tree. From its topmost branches, it was his job to make a note of the position of the stars so that the sky pirate could chart their progress and plan their next day's journey – or 'voyage', as Squall still insisted on calling it. Once Nate had scrawled down the appropriate observations in the barkpaper notebook Squall had given him, he would return to the sleeping nest and be allowed to sleep in.

From outside the nest, the unmistakeable smell of frying thousandfoots wafted in through the oakwillow and briargrass weave. Nate stretched and yawned before climbing out of his blanket and folding it into his bedding roll. Slinging it over his shoulder, he pulled the notebook from his topcoat and crawled out of the sleeping nest.

It was a bright sunny morning, with huge cumulus clouds billowing high into the sky over the distant treeline. A warm and gentle breeze rustled the broad leaves of the lufwood trees all around. Up in a tree close by, Squall and Slip were eating a breakfast of thousandfoot fritters beside the hanging brazier, while Eudoxia and the Professor were deep in conversation about the timber trade in the Midwood Decks.

Nate was about to climb the tree to join them when he noticed the banderbear. The great shaggy creature was standing some way off at the top of a nearby tree ridge, stock-still and back turned. He was sniffing the air, his feathery ears fluttering animatedly.

Nate frowned. 'What's wrong?' he called out.

Weelum turned round and stared back at him, and Nate saw that his arms were full of succulent grayleberries.

'I said . . .'

'Wuh-wuh,' the banderbear murmured distractedly, letting the grayleberries fall to the ground and turning away.

Nate glanced round uneasily. In the branches above him, the

others were oblivious to the banderbear. A twist of smoke was rising up from the brazier as Squall and Slip complimented Eudoxia on her cooking, and the Professor helped himself to another mug of tea. He turned back.

'Weelum?' he said, walking up the slope towards his friend.

Above his head, the sky was a brilliant blue and the warm morning sunshine dappled the forest floor. Just then, out of the corner of his eye, he thought he saw a flash of orange. He looked round, but there was nothing there.

'Wuh,' Weelum groaned miserably.

'What *is* it?' asked Nate. 'Are you sick?'

The banderbear looked at him as if seeing him for the first time. His eyes were wide and filled with panic and, Nate realized, the poor creature was trembling from the tops of his ears to the tips of his toes.

'Wuh-wuh,' he said, raising a single paw and bringing it slashing down through the air.

'Danger?' said Nate. 'What kind of danger?'

The banderbear turned his attention back to the forest floor ahead of them. There was another flash of orange. Nate followed the banderbear's gaze and found himself staring at a small round creature with fluffy orange fur and small unblinking eyes, standing low to the ground beneath a copperwood tree.

'Is that what I think it is?' Nate whispered, his voice trembling.

'Wig-wig!' the banderbear cried out, the fur at his neck standing on end. 'Wig-wig! Wig-wig!'

On the far side of the clearing, more of the orange creatures tumbled into view. A handful at first, then a dozen, then a hundred, their numbers rapidly swelling as more and more of them spewed out from the undergrowth. With a yelp of abject terror, Weelum turned, hoisting Nate up roughly onto his shoulders as he did so, and hurtled back down the slope. Nate clung on tightly to the thick fur at the back of his neck, ducking low to avoid the overhanging branches as the banderbear flattened everything before him.

He glanced round. The wig-wigs were close on their heels, their fur glossy and gleaming in the dappled sunlight as they scampered behind in pursuit. To his right, half a dozen of the little creatures leaped at them. As they did so, their fluffy bodies split in two, to reveal two rows of savage teeth.

'Earth and Sky protect us,' Nate gasped, gripping tightly round Weelum's neck.

One of the creatures attached itself to Weelum's elbow. Grunting with pain, the banderbear swung his arm round and dashed the wig-wig against a tree. As it dropped to the ground, several more took its place, and Nate found himself holding on for dear life as the banderbear slashed and snatched at the vicious beasts, lurching and swaying in his efforts to rid himself of the savage orange furballs that clung to his body like vicious tarryburrs.

'Help!' Nate cried out, his voice faltering as the banderbear pounded on. '*Help!*'

Just up ahead, he saw the others turn and peer down from the tree, looks of surprise on their faces. He heard a cry of dismay, then a loud clatter as they dropped what they were doing. Squall jumped to his feet. The Professor pulled his phraxpistol from his belt.

'Wig-wigs!' Eudoxia exclaimed, her own phraxpistol in her hand.

Beside her, Slip raised his blackwood bow.

A moment later, the banderbear arrived at the lufwood tree. Reaching behind his shoulders, he grasped Nate round his waist and hefted him up into the branches, before stooping down and tearing at the wig-wigs that had seized the opportunity to launch themselves at his legs.

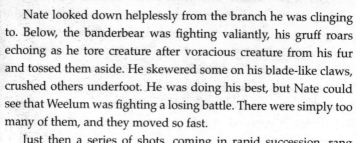

Nate looked down helplessly from the branch he was clinging to. Below, the banderbear was fighting valiantly, his gruff roars echoing as he tore creature after voracious creature from his fur and tossed them aside. He skewered some on his blade-like claws, crushed others underfoot. He was doing his best, but Nate could see that Weelum was fighting a losing battle. There were simply too many of them, and they moved so fast.

Just then a series of shots, coming in rapid succession, rang out from the branch above. Nate looked up to see Eudoxia and the Professor with steaming phraxpistols in their hands. He looked back down. The dead and wounded wig-wigs were already being

torn apart by the living – yet for Weelum, there was no respite. Five or six dead meant nothing to the great pack. If anything, the scent of blood seemed to spur the bloodthirsty creatures on, and they continued their attack with renewed vigour, clinging to his legs, his arms; crawling up his arched back and snapping at his quivering neck . . .

Nate eased his bedroll from his shoulder and slipped a hand inside it, closing his fist round the sky crystals the old sky pirate had lent him for his nightly climbs. Then, gripping a thick jutting twig, Nate swung himself down, till his legs were dangling just above the ground. A second series of shots rang out from the reloaded phraxpistols, killing a dozen more wig-wigs and sending the rest into a frenzied chaos of bloodlust.

'Good shot!' cried Squall Razortooth from the branch above, raising his own rather battered phraxmusket to his eye and opening fire.

A shower of leadwood shot peppered the pack, wounding more than it killed, but setting the blood-crazed creatures one upon the other. At the same time, Slip released a volley of arrows from his blackwood bow. Seconds later, a dozen more lay dead, maybe two dozen – yet Nate knew that even their best efforts were making little difference.

He released his hold on the branch and dropped to the forest floor. Crouching low to the ground, he brought the sky crystals he was clutching in each hand together with a loud crack. A vivid yellow flash was followed by a shower of sparks that rained down onto the seething mass of wig-wigs swarming about him. Like a forest fire hitting a field of glade barley, the orange creatures burst into flames as the sparks hit their lustrous, tinder-dry fur. In an instant, the fire travelled from one wig-wig to the next, until it formed a blazing carpet of flames.

The wig-wigs squealed and screamed as the fire engulfed them and swept on towards the swarm that covered the struggling banderbear. As the heat rose and the acrid stench of burnt flesh and fur filled the air, the wig-wigs let go of their prey and scurried away in terror – only to burst into flames as they tried to escape. Off into the depths of the forest, the pack scattered like tiny shooting stars, leaving the forest floor beneath the lufwood trees smouldering with small smudges of blackened teeth and fur.

Nate rushed over to the cowering banderbear and touched him softly on the arm. The banderbear looked round, his frightened eyes meeting Nate's gaze.

'It's over,' he said simply.

Weelum nodded slowly. The next instant, he reached forward and Nate felt the banderbear's massive arms wrap themselves around his body. He smelled the musty odour of mossy fur, laced with the tang of singeing, as he was crushed against the creature's great belly. And there the two of them remained; boy and banderbear, hugging each other gratefully in the crisp light of the Deepwoods morning.

· CHAPTER FORTY-THREE ·

Heavy rain was falling as the small group of travellers crested the ridge and looked down over the marshy valley below. It had started around midday, huge drops which had spattered down through the leaves of the trees as grey clouds darkened the sky. Now, by mid afternoon, it was a steady downpour, with the warm rain drenching Nate and his companions to the skin and making the ground slippery with claggy mud.

The banderbear, in particular, was finding the going tough. As the rain pattered down on the matted fur of his broad back, and clouds of steam rose above him, Weelum was hobbling badly. For the most part, the injuries the wig-wigs had inflicted were superficial, little more than scratches and grazes. One of the creatures, though, had bitten deep into the tendon at the back of the banderbear's ankle, and the vicious wound now throbbed painfully with every step he took.

'Wuh,' he grunted, and winced as he lumbered after the others, who slowed to allow him to catch up.

Eudoxia turned, and grimaced. 'We'll soon be there, Weelum,' she said. 'And the first thing we'll do is find an apothecary to take a look at that leg of yours.'

Falling into line, they started along a narrow track that wound down from the ridge, through pastures of gladegrass, to the valley below. To their right was an area of farmland, the fields familiar shades of yellow, green and blue, despite the unfamiliar crops that grew in them. Slip paused and crouched down to inspect the rows of bushy plants growing closest to the track. They had dark heart-shaped leaves and glistening clusters of succulent-looking fruit growing from their bulbous stems. He plucked one and turned it over in his hands.

'Never seen their like before,' he commented to himself, 'but they'd grow well in Slip's steam garden back in Great Glade . . .' For a moment his large eyes took on a faraway look, then he smiled, pushed the fruit into his forage sack, and ran to catch up with the others.

They rounded a low shrub-clad spur at the bottom of the hill and, as they did so, Nate gasped. Before him, looming out of the mist, stood a magnificent settlement, which looked curiously out of place in the humid rain-drenched forest – though no less welcome for that.

'The Midwood Decks,' said the Professor with an airy wave of his hand. 'Five weeks' hard march through the Deepwoods and here we are, halfway to Hive.' He smiled. 'Thank you, Squall, for your excellent navigation – and you, Nate, for those meticulous nightly observations.'

The Professor shook them both warmly by the hand, before turning to the banderbear.

'As for you, Weelum, our nest builder and protector. And you, Slip, with that forage bag of yours always full of delicious surprises . . . What can I say?' He embraced both of them, before turning to Eudoxia. 'And you, my companion at the brazier.' He smiled. 'I cherished our talks over the cooking pots and look forward to many more . . .'

Blushing, Eudoxia allowed the Professor to take her hand and kiss it gallantly. Then, straightening up, he turned and stood for a moment, looking at the extraordinary sight before them.

Built almost entirely from buoyant sumpwood taken from the surrounding forests, the Midwood Decks consisted of great clusters of floating cabins, log houses and timber towers, all tethered by anchor chains to the ground below. Around the perimeter of the settlement, a great timber wall of spike-topped copperwood logs had been driven deep into the marshy soil. Behind it, the towers and tall houses of the town dipped and swayed in great ripples as the warm rain clattered on their rooftops and gables, and fell to earth from long gutter spouts in fountain-like streams. But the most remarkable feature of the settlement were the decks themselves. These were great saucer-shaped platforms of floating sumpwood, like gigantic glade mushrooms, where visiting phraxships would dock and load and unload their cargoes. Like the buildings below them, they rose and fell, their anchor chains controlled by great gearwheels that seldom stopped turning.

'Stay close together,' the Professor advised the others, 'and follow me.'

They headed left along a broad track paved with a thick layer of rocks and stones that squeaked and chinked underfoot as they passed. Overhead, a steaming skybarge puttered on towards the town, while ahead of them, swathed in a fine mist that coiled up into the air, stood the tall stockade wall, standing some fifteen strides high. The top of each post had been fashioned into points, making the whole lot look like a long row of filed teeth. A broad double gateway, its doors reinforced with ornately swirling iron hinges, stood ajar.

They passed through the narrow opening and into the town. A couple of flatheads stood to the right of the entrance at the bottom of a wide staircase, which was seemingly floating in mid-air. They wore oilskin capes and broad flat hats from which the rainwater dripped, and had phraxpistols hanging from low-slung holsters at their sides.

The Professor nodded casually to them as he walked past and began climbing the stairs, then turned to Nate. 'Hired thugs,' he whispered. 'This is a frontier town. There's no law here.'

To their left and their right were modest sumpwood cabins, each one hovering above the ground at head height, anchored by the chains attached to the underside of their floorboards, gently swaying in the rain-soaked wind. As they reached the top of the staircase, itself held in place by anchoring chains bolted to each of the individual steps and which clanked softly as they climbed, it opened out onto a vast platform. Beyond it, steaming walkways snaked off in all directions. Buoyant buildings around them soared up towards the glowering sky, the tops of the highest towers swathed in cloud.

'Ah, the floating city,' Squall muttered croakily, a hand raised to shield his eyes from the driving rain as he looked about him. 'It's been a while. I'd almost forgotten how grand it looks, even in this confounded drizzle.'

'Those towers are amazing!' the grey goblin sighed. 'They're like stilthouses.' He frowned. 'Only without the stilts . . .'

All around them as they walked, streams of warm water fell from the gutters of the buildings above, drumming on the decking and forcing them to weave a path between them to avoid a soaking. The denizens of the Midwood Decks, though, didn't pay these water spouts any attention. In their great broad-rimmed hats and oilskin capes, they walked straight through the streams of water – splattering Nate and his companions as they passed by.

'It's like living inside a waterfall,' said Eudoxia. 'A warm, steamy waterfall, at that.'

They continued across a swaying bridge and took the left-hand fork of the walkway on the other side. As they went deeper into the bustling city, the buildings became grander, some with fluted pillars, gabled arches and ornately carved parapets, others with rows of lancet windows and latticed spires; all of them anchored to the saturated ground beneath by increasing lengths of chain. And above them were the huge decks themselves, stretching up into the air, each one secured by a series of chains and cables to the gear-wheels that raised them to meet the laden phraxbarges, and lowered them again once their cargoes had been unloaded.

The Professor paused and placed the flat of his hand against the wall of one of the sumpwood towers. He looked around at Eudoxia.

'You try it,' he said.

Eudoxia touched the wood herself and smiled. 'It's warm,' she said.

'Only the finest-grade sumpwood has this timber *glow*,' the Professor explained as he continued along the crowded walkway. 'It's treated with a special varnish which stabilizes its natural buoyancy, sealing in the warmth but allowing the wood to breathe . . .'

He moved aside to allow a short lugtroll who had come clattering up behind them to hurry past, the lufwood barrow he was pushing covered with a dripping square of waxed tarpaulin that concealed its load. A pair of slaughterer matrons, each with a tall angular umbrella-shaped hat upon her head, parted to let him through. Beyond them, a tall fourthling grunted irritably as he was forced to step out of the way of the approaching barrow.

'We have sumpwood furniture at our house in New Lake,' Eudoxia was saying. 'Did that come from here?'

'Possibly,' the professor said thoughtfully, 'but not if it's old furniture. Until the sumpwood stands of Midwood were discovered, sumpwood was comparatively rare – a few clusters here and there in the Free Glades . . .'

Nate smiled as he followed Eudoxia and the Professor, who were soon lost in the sort of conversation they had enjoyed together round the hanging brazier.

'During the First Age of Flight,' the Professor was telling her, 'sumpwood was used down in the Great Storm Chamber Library of Old Undertown. The librarians had lecterns and desks made of the stuff. Trouble was, the least change in humidity or temperature made them unstable. It was only with the invention of the varnish that everything changed.'

'Invented by the spindlebug, Tweezel!' Eudoxia exclaimed. 'Didn't *he* live in the Free Glades district?'

The Professor nodded. 'Only it was just the plain old Free Glades in those days,' he said. 'The other districts had yet to be settled.' He stepped aside to avoid the water gushing down from an overhead spout, and continued. 'The story goes that he experimented for years down in the Gardens of Light beneath the ironwood stands of the Free Glades. Finally, he managed to perfect the varnish that not only made sumpwood more stable, but also ushered in the Second Age of Flight.' He paused. 'If it hadn't been for him, none of this,' he said, sweeping his arm round in a wide arc, 'would have been possible.'

They had reached a broad platform, lined with stores and market stalls. Nate looked up at the crimson-feathered hammelbills that perched on the jutting gutters in huddles of three or four. The birds were scavengers from the surrounding forests, large and ungainly, hunched forward on long spindly legs, their bedraggled feathers hanging limply at their sides. Occasionally, one would lift a bald crested head and yawn, its long hooked bill gaping widely, before resuming its close watch on the bustling market square below, clearly on the lookout for scraps.

'I suggest that we split up,' said the Professor, stopping next to a decoratively carved gutter spout. 'Eudoxia and Nate, why don't you take Weelum here to have his leg seen to by the apothecary over there.' He nodded towards a cabin at the far end of the platform, connected to it by a narrow walkway. 'While Squall, Slip and I find us a bed for the night. Those timber towers over there look promising. We'll meet up there in half an hour.'

Eudoxia nodded, and she and Nate – together with Weelum, who was hobbling worse than ever now – headed towards the apothecary. Squall, Slip and the Professor set off in the opposite direction towards the row of swaying timber towers, tall ridged buildings with lanced gables and oilskin-covered balconies.

Nate and Eudoxia stepped onto the narrow walkway. It was crammed with goblins, trogs and trolls, who were shoving and jostling one another, their broad umbrella-shaped hats clashing. They squeezed their way through, with Weelum following some distance behind. Twenty strides or so along the swaying boards, they saw a glistening sign – MIDWOODS APOTHECARY (*Medicines and Elixirs from the City of Night*) – which hung above the studded door of a cabin. Nate opened it, setting a small bell jangling, and he and Eudoxia went inside.

'Greetings,' came a voice, and a small dumpy gabtroll, wearing an ochre dress and a starched white apron, came tip-tapping out of the shadows, a knotted walking stick in one hand and a lantern in the other. She examined them closely, her glistening eyeballs bouncing about on their stalks. 'And what can I do for you?' she asked brightly, and slurped as her long tongue flicked out and moistened her eyes.

'Our friend is injured,' said Eudoxia. 'He has a bite to his leg . . .'

'A bite . . . *slurp* . . . you say,' the gabtroll said, turning to the rows of shelves behind her that rose from the floor to the rafters, and were crammed with bottles, vials and jars of every description. 'Now, let me see . . . *whooah!*' she exclaimed as the banderbear crossed the threshold, setting the whole store swaying. 'By Sky and Earth . . . *slurp*,' she said, her eyestalks rigid with surprise. 'If it isn't a banderbear!'

She smiled as she looked Weelum up and down from two directions at once.

'Takes me back to the days when I used to travel the Deepwoods trails . . . *slurp* . . .' she said, 'in a covered wagon and prowlgrin . . . *slurp* . . . listening to the yodelling of your kind.' The gabtroll chuckled, then tutted softly. 'Nasty bite you've got there. A wig-wig by the look of it . . . *Slurp* . . . Lucky to be in one piece . . .'

Weelum nodded, his ears fluttering and coils of steam rising from his wet fur.

'You've come to the right place,' said the gabtroll. 'I've . . . *slurp slurp* . . . got just the thing.'

She bustled behind the overflowing counter and, her walking stick raised, began poking and pushing at the bottles and pots which crowded the top shelf.

'I'm . . . *slurp* . . . sure I had some, but . . . Ah, yes, here we are.' She tapped the side of a large stone-coloured urn twice with the end of the walking stick, before turning to the banderbear. 'If you could just lift that down for me.'

Wincing with pain, Weelum stepped forward, retrieved the urn and held it out. The gabtroll took it in both hands and, making space for it on the counter with her elbows, placed it carefully down on a reed mat at the centre. She unscrewed the lid, filling the small store with an aromatic, yet pungent, smell of herbs and spices.

'Healing balm,' she said, 'all the way from the City of Night.' Her tongue slurped noisily round her eyeballs. 'Water from the Riverrise aqueduct.' She smiled and slurped again. 'Blended with my own special ingredients.'

Using a wooden spatula, the gabtroll filled a small glass pot with the oily green paste. Then, having stoppered it, she handed it to Eudoxia.

'Apply three times a day for three days,' she said. 'And keep the wound uncovered,' she added. 'It needs to breathe.' She smiled and wiped her fingers on her apron. 'That'll be five hundred dockets.'

'Five hundred dockets?' Eudoxia repeated. The price sounded high. 'Are they anything like gladers?'

The gabtroll frowned.

'I've got some gladers,' said Nate, reaching into his pocket and pulling out a roll of damp notes.

'Dockets, gladers, waifmarks or hivegeld, I don't mind,' said the gabtroll, her face brightening up. 'Everyone's money's welcome here in the Midwood Decks.' She smiled. 'That'll be two gladers.'

Nate peeled off two notes and handed them to the gabtroll, who folded them and placed them carefully into the pocket of her apron.

'Just . . . *slurp* . . . passing through?' the gabtroll enquired.

'Yes,' said Eudoxia. 'We're hoping to take a phraxbarge to Hive . . .'

'Hive, you say?' said the gabtroll, her eyes narrowing as the stalks recoiled towards her forehead. 'There's plenty here in the Midwood Decks who'd welcome the clans of Hive with . . . *slurp* . . . open arms. Those academics from that Sumpwood Bridge Academy of theirs have helped build the settlement into . . . *slurp* . . . what it is today – what with their engineering skills and way with the sumpwood . . .'

'Really?' said Eudoxia, fascinated.

Nate could tell she would enjoy imparting anything she learned to the Professor in due course.

'Oh . . . *slurp* . . . yes,' said the gabtroll, her eyestalks extending towards Eudoxia and her tongue flicking out at them. 'Greeg Kleft the gangmaster, for example. He's the leader of the pro-Hivers. He'd have us join with Hive tomorrow if he could . . .'

'And that would be a good thing?' Eudoxia asked.

'Not necessarily,' came the reply. 'Certainly not according to the free timbersmiths. They're led by . . . *slurp* . . . Hoathly Hextree, the woodtroll Hoathly says Hive will chop down all the sumpwood they can find, and when it's gone, they'll leave Midwooders to . . . *slurp* . . . starve. He says we should fight Hive if they try to take us over, and send for help from Great Glade . . .'

'A war?' exclaimed Eudoxia, growing suddenly pale.

'That's what some folks say . . . *slurp*,' said the gabtroll. 'These are dark times here in the Midwood Decks, I can tell you. Why, *slurp* . . . there've been occasions just lately when I've thought about selling up and returning to Riverrise . . .'

Just then, from outside on the walkway, there came the sound of raised voices. Nate went to the small latticed window of the shop and peered out. A stocky woodtroll in a stained topcoat and chequerboard waistcoat was squaring up to a tall and rangy flathead in a broad-brimmed hat and oilskin cape. Eudoxia and Weelum joined him at the window and, as they watched, they saw the flathead take three steps back and sweep back the folds of his cape to reveal a pair of gleaming phraxpistols.

The bystanders fled down the walkway, leaving it suddenly deserted in the warm heavy rain. The woodtroll stood his ground, waving a fist at the flathead and shouting something about the free timbersmiths.

With a snarl, the flathead drew his phraxpistols and fired. Two billowing jets of steam spurted from the ducts in the pistol's phraxchambers. When the air cleared, the crumpled figure of the woodtroll was revealed lying at the flathead's feet.

'One of Greeg Kleft's pro-Hivers . . . *slurp* . . .' said the gabtroll behind them. 'It's getting worse by the day . . .'

Outside, the flathead pushed the body of the woodtroll off the walkway, sending it tumbling down to the marshy ground below, before striding off. A small pool of blood was left on the timber boards,

but was soon washed away by the torrential rain. A moment later, with harsh raucous cries, half a dozen hammelbills launched themselves off the guttering and, with purposeful flaps of their crimson wings, flew across the square and down to the unexpected feast lying in the mud far below.

Leaving the apothecary's store, Nate, Weelum and Eudoxia set off at a trot, the banderbear hobbling as quickly as he could. None of them wanted to spend more time out on the walkways and platforms of the Midwood Decks than they had to. After the splendour of the Deepwoods, the casual violence they had just witnessed sickened them.

'There you are!' called the Professor when they approached the timber towers on the far side of the platform. 'We've booked six sleeping cabins. They're ready and waiting for us . . .' He paused when he saw the looks on their faces. 'We heard shots,' he said. 'What happened?'

Eudoxia looked at the Professor, and Nate knew that tears were mingling with the raindrops running down her face.

'I don't want to talk about it,' she said.

· CHAPTER FORTY-FOUR ·

After the incident outside the apothecary's, Nate was glad to turn in for the night. His sleeping cabin was warm and dry, its shuttered doors opening out onto a covered balcony high in the timber tower. The cabin was lined with a mattress of soft snowbird down and had a shelf to stow his belongings away – the bedroll, waterflask, knapsack.

Nate checked the oil level on his lightbox and went through the contents of his little memory chest. He retrieved the painted medallion and turned it over in his fingers, inspecting the portrait thoughtfully, before tying the cord it hung on around his neck. Then, pulling from his pocket the sky crystals that Squall Razortooth had just made him a present of, he added them to the small chest.

'You saved our friend Weelum with these, lad,' the old sky pirate had said, pressing them into his hand when Nate had tried to return them that evening. 'They're yours now.'

Nate smiled and placed the crystals next to the 'Professor of Light' splinter from the skytavern and Eudoxia's false moustache. He closed the chest and placed it next to the lightbox in his knapsack. He was lucky to have friends like these, he thought as the gentle sway of the tower rocked the cabin from side to side.

The Professor was knowledgeable, cool-headed and, despite his career as an itinerant skytavern gambler, honourable. Nate trusted him with his life. Weelum the banderbear was steadfast and loyal, as only one of his kind could be, and the same could be said for the old sky pirate, Squall Razortooth. Nate had grown to admire his skill, both theoretical and practical – the way he could read a sky map one moment, and fashion a hanging brazier from a pinecone the next.

Nate smiled and stretched out on the bed.

Then there was Slip, the grey goblin from the mine. Who would have thought that the frightened phrax-touched little scuttler would become Nate's best friend? Observant, resourceful, and now a crack shot with his blackwood bow, Nate felt that the tables had turned, and Slip was now protecting him as much as the other way round.

His eyes closed.

And then there was Eudoxia. Eudoxia Prade, the mine owner's daughter. Nate had never met anyone like her. She could outride, outshoot, out*think* any one of them, and yet was never boastful, never proud. Despite her privileged upbringing, she'd never once made Nate feel awkward about his humble background in the rough mining camps of the Eastern Woods. In fact, quite the opposite . . .

Yes, he was lucky to have friends like these, Nate thought as he drifted off to sleep.

'Wake up! Nate, wake up!'

Nate's eyes snapped open, and he was surprised to see a chink of sunlight streaming in through the shutters. The night had passed, seemingly in the blink of an eye, and now it was already morning. He opened the doors of the sleeping cabin and stepped out onto the covered balcony, stretching as he did so. Eudoxia, dressed in a green topcoat and newly patched and mended riding breeches, stood before him, hands on her hips and her green eyes sparkling brightly.

'The rain's stopped, it's a beautiful day,' she said and laughed delightedly. 'The Professor and Slip have gone up to the decks to find us a passage to Hive on a timber barge, and Squall's looking after Weelum, insisting that he rest that leg of his. So that leaves you and me, Nate!'

'It does?' said Nate sleepily.

'Yes, so hurry up and get dressed. We're going out into the forest to see the sumpwood stands.' Eudoxia's eyes glazed over momentarily. 'After what happened yesterday, I'd like to get out of the city . . . Besides,' she said, brightening up again, 'it's such a glorious morning, and it might not last. According to the Professor, it rains every day here. And the sumpwood stands, Nate! The

Professor says they're magnificent. We can't miss seeing them . . .'

'All right, all right,' said Nate, smiling, happy to share her excitement. 'I'll throw on some clothes and see you downstairs.'

Half an hour later, leaving the town behind them, Nate and Eudoxia took a broad sloping boardwalk out into the forest. It was the major thoroughfare, used every day by those who lived in the Midwood Decks but worked in the surrounding sumpwood stands. At the centre of the boards, the wood was splintered and worn, and spattered with mud from the boots of the timbersmiths who'd passed along it earlier that morning.

Like the walkways back at the Midwood Decks, the boards had been anchored in the earth below them, with long chains keeping them in place, and that could be moved whenever the felling operations shifted from one spot to another. Far ahead of them, they caught glimpses of tiny phraxcraft darting across the sky; behind them, the Midwood Decks steamed gently in the hot sun, while all around, the mighty stands of sumpwood trees rose up from the marshy, waterlogged ground below.

'The Professor was right,' Eudoxia breathed. 'They are magnificent!'

Nate nodded. He'd never seen trees quite like them before. Tall and pointed at the top, with upturned branches covered in dense blue sumpneedles, the trees had squat bulbous trunks that were almost spherical, like phraxchambers. But more remarkable still were the roots of the sumpwood. These, in comparison to the tree above, were huge, and mostly exposed. To Nate, they resembled nothing so much as a series of huge waterfalls, tumbling down from the tree trunk, dividing and dividing again into a thousand cascades until burying themselves in the sodden earth beneath.

Eudoxia turned to Nate. 'The Professor was telling me it's the boll of the sumpwood that produces the most buoyant timber of all. Ten times more buoyant than the roots, apparently. And more remarkable still, he said that if you chop the tree down just below the boll, being careful not to damage the roots, it'll grow back again! The whole tree!'

Just then, overhead, they heard a squawking cry and the flapping of wings and looked up to see a hammelbill soaring across the sky. In the warm sun its feathers trailed behind it like glistening ribbons of crimson silk. Drawing in its long neck, the creature flew down through the air and landed, feet first, on a great vertical slab of bulbous root, where it gripped on tightly with its sharp claws.

Nate and Eudoxia watched as the bird cocked its head first to one side, then to the other, before walking up the root a couple of strides and repeating the process. Suddenly it froze. The next instant, it stabbed at the oily rootbark with such force that the tip of its bill plunged deep into the wood. It shuddered as it braced itself, its feathers shimmering with colour, then, with a sharp backward jerk, pulled its beak free – and at the end, wriggling and writhing, was a long red worm-like creature.

Eudoxia shuddered. Like Nate, the sight of the bird had reminded her of the shooting of the woodtroll the day before, and how the hammelbills had swooped down to feed on the body.

'At least here, those hideous birds do some good,' she murmured. 'It's caught a rootweevil. The Professor says the rootweevil burrows into the sumpwood's roots and kills the tree.'

The hammelbill shook its head vigorously from side to side until the rootweevil fell still. Then it flipped the lifeless creature up into the air, opened its beak and swallowed it whole. With a triumphant squawk, the bird released its grip on the bark, flapped its wings and soared off into the depths of the forest. Nate looked up at the sun, already high in the sky.

'Come on,' he said as cheerfully as he could, 'I want to see as much as possible while the weather holds.'

As they ventured deeper into the forest, the sounds of the creatures who had made their homes in the sumpwood stands grew louder. As well as the squawking of the hammelbills, there were odd stuttering cries, lone howls and the muffled chattering of flocks of riffraffs; small ragged birds that flew round and round the upper branches of the trees, snapping at the woodmidges and sumpgnats that gathered there in drifting clouds.

Suddenly Eudoxia stopped. She grabbed Nate's arm and pointed. Nate peered into the shadows.

'What?' he whispered.

'Just there,' said Eudoxia. 'Behind that knobbly root . . . *There!*'

As she spoke, there came a rustling sound, and Nate saw a flash of movement as a small grey animal abruptly emerged from the shadows and leaped across from one root to the next. It paused, sniffed at the air, and looked around, its small eyes glinting in the shafts of sunlight, then darted back out of sight. A moment later it was back, a large sumpwood seedpod clutched in its paws.

'I think the Professor said they were called ghost quarms,' said Eudoxia. 'They feed off the seedpods. Apparently, though, they're very shy, which is why they live down here among the roots, foraging for pods that have dropped down, rather than risk picking

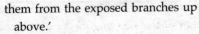

them from the exposed branches up above.'

She glanced round at Nate, only to find him grinning broadly.

'What?' she demanded.

'Nothing,' said Nate. 'Only you sound like an academic from the Cloud Quarter, or one of those fusty old librarians from the Great Library in the Free Glades district,' he said, and laughed.

'Fusty old librarians?' came a voice from behind them. 'Surely not! Your companion's far too pretty to be mistaken for an old librarian . . .'

Nate and Eudoxia turned from the sight of the quarm feeding to see a tall thin fourthling standing on the walkway a little way off, watching them with amusement. He wore a peaked funnel hat with earflaps, a short battered topcoat of green tilderleather and breeches that had been patched and repatched so many times it was difficult to tell what they'd been originally made of. A sabre hung from his belt, and the harness over his shoulder had a crossbow and a cluster of ironwood bolts hanging from it.

'Forgive me,' said the stranger, giving a small bow, 'but I couldn't help noticing from your clothes that you're from Great Glade . . .'

'New Lake,' said Eudoxia politely. 'And Nate's from Copperwood.'

'Pleased to meet you, Nate,' said the fourthling. 'And you . . . ?'

'Eudoxia,' said Eudoxia. 'Eudoxia Prade.'

'Eudoxia Prade of New Lake, very pleased to make your acquaintance,' he said, smiling broadly. 'Allow me to introduce myself. My name is Zelphyius Dax, and I'm' – he glanced at Nate, his eyes twinkling with amusement – 'a fusty old librarian from the Third Great Library of the Free Glades.'

299

Nate blushed, and Eudoxia laughed.

'Though I left the library to avoid becoming *too* fusty many years ago,' Zelphyius Dax continued, in a soft measured voice that suggested he didn't often get a chance to chat, and was enjoying this opportunity to do so. 'And I've travelled the Deepwoods ever since, compiling a treatise that never quite seems to be finished.'

He crossed over the walkway to join them, and studied the ghost quarm in the distance.

It was plump and squat, with hunched shoulders and silvery grey fur. Its limbs were long and sinewy, and its fingers dextrous. Most distinctive of all, though, were the two long yellow incisors which grew down from its upper jaw, giving it a comical bucktoothed appearance. The ghost quarm was slowly turning the pod over in its paws, its chisel-like teeth drilling a line right the way round the hard outer casing as it did so until, with a soft *crack*, the whole pod fell into two halves, which clattered away below. The creature gripped the soft inner kernel in its claws and was raising it to its mouth when, with a startled yelp, it was suddenly attacked.

In the blink of an eye, a worm-like creature with rough mottled skin had dropped down from the roots above, its huge fang-tipped jaws gaping, and swallowed the hapless ghost quarm whole. The thin end of the predator's serpentine body was wrapped around a high jutting root, anchoring it in place. Dangling in mid-air, the body grew broader as it neared the angular head with its small eyes and writhing feelers. The creature's jaws had closed, and the ghost quarm was now a large bulge that moved slowly up inside the creature's body, pushed by strong muscles that rippled as they flexed.

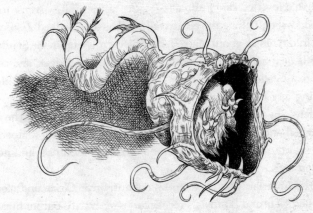

'The lanternjaw,' said Zelphyius Dax, turning to Nate and Eudoxia.

Although younger than Squall Razortooth, the librarian had the same weather-beaten complexion as the sky pirate, suggesting a long career in the skies. Despite the deep-etched lines, there was an openness in the librarian's features – his clear grey eyes, firm-set jaw and broad cheekbones – which gave him a look of honesty and trustworthiness which Nate couldn't help but like.

'Like the ghost quarm on which it feeds, the lanternjaw is found nowhere else in the Deepwoods, to my knowledge, which' – he smiled at Eudoxia – 'is extensive.'

Eudoxia smiled back. 'What brings you to the Midwood Decks?' she asked.

'My skycraft, the *Varis Lodd*, needs repairs.'

'If it's to do with the phraxchamber, perhaps I could help,' said Nate. 'I worked in a phraxchamber works in Copperwood.'

'Thank you, Nate . . . ?'

'Quarter,' said Nate.

'Thank you, Nate Quarter – but, no thank you,' said Zelphyius Dax. 'I'm a librarian of the old school. I was taught sky flight at the Lake Landing Academy. None of your phraxchambers for me – just sumpwood, varnish and spidersilk sails. I was on my way to the logging stands to purchase timber, if you'd care to accompany me.'

'We'd love to,' said Eudoxia.

They set off along the boardwalk, and as they walked Zelphyius Dax told them all about himself; how he'd grown up in the Southern Woods near a small settlement called the Farrow Ridges, and come to Great Glade to study at the Lake Landing Academy. But life in the big city had not been to his liking and, though he loved the academy, he yearned to return to the Deepwoods. Finally, he had designed and built a twin-masted skycraft of the finest sumpwood and set off on a treatise voyage of a couple of months – and never looked back.

The librarian was eager to talk about Great Glade and clearly enjoyed Nate and Eudoxia's recollections of the city, but for himself, he had no intention of ever returning. After an hour or so, the walkway began to rise higher in the air until they were almost at the height of the great bulbous trunks of the surrounding sumpwood trees. The boards snaked round to the right and, as the three of them rounded the bend, the logging stands came into view.

To the accompaniment of the shrill rasping buzz of phraxsaws, a gang of timbersmiths was working on a sumpwood tree; some of them clustered around the swollen sumpwood boll, others in small phraxcraft which hovered around the top of the tree. With half a dozen neighbouring trees already missing their boll, upper tree and most of their roots, the timbersmiths had just turned their attention to this latest tree. They were working fast, responding to the shrill whistles of the gangmaster who was orchestrating the work.

The phraxsaws they were using were long and thin, like serrated-edged sabres, three blades sandwiched together but moving independently, and a twist of steam emerging from the miniature phraxchambers at the saw's handle. At the same time, a small group of timbersmiths – five or six in number – had climbed up into the top branches of the tree, to which they were securing the hooks that hung down on ropes from the phraxvessels hovering overhead.

'*Pfweep! Pfweep!*' the gangmaster's short sharp whistles echoed through the air as, with his two index fingers lodged in his mouth, he blew twice.

With all the hooks now attached, the woodtrolls up the tree shinned hastily down.

'*Pfweep!*'

In the air above, the three phraxvessels rose slowly upwards, and the ropes went taut.

'*Pfweep! Pfweep! Pfweep!*'

At the base of the swollen boll, three of the four timbersmiths pulled their phraxsaws clear of the wood and stepped back, while the fourth continued sawing, driving his buzzing phraxsaw further and further into the narrow cut until, with a splintering crack, the whole tree abruptly floated free. Maintaining their three-point positions in the sky, the phraxvessels flew off over the crest, the upper section of the mighty sumpwood tree dangling above the treetops.

'*Pfweep!*' The gangmaster now sent the timbersmiths down into the roots, where they set about slicing through the sinuous cascades with their phraxsaws.

Beside him, Nate heard the librarian cursing quietly under his breath.

'Sky curse them,' Zelphyius Dax muttered, turning away.

'Don't they have the timber you need?' asked Eudoxia as the librarian strode off along the walkway.

He turned, his eyes blazing with anger. 'Forgive me,' he said. 'These are clearly pro-Hiver timbersmiths – one of Greeg Kleft's gangs, most likely, and I won't have any dealings with them. Look!'

Zelphyius pointed at the timbersmiths, who were bundling the roots into great stacks ready for the returning phraxvessels.

'In their greed, they take not only the upper tree and boll, but the roots as well, destroying the entire tree for ever, rather than allowing it to grow back. A sumpwood that has taken five hundred years to grow, destroyed in five minutes! I'm sorry, but I can't stand the sight of it. I'll find some free timbersmiths for the wood I need, or go without!'

Turning on his heels, the librarian strode off, pulling the earflaps of his funnel hat down to drown out the sound of the phraxsaws.

As Nate and Eudoxia stared after him, a huge

raindrop hit the walkway with a thud, followed closely by another, then another. They looked up at the sky. Coming in from the north, a bank of black and purple clouds swept towards them like a huge carpet unrolling across the sky, plunging the forest into gloomy shadow. Beneath it, streaks of dark grey cutting down through the sky at an angle showed the driving rain already falling.

'Come on,' said Nate. 'Let's head back to the Midwood Decks – before we get soaked to the skin again.'

· CHAPTER FORTY-FIVE ·

Nate and Eudoxia reached the timber tower an hour later – soaked to the skin – to find the Professor waiting for them by the front entrance. He looked them up and down and smiled ruefully.

'Take a pair of oilskin capes next time,' he advised them. 'I've taken the liberty of packing for you. There's a timber barge setting steam for Hive that'll take us if we hurry.'

Nate and Eudoxia quickly changed, grabbed their things and joined the others outside the swaying timber tower. It was raining steadily and they were all now wearing the distinctive oilskin capes – even Weelum, whose leg, Nate noticed, looked considerably better. Squall patted the banderbear on his huge shoulder and told Weelum to lean on him. But as they set off, Nate could tell it was the old sky pirate who was actually being supported.

As they climbed higher and higher on the walkways, Slip and the Professor led the way, with Eudoxia looking round anxiously at any flathead goblins in oilskin capes who passed by. Nate could tell the memory of the phraxpistol fight was still fresh in her mind.

'After what we've seen here,' she whispered to Nate fiercely, her hand clutching her holstered phraxpistol, 'I'm on the side of the free timbersmiths. I hope they *do* get help from Great Glade to stop the pro-Hivers!'

'Even if it means war?' asked Nate.

Eudoxia didn't answer.

Half an hour later, the six travellers arrived at the mooring station, one of the highest of the great circular decks, dripping with rain and sweat, and short of breath. The steam klaxon had already sounded twice, announcing *Old Glory*'s imminent departure. From the wheelhouse, the captain of the phraxbarge – a swarthy woodtroll in a green jacket, tight breeches and with a brace of phraxpistols that hung at his hips – saw his passengers hurrying across the deck towards his vessel.

'You're just in time,' he said. 'Thought I was going to have to set steam without you.'

The Professor smiled. 'We're grateful for your patience, Captain Barkscruff.'

'Better late than never, I suppose,' said the woodtroll captain as the third and final blast of the steam klaxon echoed around the decks. 'Come aboard, and look lively. We're about to depart.'

One by one, the Professor leading the way, they climbed the gangplank from the mooring deck onto the phraxbarge and gathered around the wheelhouse.

Typical of its kind, *Old Glory* was massive; some twenty strides across and at least sixty long. At its centre was a vast phraxchamber mounted on a scaffold of leadwood struts. Below it, towards the stern, was the wheelhouse, where the woodtroll captain stood. As his expert fingers worked the flight levers, clouds of steam abruptly billowed from the funnel as a jet of white-hot air blasted out from the back of the propulsion duct. It passed over the low-slung aft deck with its covered chamber and sleeping cabins. In contrast, the fore deck had been given over to cargo; a vast and valuable consignment of sumpwood timber that had been stacked in a towering mound of roughly sawn beams, boards and laths.

The woodtroll captain pulled hard down on one of the bone-handled levers, and the cumbersome phraxbarge slowly rose into the air. To Nate's right, a mobgnome crewmember was pulling in the tolley rope and twisting it round and round to form a neat coil on the deck. Behind him, he could hear the scraping of metal on metal as a stocky pink-eyed goblin hacked at the icicles that had formed around the bottom of the phraxchamber when the cold rain struck the colder metal panels.

'Sluice the hull brace!' a flathead goblin deckhand barked. 'Shackle them staves!'

As they rose in the grey afternoon sky, Nate watched the Midwood Decks open up below him, each light and lamp surrounded with a fuzzy rain-drenched halo. The town had seemed large when he was down among its tangle of walkways and clusters of towering buildings. Now, from above, it revealed itself to be smaller than the smallest Great Glade district, a mere drop in the mighty Deepwoods ocean.

The stockade that seemingly enclosed the town, he now saw, was in fact more of a timber wall of logs that ran along its western edge. In front of it lay open country of flat farmland, fields and pastures, with marsh lakes beyond that gleamed like mirrors. He saw the track the six of them had taken when they'd first approached the town, snaking its way over the rocky tree crest and down into the valley. On the other three sides of the Midwood Decks, was the natural barrier of the great sumpwood stands through which he and Eudoxia had walked that morning. He could see that, with the walkway rolled up, the town would be well fortified.

Soon, the bright haloed streetlamps had become little more than blurred smudges. Nate looked ahead at the endless forest they had yet to cross. When he looked back, the Midwood Decks had completely disappeared from view. From his post in the wheelhouse, Captain Barkscruff suggested they make their way to the passenger quarters below the aft deck.

'You go,' said Eudoxia to the others. 'I want to stay out here for a while.'

The Professor nodded, and Slip, Weelum and the old sky pirate clambered down the gangway from the wheelhouse and made their way towards the cabins. Nate hung back and crossed over to where Eudoxia stood at the starboard bow of the fore deck, staring out across the sky.

'Mind if I join you?' he asked.

'Of course not,' said Eudoxia with a smile, though she looked sad and thoughtful.

'You're worrying about your father, aren't you?' said Nate softly.

'Yes,' said Eudoxia, turning her back on the view and leaning on the balustrade. In front of her, the great stacks of sumpwood timber gently strained against their tethers. 'Though I was also worrying about all of you.'

'You mustn't worry about us,' said Nate, turning to her. 'We're all right.'

'But I can't help feeling that you wouldn't be going to Hive if it wasn't for me,' she said. 'I have to find my father, but I don't want to put the rest of you in danger . . .' She bit her lip and looked down at her feet.

'We're here because we want to be,' Nate reassured her. 'Slip, Weelum, Squall and the Professor feel the same. We're all in this together.' He took her hand and squeezed it.

'But I don't like what we've been hearing,' said Eudoxia, her eyes filling with tears. 'The trouble brewing in the Midwood

Decks, this talk of war – and now we're going to Hive, the worst place for Great Gladers, because of me!'

Nate looked into Eudoxia's green eyes. 'Together,' he said.

· CHAPTER FORTY-SIX ·

With a shrill hiss from the phraxchamber, and the rumbling sound of shifting cogs and grinding gears, *Old Glory* began its descent. Thick cloud buffeted the vessel, making it impossible to see further than a couple of strides and turning the phraxbarge's landing into a series of disembodied barked commands and muffled cries of acknowledgement, as the captain and his crew prepared themselves for docking.

Nate and his companions, dressed in their heavy oilskin capes with the hoods pulled up over their heads, stood on a gantry at the stern of the phraxbarge as Captain Barkscruff had instructed. He'd woken them an hour earlier, his heavy brow creased with concern.

'We're approaching Hive,' he'd told the Professor. 'And as you're no doubt aware, Great Gladers aren't too popular in Hive at the moment. So to avoid any unpleasantness,' the captain had continued, 'I suggest you disembark quietly at the stern, using the rudder rungs, while I keep the deck guards occupied.'

The Professor had thanked him and held out a ten-glader note.

'I'll not take your money,' the woodtroll had said. 'They pay me three times the going rate for my sumpwood, but I've no love for Hive. I'm a free timbersmith who just wants the Midwood Decks and the sumpwood stands to flourish, with the support of Great Glade. So I wish you Great Gladers well, no questions asked.'

Eudoxia had stepped forward and shaken the woodtroll's hand warmly. 'And I wish you and your magnificent forests well, Captain Barkscruff,' she'd said.

Now, standing on the gantry beside the great skybarnacle-encrusted rudder, Nate couldn't help but feel nervous. As if sensing this, Weelum laid a paw on his shoulders.

'Wuh-wurruh-wuh,' he said, his tusks glinting from beneath his hood. *Courage, Nate, keeper of light, Weelum shall walk at your side.*

As *Old Glory* came lower in the sky, the clouds grew wispier. All at once, the phraxbarge emerged from underneath the glowering blanket of grey. A sharp sour wind instantly gripped the vessel and set it listing to starboard. At the helm, the woodtroll captain, who had been humming tunelessly, corrected the tilt with a series of dextrous realignments of the flight levers.

Spread out below them, Nate saw the great city of Hive. It was a magnificent sight. The city was built on three towering tree ridges, the first two lower than the third, and divided by a great gorge through which a torrent of shimmering water flowed. This river was fed by a vast lake that lay beyond the gorge at the foot of the highest ridge.

'That's Back Ridge,' said the Professor, pointing towards the sprawling mass of closely packed buildings of typical goblin design; longhuts, hive towers, roundhouses and sprawling clusterhuts that perched on stilts at the lake's edge. 'It's the oldest part of Hive, and absolutely fascinating. It's home to grey, tufted and low-belly goblins, as well as the largest clan of webfoots this side of Four Lakes, or so I believe. Splendid head crests, they have, that glow in a kaleidoscope of colours when they talk.'

He pointed to the two ridges in front.

'The one on the left is West Ridge,' he said, 'where the goblin nobility live – the long-hairs, hammerheads, flatheads . . .'

Nate stared down at the towering tree ridge to his left. At its top was a magnificent array of palaces and fine buildings, the equal of anything in the twelve districts of Great Glade. Below them, the hive towers and longhuts became increasingly jumbled and tightly packed the further down the ridge that Nate looked, until they ended in a chaotic sprawl of workshops, factory yards and forge sheds, crammed together beside the left bank of the torrential river.

'And the one on the right is East Ridge,' the Professor was saying. 'Home to gyle goblins, underbiters, trogs, black and red dwarves, spindle-eyes, jag-ears, wormchins . . . In fact, the strangest, oddest looking goblins from the furthest corners of the Deepwoods you could ever wish to meet!' The Professor chuckled. 'We had some wild nights at the gaming tables of the East Ridge taverns in the old days, I can tell you . . .'

But Nate wasn't listening. Instead, he was staring at East Ridge. Unlike West Ridge, East Ridge had fertile farmland and vineyards spreading out at its base, while the jumble of huts, houses and towers higher up had a familiar goblin look to them. What drew Nate's gaze, though, was the astonishing cluster of buildings at the summit.

He'd never seen anything like them. They comprised great glistening spires, arches and domes, dripping with spiralling rivulets, like melted wax on a tallow candle, and piled one upon another as the whole edifice towered up into the sky. The Professor followed Nate's stare.

'Ah, I see you've spotted the Gyle Palace, residence of Grossmother Meadowdew and her seven sisters,' he said. 'It's one of the wonders of Hive, though I've never been inside . . . Magnificent, isn't it?'

Nate nodded. 'Yes,' he said thoughtfully, 'but also terrible . . . like the palaces at the top of the other ridge.' He frowned. 'They seem all the more magnificent because of the contrast with the buildings below them. Look. The lower you go, the more run-down and ramshackle the city becomes. It's almost as if . . .'

'As if, what, Nate?' said Eudoxia, turning to look at him.

'As if the palaces were feeding on the city, sucking up all the wealth and beauty, and leaving nothing for those who live below.' Nate shuddered.

'Aye, lad,' came the gruff voice of Squall Razortooth, the old sky pirate, from behind him on the gantry. 'I'm with you on that. There's something not quite right about this here city of Hive, and that's a fact.'

The phraxbarge swept down lower in the sky, passing over the great gorge that divided the city and the gushing torrent of the Hive river. Looking down, Nate saw a huge bridge spanning the turbulent water and linking the two parts of the city, east with west. It was a massive construction with a complex maze of struts, interlocking in fan-like vaults, forming its arch, and a forest of spires, ornate cloisters and crenellated towers lining its sides. Built exclusively from the finest seasoned and varnished sumpwood, the bridge glowed a deep, resonating amber, even in the grey morning light.

'Now, that *is* magnificent,' breathed Eudoxia, awestruck.

'Indeed it is,' said the Professor with a smile. 'The Sumpwood Bridge of Hive. It was built three hundred years ago from designs based on the legendary sewer library bridges of Old Undertown. A sight for sore eyes, if ever there was one . . .'

Passing over the bridge, the phraxbarge now approached the angular cranes, gantries and docking platforms of the Hive docks in the crowded slums of lower West Ridge.

'Crew to mooring positions!' shouted the woodtroll captain.

'Aye aye,' half a dozen voices shouted back as the crew took to the tolley bollards, grappling mounts and chamber station.

'Shank!' bellowed the captain.

'On my way, Cap'n,' an anxious-looking slaughterer called across as he came running along the deck, the funnel of a burnished copperwood ship-hailer in his hand.

Without stopping, he hurried past the wheelhouse and up onto the fore deck. From the stern, Nate turned and watched him as he skirted the high mounds of neatly stacked sumpwood logs and disappeared from view, only to re-emerge a moment later at the top of the phraxbarge's beak-like prow.

'*Old Glory*, phraxbarge out of the Midwood Decks, seeking permission to dock,' the slaughterer bellowed into the ship-hailer.

Nate looked down to see a stocky flathead guard in grey uniform standing at the end of a jutting gantry. Beside him stood a hefty hammerhead, the red and green ribbons on his coat and the crest on his spiked helmet singling him out as an officer. All around them on the platforms and boardwalks were a score more guards, each of them wearing the same grey uniforms and spiked helmets. Some were standing, their legs apart and braced; others were down on one knee. All of them held heavy phraxmuskets which they had trained on the incoming vessel.

'Take aim!' the flathead ordered, and Nate watched uneasily as the other guards readied themselves for the command to fire on the phraxbarge.

'Shank!' hissed the captain.

The slaughterer swallowed, put the ship-hailer to his lips again and leaned down over the side of the prow. 'This . . . this is the *Old Glory*,' he repeated. 'With a cargo of sumpwood bound for the Hive timber yards. We seek permission to land.'

The officer raised a telescope to his eye and studied the vessel for a few seconds, from bowsprit to rudder, before leaning across and speaking to the guard. The brawny flathead cupped his hands to his mouth and bellowed.

'Where did you set steam from?'

'The Midwood Decks,' the slaughterer replied, his voice, like his body, trembling with fear.

Nate saw the corporal lean across to the guard a second time. He held his breath.

'Permission granted!' the voice boomed back.

At the helm, the woodtroll captain grunted with relief. 'Thank Sky for that,' he muttered as he pushed the thrust lever forward and steadied the tiller.

Glancing back over his shoulder to the stern, he signalled to the Professor to get ready.

'Here we go,' whispered the Professor. 'Follow me, and do exactly as I do,' he told the others. 'And remember, keep your heads down and don't speak to anyone. Understand?'

They all nodded as the Professor unhooked the rope tied across the gantry and climbed onto the rungs – jutting pegs that ran the length of the phraxbarge's rudder. In the wheelhouse, the captain returned his attention to the flight levers. Above his head, the great phraxchamber began to wheeze and chug as he closed off the vents to the propulsion duct one by one, cutting the incoming air supply and slowing the phraxbarge for its final descent. Slowly, it sank down towards the docking platform, heavy icicles from the phraxchamber clattering down through the air as it did so.

The next instant, the phraxbarge juddered to a standstill. The sound of loud voices echoed back from the fore deck as the crew jumped onto the docking platform and secured the tolley ropes to the bollards while a handful of dockworkers – and as many guards again – scrambled aboard.

At the stern, the Professor was halfway down the rudder and within jumping distance of the platform. Behind him, Weelum followed clumsily, even the simple rungs proving difficult for the great hulking banderbear. Above him, Squall muttered reassurances, while Slip, Nate and Eudoxia prepared to follow him off the gantry and onto the huge rudder.

'Hold up,' hissed the Professor, stopping and raising a hand.

The thud of footsteps sounded on the platform, and a guard, phraxmusket in hand, appeared directly below them.

'Wuh!' grunted Weelum,

letting go of the rudder rungs and jumping past the Professor.

Looking up, the flathead guard's eyes opened wide with astonishment before, an instant later, the full weight of the banderbear came crashing down on him.

Just then, there came a colossal rumbling noise from the fore deck and the phraxbarge trembled and lurched. Both the Professor and Squall tumbled from the rudder rungs and landed in the banderbear's outstretched arms. The air erupted with the sound of panic-filled shouts and cries, and the heavy pounding of feet. But all these came, not from the stern of the phraxbarge, but from up near the prow.

'Good old Captain Barkscruff,' smiled the Professor as he got to his feet, and Nate, Eudoxia and Slip climbed down to join him.

Weelum straightened up, with the old sky pirate still cupped in his left arm.

'You can put me down now, Weelum,' Squall protested. 'I'm too old and creaky to be a cub!'

Weelum placed the sky pirate gently back on the boards of the platform. At his feet, the figure of the guard gave a low groan, but beneath his battered helmet his eyes remained shut.

'Good-looking weapon,' grinned Squall, eyeing the guard's phraxmusket. 'We'll make a swap, shall we?' Placing his old battered musket beside the unconscious guard, he shouldered the shiny, newly forged phraxmusket.

'Come on!' urged the Professor. 'Let's get out of here before we're spotted.

Nate and the others followed close behind as the Professor, hood pulled down low over his face and without looking back, made for the nearest staircase down from the docking platform. As they headed down the first of fourteen flights that zigzagged all the way to the ground below, Nate glanced back at the phraxbarge.

The sumpwood log cargo that had been so firmly secured to the fore deck had mysteriously broken free, and the logs were now hovering in mid air just above it. The woodtroll captain was standing with one hand on his hip and the other gesticulating wildly, hurling insults and instructions at the deckhands, who were clambering over the spilled cargo, long boathooks in their hands. They were stabbing down into the bark with them and tugging hard, in a desperate effort to prevent the logs from floating away. Above them, the dock cranes had swung round, and deckhands and dockworkers were doing their best to attach the dangling ropes to the logs – while the guards, distracted, roared with laughter.

Nate turned away and continued down the stairs, gripping the side banister and taking them two at a time. At the bottom, he saw Eudoxia and Slip looking up at him, questioning expressions on their faces. Nate smiled.

'Bit of a problem with the cargo, apparently,' he said, stepping down to the ground. 'The ropes holding it in place must have snapped.'

The Professor nodded. 'Captain Barkscruff was as good as his word.' He chuckled. 'You can always trust a woodtroll.'

Sticking close together, the group made their way downhill, through the forest of posts and girders that supported the docking gantries overhead, and emerged from the shadows on the lower dockside. Above them, the cloud cover had thickened once more, and the sky was dark and threatening. Hurrying across a deserted square, then darting down a shadow-filled alley, the Professor led the others on towards the Hive river.

Just then, from the far end of the narrow alley, there came the echoing *thud thud* of marching feet. Shouting and jeering voices rose up above anguished cries. At the Professor's signal, the group darted back out of sight, pressing themselves against the doorways and timber walls of the ramshackle buildings.

They peered out cautiously to see a long line of guards marching past the end of the alley. Dressed in the same drab uniform of the Hive Militia – grey buttoned-back topcoats and peaked funnel hats – they were escorting a line of chained prisoners. With the light behind them, casting everyone into silhouette, it was difficult to see who exactly had been arrested. It was Eudoxia who recognized them first by the cut of their clothes.

'Great Gladers,' she gasped, turning to Nate. 'They're all Great Gladers. Like you and me.' She swallowed hard. 'Like my father . . .'

As the last of them passed by, the Professor emerged and beckoned the others on. They hurried to the end of the eerily quiet alleyway. It opened up onto a broader, though equally quiet, road that ran parallel to the thunderous river. On the far side of the road was the magnificent bridge they had seen from the air, its intricate framework of honey-coloured wood seeming almost to glow in the overcast gloom.

'Here we are, the Sumpwood Bridge,' said the Professor. 'The greatest structural achievement since the days of the great architect Vox Verlix of Old Undertown.'

'And those buildings?' said Nate, looking at the long galleries that ran the length of the bridge, with their spires and towers, so elegant and well crafted compared with the simpler rough-hewn constructions back in the Midwood Decks.

'They,' said the Professor, 'house the Sumpwood Bridge Academy. I have friends here.'

Checking that the way was clear, they scurried across the road and onto the bridge. Stepping onto the timber decking – if decking could adequately describe the fantastically intricate inlaid wooden mosaic – Nate felt himself bathed in warmth. It emanated from the carved buildings, with their beading and curlicues and gleaming varnished panelling, that surrounded him on every side. Next to him, Eudoxia let out a gasp and Slip's eyes opened wide with wonder.

'Well, I never,' croaked the old sky pirate, holding up his hand to test the golden light which, like the warmth, enveloped them.

At his side, Weelum gave an appreciative growl.

'This way,' said the Professor, checking the coast was clear.

The bridge, like the rest of Hive, was remarkably quiet. The Professor stopped outside a narrow building with a low sloping roof dotted with rows of triangular jutting windows and tall spiral towers at each end. Its door, like everything else on the Sumpwood Bridge, was finely decorated, and there was a small copper plaque, green with age, screwed into the wall on the left.

i. THE ROCK CABINET

ii. THE LIGHT MAGNIFIER

iii. NATE'S SLEEPING CABIN

iv. BARKSCROLLS

v. ARCHIVES

vi. SUMPWOOD TABLE

vii. SUMPWOOD ARMCHAIRS

viii. THE HIVE RIVER

ix. ARCHIVISTS

X. FRONT DOOR

SLEEPING CABINS

iii.

THE LABORATORY

ii.

ix.

viii.

At the top, and underlined, was the word, *Archivists*. Beneath it were three names. *Klug Junkers*, *Togtuft Hegg* and *Magnus Spool*. The third name had been roughly scored through, and recently, judging by how brightly the scratches in the copper glinted through the verdigris.

'This is it,' said the Professor. He raised a fist and knocked at the door.

From inside, there came the sounds of frantic activity. Scraping chairs, rustling papers and the clatter and grind of metal, along with hushed, urgent voices. From the far end of the bridge, they heard another noise. It was the pounding of marching feet, and it was coming their way.

'Hurry up,' the Professor muttered under his breath, knocking again.

'I'll be right there,' came a voice, followed by more scraping and scuffling. 'Just coming . . .'

There was a rasping sound as a small panel, decorated with the carved head of a fromp, slid back and a wary eye peered out.

'Who are you?'

'It's me,' said the Professor. 'Ambris. Ifflix Hentadile's brother.'

The eye blinked twice, then the panel slammed shut. Nate looked round anxiously as the sound of the marching feet came closer. The next moment, there was the soft grating of metal as a bolt was pulled across, and the door creaked open. A tall mottled goblin in shabby academic robes stood in the doorway, his face taut with concern. He looked round at the small group clustered in the doorway.

'Ifflix's brother?' he said. 'And you seem to have brought some friends with you . . . You'd best come in.'

One by one, the six travellers stepped inside and lowered the hoods of their oilskin capes. The Professor stepped forward, a hand outstretched in greeting, only to be stopped by the academic, who had a finger raised to his mouth.

There was silence in the narrow but high-ceilinged chamber, its walls lined with shelves that were crammed with papers, charts, hanging barkscrolls and complicated architectural drawings.

Sumpwood furniture floated in clusters above their heads, and everywhere was bathed in a soft warm golden light.

Outside, the footsteps grew louder and, as they passed the door, the whole building seemed to ripple with the pounding of the marching feet. As they died away, the academic visibly relaxed. He took the Professor's hand and shook it.

'Forgive me, Ambris,' he said, 'but these are dark times in the city of Hive, and no place for Great Gladers.'

The Professor nodded solemnly. 'We have much to talk over, archivist Junkers.'

'Please, call me Klug,' said the mottled goblin. 'Our cities might be at daggers drawn, but we are all friends here . . .'

'Well said, Klug,' came a voice from above, and looking up, Nate saw a second academic sitting at a floating lectern high in the rafters. Tugging on its anchor chain, he descended towards the floor. 'I'm Togtuft Hegg. Welcome to our humble cloister, and please make yourselves comfortable,' said the long-hair goblin.

As the Professor introduced the others one by one to the archivists, Klug and Togtuft pulled down sumpwood armchairs for them to sit on – all, that is, except for Weelum, who settled himself comfortably on the floor beside Squall's chair.

'There is someone I think you should meet, Ambris,' said Togtuft, turning to the Professor as his colleague Klug handed round a tray of tiny sapwine glasses.

'There is?' said the Professor, intrigued. 'And who might that be?'

'Cirrus Gladehawk,' came a deep voice from the shadows in the corner of the study. 'The last person to see your brother alive.'

· CHAPTER FORTY-SEVEN ·

'This way,' said Cirrus Gladehawk, turning up the collar of his grubby topcoat and pulling down his crushed funnel hat of black quarmskin until its battered brim cast his face in shadow.

He was a tall upright fourthling with heavy-set features and clear blue eyes that sparkled from beneath a low brow, giving him an alert vigilant look. Though naturally tall, now, in his shabby and nondescript clothes, he walked with a stooped back and a shambling gait that made him appear shorter and slighter than he actually was.

Beside him, dressed in his oilskin cape with its heavy hood, the Professor fell into step as the two of them made their way across the magnificent sumpwood bridge.

'If we run into the Bloody Blades,' Cirrus cautioned, 'turn and walk the other way.'

'Bloody Blades?' the Professor said.

'Elite troops of the Hemtuft Battleaxe Legion,' Cirrus told him. 'Long-hairs, the lot of them. Brutal killers that the Clan Council uses to spread terror throughout the city. "Keeping order", the high clan chief, Kulltuft Warhammer calls it.'

At the end of the bridge, they turned left onto a pitted track which ran along the banks of the torrential Hive river, spume from its swirling waters rising in great squalls of drizzle. On the opposite bank lay the slums of the lower West Ridge, with their squat workshops, smithies and ramshackle forges, each one belching thick black smoke from tall crooked furnace chimneys. On this side of the river, low sheds and thatched huts soon gave way to the smallholdings and farmland of the lower East Ridge, lush vineyards stretching out into the distance.

Heading along the steepening track, Cirrus and the Professor climbed towards the gorge, the thunderous waterfall that bisected the city of Hive. They were about halfway up the ridge and had reached the densely populated terraces of hive towers, longhouses and clusterhuts on the right when they heard the sound of marching feet coming in their direction.

Cirrus reached out and pulled the Professor off the path and back behind a mist-drenched outcrop of black rock. At their back, the great white curtain of the gorge waterfall thundered down in a deafening roar. Crouching in the shadow of the rock, they waited, Cirrus Gladehawk's hand closing on the handle of his phraxpistol.

On the track, a regiment of tall long-hair goblin guards marched past. They wore burnished copperwood helmets, black topcoats with silver braiding and buttons, and polished phraxmuskets with large powerful chambers in their stocks. From their white double-buttoned waistcoats, clusters of leadwood bullets hung, and at their sides, each had holstered a short-handled axe. Their bare feet slapped down on the wet path percussively as they marched by in ranks of five abreast, taking up the entire width of the path.

Cirrus and the Professor waited for the regiment to pass and, with the coast clear, were about to step back onto the track when there came the sound of agonized screams, just detectable above the roar of the waterfall. The Professor looked up.

At the top of the gorge where the river burst through the deep channel between the two ridges and began its churning frothing descent, was what looked like an overhanging crane, like the ones employed in the docks to unload cargo. From its jutting crossbeam, three barrels hung from ropes, each one containing a screaming prisoner who had been tethered inside. As the Professor watched, the crane swung over the waterfall and released the barrels.

One after the other, they disappeared into the foaming torrent of water and flashed past the outcrop of rock the Professor and Cirrus were standing beside. Moments later, the barrels resurfaced, bobbing about in the seething waters of the Hive river below.

'Take aim!' The command sounded from the track below Cirrus and the Professor. 'Fire!'

The sound of fifty phraxmuskets firing cut through the roar of the waterfall. Below in the river, the barrels and their hapless occupants exploded in a mass of splintered wood and bloodstained water.

'It's called barrelling,' said Cirrus bitterly. 'One of the High Clan Chief's little innovations. It's his way of dealing with any in Hive who cause him displeasure, and strikes terror into the rest.' He smiled bleakly as they resumed their walk up the wet, slippery track. 'As well as providing the Bloody Blades with target practice.'

'I had no idea things had got this bad,' said the Professor, shaking his head.

As they drew level with the top of the waterfall, he looked across at the flat jutting rock on which the wooden crane stood. Two scruffy trogs and a malnourished-looking fourthling in the grey uniforms of the Hive militia were coiling up ropes and packing chains and manacles into sacks. They ignored the Professor and Cirrus as the two of them hurried past and continued through the high-sided, shadow-filled gorge.

All at once, emerging on the other side, the low sun struck their faces. Cirrus tugged at his funnel hat, pulling the jutting peak down low over his eyes. The Professor raised a shielding hand. In front of them, above the glistening lake of Back Ridge, a rainbow spanned the sky. As the roaring of the waterfall slowly diminished behind them, Cirrus turned to the Professor.

'I know why you've come to the Sumpwood Bridge Academy,' he said gently. He stopped and faced the Professor, and placed a hand on his shoulder. 'You want to go in search of your brother, Ifflix . . .'

The Professor nodded curtly, a painful lump in his throat and his eyes glittered brightly behind his spectacles. He returned Cirrus Gladehawk's penetrating gaze.

'You captained the phraxship *Archemax* on my brother's expedition to the Edge,' he said, shrugging Cirrus's hand from his shoulder, 'and yet you returned without him, leaving Ifflix and his comrades back there!' He gestured far off to the distant horizon. 'At the Edge . . .'

Cirrus recoiled as though he'd been struck. He pulled a handkerchief from his jacket pocket and mopped the beads of river spray from his brow.

'You . . . you don't understand,' he said, his voice low and expressionless. 'There were other factors at play. Things I couldn't control . . .'

'Yet you left him there,' said the Professor coldly. 'And now here you are, hiding out on the Sumpwood Bridge.'

'As are you, Ambris,' said Cirrus darkly.

'That's different!' said the Professor, his eyes blazing with anger.

'Not so different,' replied Cirrus, 'and if you'll listen to what I have to say, you'll understand.'

The Professor looked at him warily. 'Very well,' he said.

They continued walking along the path. Ahead of them lay the lake at the centre of Back Ridge, the stilthouse clusters of the webfoot goblins mirrored in its still surface.

'As you know,' Cirrus began, 'the High Professor of Flight, Quove Lentis, had agreed to fund the expedition, and arranged for the *Archemax* to be released from the phraxfleet for the purpose. The dean of the School of Edge Cliff Studies, Cassix Lodestone, was delighted, as was his protégé, your brother, Ifflix.'

The Professor nodded, thinking back to his encounter with the disappointed former dean in the Long Gallery of the Lake Landing Academy.

'He, together with three experienced colleagues, were intent on completing the greatest descent of all time, to dispel the myths and superstitions once and for all, and to discover what truly lies at the foot of the jutting Edge cliff.'

As they neared the great Hive lake, Cirrus and the Professor found that they were no longer the only ones on the path. Webfoot goblins of all ages were out and about, visiting each other's stilthouses, or returning dripping wet from swimming in the lake. Just up ahead, their arms linked together, two large webfoot matrons promenaded, their crests glowing blue and green as they chatted, while attached to their aprons by lengths of string were clusters of tiny hatchlings, trilling delightedly.

'I was as excited as everyone else. As captain of the *Archemax*, I'd just about had my fill of patrolling the skies over Great Glade, chasing rogue phraxvessels,' Cirrus said as they continued walking, 'or supervising the transportation of phraxcrystals from the mines of the Eastern Woods. As an experienced captain, I wanted a challenge, and that's just what your brother's expedition promised to give me.'

Cirrus Gladehawk and Ambris Hentadile made their way round the great sweeping curve of the lake, past a cluster of webfoot stilthouses with their woven sides, wateroak stilts and thatched roofs covered in meadow turf. Judging by the rowdy noise coming from them, the webfoots had brought home a welcome harvest of lake eels, and a communal feast was well underway. Then, at the far side of the lake, just beyond a spreading lullabee tree, where a caterbird cocoon dangled down from an upper branch like a discarded sock, the path divided into two.

The left fork continued round the Hive lake. The right fork led away from Back Ridge and up into the forest beyond.

'It's this way,' said Cirrus, taking the right-hand fork.

'*What's* this way?' said the Professor, surprised. 'Where exactly are you taking me, Cirrus?'

'All in good time,' the captain replied. 'All in good time.'

As they slowly climbed the hill behind the lake, the low sun pierced the dappled forest with shafts of golden sunlight. Above their heads, a flock of emerald-green skullpeckers flickered across the sky, searching for somewhere to roost for the night.

'The *Archemax* set sail at daybreak,' Cirrus told him. 'The weather was cold and crisp and clear, with a light westerly wind blowing – fine weather that, according to the skywatchers, was set to hold. We soared over the Deepwoods towards the rising sun, and as it rose above our heads and sank behind us, we carried on through the

329

night, plotting our route instead by the East Star that shone brightly ahead.

'Several days later, the golden glow of the Twilight Woods was before us.' He shook his head. 'What a strange, hypnotic place that is,' he said, his voice suddenly low and hushed. 'Even on board the *Archemax*, far, far above the tops of the trees, we were beguiled by its strange beauty. The sights we saw, Ambris! Great storms tumbling in from the Edge and disgorging their lightning down into the forest's glowing depths . . . It was incredible, yet the risk of storm damage drove us on. Then,' said Cirrus Gladehawk, 'we came to the Mire.'

'Now that,' said the Professor, 'is a sight *I'd* like to see. Not a tree in sight. Just a barren expanse of bleached mud and poisonous blowholes stretching away into the distance. It's where the First Age of Flight came to an end, you know, with the scuttling of the sky pirate fleet at the Armada of the Dead . . .' His eyes took on a faraway look.

'Actually,' said Cirrus, 'the truth couldn't be more different. These days it's a vast plain of lush swaying bladegrass, home to great flocks of the strangest birds I've ever seen. The mighty Edgewater river now flows through it uninterrupted towards the Edge itself.'

'Remarkable,' said the Professor. 'Quite remarkable.'

'Finally,' Cirrus continued, 'we reached the outskirts of what we took to be the ruined city of Old Undertown. Moss-covered boulders, ruined arches and rubble – all overgrown with huge thornbushes and dense tangles of briars. Here and there, strange plants I'd never seen before seemed to have seeded themselves and were growing up through the surrounding vegetation. Black-stalked shrubs with huge flat leaves the size of decking platforms, and mounds of mottled moss and lichen, higher than a hammelhorn. A strange, eerie place . . .'

Cirrus shook his head at the memory. As he'd been speaking, he had continued to lead the Professor up through the forest behind Back Ridge. To their west, the sun had turned blood-red and slipped down to the horizon. All round them, the sounds of the night creatures were starting up, whooping and screeching as they emerged from their roosts and dens in search of food.

'We reached the Stone Gardens a little while later – not overgrown like the ruined city, but just bare rock, the boulder stacks which once had studded its surface now eaten away and crumbled to dust. Colonies of roosting birds had made their nests in the barren landscape – though not the fabled white mire ravens,' he added thoughtfully. 'Instead, these birds were similar to the ones in the grasslands of the Mire, long-legged and sharp-beaked, with piercing, screeching calls. By the vicious way they mobbed each other and fought over the scraps of what we imagined must be prey, we knew they were dangerous and decided to keep our distance.

'At last we came to the jutting tip of the Edge cliff itself, with the almighty Edgewater river cascading over it into the abyss. It was one of the most spectacular sights of the voyage so far. I brought the *Archemax* down low to the cliff edge and moored her with grappling hooks. Ifflix and his colleagues were eager to set off, already clambering over the side, their phraxpacks strapped to their backs and ropes in their hands as I left the wheelhouse.

'"This is it, Cirrus," Ifflix called up to me as he followed the others descending the cliff face. "Wish me luck." And I did, with all my heart.

'They carried supplies enough for two weeks' descent and two weeks' climbing back, and I agreed to wait for them for six weeks, no matter what. The crew and I watched them go, down through the clouds and into the gloom far below, until they disappeared from view, and then . . .'

331

'Then, what?' asked the Professor, watching Cirrus intently.

'We waited,' he replied. 'I took a small landing party into the ruined city where we hacked our way through the undergrowth and located what we believed to be the remains of the magnificent Palace of Statues, now just a heap of shattered rubble. Amongst the shards, I found the head of one of the statues and we returned with it to the ship. I knew it would make a fine gift for the High Professor of Flight, who prides himself on being a descendant of scholars from the First Age . . .'

'And *then*?' said the Professor.

Cirrus sighed and shook his head. 'Three months we waited, Ambris,' he said, his voice low and grim. 'Three whole months. That was how long we remained there, moored to the Edge cliff, waiting for your brother to reappear. And it wasn't as though we did nothing. I led a party down the cliff face myself, in search of the expedition. We descended as far as our ropes and our limited skill allowed, but found nothing. I even took one of the *Archemax*'s phraxlighters down below the cliff, but was forced back by the treacherous gale-force winds. Finally, we were running out of provisions ourselves, so we decided to return to the Mire in search of game.'

The Professor turned and looked at the captain, his brow furrowed. He said nothing. High up behind Hive now, they had come to a clearing, bathed in shadows from the full moon, which had risen as the red sun sank.

'We set off the following morning, but vowing to come back to the Edge to undertake a more thorough search just as soon as we'd replenished our stores.' Cirrus Gladehawk's lips pursed at the memory of it all. 'That journey proved to be a nightmare,' he said.

'Almost immediately we ran into a huge storm that drove us out over the Mire. There, flying low to avoid the worst of the hurricane winds, we were struck by a jet of mud that exploded from a blowhole below us, hitting us broadside and damaging the hull weights. Before we knew it, we were over the Twilight

Woods and out of control. As the storm condensed around us, a stray bolt of lightning hit the phraxchamber, cracking the outer casing and almost causing a catastrophic explosion. The storm released its energy and broke up, but by this time, the *Archemax* was barely skyworthy. So I made the only decision I could in the circumstances. I set a course for Great Glade and limped home for repairs . . .'

He shook his head grimly. The Professor turned to him, his eyes full of questions.

'When we finally got there, several weeks later, I discovered that the Society of Descenders had been outlawed,' Cirrus explained, 'while all funding for the School of Edge Cliff Studies had been cut. What was more, although the pompous barkslug was delighted with the stone head I gave him, Quove Lentis then betrayed us all by taking back the *Archemax* and banning all future trips to the Edge . . .'

'That's typical of the academics of the Cloud Quarter,' the Professor muttered. 'It's why I left the Academy. I only wish my brother had done the same.'

Cirrus shrugged. 'He was a brave scholar, your brother,' he said, 'and I was determined not to abandon him. That night, I crept unnoticed into the phraxshipyard where the *Archemax* was being repaired and, singlehandedly, stole her right from under the noses of the phraxmarines. I knew that if I was ever to mount a rescue attempt, I had to find help, so I set steam for Hive.' He sighed deeply. 'I hadn't reckoned on the upheavals taking place in this once great city. No sooner had I docked than the *Archemax* was seized by the guards of the Hemtuft Battleaxe Legion. Of course, they weren't interested in the skyship at all, it was the crystals they were after. They smashed their way into the phraxchamber and removed the phraxcrystals . . .'

The pair of them had come to a clearing, high up at the top of the ridge behind Hive. The moon shining down, bright and white, illuminated the grassy earth and the surrounding circle of trees.

'And the *Archemax* herself?' asked the Professor. 'What happened to her?'

'See for yourself,' said Cirrus Gladehawk, and pointed.

The Professor followed the line of Cirrus's outstretched finger to a tall tree at the edge of the clearing. He looked up. And there, the varnished wood of her mighty hull glinting in the silvery moonlight, was the wreck of the once proud phraxship, the *Archemax*, skewered at the top of an ironwood pine.

· CHAPTER FORTY-EIGHT ·

Nate put down his spoon and stared forlornly at the remains of the watery gruel in the bowl in front of him. Eudoxia nudged him gently and, remembering his manners, he looked up at the two archivists at the other end of the sumpwood table.

'That was excellent, Klug,' he said.

'Delicious,' added Eudoxia.

The mottled goblin smiled sadly. 'You're very polite,' he said, 'but bluebean porridge is no meal for guests.' He checked himself, his blushing face turning a deeper shade of red. 'But times being what they are, it's all we can afford.'

'We're very grateful for your hospitality,' said Eudoxia.

'It's the least we could do,' said Klug, 'considering how badly some in Hive are treating Great Gladers.'

'You shared what little you had,' said Squall Razortooth. 'And now it's time for this old Great Glader to return the favour.' He climbed to his feet, pulled a roll of gladers from his pocket and flicked through them with his thumb. 'Do you think they'll take these in Hive?'

Togtuft snorted. 'Take them?' he said. 'But of course. Gladers are worth five times what Hivegeld's worth. But you must be careful, Captain Razortooth. If you intend to visit the markets here in Hive, stick to the ones in Low Town. East Ridge, near the bridge.' He added, 'And return immediately at the first sign of trouble.'

'Slip'll come too, said the scuttler, collecting his forage sack and oilskin cloak from the row of hooks by the front door.

'Wuh-wuh-wurrah,' said the banderbear, picking up his own cloak and pulling it on.

Squall grinned as he fastened the collar of his cloak and raised the hood. 'It's a peculiar language you speak, my friend,' said the old sky pirate, opening the door for the banderbear, 'but I think I'm beginning to pick it up.'

As the door closed behind the three of them, the cloister swayed and there was a loud clatter as something heavy fell to the floor. Klug and Togtuft exchanged glances.

'One of the drawbacks of living in a sumpwood building,' said the long-hair goblin as the pair of them got up from the table and went through to the other end of the long chamber.

Nate and Eudoxia got to their feet and followed them. The four of them stared down for a moment at the upturned cabinet which lay on the wooden floor, the collection of rocky shards it had contained strewn across the floorboards.

'No harm done,' said Klug, relieved. 'We'll just need to sort through them,' he added, crouching down and righting the metal cabinet.

'It's my fault,' said Togtuft. 'I keep meaning to fix it to the wall, but somehow I never get round to it.'

He bent down beside his friend, and the pair of them began gathering up the small pieces of rock, quickly inspecting them one by one, before returning them to the small labelled compartments in the cabinet they had come from. Spotting a small stone, flat and glittering, at her feet, Eudoxia bent down and picked it up.

'What are they all for?' asked Nate, standing hands on hips and looking around at the small shards and slivers of rock strewn across the dusty floor.

'To study, of course,' said Togtuft, glancing back over his shoulder. 'These are samples of rock taken from all over the Edgelands.' He sat back on his heels and, reaching round, held up a small grey piece of stone. 'This, for instance, is from the Edgeland pavement.'

Nate took it and held it to the light.

'It doesn't look much right now,' the long-hair archivist conceded, 'but, in cold damp conditions it gives off curious wisps of vapour. For centuries, it was thought that the Edgelands were home to wraiths and spirits. By studying this rock, we now believe that it is the rocks themselves, coupled with the feverish imaginations of those who ventured to so desolate a place, that gave rise to the superstitions.'

Klug pointed to a small orange-tinged shard of stone lying in the shadows of the workbench. 'That one's interesting too,' he said. 'Have a look.'

Eudoxia bent down and grasped the fragment of rock. When she tried to pick it up, though, her fingertips slipped uselessly from the edges. She tried again, and then a third time – but the stone seemed impossible to move, as if it had been stuck to the floor. She looked up to see the faces of the two Sumpwood Bridge academics creased up with amusement.

'I recognize that,' said Nate. 'It's compacted mud from the mine workings of the Eastern Woods.'

Klug laughed out loud. 'Well spotted,' he said. 'It contains a minute speck of phraxcrystal. That's what makes it so immensely heavy.' He laughed. 'To be honest, we were lucky it didn't make a bigger dent in the floor when it fell.'

'And what's this,' Eudoxia asked, holding out her hand to reveal a glittering sliver of polished rock in her palm.

'This,' said Klug, taking the rock and scrutinizing it closely for a moment before looking up and smiling, 'is the most remarkable rock of them all. Follow me and I'll show you.'

With the rock held carefully between his thumb and index finger, Klug crossed the chamber and went through a low door at the far end. Eudoxia and Nate followed, and found themselves in an untidy laboratory.

Jugs, filters and funnels, and an array of tools hung from the ceiling on hooks, while the windowless walls were lined with bulging cupboards and bowed shelves laden with leather-bound books, yellowing scrolls and stacks of thick parchment-filled folders. Standing against the wall to the left of the room was a long sumpwood table, its surface crammed with gleaming apparatus and intricately connected paraphernalia: balance scales, with racks of weights; miniature stoves, ice cabinets and centrifuges – and, at the very centre of all the clutter, a large black and brass light magnifier,

its dials polished and lenses sparkling.

Klug pulled down on a small lever, switching on the phraxlight, which threw a great circle of brightness across the shadowy ceiling above. Then he took a glass slide from a stack, placed the sliver of polished rock carefully upon it and secured the whole lot beneath the holding clips at the base of the magnifier. The light was instantly doused. Klug lowered the lens funnel, bent forward and looked through it, turning the focusing dial as he did so.

'There,' he said. 'Take a look, Miss Eudoxia.'

Eudoxia stepped forward. A moment later, she took a sharp intake of breath.

'What?' said Nate. 'What can you see?'

'Thousands of tiny lights,' she said. 'They're glowing . . .' She pulled away and turned to the archivists. 'What *are* they?' she asked.

'Glister fossils,' said Klug. 'This is a sliver of Edge cliff rock.'

'Quarried from the cliff face itself by members of the Society of Descenders,' said Togtuft.

'Let me see,' said Nate.

Eudoxia moved aside for her friend. He put his eye to the lens funnel and focused in on the magnified sliver of rock. The tiny fossilized glisters sparkled like stars in a night sky.

'We believe,' said Togtuft, 'that this rock contains the very seeds of life.'

'Blown in from Open Sky,' added Klug, 'and preserved in the cliff rock.'

'. . . Which is how rocks once germinated and grew in the Stone Gardens of Old Undertown.'

Nate looked up from the light magnifier and saw the archivists' flushed excited faces staring back at him.

'While most of the academics of Great Glade study the power of phraxcrystals, and our colleagues here on the bridge devote their time to the uses of sumpwood, Klug and I study the greatest mystery of all . . .'

'And what's that?' asked Eudoxia, fascinated.

Togtuft smiled. 'How life itself began,' he said.

· CHAPTER FORTY-NINE ·

Nate, Eudoxia and the archivists emerged from the darkened laboratory to find Slip, Weelum and Squall returning from their expedition. They came in noisily, looking short of breath and sparkle-eyed with excitement.

'We didn't go far,' said the old sky pirate, throwing off his cloak to reveal a heavily laden forage sack. He crossed to the sumpwood table and emptied the contents onto its glowing amber surface.

Beside him, Weelum and Slip did the same.

'Just the local market in the square at the end of the bridge. You were right.' Squall grinned. 'They did seem happy to take our gladers, and this is what we got in return . . .'

The two archivists stared in silence at the mound of provisions on the table before them.

'Black bread and white bread,' Squall announced. 'Shoulder of hammelhorn. Spiced tilder sausages. Four, five . . . six bottles of finest Hive sapwine. Pickled snowbird eggs. Hammelhorn curds. Glimmer onions, smetterlings and nibblick . . .'

Klug licked his lips appreciatively and Togtuft chuckled with glee.

'Woodapples, sweetgourds . . .' said Squall. 'Squabfruits . . .'

'Oh, and pickled tripweed!' Eudoxia exclaimed, her eyes sparkling mischievously as her gaze fell upon the tightly packed jar of green and yellow fronds. 'That's Nate's favourite!'

Nate made a face at her and laughed, only to stop when he saw the look on Slip the scuttler's face.

'Slip, what's wrong?' he asked.

The grey goblin looked down at the pile of sumptuous food on the table and shook his head.

'The market stalls were full of good things to eat, friend Nate,' Slip said in a quiet voice. 'But only the rich folk from High Town seemed to be buying anything. All around, Slip saw hungry faces, desperate faces. Young'uns begging for food, fighting over scraps . . .' He clenched his fists in anger. 'It just wasn't right, friend Nate!' he said fiercely.

'Slip here gave away what he could,' Squall admitted, 'but I had to stop him when the militia showed up. That's when we came away.'

Eudoxia crossed the study and hugged the grey goblin. 'I'm sorry for bringing you to this place,' she said, tears springing to her eyes. 'Truly sorry.'

'No, Miss Eudoxia,' Slip protested. 'You've nothing to be sorry for. Slip's here because he wants to help you find your father, just like friend Nate!'

'Thank you,' said Eudoxia, wiping her eyes.

Behind her, Weelum gave a low growl and put a massive paw on her shoulder. Eudoxia glanced round.

'And you, Weelum,' she smiled.

They set to work in the galley of the sumpwood cloister, with its huge wrought iron oven whose twisting chimney led up into one of the building's spiral towers. Soon, the top of the stove was covered in bubbling pots and pans of all shapes and sizes, with coils of steam rising up into the air and gathering in clouds at the low ceiling. Behind heavy iron doors below, the shoulder of hammelhorn was roasting, while the tilder sausages sizzled and spat in a pan on the hob above.

Squall Razortooth revealed himself to be an excellent cook, ably assisted by Eudoxia. Nate peeled and chopped the vegetables, while Weelum – with a stone pestle grasped in his huge paws – carefully ground the herbs and spices that Slip kept adding, little by little, to the mortar in front of the banderbear.

A full moon had risen over the torrid waters of the Hive river by the time the Professor and Cirrus Gladehawk finally returned to the archivists' cloister on the Sumpwood Bridge. They both looked drawn and tired, and their boots were crusted with dark forest mud – but they brightened up when they saw the sumpwood table laden with delicious dishes.

They all sat down at the floating table. Togtuft and Klug both proposed toasts to their guests and praised the cooks, before everyone started tucking in. Next to Eudoxia, the Professor was pensive and quiet, and while the others ate, he seemed barely to touch his food.

'Are you all right?' asked Eudoxia quietly, touching the Professor's arm.

'Forgive me, Eudoxia,' the Professor replied, taking off his spectacles and pinching the bridge of his nose. 'It's been a long day, and I've learned that mounting a rescue mission for my brother seems, in the present circumstances, all but impossible.'

Replacing his spectacles, he looked across at Cirrus Gladehawk, who nodded grimly.

'But if I can't help my brother,' the Professor said, 'then, by Earth and Sky, I intend to find your father, Eudoxia, and provide him every assistance it's in my power to give!'

Nate raised his tumbler of sapwine. 'Here's to finding Eudoxia's father!'

Around the table, everyone echoed his toast.

'Thank you,' said Eudoxia, her eyes sparkling. 'Thank you . . . When can we start?'

'Tomorrow morning,' said the Professor firmly. 'At dawn.'

· CHAPTER FIFTY ·

After supper, Klug and Togtuft took their guests up a small staircase to their sleeping quarters in the broad roof of the cloister. The room was long and square, with angled ceilings and a boarded floor. A row of small doors lined the wall at the far end.

'Sleeping closets,' Klug announced, opening the first of the double doors set into the sloping pitch of the roof.

'Take whichever you please,' said Togtuft. 'But you, Weelum, might be more comfortable in the gable end closet. It's the largest.'

Thanking the archivists and bidding them goodnight, Nate and the others climbed into their respective closets.

'I'll wake you,' Eudoxia whispered to Nate, before disappearing inside her own sleeping closet. 'Early!'

Nate pulled the small doors towards him and they closed with a soft *click*. He quickly undressed. The small chamber was similar to the cabin in the timber tower of the Midwood Decks, but the sumpwood here had a richer glow and a comforting warmth that the other lacked. As Nate lay down on the soft bedding and dimmed the small lamp fixed to the panelled wall, another sensation overwhelmed him. The smells of fragrant wood lavender and earthy sumpwood filled the air of the sleeping closet, and Nate realized that the blanket and pillow had been impregnated with their fragrance.

He felt warm and heavy, cocooned in the sweet-smelling sleeping closet, and was lulled by the faint rushing sound of the river water sweeping along far beneath him, which sounded so much like the soft wind rustling through the leaves of the forest. His eyelids flickered for a moment as drowsiness overwhelmed him. And, as he closed his eyes, Nate was no longer in the bewildering troubled city of Hive, but safe in a banderbear nest in the vast expanse of the mighty Deepwoods . . .

When Nate awoke, a shaft of daylight had pierced the shutters of the small triangular window at the foot of his bed. Rolling over, he pushed the shutters open and stuck his head outside.

Far below him, the swirling torrent of the Hive river thundered past, throwing up a fine refreshing spray. Nate wiped his face with his sleeve and gazed at the two ridges that towered before him.

The central area of West Ridge was swathed in mist, while the spires of the palaces and fine buildings at its summit poked up through the cloud. Nearest to the Sumpwood Bridge, the slums around the Docks were already stirring; chimneys smoking, forge fires glowing and timber barges steaming slowly into the docks.

In the jumble of huts and longhouses on the ridge opposite, the lights of Low Town also shone at the windows as the inhabitants rose early, ready for a long day in the fields and vineyards. High up at the top of East Ridge, Nate could see the extraordinary fluted towers and glistening domes of the Gyle Palace, picked out by the early light of dawn.

Somewhere in this vast woodanthill of a city, his friend Eudoxia hoped to find her missing father. As Nate gazed at the maze of streets, terraces and winding paths in front of him, it seemed like an impossible task.

'Nate? Nate? Are you awake? It's dawn. Time to go.' Eudoxia's voice sounded from the other side of the door.

'I'll be right with you,' Nate said sleepily, and began to pull on his shirt. Next he jammed his arms into the sleeves of his undercoat, pulled on his breeches, noting a number of fraying patches, and fumbled with the buttons of his waistcoat. Pulling on his topcoat, he grabbed his tilderleather boots, their toecaps scuffed and worn, and stepped out of the closet.

Eudoxia was waiting for him, her face flushed with a mixture of excitement and anxiety.

'Come on, Nate, you're slower than a giant tree fromp! Put your boots on,' she urged. 'Everyone else is up! Cirrus Gladehawk is going with Squall and Weelum to the docks to ask around, while you, me, Slip and the Professor are going to the Hive towers of West Ridge . . .'

'We are?' said Nate, stumbling down the stairs after Eudoxia.

'Yes,' she said. 'According to the Professor, it's where my father would have gone to recruit the hammerheads for the New Lake thousandsticks team.'

In the chamber, the others were waiting for them.

'Remember,' said Cirrus Gladehawk as they made for the door. He jammed his crushed funnel hat down on his head. 'Be careful who you speak to, and avoid the Bloody Blades at all costs.'

Togtuft and Klug wished them luck in cheery voices, but it was plain by the looks on their faces that the two archivists were concerned for their safety.

They crossed the Sumpwood Bridge to West Ridge, then split up. Cirrus Gladehawk, Weelum and Squall headed for the docks, while Nate and the others followed the Professor on the long climb up Hive's West Ridge.

They skirted round the docks area, the smoke-filled air already loud with the business of loading and unloading, and continued along a narrow winding road that zigzagged its way up the steep hill behind. To their left and right, the pitted track was lined with ramshackle shacks and humble dwellings, with cracked walls and tiny windows, where the dockworkers and their families lived in cramped dirty conditions. The sound of squalling young'uns and screeching goblin mothers echoed round the blocks, and the air was ripe with the stench of waste and decay.

As they climbed higher, the ramshackle and dilapidated housing gave way to older and more traditional buildings. And instead of lining the road, the goblin dwellings had been laid out in 'villages' – circular clusters, linked one to the other with connecting paths, their individual design reflecting the traditions of those who dwelled in them.

The long-hairs lived in villages with a central open-sided clan hall which was built on a raised mound. Radiating out from this hall were narrow pathways, at the end of which were more modest buildings, each one surrounded by a deep moat and housing an extended family of some twenty or so goblins. Further on, they came to a typical thatched longhouse favoured by the lop-eared goblins, with its circle of squat roundhuts about it, and a tall wooden post given pride of place.

'It's called an ancestor tree,' said the Professor as they passed it. 'Cut down and brought with the tribe when they first settled in Hive, to remind them of their Deepwoods roots.'

The post was intricately carved with scenes that, Nate could only suppose, came from stories handed down through the generations, and he would have loved to study it in detail, but Eudoxia was clearly anxious to press on. Beside him, Slip, wide-eyed, shared his fascination, but he too was aware of Eudoxia's anxiety.

Keeping to the tracks, the four of them made their way through the various goblin districts. They passed by the sunken pithouses of the tusked goblins, the painted roundhouses of the mottled goblins, and a stand of original ironwood pines, where a colony of diminutive treegoblins had secured their woven cabins to the upper branches. Scraggy woodfowl strutted about, scratching and pecking at the ground; a mangy-looking hammelhorn stared at them for a moment before trudging away. Eventually, through the thickening cloud mist, they saw the distinctive shapes of the hive towers of West Ridge silhouetted up ahead.

They were huge, each conical tower with its three-cornered roof windows housing up to twenty extended families. Looming up out of the mist, the towers looked as forbidding as the war-like hammerhead goblins who lived in them.

'Let me do the talking,' said the Professor as they approached the first of a dozen or more towers.

Up close, Nate could see its massive walls were constructed of woven woodwillow, with a coating of black pine pitch. Hoods pulled down low over their faces, Eudoxia, Slip and Nate followed the Professor through the open entrance of the hive tower into the gloom inside.

The air was thick with woodsmoke from numerous open fires, and the roof windows high above their heads in the conical roof allowed only the minimum of light into the huge enclosed space. Dozens of tall wooden pillars, as thick as tree trunks and with red and black horizontal stripes painted from top to bottom, supported a mass of roof beams above, with hammocks and sleeping nets strung out across them. There were no walls, the pillars marking out areas of the floor occupied by different family groups.

To their right, half a dozen elderly hammer-head matrons sat on rocking stools around a bundle of willow branches, weaving elaborate-looking bowls and baskets with their gnarled fingers. Further on, to their left,

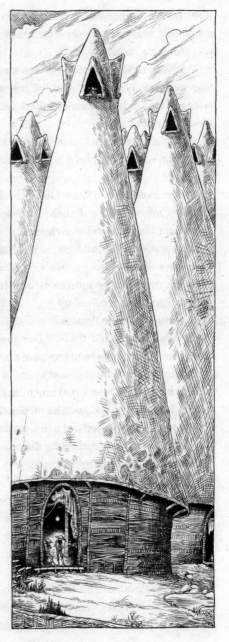

three young'uns played a wrestling game of rough-and-tumble near a smoking brazier fire, over which their exhausted-looking mother was stirring a cooking pot.

As Nate looked around, he was struck by the fact that all the hammerheads he could see in the tower seemed to be either very young or very old, or nursing mothers. Of the war-like hammerheads, there was not a trace.

'What do you want?' came a gruff voice, and the four of them turned to see a tall, powerfully built hammerhead eyeing them warily.

'We're looking for a Great Glader by the name of Galston Prade,' said the Professor, 'who we believe visited the hive towers to recruit players for his thousandsticks team . . .'

'Thousandsticks?' said the hammerhead, his wide-spaced eyes narrowing. 'Last recruiters we had round here were a couple of webfoots, who paid handsomely as I recall. That was a good six months ago, before the call up.'

'Call up?' said the Professor.

'That's right. You'll find all our finest thousandsticks players serving in the hammerhead legion of the Hive Militia now,' said the hammerhead. 'So if this Galston Prade of yours did come to the hive towers, he wouldn't have had much luck.'

The Professor pulled aside his oilskin cape, reached into the pocket of his topcoat and pulled out a five-glader note. The hammerhead's eyes widened and he reached for the note with a badly scarred hand that lacked several fingers. His other arm, Nate noticed, was missing from the elbow down.

'Ask round the towers whether anyone has seen Galston Prade,' said the Professor, placing the note in the hammerhead's open palm. 'If you learn anything, there'll be twenty gladers more coming your way. You'll find me at the splinters table in the Winesap Tavern in East Ridge later this afternoon.'

'Twenty gladers!' said the hammerhead in amazement. 'That's a fortune to an old legionary like me, wounded in the service of his city.' He deftly folded the five-glader note into a tiny square and placed it in the pocket of his grubby triple-breasted waistcoat. 'It'll take a few hours,' he added as they turned to leave.

'I'll be waiting,' said the Professor.

Nate and Eudoxia followed the Professor back towards the entrance of the hive towers, only for Eudoxia to pause and turn back to the hammerhead.

'These webfoot recruiters you mentioned,' she said. 'Did they say who they worked for?'

The hammerhead scratched his broad head. 'Let me see . . . er . . . yes . . .' he said. 'An associate of theirs in Great Glade by the name of Felftis Brack.'

Leaving the hive towers, they continued through West Ridge until they hit the gorge path, then turned right towards the lake in the Back Ridge district of Hive.

'We can take a webfoot ferry across to East Ridge and then the cliff road above the caves to the Winesap Tavern,' the Professor told them, scanning the path ahead for any signs of the Bloody Blades.

'What do you think my father was *really* doing in Hive?' Eudoxia asked, falling into step with the Professor. 'If Felftis Brack had already recruited the thousandsticks players for New Lake, my father had no reason to come here himself,' she said. 'Unless . . .'

'Unless what?' asked the Professor.

Eudoxia frowned. 'What if he was here on some other business?' she said quietly. 'Such as . . .' She hesitated. 'Supplying the High Council with the phraxcrystals that Great Glade has been denying them?'

They got to the top of the gorge where the mighty waterfall began its thunderous descent towards the Sumpwood Bridge, far below in the distance.

'Do you think he's capable of such a thing?' asked the Professor.

Behind him, Nate and Slip exchanged glances.

'My father is a good man,' said Eudoxia slowly, her voice thick with emotion. 'But he can also be ruthless and ambitious. How do you think he became a mine owner in the Eastern Woods? It's a tough brutal life, and you have to be strong to survive – do things that you think are necessary . . . That's what he always told me.'

Nate thought of his own father, honourable and scrupulously fair in his dealings.

'And did you agree with your father?' he asked quietly.

Eudoxia turned on him, her green eyes blazing. 'Yes! . . . No! . . . I mean . . .' Her face crumpled and she buried it in her hands. 'I don't know, Nate,' she sobbed. 'I just don't know.'

· CHAPTER FIFTY-ONE ·

The Winesap Tavern was a shadow of its former glory. Once it had been the most famous tavern in the great city of Hive, a place where traders, travellers, merchants and phraxpilots had rubbed shoulders with the denizens of this, the most diverse of the districts of Hive. In the crowded longhuts and roundhouses of the slopes of East Ridge, some of the oddest and least-encountered goblins had made their homes, and a fair number of them were to be found each evening in the Winesap Tavern.

There were the so-called wormchins, white goblins from the depths with long glistening tendrils, three feet long, snaking from their heads; snagjaws, tusked goblins from the Western Woods; red and black dwarves, tiny beaked goblins with taloned feet and nervous dispositions – all of them, and a hundred more, to be found nestling at the tavern's drinking troughs and wine fountains.

But not any more.

With the rise to power of High Clan Chief Kulltuft Warhammer and his Bloody Blades, the citizens of Hive had started to avoid public places. And as the trade with Great Glade dropped away, so the tavern had also emptied of merchants and travellers. Then the call up had been announced, and business in this once bustling tavern slowed to a trickle.

At the splinters table where, in the old days, he'd once played hands of splinters with forty fellow gamblers, the Professor drained his glass. Beside him at the table sat Nate, Slip and Eudoxia, her face streaked with tears.

'Try not to worry, Eudoxia,' said the Professor. 'Let's concentrate on finding your father first, and we can ask questions later.'

'But what if he doesn't *want* to be found?' said Eudoxia, looking

down at the untouched glass of squabfruit cordial in front of her. 'What if he's changed sides and become a pro-Hiver?'

'Then he can tell you that himself to your face,' said Nate, 'when we find him.'

The tavern was a low-beamed longhut with galleries running the length of one wall and great round wine barrels running along the other. In days gone by, tavern hands had pumped the bellows beneath each barrel to send jets of sapwine bubbling through pipes from the barrels to the wine fountains that stood in front of them. From these, jugs were filled and delivered to the crowded tables in the galleries above. Now, a single low-bellied goblin stood propped up against a barrel in the corner, one foot resting on a pair of bellows as he polished a jug.

Upstairs in the gallery, Nate and his companions were alone, except for a couple of sharp-nosed treegoblins in the corner, whose mottled greenish colouring blended with the wood panelling, rendering them virtually invisible, apart from their large yellow eyes.

Just then, the doors to the tavern opened and five bedraggled members of the Hive Militia trooped in, their grey topcoats and breeches crumpled and caked in mud. Calling to the low-belly for jugs of sapwine, they tramped up the stairs and slumped down round a table. With two fourthlings, two grey trogs and a pink-eyed goblin, each one thin, exhausted-looking and footsore, the group was a sorry sight. They shrugged off their knapsacks and stacked their phraxmuskets against the wall. The low-belly placed a jug and five glasses on the table in front of them, and returned to his barrel.

'Here's to two days' leave,' said one of the fourthlings, raising a glass of the golden sapwine. 'Who knows when we'll get any more.'

'Two days' leave,' the others chorused, and drained their glasses.

The pink-eyed goblin sat back, his muddy feet perched on the corner of the table. 'Won't be long now, lads,' he said, his pale eyes darting round his companions' faces. 'The big one's coming, and that's a fact. Why else would those flathead drill sergeants be marching us into the ground?'

'Hush now, Spig,' said the grey trog next to him, glancing up and catching the Professor's eye. 'You know what they says about careless talk. Never knows who might be listening . . .'

All five soldiers turned in their chairs and stared at the Professor and the others.

'Time to go, I think,' muttered the Professor, climbing slowly to his feet and wrapping his oilskin cape around him.

Nate, Eudoxia and Slip did the same. Crossing to the stairs, they walked down them as casually as they could, Nate aware of the five pairs of eyes boring into the back of his head.

'Lost some of its charm since I was last here,' said the Professor, opening the tavern door and ushering them out.

From upstairs in the gallery, loud laughter erupted and raucous calls rang out for more jugs of sapwine. The door slammed shut behind them and the voices became muffled. The Professor gathered his cloak around him and went down the tavern steps.

'Oi! Not so fast!' came a gruff voice from just along the street.

The four of them froze, the Professor's hand going instinctively to the phraxpistol beneath his cloak.

'You said you'd wait.'

Turning, Nate saw with relief the hammerhead from the hive towers hurrying along the street towards them.

'Do you have any information?' the Professor asked.

The hammerhead held out his maimed hand. Reaching into his cloak, the Professor produced two ten-glader notes.

'I asked all round the hive huts,' the hammerhead told him, taking the notes, 'and a friend of mine – a thousandsticks trainer by the name of Deggut – did hear something about a Galston Prade. But you won't find him in the hive huts . . .'

'Then, where?' said Eudoxia, unable to contain herself.

'According to Deggut, Galston Prade's in the Gyle Palace.' The hammerhead grinned, revealing two rows of sharp yellow teeth. 'He's a guest of the grossmothers.'

· CHAPTER FIFTY-TWO ·

To the east, the sky was deep indigo and studded with stars that sparkled like glister fossils in cliff rock; to the west, the sun had just set below the horizon. As they reached the East Ridge end of the Sumpwood Bridge, the two figures – one huge and shaggy, the other short, wiry and agile – were cast in stark silhouette against the glowing sky.

The short one looked round and held a finger to his mouth for a moment, before turning back and scuttling off along the bank of the river. His huge companion followed, his body stooped forward as he loped along. Behind them, sumptoads croaked a discordant chorus from the clumps of riverweed at the edge of the turbulent river.

The two figures headed left. They took a track that skirted round the cluster of ramshackle hovels and tumbledown shacks on the edge of the farmland, then up into the main part of Low Town as the moon, full and yellow and low in the sky, appeared above the rooftops.

'Another brazier stone!' shouted the hulking grey trog as he stretched out in the lufwood tub. 'The water's getting cold.'

His companions, a small tufted goblin and a sallow-faced fourthling, nodded in agreement.

'Nothing like a hot herb bath after a hard day's drill,' said the tufted goblin.

'And this is nothing like a hot herb bath!' retorted the grey trog irritably. 'Where's that vat keeper?'

The three of them were sitting in a large circular tub the size of a sapwine barrel, which was filled to the brim with greyish-blue water.

The tub was situated on the edge of a small terrace, with views over the jumble of Low Town rooftops, and the farmland and vineyards beyond. Behind them was a barn-like building, its double doors open wide and a large brazier glowing inside.

The brazier illuminated the white plaster walls of the building's interior, which were studded with hooks from which various items of clothing hung; light grey topcoats, dark grey breeches, burnished copperwood helmets and white waistcoats. Below them, three shiny, new-looking phraxmuskets leaned against the wall. From the low roof beams that crisscrossed overhead, bundles of dried herbs hung down in bushy clusters, while in the corner was a pile of smooth round stones the size of dinner platters.

From the shadows at the back of the building, an elderly mobgnome in a large padded cap and a long apron festooned with small pouches and bundles wrapped in cloth came shuffling forward. She wore large protective gauntlets and gripped a set of fire tongs, which she used to retrieve a glowing stone from the centre of the brazier. Holding it at arm's length, she shuffled out across the terrace and over to the tub.

'Watch your toes, boys!' laughed the fourthling. 'Old Mother Hivewater's got a present for us.'

'About time, if you ask me, corporal,' muttered the grey trog as the mobgnome reached over the bathers and dropped the brazier stone into the tub.

There was a loud hiss, followed by a cloud of aromatic steam, and the greyish-blue water began to bubble. The aged mobgnome wiped her brow on her apron.

'More seasoning, I think,' she croaked, taking off her gloves and unpinning a cloth bundle from her apron. She untied the string that bound it and sprinkled the contents of the pouch into the bubbling water.

With a sigh, the grey trog leaned back contentedly in the tub and closed his eyes. His companions did the same. Chuckling to herself, the mobgnome shuffled back inside.

A few moments later, two figures – one huge and shaggy, the other short, wiry and agile – crept across the terrace. While the large figure stood guard at the door to the building, his smaller companion scuttled inside, re-emerging a few moments later with a bundle of clothes, helmets and three phraxmuskets. Sharing the spoils between them, they slipped away into the night.

From the steaming herb bath came the deep rumble of snores.

· CHAPTER FIFTY-THREE ·

The burnished copperwood helmet was several sizes too big for Nate, and its visor kept slipping down over his eyes, making it difficult to see ahead. The phraxmusket on his shoulder also felt heavy and unfamiliar, as did the voluminous grey topcoat. As for the dark grey breeches, they were baggy and uncomfortable and he kept having to hitch them up.

Pushing back his helmet, Nate glanced round at Eudoxia, who was marching alongside him.

With her long blonde hair swept up and piled on top of her head, Eudoxia's helmet fitted perfectly, as did her topcoat and breeches, though she clearly found the phraxmusket as burdensome as Nate found his own. Despite this, Nate had to admit, she looked the part – every inch the fresh-faced recruit to the Hive Militia.

None of this was surprising, as Eudoxia's uniform had belonged to a small tufted goblin, while Nate's had been worn by a much bigger grey trog.

Ahead of them, perfecting what Nate took to be a military swagger, marched the Professor, in the uniform of a corporal. Stitched to the sleeves of their grey topcoats were lozenge-shaped patches of cloth bearing the words *2nd Low Town Regiment* in the heavy curlicued script favoured in Hive.

'Halt!' ordered the Professor with a bark worthy of a drill sergeant, and Nate suspected that he was rather enjoying his role.

They had reached the Peak, at the very top of East Ridge, and were surrounded by terrace gardens, fountains and spacious villas built in the Hive style – conical roofs, tall towers and long balconies of carved timber. The rich citizens of Hive passed them by without a glance, exercising milk-white prowlgrins or promenading in gaudy topcoats and gowns at the head of long processions of servants in green livery.

In front of them, the magnificent Gyle Palace towered up into the morning sky. Up close, Nate marvelled, it was even more spectacular than from the phraxbarge or the window of the Sumpwood Bridge.

Unlike the black hive huts of the hammerheads, or the carved clan halls of the long-hairs, the glistening pink-tinged palace of the gyle goblins didn't rely only on timber for its construction. Instead, the Professor had told Nate and Eudoxia on the long march through East Ridge to the Peak, the gyle goblins built in wax – milchwax, to be precise.

This extraordinary building material, both malleable and incredibly strong, was produced by the huge milchgrubs that fed on the glowing fungus beds in the vast cellar gardens below the palace. As well as this wax, secreted from glands in the creatures' translucent heads, the milchgrubs produced a sweet, sickly honey on which the gyle goblins exclusively fed.

As befitted a palace constructed of wax, its magnificent towers, buttresses and high walls had a soft, almost liquid appearance, with intricate traceries of droplets and rivulets seemingly running down its surfaces, collecting on lintels and gables and flowing round doorways. It was as if the Gyle Palace was both growing and melting at the same time. The effect was mesmerising, and it was all Nate could do to take his eyes off it when the huge wooden doors in the great dripping archway at the entrance opened, and a trio of gyle goblins marched out.

All three of them were of identical appearance; short and thin, with bow legs and long tremulous fingers which they held up in greeting. With their bulbous noses and heavy-lidded eyes, the gyle goblins looked comically sleepy, an impression heightened by their expensive-looking clothes; embroidered topcoats, triple-breasted waistcoats and crushed funnel hats – all of which looked as if they'd been slept in and were stained with honey.

'What be you wanting?' the first of the goblins asked in a flat voice that betrayed almost no interest.

'We have orders from the High Council to escort Galston Prade to the Clan Hall in High Town,' the Professor barked, saluting the gyle goblin theatrically.

He flourished the barkscroll that the archivists had carefully forged in front of the goblin's bulbous nose. Ignoring it, the goblin turned to his companion.

'The High Council be wanting Galston Prade,' he said.

The gyle goblin nodded and turned to the gyle goblin next to him. 'The High Council be wanting Galston Prade,' he repeated.

The third gyle goblin turned to the open doorway and, cupping his hands to his mouth, called in a flat sing-song voice. 'The High Council be wanting Galston Prade.'

The cry was taken up by unseen goblins in the halls and corridors inside the palace, passed on one to another until it faded out of earshot. Nate, Eudoxia and the Professor waited. Then, in the distance, but getting louder as it proceeded back along the chain, came a reply.

'Galston Prade, central tower, top balcony.'

The third gyle goblin stepped aside and ushered them in.

'Galston Prade, central tower, top balcony,' he said, his heavy-lidded eyes staring expressionlessly.

As Nate and Eudoxia followed the Professor through the entrance, the three gyle goblins pushed the door shut behind them and resumed their positions at three small peepholes.

'Which way?' asked the Professor, but the gyle goblins, their backs turned, ignored him.

'Never mind,' he muttered. 'You two, follow me.'

They strode off up a long narrow corridor that rose at a gentle incline. It was warm and stuffy in the palace, and the waxen walls gleamed with a flickering light thrown out by the brazier torches that hung down from the curved ceiling above. Nate trailed his hand along the wall and found it soft and smooth to the touch. He held his fingers to his nose, and recoiled at the intense sickly-sweet smell, so overpowering it made him feel light-headed.

'Come on, Nate!' the Professor muttered. 'This isn't a sightseeing trip!'

After some twenty strides or so, the corridor abruptly opened up into a vast vaulted hall. Towering high above them, and plunging down deep into the depths of the palace, the hall was immense, crisscrossed both above and below with drip-streaked walkways of wax. The corridor split into three walkways which snaked upwards around the circular walls of three huge towers.

'This way,' said the Professor, taking the central fork along the curved aerial balcony which led up towards the central of the palace's towers.

Nate followed Eudoxia and the Professor, a raised hand holding the oversized helmet from slipping, scarcely daring to look down over the edge of the walkway as it spiralled higher and higher round the sides of the tower. All around them, balconies and walkways of glistening wax connected and interconnected, leading to chambers, ledges and alcoves which had been moulded and sculpted from the thick waxen walls. Nate pushed back the visor of his helmet and stared around him.

There were gyle goblins everywhere. In the chambers, on the walkways, heading up and down slippery stairs; all identical, and all engaged in carrying, sorting through, grading and chopping vast sackfuls of vegetables and fruit. As Nate, Eudoxia and the Professor marched ever higher, lines of gyle goblins would jostle past them, carrying baskets of pulp which they tipped over the balustrades of the balconies and sent spinning down into the palace depths.

'They're feeding the gardens, which feed the milchgrubs – which feed *them*,' explained the Professor as they reached the halfway point in the walkway's spiralling climb up the tower.

Just then, a large cauldron filled to the brim and dripping with pink honey rose past them. It was connected by a chain to a crane which jutted out from a balcony ahead. Nate edged as close to the side of the walkway as he dared, and looked down. Just visible far below, glowing in the cellars of the palace, were the fungus beds, laid out like a patchwork quilt. Looking up again, he saw thirty or so gyle goblins carefully unhook the cauldron and carry it off the balcony and into the chamber beyond.

As Nate and Eudoxia marched past, they peered inside what appeared to be a vast kitchen. Huge steaming vats were perched on tall stoves, surrounded by twisting pipes and covered in gauges and levers. The air was impossibly sweet, warm and moist, and almost made Nate gag. An army of gyle goblins in stained aprons were pouring heated honey from a vat into a funnel embedded in the floor. From a chamber just below, the chants of waiting gyle goblins could be heard – animated, excited and shrill.

'Honey! Honey! Honey!'

Suddenly, from out of the shadows, a huge gyle goblin grossmother waddled into view.

Nate had never seen anything like her. Dressed in a flowing gown the size of a skyship sail, encrusted in mire pearls and with an elaborately tied and knotted turban of finest woodspider-silk on her great head, the huge grossmother seemed to flow across the

362

kitchen chamber like melted milchwax. As she moved, her eight chins wobbled and her tiny eyes glistened in the fleshy folds of her face like marsh gems in Mire mud.

'Patience, my darlings,' the grossmother trilled in a high-pitched fluting voice. 'Your honey is coming.'

With a wave of a massive wobbling arm, the grossmother directed the gyle goblins to empty more vats into the funnel, before taking hold of a large brass lever and, her face glistening with sweat, pulling back. There was a great whooshing sound and, in the chamber below, the chanting gave way to shrieks of excitement and then the contented sounds of slurping.

Tearing his gaze away, Nate shouldered his phraxmusket and hurried after Eudoxia and the Professor, narrowly avoiding a shower of oakapple shavings cascading down through the air as he did so.

'How much further?' he gasped, catching them up.

He was hot and thirsty, and the sweet sickly odour of the palace was making his head swim.

'Just up there,' said the Professor, nodding towards the top of the conical tower where the walkway reached a small balcony, a wax-fringed doorway on its far side.

As they reached the top balcony of the central tower, Eudoxia sprang forward, only for the Professor to take her arm.

'Stand to attention,' he said firmly, straightening the phraxmusket on Eudoxia's shoulder and adjusting the helmet on Nate's head. 'Until we know what's on the other side of that door, we're soldiers of the Hive Militia. Is that clear?'

Eudoxia and Nate nodded. The Professor turned and rapped briskly on the door.

'Come in,' replied a low voice from inside.

· CHAPTER FIFTY- FOUR ·

The Professor turned the handle of the lightly varnished gladeoak door, and entered. Behind him, Nate and Eudoxia peered out from behind the low visors of their copperwood helmets, their phraxmuskets braced at their shoulders.

Nate had expected to see some sort of cell, or cage with barred windows and chains bolted to walls. Instead, they found themselves standing in a spacious elegant chamber. The circular walls were painted with curling tendrils of Deepwoods plants with luxuriant foliage and heavy-headed flowers, their deep colours echoed in the elaborate woodsilk drapes at the high window and the heavy quilts and pillows on the large floating sumpwood bed. In the middle of the chamber, at a circular desk and attended by three expensively dressed gyle goblins, sat a figure. He was stooped forward, head down, over a bundle of barkscrolls.

The figure looked up, and from beside him Nate heard Eudoxia give a low gasp. Tall and elegant-looking, he was a fourthling with dishevelled grey hair and side-whiskers and a tired careworn face. He was dressed in a topcoat of the finest quality, edged in quarm fur, and had a carved fromp-head cane propped against the table beside him. There was no mistaking that this was Eudoxia's father. She had his features and bearing, but where her eyes were a deep green, Galston Prade's were a startling blue.

As he looked wearily at the three guards from the Hive Militia standing before him, he stifled a cough, wisps of breath visible despite the warmth of the chamber. Nate had seen this all too often before, down in the mines. The blue eyes, the clouds of breath, the cough . . . Galston Prade's eyes and lungs, he knew, had been affected by phraxdust, probably from his days as a miner in the

Eastern Woods. He'd clearly worked at the phraxface himself, and must have clawed his way up to become the rich mine owner he was today. But at what cost?

'I've been expecting you,' Galston Prade said drily. 'Or at least, someone like you. Once I did as Felftis Brack wished and signed over my mine to him, I knew my days were numbered. My own stupid fault for falling into this trap of his . . .' He coughed softly, the clouds of breath rising up in wispy twists. 'Now I suppose you're taking me to be barrelled.'

He knocked the barkscrolls off the desk with a despairing sweep of his arm and Nate saw, for the first time, that Galston Prade had shackles on his wrists, a single chain connecting one to the other. Nate glanced at Eudoxia. She was trembling, he saw, and her knuckles showed white where she gripped the phraxmusket at her shoulder.

'But none of it matters, so long as that slimy lakescum honours his word and ensures no harm befalls my daughter.'

Galston Prade got to his feet shakily, one shackled hand leaning heavily on the cane for support. At his side, the gyle goblins stared at Nate, Eudoxia and the Professor with heavy-lidded indifference.

'You have orders?' said the first gyle goblin.

The Professor saluted and handed him the barkscroll he carried. 'To take Galston Prade to the Clan Hall in High Town,' he said crisply.

'He has orders,' said the gyle goblin to his companions.

'He has orders,' they repeated in turn as they looked at the document, before handing it back to the first goblin.

'We must tell the grossmothers,' he said, walking towards the door.

'Tell the grossmothers,' his companions nodded behind him.

Opening the door, the goblin leaned out and shouted. 'Tell the grandmothers that . . . *unkhh!* . . .'

The Professor swung the barrel of his phraxmusket and connected with the back of the goblin's head. Taking their cue, Eudoxia and Nate dropped their phraxmuskets and sprang on the two startled goblins in front of them, grasping them by the collar and clamping a hand over their mouths. The Professor strode over to the window, tore down one of the drapes and spread it on the floor. Nate and Eudoxia dropped their goblins, kicking and struggling, onto the embroidered silk, which the Professor tied into a knotted bundle.

Outside, the cry of 'Tell the grossmothers that . . . *unkhh!* . . .' echoed through the corridors and passages of the colony.

'I . . . I don't understand,' wheezed Galston Prade as the Professor took him by the arm.

'We'll explain later,' the Professor said, 'but for now, we have to get you out of here.'

Nate and Eudoxia picked up their phraxmuskets and fell in behind the Professor and Galston Prade, who'd stepped over the body of the unconscious gyle goblin at the door and were making their way back down the walkway. Nate could tell from the look in her eyes that Eudoxia was desperate to fling off her helmet and embrace her father, but they both knew that that would have to wait until they reached the safety of the Sumpwood Bridge Academy. Right now, they were too busy playing the role of guards, marching briskly behind the stooped and shackled figure of Galston Prade, phraxmuskets at their shoulders, while ahead of them the Professor barged gawping gyle goblins aside.

They made their way quickly down the hot humid walkway, past the teeming chambers of busy goblins on either side, while the cry of 'Tell the grossmothers that . . . *unkhh!* . . .' died away far below – to be replaced with a chorused response.

'Tell the grossmothers what?'

Growing louder all the time, the cry approached, then overtook them and echoed up the central tower towards the top balcony.

'Tell the grossmothers what? . . . Tell the grossmothers what?'

They had just reached the bottom of the tower and were back in the huge hall at the centre of the Gyle Palace when there came an urgent shout from high above. The gyle goblin the Professor had stunned had come to his senses.

'Galston Prade is escaping! Galston Prade is escaping!'

'*Seize them!*'

The high-pitched scream cut across the gyle goblins' cries, and Nate turned to see two huge grossmothers waddling towards them from the opposite side of the hall. Behind them came a phalanx of furious-looking gyle goblins, the honey from the interrupted meal dripping from their bulbous noses and down the fronts of their embroidered topcoats.

On the thousandsticks field, Nate had faced this situation a hundred times. Only this time, the thousandsticks track was a walkway of glistening milchwax, and instead of a flying wedge of New Lake players, Nate was facing a phalanx of gyle goblins with two of the biggest blockers he'd ever seen. In his hands, he gripped the phraxmusket as if it was his trusty thousandstick and set off at full pelt towards the oncoming goblins. Behind him, the Professor and Galston Prade were hurrying down the corridor towards the

entrance to the Gyle Palace. Eudoxia turned back.

'Nate! What are you doing?' she shouted in alarm.

Nate ducked low and slid along the waxy surface, sweeping his phraxmusket in rapid movements low to the ground in front of him. It was a move called the 'Barley Cutter', and he'd only ever used it in practice before – and then, with limited success.

This time, it was different. The barrel of the phraxmusket clipped first one heel, then the other, of the two grossmothers as he slid through the chink of light separating their huge wobbling bodies and ploughed on through the phalanx of goblins following. Like a scythe cutting through glade barley, the phraxmusket sent the goblins sprawling. Behind him, the two grossmothers had lost their balance and, with gurgling cries of terror, toppled off the walkway and down towards the cellar gardens far below, followed by dozens of shrieking gyle goblins.

Moments later, there came the sound of two huge glutinous *splats* followed by smaller *plops*. A wailing cry echoed up from the gardens – 'The honey's spoilt! The honey's spoilt!' – followed by the grossmothers' indignant calls for help.

With the Gyle Palace in uproar, Nate scrambled to his feet and came running back to where Eudoxia was standing, open-mouthed.

'What was that?' she said, her eyes wide with astonishment.

'Just something I picked up in thousandsticks training,' Nate smiled. 'Come on, we'd better get out of here before any more grossmothers show up – and catch up with the Professor and your father.'

They turned and hurried down the corridor towards the doors of the Gyle Palace. The three gyle goblin doorkeepers looked at each other, bewildered.

'What should we do?'

'I don't know, what should we do?' they repeated in confusion as Nate and Eudoxia elbowed them aside and hurried out of the stifling building and into the overcast gloom outside.

The heavy door clanged shut behind them. Eudoxia sighed with relief. Nate, his copperwood helmet slipping down over his eyes, paused and drew in a lungful of fresh cold air.

'And where do you think you two are going!' came a low growling voice.

· CHAPTER FIFTY- FIVE ·

As darkness began to fall, the going got harder. On the forest floor, the thin covering of leaf fall and needledrop obscured the crimped knots of tree root radiating out from the trees and the jagged rocks embedded in the mud. Eudoxia stumbled forwards, but managed to right herself. She glanced round at the other recruits in the marching column, wondering whether she was the only one having difficulties.

There were a hundred recruits in all, marching three abreast, with her, Nate and a hard-faced tufted goblin forming one rank near the back of the column. Each of them was dressed in the same uniform: dark grey breeches, white waistcoat, burnished copperwood helmet and light grey topcoat, with a patch stitched onto the sleeve that read, *2nd Low Town Regiment*.

On their backs, they each carried a pack made of canvas and tilderleather constructed on a buoyant sumpwood frame. Although bulky and containing kit, ammunition, bedroll and rations, the sumpwood frame made the backpacks virtually weightless. They didn't, however, make the conditions underfoot any easier.

'How much further?' Eudoxia groaned, stumbling again and gripping Nate's arm for support.

Nate shrugged, tipping his oversized helmet forward as he did so.

'Till we can't see our hands in front of our faces, like as not,' came a gruff voice from the rank just in front of them, and a grey trog turned, his large bulbous nose and tiny eyes screwed up in a look of utter weariness.

'Silence in the ranks!' the company sergeant barked, waving the vicious-looking cane of woodwillow above his head and glaring back along the line.

The brutal flathead sergeant was in command of the second of the three infantry companies that made up the three-hundred-strong Second Low Town Regiment and, like the other two company sergeants, he kept his recruits in line through constant vigilance – and the occasional savage flogging.

Ever since Nate and Eudoxia had stumbled out of the Gyle Palace into the daylight, and heard that growling voice – '*And where do you think you two are going?*' – their only thought had been one of escape.

The voice had belonged to the company sergeant, who was dressed in the light grey topcoat of the Hive Militia, the woodwillow switch beneath his arm. He had no interest in who they were as individuals, having eyes only for the uniforms they wore; uniforms which matched his own and bore the patch of the Second Low Town Regiment.

'Fall in!' the sergeant had barked, lashing out with the woodwillow cane, and Nate and Eudoxia had found themselves tramping back through East Ridge in a column of other dejected grey-coated recruits towards the Low Town barracks.

'But my father and the Professor . . .' Eudoxia had whispered desperately to Nate as they entered the cramped and dingy barracks courtyard.

'Silence in the ranks!' the sergeant had barked.

It would be the first of many times they would hear that order in the days to come.

'As soon as we get a chance, we'll ditch these uniforms and slip away,' Nate had whispered.

'*Silence*, I said!'

In the courtyard, they were each handed the impossibly heavy-looking backpacks, which they struggled into, and were amazed to find how light they were. Not that there was much time for amazement. Under the barked commands of the three flathead sergeants, the recruits were ordered outside and formed into company columns. A long-hair goblin officer in a stylish grey topcoat bedecked in gold braid and medal ribbons appeared, and walked up and down the ranks, giving the new recruits to the Second Low Town Regiment a cursory inspection. Satisfied, he mounted his skittish-looking black prowlgrin and led the regiment out of the city and into the forest.

That had been six hours earlier. Apart from one break to replenish their waterflasks from a stream, and another when a fourthling corporal had bagged a squealing woodhog, they hadn't stopped at all. Now they were quite some distance from Hive and it was beginning to get dark.

As they went deeper into the forest, and the cackle and screech of the night creatures started up, the trees became older and larger, though there were fewer of them. The dense canopy above them shut out even the brightest day's sunlight, plunging the forest into a darkness that starved the smaller weaker saplings and shrubs, and nipped growth in the bud. The going underfoot became easier and, as the trees thinned, other columns could be seen around them, making their own way through the Deepwoods.

To their right, in the fading light of evening Nate saw a regiment, like their own, about three hundred strong, trudging parallel to them. Their grey uniforms camouflaged them well, but he would occasionally glimpse the gleam of a phraxmusket or the glint of a helmet spike. And all the while, as the soft breeze blew through the branches, he could hear their marching feet stirring up the carpet of fallen pine needles and leaves. It sounded like a stream rushing along through the forest beside them.

'Look over there,' Eudoxia whispered, nudging Nate softly in the side.

To their left, through the trees, was a long row of sumpwood limbers – varnished wooden sleds that hovered above the ground – each being drawn by prowlgrins. The air was shot with their soft whinnying and occasional yelps. Some of them were buckled in between the shafts of covered limbers; some were harnessed in fours, and even eights, when the weight of their burden called for it. The larger limbers supported massive cannon, with bulging phraxchambers and barrels like tree trunks, while the smaller covered limbers carried the missiles they would fire: phraxshells of various shapes and sizes.

The whole column, Nate realized, represented an awesome display of power and a huge expenditure of resources. The massive phraxcannon and the shells they fired required more phraxcrystals than an entire fleet of skyships, while the sumpwood used to transport them must have left half a forest depleted. This was clearly where the clan chiefs of Hive had used up their city's wealth.

Beyond the line of artillery were yet more flashes of black, sky-blue and grey, where other regiments marched through the Deepwoods in silence, whatever thoughts they were thinking, locked up inside their heads. And there were probably more Hivers still, it occurred to Nate, marching beyond those he could see, and all in the same direction.

It was little wonder, he thought, that the streets of Hive were so empty.

'Company halt!'

A sigh of relief went up as the company sergeant's command echoed back along the line. Up ahead, he was standing in a small clearing, a phraxlamp illuminating him now as the last glimmers of the long day were snuffed out.

'Recruits to sleep up there!' He pointed behind him to a majestic lufwood, thick with dark foliage and broad sweeping branches. 'Corporals to post guard beneath! Now, get the brazier up and working, and let's roast that hog!'

Nate and Eudoxia pulled the backpacks from their shoulders and sat them down on the forest floor. They looked at one another, then at the surrounding trees, a questioning expression in both their eyes.

Should they try their luck, and sneak quietly away into the shadowy forest?

As if in answer, the company sergeant loomed up in front of them.

'First I find you loitering outside the Gyle Palace,' he snarled. 'Now I catch you eyeing the forest.' His voice became low and menacing. 'I've seen fresh-faced recruits like you two before, looking out for any opportunity to scarper back to your mothers. Well, be warned . . .' The sergeant stuck his willow cane under Eudoxia's chin and raised her head. A strand of golden hair slipped free from under her copperwood helmet. 'I'll be watching you!'

He turned and strode back to where the brazier was being stoked and lit. Eudoxia kicked her backpack with frustration. Despite the buoyant sumpwood frame, the tilderleather and canvas pack was solid and felt heavy to the touch. Nate knelt down, undid the straps on his own pack and opened it.

It was stuffed with smooth sharp-tipped leadwood bullets, each one threaded to a cord, forming clusters of twenty. These were placed in pouches and attached to the hooks on their waistcoats, ready to be pulled off the cluster and loaded into the shiny new phraxmuskets each recruit carried. Then the musket could be aimed, the trigger at its phraxchamber squeezed, and the shard of phraxcrystal inside would create an explosion that would send the bevelled lump of leadwood flying from the barrel with deadly accuracy. Once, twice, a thousand thousand times the shard of phraxcrystal in the musket would do its work before needing to be replenished. And the backpack contained an ample supply of bullets to keep it busy.

'You know what this means?' Nate said.

Eudoxia nodded. 'War,' she said.

'War,' Nate repeated. 'We're heading off to war.' He swallowed heavily. 'Against . . .'

'The free timbersmiths of the Midwood Decks and their friends, the Great Gladers,' said a small treegoblin, placing his backpack next to Eudoxia's. He looked up. 'Twill's the name,' he said chirpily. 'I was a barrel maker by trade before the call up.'

He stuck out his small long-fingered hand and shook Nate and Eudoxia's hands.

'I'm Nate, and this is . . . Dox . . . We're apprentices,' said Nate carefully.

'From the Sumpwood Bridge Academy,' Eudoxia added.

'Ah, learned types!' chuckled the treegoblin. 'Well, welcome to the Second Low Town – the sorriest bunch of misfits in the Hive Militia. Not counting the *First* Low Town, that is!' He laughed at his own joke, before picking up his musket and backpack again. 'Come on,' he said, 'grab a leaf. Let's get in line for supper before it's all gone!'

He gave them each a broad barksorrel leaf he'd picked from a nearby bush, and Nate and Eudoxia followed Twill to the brazier, where a woodhog was being roasted and turned on a spit.

''Ere we go,' said a red-faced mobgnome when they finally got to the head of the line, carving off a large hunk of dripping meat and dropping it onto Eudoxia's outstretched leaf.

He wiped his hands on his greasy waistcoat, turned back to the smoking carcass and plunged the serrated blade through the hard glistening skin of the woodhog. Less than half the company had been fed, yet most of the hog was already gone.

'Thanks,' said Nate as a portion was dropped on his own leaf, and he and Eudoxia found themselves being jostled out of the way as the recruits behind them elbowed their own way forward.

'Now, let's find a comfortable branch before they're all taken,' said Twill, folding his supper up in the leaf and carefully placing it in the pocket of his waistcoat.

Following suit, their stomachs rumbling, Nate and Eudoxia stumbled after the little treegoblin and began to climb the majestic lufwood tree – under the ever-watchful eye of the company sergeant below.

CHAPTER FIFTY-SIX

'Seven mouths to feed, you say,' said the grey trog, nodding his head thoughtfully. He was lying on his side, strumming his spatula-like fingers on the helmet which lay next to him. 'That's a large family, Twill, so it is.'

The treegoblin nodded. 'And they're hungry little nestlings, Sky love 'em,' he said, 'and with only my wife to care for them now . . .'

Around them, in the branches of the lufwood tree, many similar conversations were taking place between the members of the Second Company of the Second Low Town Regiment. Nate, Eudoxia and Twill the treegoblin had joined a grey trog and a red-haired fourthling on a broad branch halfway up the tree's massive trunk.

'What . . . about . . . you, Gorlan?' asked Nate as he licked the tips of his fingers clean of the woodpork juices.

'Me?' said the grey trog, his large brown eyes taking on a faraway look. 'Oh, there's just me and Merla.'

'No young'uns, then?' said the treegoblin.

Beside him, the fourthling reached out for the half-empty bottle of woodgrog that stood beside him on the branch. He pulled out the cork, raised the bottle to his lips and slurped the pungent liquid noisily.

'No young'uns, Twill,' said Gorlan in answer. 'Merla and I haven't yet been blessed. Mind you,' he added, 'I sometimes think that that's a blessing in itself.' He shook his head and lowered his voice to a hushed growl. 'Hive's no place to be raising young'uns these days.'

'And what do you do?' Nate asked him.

'Do?' said the grey trog, looking up at him, his brown eyes narrowing. 'I march. But if you want to know what I *did*, well, I used to work in the caves. I was a cellar keeper.'

'Best sapwine cellar in all the Edge,' added Twill.

The grey trog nodded, his eyes twinkling. 'I like to think so,' he said. 'I had barrels in my cellar that were filled in the Second Age of Flight,' he told them, 'when Hive was a tiny hamlet, sitting on the edge of the great gorge.' He pulled himself up and sat looking round the group, his hands resting on the branch below him. 'My father was a cellar keeper, and his father before him. At one time all three of us were working the caves together, side by side. We'd be up before daybreak when the sapgrape harvest came in from the vineyards, and be pressing and barrelling till well after sunset.' The grey trog's small eyes glistened. 'Like Twill says, best sapwine cellar in the Edge, it was,' he concluded proudly. 'Until they came and took it all away from me.'

'Who?' asked Eudoxia, peering out from beneath her helmet.

'Why, young Dox,' Gorlan smiled sadly, 'the Bloody Blades, of course. "On the orders of the Clan Council", they said, my barrels were needed for trade. They seized the lot of them.'

The red-haired fourthling gave a bitter laugh. His name was Oakshank and, judging from his name and his features, he had woodtroll and slaughterer forebears.

'On the orders of Kulltuft Warhammer, more like!' he scoffed. 'Seizing your sapwine to trade for phraxcrystals most likely, and now seizing *us* to fight for him.'

He took a deep breath and sank his head into his hands. The others watched him uneasily.

'The thing is, I blame myself,' Oakshank said, taking another swig of woodgrog. His voice was slurred, but his words were coherent enough. 'I was one of them who trusted Kulltuft Warhammer. I was there at his rallies, cheering him on and picking fights with any who disagreed with him. I believed what he had to say about dealing with Great Glade from a position of strength. I believed his lies about how they wanted to bring us Hivers to our knees . . .'

'Shhh,' Gorlan reminded him as, in his rising anger, Oakshank's voice was beginning to grow louder.

'I was one of the thousands who helped sweep him to power,

replacing the old council with him and his bunch of clan chief cronies. And by the time we realized we'd all been misled, it was too late. Kulltuft Warhammer was safely ensconced in the Clan Hall, protected by those Bloody Blades of his.'

He looked round at the others on the branch, his eyes glittery and unfocused. His face hardened.

'I used to be a shipbuilder,' he said, 'but when the Bloody Blades confiscated all the phraxcrystals, there was no more shipbuilding in Hive and I lost my job. I never found another. My wife, heavy with child, got sick with the sweating fever. I nursed her best I could, but I couldn't afford the expensive medicines from the City of Night she needed – and she died in childbirth.' He hung his head. 'The young'un didn't survive neither.'

Nate heard Eudoxia take a short intake of breath. The fourthling shook his head.

'And it was my fault. All my fault.' He snorted. 'When the call up came, I welcomed it with open arms. I was being punished, and I deserved to be . . .' He climbed slowly to his feet. 'Not that I want to go to war,' he said. 'But then again, what else is there left for us Hivers to do? And at least we get fed.' He looked down, and noticed the bottle of woodgrog and seized it in his shaking hand, '. . . and watered.'

He staggered off along the branch, almost falling, until he got to the trunk, where he slumped down and pulled his blanket over his head. Twill the treegoblin and Gorlan the grey trog watched him sadly.

'He'll be lucky to survive this march,' said the grey trog, shaking his head before climbing to his feet. 'I think I'll turn in as well.'

'And me,' said Twill.

The two of them joined the fourthling on the widest part of the branch, their backs against the massive tree trunk and their blankets pulled around their shoulders. Alone, Eudoxia turned to Nate.

'What are we going to do, Nate?' she asked.

Nate looked down at the base of the huge tree, where the figure of the sergeant prowled in the flickering brazier light, woodwillow cane in hand.

'There's only one thing we can do, Eudoxia,' he said, looking up and seeing in her eyes the despair of finding and then losing her father again. 'And that is, to wait . . .'

· CHAPTER FIFTY- SEVEN ·

A nd so they'd waited. For four long weeks, as the Second Low Town Regiment marched through the Deepwoods, Eudoxia and Nate had waited for the chance to escape. But under the vigilant eye of the company sergeant that chance never came.

Every day was the same. At dawn, they would be woken by the company sergeant, eat a meagre breakfast of boiled barley porridge and, if they were lucky, some Deepwoods fruits or roots that had been identified as edible, and washed down with tea made from whatever herbs or aromatic plants grew close by. Then they would march, for ten hours – or eleven or twelve if the company sergeant felt they hadn't made enough progress – until, as evening fell, he finally called a halt.

There, in whatever clearing or thicket the company sergeant had selected, they would eat whatever had been caught that day under the company sergeant's supervision, before retiring to the branch of whatever tree the hundred-strong regiment had been ordered to sleep in by the company sergeant. There, they would sleep fitfully, wrapped up in their musty blankets, with the company sergeant and his corporals keeping guard below.

The company sergeant! The company sergeant! The company sergeant!

By the fourth week of the march, Nate had begun to see the flathead sergeant with that woodwillow cane of his watching him in his dreams. There seemed no escape.

'Here, I got you this,' said Nate, handing Eudoxia an extra oatcake he'd managed to snatch from the skillet over the brazier and return with, unbroken, through the scrum of ravenous recruits.

'Thank you, Nate.' She nibbled at the corner of the tasteless biscuit. 'Just what I needed,' she said, her eyes dull and lifeless, tinged with dark rings beneath.

'Company, prepare to move out!'

The company sergeant's deep commanding voice echoed through the air, and the recruits fell into line. Nate helped Eudoxia on with her sumpwood backpack and then she returned the favour. Without a word being spoken, they found the places in the great column that they always took, with the same neighbours left and right, back and front.

'Company, forward march!'

Nate turned to Eudoxia as the pair of them started forward.

'Hair,' he whispered, nodding towards a long golden tress that must have slipped free from the topknot inside her copperwood helmet and now dangled down limply over the wet shoulder of her topcoat.

Eudoxia frowned and pushed the telltale hair back into place as discreetly as she could.

'That's better,' said Nate, glancing round a moment later.

'Silence in the ranks!' the company sergeant barked for the thousandth time.

Eudoxia looked around her, checking to see whether anyone had noticed the hair. No one had. The day's march had begun and, with their heads down and bodies stooped forward, the goblins, fourthlings, trogs and trolls of the second company, Second Low Town Regiment, were marching with weary intent, oblivious to anything or anybody around them. Eudoxia's gaze fell on a gap in the line, three ranks back. She frowned and turned to Nate.

'Oakshank's missing,' she hissed.

'Yes, I know,' said Nate.

'Did he . . . ?' Eudoxia said, her face suddenly bright with hope.

Nate shook his head. 'He fell out of the tree in the night,' he told her, his voice hushed and low. 'Broke his neck when he landed . . . Twill told me when I was getting the oatcakes.'

Eudoxia's eyes filled with tears.

'Silence in the ranks!' the company sergeant barked angrily.

382

On this march, the days could prove just as hazardous as the nights, Nate knew. The company had lost several recruits to forest ague – a shivering fever that caused collapse and death in less than two days. Then, just the previous week, a hulking cloddertrog, his waterflask empty and throat parched, had reached out, plucked a juicy-looking fruit from an overhanging branch and sunk his teeth into its sweet flesh – only to drop dead on the spot. Perhaps strangest of all was the case of the flathead sergeant of the third company, which marched alongside them. He had disturbed a hover worm. Hissing furiously, the glistening snake-like creature had lunged at him, its tentacles sinking into his neck and pumping him full of venom. The hapless sergeant had blown up like a balloon and, mumbling incoherently, floated up into the air, through the forest canopy and away across the sky – though it has to be said, few tears were shed as the recruits saw him go.

Nate calculated that of the hundred recruits who had left Hive, only ninety-three remained in the second company. He glanced round at Eudoxia, her expression still crestfallen by the news that Oakshank the red-haired fourthling had died rather than escaped. He reached out and touched her arm. She turned and smiled bravely. Nate smiled back, but he understood only too well her feelings of hopelessness and frustration. If they didn't find a chance to escape soon, it might be too late. A great battle was looming, and the whole regiment knew it.

As they'd marched on through the morning, the drizzle had turned to rain, which grew heavier and heavier as the time passed until now, a little shy of six hours after they'd set off from their last camp, it was torrential. It had soaked into their topcoats, making the thick material heavy and stiff, and through to the jackets and waistcoats beneath. More rain sluiced down their necks, driven into the tiny gap between the tops of their raised collars and the backs of their copperwood helmets by gusting winds.

This torrential rain, warm and clammy, could mean only one thing, Nate realized. They must be approaching the forests around the Midwood Decks.

Underfoot, the ground had grown wetter and wetter, first turning the covering mattress of leaves and needles spongy, then – as the trees had begun to thin out – being churned up by the passing recruits so that, in their position far down the line, Eudoxia and Nate found themselves ploughing through thick sucking mud that made each step an effort.

Nate looked at the bare feet of the marching goblins and trolls all around him. 'I envy them,' he said.

Eudoxia shrugged. 'They've got soles as hard as strips of leadwood,' she said. 'We wouldn't last ten minutes barefoot.'

'All the same . . .' said Nate, hopping forward on his left leg, his right leg raised up behind him.

Eudoxia looked down to see muddy water gushing out of the top of his boot. She smiled – then, her attention drawn by a movement to her right, her brow furrowed and she pointed.

'Look,' she whispered.

Nate turned and saw a column of marching soldiers, some fifty strides to their right. Unlike the ramshackle recruits of the Second Low Town, this regiment was marching smartly, backs straight and shoulders back. They were each wearing long oilskin cloaks and their helmets had canvas covers to ensure that the gleaming silver beneath would not tarnish. Heavy phraxmuskets rested on their shoulders, while short-handled axes could just be glimpsed beneath the swinging folds of their cloaks, their razor-sharp blades glinting as they marched. A company sergeant, the long hair on his face spiked into tufts by the rain, glanced across at his opposite number at the head of the Low Towners and bared his fangs in a haughty grimace of contempt.

Nate saw his company sergeant flinch as if he'd been physically struck as the long-hair sergeant strode past.

'The Bloody Blades!' someone muttered in the ranks of the Second Low Town Regiment. 'They got us into this and, by Earth and Sky, let's hope they can get us out!'

This time the company sergeant said nothing.

Beyond the Bloody Blades was a second, and then a third, great column of goblins – the Hammerhead and Flathead Guard, their sky-blue coats half camouflaged by the drenching rain, and their narrow-topped funnel helmets rising and falling in unison as they strode resolutely on.

From all sides, the various regiments of the Hive Militia were converging through the thinning trees. The view on both sides was unbroken now, with the forest all but behind them and only a few sickly-looking lufwoods or stunted ironwoodpines remaining on the forest fringe.

To their left, the buoyant sumpwood limbers glided effortlessly above the mud as the prowlgrins that pulled them trudged on. The phraxcannon mounted upon the limbers were now in plain sight. They were truly vast weapons, each one at least as large as the *Thunderer*, the mighty cannon Nate had seen being ceremonially fired in the Old Forest district of Great Glade. Their phraxchambers were as large as those of any phraxlighter, and the barrel of the cannon jutted out some twenty strides in front.

To Nate's right, the other two companies of the Second Low Town Regiment had fallen into step with them, followed by the three companies of the First Low Town Regiment marching close behind. And far off to their right, but rapidly converging, were the High Town Regiments – servants, scriveners, cooks and cleaners who, like their comrades from Low Town, had been forced into military service in the great call up.

Nate looked away from the growing swell of infantry and artillery, and concentrated on not losing a boot to the sucking mud. He staggered on, eyes fixed on the ground as, to the growing noise of whinnying prowlgrins and squelching feet, the mighty Hive army streamed out of the forest all around him.

'Nate!' Eudoxia gasped, suddenly grabbing at his arm. 'Nate, I think we're here!'

· CHAPTER FIFTY- EIGHT ·

'Form column!' the company sergeant bellowed, a thin strand of drool trickling from the corner of his mouth and his lips flecked with foam.

He was clearly as exhausted as the rest of the company by the march between the marsh lakes, tramping in single file through the claggy cloying mud. But now, out on the flat featureless marshland beyond, with the settlement of Midwood in the distance and the rest of the regiments of the Hive Militia forming up for battle all around, the flathead sergeant's blood was up.

'Form column, I said, you Low Town dawdlers, not stop to admire the view!' he barked, his small eyes bulging beneath his low brow.

Any moment now, Nate thought miserably, the sergeant would start lashing out with the vicious woodwillow switch cane he carried clamped under one arm. Next to him, in the front rank, the same thought had obviously occurred to Eudoxia, for she now straightened up from her crouching position, where she'd been gulping down lungfuls of air, and shouldered her phraxmusket. Nate did the same, cursing the oversized copperwood helmet that slipped down over his eyes as he did so.

The company sergeant strode through the ranks, the switch twitching under his arm.

'Drop your packs!' he ordered in a low growl. 'Ammunition and waterflasks only, and check those phraxchambers. I want no misfires!'

Nate undid the straps to the sumpwood backpack and allowed it to float to the ground behind him. He patted the leather pouch of leadwood bullets that hung from his waistcoat and shook the flask strapped to his belt. Half full, but it would have to do. Glancing down, he checked that the lamp in the phraxchamber of his musket was glowing, and that the steam duct wasn't blocked by mud. The rain had eased off, but the ground was still saturated. From all around him, there came the squelching sound of falling packs and the clinking of phraxmuskets as the rest of the company did the same.

'Company, prepare to advance!'

Nate peered out of the corner of his eye along the line. The Hive Militia had formed up for battle and now stretched out across the sodden turf and gladegrass tuffets of the Midwood marshes in columns, three companies wide. Nate and Eudoxia's company was on the extreme left, alongside the other two companies of the Second Low Town Regiment, their light grey topcoats and dark grey breeches as mud-spattered and dishevelled as their comrades'.

Looking past them, Nate could see the Hemtuft Battleaxe Legion – the Bloody Blades – standing proudly at the centre of the line, their polished silver helmets and crisp black topcoats now revealed from underneath discarded muddy cloaks and helmet covers. Beyond them, just visible, were the Hammerhead and Flathead Guard in sky-blue and, at the end of the line, on the extreme right, the First and Second High Town Regiments, their topcoats a smudge of light grey in the distance.

Nate had to admit that it was a magnificent sight. Behind them, to the right, came the sounds of whinnying and barking prowlgrins as the phraxcannon arrived and started to unlimber. Around the great gleaming brass guns, the black-uniformed figures of the Bloody Blades artillery swarmed, preparing the cannon for action. Ahead of them, across the marshes, the Midwood Decks nestled behind the stockade wall, seemingly oblivious to the mighty army facing it.

'The phraxcannon will turn that wall of theirs to splinters,' whispered Twill the treegoblin from behind Nate. 'Then the Bloody Blades and the Guards will go in and teach them a lesson . . . They'll only need us and the High Town lads to clear up, I reckon.'

Eudoxia stared ahead at the familiar settlement, the great circular decks swaying in the humid air. 'Who'd have thought we'd be back here like this?' she murmured beside Nate, her green eyes dulled by a mixture of sadness and exhaustion, 'fighting on the wrong side . . .'

'No talking in the ranks!' the company sergeant bellowed from the front of the column.

Just then, Eudoxia gave a little gasp. 'Nate, look!' she whispered urgently.

Nate pushed back the helmet on his head and followed Eudoxia's gaze. There, flying high over the sumpwood stands, appeared first one, then two, then dozens of phraxships. They were in full steam and making for the Midwood Decks.

'It's the phraxfleet from Great Glade,' she said, her voice low and excited as the phraxships started coming in to dock.

As they did so, Nate could see that they were packed full of uniformed figures, who poured off the ships and across the decks the instant they landed. A low murmuring spread through the company.

'I said, "no talking!"' barked the sergeant, hitting out with his woodwillow cane.

Just then, a prowlgrin came bounding along the line, ridden by the colonel of the Second Low Town Regiment, a long-hair goblin by the name of Henten Boltrage. He leaned down low in the saddle and muttered a few words to the sergeant, before spurring his prowlgrin on and galloping back towards the centre of the line.

'Colonels!' muttered Twill the treegoblin. 'Always at the back when there's fighting to be done . . .'

'Listen up, lads!' shouted the sergeant, plainly disappointed by his orders. 'Stand at ease. We'll not be wanted just yet.'

Along with the rest of the company, Nate sank gratefully to his knees, cradling his phraxmusket under one arm – though, under the steely gaze of the sergeant, he was careful not to break formation. Glancing back along the line, he could see the barrels of the phraxcannon being cranked up until they pointed skywards. Clearly, their target was no longer the stockade wall in front of the Midwood settlement, but the decks above the town.

Beside him, Eudoxia shook her head in disbelief. 'Knocking

down the wall is one thing,' she muttered to Nate, not wanting to be overheard, 'but firing on the town itself . . . Think of all the poor innocent young'uns living there.' Her green eyes blazed. 'It's – it's madness, Nate! They risk destroying the entire settlement . . .'

Nate nodded sadly. 'I don't think the clan chiefs care,' he said, 'so long as it means victory over Great Glade.'

As if in answer, there was an earsplitting roar as first one, then another, of the huge cannon opened fire. It spread down the line as all twenty phraxcannon discharged their phraxshells in a huge cloud of steam. The shells whistled overhead, wispy vapour trails marking the progress of their arcing flight. In the ranks of the Hive Militia, all eyes gazed skyward after them.

Down they came, closer and closer to the mass of phraxships and jostling figures on the distant decks . . .

'I can't bear to look,' said Eudoxia quietly, hunching over and staring down at her mud-caked boots.

In the distance, there was a series of white flashes, followed by the sound of explosions: short, sharp cracks, one after the other, like a sap-rich log crackling in the heart of a brazier. Plumes of black smoke began to rise from the decks, and the timber towers and bobbing cabins beneath. Nate peered at the town in the distance. Phraxships, he could see, were still arriving, some circling the decks while others, obviously hit, were shooting off into the surrounding forest, trailing smoke and steam as they went.

At the centre of the line, the phraxcannon were being reloaded. Nate counted down the seconds, willing the phraxships in the distance to land, unload and take off as quickly as possible. The heavy phraxshells were hefted up into the brass barrels.

Several phraxbarges landed and figures leaped from their sides. The phraxcannon's muzzles were cranked up to maximum elevation. The phraxbarges began to rise up in the air from the burning decks. The gunnery corporals set the sights; the bombardiers pulled on the firing pins. Two of the phraxbarges rose clear.

With a colossal roar, the phraxcannon fired. The decks disappeared in a white flash of explosions. When the smoke cleared, both phraxbarges had disappeared, their wreckage scattered across the sumpwood stands behind the town.

Nate looked away.

The bombardment of the Midwood Decks continued for the next half hour until, amidst the smoke and fires and white flashing explosions, the last phraxship of the Great Glade had run the gauntlet and delivered its cargo of militia – or been destroyed in the attempt.

As the Midwood Decks blazed in the distance, the company sergeant was in high spirits. He marched up the line, the woodwillow switch slashing at the air ahead.

'Now, lads, we move in for the kill! Form column!' he roared.

Nate, Eudoxia and the rest of the second company rose to their feet.

'*Advance!*'

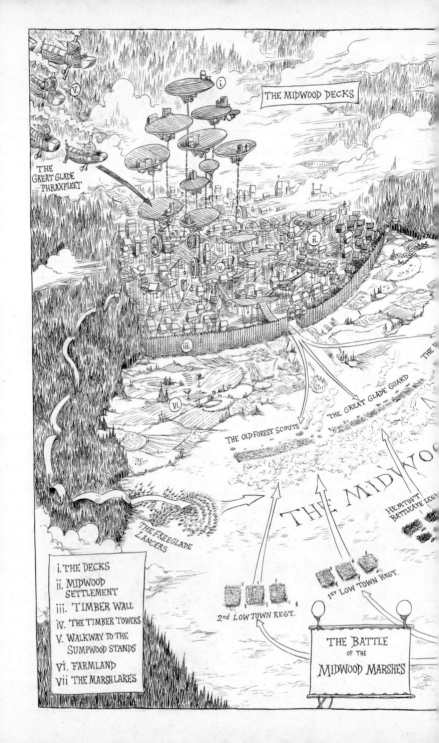

THE MIDWOOD DECKS

THE GREAT GLADE PHRAXFLEET

i.

v.

ii.

iv.

iii.

vi.

THE OLD FOREST SCOUTS

THE GREAT GLADE GUARD

THE

THE FREEGLADE LANCERS

THE MIDWOO

HEMTUFT BATTLEAXE LEG

i. THE DECKS
ii. MIDWOOD SETTLEMENT
iii. TIMBER WALL
iv. THE TIMBER TOWERS
v. WALKWAY TO THE SUMPWOOD STANDS
vi. FARMLAND
vii THE MARSHLAKES

2nd LOW TOWN REGT.

1st LOW TOWN REGT.

THE BATTLE
OF THE
MIDWOOD MARSHES

HIVE MILITIA

1. THE SECOND LOW TOWN REGT.
2. THE FIRST HIGH TOWN REGT.
3. THE HAMMERHEAD GUARD
4. THE FLATHEAD GUARD
5. THE HEMTUFT BATTLEAXE LEGION
6. PHRAX CANNONEER

MARSHES

2 HIGH TOWN REGT.

1 HIGH TOWN REGT.

FLATHEAD GUARD

HAMMERHEAD GUARD

(vii)

1. THE OLD FOREST SCOUTS
2. THE PHRAX-MARINE
3. THE GREAT GLADE GUARD
4. THE FREEGLADE LANCERS

GREAT GLADE MILITIA

· CHAPTER FIFTY-NINE ·

They set off at a slow trot across the spongy moss-covered ground, their feet squelching deep into the waterlogged earth with every step. It was, Nate thought, like walking across a vast snowbird down quilt that had been left out in the rain – soft and damp and hugging tenaciously at his boots. Overhead, large grey clouds closed in, and before long a warm drizzle was falling steadily. To their right, the First Low Town Regiment was keeping pace with them, while in the centre of the line, the disciplined ranks of the Bloody Blades and the Hammerhead and Flathead Guard had forged on ahead.

Nate glanced over at the tree ridge to the left of the company, and Eudoxia nudged him with her elbow and nodded in unspoken agreement. As soon as they got the opportunity, they would slip out from under the watchful eye of the company sergeant and make a dash for the forest. Although there had been no such opportunity in the whole of the long march from Hive, Nate hoped that once the shooting got underway, the sergeant's ever-vigilant gaze would be elsewhere.

One thing was for certain, he told himself, whatever happened, he would never open fire on a fellow Great Glader.

Half an hour later, Nate's boots were caked in claggy marsh mud, and from the ranks around him came the sound of heavy gasping breaths and grunts of exertion as the Second Low Town Regiment tried to stay in formation. Behind them, in the distance, he heard the whinnying of prowlgrins and the bark of commands as the phraxcannon limbered up and moved forward in support.

As they neared the centre of the marshes, the rain grew steadily heavier. Nate looked up to see that the stockade gates of the now smouldering town had been thrown open, and a steady stream of Great Glade Militia were pouring out.

'Keep in formation!' roared the company sergeant as they continued to march forward, phraxmuskets now clasped across their chests.

Ahead, advancing to meet them in three great columns, several thousand strong, came the dark green topcoated Great Glade Militia. In the centre marched the Great Glade Guard, their funnel hats garlanded with sprigs of lullabee leaves; on the right, the phraxmarines, in short topcoats and tall black funnels; and on the left, the Old Forest Scouts, in distinctive caps of grey frompskin. Rapidly, the columns spread out in long lines, six deep, blocking the advance of the Hive Militia.

To his right, Nate saw the ranks of the Bloody Blades shoulder their phraxmuskets, draw their battleaxes and, with a heart-stopping roar of battle rage, break into a disciplined run.

'The Bloody Blades are going in with their axes!' Twill the treegoblin murmured in admiration. 'Just like the olden days . . .'

Some way ahead of them, the front rank of the Great Glade Guard fell to the ground. The second rank went down on one knee behind them, and the third rank stepped crisply forward.

'Fire!' came a distant command, and the three ranks disappeared in clouds of steam as they discharged their phraxmuskets simultaneously.

Like buzzing woodwasps, white-hot leadwood bullets cut through the air, and smashed into the Hemtuft Battleaxe Legion, punching holes in the ranks of the black-coated Bloody Blades. The three ranks of the Great Glade Guard fell flat in the soft marsh mud, to reveal three more behind, and again the phraxmuskets fired in a deadly volley.

With a low groan, the Legion staggered, no longer in ordered company columns of a hundred strong, but now thinned out by their losses into ragged groups of twenty or thirty. To their right, the Hammerhead and Flathead Guard were also attacking, pressing on into the withering fire of the phraxmarines, while the grey ranks of

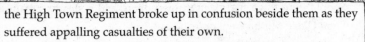

the High Town Regiment broke up in confusion beside them as they suffered appalling casualties of their own.

Pushing back his helmet, Nate saw that the Second Low Town Regiment was advancing towards the ranks of the Old Forest Scouts, who now knelt in a long green line ahead of them and levelled their phraxmuskets. As the grey-topcoated ranks continued to trot forward over the heavy marsh, Nate gripped his phraxmusket tightly, both fists clenched, his stomach knotting and churning with awful anticipation. The terrible screams and cries of the wounded sounded to the right, where the bloody battle was raging.

'Fix spikes!' roared the company sergeant, and Nate, along with the rest of the regiment, unsheathed the long knife from his belt and thrust it into the muzzle of his phraxmusket.

'We're going in the old way,' breathed Twill the treegoblin, fear and excitement mingling in his voice, 'in a phalanx of spear spikes!'

'Charge!' yelled the company sergeant, unable to contain his battle rage a moment longer.

He sprang forward, phraxpistol in one hand, woodwillow cane in the other, and with a throaty roar the regiment surged after him.

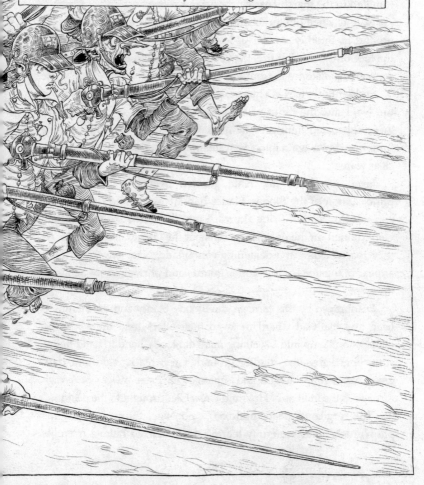

They hadn't gone more than half a dozen steps when the command sounded in the Forest Scouts ahead.

'Fire!'

A great cloud of steam billowed across the ranks of green in front of Nate, like a storm rolling over the Deepwoods, out of which spat leadwood bullets with the now familiar whine of angry woodwasps whose nest was under attack. Just ahead of him, the company sergeant staggered and fell, the back of his grey topcoat blossoming with four crimson stains. Around Nate, trogs, goblins and fourthlings reeled back, flinging phraxmuskets in the air as they tumbled to the marshy earth.

Nate reached out, grabbed Eudoxia and hauled her down to the ground as another swarm of leadwood bullets flew overhead. In the face of the musket fire, the Second Low Town Regiment melted away like hailstones in front of a forge fire.

Suddenly, there was a huge explosion just ahead of them. Looking up, Nate saw the ranks of the Old Forest Scouts split apart, with green-topcoated figures being hurled high in the air, only to come tumbling down again into a vast steaming crater, rapidly filling with clear water.

From where he lay, Nate glanced over his shoulder. The phraxcannon of the Bloody Blades had advanced and unlimbered, and now, instead of firing skyward into the Midwood Decks, they were trained on the dark green ranks of the Great Glade Militia. As they roared again in a deafening cannonade, Nate saw great holes appear in the lines of the scouts, guards and phraxmarines all along the front.

Encouraged by this carnage, the Bloody Blades and the Hammer-head and Flathead Guard renewed their attack, and the Midwood marshes broke up into a seething mass of bloody hand to hand fights, sprawling across the muddy ground. Grey, black, blue and dark green ranks now merged and separated in great mêlées of savage carnage as the militias of Hive and Great Glade fought to the death.

'The sergeant's dead, Eudoxia,' said Nate, throwing away his phraxmusket and gratefully tearing the oversized helmet from his head. 'Let's make for the tree ridges!' He climbed to his feet, the shrieks and cries of the wounded mingling all round with the crash of phraxmuskets and clash of blades. Great clouds of steam drifted across the marshes, billowing up from the craters made by the phraxshells and covering the battlefield in an eerie swirling mist. He glanced around him, dazed and trembling, at the terrible battle raging across the Midwood marshes.

The Second Low Town Regiment was in disarray. There were bodies lying all about him on the ground, writhing in the mud like stranded oozefish, their low groans and echoing cries seemingly disembodied – or more terrible still, motionless and silent. Nate stared down mutely at the appalling injuries inflicted upon his fallen comrades.

Before him was a tufted goblin, face down in the mud, the shell that had struck him leaving a gaping hole through his chest so large that a pool of water had collected where he lay. Next to him, a cloddertrog was recognizable only from his size and stature, for his head was no more than a mangled pulp of bloody flesh and splintered bone. And beside him, already half buried in the thick mud, lay an arm ripped from a long-hair guard. The battleaxe it had been brandishing was still gripped tightly in its bloodless fingers, while its owner staggered off blindly into the coiling mist, tripping over his fallen comrades and bellowing with pain.

Nate looked away, aghast, and clamped his hands over his ears. But there was nothing he could do to shut out the gory sights and sounds of battle. The dead and the dying were everywhere. Broken goblins and shattered trolls; a mobgnome, both his legs shot away at the knees, and innumerable other mutilated corpses bearing witness to the appalling damage phraxweapons could inflict on flesh and blood.

He and Eudoxia had to get away from the horror. He knelt down next to his friend, who was still curled up in the mud, her hands clasped over her helmeted head, and shook her by the shoulder.

'Come on,' he said. 'We've got to make a run for it . . .'

Just then, to his left, amongst the countless unknown soldiers

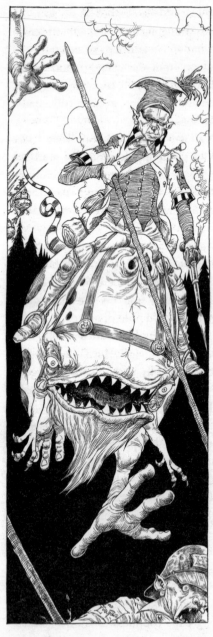

strewn across the mud, Nate saw someone he did recognize.

It was Twill, the treegoblin. He was kneeling on the ground, cradling the head of a fallen grey trog in his bony lap. The treegoblin stared down at the trog, tears in his eyes, stroking the side of his face and whispering words of comfort as he did so.

'It's all right, Gorlan,' he was saying. 'You're going to be all right ... But you've got to hold on. Just a little bit longer. Hold on ... for Merla,' he said, reaching up and brushing tears away from his mud-smeared face. 'For me ...'

Yet even as he watched, Nate knew it was too late. His friend and comrade, Gorlan the grey trog, was fading fast, and as his life slipped away, so too did his hopes and dreams for the future – for the coming harvest, for the recovery of his sapwine cellar, for the family he'd always longed to have with his beloved Merla ...

All around him, Nate

heard the groaning and moaning and blood-choked coughs that swirled through the air, the hideous noises rising to a terrible crescendo – before fading once more as, one by one, the stricken soldiers breathed their last. Before him, Gorlan closed his eyes and, with a low breath rattling at the back of his throat, the trog slipped away.

'Open Sky take your spirit,' Twill whispered. He hung his head, then turned to Nate, his eyes blazing and nostrils flared. 'They'll pay for this,' he said bitterly. 'Kulltuft Warhammer, Firemane Clawhand and the rest. They'll pay.'

Suddenly, a strident trumpet call sounded far ahead. On his knees beside Eudoxia, Nate turned to see wave after wave of prowlgrins emerging from the tree line, rising up into the air and coming down, landing amid the depleted ranks of the Second Low Town Regiment. Their riders wore white topcoats with green and white chequerboard collars and carried thornwood lances under their arms.

'The Freeglade Lancers!' breathed Nate, his hand shooting involuntarily to the medallion that hung at his neck.

He shook Eudoxia excitedly by the shoulder once more, only for her to roll over in the mud with a strangulated sigh. The side of her copperwood helmet had been shattered by a bullet and her golden hair was covered in blood.

Around him, the Second and First Low Town Regiments were in full flight, bundling into the Bloody Blades and goblin Guard as the Freeglade Lancers slammed into their flank, and began rolling up the line. A prowlgrin shot past him and, as it did so, the heavy butt of a thornwood lance dealt Nate a savage blow to the side of his unhelmeted head, and he slumped forward into oblivion.

· CHAPTER SIXTY ·

'Nate . . . Nate . . . Nate Quarter . . .'

Nate opened his eyes. Above him, two great white sails billowed up into a blue sky dotted with huge clouds. Wind was ruffling his hair, the air rushing past his ears, while beneath him the ground swayed and shivered like a sumpwood bunk.

'Where . . . Where am I?' he croaked, his throat dry and sore.

Squinting into the bright daylight, he saw a familiar-looking figure standing above him. He held a rudder lever in one hand, a coil of rope in the other, and was gazing over Nate's head into the distance.

'Do I know you?' Nate asked, propping himself up on one elbow. He was suddenly aware of a painful throbbing at his temples and, raising a hand to his forehead, found it heavily bandaged.

'Only slightly,' said the figure. He was wearing a peaked funnel hat with earflaps and a worn topcoat of tilderleather; his breeches were a patchwork of carefully stitched repairs. 'I'm Zelphyius Dax, librarian scholar. We met in the sumpwood stands,' he said, without looking at Nate. He adjusted the rudder lever and played out some rope with his other hand. 'And you're aboard my skycraft, the *Varis Lodd*.'

'But . . . but how?' Nate said, suddenly feeling very weak and equally dizzy.

Looking down, the forest was an unending sea of green far below, while on either side of him, on outstretched cradles of sumpwood, two masts stretched up into the sky, each with a billowing white sail. Nate was lying at the feet of the librarian scholar on a narrow deck no wider than a New Lake coracle. In front of them, a long thin prow stretched up into the sky. At its tip was a carved figurehead of a striking fourthling female, dressed in the flight suit of a librarian knight from the Second Age. Behind, on an equally thin sumpwood board, was a tiny covered cabin, a lamp attached to its roof and a three-pronged fork rudder secured to the back.

'I found you on the battlefield and recognized you,' Zelphyius Dax said simply, 'though I hardly expected you to be wearing Hive grey . . .'

'It's a long story,' mumbled Nate. 'And where's Eudoxia?'

'Your friend?' said the librarian, his eyes fixed steadily on the horizon. 'She, like you, had been left for dead. Though for her, alas, that was nearer to the truth . . .'

'What do you mean?' said Nate slowly as the horror of those final moments in the Midwood marshes replayed themselves in his mind. 'Where is she?'

'Eudoxia is back there.' Zelphyius Dax nodded over his shoulder.

'At the Midwood Decks?' Nate asked, sitting up and gripping one of the sumpwood struts that supported the decking.

'No, in the stern cabin,' Zelphyius replied, smiling grimly. 'But she's badly wounded. A leadwood bullet has lodged itself behind her right ear.'

Nate pictured the scene in the marshes, Eudoxia's fair hair covered in blood. Had they really come so far, endured so much, only for it to end like this? he thought bitterly.

'Is there anything you can do for her?' he asked the librarian.

'Her wound is far beyond my limited skills as a physician, I'm afraid,' Zelphyius Dax admitted ruefully. 'But I'm taking you to the one place where you might find help.'

'Where's that?' asked Nate, his mouth dry and his head throbbing.

'Riverrise,' said Zelphyius Dax. 'The City of Night.'

· PART THREE ·

RIVERRISE

SOUTH CLIFF

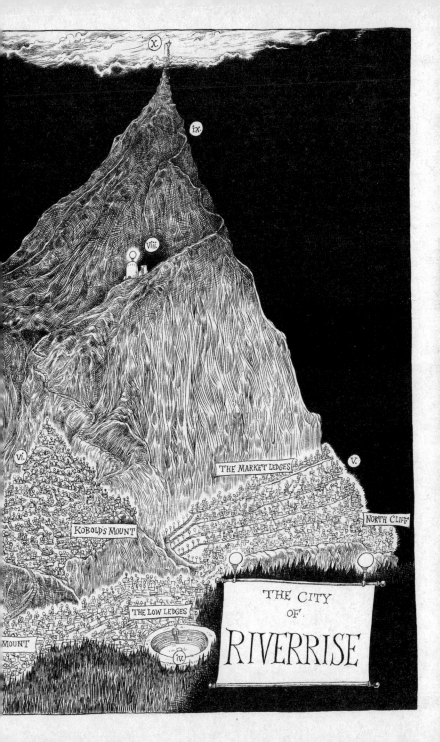

X.

i.

ii.

iii.

MAST DECK

TILLER DECK

iv.

i. FIGUREHEAD
ii. STORES
iii. TILLER
iv. HULL WEIGHTS
v. LOW MAST
vi. STERN CABIN
vii. RUDDER
viii. STORES
ix. HIGH MAST
x. SPIDERSILK SAIL

RUDDER DECK

MAST DECK

THE
VARIS LODD

'Secure the nether sail, Nate,' said Zelphyius Dax, his voice calm and measured as ever.

Nate, who had been perched on the narrow sumpwood deck of the *Varis Lodd* staring out over the forest, looked up to see that one of the two sails on the starboard mast had folded back on itself and was fluttering uselessly in the wind. He scrambled to his feet and edged across the cradle of sumpwood struts until he reached the foot of the mast. Reaching out, he grasped the swaying sail rope. Then he unhitched the slide knot – just as Zelphyius had shown him how to – and pulled hard. The rope went taut, and the sail above instantly filled with wind, billowing out in front alongside the loft sail.

'Well done,' said Zelphyius, pulling on the rudder, his unblinking gaze fixed ahead as the skycraft gathered speed once more.

Like a great bird, the *Varis Lodd* flexed and bowed as the wind carried it across the sky, its slender masts and sumpwood timbers bending into each gust. And, as they did so, the whole vessel bucked and shuddered, movements that Zelphyius seemed to anticipate, never losing his balance – unlike Nate.

'The timbers give with the wind,' he'd explained as Nate stumbled and gripped the slender sumpwood struts of the mast cradle beside him for dear life. 'You'll soon get your skylegs. We've got a long voyage ahead.'

The librarian was right. After eight hours of flight, Nate had begun to get used to the constant movement of the skycraft beneath him. It felt, he thought, almost as though he was riding Tallix as he galloped over the forest canopy, and that, instead of a construction of sumpwood timber and sailcloth, the *Varis Lodd* was in fact a living creature moving beneath his feet.

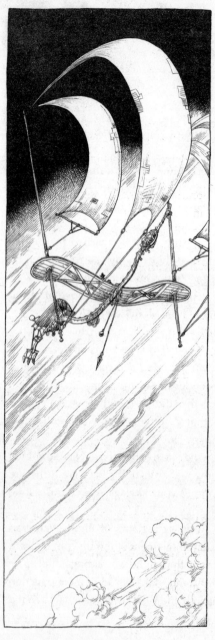

It was all a far cry from the mighty phraxvessels like the *Deadbolt Vulpoon*. The skytavern, with its humming phraxchamber, its roaring propulsion duct and great funnels billowing steam, powered its way through the skies with a brute force that seemed to defy the buffeting winds and swirling air currents. *Old Glory*, the great timber-laden phraxbarge Nate had taken from the Midwood Decks to Hive, was the same. Slow and lumbering, it had ploughed through the turbulent air, reliant on the awesome power and buoyancy of its phraxchamber to stay aloft.

The *Varis Lodd* was different. Guided by Zelphyius Dax's steady hand, it used the winds and air currents rather than fighting against them. Once Nate had become accustomed to the feel and rhythm of its flight, the effect was exhilarating.

Nate glanced up at the librarian scholar. He was standing upright, perfectly balanced, with his head back and legs apart, surveying the mighty expanse of sky before him from beneath the jutting peak of his funnel hat. His earflaps fluttered as, with one hand on the sumpwood tiller and the other on the sail ropes, he steered a course through the air, heading due west.

Nate watched in awe as the librarian scholar's long thin fingers played out more rope to the sails and realigned the tiller, making constant tiny re-adjustments as the air eddied and swirled about them. It was, Nate thought, as if Zelphyius Dax himself was a part of the vessel.

Slowly and expertly, the librarian scholar brought the skycraft round until the low orange sun was directly ahead of them. Nate raised his hand to shield his eyes. Beside him, Zelphyius tugged at the peak of his hat, casting his eyes into shadow, before returning his hand to the bone-handled tiller. Nate turned away, and looked down at the blur of green forest speeding along below him.

This was the second time, he realized, that he'd crashed into unconsciousness, only to wake and find his world turned upside down. The first had been his fall from the High Pine during the mock battle of thousandsticks, when he'd woken to find that his life in Great Glade was at an end. The second time, the battle had been all too real, though now the carnage on the Midwood marshes seemed more like a waking nightmare.

And here he was again, he thought, waking up to find himself heading across the Edgeland skies towards another great city. This time, though, it wasn't his life that was in danger; it was Eudoxia's.

She now lay in the tiny stern cabin of the *Varis Lodd*, racked with fever, her face crimson and her breathing shallow and rasping. With the leadwood bullet lodged in her skull behind her ear, she was hanging onto life by a thread.

'Do you see those clouds, there?' said Zelphyius, stirring Nate from his thoughts.

He pointed towards a small cloudbank up ahead, its flat top tinged with a twilight glow. Nate nodded.

'That's what the librarian knights of the Second Age called

Kobold's Anvil,' Zelphyius said, 'and it's what every skycraft pilot looks out for. The flat top is formed by powerful air currents above,' he explained, 'which we can use to ride clear across the central Deepwoods and down towards the west.' Stooping slightly forward, a look of intense concentration on his face, he cranked up the hull weights until they nestled beneath the sumpwood deck. Then, with a slight realignment of the rudder, the *Varis Lodd* soared up towards the flat-topped cloud. The sails flapped for a moment, before billowing hard; the masts creaked as they bowed forward.

Nate gripped on tightly to the struts of the mast cradle.

'Mind you,' said Zelphyius thoughtfully, 'the weather's been unpredictable of late, even for an old hand like me. Odd cloud formations, unpredictable currents . . . It's almost as though something strange was brewing out in Open Sky.' He pulled the rudder further to starboard. 'But if I'm right about Kobold's Anvil, then it's all a matter of . . .' He realigned the hull weights, bringing the *Varis Lodd* round. 'Of entering the current of air at . . . the right angle . . .'

As he spoke, Nate could feel the skycraft buck and sway beneath him. Zelphyius played out more rope to the sails, and pulled hard on the tiller. The skycraft stopped rising and, for a moment, hovered in one place. He turned to Nate and winked.

'Any second now . . .' he said, glancing down at the curiously shaped cloudbank almost directly below them.

The next moment, and with a colossal lurch, the *Varis Lodd* was seized by a powerful current of air and propelled through the sky with such speed that Nate was left gasping for breath. He gripped the mast cradle with white-knuckled ferocity as the skycraft sped through the evening sky in a huge sweeping arc. Below them, the forest became a green smudge; above, the sails strained at the slender masts.

'Now, this is what I call skysailing,' said Zelphyius, his face flushed and eyes twinkling with excitement as he glanced round and smiled.

Nate – who was surprised to discover that he'd been holding his breath – breathed in deeply and smiled back. 'It feels very fast,' he said.

'Oh, it is, Nate, it is,' said Zelphyius. 'Up here in the high skies, we'll cover a thousand strides in the blink of an eye. I tell you, when you ride the air currents in a sleek skycraft like the *Varis Lodd*, it's possible to cover vast distances in days rather than weeks. There isn't a phraxcraft built that can match her! We'll be at the Thorn Gate in no time . . .'

'The Thorn Gate?' said Nate, puzzled. 'But I thought we were going to Riverrise.'

'That's right, Nate,' said Zelphyius, tugging on the tiller and securing all four of the sail ropes. 'But we can't fly all the way there.'

'We can't?' said Nate.

'Certainly not,' said Zelphyius with a shake of his head. 'In the old days, during the First Age of Flight, the sky galleons learned that the hard way. The sky changes over the Nightwoods. It becomes wild and unstable, prone to funnel storms, maelstroms and worse. Many spent their lives trying to reach the fabled Riverrise peak, only to be beaten back. No,' he said, his eyes fixed on the distant horizon, 'the only way to Riverrise is on foot, through the Thorn Gate.'

Nate nodded as the *Varis Lodd* continued its westerly flight, swaying gently, now in the grip of the powerful air current.

'I think I'll go and check on Eudoxia,' he said.

'Good idea, Nate,' said Zelphyius.

Nate climbed to his feet and made his way carefully along the curved sumpwood spine of the skycraft to the tiny cabin at the stern. He crouched down and crawled in on hands and knees.

Placing a hand on his friend's brow, Nate felt his stomach give a sickening lurch. Eudoxia was freezing cold. The burning fever was gone, and now she was shivering violently, her skin blue and cold to the touch and her teeth chattering. He pulled her light grey topcoat up over her and removed his own topcoat and laid that over it. Then, leaning forward, he gently swept the strands of lank golden hair from Eudoxia's face and checked the bandage that swaddled her head.

'You've been so brave,' he told her. 'I couldn't have survived the march to Midwood without you by my side . . .'

Eudoxia's husky breathing continued, low and faltering.

'You're strong,' Nate continued, and swallowed hard. 'And you've come this far. Don't give up, Eudoxia. Hold on until we get to Riverrise . . .'

Shivering, he reached out and unhooked a waterflask from the cabin strut above Eudoxia's head and held it to her lips – but he couldn't get her to take more than a sip. Replacing the flask, he noticed a green tilderleather jacket stowed neatly below it. Nate picked it up and put it on, before crawling back out of the cabin and returning to the sumpwood deck where the librarian stood.

'She's a fighter, that one,' said Zelphyius Dax, his hand playing rope to the billowing sails. 'I could tell that the moment I first clapped eyes on her. But that nasty wound she's got . . .' He turned and looked at Nate, then smiled. 'I see you found a new jacket,' he said.

'Oh, yes,' said Nate looking down at it, a little embarrassed. It was long in the body and tight in the arms, with several pleated pockets and a line of copperwood buttons that did up to the neck. 'I'm sorry,' he said, 'I should have asked . . .'

'Don't apologize, lad,' said Zelphyius Dax. 'It's yours,' he added generously. 'And I've got to say, I much prefer to see you dressed in my old jacket than in that terrible grey topcoat.'

Nate smiled. 'To tell you the truth, I'm glad to be able to take it off at last,' he admitted, looking back across the darkening forest the way they'd come. 'And there were many Eudoxia and I marched with in the Hive Militia who I'm sure would feel the same.'

'I don't doubt it,' Zelphyius Dax said grimly. 'Perhaps, after the defeat at the Midwood marshes, they'll take off their topcoats too.'

He returned his attention to the skycraft, trimming the sails and readjusting the hull weights as he peered out from under the peak of his funnel cap. Far in the distance, the sun was down on the horizon now, a giant crimson ball that seemed almost to wobble the lower it sank. The air current filled the sails and, as he looked up, Nate saw that the few clouds there had been had turned to wisps and dissolved, leaving the sky empty of everything but the first stars of night, which were beginning to shine in the gathering dusk.

'Look at that sky,' said Zelphyius Dax, his voice hushed with awe. 'It's going to be a magnificent night . . .'

· CHAPTER SIXTY-TWO ·

It was a dark moonless night, and the stars patterning the great vault of the sky seemed brighter than Nate could ever remember. Next to him on the narrow deck, Zelphyius Dax stood, as usual, with one hand on the tiller and the other playing out rope to the billowing sails. With his legs planted apart and flexing from the knees, the librarian scholar seemed to anticipate every buck and sway of the skycraft beneath his feet.

'Might as well get some sleep, Nate,' Zelphyius said, without taking his eyes off the stars overhead. 'We'll be riding this current till sunrise.'

'I don't feel like sleeping,' said Nate, which was true. Although he was tired from the long day's sailing, he was too worried about Eudoxia to sleep. 'I'd rather talk . . .'

'Ah, talk,' said Zelphyius with a low chuckle. 'That's a rare treat for an old librarian scholar like me. Many's the night I've spent up here in the high skies with only the wind and the stars for company. Mind you, that's generally the way I like it. I can't be doing with the ways of the earthbound folk in their settlements and great cities . . .' He shook his head. 'For all their phraxships, factories and fine buildings, they never seem to be content – always finding some reason or other to fall out and go to war. Take this business over the Midwood Decks, for instance . . .'

Nate shuddered. The horrors of the battle in the marshes were still fresh in his mind; the thunder of the phraxcannon, the crack of the phraxmuskets and the screams of the wounded and dying.

'If the *Varis Lodd* hadn't needed a new bowsprit, I would have left the Midwood forests weeks ago. As it was, I was kicking my heels in the sumpwood stands when your lot came marching out of the woods . . .'

'They weren't *my* lot,' said Nate indignantly. 'I told you, Eudoxia and I were caught in Hive and forced into their militia.'

'Which just goes to prove my point, Nate,' said Zelphyius, playing out some rope to the sails as the skycraft trembled beneath them. 'That's what happens in these great cities. You get caught up in events beyond your control. That's why I decided to leave the library in Great Glade. I wanted to get away from the intrigues and rivalries of the academics and under-librarians and chart my own course through the Deepwoods before it was too late.'

'What do you mean,' said Nate, 'before it was too late?'

'The Edgelands are changing, Nate,' said Zelphyius bleakly. 'It began with the dawn of the Third Age of Flight, five hundred years ago, when the master of the Lake Landing Academy, Xanth Filatine, built the first phraxchamber. Ever since then, the Deepwoods has been in retreat as the first settlements grew into the three great cities, and phraxships took over the skies. Now there are a dozen more settlements that'll soon be as big as Hive or Great Glade – from the Midwood Decks in the east to Four Lakes in the west; New Hive, Gorge Town, the Farrow Ridges and all the others. Each one consumes the forest around it and competes with the others as it grows, causing skirmishes and unrest that erupt into wars. And at the heart of it all, driving this expansion on, is the curse of phraxflight.'

Zelphyius fell silent for a while, standing motionless, a dark shape against a glittering backdrop of stars.

'I was a phraxminer in the Eastern Woods,' said Nate quietly. 'And I worked in a phraxchamber works in Great Glade. I've always thought of phraxcrystals as something precious, something good . . .'

'Are the phraxcannon used by the Hive Militia good?' said Zelphyius. 'Or the phraxsaws used by pro-Hivers to decimate the sumpwood stands? What about the phraxmusket that embedded a leadwood bullet in your friend Eudoxia's head? All of them were made possible by those precious phraxcrystals of yours.'

'But there are good people out there!' Nate protested. 'Phraxminers who I was proud to call my friends, factory hands I played thousandsticks with, and honest souls forced – like me – to march in the Hive Militia with phraxmuskets on their shoulders. *They* didn't cause this war. Their leaders did!'

'Maybe you're right, Nate,' Zelphyius said.

In the darkness, Nate couldn't make out the expression on his face, but he sounded tired and disappointed.

'I'm a lonely old librarian,' he said. 'I chose to retreat from the world into a dream from the Second Age of Flight, where rope, sail and varnished wood were the only tools with which to take to the skies. You're different, Nate. You belong in this Third Age we live in, and perhaps you and these friends of yours will make a difference.' He paused to make an adjustment to the tiller, and when he spoke again, the librarian scholar seemed more cheerful. 'Certainly,' he conceded, 'from what I saw on the battlefield of the Midwood marshes, that long-hair legion . . .'

'The Bloody Blades, they're called in Hive,' said Nate.

'The Bloody Blades,' Zelphyius continued, with a nod of the head, 'will not be terrorizing Hive any more. They were pretty much destroyed by the Freeglade Lancers along with their phraxcannon. I stepped over countless black-topcoated dead before I stumbled across you and your friend. As for the rest of the Hive Militia, they'd disappeared back into the woods as a disorganized rabble, and will be halfway back to Hive by now, I'd wager. The Midwooders were doing their best to care for the wounded of both sides,' he added, 'but one look at your friend convinced me that her only hope lay in Riverrise.'

'I'm very grateful to you, Zelphyius,' said Nate, patting the smooth sumpwood decking. 'And to the *Varis Lodd*, for helping Eudoxia and me like this. I don't know what we'd have done without you and your skycraft from the Second Age of Flight.'

The librarian scholar stood as motionless and impassive as ever at the tiller of the *Varis Lodd* as they sailed on through the dark star-filled sky. When he spoke, his voice was hoarse and constricted with emotion.

'I only hope, for young Eudoxia's sake,' he said, 'that this voyage of ours will not have been in vain.'

· CHAPTER SIXTY-THREE ·

'Check the logbait, Nate,' Zelphyius Dax said, his silhouetted figure black against the rosy dawn sky, 'and let's see what we've caught for breakfast.'

On the narrow sumpwood deck, Nate rose to his feet, flexing from the knees to accommodate the swaying motion of the skycraft. The brazier he'd just lit, a small burnished copper globe with sturdy tripod legs, had caught and was crackling as the flames sped through the scentwood kindling and began to bite at the larger lufwood logs, filling the air with a soft woody aroma.

'Aah, the smell of scentwood,' said Zelphyius as the twists of aromatic smoke blew back past him. 'There's nothing like it after a long night in the high skies.'

The librarian yawned and stretched before resuming his stance, legs braced, one hand on the tiller and the other grasping a length of sail rope. Nate didn't know how he did it. At first, he'd assumed that Zelphyius never slept. But after watching him over several nights, Nate realized that, in the moments between the swells and eddies of the air currents, when the sails were full and the tiller set, the librarian did in fact close his eyes. These moments – naps of no longer than three or four minutes at a time – seemed to be enough for Zelphyius, who'd remained at his post on the sumpwood deck for the entire voyage. He clearly appreciated having Nate on board, however, to secure ropes, fetch water from the mist catchers at the base of the masts and to perform routine errands like raising the logbait.

Nate paused on the mast cradle, where a thick rope was tethered to one of the sumpwood struts. He crouched down and, with one hand holding onto the mast, reached over the side with the other. His fingers closed round the rough damp fibres of the rope and gripped tightly. He gave a sharp tug.

'Feels promising,' he grunted as the heavy load swung below him.

Hand over hand, he pulled the rope up through the air, before hefting the whole lot onto the narrow deck behind him. Tied to the end of the rope was a length of lufwood log, gnarled and wormy, which landed on the sumpwood boards with a *thud* and a soft *crunch*. And clinging hold of the log, their claws and suckers sunk into the timber, was a writhing mass of airborne creatures that had been lured to the bait during the night.

There were windsnappers with curved claws, whiplash feelers and broad white shells; whiskered skyworms, their slimy bodies glistening as they writhed; and mist barnacles, huddled together in transparent clusters, their soft shells fringed with long hair-like tentacles. Nate pulled his knife from his belt and began prising

the creatures from the log, dispatching the edible specimens with a swift blow or knife cut, and allowing the others to scuttle across the deck and disappear back into the dawn sky. The sumpwood deck on which he worked was scored with knife marks that attested to its use as a chopping board for many such feasts in the past.

He glanced round at the stern cabin, where Eudoxia seemed to be sleeping a little more peacefully. Nate had spent most of the night helping her fight another of the fevers that had tormented her for most of the three days and three long nights of their voyage. He felt so helpless as he mopped her brow and got her to sip water from the flask, aware that neither he nor Zelphyius possessed the skill to remove the leadwood bullet that was slowly killing her.

'Hold on, Eudoxia,' he'd whispered to her as she tossed and turned. 'Just hold on . . .'

Turning to the brazier, Nate lifted its lid to reveal a griddle nestling over the now glowing embers of lufwood. Scooping up handfuls of skyworms and mist barnacles, he piled them onto the griddle and replaced the lid on the brazier.

Fire and varnished sumpwood, Zelphyius had impressed upon Nate, didn't mix, and every care had to be taken with a lit brazier.

Beneath the copperwood lid, the skyfare sizzled enticingly, giving off a mouth-watering aroma and causing Nate's stomach to rumble with hunger. Nate checked it every so often, lifting the lid and turning the sizzling morsels with his knife until they were browned on both sides.

When he was satisfied that they were done, he pulled a couple of thorn needles and a length of greased twine from the pocket of his topcoat and opened the brazier once more. Quickly, he skewered the juicy chunks of skyfare with the thorn needles and threaded them onto the greased twine, which was knotted at the other end, before extinguishing the lufwood embers by closing the ventilation holes in the brazier's lid. Then he turned and handed Zelphyius one of the steaming strings of skyfare.

'Breakfast,' he said.

The librarian scholar took it with thanks, raising the string to his lips and pulling off chunks with his teeth – his other hand never leaving the tiller.

As Nate turned and made his way back towards the stern cabin, he couldn't help but marvel at how self-sufficient the *Varis Lodd* was. Drinking water was collected in the mist catchers, two small containers attached to the bottom of each mast. These caught the condensed vapour of the clouds which formed on the masts and trickled down. Small light lufwood logs were kept in a net that hung down beneath the mast cradles and served as fuel. The wood was light, but not the lightest available.

'I refuse to burn sumpwood root logs, no matter how light they are,' Zelphyius Dax had told Nate. 'It's a crime, those pro-Hivers destroying the sumpwoods, and I for one won't be a party to it.'

As for food, apart from the skyfare hauled up each morning from the logbaits, the hooks along the curved prow of the *Varis Lodd* were festooned with oilskin sacks containing dried or cured provisions. There were chunks of woodapple, gladeonions and steam celery, strips of hammelhorn and tilder, while rings of smoked lake eel could be found dangling from hooks set into the sumpwood prow below the carved figurehead.

At the stern, Nate ducked down and crawled into the tiny cabin. Eudoxia was lying on her side, the two topcoats that had been covering her now lying in a heap at her feet. There was a watery stain on the bandage at her neck. He leaned forward and rested the backs of his fingers against her forehead. It was hot to the touch, though nowhere near as hot as it had been in the night, and her breathing – which had been rasping and faltering – was low and regular.

'I've brought you some food,' he said softly, reaching down and shaking her shoulder gently. 'Eudoxia,' he said. 'A little something to eat.' She didn't stir. 'Come on, now,' he told her. 'Just a mouthful or two, to keep your strength up.'

Eudoxia's eyelids flickered, then snapped open. For a moment, she looked round her wildly, before her gaze focused on Nate's face and a smile plucked at the corners of her mouth.

'Nate,' she said. 'Is it time to march . . . ?'

'I've brought you some food,' he repeated. He hooked the string of skyfare to the cabin strut beside the waterflask and, leaning forward, helped her to sit up a little, wincing at how thin and light her body had become. He wedged one of the folded topcoats behind her shoulder, then pulled off a piece of grilled mist barnacle.

'Here,' he said, putting the morsel to her lips.

She took it and chewed slowly, her eyes dull and glassy-looking. She swallowed finally, with difficulty, and when Nate offered her another piece, she turned her head away.

'We've got to fall in, Nate. The sergeant's waiting . . . So tired, Nate . . . So . . . tired . . .'

Eudoxia closed her eyes and drifted off again into a troubled sleep.

Gently, Nate laid her back down on her side. Leaving one of the topcoats as a pillow, he pulled the other one up to her shoulders. He looked at the bandage again. Moving her must have disturbed the wound. The watery stain had spread, and was edged now with a line of dark red.

'Let me just see to this,' he said softly, reaching behind him for the small tethered sumpwood chest floating in the corner, with its bandages, lint and salves.

He unknotted the bandage and, slipping his hand under her partly raised head, unwound it. The wound beneath her ear looked angry – the flesh about it bright red and raised – with a yellow centre, thick with pus. He wiped it clean as best he could with a moist cloth. Then he reached into the chest for a small pot, unscrewed the lid and scooped out a large green dollop of fragrant hyleberry and feverfew salve, which he smeared gingerly over her burning skin. Eudoxia flinched in her sleep and groaned softly.

'Nearly done,' said Nate. He took a square of fibrous lint and placed it on the wound, then wrapped a clean length round her neck and head, before tying it off at the end.

He sat back on his heels and looked at her. Her eyes were dark-ringed and sunken, and she was painfully thin. Beneath the fresh bandage and soothing salve, the deadly leadwood bullet still lay embedded behind her ear. They couldn't get to Riverrise too soon, Nate thought, his stomach knotted with an unspoken dread.

'Nate,' Zelphyius called from the helm. 'Nate, this is something you should see!'

As he crawled out of the stern cabin, the dazzling low sun struck him in the face, all but blinding him. With one hand raised to shield his eyes, he picked his way back along the narrow deck.

'There,' said Zelphyius, pointing ahead.

Nate gripped the side of the helm and peered into the distance. Like a handful of great silver coins, clustered together and gleaming brightly against the backdrop of dark green forest and emerald grassy glade, were four mighty lakes, fringed with clusters of cabins and towers with landing decks. Here and there, lone chimneys belched thin spirals of smoke, and small coracles and oared boats, like waterbeetles, paddled across the glistening waters.

'That,' said Zelphyius with a smile, 'is the settlement of Four Lakes. One day, it too will be a great city. It is home to the webfoot goblin clans,' he said. 'The crested, the tusked, the red-ringed and the white . . . And these are their magnificent lakes, the largest and most ancient in all the Deepwoods. That one, there,' he said indicating the nearest of the four, 'is called the Silent One. The one next to it is the Shimmerer. And that,' he said, pointing to the most distant lake, whose waters appeared milky white, 'is called the Lake of Cloud.'

'And that one?' said Nate, pointing to the wide expanse of the third lake, its surface reflecting the forest all round it.

'That,' said Zelphyius, 'is the most miraculous of the lakes. It is called the Mirror of the Sky and its waters are home to the Great Blueshell Clam, one of the most ancient living beings in the whole of the Edgelands. Apart from the crested webfoots who tend it, the Great Blueshell Clam has only ever been seen by one person . . .'

'Who?' said Nate, intrigued.

'Keris Verginix,' said Zelphyius, leaning on the tiller and bringing them down lower in the sky. 'Granddaughter of the great Maris, founder of the Free Glades in the First Age, daughter of the legendary sky pirate captain, Twig. Hers was a truly remarkable story . . .'

'Go on,' said Nate, staring out at the glassy waters of the Mirror of the Sky in the distance.

Playing out the sail rope of the portside mainsail, Zelphyius continued.

'Keris Verginix was born and raised in a slaughterer village far off in the northern Deepwoods,' he said. 'Her father, Twig, had left shortly after her birth to rescue his crew, who were stranded at Riverrise. But back then, in the First Age of Flight, his task proved impossible. Years later, Keris heard of the Great Blueshell Clam from webfoot traders and set off to journey to Four Lakes to seek an audience with it, hoping that it could tell her if her father was still alive.'

Zelphyius smiled to himself.

'As a young librarian, I once found a dusty barkscroll in the Great Library with an account of her epic journey.' He glanced round at Nate. 'The perils, the wonders and more . . .'

'So she saw the clam?' Nate asked.

'Yes, the only outlaker ever to do so,' said Zelphyius, 'and it sent her to the Free Glades, where she seeded the South Lake with clams, and met Maris, her grandmother.'

'And did she ever find out what happened to her father?'

'Alas, no,' said the librarian scholar with a shake of his head. 'But her son, Rook Barkwater, did . . .'

'Rook Barkwater,' breathed Nate, reaching up and feeling through the material of the high-buttoned jacket to the oval-shaped portrait that hung round his neck.

'Yes, at the beginning of the Second Age,' said Zelphyius. 'Rook Barkwater met Twig and the pair of them sailed the last of the sky galleons together to old Undertown. Twig was mortally wounded and was last seen being carried away by a great caterbird over the horizon . . .'

'To Riverrise?' said Nate.

'So the legend goes,' said Zelphyius. 'Certainly Rook always thought so, which is why he travelled to Riverrise many years later, only to disappear himself . . .'

'I'd love to read that barkscroll,' said Nate. 'It sounds amazing.'

'One day, Nate, I'll show you round the Great Library,' said Zelphyius. 'But for now, we must make our descent to the Thorn Gate.'

He turned back to the tiller, his face set in a mask of concentration that Nate had seen many times on their voyage. As the lakes came closer, Nate peered down from the sumpwood deck at the approaching settlements of Four Lakes. He could see the various inhabitants going about their business. There were groups of tusked webfoots mending their nets on the northern shores of the Shimmerer; seated white webfoots sharpening their harpoons beside the Lake of Cloud, while on the still waters of the Mirror of the Sky, three small coracles bobbed about the eel corrals – the great circular cork and rope enclosures which held the giant lake eels that the crested webfoots farmed. To their left were the huts they lived in, with their reed-thatched roofs and tall stilted platforms, which jutted out over the water.

Behind the main settlement, and looking out of place in the lakeside setting, were the docking cradles – towering wooden structures with tall cranes, pivoting gantries and aerial jetties, each one with a phraxbarge moored to it. At the tiller, Zelphyius pulled hard on the sail ropes, which unfurled and collapsed as the skycraft suddenly rose steeply in the sky.

Soon, the four great lakes were behind them. Riding the powerful air currents, the *Varis Lodd* sped across the sky, forest ridges and grassy plains passing below them in a blur of brown and green. The sun had by now passed its zenith and was dropping down through the sky before them. From the cabin at the stern, Nate heard the sound of Eudoxia moaning softly, and he was about to return to check on her once more – and see if he could get her to drink a little water – when Zelphyius Dax turned towards him, his face drawn and tense.

'Secure the sails tightly, Nate,' he said urgently, 'and as quickly as you can. Then hold on fast and keep your head down. The skies over the thorn forests are unforgiving.'

Nate hurried to do as the librarian scholar had instructed, before returning to the narrow deck, as the *Varis Lodd* began to buck and sway more violently than ever.

Ahead of them, in the distance, the horizon was black, as if a curtain had fallen across the sky, and all around the skycraft there was the crackle of lightning and deep rumbles of thunder. At the tiller, his feet set wide apart, Zelphyius stared ahead, giving the movement of his skycraft his full attention as it swayed from side to side and rose and fell in dipping swoops. And, as he brought the vessel down lower, the air turned dark and oppressive. Nate looked ahead, to see that the sky above the thorn forest and beyond was curdled and churning. Borne on a maelstrom of high, turbulent winds, writhing columns of black and purple cloud tumbled over each other, dazzling jagged spikes of fork lightning leaping between them as they did so.

Suddenly, Nate understood all too well why Riverrise itself could never be reached by air.

The black curtain grew closer, and dark rain-tinged clouds closed in around them like a clammy shroud. Flexing his legs from the knees, Zelphyius pushed up on the tiller and, with his stomach giving a sickening lurch, Nate felt the *Varis Lodd* drop down out of the sky in a spiralling dive.

Seconds that felt like hours passed as the skycraft fell through the dense grey cloud, the masts bending and sumpwood timbers straining – until, all at once, they were clear, and swooping down towards the most astonishing sight Nate had ever seen.

· CHAPTER SIXTY-FOUR ·

Nate stood, head down, clutching the sumpwood struts of the mast cradle for a moment, waiting for his stomach to settle and his head to stop spinning. The hair-raising descent out of the gloomy sky had left him breathless and shaken up, his legs like jelly.

'Come on, Nate,' he heard Zelphyius Dax saying, and he looked up to see the librarian scholar standing before him, beaming. 'Nothing like coming in to Thorn Harbour to get the pulse racing,' he said.

'That . . . was . . . terrifying!' Nate gasped.

Zelphyius patted the smooth sumpwood figurehead. 'We were in safe hands, Nate. The *Varis Lodd* has never let me down yet,' he said proudly, and frowned as he noticed one of the sail tethers dangling limply from the slender mast. 'Mind you,' he said, 'she could probably do with a few running repairs before the return journey.'

Zelphyius quickly secured the nether sails and clicked the rudder lock into place. Then, leaving the skycraft bobbing in the air, he jumped onto the platform, tolley rope in hand, and tied the *Varis Lodd* to the mooring ring beside them.

Nate looked around, still clutching the mast cradle. All about them, moored to the neighbouring platforms, were phraxbarges, with heavily built brogtrolls and diminutive waifs engaged in loading and unloading – the brogtrolls bellowing to one another while the slightly-built waifs moved among them in silence. Below and behind the docks were dozens of simple wooden cabins with pitched roofs and gable lamps. Some were windowless warehouses, clearly used to store merchandise and cargo; others had balconied windows that blazed with light, where the captains and their crews could rest the night before embarking on the long difficult voyage back to the great cities of Hive and Great Glade.

'Welcome to the settlement of Thorn Harbour, Nate,' Zelphyius said, reaching out a hand to steady the trembling youth. 'What we need now are the services of a waif guide. There should be one hereabouts.'

Nate grabbed his arm and stepped onto the boards of the mooring platform. After so long up in the air, balancing as the skycraft pitched and swayed, it felt strange standing on something that didn't move, and he teetered about unsteadily, arms outstretched and head down watching his feet.

Zelphius smiled. 'It'll take a few moments for those skylegs of yours to wear off.' Holding Nate by the arm, he set off towards the broad staircase at the back of the platform. As he went, Nate's legs gradually stopped wobbling and Zelphyius let go of his arm. Nate looked up – and stopped in his tracks. There it was. The extraordinary sight of the thorn forests he'd glimpsed as they'd come in to land.

Towering high above the settlement of Thorn Harbour, 'forest' was not a sufficiently impressive word to convey the sheer immensity of the impenetrable-looking wall of thorns that stood before him. There were great gnarled trunks and branches, intertwined one with the other and bristling with immense dagger-like thorns that stuck out in all directions, like the spiked bars of a savage cage. At the tip of each thorn were droplets of dew, each one glinting menacingly despite the gathering gloom, and making it appear as though the great thorn bush had constellations of stars trapped within its depths.

'It's one of the most spectacular sights of the Edgelands, Nate,' said Zelphyius. 'And for thousands of years it separated the Waiflands and the Nightwoods from the rest of the Edge. Century after century, waifs attempted to escape from their dark home, but for every one who got through, hundreds died in the attempt, and to this day their bones are strewn throughout the forests of thorn. Now, in the Third Age,' he said, turning and pointing to his right, 'we have the Thorn Gate.'

Nate stared at the tall arched opening in the impenetrable wall of thorns, black against the glittering brown of the thorn forests themselves. The Thorn Gate disappeared into the heart of the tangled mass of glistening thorns like the dark maw of a logworm, swallowing up the long column of travellers entering it. From his vantage point on the mooring platform, Nate saw that there were denizens from every part of the Deepwoods – trogs, goblins, trolls and fourthlings of every type, some with sumpwood backpacks, others with sumpwood sleds, all heavily laden with boxes, crates and huge misshapen bundles.

'The beginning of the Waif Trail,' said Zelphyius. 'The only way to get to and from Riverrise . . .'

'*You are looking for a waif guide,*' a sibilant voice sounded in Nate's head.

He spun round to see a small waif with huge eyes, long fluttering ears and a pale grey complexion climbing the staircase towards him. He wore simple grey robes, with a hooded cloak of a dark shimmering material over his narrow shoulders. In his left hand, he carried a staff, on top of which was a glowing lamp. He tilted his head to one side, his large eyes wide with concern.

'*My apologies,*' Nate heard him say, his thin lips unmoving. '*I did not wish to startle you. My name is Felderforth, and I hear you're looking for a guide . . .*' He blinked twice as he probed Zelphyius and Nate's thoughts '*Your companion is very sick,*' he said, '*and you need to travel swiftly to the City of Night.*'

He turned to Zelphyius and nodded, the barbels at the corners of his mouth trembling as they agreed terms wordlessly with their thoughts.

'How much?' Nate asked Zelphyius.

'*Sixty gladers,*' the waif's sibilant voice sounded in his head, '*for the three of you. The journey along the Waif Trail will take three days if we don't stop.*'

Nate looked into the waif's large unblinking eyes. The only other waif he'd ever encountered was the tavern waif back at the Hulks in the Eastern Woods – a tiny timid creature with sickly yellowish skin and frightened-looking eyes who kept his thoughts to himself.

Nate hadn't really noticed him, but now it occurred to him that the tavern waif had probably wanted it that way, and had listened in on Nate's thoughts – and those of the other miners – for any information that he might sell to the mine sergeant.

Felderforth seemed different. His posture was upright and his bearing confident – and there was something about the understanding look in his eyes that made Nate feel he could trust him.

The waif smiled. '*I shall go and fetch a sumpwood stretcher for your companion,*' he said, the words clear in both Zelphyius and Nate's heads. '*And we shall set off without delay.*'

As the grey waif turned and descended the stairs, his cloak flapping and lampstaff held high, Zelphius Dax turned to Nate, nodding.

'I think we've found a trustworthy guide in Felderforth,' he said.

'Yes,' said Nate, 'that's what I was thinking . . .'

'Come, Nate, we'd better prepare Eudoxia for the journey ahead.'

Zelphyius and Nate retraced their steps to the skycraft and, climbing on board, made their way to the little cabin at the stern where Eudoxia lay sleeping. Nate gathered the waterflask, spare topcoat and sumpwood medical box from the cabin struts, while Zelphyius picked up the feverish Eudoxia in his arms and carried her out to the mooring platform. Nate joined him.

'Zelphyius,' he began, 'I want to thank you for everything you've done for Eudoxia and me. I don't know what would have become of us if you hadn't found us on the battlefield . . .'

'Don't mention it, Nate,' said Zelphyius, his face colouring as he held the sleeping Eudoxia in his arms. 'It is the duty of every librarian scholar to help those in need.'

'But now I must ask you to do something else for us, Zelphyius,' said Nate. 'Something of the utmost importance.'

'Anything,' said Zelphyius. 'Just name it.'

'I want you to leave us here . . .'

'Leave?' said Zelphyius, puzzled.

'Yes,' said Nate, 'and set sail for Hive. There, I want you to go to the archivists' cloister of the Sumpwood Bridge Academy, where you'll find Eudoxia's father, Galston Prade, and tell him what has become of us.'

'Galston Prade?' the librarian scholar said, taken aback. 'The owner of the largest phraxmine in the Eastern Woods?'

'Yes,' said Nate hesitantly, as it dawned on him that Zelphyius Dax had made his hatred of phraxcrystals clear to him on a number of occasions.

The librarian scholar looked down at the injured girl in his arms, and then back at Nate. He held Nate's gaze for a second, then he nodded.

'Consider it done, Nate,' he said solemnly.

'You mean it?' said Nate. 'Oh, thank you, Zelphyius, thank you. I'll never forget what you've done for us. Never.'

Zelphyius handed Eudoxia to Nate. 'You look after her, you hear,' he said. 'You'll be in safe hands with Felderforth.' He smiled. 'Here he comes now.'

Nate looked round to see the grey waif walking towards them, the lampstaff raised in one hand and, in the other, the leading rope of a broad sumpwood sled, which had a curved headboard at one end and was loaded with two sumpwood backpacks and a second lampstaff.

'*My apologies for the delay,*' Felderforth's voice sounded in Nate and Zelphyius's heads.

In Nate's arms, Eudoxia moaned softly and grimaced. The waif looked down at her. He winced.

'*Oh, she is indeed in need of the sort of help only the City of Night can provide,*' he said. '*We must travel the Waif Trail with the utmost speed.*' He turned to the others. '*Let us get her on the stretcher.*'

Nate carefully lowered Eudoxia onto the buoyant sumpwood stretcher. She didn't stir.

'There has been a slight change of plan,' Zelphyius said.

'*I understand completely,*' said the waif, nodding.

The librarian scholar turned back to Nate. 'Take care, Nate,' he

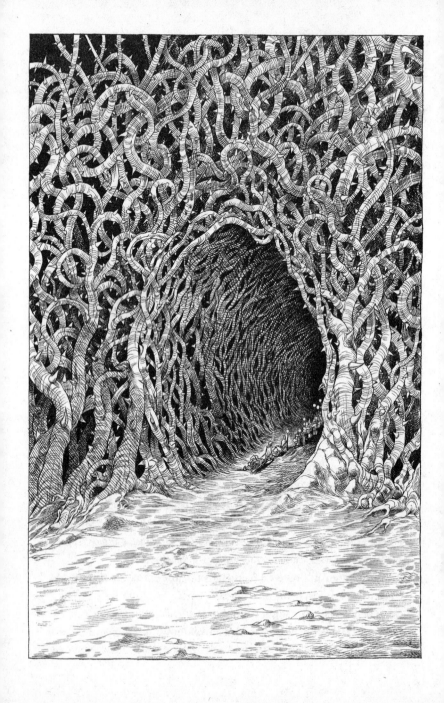

said. 'And maybe one day we'll meet again, you and I. I can show you around the Great Library, and we can find that barkscroll I mentioned about the young fourthling from the slaughterer village, Keris Verginix . . .'

Nate nodded, smiling. 'I'd like that,' he said. 'I'd like that very much.'

'Until that time,' he said, 'fare you well.' He gripped Nate's hand with both of his own, and pumped it up and down, then looked back down at Eudoxia, tucked up on the sumpwood stretcher beneath the grey topcoats. 'Earth and Sky be with you both!'

With that, he turned away. Nate watched him stride back to the *Varis Lodd* and climb on board – then pause thoughtfully before turning to inspect the sail ropes, one by one.

'*Are you ready to depart, Nate Quarter?*' asked Felderforth, his voice soft and questioning in Nate's head as he slipped one of the backpacks onto his shoulder and held the other one out.

Nate turned to him and nodded. 'Yes, I'm ready,' he said.

He pulled the almost weightless sumpwood pack onto his back, then leaned down and seized the thick rope attached to the front of the floating stretcher. He tugged it gently and the buoyant sumpwood glided through the air after him as easily as a feather floating on a breeze. They went to the end of the mooring platform and joined a line of other arrivals with backpacks, lampstaffs and sleds of their own, who were making their way down the broad stairs to the shadow-filled earth below.

Away from the bright lamps that illuminated the mooring platform, Nate found himself in the eternal gloom of Thorn Harbour's broad main street, along which the column of travellers was steadily moving. Up ahead loomed the forbidding thorn forests and the cavernous opening of the Thorn Gate.

They fell in behind other travellers at the back of the line. There was a lugtroll mother, a pale wheezing young'un swaddled up in the sumpwood basket which hung at her side. There was a cloddertrog merchant, barrels of tripweed and sides of salted hammelhorn laid out on his rough-hewn sledge. A family of gnokgoblins clustered together, their own possessions – meagre in comparison to those of the cloddertrog merchant – gathered together on a small sled, which was decorated with ornately carved fruits and flowers; and just to Nate's left was a couple of gabtroll old'uns, both bowed under large backpacks. Each of them was accompanied by a diminutive waif guide.

As they fell in with the steady rhythm of the marching feet, the Thorn Gate loomed closer, towering far, far above their heads. Nate turned and looked back at the scaffold of mooring platforms. There, her four sails billowing, was the *Varis Lodd*, rising from the jutting platform of wood and soaring up into the dark gloomy sky.

Nate raised his free arm and waved – then looked away, his face troubled. If only there had been more time, he'd have asked the librarian scholar to tell Eudoxia's father that he wouldn't let anything happen to her, that no matter what, he'd get her the care she needed and watch over her until she got better. If only he'd been able to tell Zelphyius . . .

'*He knows.*' Felderforth's voice cut through his thoughts.

Nate shook his head. 'He doesn't,' he said. 'I didn't have time to tell him.'

'*Believe me, Nate, he does know,*' the waif's reassuring voice whispered inside his head. '*I just told him.*'

· CHAPTER SIXTY-FIVE ·

As the great opening of the Thorn Gate receded behind them, Nate fell into step with Felderforth the waif guide, while pulling the sumpwood stretcher bearing Eudoxia behind him.

In front of him were two lugtrolls, bulging sumpwood-framed backpacks on their shoulders, and a slaughterer, his buoyant sled piled high with cured pelts. Half a dozen cloddertrogs marched just ahead of them, each one pulling a huge rough-hewn sumpwood sledge laden with barrels, crates, casks and haunches of salted tilder that peeked out from the waxed tarpaulins stretched over them. As they marched behind these merchants and their waif guides, Nate and Felderforth passed slower moving groups of the sick and infirm.

There was the lugtroll mother Nate had seen earlier, her pale wheezing infant now clasped to her chest. She was followed by a pair of pink-eye old'uns, stooped and hobbling. There was a blind woodtroll, a crippled flathead matron, and a mobgnome, paralysed from the neck down, lying stiffly on a sumpwood stretcher that was being pulled by an older brother or friend; there was a shuffling brogtroll, his skin covered with boils and cankers, and a gaggle of webfoot young'uns, clutching to the broad skirts of their spawn mother, each of them racked with hacking coughs . . .

Nate looked over his shoulder at Eudoxia. She was still asleep, beads of sweat lining her feverish brow.

'That's it,' he told her softly. 'You rest, Eudoxia. It'll do you good. I'll wake you when we reach Riverrise . . .'

'Her condition appears to be . . . *slurp* . . . serious,' came a concerned voice at Nate's shoulder, and he turned to see the old gabtroll couple he'd noticed as they'd approached the Thorn Gate.

'It looks like . . . *slurp* . . . a fever to me, Gilmora,' said one of the gabtrolls, and his eyestalks, sticking out of two holes in his funnel hat, swung round. He raised the lampstaff clasped in his hand, bathing Eudoxia's glistening face in light.

'And wet lung . . . *slurp slurp*, Gomber,' his wife replied, her pointed bonnet wobbling on her head as she leaned forward. 'Listen to how her breathing rasps . . .'

'It's a leadwood bullet,' Nate said, interrupting their musings, 'lodged behind her ear.'

The two gabtrolls gasped, slurping loudly as their long tongues licked their startled eyeballs.

'A leadwood bullet,' Gilmora repeated, her hand shooting up to the tangle of talismans and charms clustered at her neck. 'Sky above,' she murmured. 'But . . . but how . . . *slurp* . . . did it happen?'

'It's a long story,' said Nate, shaking his head. 'In short, we were at the battle of the Midwood marshes,' he told her, 'and Eudoxia was wounded . . .'

'A battle? But . . . *slurp* . . . that's terrible,' said Gilmora, tutting sympathetically as she fell into step with Nate. 'Absolutely terrible.' She leaned across and fussed with the topcoat that lay across Eudoxia's sleeping body. 'The poor little mite . . .' She peered up at Nate with her stalk-like eyes. 'You're taking her to the right place,' she said. 'The City of Night is justifiably famous for its gifted physicians and apothecaries – not to mention the healing properties of the sacred water from the Riverrise spring.'

Her husband tapped Nate on the arm. 'Do you mind if we walk with you?' he asked. 'You're setting a good pace.'

Felderforth must have said something, for the old gabtroll nodded.

'Much obliged,' he said, and smiled, his eyestalks quivering as the small group continued their march deeper into the thorn forests.

The tunnel through the thorns was broad, straight and cavernous. The sides had been crudely created by hacking away at the thorn trees, leaving the ends of the chopped branches ragged and splintered. Droplets of water clung to the sharpened tip of every thorn, glittering like a treasure trove of black diamonds. The air was heavy and still, laden with a sweet peppery odour – and, given the hundreds, possibly thousands, of travellers making their way in both directions, oddly quiet.

Tearing his gaze away from the tangled depths of the thorn forests, Nate noticed that Felderforth was looking at him, a smile playing on his thin barbelled lips. He guessed that the guide had been listening to his thoughts. The waif smiled apologetically and flapped a thin bony hand before him.

'*It is always fascinating to experience the thorn forests through the senses of someone experiencing them for the first time,*' he said softly. '*I confess, we waifs have always found it a dark and terrifying place . . .*'

'It is . . . beautiful,' Nate breathed as the thorns gathered around them.

'*Yes,*' said the waif, his large black eyes looking around as if seeing it all for the first time, '*I suppose it is.*'

For hours they marched on, the trail beneath their feet now hard and stony, now soft and marshy, rising and falling as they trudged down shallow valleys and heaved themselves up over low hills. Whatever the terrain below, the cavernous tunnel continued unbroken, its lofty arch far above their heads looking, to Nate at least, like a great vaulted ceiling.

'*We waifs contend that the Thorn Tunnel is every bit as mighty a construction as the bridges and buildings of Great Glade or Hive,*' the waif told him.

Nate nodded. How long, he wondered, had it been here?

'*It was first constructed almost five hundred years ago,*' the waif responded, reading his thoughts, '*though of course it has to be constantly tended. The thorn forest is tenacious and grows fast, forever trying to heal the rift running through its heart . . .*'

But the tunnel was huge and the waifs seemingly so small and frail, Nate thought.

'*We waifs did not build it,*' Felderforth's voice sounded in his head. '*It was built by the red and black dwarves and their slaves, the nameless ones.*'

Nameless ones, Nate thought. Those strange creatures of the Nightwoods, uncategorized by the librarian scholars and seldom seen in the sunlit Deepwoods. What must they be like?

'*If you look over there, you'll see,*' said Felderforth, nodding to his left as they marched on at a steady pace.

Following his gaze, Nate found himself staring at three gigantic lumpen individuals up ahead, who were standing high up on broad sumpwood ladders propped against the side of the tunnel. They each had huge pairs of shears in their hands, and were busy trimming back the encroaching twigs and branches, while a fourth gargantuan individual gathered the cuttings together in piles beneath them. As they drew closer, Nate looked more closely at the four enormous, lumbering creatures.

So these were the nameless ones . . .

'*Yes, they are,*' he heard Felderforth confirming in his mind.

Nate was shocked. One was broad-shouldered, its leathery grey skin crisscrossed with scars, and it had a long, jutting lower jaw set with serrated tusks. Another was tall and curiously gangly, its spine crooked and head misshapen. Both of them were draped in tattered rags of what once must have been rudimentary garments, now torn and shredded beyond recognition by the savage thorns. Nate's gaze fell on the third nameless one – a low-browed, earless creature with a barrel chest and squat bowed legs – and what looked like a stubby tail sticking out from the seams of the threadbare breeches it wore.

On the ground, the fourth nameless one grunted and growled miserably as it raked the thorny clippings together in piles with its chipped claws. It had a bulbous neck, twice the thickness of its head, while its arms were so long that, even when it bent them at the elbows, its knuckles still grazed along the ground. It turned to reveal a monstrous face, tiny eyes sunk deep in cratered sockets and gaping nostrils set into a broad ridge of bone. Beneath them was a lipless mouth, the lower fangs so large and irregular that its jaw hung open, strands of dripping drool glinting in the yellow lamplight.

As Nate watched, he saw the nameless one's brutal features convulse with spasms of pain. It was only when he looked more closely that he realized why.

Perched on the creature's shoulder was a tiny red dwarf – a

diminutive beaked goblin from the depths of the Nightwoods, a glinting spike in its grasp. This one was typical of its kind, with blistered red skin and a bloated body set upon spindly legs. Between small wide-set eyes, its beak-like nose jutted out over its protruding jaw, while its tufted ears twitched every time it stabbed with casual brutality at the hapless nameless one in its charge.

'*They have to be harsh,*' said Felderforth in answer to Nate's thoughts, '*to keep the nameless ones working.*'

Nate looked up at the others, still ceaselessly chopping at the thorny twigs and branches which had encroached into the tunnel, and he realized that each of them, too, had one of the tiny red or black dwarves clinging to them. Every time the great lumbering creatures paused in their efforts, even for a moment, the dwarves would jab them with their vicious spikes in those soft sensitive places behind their ears or in the delicate membrane inside their noses, until they started working once more.

'*I sense you find this brutal,*' the waif whispered in his head. '*But . . .*' He hesitated, and for an instant, Nate thought he felt an element of doubt in the words inside his head. '*But how else can we waifs ensure the tunnel is kept open for visitors to our great city; visitors such as yourself?*'

Nate turned from the enslaved nameless ones and increased his pace to keep up with the waif guide, suddenly aware of how weary he had become. Here, in the constant gloom of the Thorn Tunnel, it was impossible to tell the time of day, and Nate had no idea how long they had been marching. Certainly it felt like hours.

'*We have marched through what you call the night,*' the waif told him. '*But there are still many hours left to journey. We must maintain our pace, for we cannot get to Riverrise too soon for your friend, Nate.*'

Head down, his hand grasping the stretcher's tether rope, Nate pressed on, urging his legs forward, one step after another after another. His eyelids became heavy and, as his head began to swim with tiredness, he wondered once again how Zelphyius Dax had managed to keep going with so little sleep.

A while later, Nate was stirred from his waking reveries as he

444

heard loud cries and the sound of shouting voices – both inside *and* outside his head – coming from up ahead. Felderforth's pace didn't slacken for a moment, and as Nate and the gabtrolls struggled to keep up, he saw two large bowers had come to a halt beside the trail. They each had purple velvet curtains and tasselled canopies, and were surmounted with a golden spike carved in the shape of the Riverrise mountain itself. Long lufwood hefting staves stuck out back and front. Beside the bowers, in white uniformed topcoats, a group of heavy-set brogtrolls – who had been carrying the curtained chairs – gathered round a cowering waif guide

'What's happening?' Nate asked directly, and in his head he heard the sound of Felderforth sighing.

Nate turned to see him stricken with fear. His trembling ears hung limply down, while his face had drained of all colour.

'They are the custodians,' he said without breaking step, *'and their guards.'*

As they approached the bowers, Felderforth quickened his pace.

'The custodians are our wise and venerable leaders,' Felderforth told Nate, though even as he heard the waif's sibilant words, he was aware of a second, deeper voice, underlying it. ***They rule Riverrise with an iron fist, allowing neither disobedience nor dissent. Any who think of opposing them are dealt with without mercy.***

Nate turned and looked at the waif, his eyes wide with confusion.

The waif continued. *'And Custodian General, Golderayce One-Eye, is the most wise and venerable of them all,'* Nate heard. *I am communicating my underthoughts to you, Nate Quarter ... Yes, underthoughts. From birth, every waif learns to conceal his true thoughts by underthinking. But on occasions, a waif – particularly the young and foolish – will forget, and inadvertently reveal their true feelings ...*

'I ... I don't understand,' Nate said.

The custodians caught one of their retinue – a waif guide – harbouring negative thoughts about them ...

All at once the distant-sounding cacophony of voices inside

Nate's head fell still. The waif shook his head.

And he has been dealt with.

'Dealt with?' said Nate.

'Long live the wise custodians!' Felderforth nodded grimly. ***Without mercy.***

As they passed the two bowers and the uniformed brogtroll guards, Nate glanced over at them and swallowed hard. Impaled upon the vicious wall of thorns was the body of the young waif guide, blood dripping down onto the ground below him. He had clearly been thrown at it violently, remaining fixed to the spot where he'd landed, his body twisted and arms and legs akimbo. Sharp spikes stuck out at all angles from his body, the thorns piercing his ribs, a knee, an eye . . .

'Without mercy,' Nate repeated, his voice low and tremulous.

'Our custodian leaders are indeed venerable and

wise,' he heard Felderforth saying, followed by a low shudder. *Their brutality knows no bounds.*

They continued their march at an unvarying pace, Nate glad that his growing exhaustion distracted his mind from thoughts of what he'd just seen. Far above his head, through the tangle of terrible thorns, the glowering sky seemed to be a shade lighter and he wondered for a moment whether this was what passed for daylight in the Thorn Tunnel.

If it was, then was this the second day of their endless march? he wondered. The third? He shrugged. Since his head was reeling with tiredness, the apparent lightness in the stormy sky beyond the upper reaches of the thorny tunnel might be no more than a figment of his imagination. He returned his attention to the seemingly endless Waif Trail before him, the lamp glow spilling out across the uneven ground and, as he did so, he heard Felderforth penetrating his thoughts once more.

'*There,*' the waif guide told him, nodding ahead, '*is the Night Gate – the end of the Thorn Tunnel.*'

Nate peered ahead, to see the dark arch give way to an area of even denser darkness beyond. A broad smile spread across his face.

'The end of the Thorn Tunnel,' he repeated. 'At last . . .'

'*Yes,*' said the waif. '*Now our journey becomes more difficult.*'

They emerged from the Night Gate into a cold dank forest, so dark that the gnarled trees – each one encrusted with thick shaggy moss and glistening clumps of wormy fungus – disappeared into endless blackness beyond the range of the lamps. Nate turned to Felderforth.

'*These are the Nightwoods,*' he heard him say. '*The beginning of the Waiflands. Wild waifs still inhabit the forest,*' he said. '*Leechwaifs, copperwaifs, bloodwaifs, waterwaifs and ghostwaifs who would like nothing better than to lure travellers from the trail and to their deaths. But fear not, Nate Quarter, as a waif guide I am sworn to protect you until you reach our great city . . .*'

As he spoke, Nate suddenly became aware of something flapping round his head. He swatted at the air, his fingers grazing the tips of leathery wings. Beside him, he felt the stretcher tilt and sway and, looking round, saw to his horror that four leathery winged creatures with flat faces and tiny fangs were perched on Eudoxia's sleeping body.

'Felderforth!' he gasped.

But the waif had already noticed and, his eyes blazing and barbels at his mouth quivering, he stared at the tiny creatures. Whatever his thoughts, the waif guide certainly had an effect for, as Nate watched, the creatures let out rasping screams and instantly scattered, flapping off into the pitch black of the surrounding Nightwoods.

'Flitterwaifs,' Felderforth said. '*Some in Riverrise keep them as pets,*' he added, the voice in Nate's head laced with disgust. '*But out here, they are untamed – and always hungry.*'

They continued walking, with Felderforth in front setting the pace, Nate behind pulling the floating stretcher, and the old gabtroll couple tramping doggedly after. Underfoot, the going was soft and marshy, and the air smelled stagnant and rank. Up ahead, silhouetted in the lamp glow, Nate saw others defending themselves against the flitterwaifs. Their arms waved frantically as they used clubs and cudgels to beat the creatures off, and the dank air hissed with the sound of the furious flitterwaifs as their ferocious attacks were thwarted.

Nate glanced at Felderforth, grateful to have the services of such an attentive waif. Time after time, he had leaped forward – often before Nate was even aware of any danger – and scattered the attacking flitterwaifs with the power of his thoughts. As they travelled still further into the dark forest, though, their numbers increased, gliding through the shadows and alighting on the knobbly branches, where they hissed and squealed.

Nate stared into the oppressive gloom, trying to make out the shifting forms in the shadows. The trees seemed to squirm and writhe, their trunks and branches dripping with thick viscous liquid which oozed from the bark. Dense skeins of cobwebs spanned the bone-like twigs, each one beaded with droplets of condensed mist that seemed to stare back at him like eyes – until with a sudden jolt he realized that, in amongst the tangle of branches, there *were* eyes there.

Large and small eyes. Red eyes. Yellow eyes. Eyes that were narrowed to razor-like slits; wide, round eyes that never seemed to blink. They were all around the steady stream of travellers on the Waif Trail, menacing and predatory, waiting for one of the old or weak to stumble and slip unnoticed, so that they might pounce. Occasionally, Nate would see more than just their eyes reflected in the light. Once, the lamp glow glinted on the green scales of a thin creature with a broad mask-like face; once he caught a glimpse of the dripping fangs of a tall emaciated-looking creature that, even as he was watching, slipped silently behind the moss-encrusted trunk of a crumbling tree and disappeared.

'*The denizens of the waiflands are many,*' he heard Felderforth saying, and was comforted to hear the familiar voice. '*Bark demons, slime steppers, gulpers and snatchers . . . And all with the gift of reading your thoughts.*'

Nate stumbled on. His feet were blistered; his body felt as though it had been stretched on a rack. And all the while his tiredness intensified, blunting his senses and filling his head with strange unsettling thoughts.

'*Come this way,*' they seemed to be hissing. '*The path over here is easier, quicker. We can show you . . .*'

'*Don't listen to them,*' Felderforth's voice told him.

'I'll try not to . . . But I'm so tired . . .' said Nate.

'*Concentrate on the trail,*' the waif told him. '*And on my voice – and no others . . .*'

The waif guide scanned the forest about him, his barbels quivering violently. All around, unseen creatures squeaked and squealed as they flapped away or scuttled off, retreating in alarm from the waif guide's threatening thoughts.

Nate had no idea how long he'd been walking when he first heard the trickling water far ahead. Hours? Days? Time had lost all meaning in the Nightwoods. The tiredness had reached such a pitch that his head felt foggy and numb, while his body felt almost as though it belonged to someone else.

As the sound of the running water became louder, the ground beneath his feet grew marshy. The going was increasingly difficult, and more than once Nate stumbled forward as the sucking mud tried to hold him back. Behind him, the gabtrolls were having an even harder time of it, their aged bodies battling to keep going. He heard them stumble and trip repeatedly, their breath coming in short wheezy gasps as they staggered on, trying hard to keep up with Nate and Felderforth.

'Oh, Gomber!' Gilmora cried out, her cry followed by a soft *splash*, and Nate turned to see the hapless gabtroll matron sprawling in the mud, Gomber behind her, struggling hopelessly to help her to her feet.

'Take this,' he said to Felderforth, handing him the rope tether for Eudoxia's stretcher.

Though close to exhaustion himself, Nate reached down, seized the stout gabtroll matron beneath her arms and, using reserves of strength he didn't even know he possessed, hoisted her up to her feet. She stood there unsteadily, her eyestalks trembling.

'Oh . . . *slurp* . . . thank you so much,' she said as her eyes slowly focused on the youth standing before her. 'These tired old bones of mine . . .'

'Let me take your backpack,' said Nate, holding out a hand. 'And yours,' he added, turning to Gomber.

The two gabtrolls put up no resistance as he helped them pull the straps from their shoulders, and he returned to the stretcher, the two sumpwood packs under his arms. With Eudoxia curled up in a ball beneath the military topcoats, there was more than enough space for the backpacks, and he secured them at the base of the carved headboard.

They set off once more, with the gabtrolls walking along beside him, their gait less unsteady now and their breathing more even.

'This is indeed . . . *slurp* . . . a kindness,' said Gilmora, her long tongue flicking out over her eyeballs. 'A great kindness . . .' She hesitated, her eyestalks swinging round and looking at him quizzically. 'I don't believe you told us your . . . *slurp* . . . name.'

'Nate,' said Nate. 'Nate Quarter.'

'Well, thank you, Nate Quarter,' she told him.

'Yes, thank you,' added Gomber as he squelched along beside them, using his lampstaff to negotiate the spongy mud.

'And what is the name of your companion here?' Gilmora continued.

'Eudoxia Prade,' said Nate, and shook his head, suddenly overwhelmed by tiredness. 'She's . . . she's been a true and loyal friend and . . .' He swallowed hard. 'I just hope that I can find the help she needs in the City of Night.'

'Oh, to be sure, you're doing the right thing,' said Gilmora, nodding enthusiastically. 'As I . . . *slurp* . . . told you . . . *slurp* . . . before, Nate Quarter, the city is full of highly skilled physicians and the most inventive of apoth-

ecaries in all the Edge. Isn't that right, Gomber?' she said, turning to her companion.

'Indeed it is,' he replied.

'The City of Night is a truly wonderful place,' Gilmora went on, waving an arm expansively, 'where many find cures for what ails them.' Her eyeballs contracted on the stalks. 'Though it is not without its troubles . . .'

Alerted by the gruff sound of Gomber clearing his throat, Gilmora fell silent. Nate looked at first one gabtroll, then the other. His brow furrowed.

'Troubles?' he said.

'I think I should . . . *slurp* . . . tell him,' said Gilmora, talking across Nate to her companion.

'It isn't wise,' he said, his leathery face crumpling with concern as he continued to stride down the trail alongside Nate.

'But he's been so kind to us,' Gilmora hissed back, careful to keep up. 'It's . . . *slurp* . . . the least we can do.'

The gabtroll old'un shrugged, and looked round over his shoulders furtively. Gilmora turned to Nate, her eyes misty with sympathy.

'I can trust you, Nate Quarter,' she said and slurped, 'can't I?'

'Y . . . yes,' said Nate, puzzled. 'Of course.'

'We are the personal servants of the Custodian General,' Gilmora said, her voice low and hushed. 'We prepare his meals, clean . . . *slurp* . . . his living chambers, wash his clothes . . .' She slurped twice in succession. 'Golderayce One-Eye, his name is, and . . .'

'He's a wonderful leader. *Slurp* . . . Riverrise's finest!' said Gomber loudly and enthusiastically. 'Venerable and wise, and . . . *slurp* . . . generous to a fault. And he certainly appreciates all that we do for him.'

'He is an evil tyrant,' Gilmora whispered in Nate's ear, 'He rules . . .'

This is very dangerous, Felderforth whispered urgently inside all their heads. ***For all of us . . .***

Gilmora turned to him and nodded. 'I know,' she said, 'but Nate

Quarter should hear this . . .' She turned back to Nate. 'He has ruled Riverrise for . . . *slurp* . . . hundreds of years,' she whispered. 'Sky love him,' she added loudly, her eyestalks peering wildly around her.

Nate frowned. 'Hundreds of years?' he whispered back.

Beside him, Gomber nodded, his trembling eyestalks betraying the agitation he was feeling.

'While . . . *slurp* . . . the city of Riverrise has to rely on the meagre trickle of water that falls into the great aqueduct below the Riverrise spring . . . *slurp* . . . for its medicines and cures,' she explained, her voice hushed and urgent, 'Golderayce the Custodian General has access to . . . *slurp* . . . the pure life-giving water at the spring's source.' She leaned in still closer to Nate. 'Pure Riverrise spring water from the source is the most powerful cure in the entire City of Night,' she said, 'but Golderayce guards it jealously and keeps it only for himself . . .'

'*Enough!*' Felderforth's voice sounded in all their heads.

The waif guide, who had been trying his best to mask the seditious thoughts of his travelling companions with prattling thoughts of his own, turned to them now. His wide eyes were sparkling and the barbels at the corners of his mouth trembled with anger. He raised his lampstaff and pointed ahead.

'*The end of our long journey is near,*' he said. '*Take care as we descend.*' He turned to the gabtrolls. ***And in future, you should take care what you think.***

'Waifs aren't the only ones who can underthink,' Gilmora told him. 'How else do you think Gomber and I have remained in the Custodian General's employ for so many years?'

Nate looked round the dark forest, scarcely able to believe that their destination was approaching. For hours now, it had been like walking through a dream, the air like treacle and his head constantly playing tricks. Now the Waif Trail had started to descend, with the track becoming both narrower and steeper, and Nate found himself continuing downhill in a series of zigzags as the track made its way down a long and precipitous drop of shifting gravel and treacherous scree.

Nate moved to the front of the stretcher, gripping on tightly to the rope tether while Felderforth steadied it from behind. The two gabtrolls slipped and skidded down the track behind them, arm in arm, clutching onto one another for support. The sound of trickling water that Nate had heard for several hours – sometimes aware of it, sometimes not – became louder now, impossible to ignore as it splashed down into some unseen pool close by. And as the column of travellers went deeper down into the great gulley, a thin swirling mist spiralled up from the cold wet ground, wrapping itself around their ankles, then their legs, then coiling slowly up around their bodies.

'*Not far now,*' Felderforth whispered encouragingly.

'Soon be there, Eudoxia,' Nate said, hardly able to believe it himself as he glanced down at her pale face peeking out of the swaddling topcoats.

All at once, having struggled down a particularly treacherous stretch of path, loose jagged rocks threatening to send him sprawling with every tentative step, Nate looked up to see something ahead. He blinked, once, twice; he rubbed his eyes. There was no doubt. This was no dream, no figment of his imagination brought on by lack of sleep. No, before him lay the most extraordinary city he had yet seen.

'*We have reached our destination,*' Felderforth whispered inside his head. '*Riverrise, the City of Night.*'

· CHAPTER SIXTY-SIX ·

'In the sixth quadrant there are four clusters made up of . . .' Klug Junkers squinted down the lens of the light magnifier, counting softly under his breath. 'Six . . . no, seven glisters,' he said.

'Four clusters,' Togtuft Hegg repeated, making a note in the barkscroll ledger with a scratchy snowbird quill. 'Seven glisters in each cluster.' He looked round. 'Seven, eh?' he said. 'So they're fused together to form a larger entity . . . Fascinating.'

The pair of them were working in the small laboratory they had set up in their academic cloister. Togtuft was perched on a high stool, the barkscroll ledger in which he was recording their findings laid out on the tall sumpwood bench before them. Klug stood beside him at the light magnifier, the sleeves of his brown robes rolled up, his body stooped forward and dust dancing in the shaft of light around his face.

'If our theory is correct,' mused Klug, 'then these glisters, fossilized in the cliff rock, were once seeds of life, blown in from Open Sky.'

'In a Mother Storm,' Togtuft added. 'Perhaps the very storm that first seeded the Edgelands with life at Riverrise.'

'This tiny piece of Edge cliff rock has yielded so much,' Klug said, his eyes pressed to the light magnifier. 'But just think, Togtuft, what we could discover with more samples – larger, and from further down the cliff face . . .'

'Before we get too carried away with thoughts of better samples, Klug my friend,' said his companion, 'let us continue the examination of the sample we do possess . . .'

Togtuft had fashioned a grid from fine wire, which they'd placed over the tiny rock sample, dividing it up into twenty-four separate squares which Klug was now systematically examining, one by one.

'Seventh quadrant,' said Togtuft. His pen, freshly dipped in the pot of blackwood ink, was poised. He frowned and turned to his colleague. 'Seventh quadrant?' he repeated.

'Yes . . . I . . .' Klug paused. 'There's something strange here, Togtuft,' he said, readjusting the focus of the light magnifier. 'I think I've found a new type of glister,' he said, his voice hushed with excitement. 'A *red* glister . . .'

'A red glister?' Togtuft said.

'Take a look,' said Klug, straightening up and groaning as the bones in his spine softly cracked. 'In the bottom right-hand corner of the quadrant. Dark and misshapen . . .'

Togtuft slid down from the stool and put his eye to the lens. For a moment he was silent. Then, a broad grin spreading over his hairy features, he looked round.

'You're right,' he said breathlessly. 'It *is* a red glister.' He frowned. 'If these *are* seeds of life, then what in Sky's name might this red glister have become . . . ?'

Just then, there was a loud clattering in the room behind them and the sound of familiar voices talking animatedly.

'Squall and Weelum are back,' said Togtuft to Klug, who nodded. 'Perhaps they have news.'

The pair of them hurried across the cluttered laboratory and out through the door. Weelum the banderbear had just entered the cloister, lowering the hood of his heavy oiled leather cape and struggling to unfasten the clasp at the neck. Squall Razortooth had removed his ochre topcoat and was hanging it on a hook by the front door.

'And did you hear anything of friend Nate or Mistress Eudoxia?' Slip the grey goblin scuttler was asking them, his huge black eyes darting optimistically from the banderbear to the sky pirate, and back again.

'Wuh-wuh,' said Weelum, shaking his head, the claws of his left hand touching his chest and fluttering away. *We spoke to many, but found no answers.*

'All too true, I'm afraid, old friend,' said Squall. 'We tried the Low Town markets, and Mid Town in both East and West Ridge, just like yesterday and the day before that, *and* the day before that . . . The city is full of returning militia, and everywhere there is talk of rebellion . . .'

'I don't blame them. They feel let down by the Clan Council – and Kulltuft Warhammer especially,' said Klug, his mottled features creasing with concern.

Squall shrugged and nodded towards the light grey topcoat hanging from a hook between Weelum's cloak and his own embroidered topcoat. It was the militia coat that the Professor had disguised himself in when he, Nate and Eudoxia had rescued Galston Prade from the Gyle Palace.

'We spoke to as many of the greycoats as we could find, but no one could tell us anything of our brave young friends. But one thing they all agreed on,' the old sky pirate said darkly, 'is that the whole of the Hive Militia took a terrible mauling at the battle of the Midwood marshes.'

From the shadows, there came a low despairing groan, followed by a hollow cough. Wisps of vapour twisted up into the air from the buoyant leather-bound chair.

'I'm sorry, Galston,' said Squall, turning to the mine owner and trying hard to look optimistic. 'But we'll keep asking. There are more militia arriving back with every day that passes . . .'

'Ten days,' the old man wheezed. 'Ten days since the battle, and not a word . . .'

'We mustn't give up hope,' said Squall. 'Nate and Eudoxia disappeared wearing the grey topcoats, but who's to say they didn't find a way to escape the militia and, even now, are making their own way back to Hive?'

Suddenly, there was a loud and insistent pounding at the door. Klug and Togtuft exchanged anxious glances.

'The School of Archivists seldom has visitors,' murmured Togtuft.

'Who is it?' Klug called out.

457

'The High Academe,' came an urgent voice. 'Let me in . . .'

Klug strode forward and opened the door. Before him stood a gaunt-looking tufted goblin in the thick green velvet gown and black silk nightcap of the Sumpwood Bridge Academy.

'Arch-Professor Ignum Spave,' said Klug, his eyebrow raised in surprise. 'It's been a long time since you graced our humble school with your presence.'

'For which I'm most heartily sorry,' the professor blustered. 'Matters of high politics, Archivist Junkers.' He glanced round furtively. 'Can I come inside?'

Klug Junkers stepped aside, and the harassed-looking High Academe hurried into the high narrow cloister hall, his gown flapping behind him and the sumpwood soles of his sandals clattering on the floorboards. Klug closed the door behind him and pushed the bolt securely into place.

'To what do we owe the honour?' asked Togtuft, his voice laced with disdain.

'Ah, Archivist Hegg, good morning,' the professor said, nodding at the long-hair goblin. He looked round uncertainly at the others in the room, his gaze resting for a moment on the faces of the banderbear, the grey goblin and the craggy sky pirate. He frowned, and turned back to Klug. 'I wasn't aware you had visitors . . .'

'These are our friends,' said Klug. 'Anything you wish to say to us, you can say in front of them.'

The High Academe nodded earnestly and took a deep breath. 'I realize now that I've treated you archivists in the School of Restoration badly,' he said, his words tripping over one another, 'ignoring your field of study, starving your school of funds and resources.' He shook his head. 'I confess, I was seduced by the wealth and prestige that the clan chiefs promised me,' he said, searching the two archivists' faces for a glimmer of forgiveness. 'Which is why I devoted all the academy's energies to the development of phraxcannon and sumpwood limbers . . .'

'And you said nothing when the Bloody Blades arrested our colleague, Magnus Spool, for speaking out against the Clan Council?'

said Klug, his eyes flashing defiantly.

The third name on the small copper plaque screwed to the wall beside the School of Archivists' door bore witness to this fact, the ornate lettering crudely scored through with the tip of a razor-sharp battleaxe.

The High Academe nodded sorrowfully. 'That was my greatest shame,' he conceded. 'When they came for the High Professors on the Academy Bridge, I did nothing. When they came for the under-professors, I did nothing. Then, when they came for me, there was no one left to speak out . . .'

'They came for *you*?' said Klug, frowning. 'When?'

'You didn't know?' said the High Academe. 'But then, why should you? You archivists keep yourselves to yourselves. It was when the first news of the disastrous defeat began coming back from the Midwood Decks.

Firemane Clawhand, the High Clan Chief's henchman, and half a dozen hand-picked guards of his broke into the High Cloister, ransacking our libraries and laboratories. They burned our books and barkscrolls. They smashed our scientific apparatus against the walls.' He scowled angrily. 'Apparently, our great Clan Chief had decided that the sumpwood limbers we'd designed for his precious phraxcannon were faulty, and that we at the academy were somehow to blame for the Hive Militia's defeat . . .'

He shook his head, his gaze fixed on the floor.

'In the course of ten minutes,' he said gravely, 'the accumulated knowledge of more than a hundred years of research was destroyed.' He looked up. 'I've spent the last few days going through the wreckage, trying to salvage what I can, but it is proving a hopeless task – which brings me to the reason for my visit . . .'

'You need our archives,' said Togtuft and Klug together.

Arch-Professor Ignum Spave nodded. 'Working together, we can recover what has been lost, and restore this great academy of ours to its former glory.'

'We have made copies and catalogued the work of the academy as best we could – with no encouragement or help from you,' Klug replied. 'And much of your work in the High Cloister *can* be recovered,' he confirmed. 'But what is to stop you going back to your old ways, doing the Clan Council's bidding?'

'The days of Kulltuft Warhammer and his Clan Council are coming to an end,' said the High Academe fiercely. 'Already, by all reports, his henchman Firemane Clawhand has received his comeuppance. He was drinking in the Winesap Tavern and started berating the members of the Hive Militia he saw there, calling them traitors and cowards. But without the Bloody Blades backing him up, Firemane soon found out that no one was afraid of him or his master any more.'

'What happened?' asked Klug.

'Four goblins from the Flathead Guard grabbed him and shaved his head, then they sent him packing, back up to High Town to tell Kulltuft Warhammer that his days are numbered.

There is a new council being formed, representing all of Hive, and it wants to put an end to the fear and bloodshed of the past. It'll be a new beginning for us all!'

The High Academe held out his hand to the two archivists. 'Can you find it in your hearts to forgive me,' he said humbly, 'and work with me and my apprentices to restore the Sumpwood Bridge Academy?'

Togtuft and Klug exchanged glances, then stepped forward and shook the High Academe's hand.

'You can count on us,' they said solemnly.

'Thank you, thank you,' said Arch-Professor Ignum Spave, relief flooding his gaunt features. 'I shall not let you down again, I swear!'

He strode back towards the door, seized the handle and pulled it open – only to start back with surprise as he was confronted by two tall fourthlings standing before him. One was a dour-looking individual in a crushed funnel hat and a short topcoat, the other wore a long, grubby coat and a broad-rimmed quarmskin hat.

'More of your friends, I see,' Spave observed, turning back to Togtuft and Klug. 'As I said, changes are afoot in Hive. Huge changes.'

With that, he turned and left, his sumpwood soles tap-tapping on the boards of the Sumpwood Bridge. The Professor and Cirrus Gladehawk stepped inside and pushed the door to.

'Professor! Captain!' came a weak voice from the corner of the room as Galston Prade struggled to his feet. He coughed weakly, a cloud of mist clinging to his tousled hair and unkempt side-whiskers. 'Any . . . news of my daughter?' he wheezed, looking searchingly into the faces of the two newcomers.

'I'm afraid not, Galston,' said the Professor softly.

'Ah,' said the mine owner wearily, the sound of his sigh like air escaping from a deflated trockbladderball. He collapsed back into the chair and buried his head in his hands.

'But there is other news,' said Cirrus Gladehawk, his clear blue eyes darting round the expectant faces in the room. 'Wherever we went, we found stirrings of dissent.' He shook his head. 'You mark my words,' he said, 'huge changes are coming to Hive . . .'

'That's just what that the High Academe was saying,' said Squall Razortooth.

'Was he now?' said the Professor, his dour expression barely lightening even for a moment. 'Good news, I suppose, though for the time being it does nothing to help us with our problem . . .'

'You weren't able to find any then?' said Togtuft.

The Professor shook his head gloomily.

'It seems there isn't a phraxcrystal to be had in all of Hive,' said Cirrus Gladehawk glumly.

'Every gloaming one has been used to arm phraxmuskets and phraxcannon. And what for?' added the Professor bitterly. 'Sky above, what I wouldn't give to get my hands on just one crystal . . .'

'Of course, there are plenty enough to be had in Great Glade,' Cirrus Gladehawk broke in. 'But it'll be months before trade is resumed between Hive and Great Glade, whatever happens with the Clan Council.'

'So we're stuck,' said the Professor.

Cirrus Gladehawk pushed back his crushed funnel hat and surveyed the others seriously. 'It seems so,' he said. 'There's plenty of sumpwood in Hive, so I'm confident we can make repairs to the bow and stern,' he said. 'Rebuild the rudder . . . And Squall here can retool the phraxchamber. But without a phraxcrystal to power her, then the *Archemax* will never be able to take to the skies again . . .'

Slip the grey goblin turned and crossed the room unnoticed, and hurried up the stairs at the far end. The Professor went over to Galston Prade and sat down on the buoyant chair beside him. He reached out and placed his hand on the old man's bony arm.

'There is nothing worse than being powerless to help those we love,' he said, and squeezed the mine owner's wrist reassuringly. 'I haven't given up hope. And you mustn't either, Galston. Just as I believe my brother Ifflix is out there somewhere, I know Nate and your daughter Eudoxia are still alive, and that we will find them . . .'

Galston Prade's face hardened, his eyes narrowing and lips growing thin. Beneath his hand, the Professor felt the mine owner's tendons tense like cables as the old man clenched his fist.

'Felftis Brack.' He spoke the name slowly and deliberately, a cold anger in his eyes. 'He shall pay for the grief he has caused me and my family. When I get word to the High Council in Great Glade, Felftis Brack will be dealt with . . .' He clicked a finger and thumb together. 'Like that!'

The Professor nodded grimly. 'If anyone deserves what's coming to him, it's Felftis Brack . . .' He paused, noticing out of the corner of his eye the grey goblin, who was standing at his elbow, a heavy-looking knapsack clutched in his outstretched arms. 'What's that, Slip?' he asked. 'Aren't they Nate's belongings?'

The grey goblin nodded. 'They are,' he said. 'But Slip doesn't think friend Nate will mind,' he added. Placing the knapsack down on the floor at his feet he stooped down, undid the straps and removed a small chest. 'There's something you should see, Professor,' said Slip enthusiastically. 'It could be the answer to all your problems . . .'

The Professor had opened the small chest and was peering down at the bits and pieces inside. 'Epaulettes,' he said. 'A scroll, a spoon . . . A bit of fur?' He looked up, confused.

'Not that one,' said Slip, retrieving Nate's lightbox and swapping it for the little box of memories. 'This . . .'

Just then, there came a loud hammering at the door. The Professor looked up. The others turned, and Klug went to answer it. Before he reached the door, it burst open and a tall gaunt figure strode inside. Laying the lightbox aside, the Professor climbed to his feet, his hands hovering above the pearl handles of the phraxpistols at his belt. He surveyed the stranger, taking in the old-fashioned flap-eared funnel cap and heavily patched tilderleather breeches he wore.

'Who, in the name of Earth and Sky, are you?' he demanded.

'Forgive my intrusion,' the stranger began, 'but where might I find the phraxmine owner, Galston Prade?'

The bowed and shrunken figure of the mine owner looked up at the stranger from his buoyant chair, unease in his startling blue eyes and trails of misty breath seeping out between his thin lips. 'I am Galston Prade,' he said, his voice low and tremulous.

The tall figure seemed visibly to relax. He bent down and extended a hand in greeting. 'My name is Zelphyius Dax,' he said, 'and I have news of your daughter . . .'

· CHAPTER SIXTY-SEVEN ·

Although it was a warm and cloudless morning in Hive, the streets of High Town, far up at the top of West Ridge, were eerily deserted. None of the goblin matrons in their silk skirts and fur-trimmed coats were out walking their pet lemkins and fromps. No money lenders or factory bosses were on the sidewalks, twirling bone-handled canes as they strode importantly along, or riding in sleek prowlgrindrawn carriages. There were no married old'uns strolling or young couples walking arm in arm, no cloddertrog merchants or lugtroll porters, no young'uns out playing dodger or ragtag or stick-and-hoop.

'Where is everyone?' muttered Clan Chief Kulltuft Warhammer impatiently from his throne in the Clan Hall's magnificent council chamber. 'Where are they all?'

He looked across at the five-sided table and the empty clan chairs which stood around it. There was the tall-backed leadwood throne where Turgik, clan chief of the hammerheads, normally sat; the ornately carved pinewood chair of Ragg Yellowtooth, the wily leader of the tusked goblin clans, and the broad reinforced sumpwood settle, where Grossmother Meadowdew would rest her massive body. And, of course, the padded rocking chair that had belonged to Leegwelt the Mottled – until his unfortunate accident . . .

Kulltuft's eyes narrowed. 'I've disciplined clan chiefs before,' he muttered grimly, 'and by Sky, I'll do it again if I have to.' He sighed, and sat back in his arch-backed throne, which was perched high atop the heap of gurning skulls at the centre of the great octagonal clan hall. His right foot tapped impatiently against the smooth yellow surface of Hemtuft Battleaxe's skull. 'It was different in your day,' he said, addressing the skull as the big toe of his right foot slid round and round one of the eye sockets. 'Back then, the clans were proud warriors, happy to lay down their lives in battle for their high clan chief.'

Kulltuft brought his left foot up and placed it next to his right, and rubbed both feet back and forwards over the ancient yellowed bone. Normally, just having contact with the skull was enough to calm him down, to fill him with a sense of destiny and invigorate him with the power of Hemtuft Battleaxe, as if the greatest clan chief of all was speaking to him directly from the spirit world of Open Sky beyond.

Not today, though. Today, the skull felt cold as marble and remained as silent as death itself.

'More militia arriving back every day,' Kulltuft muttered through clenched teeth. He leaned forward and preened the feathers of his cape absentmindedly, then looked up, his eyes blazing with rage. 'Yet still I must wait for the return of my Bloody Blades!'

The words echoed round the octagonal clan hall. Kulltuft looked up, wondering for a moment whether the voice he could hear might belong to someone else. Yet as it faded away, he recognized it for what it was – his own impotent anger rattling round the rafters overhead. He kicked viciously at the skull, sending it arcing through the air from the top of the great pile to the paved floor far below, where – with a sharp *crack* – it split into two halves.

Outside, the sound of heavy footfalls echoed along the empty streets as a lone figure dressed in an ornate fur-trimmed topcoat and breeches, the metal hook at the end of his left arm glinting in the sun, approached. His face was red and there were beads of sweat on his smooth brow. He glanced up at the magnificent Clan Hall ahead of him, and as he strode towards the door he rubbed his hand round his unfamiliar stubbly jaw, his eyes narrowing coldly as he did so. For a moment he hesitated, gathering himself, then, reaching forward, he seized the door, his eyes blazing, and pulled it open.

'So, there you are!' Kulltuft Warhammer said, climbing to his feet as Firemane Clawhand strode into the main hall. 'What news?'

'News?' said Firemane Clawhand.

'Of my Bloody Blades!' he said. 'When can we expect their return?'

Firemane left the shadowy doorway and crossed the stone floor. Bright shafts of sunlight sliced down from the tall windows to the east, sweeping up his body as he approached the high throne, illuminating his filthy bare feet, his tilderleather breeches and tooled high-buttoned jacket – and his head. Kulltuft's eyes opened wide.

'Earth below and Sky above!' he exclaimed.

Firemane Clawhand's good hand shot upwards. It passed briefly over his badly shaven skull and round the hairless features of his face, the skin scraped and cut.

'What is the meaning of this?' said Kulltuft. 'What's happened to you?'

'Isn't it obvious?' Firemane Clawhand replied icily. 'I've had a close shave, Kulltuft, at the hands of your beloved Hive Militia.'

Kulltuft's heavy brows drew together. 'They did this to you?'

'Only because they couldn't lay their hands on you, Kulltuft, hiding away here in High Town,' Firemane replied sharply.

'How . . . how dare you, Firemane!' the clan chief shouted, his anger getting the better of him. He jumped to his feet and glowered down at his insubordinate underling.

'Dare?' said Firemane Clawhand, looking back at Kulltuft levelly. 'I'll tell you how I dare. You, the High Clan Chief, Kulltuft Warhammer, said we couldn't fail. You said that our militia was invincible; that it would march into the Midwood Decks and claim the sumpwood stands for Hive, with your Bloody Blades and their phraxcannon leading the way. Remember?' He shook his head and laughed humourlessly. 'Oh, they led the way, all right,' he sneered, 'straight into the Great Gladers' trap. Destroyed by the Freeglade Lancers, along with all your precious phraxcannon.'

Kulltuft Warhammer's jaw dropped. 'Destroyed?' he said. 'But you told me that we'd suffered a minor setback, that the Bloody Blades were on their way back to Hive to refit and rally the militia for battles to come . . .'

'Battles to come!' Firemane interrupted him, his contempt echoing around the hall. He snorted. 'I simply told you what you wanted to hear. I learned the truth last night in the Winesap Tavern as those flatheads shaved my face. There won't be any battles to come, not for the Bloody Blades, or you . . .'

'I . . . I . . .' Kulltuft blustered. He strode down the pile of skulls, his heavy staff knocking hollowly against the bone. 'I've done everything I can to—'

'*I'll* tell you what you've done,' said Firemane. 'You've used every phraxcrystal Hive possessed to equip your precious army with phraxmuskets and phraxcannon, and you've destroyed the sumpwood trade . . . What was it you used to say? "We shall deal with Great Glade from a position of strength." A position of strength! By Sky, you have brought the once great city of Hive to its knees – and I have helped you. Well, not any more.'

Kulltuft strode towards Firemane, feathered cape flapping and skull-mounted staff clacking on the stone floor. His eyes blazed with rage. 'Silence!' he roared. 'I've had just about all I—' His gaze fell on the glint of metal as the shaven long-hair pulled his battleaxe from his belt. 'What – what are you doing, Firemane?'

'You've destroyed Hive,' Firemane said, his voice calm once more. '*You!*' The axe glinted in one hand, the hook at the other. 'And the Hive Militia took out their anger on me, as you can see, Kulltuft. As you can see . . .'

Kulltuft Warhammer stared at his chief guard, at the cut and hairless face, at the few glistening tufts of hair on his skull that his attackers had missed.

'You,' said Firemane. 'You did this.'

From outside the Clan Hall came the sound of raised voices and pounding feet. Kulltuft Warhammer stepped back uncertainly, his heels knocking against the broken skull of Hemtuft Battleaxe . . .

The citizens of Hive knew that change was in the air. They had been gathering down on the Sumpwood Bridge since daybreak, arriving from Low Town and the Peak, from the Caves and the Docks, as word had gone round that Kulltuft Warhammer had called a meeting of the Clan Council. There were returning militia, artisans and stevedores, and the shambling ranks of beggars, pauperized by the council's policies, all of them wearing garlands of sapvine leaves or sprigs of grapes, to symbolise their support for change.

Rallying together, they had risen up against their leaders who had led them into a disastrous war, and were marching on the council chambers of High Town. In their midst were the three high councillors themselves, intercepted on their way to the Clan Hall, each one trussed up in lengths of straw matting that pinned their arms to their sides and made escape impossible.

Turgik, the young furrow-brow clan leader of the hammerheads, was looking even more worried than normal. Ragg Yellowtooth, clan leader of the tusked goblins stared around him, his stained teeth glinting in the early sunlight as his gaze fell on the circle of scornful faces. He was trying his best to explain to them that the decisions taken by the Clan Council had not been his; that he'd been forced against his will to support the war – but to no avail. None in the gathering crowds believed a single word the hulking tusked goblin had to say.

'Where were you when we were dying in the Midwood marshes?' a cloddertrog in a grey topcoat shouted, pushing his face into Yellowtooth's own as the tusked goblin staggered forward.

'Living the life of luxury in your mansion in High Town,' added a treegoblin in the bloodstained uniform of the Second Low Town Regiment, shaking his fist.

'While our young'uns starved,' another voice went up. 'And our crops rotted in the fields.'

The crowd surged forward, off the bridge and up the steep winding road of West Ridge.

'Help me! Where are you, my gyles?' wailed Grossmother Meadowdew, tears of self pity gathering in the corners of her eyes and trickling down over the great rolls of fat that hung down her cheeks and jowls. 'Where are you now your grossmother needs you?'

But the crowd around the vast trussed-up figure being forced to climb the steep hill was having none of it.

'The gyles have joined us, Meadowdew!' voices shouted.

'The Gyle Palace has opened its doors and is already sharing its honey!'

Closing her tiny eyes for a moment, Grossmother Meadowdew could almost imagine that she was back in her golden carriage, when adoring crowds had surrounded her every time she set forth for the Clan Hall. They had loved her then, worshipped her, striving to touch one of her wobbling folds of fat for good luck and raining down praise and adulation upon her head.

'May gyle honey drop into our poor mouths,' they had cried out. 'May the golden blessings of the colony flow down to us all.'

But not any longer. Now, she tottered on her gigantic legs, trussed up and bound, scarcely able to understand the change that had come over the citizens.

'But . . . I'm not to blame,' she whispered breathlessly. 'I only did as I was told . . .'

'You could have stood up for us. The poor of Hive. But you didn't!' a harassed-looking crested goblin cried out, her face looming up before the grossmother's. 'Riding among us in your golden carriage, while keeping the doors of the Gyle Palace barred to the needy.'

The crested goblin's face disappeared, to be replaced by another, and then another, their accusing voices full of disappointment and contempt.

'Sky forgive me,' Grossmother Meadowdew murmured softly, the tears coursing down her face. 'I've let you all down . . .'

A loud cry went up as the Clan Hall came into view. It towered above the surging crowd, tall and magisterial, like a vast crown studded with crystal. The carved timbers were silhouetted against the clear blue sky, the windows gleaming in the rising sun.

Once, the mighty goblin Clan Hall had stood for everything that was great about Hive – its industriousness, its clan kinship and co-operation – and the council that had sat within its glazed walls had ruled wisely, bringing stability and prosperity to every one of its citizens. But all that had changed when Kulltuft Warhammer had seized power and turned the city's energies to preparing for war and conquest.

All at once, a dozen or so hammerhead guards appeared from the shadows, phraxmuskets raised. They stood before the great building, staring back at the crowd, which had come to a nervous halt before them.

'Guards!' Ragg Yellowtooth shouted to them. 'Release us!'

One of the guards raised a phraxmusket to his eye and trained it on a tall cloddertrog standing right at the front of the crowd.

'Do what you have to do!' bellowed Ragg.

The guard's finger tightened on the trigger – then relaxed. He tossed the weapon aside and, one by one, the others did the same.

A triumphant roar went up from the crowd. As one, they surged forward once more, swallowing up the guards in their midst as they continued marching on up the steep hill.

'Let us take back what belongs to all of us!' someone shouted. 'Not just the clan chiefs!'

'It is time for a new council!'

'A council for all, not just the few!'

As the rallying cries went up, determined and optimistic, the inhabitants of High Town streamed from their clan huts and longhouses or, pushing tilderleather drapes aside, hung out from overlooking windows, cheering the crowds below. Matrons and money lenders, married old'uns and young couples, and young'uns, their voices high-pitched with excitement, joined the gathering throng as they completed that last stretch of road to the Clan Hall.

'Open the Clan Hall to us!' loud voices demanded, those at the front of the crowd hammering on the tall arched doors, while those at the back surged forward.

'Open the Clan Hall to the New Council!'

'The New Council! The New Council! The New Council!' the cry went up through the crowd at the Clan Hall's great doors.

All at once, cutting across the pandemonium, there came a bloodcurdling scream from inside.

The crowd fell silent, and in the long seconds that followed, individuals exchanged puzzled glances or craned their necks, trying to get a glimpse of what was happening.

Then, out of the unnatural stillness, there came a clatter of wood on metal, followed by a resounding *clang* as the great ironwood bar that had been holding the Clan Hall secure was removed and tossed to the floor. The doors creaked slowly open, and Firemane Clawhand emerged.

'Citizens of Hive,' he called out, ignoring the catcalls and whistles that greeted his words. 'The tyrant, Kulltuft Warhammer, is dead!'

As he spoke, he swung his left arm out from behind his back and held it up high in the air above his shaven head. And there, skewered on the end of his glistening hook, dangled the severed head of Kulltuft Warhammer. The hair was matted and thick with blood, ribbons of leathery skin hung from the neck, while the eyes – those dark deep-set eyes that had filled those whose gaze they fell upon with such fear and dread – stared blindly at the gawping crowd as Firemane twisted the skull round at the end of his hook.

If he had expected cries of joy and gratitude to greet his announcement, the chief guard was to be disappointed. A dark silence hung over the crowd as they stared back. Blood dripped down from the severed head and splashed on the stones below.

'I have killed the High Clan Chief,' Firemane declared, his voice breaking with sudden uncertainty. 'For you, citizens . . . I did it for you . . .'

A goblin corporal stepped forward, the light blue topcoat of the Flathead Guard uniform he wore stained with mud from the battlefield and the blood of his comrades and friends. Firemane recognized him at once as one of the soldiers who had dealt with him so ignominiously in the Winesap Tavern the night before.

'You have learned nothing, Firemane Clawhand,' the flathead goblin declaimed, his deep voice echoing round the gathered crowd, who muttered in solemn agreement.

'But . . . but . . .' the chief guard began.

'The days of summary execution and bloodshed are over in Hive,' the flathead continued, stepping forward and taking Firemane's

arm. 'You shall have a fair trial in front of the New Council.'

'Trial?' blustered Firemane, bewildered, his eyes wide with panic. 'But on what charge?'

The flathead pointed to the severed head dangling from Firemane's hook.

'Murder,' he said.

· CHAPTER SIXTY-EIGHT ·

'It's warm,' said Cirrus Gladehawk, pulling the crushed quarmskin funnel hat from his head and wiping a sleeve across his sweating brow.

'Certainly is,' said the Professor. Undoing the top buttons of his short coat, he looked up at the high sun shining down out of a clear blue sky. 'It's a beautiful day.' He turned to the grey goblin scuttler, who was trotting along behind them. 'Are you sure you're all right with that knapsack, Slip?' he asked.

'Slip's absolutely fine,' the grey goblin replied, his large eyes widening as he nodded enthusiastically. He patted the straps at his narrow shoulders. 'Slip'll take care of friend Nate's knapsack,' he said, 'until he comes back for it himself.'

The three of them left the Sumpwood Bridge behind them and continued along the pitted track, the turbulent river some way to their left, before cutting up through the outer reaches of Low Town. The narrow streets were thronging. It seemed as though everyone in East Ridge was out and about.

They passed through a market square which only the week before had been all but empty, the couple of pinch-faced stallholders there having almost nothing to sell. Now, with the returning militias back tending their fields, the cluster of stalls, with their broad canopies and tasselled umbrellas, were overflowing with local produce, aproned goblins and trogs cheerfully hawking their wares to the bustling crowds buying them.

'Honeybeets, three hivers a bag!'

'Punnets of bluecurrants! Punnets of bluecurrants!'

'Sapgrapes! Sweet juicy sapgrapes. Get your sapgrapes here!'

There were webfoots selling lakefish, slaughterers with glowing braziers selling hammelhorn steaks and tilder sausages, and a gabtroll with boxes of teas and infusions, which she would mix to taste and wrap in brightly coloured paper cones. There were lugtrolls and mobgnomes sitting cross-legged on woven mats, surrounded by rolled-down sacks of pulses and beans; a gnokgoblin matron, her mouth-watering display of honey-drenched pastries glinting in the sunlight.

The Professor paused at a low stall, the tabletop crammed with plump fruit and succulent vegetables, and selected a large juicy-looking red woodapple. Polishing it on his sleeve, he looked across at the grey trog on the other side of the counter.

'How much?' he asked, reaching into the pocket of his breeches.

'For one woodapple?' said the grey trog and smiled. 'Take it, friend.'

'I thank you,' said the Professor, nodding appreciatively and biting into it.

On the far side of the market square, they headed up along a winding cobbled street. There was laughter and song in the air, and the sound of happy voices spilled out from the thatched low shacks and timber longhouses they passed, the shutters of every building flung wide open. A flathead, leaning out of her window to hang up wet washing on the jutting drying racks, waved down at them as they passed by. Twenty strides further on, a couple of cloddertrogs walking down the hill towards them, wished them a cheery 'good day'.

They passed the bathing tub, where a dozen red-faced individuals were luxuriating in the hot fragrant water, chatting animatedly as they were tended to by a family of mobgnomes, who scurried back and forth with glowing brazier stones and cloth pouches of herbs, whistling as they worked.

'Wouldn't mind a bit of a soak myself,' said Cirrus Gladehawk, 'on the way back this evening.'

The Professor smiled and swallowed the mouthful of woodapple he'd been chewing. He pointed up ahead to the Winesap Tavern.

'That's where you'll find me,' he laughed. 'Trying my hand at the gaming tables, just like the old days.'

The inn was heaving, with customers spilling onto the streets outside. As they walked past it, the arched doors swung open and the sound of foot-tapping music from inside abruptly filled the air – above it, the unmistakable cries of an animated game of splinters. A group of flatheads turned towards them, tankards of frothing ale in their hands, which they raised as one.

'To your very good health!' they chorused.

As the three of them continued up the hill, the streets grew narrower and the buildings fewer and farther between. They rejoined the pitted river track just below the gorge, rushing water cascading over the high drop, and looked up to see a small party of Hive Militia standing on the jutting rock above them. The sinister overhanging crane, silhouetted against the sky beyond like a hangman's gibbet, was being swung round. At the end of its jutting crossbeam, a single barrel hung from a length of rope.

Cirrus Gladehawk frowned. 'What's going on?' he said. 'I thought the days of barrelling were over in Hive.'

'So did I,' said the Professor grimly, tossing the woodapple core into the foaming waterfall.

They kept on up the track, arriving at the top of the gorge a minute later, and looked out from behind a tall jagged boulder to where the sound of a commanding voice was coming. There were six uniformed guards in all on the flat rock, their faces glum and sombre. Three were gnokgoblins in the topcoats of the Second Low Town Regiment, two were from the Flathead Guard, while the sixth – his back turned towards them – was a long-hair goblin corporal who, though he still bore the insignia of the Hemtuft Battleaxe Legion, wore it on the sleeve of an underjacket, rather than the sinister black topcoat of the feared Bloody Blades. All of them wore sapvine leaves in their funnel hats and copperwood helmets, the symbol of the New Hive Militia.

It was the long-hair who was talking, his gruff voice ringing out above the background roar of the surging water.

'Firemane Clawhand,' he announced, reading from a length of yellowed barkscroll, 'after a fair trial, you have been found guilty of murder and sentenced to barrelling.'

From inside the barrel, there came the sound of muffled whimpers and pleading cries for mercy.

'By the powers vested in me by the New Council,' the long-hair continued, 'the sentence will now be carried out.'

The pleading became louder. The long-hair rolled up the scroll.

'Release the barrel,' he barked.

The hammerhead stepped forward, his face a frozen mask. He seized the lever on the side of the crane gantry and tugged hard. The rope jerked and the barrel fell. It hurtled down the mighty waterfall, gathering pace as it dropped, until with a loud splintering *crack* it smashed to smithereens on the rocks below. For an instant, the rapids foamed pinky-red, before the water rushed on, sweeping the blood and the dead body of the shaved long-hair along with it.

The corporal straightened up, his face grim. He turned to the others in the small party.

'Dismantle the crane,' he said. 'That's the last barrelling there'll ever be in Hive.'

'The last one, sir?' said a young gnokgoblin as his comrades set to work.

He looked fresh-faced and keen, his uniform smart and new, with polished buttons on his jacket and his breeches, sharply creased. The long-hair turned to face him, his hands on his hips.

'The last one, Tag,' he said earnestly. 'Earth and Sky willing. Firemane Clawhand has paid for his misdeed and it is time now to look to the future.'

'I'm glad to hear it,' said Cirrus Gladehawk as he, the Professor and Slip resumed their journey, leaving the new militia behind.

'Hive is already transformed,' said the Professor, glancing over his shoulder as the terrible barrelling crane came crashing to the ground. 'You can see it in the streets of Low Town and Mid Town. And as for the former clan chiefs . . .' He smiled. 'I hear that Ragg Yellowtooth has had his phraxmusket exchanged for a broom, which he now uses to sweep the streets of High Town. Turgik the furrow-browed, who it transpired was hoarding vast quantities of sapwine, has returned it all to the cave cellars he stole it from, and is out working the vineyards below East Ridge . . .'

'And up at the Peak,' said Cirrus Gladehawk, joining in with his companions' laughter, 'your old friend, Grossmother Meadowdew, and her sisters have opened the Gyle Palace to the poor and needy.'

'Slip knows,' said the grey goblin enthusiastically. 'Slip was there yesterday, collecting a vat of gyle honey for poor Master Galston. Never seen anywhere as grand.'

The Professor nodded, ill-concealed amusement plucking at the corners of his mouth as the three of them continued on towards the glistening lake of Back Ridge.

'It seems they have learned a lesson after all,' he said as they approached the thronging lakeside path. 'I have high hopes for the future of Hive.'

Cirrus nodded. 'A future grounded in the principles of the past,' he said, 'with the clans working together as equals for the good of all the citizens. Why, on a day like today, I could almost imagine retiring here myself, to a nice lakeside mansion with good fishing and a full wine cellar . . .'

The Professor laughed. 'First things first, Cirrus,' he chuckled. 'We've still got work to do!'

As the sun rose above their heads, they continued round Hive lake, its stilthouse-lined shores peppered with whistling webfoot fishermen, dragging in their catch, and young'uns laughing and shouting as they splashed in the shallows and skimmed stones. Taking the right fork at the back of the lake, they headed up into the forest that lined the slopes of Back Ridge, Cirrus removing his hat to mop his brow for the twentieth time and Slip shifting the knapsack on his back.

The track grew narrower, with low branches scraping at their heads, arms and shoulders as they climbed higher. From up ahead, there came the sounds of sawing and hammering and the low mumble of voices, which grew louder as they approached until, emerging in

479

a broad clearing high up at the top of the ridge, a scene of busy industry – out of place in the quiet forest setting – opened up before them.

Directly in front of them was a tall pile of sumpwood boards with the banderbear Weelum, his back turned, sawing them into different lengths. Ropes lay beside him, each one neatly coiled, while a length of hull rigging dangled from the branches of a large broad-leafed bush. Arch-Professor Ignum Spave, High Academe of the Sumpwood Bridge Academy, had been as good as his word, furnishing the archivists with all the materials they'd requested.

Opposite them, on the far side of the clearing, was a tall ironwood pine and, far up at its top, was a skewered phraxship, gleaming in the sunlight. The soft chinking sound of metal on metal blended with the hammering coming from inside the battered timber hull.

480

Cirrus Gladehawk and the Professor stared up at the *Archemax*, noting the changes that had taken place since their last visit. Slip trotted over to greet Weelum.

'Wuh-wuh,' he grunted happily, rolling his paws over and over to show just how busy he had been, then turned to greet Cirrus and the Professor, who nodded back.

'She's certainly coming along,' said Cirrus Gladehawk to the Professor excitedly.

The Professor nodded.

There was still a huge hole in the hull, where the top of the tree had lanced the skyship's hull timbers, but the fore deck had been repaired and the beak-shaped prow restored; and high up above its central deck, the phraxchamber was being worked on. Several of its curved upper panels had been removed to reveal its inner workings, and a spray of jointed struts of bevelled metal glinted in the bright sun.

All at once, a stocky figure in a dark jacket straightened up, a bolt-driver in one hand and a wrench in the other. He reached up and straightened his crumpled funnel hat – and noticed the newcomers down below as he did so.

'Cirrus, Professor, Slip,' Squall shouted down, his deep voice loaded with pride. He laughed throatily. 'Welcome to my new workshop!'

'How's it coming along?' Cirrus called back, his eyes glittering with excitement.

On the aft deck, the mottled and the hairy heads of Klug Junkers and Togtuft Hegg the archivists appeared over the port bow, and beamed down.

'The timberwork's nearly complete,' said Klug. 'We can finish off the last few sections when we've got her airborne.'

'*If* we get her airborne,' said Squall Razortooth. 'Have you got them?'

'Slip's got them here!' said the grey goblin excitedly, shrugging the knapsack from his shoulders.

'Well, what are you waiting for?' said Squall. 'Not much use down there, are they?'

Slip hurried across the clearing to the foot of the ironwood pine and started to climb the tall tree. Cirrus and the Professor followed, leaving only Weelum down on the ground, looking up at them.

'Wuh-wuh,' he murmured. *May Nate's gift bring life to the great skybird.*

High in the upper branches, Togtuft Hegg reached down to help Slip over the port bow and onto the deck. Cirrus and the Professor scrambled aboard after him. They looked around.

'It feels good to be back on board,' Cirrus Gladehawk purred. He stared at the freshly varnished boards, at the gleaming brass bolts, tolley mounts and cleating bars, and the thick white ropes of the hull weights that were threaded through the system of pulleys and cogs beneath the polished bone-handled flight levers. 'She's looking almost as good as the day they launched her, all those long years ago, at the Ledges shipyard.' He reached up and ran a hand lovingly over the bottom of the phraxchamber, a broad grin on his face.

'Come on, then,' said Squall Razortooth. 'Let's see if we can't breathe life into the old girl.'

Slip looked up and nodded, before completing the short climb up the scaffolding supports of the phraxchamber, joining the old sky pirate on a narrow platform. He looked inside the open chamber, his eyes wide with amazement.

'It all looks very complicated,' he said.

'Not to an old engineer like me,' said Squall. His gnarled hands reached inside the innards of the chamber, touching the various parts, one after the other. 'It's a beautiful bit of machinery. Just look at the workmanship in these buoyancy rods,' he said, his fingertips trailing over the metal struts. 'They're hollow and are fixed in position between the cooling plates outside and the explosion chamber at the centre. A thing of beauty . . . This pipe leads to the propulsion duct,' he said, 'and that one to the funnel. And just there is the finest, most delicately tooled phraxlamp you'll ever see,' he said, pointing to a small glowing light screwed into place beside the explosion chamber. 'It ensures that the chamber remains buoyant. And that,' he added, 'is the piston, without which there would be no thrust . . .'

'And where do the phraxcrystals go?' asked Slip.

'Inside the explosion chamber of course,' said Squall Razortooth.

He pushed his right hand deep inside the chamber and unscrewed a couple of bolts on the side of a round globe. A moment later, with a soft *click*, the whole globe came away. He pulled it out into the light and, with Slip peering down at it in wonder, Squall pointed out the different parts.

'This side is solid metal,' he explained, 'with this hole here leading to the thrust pipe. The other side is, as you can see, perforated with tiny holes so that the phraxlamp can shine through, keeping the crystals in a permanent glow . . .' He looked up. 'Shall we put them into place?'

Slip nodded, as excited as a young'un. He held up the knapsack and, with clumsy fingers, undid the buckles. He pulled out the small lightbox, the light of the lamp within glowing through the crack at the closed lid. With trembling fingers, Slip released the catch of the box.

Klug and Togtuft, Cirrus and the Professor looked up from the deck. Far below them all, Weelum yodelled questioningly.

'Patience, old friend,' Squall called down to him.

Slowly, hardly daring to breath, Slip opened the lid of the lightbox. As he did so, the bright sun glinted on the shining crystals and, for a moment the lightbox became all but weightless in Slip's hands. Squall Razortooth removed his hat and held it over the crystals which nestled at the bottom of the box like two chiselled spear tips, casting them in shadow, and Slip felt the phraxcrystals grow heavier. Squall peered down to inspect the crystals more clearly.

'They're magnificent,' he breathed. 'The finest phraxcrystals I've ever seen . . .'

'You think they'll do, then?' the Professor called up from deck.

'Do?' said Squall Razortooth. 'They'll more than do. These two beauties have enough power in them to give the *Archemax* speed and manoeuvrability such as she has never known before – and will easily last for a hundred years!'

'So, what are we waiting for?' cried Cirrus Gladehawk, barely able to contain his excitement. 'Let's try them out.'

Squall Razortooth smiled. Reaching forward, he carefully picked up the first of the phraxcrystals and placed it in the metal globe. Then he placed the second crystal beside it and, tilting the whole globe so that the perforated metal pointed upwards, secured the other half into place and tightened the bolts. Satisfied, he reached back inside the phraxchamber and attached the globe firmly to the central framework. He bent down and retrieved the first of the curved pieces of burnished metal that lay at his feet, and after ensuring that the buoyancy rods were positioned over the holding slots, bolted it into place – then reached down for the second piece . . .

With a grunt of exertion, Squall tightened the last bolt on the final section of the outer casing. Then, having given the duct and funnel, the cooling gears and cooling plates, and everything else one final inspection, he looked down at the others.

'Let's fire her up,' Cirrus Gladehawk said as Squall and Slip climbed down from the phraxchamber.

He turned his attention to the flight levers mounted at the bottom of a series of pipes directly beneath the phraxchamber. It felt good to be standing back at the helm of his phraxship once more. He pulled the left-hand lever towards him. As he did so, there was a muffled explosion from deep inside the great metal globe. A moment later, that single explosion had become a thousand, and the sound a low and sonorous hum. Pushing his funnel hat back on his head, Cirrus seized the central lever . . .

Frowning with concentration, he bit his top lip as he eased the lever slowly back. Steam began to billow from the upper funnel and the hum grew louder. The Professor held his breath. Togtuft and Klug exchanged nervous glances, while Slip – his eyes wide with a mixture of fear and excitement – gripped the side of the bow as the *Archemax* began to tremble and lurch. All at once, there was the sound of creaking wood on wood, and the Professor looked across to see that the top of the great ironwood pine was beginning to disappear through the deck beside him.

'We're rising,' he said.

The ironwood trunk and branches continued to disappear through the shattered boards of the deck as the *Archemax*, quivering and juddering, slowly rose.

'Easy does it,' murmured Squall, his head wreathed in the steam billowing from the funnel.

All at once, with a soft grating sound, the upper needles of the towering trunk grazed the underboards of the hull, the flight weights swung free, and the phraxship finally cast off the tree that had skewered it for so long and soared up into the sky where it belonged.

'She's skyworthy,' Cirrus Gladehawk, captain of the *Archemax* breathed, 'but our work is only just beginning . . .'

· CHAPTER SIXTY-NINE ·

Felftis Brack sat back in the padded sumpwood chair with a contented sigh. Through the high arched doors of the elegant sitting room, he gazed out across the shimmering waters of New Lake. The old Prade Mansion – or rather, the new Brack Mansion – had the most magnificent views.

Hardly surprising, thought Felftis, when you considered that the luxurious villa, with its twenty rooms, lakeside jetty, stables and extensive grounds, was situated in the most sought after location in the whole of the New Lake district. How considerate of his former employer, Galston Prade, to sign this magnificent mansion over to his most faithful chief clerk, together with the phraxmine in the Eastern Woods.

After all, as Felftis had so carefully explained to the Great Glade Council, Galston Prade had no need of the mine *or* the mansion after his sudden retirement to the Gyle Palace of Hive. A smile played over his green-tinged features as he remembered his persuasive words. Why, everyone knew that the restorative powers of gyle honey could work wonders for chronic phraxlung – that and absolute rest, away from the pressures of running the richest phraxmine in the Eastern Woods.

Felftis stretched and yawned extravagantly, his snailskin topcoat creaking as he did so.

What a pity poor Galston Prade's retirement would prove to be so brief, he thought. Any day now, he expected his close associate, Grossmother Meadowdew, to send word confirming that the eminent mine owner had passed away 'peacefully in his sleep' as arranged. Why else had Felftis gone behind his employer's back, fiddled the accounts and supplied the grossmother with phraxcrystals, despite

486

the Great Glade embargo? Now, in return, she would have disposed of the mine owner in that peculiar way they had in the city of Hive, by pushing him over that waterfall of theirs.

What did they call it? Ah, yes . . . Felftis smiled. 'Barrelling', that was it.

'Why Felftis Brack, you sly old lake snail!' He chuckled to himself. 'He never saw it coming . . .'

And why should he? Felftis had worked hard to avoid attention, to fade into the background while making himself indispensable through his administrative skills and attention to detail. Inch by inch, year by year, he'd plotted and schemed and slowly accumulated wealth and power, like a lake snail grazing the silt for mudworms.

And those years of scheming had paid off. First organizing the smuggling of phraxcrystals in the Prade mine, then gaining promotion to chief clerk and making excellent contacts in Hive. Not that he hadn't been busy here in Great Glade. He smiled. Taking that young fool, Branxford Drew, under his wing had proved unexpectedly profitable.

The spoilt brat had sold his birthright to Felftis for a thick wedge of gladers, and one unfortunate accident later, Felftis was the proud owner of a phraxchamber works in the Copperwood district. And now, he thought triumphantly, he also owned the Prade mine – *and* this beautiful mansion. What was more, he had it all to himself, for Galston Prade's troublesome daughter had done him the favour of disappearing with the young lamplighter that Branxford had been so anxious to frame for his father's murder.

Things couldn't have worked out more perfectly.

Why, even this latest dispute with Hive over the Midwood Decks looked as if it would be good for business. With the defeat of the Hive Militia, Grossmother Meadowdew and the other clan chiefs would be desperate for more phraxcrystals to re-arm their forces. Felftis could name his price and, with his smuggling operation set up, the fools in the Great Glade Council would be none the wiser.

Felftis tweaked the tuft of hair that rose like a spike from his forehead with his right hand, and folded his left arm behind his head as he gazed out over New Lake. Yes, life was good . . .

Suddenly, a large cloddertrog appeared in the arched doorway, blocking Felftis's view. He wore the low peaked cap and sapgreen topcoat of a cloddertrog constable and was carrying a stout phraxpistol in one massive hand and a barkscroll in the other.

'Felftis Brack?' the constable enquired.

The chief clerk composed his pale features into a look of polite concern.

'I'm Felftis Brack,' he said, getting to his feet. 'What can I do for you, Constable?'

Behind the cloddertrog were two more in constabulary uniform, together with a tall thin fourthling in the tilderleather topcoat of a librarian scholar.

'I have a warrant for your arrest issued by the Great Glade Council,' the cloddertrog announced, stepping into the sitting room.

'Arrest?' said Felftis coolly, backing away. 'On what charges?'

'Charges of fraud, embezzlement, blackmail, smuggling, false imprisonment, conspiracy to commit murder . . .' the cloddertrog read from the barkscroll in his hand.

'I . . . I don't understand . . .' said Felftis, edging towards the door opposite. 'Galston Prade signed everything over to me. I have the documents signed in his own hand, just before his sad death in Hive—'

'Galston Prade,' said the librarian scholar, stepping into the room, followed by the other two constables, 'is very much alive, and has asked me to inform you that your services as chief clerk are no longer required.'

Felftis's hand closed round the door handle. In an instant, he pulled it open and darted out of the room and down the broad hallway. With the tails of his snailskin topcoat flapping wildly behind him, Felftis Brack, former chief clerk, burst from the front door of the old Prade Mansion and clattered down the white lakestone steps – only to run into a phalanx of burly flathead goblins, thousandsticks in hand.

Seizing the former chief clerk, they hoisted him high above their heads and pounded down the mooring deck which jutted out over the waters of New Lake. At the end of the wooden jetty, with a mighty roar, they threw Felftis Brack high in the air and out over the lake. Moments later, he plunged into the clear waters of New Lake with a resounding *splash*. When he surfaced, coughing and spluttering, his tuft of hair plastered flat across his green-tinged face, Felftis looked up to see the cloddertrog constable approaching the end of the jetty through the throng of cheering flatheads. The constable raised the arrest warrant.

'. . . And non-payment of the New Lake thousandsticks team,' he read.

· CHAPTER SEVENTY ·

'Is somebody there?' came a cracked and ancient voice, and the gaunt figure who had uttered the words paused on the rocky slope rising up from the fringes of the Garden of Life at Riverrise, and looked stiffly around him.

He was sure he'd heard someone. Or something. What was more, it had sounded familiar, cutting through the centuries and stirring long-forgotten memories. He reached up, pushing aside the white beard that hung down over his bony chest, and rubbed his shoulder, which would twinge with pain whenever something reminded him of the past, so long ago and far away.

'I said, is somebody—'

All at once there was a great flurry of wings, and as he looked up, a mighty caterbird swooped over the crest of rock ahead and landed on one of the circle of pointed pinnacles that surrounded the turquoise lake below. He stepped forward, his limpid green eyes gleaming brighter than they had for hundreds of years.

'You,' he whispered.

'Yes, it is I,' the caterbird replied. It folded its vast wings, the black feathers gleaming blue and purple in the bright sunlight, as its long tail feathers – striped black and white – balanced its perch. It turned its head till the hooked bill and ridged crest were silhouetted against the bright sky, a single beady eye staring.

'You have come back,' the figure stated.

'I have come back,' said the caterbird, nodding. 'You were at my hatching, and I have watched over you always . . .'

· CHAPTER SEVENTY-ONE ·

The City of Night it may have been called, but though it was enfolded in the permanent darkness of the surrounding Nightwoods, the constellations of brightly shining lamps that covered the Riverrise mountain ensured that the inky blackness was kept at bay.

Huge globes mounted on tall, elegantly carved posts lined every street and walkway and formed serpentine ribbons of brightness that meandered through the city's crowded ledges. Countless more lamps – vast opalescent glass spheres, glowing with the intensity of miniature suns – crowned the roofs and gables of every building, while the spaces between them were festooned with yet more, dangling from thick vinerope cables. And from the buildings themselves still more light streamed out from the tall arched windows, each one lit up by the multitude of lamps blazing inside.

High up at the mountain's peak, obscured from view by dark, swirling clouds, was the fabled Riverrise spring, situated in the Garden of Life. Kobold's Steps, an ancient winding staircase hewn from the rock, led up to this forbidden place, its lower reaches guarded by the massive fortress known simply as the keep.

Below, on the rock ledges and lower slopes, the twinkling clusters of lamps marked out the various districts of this, the third of the three great cities of the Edge. There was Kobold's Mount, home to the gabtrolls, with its magnificent lamphouses; the Market Ledges, with their bustling shops and candlelit stalls; the waif districts of North and South Cliff, each of them decked out with forests of lantern posts; and the bustling cosmopolitan districts of Under Mount and the Low Ledges, their streets lined with guesthouses and hospices, and home to the city's most diverse communities. These lower districts fringed the Nightwoods on the mountain's western slopes below Kobold's Mount, with the vast bowl of the stone amphitheatre nearby.

For centuries, in this huge open air auditorium, it had been the custom for the waifs, gabtrolls and other Riverrisers to congregate. Here, grievances had been aired, disputes settled and issues debated. But today this was the one place in the great lamp-filled city that lay unlit and empty, such was the all-pervasive power of Golderayce One-Eye and the custodians of Riverrise.

But it wasn't the tall lantern posts, the magnificent lamphouses, or even the great dark amphitheatre that commanded the attention of the visitor to Riverrise. The most extraordinary sight in this most extraordinary of the three great cities was the Riverrise waterfall, which flowed down out of the darkness like a glistening strand of spidersilk. Falling from the lip of the lake that was fed by the Riverrise spring far above the dark clouds, this glowing column of water cascaded down the east face of the mountain into the aqueduct below.

Of all the strange and magnificent buildings in the City of Night, the aqueduct was the most important, for it was here that the life-giving waters were collected and dispensed to the inhabitants of Riverrise. Once, the waterfall had flowed in a constant steady stream, and the city had grown and prospered with the arrival of visitors desperate to avail themselves of its healing properties. But Golderayce One-Eye had not been slow to grasp the power that control of the waters could give him and, with his feared custodians, had strictly regulated the flow.

After all, the Custodian General reasoned, the Riverrise spring was his to do with as he saw fit, and any Riverriser who didn't like this fact could leave. And if they didn't, well, then there were other ways to deal with troublemakers: Golderayce's hand-picked waif assassins, for example . . .

The latest visitors to Riverrise, a small party consisting of two gabtrolls, two fourthlings – one lying on a sumpwood stretcher – and a waif guide, passed through the towering Nightwood Arch and entered the city. The waif guide bowed low and, bidding his charges a soundless farewell, hurried off, back the way he'd come. With the two gabtrolls leading, and one of the fourthlings – the tether of the buoyant stretcher still tightly clasped in his hand – following close behind, the four weary travellers left the great illuminated archway behind them and headed along the lamp-lined road into the City of Night.

Nate Quarter was more tired than he had ever been in his life. His legs felt as heavy as leadwood; his head, lighter than sumpwood.

The streets were thronging. There were waterwaifs, ghostwaifs, mottled and grey waifs, blackwaifs and bloodwaifs scurrying silently past, lamps glowing from the ends of stout staffs or dangling from their belts, or sometimes strapped to their chests. Despite the crowds, it was eerily quiet for a non-waif visitor. For though the waifs clustered together round stalls, in doorways, or walked side by side in twos and threes, their heads nodding as if deep in conversation, Nate heard not a single word.

It felt, he thought, almost as though he was walking through a dream.

Even as that thought formed in his head, he noticed how the ears of the waifs he passed trembled and flexed; how some of them turned their heads towards him, looks of wry amusement on their flat wide-eyed faces. And Nate knew that they could hear his thoughts as clearly as if he'd shouted them from the lamp-lined rooftops.

The four travellers skirted round the foot of a vast building constructed of hundreds of stone pillars and vaulted arches. Nate looked up to see a twisting thread of water, seemingly emerging out of the darkness far above his head and splashing down into the long causeway which the stone pillars supported. Spouts branched out from this ornately carved trough at regular intervals, channelling the precious water into vast stone vats beneath, with shining brass taps in the form of grinning flitterwaif heads at the base. By each of these taps, surveying the long queues, stood a diminutive waif custodian in dark shimmering robes, clutching a long blowpipe.

'The great aqueduct gets crowded at highflow,' whispered Gomber as they hurried past.

Everywhere, there were lamps and, Nate realized, it wasn't only light they were giving off, but also warmth – soft comforting warmth which gradually dispelled the chill that had set into his bones in the cold dank Nightwoods.

Shortly after the aqueduct, the gabtrolls turned left. Nate found himself on a steep path that wound its way up the mountainside between glowing lamphouses – tall spacious mansions of glass held together by a pale tracery of timber struts and arches. Each one glowed from within, lit by clusters of lamps, like bunches of sparkling sapgrapes.

'This is . . . *slurp* . . . Kobold's Mount,' said Gilmora, panting slightly as she turned to Nate, her lampstaff raised. She gestured towards the buildings all round them. 'It is home to the gabtroll apothecaries, and is where the finest medicines of Riverrise are . . . *slurp* . . . concocted. Potions and tonics. *Slurp slurp*. Unguents, balms . . .'

'Have gabtrolls always lived in the Nightwoods?' asked Nate, staring at the pathways full of the stooped and stalk-eyed trolls, carrying covered baskets and lampstaffs.

'No, no,' said Gomber, nodding in greeting to a young gabtroll as she passed them by, a basket overflowing with herbs hanging from the crook of her arm. 'We were daylighters originally, but we settled here once the Waif Trail was completed.'

'We gabtrolls have always understood the art of healing,' Gilmora told him. 'Our apothecaries and . . . *slurp* . . . apothecaresses once travelled the Deepwoods in prowlgrindrawn wagons, dispensing medicaments to all who needed them. When the route to Riverrise was created, however, my ancestors . . . *slurp slurp* . . . made a permanent home here – and, thanks to the restorative waters, the medicines and cures they produce here are . . . *slurp* . . . ten times more efficacious. Or rather,' she added under her breath, slurping as she spoke, 'they *were*, before that Custodian General, Golderayce One-Eye, began to limit the supply . . .'

'Gilmora,' Gomber chided his wife, his eyestalks swinging round warily as he looked to see whether any waifs might have overheard her seditious thoughts.

'Well!' she muttered, and slurped indignantly. 'It's a disgrace, so it is . . .'

'The name . . . *slurp* . . . of the district has an interesting origin,' Gomber broke in a second time, anxious to move the subject on to something less contentious. 'You may have heard of . . . *slurp* . . . Kobold the Wise,' he ventured.

Nate shook his head.

'I must say, you surprise me, lad,' said Gomber, shaking his own head in turn. 'Kobold the Wise was the legendary leader who united the Deepwoods into "the thousand tribes" and, or so the story goes, discovered the Riverrise spring and built the original Garden of Life around it. That was long before even the First Age of Flight, but it was a time, according to fireside tales, of peace and harmony . . .'

'Not like these days,' muttered Gilmora, 'when Golderayce claims the spring as his own . . .'

Tutting softly under his breath at his wife's indiscretion, Gomber raised his lampstaff and pointed to a mansion just up ahead. Unlike all those surrounding it, it was dark inside.

'Here we are,' he announced, stepping forward to open the circular door of pale, polished wood and ushering Nate inside. 'Welcome to our humble lamphouse.'

'I'll just see to the lamps,' said Gilmora, following them in and closing the door behind her.

Letting go of the stretcher tether, Nate watched as the gabtroll scuttled round the magnificent lamphouse, firing up the clusters of globe phraxlamps, setting the huge central darkelm oil lamps ablaze and lighting the forest of tall tallow candles that ringed the upper gallery.

Supported on a series of thin elegant pillars, the lamphouse was tall and hexagonal. Each of its six walls was glazed with a tall arched window, the angled walls between them lined with cupboards and ledges. A spiral staircase was set into the centre of the spacious timber floor.

As Gilmora slowly climbed the wooden steps, she lit the jutting

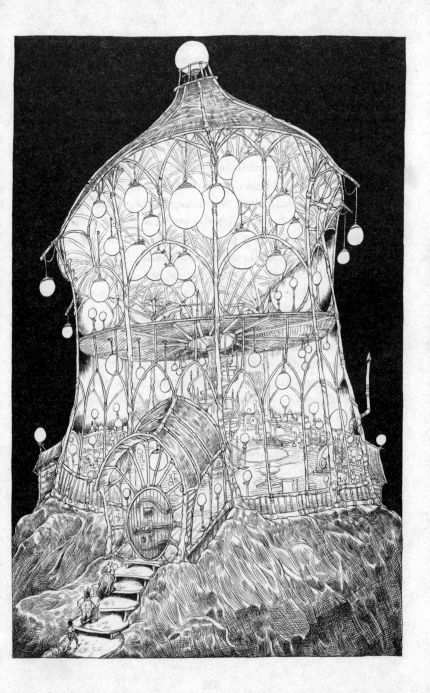

lamps that clung to its central column, one by one, illuminating the intricate joinery of the turning stairs, the circular upper gallery and the complex fan vaulting in the ceiling high above. The whole building – as well as the simple furniture that filled it – had been constructed from the same timber, gathered from the surrounding Nightwoods. Clearwood, Gomber called it. It was hard and, Nate saw as the light caught it, almost translucent.

Behind him, Gomber had removed his and his wife's sumpwood backpacks from the stretcher and placed them on a low table. Then, taking up the tether, he had pulled the stretcher to the far side of the great six-sided chamber, where a pot-bellied stove nestled in a shallow hollow in the floor. Gomber tied the stretcher to a curved hook on the wall beneath a large glowing lamp and stood gazing down at Eudoxia. Despite the lamp glow, she didn't stir from her deep sleep and, Nate saw with a renewed pang of unease, she looked thinner and paler than ever.

'I've prepared a sleeping chamber . . . *slurp* . . . for young Nate,' Gilmora announced as, with one hand gripping the sweeping banister, she headed back down the stairs. 'I'll get the stove lit . . . *slurp* . . . and see about something to refresh us all.' She turned to Gomber. 'Why don't you go and call on the healer. It's late,' she added, 'but . . . *slurp slurp* . . . if you tell him we have urgent need of his help . . .'

'I'm already on my way,' said Gomber, slurping noisily as he crossed the floor.

As the gabtroll old'un closed the door behind him, Gilmora turned to Nate.

'How's . . . *slurp* . . . our patient doing?' she asked.

Nate shrugged. 'It's hard to tell,' he said wearily.

'A nice cup of bristleweed tea, that's what we need,' said the gabtroll.

Nate nodded – but suddenly found himself yawning, long and deep. He rubbed his eyes.

'Oh, but you must be exhausted, Nate,' Gilmora said. 'Why don't you go and lie down.' She smiled. 'You've proven yourself to be a true and loyal friend, Nate, but really there's nothing more you can do until the healer's looked at her.'

Nate made no argument. Crossing the room, he said goodnight to Gilmora, who laughed.

'There's no day or night to mark the passing of the hours here,' she chuckled. 'In the old days, we used the burning down of a tallow candle, but now it's the Riverrise spring we set store by . . . I'll wake you at highflow!'

Too tired to reply, Nate dragged himself up the circular stairs. All round him, the multitude of lamps hissed and fizzed, and the air was laced with the smells they gave off – the sweet aromatic fragrance of burning darkelm oil and the tang of toasting almonds from the phraxlamps. It was so bright that, as he climbed those last few steps to the circular balcony, with the light streaming out of the arched windows round him, Nate felt as though he was inside a giant lantern.

'Your sleeping chamber's to the right,' Gilmora called up to him. 'Good sleep, Nate Quarter, and pleasant dreams . . .'

The chamber was in an alcove off the landing of the upper gallery, and had hooks behind the circular door to hang his clothes on. Nate pulled off his boots, his breeches and the green tilderleather jacket that Zelphyius Dax had let him keep, and hung them up, before climbing into the low sumpwood cot that hovered above the floor. On the soft patchwork quilt, he found a black sleeping cap, which he placed on his head and, pulling it down over his eyes to shut out the lampglow, Nate let his head sink down into the pillow. Stuffed with woodduck down and dried herbs, whose heady aroma was released as the fragments of leaf and seed were crushed beneath his head, it was sweet and fragrant and soft; so very very soft . . .

When Nate awoke from a deep dreamless sleep, he felt refreshed and clear-headed. Leaning up on one elbow, he looked out of the arched upper windows of the lamphouse at the glittering lights of Riverrise outside. High overhead, beyond the glow of the city, was the blackness of the unending night.

He became aware of whispers coming from downstairs, urgent and sibilant.

'Eudoxia,' he breathed.

Getting up, Nate dressed quickly and hurried down the stairs into the brightly lit chamber below. Eudoxia was lying on the sumpwood stretcher over by the pot-bellied stove, which was now softly glowing, a large cauldron of steaming water bubbling on its top. Clustered round her were three stooped figures; Gilmora and Gomber, the old gabtrolls, and a third individual, who Nate had not seen before, who was wrapping a length of bandage around Eudoxia's head.

'Ah, Nate,' said Gilmora, looking up. 'You were sleeping so peacefully, I didn't have the heart to wake you.'

'How is Eudoxia?' Nate asked.

Gilmora took his arm and patted it reassuringly. 'Healer Barkscale is one of our city's most respected metaphysicians,' she said. 'He has done all he can for your young friend . . .'

On hearing his name, the healer straightened up and turned, and Nate found himself looking at a short stout waterwaif with scaly green skin, huge fanned ears and pale orange eyes that were magnified by the wire-rimmed spectacles perched at the end of his stubby upturned nose. Beneath his bloodstained apron, Nate saw that he was wearing neatly pressed calf length trousers and a black waistcoat. A long gold chain attached to one of the waistcoat's bone buttons disappeared into an upper pocket

'This is . . . *slurp* . . . the visitor I was telling you about, Healer Barkscale,' said Gilmora. 'Nate. *Slurp*. Nate Quarter.'

Barkscale nodded, the lamplight glinting on the glass of his spectacles. '*You have travelled far to bring young Eudoxia here*,' he said, the voice in Nate's head soft and soothing. He wiped his hands on his apron.

Nate nodded.

'*And you have tended to her diligently and tirelessly on the journey*,' the healer acknowledged, the barbels at the corners of his mouth twitching, '*keeping the wound clean and well bandaged*,' he added. '*If *it hadn't been for you, Nate, Eudoxia would not have survived the Battle of the Midwood marshes.'* The waif healer shook his head. *'As it is, it's still touch and go.'*

Nate swallowed hard. This was not what he had wanted to hear.

'I have removed the leadwood bullet,' Healer Barkscale's whispering voice continued, *'that was slowly taking her life.'*

He reached round for a small bowl perched on the jutting ledge behind him, and held it out. Nate looked down at the gleaming piece of metal, its pointed end blunted and its casing still bearing traces of blood – Eudoxia's blood – and his stomach churned.

'But it has caused much damage,' the healer was saying, removing his spectacles and polishing them thoughtfully on a corner of his waistcoat, before returning them. *'Damage which will not be easy to heal,'* he added. *'I have looked deep into*

Eudoxia's mind,' he said, tugging at the gold chain and pulling a round timepiece from his waistcoat pocket, which he squinted at short-sightedly, *'where her spirit – her life force – has retreated from the terrible pain, like a forest creature seeking refuge from a raging storm . . .'*

'She's going to be all right, isn't she?' Nate interrupted.

'Only time will tell,' said the healer, glancing down at his patient, before looking back at Nate. *'Her life force is very weak, but if the healing powers of the medicines here in Riverrise ease the pain, Eudoxia might return to us.'*

'I'll do anything,' said Nate. 'Just tell me . . .'

'It's all right, Nate,' Gilmora reassured him. She pulled a small piece of barkscroll from her apron and held it up in the lamplight. 'Healer Barkscale here has already suggested a course of treatment.' She frowned and squinted at the list. 'Hylesalve,' she read out. 'Tincture of nightoil. Bitter woodaloes – for her fever. And of course,' she added, looking up, 'a vial of spring water from the aqueduct.'

'I'm afraid such things are expensive,' said the healer, the dark green barbels twitching uncomfortably, *'but these days, all medicaments requiring spring water are increasingly costly . . .'*

'I'll pay, whatever the cost,' said Nate stoutly. He reached into the pocket of his dark grey military breeches and pulled out a thin folded bundle of notes, the last of his gladers.

'Now you put that away at once, Nate Quarter!' said Gilmora indignantly. 'After the kindness you showed to me and Gomber on the Waif Trail, we wouldn't dream of letting you pay so much as a single brass glimmer.'

'But . . . but what about Healer Barkscale's services?' Nate protested. 'I can't expect you to—'

'The healer's fee has already been taken care of,' said Gomber, and at his side the waterwaif nodded earnestly as he patted the lower pocket of his waistcoat.

'Besides,' Gilmora added, 'Healer Barkscale, like all the best metaphysicians in Riverrise, charges only what he senses his patients can afford for his services – unlike those custodians . . . So you put that money of yours back in your pocket, and let's the pair of us go into the city and see about these medicines Eudoxia needs.'

She seized a thick shawl from the back of a straight-backed chair and wrapped it round her shoulders, picked up a basket with a tilderleather cover from the floor and a glass vial from the shelf, then strode purposefully across the pillared chamber to the door. Nate held back a moment, stealing one last look at his sleeping friend. Her face seemed to have more colour in it now, and her breathing was low and even. He turned and, reaching out, shook the waterwaif healer's hand, surprised by how warm and dry it felt.

'Thank you,' he said.

The healer smiled, his pale orange eyes glistening. '*I've done all I can,*' he said. Reaching round behind his back, he untied the strings and pulled the bloodstained apron up over his head. '*The rest,*' he said, looking at Nate, '*is up to your friend.*'

Nate nodded, trying not to let the worry show on his face, then turning on his heel he crossed the floor and followed Gilmora out of the lamphouse and onto the bustling pathway outside. As he turned to shut the door behind him, he heard Gomber calling to him from the other side of the room.

'And mind what you're thinking out there in the city, Nate Quarter,' he said, and slurped. 'As we say here in Riverrise, "thoughts speak louder than words".'

With Gilmora the gabtroll bustling along by Nate's side, the basket swinging from her arm, the pair of them made their way down the winding lamplit path through Kobold's Mount. All round, the pathways were busy with waif healers, gabtroll apothecaries and others; lugtroll porters, gnokgoblin merchants, grey trog traders, all going about their business.

'We should head to the aqueduct first,' said Gilmora. 'Before . . . *slurp* . . . the queues get too long.'

They turned right at the bottom of the mount then, after a short way, right again and began climbing a series of wide, yet shallow, steps. On one side, Nate saw clusters of tall elegant lamphouses with covered balconies – and as he climbed higher, he soon found himself drawing level with their rooftops, the huge globes of

503

dazzling light mounted upon the ridge tiles and gables too bright to look at directly. On the other side of the steps, the arched pillars of the vast water channel he had seen before rose up and towered over them. A rusting plaque high above Nate's head bore the words,

Erected by the Grateful Engineers of Great Glade and Hive, in Thanks to the Healers of Riverrise, in this, the 247th Year of the Third Age.

Beneath the channel, on a vast terrace, long queues had formed in front of the stone vats that collected the water. Grabbing Nate by the arm, the gabtroll chose a queue seemingly at random and joined the end of it.

'Once, the Riverrise spring flowed freely down the mountain,' whispered Gilmora sadly. 'These days, though . . .' She shook her head. 'The water is strictly rationed by the custodians, and,' the gabtroll said, her voice low and hushed, 'Golderayce One-Eye. Sky love and protect him,' she added loudly.

Nate stood on his tiptoes and looked over the heads of the waifs, trogs, goblins and trolls who were standing patiently in line before them. 'This is a *short* queue, is it?' he said.

'As short as it ever gets these days,' said Gilmora with a sigh. 'Sometimes it extends all the way down the steps and back along the road halfway to the amphitheatre . . .'

Slowly – painfully slowly – the two of them shuffled forward as newcomers joined the line behind them. Gilmora reached out and took Nate's hand in her own, and squeezed it. She peered into his face, her eyes trembling at the end of their stalks.

'Your friend, Eudoxia, is strong, Nate,' she said gently. 'She must be to have stayed alive so long. She won't leave us without a fight.'

Nate nodded, hoping that the gabtroll was right. They shuffled forward another half stride . . .

Tall globe lamps, their stanchions richly ornamented with fluted struts and twisting curlicues, lined the wall of the aqueduct, testifying to a grander past. Now, as they shone down on the paltry flow of water that trickled from the spouts into the vats, they served only as a reminder of all that had changed.

All at once, the still and brittle air exploded with squabbling voices, and Nate peered over the heads in front to see two gabtrolls squaring up to one another.

'It's not too big . . . *slurp* . . .' one of them was complaining. 'My little pot is . . . *slurp* . . . exactly the right size.'

'*Little* pot!' the other exclaimed. 'It's . . . *slurp* . . . twice the size of mine – which holds *precisely* the amount of water we're . . . *slurp* . . . allowed . . .'

'*Silence!*' hissed a furious voice inside Nate's head – and everyone else's – and he saw a waif custodian striding towards the bickering gabtrolls, his long shimmering robes sweeping over the stone flags, a blowpipe in one hand and a lampstaff in the other.

'Uh-oh,' muttered Gilmora. '*Slurp* . . . Watch your thoughts!'

The custodian thrust his glowing lampstaff into the terrified faces of the two gabtrolls. He looked at one of them, then the other, their eyestalks retracting as he did so.

'*How dare you raise your voices!*' he demanded.

'It was her!' one of them squawked. 'Her pot's too big . . .'

'Me? She's just jealous because I know the rules . . .'

'*SILENCE!*' The cry was so loud it left Nate's head spinning. '*To the back of the queue,*' the waif custodian told them. '*Go, the pair of you!*' he said to the distraught-looking gabtrolls. '*In silence!*'

The pair turned and Nate watched them, their faces downcast as they shuffled past him and Gilmora on their way to the back of the line.

Finally, half an hour later, Gilmora and Nate reached the front of the now completely silent line. The gabtroll knew the procedure, and Nate stood back as she pulled a wad of waifmarks from beneath the folds of her shawl, peeled off ten and placed them in the outstretched palm of the waif custodian who sat on a low stool beside the stone vat. The waif kept his hand out. Gilmora counted off more notes, adding a further three, four, five waifmarks before the custodian was satisfied. Then, crouching down, she removed the glass vial from her basket, placed the neck of it under the lip of the grinning waif head that jutted out from the

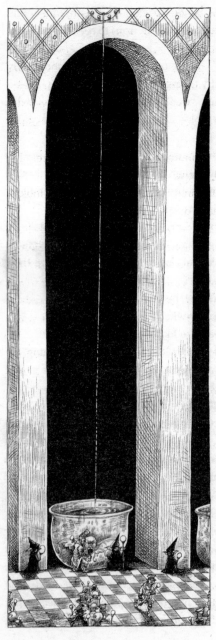

bottom of the vat, and the custodian pulled down on a brass barbel at the mouth.

A thin trickle of water poured down into the vial, the tinkling sound rising in pitch as it slowly filled. Nate watched, holding his breath as the precious healing water rose to the top. When it was full, the custodian turned off the barbel-shaped spigot. Gilmora put a cork stopper in the vial and straightened up.

'Come, Nate,' she whispered, beaming happily as she returned the small glass bottle to her basket and pulled the tilderleather cover back in place. 'May the custodians . . . *slurp* . . . be praised for their generosity.'

The waif dismissed them with a wave of his thin pale hand, barely tolerating Gilmora's whispered blessing. Seemingly oblivious to this, the gabtroll strode onto the end of the aqueduct terrace and, where the path divided, took the right-hand fork.

Narrow and all but deserted, this track, hewn from the solid stone below, took them over a massive bluff of rock so sheer that nothing had been built upon it. Below them were the glowing roof lamps and gable lanterns of Kobold's Mount, while far above their heads, Nate noticed a huge beacon of light blazing from the top of a tall round windowless fortress, an adjoining tower behind it.

'That's the keep,' said Gilmora, following Nate's gaze. 'It's *slurp* . . . where Gomber and I work.'

Her eyestalks swung round in different directions as she looked to see if they were being observed.

'Golderayce One-Eye, our . . . *slurp* . . . beloved master, lives up there,' she announced in a brittle bright-sounding voice. 'From the keep, he rules our great city as wisely as the legendary Kobold himself, allowing . . . *slurp slurp* . . . no one to pass beyond it to the Garden of Life, on pain of death.' Satisfied there were no waifs in sight, Gilmora added in a whisper, 'Keeps the most potent water – from the lake's edge – strictly for . . . *slurp* . . . himself.'

'But the aqueduct water is good, isn't it?' said Nate with a frown.

'Just what the healer ordered,' said Gilmora, taking Nate by the arm and smiling reassuringly.

On the far side of the bluff, the narrow track fanned out into a series of broader paths, some leading up to the left, where lamphouses and rambleshacks clung to the steep sides of the mountain; some returning down to Kobold's Mount – while some continued into a bustling area of stepped terraces, each one clustered with buildings with pointed arch windows and broad sweeping roofs, and ablaze with huge globelamps.

Gilmora took Nate's hand and led him up a narrow staircase from one terrace to another, and then up to the next. At the fifth terrace they came to, she paused and looked round, her eyestalks quivering inquisitively as they swung this way, then that – before focusing in on Nate's face.

507

'This is the one,' she said. 'Some of the markets . . . *slurp* . . . sell only goods brought into Riverrise by merchants and traders from the Deepwoods,' she explained. 'This one, the Waif Terrace Market, is devoted solely to those waifs . . . *slurp* . . . who have produce to sell.'

Nate looked up – and his jaw dropped open in surprise.

Fringing the bustling market square were lines of highstalls, each one mounted precariously upon clearwood timber stilts, and with a narrow wooden flight of translucent stairs leading up to their individual wooden shelves. Glistening canopies fluttered in the light breeze above the highstalls, their shelves full of merchandise.

The air was heavy with pungent aromas – from the acrid tar-like odour of pine resin to the overpowering fragrance of moonflowers, sooty toadflax and mossy feverfew, bristleweed and soapwort, and the intense peppery smell of firenettle; all of them mixing together in ever-shifting combinations . . .

Yet it wasn't the sights that bewildered Nate, nor the swirling array of smells, but the din! A hundred different waif voices filled Nate's head.

'*Finest healing balm!*'

'*Soothing cough syrups, second to none!*'

'*Tonics, cordials and herbal infusions! Tonics, cordials and herbal infusions!*'

'*Patent ague embrocation!*'

Nate clamped his hands over his ears, only for the insistent voices inside his head to grow even louder.

'This way,' said Gilmora, shouting above the cacophony of voices. She pointed to a highstall in the far corner. 'We'll find just . . . *slurp* . . . what we need there.'

They crossed the market square, pushing their way through the crowds of goblins and trogs who were, themselves, struggling to hear one another above the waif voices in their heads. Nate looked up as they reached the highstall, to find himself behind several gnokgoblins, a mobgnome and a portly cloddertrog matron. Trying to ignore the cacophony in his head, Nate hummed tunelessly to himself as they waited to be served.

'*Gilmora.*' The voice of the ghostwaif stallholder sounded in both their heads when their turn came. '*I haven't seen you for an age! You've brought a friend, I see.*'

'I've been in the daylight, Garrafuce,' Gilmora replied. 'Visiting . . . *slurp* . . . relatives in the Deepwoods. This is Nate. He is a visitor with a sick friend,' she said, slurping twice as she pulled the healer's barkscroll note from her apron and handed it to the ghostwaif.

He blinked at it once, then smiled.

'*Healer Barkscale,*' he said to Nate. '*Your friend is in good hands, daylighter.*'

Quickly and efficiently, his long thin fingers darting up to the shelves around him, the ghostwaif assembled the items on the list.

'*Tincture of nightoil, hylesalve, bitter woodaloes . . .*' his sibilant voice sounded in Nate's mind. '*Of course, you have water from the spring?*'

Nate nodded, and Gilmora pressed a handful of waifmarks into the ghostwaif's outstretched hand.

'*Golderayce One-Eye and the custodians be praised!*' the ghost waif's voice sounded in Nate's head, together with an under-thought, low but distinct. ***May he choke on the chine that preserves him!***

Nate and Gilmora climbed down the ladder, their places taken by a couple of pink-eye goblin parents, the husband clutching a young'un, nothing but skin and bones, tightly to his chest.

'It's our Tallis,' he heard the mother saying. 'He won't eat . . .'

Nate turned to Gilmora. 'What is chine?' he asked as they hurried back in the direction of Kobold's Mount.

'Chine is the sparkling sediment found on the shore of the Riverrise lake,' said Gilmora, clutching the basket tightly. 'It's what makes the water gathered there so potent . . .'

'And this potent water,' Nate continued, his eyes glistening, 'could it cure Eudoxia?'

Gilmora stopped in her tracks and seized Nate by the shoulders, her eyes on the end of their stalks staring at him intently from both sides.

'Water from the Riverrise lake could save Eudoxia's life,' she whispered. 'But getting it would cost you yours!'

· CHAPTER SEVENTY-TWO ·

Nate hurried through the crowded streets at the foot of Kobold's Mount. They were as eerily quiet and brightly lit as all the other parts of this strange city, but because this was a district given over to visitors or 'daylighters', there were few waif whispers to invade his thoughts.

So different, Nate realized, from the constant clamour that filled his head in the Market Ledges high above, or at times in the queues at the aqueduct.

Though few in the great city ever spoke louder than a whisper, the waif voices that filled Nate's head in the other districts of Riverrise proved far more tiring than the clatter of the Copperwood stiltshops of Great Glade, or the cries of the market traders of Hive.

'You'll get used to it, my dear,' Gilmora had reassured Nate.

But he didn't think he ever would. Though, in recent highflows, he'd had plenty of practice as he queued for the Riverrise water and haggled for medicaments in the Market Ledges.

That was another thing Nate had struggled with. The fact that there were no days or nights in Riverrise, where the constant darkness was kept permanently at bay by a million lamps. Instead, there were 'highflows' when the waterfall flowed down into the aqueduct at a higher rate, and 'lowflows' when it slowed to the merest trickle, as the custodians of the Riverrise spring opened and closed the sluice gates, high up above the city. At lowflow the Riverrisers tended to sleep, while at highflow – such as it was – the streets filled with the strangely quiet crowds and the constant chatter of waif whispers. Nate had endured a week of this endless brightly lit night as Eudoxia's condition remained as unchanging as the lamp glow.

'No better,' said Gilmora, sending Nate out once more into the streets to collect water and medicine, 'but thank Sky and Earth, no worse.'

Nate bobbed and weaved in and out of the crowds in the lamp-lit streets. They came from all four corners of the Edgelands. There were strange mobgnomes from the Northern Reaches with coils of purple-tinged hair plaited and piled high on their heads; bark gyles from the Edgeriver swamps, their faces as gnarled and grainy as waterlogged timber; curious long-faced tree trolls from the distant west, with their huge spider-like fingers and intricately knotted shawls; and a thousand more . . .

Some took their cures and returned to their far-off homes, while others stayed and settled in this strange city for reasons Nate could only guess at. They congregated in the Under Mount and Low Ledge districts, which lay closest to the Nightwoods, and so were less popular with the waifs and gabtrolls who formed the majority of Riverrise's population. Their lamphouses and clearwood cabins were shabby by comparison with the buildings on Kobold's Mount and the Higher Ledges, but at least here there was a respite from the intrusive waif whispers.

Nate reached the end of Low Ledge, and was about to climb the steep path that led up towards Kobold's Mount when he paused. On the other side of the paved street, steps led down to the great bowl of the amphitheatre which, Nate saw, was now illuminated by thousands of shimmering, swaying lampstaffs.

Nate had passed the amphitheatre regularly on his way back to Kobold's Mount at the end of highflow, but the ancient gathering place – where, before the tightening power grip of Golderayce One-Eye and his feared custodians, the waifs and daylighters of Riverrise had met in the forum to discuss and debate – had always been dark and empty. Now it was as if the great open air auditorium had been invaded by a swarm of fireflies. Intrigued, Nate raised the lampstaff he carried – Gomber's second best – and descended the steps.

The eight stone tiers of the enormous amphitheatre were bustling with waifs from all over the city, their huge feathery ears fluttering, whiplash barbels quivering and enormous eyes flitting from face to face. Apart from the swishing of robes and the agitated tapping of lampstaffs, the whole place was silent. Nate found a place next to several gabtrolls and a hunched creature with tiny eyes and vivid black and white blotches covering his face and hands.

Unlike the Market Ledges, where the waifs broke into the thoughts of passers-by to sell their potions, here in the amphitheatre, the situation was quite different. The waifs seemed intent on reading only each other's thoughts, speaking directly, yet secretively, one to the another, in what they called 'waif whispers'. Daylighters were excluded from this, and had to rely on friendly waifs to keep them informed of how the meeting was progressing. Every so often, in the silence, ripples of light would shimmer through the crowd as the waifs shook their lampstaffs, either in agreement or dissent – though Nate couldn't tell which.

'What are they saying?' Nate whispered to the blotch-faced individual next to him, and noticed the gold collar and chain round his neck. The other end of the chain was being held by a tiny ghostwaif with the biggest eyes Nate had ever seen.

'*He can't talk. He's a nameless one,*' a light musical whisper sounded in Nate's head. '*Though I call him Gelve.*'

Nate glanced back at the blotchy creature. The waif's eyes narrowed.

'*A daylighter I see, seeking a cure – and none too successfully,*' she said, reading the depths of Nate's mind swiftly and efficiently. Nate shuddered involuntarily as he felt the waif's thoughts inside his head. '*You have been through much and travelled far . . .*' She nodded thoughtfully, her ears fluttering as she looked into his face. '*But you are honourable, and have a good heart . . . And you are a lamplighter!*'

Nate smiled weakly.

'*We are discussing the provision of new lamps for the Higher Ledges.*' Her eyes narrowed. **We are discussing the custodians and their grip on power in the city,** added the ghostwaif, revealing her underthoughts to Nate quietly.

Nate turned to her, wondering why this waif stranger was telling him so much.

Because, Nate Quarter, I have seen that I can trust you – and, more importantly, because this is something you need to know . . .

Nate frowned, puzzled, but the ghostwaif continued.

'We have so much to be thankful for,' she said, 'not least the generous glow of the larger lamps that have been fitted.' *Golderayce One-Eye is cutting the highflow by another two hours, and there are many who resent his high-handed actions!*

Below, at the centre of the amphitheatre, a tall waif with shimmering black scales and long barbels curling from his brow and lower jaw strode out and raised his lampstaff high. Around Nate, a shiver of excitement rippled through the seated waifs.

'I shall not underthink,' the blackwaif whispered in spoken words of shocking clarity. 'I shall speak out, so that waif and daylighter alike may hear – and yes, even Golderayce One-Eye and his spies!'

The lampstaffs throughout the amphitheatre bobbed and dipped like glowworms in a gale.

'The cutting of the highflow means one thing and one thing only. More shall die through lack of the healing water! The Riverrise spring should benefit all – not just the custodians, who treat the sacred water as if it is a commodity to buy and sell. It should be free to all on the basis of need!'

The lampstaffs signalled their agreement.

'If we stand together,' the blackwaif said, 'we have nothing to fear but—'

Suddenly, the blackwaif staggered back, his large eyes rolling alarmingly in his head and a hand clutching at the thorn dart embedded in his throat. With a soft sigh, he toppled forward and his lampstaff shattered on the stone paved floor of the amphitheatre and went out.

'*Waif assassin!*' the ghostwaif's voice sounded in Nate's head, panic-stricken and shrill, no longer a concealed underthought.

Everyone looked around and listened, scanning the gathering of waifs and daylighters for the individual who had been responsible for taking the blackwaif's life. There was not a sign. The next moment, like an unfurling luminous thousandfoot, the bobbing trail of lampstaffs began flowing quickly from the tiers of the amphitheatre and out into the streets as the terrified waifs fled.

Shocked, Nate went with the crowd – though not before glancing over his shoulder to see a small black-hooded figure dart out into the centre of the amphitheatre below and crouch down beside the body of the blackwaif. In its hand, the cloaked individual clutched a long clearwood blowpipe, the chosen weapon of the waif assassin.

High above, four waifs dressed in the luminous white silk robes of the custodians stood beside the entrance to the amphitheatre as the frightened crowd streamed out. Their ears fluttered as they probed the thoughts of the minds that passed them.

'*Enjoy the new lamps on the High Ledges,*' they sneered wordlessly, '*with the compliments of the Custodian General, Golderayce One-Eye!*'

516

· CHAPTER SEVENTY-THREE ·

By the time he'd climbed the steps up to Kobold's Mount and was approaching the gabtroll's lamphouse, Nate was bitterly regretting his impulsive decision to visit the amphitheatre. It was two hours into lowflow, he was hot and tired, but worse than that, he had yet to deliver the precious Riverrise water he'd been sent out to collect – and Nate knew that Eudoxia was in desperate need of it.

As he stepped through the circular door into the beautiful glowing interior, Nate realized instantly that something was very wrong.

Barkscale the healer was standing over Eudoxia's bed beside the high arched window, his cantilevered medical trunk open and its contents spread out before him. On either side of him stood Gilmora and Gomber, their eyestalks swaying from side to side in distress, silently wringing their hands.

'What's wrong?' Nate blurted out, conscious that his voice sounded loud and raw in the hushed atrium of the lamphouse. 'I've got the water, and fresh nightoil and woodaloes . . .'

'Eudoxia's taken a turn for the worse, my dear,' said Gilmora, rushing up to Nate and hugging him. 'Healer Barkscale has done everything he can for her . . .'

'Everything?' Nate said, his voice cracking.

Barkscale turned from Eudoxia's bedside, and his black eyes scanned Nate's face.

'*I have looked deep into her mind,*' Barkscale's gentle voice sounded inside Nate's head.

Unlike the thoughts of the other waifs, Nate usually found those of the healer calm and soothing. Now, though, as he listened to the soft words, he became aware of a tight knot of fear building in the pit of his stomach.

'*She has begun the journey away from the terrible pain that afflicts her,*' he said, '*and is travelling towards the light . . . I fear she is leaving us, Nate.*'

'Is there nothing you can do?' Nate murmured, tears filling his eyes. 'I . . . I have water from the aqueduct,' he added desperately.

On the sumpwood stretcher, Eudoxia lay still. Although her skin was as pale and translucent as the clearwood window arch, she looked strangely peaceful. Nate knelt down slowly beside her.

'Are you really leaving me, Eudoxia?' he whispered, taking her hand and squeezing it softly.

Behind him, Gomber cleared his throat. 'Thank you, Barkscale, for all you've done,' he mumbled. 'Gilmora will show you out.'

Nate's eyes filled with tears. 'Don't go, Eudoxia,' he begged. 'Hang on, just a little while longer . . .'

He felt the gabtroll's hand on his shoulder. 'There is perhaps one last thing we could try,' Gomber whispered softly. 'But, no . . . it's too dangerous.'

Nate looked up at him. The gabtroll's eyestalks had shrunk back into his head, and he was visibly trembling.

'Anything, Gomber,' said Nate, climbing to his feet.

'You could take water direct from the Riverrise spring – from the shore of the lake in the Garden of Life . . .'

'The Riverrise spring?' said Nate. 'But how would I get up there? The keep bars the way, and Golderayce's custodians stand constant guard. Everybody in Riverrise knows it is certain death to trespass in the Garden of Life.'

'Nobody has ever succeeded before, I grant you,' said Gilmora, returning from the door and wiping her hands agitatedly on her apron. 'But we have no other choice,' she said. 'And besides, you're forgetting one thing in our favour . . .'

'What's that?' asked Nate, wiping his eyes.

The two gabtrolls exchanged furtive glances with one another, their eyestalks quivering.

'We work for Golderayce,' they whispered together.

· CHAPTER SEVENTY-FOUR ·

The closer they came to the keep, the more imposing it appeared. Its huge globelamp glowed like a dazzling beacon high above the other lamps of Riverrise below, while above it was the inky blackness of the permanent night. Nate glanced up at the keep from below the hood of the black cape he was wearing and swapped the lampstaff from one hand to the other.

Light, he thought. Lamplight, glowing . . .

Beside him, Gilmora and Gomber wheezed and gasped.

'Oh, it's a dreadful climb,' said Gilmora, the laden basket heavy on her arm. 'And it . . . *slurp* . . . doesn't get any shorter. And what with these old legs of mine, *slurp slurp* . . . it's more of a struggle every time. Isn't that right, Gomber?' she said, her eyestalks peering round at her husband.

'Certainly is, Gilmora,' the gabtroll on Nate's other side wheezed. The pointed end of his lampstaff crunched irregularly in the gravel as he lurched unsteadily forward. 'And we're neither of us . . . *slurp* . . . getting any younger.'

'Unlike *some* I could mention,' Gilmora said cheerfully. 'Forty-five . . . *slurp* . . . years we've been tending to the Custodian General's needs, and while we've been busy ageing, Golderayce One-Eye seems . . . *slurp* . . . more sprightly than ever – may Sky and Earth preserve our generous master!'

She gathered her skirts about her so that she could watch where she was treading as the three of them picked their way up a particularly rock-strewn stretch of path, their lampstaffs tilted forward to light the way. The flickering orbs of light cast strange confusing shadows from the jagged rocks that made the going difficult and, with the sheer drop to their side, increasingly hazardous.

'May Sky and Earth preserve him indeed!' Gomber agreed loudly. 'Tending to the Custodian General's needs gives our poor worthless lives a meaning. Isn't that right, Gilmora, dear?'

'You speak the truth, Gomber dearest,' Gilmora replied, pausing to regain her breath. 'Indeed you do!'

The keep loomed up in front of them. It was comprised of two buildings; a vast fortress with curved walls and high tiny windows at the front and, adjoining it behind, a squat tower. A huge globelamp was mounted at the top of the fortress, bathing the air in dazzling light and making the keep stand out against the pitch black of the eternal night all round it.

Look at the light.

That was what Healer Barkscale had told Nate, his voice at once patient and persuasive.

'*Think of the lamp,*' he'd said. '*Fill your thoughts with light, just light . . . Only light . . .*'

Eudoxia had a raging fever, and the healer was at her bedside tending to her far below in the lamphouse on Kobold's Mount.

'*Of course, a fourthling like you could never learn to underthink,*' Barkscale had told Nate a few hours earlier, the voice in his head soft and understanding. '*Not properly. Proper underthinking is something only waifs can do . . . But don't despair, Nate Quarter,*' he'd continued, his large fan-like ears trembling as they detected the feelings of hopelessness that had overwhelmed the young lamplighter. '*There is something you can do that will work almost as well . . .*'

Behind him, the two old gabtrolls had nodded.

'It's something we do . . . *slurp* . . . the whole time,' Gilmora had said, 'when we're up looking after old . . . *slurp* . . . Golderayce.'

'*It's called overthinking,*' Barkscale had told him. '*You have to think of one thing, and hold onto that thought to the exclusion of all other thoughts.*'

'One thought,' Nate had said. 'You mean like this?'

He'd closed his eyes and concentrated.

'*Oh, no, no, no. That'll never do,*' the waterwaif had said at once, shaking his head.

'But . . . it's one thought,' Nate had said, disappointed as the memory of his father's smiling face faded away again, 'just like you said.'

'*Yes, Nate, and if you were walking through the amphitheatre trying to mask your thoughts, it would be fine. But you won't be in the amphitheatre or Kobold's Mount, or up at the aqueduct – you'll be at the keep, and there such a thought would give you away in an instant.*'

'I . . . I don't understand,' Nate had said, confused.

'It isn't easy to grasp,' Gilmora had told him kindly. 'Not at first.' She'd paused. 'You need to blend in, Nate. *Slurp slurp*. To become invisible.'

'Imagine your thoughts are a voice,' Gomber had said. 'Imagine you're in the forest hunting, and want to remain hidden, but all the time you're shouting out, "My father!", "My father!". Do you see? No, to conceal yourself, you need to mask your own sounds – your footsteps, your breathing and the like – with the sound of, I don't know, birdsong . . .'

'Or rainfall,' Gilmora had suggested.

'Or the wind . . . *slurp* . . . whistling through the leaves.'

'*Do you understand now?*' Barkscale's voice sounded inside Nate's head once more. '*It can't be a person. Or a place. Not up at the keep. It has to be something . . . yes, that's right,*' he said as Nate imagined himself staring down at the glistening surface of a clear lake. '*Yes, that's much better.*'

Nate had held on to the thought of the water, splashing against a muddy bank and sparkling in the low sunlight. It was cool. It was swirling. It had the power to revive his ailing friend, Eudoxia, and . . .

'*No, Nate,*' healer Barkscale's voice had sounded gently and Nate knew at once that he'd let his thoughts stray. '*It was the right idea,*' said the waterwaif, his green scales glinting in the lamplight, '*but . . .*' He'd paused, and a moment later Nate heard a voice in his head. '*You're a lamplighter,*' Barkscale had said simply.

'I used to be,' Nate had replied. 'In the phraxmines of the Eastern Woods, and the phraxchamber works of Coppertown . . .'

'*Then that's it*,' Barkscale had told him. '*That's the thought you must hold onto. Not water, but light. Bright light. Enveloping light. Can you do that, Nate?*'

And even as the waterwaif had spoken, Nate could see a lamp shining brightly inside his head.

'*Think of the lamp*,' Barkscale's voice said softly. '*Fill your thoughts with the light . . . Just light. Only light . . .*'

Up ahead, the bright light of the huge globelamp mounted at the top of the keep filled Nate's vision and, when he blinked, he could still see it. The light filled his head, warm and honey-like, filling every crack and crevice of his mind, leaving no corner for other thoughts to form.

Just light . . . Only light . . .

'Here we are, Gomber dearest,' Gilmora was saying, her eyestalks looking round her nervously. 'Back at the keep that guards the path to the Garden of Life. None shall pass but our generous master, for the keep is strong, the keep is high!'

'So it is, Gilmora dear,' wheezed her husband. 'Earth and Sky be praised!'

He pointed to a rock by the cliffside, then up to a tiny window directly above it, high up near the top of the keep. Nate nodded, dispelling the slight tremor of unease which came into his mind and replacing it with lamplight. A set of steps led directly up from the path to a broad-arched leadwood door in the fortress. Far above it, four small upper windows studded the great curving frontage.

Nate crouched down behind the jagged rock, his body wreathed in shadow, while inside his head the light continued to glow steadily. From the top of the steps, he heard Gomber raise his lampstaff and strike it against the hard wood, the sound echoing through the cavernous hallway beyond. He heard bolts grinding as they were slid across and a low creak of unoiled hinges as the heavy door swung open, followed by the low murmur and slurp of the gabtrolls' voices.

'*Ah, it's you*,' he heard, and peered round the rock to see a waif custodian standing in the doorway, his white robes shimmering and

a long blowpipe in his hand. *'At last. The master has missed you.'*

There was more murmuring, low and apologetic, and a loud *clang* as the door slammed shut behind them. Nate sank back on his heels, and waited. The air was silent but for the soft whispering of the wind blowing round the curved sides of the keep. It was all Nate could do to prevent himself thinking about what might lie ahead – but he knew he must not. Second guesses and suppositions were not allowed in his head. Not now. Only the light. The warm, golden light that masked his presence in this strange eerie fastness, halfway up the steep mountainside.

'Psst!'

The faint hissing sound broke through the light. Nate acknowledged it, then pushed it aside, filling his head with the light once more as he emerged from his hiding place and looked up.

Far above his head, he saw that the latticed shutters on the tiny window closest to the sheer mountain behind were open. Gilmora's head was sticking out. Then, as Nate stepped forward, a rope came tumbling out of the window, one end fixed at the top, the other dangling down at Nate's side. He seized it and began to climb.

The light, he thought inside his head. Fill your head with the light. Just light. Only light . . .

Hand over hand, with his feet tightly gripping the rope, Nate pulled himself up the rough surface of the building. It was a long climb, an exhausting climb. Once, he glanced round to see how far he'd already gone, and a tremor of fear rippled through his head as he was shocked to see how far above the rocky ground he was.

The light, he told himself, resuming the climb. Only the light . . .

Just then, Nate felt a flapping close to his ear. He froze, his feet and hands gripping hold of the rope and heart pounding. The next moment, it was gone.

Only the light . . .

'Just opening the window,' Gilmora said to herself cheerfully, 'to let the cool night air into this stuffy old storeroom.'

Down in Golderayce's chamber, the Custodian General was sitting at his dining table, the lampstaff propped up against his chair. He looked up from his meal and eyed Gomber suspiciously. Superficially, there was nothing different about the old gabtroll. He was pottering around the room just as he always did; tending the lamps, dusting the shelves and tidying the disorder that had resulted from the old waif being left untended for a whole month. And yet . . .

'*It's so good to have you and Gilmora back with me once more,*' he said. '*That gnokgoblin you left me with was a poor substitute. Nowhere near as attentive to my needs.*' His eyes narrowed. **What are you hiding? What is it lurking there, furtive and hesitant, beneath your cheerfulness?**

'It's good to be back,' Gomber told him, pulling the cork from the opened bottle of sapwine and refilling Golderayce's glass with the sweet ruby-coloured liquid. 'I hope you like the sapwine, sir. Gilmora brought it all the way from the Deepwoods, especially for you.'

'*The sapwine is excellent,*' said Golderayce, his barbels quivering as what passed for a smile stretched his thin lips. He took another sip. '*Where is Gilmora? I should like to thank her myself.*'

'She's fetching fresh candles for you from the upper store,' said Gomber.

'*Very thoughtful of her,*' said Golderayce, staring at Gomber intently as he detected that slight furtiveness in his thoughts once again. **She's been gone ages. Where is she?**

He listened to the sounds of the keep – the scuttling of rock beetles, the idle musings of the custodian guards at the front entrance . . .

Ah, yes, there she was. The old gabtroll's thoughts were as tedious as they were unmistakeable. She *was* in the storeroom, and her head was indeed full of thoughts of the candles clutched in her hand, and how she would set them in Golderayce's silver candlesticks and fill his chamber with light . . . Just light . . . Only light . . .

Up in the storeroom, Gilmora flinched as she felt the Custodian General probe her thoughts. She pushed the candles down inside the woven bag that hung from her shoulder.

'Soon have that lovely chamber glowing bright and lovely for

526

the master,' she muttered to herself as she helped Nate over the windowsill, pulled the rope up and closed the shutters.

Nate found himself in a dusty ill-lit room, the walls lined with huge vats, familiar to him from the aqueduct but far, far larger. They were old and covered in a fine lace of nightspider webs and dated from a time when the waters of Riverrise had flowed uninterrupted from the lake in the Garden of Life down to the city below.

Just light . . . Only light . . .

Gilmora beckoned.

They crossed the floor, leaving footprints in the thick dust, and went out of the low leadwood door on the other side. Gilmora stepped through, pulled it shut behind them and, selecting one of the large iron keys that hung in a cluster from her belt, turned it in the lock. She beckoned a second time.

The light glowed brightly in Nate's thoughts as he followed the old gabtroll along a lamp-lined corridor.

They hurried over the tiled floor to the far end, and down some steps. Then, taking a second, narrower corridor, Nate peered out through one of the thin unglazed slits in the wall to find that they were crossing over a bridge that joined the curved fortress to the squat tower behind. On the far side, a brightly lit staircase zigzagged down, which they started to descend. After two flights, Gilmora raised a hand agitatedly and the two of them slipped into the shadows.

'Who goes there?' The thoughts of the custodian guard standing on the landing below sounded in Nate and Gilmora's heads.

'It's just the gabtroll . . . fetching candles,' his fellow guard's thoughts sounded in reply.

Light, just light . . . Only light . . .

The guards chuckled. *'For our master . . .'*

They shouldered their blowpipes and continued their rounds. Gilmora waited for the shuffling footsteps of the custodians to recede, before turning to Nate and nodding.

They continued down the stairs, passing low doors – some open, some closed – which led off into the sleeping chambers of

527

the resident guard. At the bottom of the tower, while Gilmora was fumbling with the keys a second time, Nate looked around him. The hall they were in was low-ceilinged, with an uneven stone floor and roughcast walls lined with hooks and racks that were filled with glistening waif overrobes and lines of blowpipes. Above them, on shelves, were bunches of the deadly darts they fired . . .

The lamp, Nate told himself. Just light . . . Only light, filling every crevice of my mind with its glow.

'Must get these candles to my master, Sky and Earth bless him!' said Gilmora, turning the key in the lock and easing the heavy leadwood door open.

Nate stepped outside and held his lampstaff up. The light streamed out along the path before him – the path that would take him directly to the Garden of Life. He patted the glass vial nestling in the pocket of his tilderleather jacket. To the precious lake water that would make Eudoxia well again . . .

Just light! Only light!

Nate started along the path, pushing down the sense of anticipation threatening to bubble up from the recesses of his mind and replacing it with the light. Leaving the squat tower of the keep behind him, he increased his pace, his heart pounding in his chest as the ascent became steeper.

'*There you are!*' Golderayce's sharp voice sounded in Gilmora's head as the old gabtroll stepped back into her chamber.

'Here I am,' she said brightly and began fussing with the candles, pulling them from her bag, dusting them on her apron and pushing them down into the guttering remains of the spent candles. As the Custodian General's chamber slowly filled with flickering golden light, she turned to him. 'Now isn't that much better?' she said. 'All bright and friendly . . .'

'*Just like you, my dear Gilmora,*' said Golderayce, his voice soft and insidious. **What is it you're trying to conceal, you tedious creature?** he asked himself.

Nate had gone no more than a hundred strides or so when he heard wings flapping near his head a second time. He looked round

528

to see a tiny flitterwaif, its angled wings black against the distant lights of the town far below.

'What's this? What's this?' a savage squeak sounded in Nate's head. 'Light? Light! . . . No! . . . An intruder!'

Red eyes stared back at Nate as the creature swooped past him. Then, with a high-pitched screech, it wheeled round in the air and flew back towards him, its fangs bared in a grimace of hatred. Without thinking, Nate raised his lampstaff and swung it above his head.

As the lamp struck the creature, the orb of glass shattered and, in a burst of flame, the flitterwaif was sent spiralling out into the blackness, its wings on fire. Like a shooting star, the tiny creature blazed down towards the constellation of lights below, screeching in a death wail.

'Aaaiii!'

Golderayce let go of his goblet of sapwine,

sending it crashing to the floor. Gomber spun round, his face white with dread. Gilmora dropped the taper she'd been lighting the candles with. Both of them put their hands to their ears, though there was nothing either of them could do to keep out their master's thoughts.

'*He's dead,*' the Custodian General hissed. '*My little flitterwaif is dead – and by the hands of an intruder. Someone has breached the keep, and is now on Kobold's Steps. Someone who was helped by—*'

He spun round and fixed his gaze on the two quivering gabtrolls who stood before him.

'No, no,' cried Gomber and Gilmora together.

Inside their heads, both aged gabtrolls could feel the Custodian General furiously prodding and probing, tearing down their thoughts and delving deep into their minds with razor-sharp talons. Gilmora fell to her knees.

'No, master . . .' she pleaded. 'No . . .'

Gomber collapsed beside her, his arms clasped round his head as he writhed on the floor.

'*A visitor! . . . A lamplighter . . . You brought him to the keep . . .*'

'Yes,' Gilmora whispered, the pain inside her head now unbearable as the waif dug ever deeper.

'*The Riverrise spring! He's after the water . . .*'

'Yes,' groaned Gomber.

'*TRAITORS!!*' Golderayce's thought exploded in the gabtrolls' heads.

Seizing his lampstaff, Golderayce stepped over the bodies of the two unconscious gabtrolls and strode towards the door. He made his way through the fortress and across to the tower.

'*Guards! Remain at your posts. There is no problem,*' he reassured the custodians who had heard the commotion. *I mustn't appear weak! Fooled by my own ignorant servants! No one must find out! I shall slit their throats and cut off their eyestalks . . . But first, the lamplighter . . .*

Reaching the bottom of the tower, he looked around him. He pulled two darts from the shelf above the hooks and pushed them into a top pocket, then took a blowpipe from the rack below. Checking that no one was about, he unlocked the door and strode from the building out onto the path.

'*I shall visit the Garden of Life,*' he thought for the benefit of the guards. *Once word gets out that one got past the keep, then all will try . . .*

He paused and cocked his head to one side, his ears trembling as he listened to the sounds in the darkness.

'*A lamp . . .*' he whispered. *So there you are!* A smile flickered over his lips as his grip tightened on the carved blowpipe. *Not for the first time,* thought Golderayce One-Eye, as he made his way silently up Kobold's Steps, *the Garden of Life shall be visited by death . . .*

· CHAPTER SEVENTY-FIVE ·

Nate trembled with fear. Behind him, in the darkness, a waif was reaching out and entering his mind.

'*Yes, little lamplighter, I know you're there,*' Golderayce's vicious hissing voice sounded in his head. '*Did you seriously think you could reach the Garden of Life without my knowing? Did you? You little fool! Now you shall pay for your impudence.*'

Swallowing hard, Nate stumbled on up the rough rocky track, trying in vain to shut out Golderayce's jeering voice. His lampstaff was broken and, though it helped him to walk up the steep slope, it could no longer illuminate the way. Time and again on the treacherous path, he slipped and skidded on unseen rocks beneath his feet that threatened at any moment to turn his ankle or send him tumbling. His breath wheezed loudly in his ears; his heart was racing, and inside his head, the light had faded, to be replaced with a single word that echoed repeatedly.

Faster! Faster!

Behind him, he could hear the Custodian General, and not just in his thoughts. No, it was his footsteps he heard now, and the *click* and *clack* of two staffs in his hands, one heavy and one light, as he drove himself on up the path.

Faster! Faster! Faster . . .

'*Your friends will have their eyestalks cut off and their throats cut. They will die slowly, and in agony,*' the Custodian General whispered inside Nate's head. '*But not as slowly as I shall kill you, lamplighter . . .*'

Nate started back. The voice sounded closer than before.

'*Oh, it is closer, lamplighter,*' hissed Golderayce. '*Much, much closer . . .*'

Nate scrambled on, the words spurring him up the steep incline.

Although even as he did so, he was aware that while his own eyes were barely able to make out a thing, the waif's huge black eyes were designed for penetrating the blanket of darkness.

'*Precisely, lamplighter,*' Golderayce sneered, '*and any second now, my gaze shall fall upon you. First I shall paralyse you, and then I shall skin you slowly, a limb at a time . . .*'

As Nate struggled on, his chest aching with exertion, the air about him began to change. The darkness thickened and curdled, and he found himself enveloped in a warm moist swaddling of mist.

The clouds, he thought. I've reached the clouds . . .

'*It won't help you,*' came Golderayce's contemptuous voice. '*You shall watch helplessly as I cut out your beating heart and hold it in front of your eyes.*'

Below his feet now, Nate felt steps, carved out of the solid rock. He ran up them blindly, the fingertips of one hand trailing the side of the rock which rose up beside him.

Keep going, he told himself. Just a little further . . .

Already, as the cloud thickened, so the darkness was beginning to recede. The swirling fog turned from black to grey and, by degrees, to a dense blanket of white. Then, as he ran, he suddenly realized that he could actually see the broad steps cut into the rock beneath his feet and, looking up, the tall rocky chimney he was ascending. The fog continued to thin. Ahead of him, through the twists of mist, he saw the sky, blue and cloudless, with a warm sun shining down out of it into his upturned face. A moment later, just ahead, a great stone archway appeared.

'*So near and yet so far, lamplighter,*' came a whispered voice inside his head, and Nate spun round to see the thin ancient-looking Custodian General standing before him, his one eye blazing. '*Didn't I say you wouldn't make it? Didn't I promise that I would make you pay for your impudence?*' Golderayce gave a low wheezing chuckle. '*Now it is time to complete the rest of my promise . . .*'

He raised the blowpipe to his mouth and shot the paralysing dart.

At that moment, from overhead, a great black bird soared up over the stone archway and down over Nate's shoulder, its mighty wings stirring up a ferocious whirlwind around it. For an instant, the dart from the blowpipe froze in mid-air, inches from Nate's terrified face, before turning and hissing back the way it had come. With a tiny glint, the dart embedded itself in the Custodian General's neck.

In front of Nate, Golderayce One-Eye dropped his blowpipe and his lampstaff, and clutched desperately at his throat. As Nate watched, the skin on the waif's face, legs, arms, fingers and neck turned darker and tougher, tightly constricting round the bones beneath it. His cheeks hollowed, his barbels withered and his ears turned ragged and drooped like tattered fragments of cloth. The one good eye, black and glinting, that only moments earlier had seemed almost to be boring right inside Nate's skull, suddenly turned as dull and opaque as its neighbour. And all the while, the Custodian General seemed to be shrinking in on himself, his body growing stooped and gnarled as centuries of the rejuvenating properties of the water of life evaporated in seconds with the dart's paralysing venom.

'He . . . e . . . elp me . . .' an ancient faltering voice stammered inside Nate's head. 'I . . .'

The voice quavered weakly and fell silent. And before Nate's eyes, the ancient waif fell to the ground in a heap of yellowed bones and tattered skin that, as he watched, crumbled to a fine powdery dust and blew away on the wind. Finally, there was nothing left where Golderayce had been standing but the lampstaff, the blowpipe and the glistening black robes of the former Custodian General, which lay in a small crumpled heap.

'What in Earth and Sky . . .' Nate murmured.

The great black bird hovered above him for a moment, its wingbeats stirring up the swirling mist. Nate knew what it was. It had a large hooked bill and curved crest, black and white striped tail feathers and black plumage, so dark it gleamed purple in the sunlight. Nate had heard of the creatures, but this was the first caterbird he had ever seen. Then, just as he was marvelling at its magnificence, the caterbird soared upwards, its outstretched wings catching thermals which spiralled up high into the air above.

'Wait,' Nate called after it. 'Come back . . .'

'So,' said a voice behind him, 'you've come at last.'

CHAPTER SEVENTY-SIX

Nate looked round. In front of him were two gaunt figures in dark shimmering waif robes. They were standing on a broad terrace of white marble. Behind Nate was a high archway of stone, the entrance to this, the Garden of Life.

Below the archway lay the remains of Golderayce One-Eye; his lampstaff, blowpipe and black robes peppered with dust. In the clear, sunlit sky high overhead, the black outline of the mighty caterbird grew smaller by the second.

On the other side of the terrace, a stone staircase led down to the lush vegetation of the garden that fringed the turquoise waters of the Riverrise Lake, while eight pinnacles of rock rose up around it. In the centre of the vast lake was a spike of rock which ascended in fluted columns to a jagged point, the highest in all the Edgelands. The waters of the Riverrise spring bubbled up from fissures in the flutes and flowed down in steady trickles into the lake below.

Opposite the spring, on the far side of the lake, a stone ledge jutted out from the garden and over the abyss below. This was the Riverrise waterfall, its flow controlled by a pair of heavy iron sluice gates at the side of the lake, their black winding mechanism disfiguring the beauty of the surrounding garden.

'You have come, as the caterbird said you would,' one of the gaunt figures said, his voice cracked and ancient-sounding.

He had a long, flowing white beard, and thick white hair pulled into tufts and knotted in the style favoured by wood-trolls of the First Age. By contrast, his companion was clean shaven, his steel grey hair oiled and combed in the way favoured by the librarians of the Second Age. Both of them seemed to shimmer

and shine from beneath their dark robes, making it difficult for Nate to look directly into their faces.

'Walk with us, down to the lake,' the bearded figure said, holding out a shining hand, 'visitor from the Third Age.'

Nate climbed to his feet and followed the two figures down the long stone staircase and into the Garden of Life. At the edge of the lake, they stopped and sat on the great stump of a silver-grey lufwood tree. A little way off was a small stone slab embedded in the mossy earth, with words that had been painstakingly carved into its surface: *Maugin, The Stone Pilot.*

'Are you custodians?' Nate asked uncertainly, fingering the glass vial in his jacket pocket. 'I . . . I meant no harm. I came here to get water from the spring to cure my friend . . . She's dying . . .' He frowned. 'Golderayce followed me. He was going to kill me.'

The clean-shaven figure turned his glowing face towards Nate.

'So you managed to get past the keep?' he said, with a bitter laugh. 'That is something in all these long years we have never managed to do. No, we are not custodians,' he said, in answer to Nate's question. 'Rather, we are prisoners here in the Garden of Life. Though, those who guard us speak of us, in whispers as' – he smiled – 'the Immortals.'

· CHAPTER SEVENTY-SEVEN ·

The *Archemax* steamed on through the howling winds, the sky overhead boiling with dark swirling clouds.

'Keep the chamber gears free of ice,' Cirrus Gladehawk shouted. 'We're going to need all the power we can get to ride out this storm.'

'Aye aye, Captain,' replied Squall Razortooth. 'Weelum and I are right on it!'

'It's worse than any storm I've ever seen!' said the Professor, emerging from the cabins below the aft deck and clutching hold of his funnel hat as he did so. 'Should we put in at Four Lakes?'

'Not if Galston's going to have any hope of seeing his daughter again,' said Cirrus bleakly. 'Slip says he's fading fast.'

Above the phraxship, the mighty storm seemed to be gathering pace, huge cloud banks merging into swirling eddies of lightning flashes and thunderclaps, the winds growing stronger by the second.

'We'll have to battle through it all the way to the Thorn Gate,' said Cirrus grimly. 'This is no ordinary storm. It's like three storms in one. I've never known anything like it.' He frowned. 'The swirling eddies and cloud eruptions indicate a white storm, but the copper-coloured hues and cursive swirls are classic signs of a sepia storm. Then again, at its heart is a build up of energy that suggests a storm from the furthest reaches of Open Sky. And judging by its course, there is only one place it can be heading for . . .'

'You mean,' said the Professor, staring up at the dark turbulent sky.

'Yes,' said Cirrus. 'Riverrise.'

· CHAPTER SEVENTY-EIGHT ·

The first time I came to Riverrise,' said Twig, 'I was little older than you are now, Nate. I was a Sanctaphrax academic *and* a sky pirate captain, and I'd come to rescue the last member of my missing crew, the stone pilot Maugin.'

His eyes lingered on the small gravestone by the lake.

'I left here, strapped to the blazing trunk of this very tree – my apprentice, Cowlquape, by my side – and rode it all the way to the very Edge itself . . .'

His green eyes went dreamy as the old sky pirate captain was momentarily lost in thought. He looked back at Nate.

'The second time, sixty years later, I was carried here by the caterbird, the mighty creature who has watched over me since its hatching. I was close to death, the crossbow bolt of a Guardian of Night lodged in my back. I remember opening my eyes and seeing the Riverrise waterfall glistening in the sunlight as we approached, and there on the very lip of the jutting rock was Maugin, still waiting as she'd promised to do, for my return. As we came closer, I saw her throw up her arms in joy – and then crumple to the ground . . .

'We swooped low over the lake and I heard the waif voice for the first time in my head. *"You shall never be reunited."*

'Above me, the caterbird shuddered as darts whistled past my head and struck its wings – and the next thing I knew, I was falling down towards the lake.

'When I came to my senses, I was lying by the shore, Maugin's lifeless body beside me. I'd spent a lifetime trying to return to her, and now finally I had – and she was dead. I drank from the spring and felt the life return to me, but it was too late for Maugin. I buried her body beside this tree stump and waited for the caterbird to return . . .

'But he didn't return,' he added softly. 'Instead, I felt the waif probing my thoughts, reading my mind and sifting through my memories.

'What strength I had, as an old sky pirate, returned to me, but I knew that I was trapped, just as Maugin had been before me. I was too old to survive a second skyfiring – and anyway, it had been Maugin herself who had calculated the angle of flight on that previous occasion. Left to my own devices, I would probably have fired myself off into Open Sky.' He shrugged. 'And as for travelling on foot, I knew that far below me, in the darkness of the Nightwoods, there lurked the murderous waif and thousands of his kind.

'Why he didn't kill me, I didn't understand. At first. But over the years that followed, I realized that the waif enjoyed reading my thoughts, just as he must have once enjoyed reading Maugin's.

'In those early days I spent at Riverrise, I never saw him. But bit by bit, the waif grew bolder. He would emerge from the darkness below and lurk by the gateway to the garden, his blowpipe in hand. He was young back then, and ambitious. As I got to know him – always from a distance and only through those thoughts he allowed me to hear – the awful truth began to dawn on me.

'The pathetic creature had made his home on the mountainside below, and had been drawn up towards the peak by Maugin's thoughts, like a woodmoth to a candle flame. He had fallen in love with her from a distance, in the shadows, reading her thoughts and hoarding them in his mind.

'What passed between the two of them in their minds, I can only guess at, but I believe the waif's love curdled into a malevolent jealousy when he realized that Maugin remained loyal to me. And when I returned, that jealousy turned to murderous rage – and poor Maugin paid with her life . . .

'How I would have loved to avenge her death, but the waif read my thoughts and never let his guard down for an instant, content instead that I was a prisoner here in the garden.

'And so the hours, the days, the years passed,' Twig said, his face glowing brightly in the sunlight, 'until . . .'

'*I* came,' said Rook Barkwater.

· CHAPTER SEVENTY-NINE ·

'Ever since I watched Twig, the last of the sky pirates, being carried from the Tower of Night over the horizon in the talons of the mighty caterbird,' said Rook, 'I wondered what had become of him. I left old Undertown and settled in the Free Glades – and only then did I discover that the sky pirate captain was in fact my grandfather.

'That only fuelled my burning ambition to travel to Riverrise to discover his fate. But there were other things burning back then in the Second Age. The Great Library for one, in the War for the Free Glades . . .

'I fought hard in that war – and the wars that followed, proud to be a Freeglade Lancer. I saw the beginning of the Third Age of Flight, and the growth of the great cities of Hive and Great Glade. And as my days drew to a close, I was proud of the life I had lived. I had five sons, all now grown to adulthood and with young'uns of their own. I had overseen the establishment of the Freeglade Lancers in Old Forest. And I had seen my great friend, Xanth Filatine, not only become head of the Lake Landing Academy but also the father of phraxflight . . .

'When Magda my wife died, though, followed less than a year later by Xanth, I sought solace in the Gardens of Thought in Waif Glen with one of my oldest friends, Cancaresse the waif . . .

'Cancaresse the Silent,' he mused. 'Keeper of the Garden of Thoughts . . . Such a wonderful individual. She tended the healing gardens for decades, helping me on so many occasions to deal with pain or come to terms with my loss. Finally, though, she announced that she wished to return to her home in the Nightwoods below the Riverrise mount before she died, a journey believed to be almost impossible, even in the early years of the Third Age. And she asked me to accompany her.

'I had nothing to lose, and was pleased to accept this great challenge so late in my life. I agreed to go with her. Before I left, I handed the portrait miniature of my great grandfather, Quintinius Verginix, to my eldest son, for him to pass on to his son or daughter when the time came. Then I set off, my head full of thoughts of Twig.

'That journey was one of the longest and hardest of my life, but through it all I was sustained by the thoughts of my friend, Cancaresse, one of the finest and noblest of her kind who has ever lived. The memories of that last march through the hell of the thorn forests will never leave me, but, thanks to Cancaresse, we made it to the great pool at the foot of the Riverrise mount.

'The Nightwoods were a cruel and savage place, and the barren slopes of the mountain little better. Cancaresse had used up the small amount of energy her frail body still possessed in reaching the pool and, although I bathed her in its rejuvenating waters, they lacked the potency of the water at the mouth of the spring far above.

'I found the ancient steps that Kobold the Wise had once taken, and carried my friend up the winding path, through the blackness. It was only when we emerged from the clouds and into the daylight that I realized she had died, peacefully in my arms, with a smile on her pale translucent face.

'I continued up to the Riverrise spring, and stepped through the gateway. I didn't see the waif, Golderayce, but I felt the sting of the dart from his blowpipe searing into my back. At the time, my thoughts were full of Cancaresse, my sorrow mixed with feelings of joy and thankfulness for her long life spent helping others – and this must have thrown Golderayce off his guard, for I was able to spin round and fire my crossbow in his direction before I passed out with pain.

'When I opened my eyes, I saw my grandfather bending over me and tending to my wound with the miraculous waters of the Riverrise spring. It was one of the strangest and most wonderful moments of my life.

'A few days later, after making preparations for the arduous journey back to the distant world of the Deepwoods, Twig and I set off down Kobold's Steps, only to find our way blocked by Golderayce and his waif accomplices. His eye was heavily bandaged, and I realized that I'd caused him injury. I could hear his murderous thoughts of revenge in my head. But he could also read my thoughts of Cancaresse and knew, as did his followers, that I was a friend to waifkind.

'That was probably what saved my life – together with the fact that I didn't care whether I lived or died. In Golderayce's twisted mind, he had already calculated that keeping me a prisoner in the Garden of Life was a better revenge for the loss of his eye than a quick death, so that is what he did.

'The years passed, turning to centuries, and the power of Golderayce One-Eye and his custodians grew. They organized the building of the Thorn Gate, the Waif Trail and the city of Riverrise itself. Below us, in the darkness, I saw the lights of the city grow ever brighter and more numerous, and the keep that he'd had built become more formidable, confining us to the Garden of Life. Finally, Golderayce had the sluice gates constructed by blindfolded brogtrolls, their every move directed by his thoughts, so that he could personally control the flow of the Riverrise spring down to the city below . . .'

He shook his head wearily.

'And we, "the Immortals", have endured this imprisonment for all these years with just each other for company, and the belief that some day, someone from below – some brave adventurer from the Third Age – might make it past the keep and discover our fate . . .

'And now you have, visitor from the Third Age,' Rook concluded, 'just as the caterbird has finally returned.'

'While I lived here in the Garden of Life, beyond the reach of death,' Twig said softly, 'the caterbird – bound, as it was, to watch over me – could not intervene. But now the end is drawing near, and that has allowed it to come back once more . . .'

'Our time is almost over,' said Rook.

'It is?' said Nate, staring into Rook Barkwater's glowing face, his hand fingering the portrait miniature on the cord round his neck.

What had this ancient Freeglade Lancer said? He'd handed the portrait miniature of Quintinius Verginix to his eldest son, to pass on to his son or daughter . . . And on and on, down the family line . . .

Nate Quarter . . . Quarter . . . Bar-quarter . . . Barkwater . . . His head was swimming.

'We have lived long lives,' Twig was saying as he and Rook stood up from the lufwood tree stump and stared down at him. 'But not here in the Garden of Life. This has been no more than a waking dream. The waters of the spring have kept us alive, but we are wearing thin as you can see . . .'

The sky pirate captain raised a glowing hand in front of his face, and Nate could almost see through it.

'Now that Golderayce is dead, you can leave,' said Nate, 'with me. We'll get though the keep together and . . .'

'No,' said Rook Barkwater with a smile. 'According to the caterbird, our path lies another way, visitor from the Third Age.'

'Where?' breathed Nate.

'There,' said Twig, pointing a translucent finger to the sky.

· CHAPTER EIGHTY ·

Nate looked up. Far above his head, the sky was growing dark. A black bank of cloud was sweeping in from Open Sky far to the east, gathering in magnitude and turbulence with every passing second.

The clouds were immense, and so dark they looked almost solid, like a rock slide of massive boulders tumbling over one another as they hurtled across the sky, coming ever closer. And as they did so, the air filled with the echoing din of deep rumbling thunder. Lightning flashed and crackled as fizzing bolts leaped from cloud to cloud in dazzling zigzags of white light, or exploded inside the clouds themselves, illuminating them from within.

As the storm approached, the wind rose to a howling gale, driving into Nate's face and threatening to knock him off balance. Bracing himself, he turned and saw the two Immortals standing by the lakeside, their heads raised and eyes staring up at the sky as their waif robes billowed out behind them.

The two figures were beginning to glow brighter as the pale luminescence intensified within them, until both were shining against the darkening sky, their bodies enclosed in a pulsating blur of light.

All at once, the mountain summit was cast into eerie shadow. Tearing his gaze from the Immortals, Nate looked up to see that the mountainous banks of rolling cloud were directly overhead, blotting out the sun. They curdled and coalesced and, as he watched, became a vast whirling vortex that spun round and round, high above the circle of Riverrise pinnacles. Thunder roared and the wind howled, and as the vortex spun ever faster, a dark circle formed at its centre, like a huge eye staring down out of the sky.

The lightning was coming in blinding flashes now, one following the other in rapid succession, and so bright that Nate had to shield his eyes. The deafening thunder that followed made the Riverrise peak shake, and seemed to leave the air trembling with anticipation of the next colossal explosion. Nate's ears rang, and when he blinked his vision was filled with a curious pink-green afterglow of the intense light. His nose twitched at the faint burnt smell it could detect, lacing the air like the scent of toasting almonds.

The swirling vortex of black cloud hovered directly above the Riverrise peak, setting the turquoise water of the Riverrise lake in motion. Jagged peaks formed across its surface, and the whole lake began slowly to turn, like fine sapwine being swirled round a giant goblet.

Slowly, but deliberately, the two Immortals stepped from the shore and strode out across the spinning turquoise lake, their feet gliding over the surface as if the water was solid marble. When they reached the Riverrise spring, that great jagged needle of rock which pointed up towards the eye of the storm, the Immortals paused.

Suddenly the sky filled with hailstones, lumps of ice the size of snowbird eggs, which rained down from the spinning vortex in a hailstorm so thick and so dense that the glowing figures were lost from view. Nate bent double, his arms raised protectively above his head as the hail pummelled his shoulders and arms. The air around him became icy cold, yet the earth was still warm, and where the hailstones landed, they melted into the ground instantly and disappeared.

A few minutes later, the ice turned pulpy, like cold oozy mud which soaked into Nate's hair and trickled down the back of his neck. He looked up warily a moment later, to find that the hailstones had turned to rain, which was pouring down on the Garden of Life with the same ferocity as the hail it had replaced. Like a mighty waterfall, it cascaded down from the vortex of black cloud above, soaking Nate to the skin.

He straightened up and, shielding his eyes with a raised hand, looked out over the lake. Its spinning waters had now formed a whirlpool of unimaginable depth, sinking down into the dark interior of the Riverrise mountain, seemingly for ever, and sucking down the torrential rain with it. Hovering now in midair by the thin needle of rock at the centre of the whirlpool and glowing more brightly than ever, were the two Immortals.

As Nate watched through the crashing blanket of rain, he could see that the glow was growing still more intense, forming two pulsating spirals of light that rose up from the Immortals towards the dark vortex above.

Nate wiped his face on a saturated sleeve and, blinking away the drops of water from his eyelashes, peered up at the swirling clouds. From out of the centre of the vortex, a ball of lightning was descending, white flashing tendrils fizzing and sparking in the air around it. The ball of lightning hovered over the spiked tip of the Riverrise spring as the spirals of light from the Immortals below connected with it.

As they did so, the rain became even more torrential, and Nate struggled to see through the thunderous downpour. The glow of the Immortals shimmered and glittered through the curtain of driving rain.

He never knew how long he stood there. An hour? Two? Six? The battering rain and howling wind – and the sight unfolding before his eyes – drove all thought from Nate's mind.

The two glowing figures rose slowly towards the ball of lightning above the Riverrise spring, seemingly pulled by the spirals of light like golden edgesalmon on the end of a line. As they merged with the lightning, there was an immense flash of dazzling light, followed by a clap of thunder so loud that Nate felt the air pressing in on his eardrums. Instinctively, he curled up into a ball, his hands over his ears and his body tensed. The rain abruptly stopped and, looking up once more, Nate gasped.

The whirlpool had ceased, and the waters of the brimming Riverrise lake had become still once more. Twists of steam rose from the turquoise water and seemed to plait themselves together, until the whole lake was wreathed in a glittering blanket of soft mist that

swirled around the central spike of the Riverrise spring. The vortex of black cloud had stopped spinning overhead and the howling wind had fallen to the lightest of breezes, while the ball of lightning above the spring had ceased fizzing and crackling and now glowed with a warm soft light, like a great phraxlamp.

Nate screwed up his eyes and shielded them with his hand. There were shapes within the light, *three* of them. As his eyes grew more accustomed to the golden glow, Nate began to see them more clearly.

They were the figures of three youths, no older than himself. One wore a spiked waistcoat of fur, and his hair was tufted and knotted in the style of a woodtroll.'

'Twig,' breathed Nate.

Next to him was a figure in a chequerboard collar and white tunic emblazoned with a banderbear badge.

'Rook,' Nate murmured, recognizing the old-fashioned uniform of the Freeglade Lancers. 'And . . .'

Nate swallowed hard, his hand reaching for the portrait miniature around his neck. He pulled it from his tunic and stared down at the familiar image, before gazing back at the third figure hovering above the spring in the ball of light.

He wore the armour of an ancient knight academic from the First Age, seemingly too big for him, and his dark hair was tousled and unruly, but the face . . . Nate knew that face so well. It had always reminded him of his own father. It was the face in the portrait, handed from father to son down the generations for hundreds and hundreds of years, until it had come to him. Now, here Nate was, staring at this familiar figure hovering before him.

'Rook's great grandfather . . . Twig's father . . .' he said in awe. 'Quintinius Verginix.'

Nate felt a surge of emotion overwhelm him. He, a humble lamplighter from the mines of the Eastern Woods, was connected to these three legendary figures from the distant past, proof of which hung from the cord at his neck: the lufwood portrait. Their stories had passed into legend, recorded in barkscrolls and recounted around blazing fires; stories that would live on for ever. Now Nate's story was entwined with theirs. Surely this, rather than that faded never-ending existence conferred by the Garden of Life, was true immortality.

Suddenly, the light grew dazzlingly intense, and Nate was forced to look away. When he returned his gaze, the ball of light had risen into the black clouds above. Around him, by the lake shore, strands of glittering sand were spiralling up into the clouds after it, making the air sparkle. Slowly, as a warm wind got up, the mighty cloud bank began to drift away, becoming whiter and wispier as it dispersed into the open sky.

For a moment, Nate stood on the edge of the lake as a warm sun began to shine. Deep down in the mountain there was a rumbling sound that grew steadily louder until, with a gurgling roar, the flutes of the Riverrise spring spouted jets of sparkling water.

Nate pulled the glass vial from his inside pocket and crouched down at the water's edge. Unstoppering the tiny bottle, he thrust it into the turquoise water. A stream of bubbles floated to the surface as it filled. When the bubbles stopped, he climbed to his feet, pushed the cork back into place and held the full bottle up to the light.

The liquid it contained sparkled with tiny specks of chine. A smile played over Nate's lips.

'At last,' he whispered.

He pushed the bottle inside his jacket and started back across the garden, hurrying towards the staircase carved into the rock on the other side. A soft warm breeze was blowing, stirring the leaves and needles of the surrounding trees and filling the air with the perfume of the sweet-smelling flowers. But Nate scarcely noticed them, his head reeling with the event he had just witnessed. He paused and glanced back at the Riverrise spring.

The Immortals had gone, released at last from the extraordinary Garden of Life that Golderayce One-Eye had turned into a prison. Nate paused. Yet this was a wonderful place – a place of miraculous healing waters that should be shared by all, not hoarded by the custodians . . .

His head suddenly filled with images of all those he'd seen on his journey through the thorn forests: the pale wheezing infant clasped to the chest of its desperate lugtroll mother, the hobbling pink-eye old'uns, the blind woodtroll, the crippled flathead matron, the paralysed mobgnome and the cankerracked brogtroll . . .

Jaw clenched, he strode round the shore of the brimming lake, stopping only when he came to the heavy ironwork sluice. He jumped up onto the jutting side and seized the great wheel set into its top. Then, gripping it tightly in his hands, he tugged sharply to the right.

There was a soft grinding sound as cogs turned and ratchets shifted and, before him, the two great iron gates slowly began to open.

The trickle of water grew in volume as the gap between the gates became wider. Nate kept turning. The gates swung further

and further back until they were fully opened, and the trickle between them was a surging torrent of frothing water which roared through the gap between, onto the jutting lip of rock and gushed down towards the dark air far, far below.

Nate stared at it, his heart racing as he realized that for the first time in centuries, the fabled waterfall of Riverrise was flowing unchecked, restored to its former glory. He had done all he could.

Turning on his heels, he jumped down from the iron sluice and dashed back round the lake to the carved staircase in the rock, which he started down, taking the stone-cut stairs two at a time. There was one thought in his head now, and one thought only . . .

Eudoxia Prade.

PART FOUR

THE EDGE

· CHAPTER EIGHTY-ONE ·

Eudoxia looked around at the great Thorn Tunnel, her bright green eyes flashing and face flushed with excitement as she took it all in – the tangled mass of thorn trees, the dew-tipped thorns glinting in the glow of the travellers' lampstaffs, and the endless darkness beyond the tunnel of light carved through the savage forest. She turned to Nate, a smile playing on her lips.

'This is incredible,' she murmured. 'Absolutely incredible . . .' A frown plucked at the centre of her forehead. 'To think I travelled through this amazing thorn forest without noticing a thing . . .'

'You were so ill, Eudoxia,' Nate said, as the painful memories came flooding back. 'There were times when I really thought that you weren't going to make it.'

'But I *did*, Nate,' said Eudoxia, running ahead and walking backwards before him, smiling into his troubled face. 'I did make it. Look at me! I've never felt better in my life – and it's all thanks to you, Nate! You saved my life.'

Nate nodded, a smile spreading across his face as he looked at Eudoxia. She was the picture of glowing health, and as elegant as ever, despite the old grey topcoat of the Hive Militia that she insisted on wearing over the new underjacket and fine barkfelt breeches she'd purchased on the Market Ledges of Riverrise. She reached out her hands towards Nate, which he grasped and squeezed tightly.

'I couldn't have done any of it without Zelphyius Dax,' he said, shifting the sumpwood backpack on his shoulders and striding forward. 'Or Gomber and Gilmora . . .'

Eudoxia fell into step beside him and the two of them strode on through the tunnel towards the Thorn Gate.

'Or Felderforth, our guide,' added Eudoxia with an infectious giggle.

'*You're too kind,*' came Felderforth's voice in Nate and Eudoxia's heads as the waif guide caught up with them, his barbels quivering with exertion. '*The Riverrise water has certainly put a spring in your step, Miss Eudoxia. At this pace, we'll be at the Thorn Gate in one and a half tallow candles' time . . .*'

Nate and Eudoxia had encountered the waif at the Nightwood Arch some three tallow candles before. Since Nate had opened the sluice gates, and news of Golderayce's death had spread through the city, highflow and lowflow had been abolished, along with the power of the custodians. Now the citizens of Riverrise met openly in the amphitheatre, there was spring water for all, and the days and nights were once more measured in the burning down of tallow candles.

'*I'd know those thoughts anywhere,*' Felderforth had joked when they'd met at the glowing archway. The waif had reached out to Nate and shaken his hand warmly. '*And you must be Eudoxia,*' he'd said, turning to the girl by Nate's side. '*And your eyes are green, I see.*' He'd shaken her hand too. '*Now the pair of you need a guide on the Waif Trail.*'

'If you wouldn't mind,' Nate had said.

'*It would be my pleasure to guide you back to Thorn Harbour,*' the waif had replied. '*After the great service you have done the City of Night, Nate, you will live long in our thoughts.*'

They'd set off almost at once. Earlier that morning, Gomber and Gilmora had packed Nate and Eudoxia's sumpwood backpacks full of provisions for the journey ahead, and all that had remained was to bid them farewell. Gilmora had sobbed, her eyes at the end of their stalks full of sadness as she'd hugged both Nate and Eudoxia tightly. Gomber had stood to one side, his face betraying little, though the eyestalks that stuck out through the holes in his funnel hat had trembled with emotion.

'You've both brought a light into our lives,' the old gabtroll had said, 'and given us a brighter future.'

'Take care of each other,' Gilmora had called out as they'd set off. 'And come and visit us again . . .'

As their voices faded, Nate had glanced back over his shoulders to see the two ancient gabtrolls, their eyes glistening in the light from the lampstaffs they carried, leaning together, their arms wrapped tightly round one another. He raised his cupped hands to his mouth.

'We shall!' he called back. 'I promise!' He turned to Felderforth. 'Do you think they heard me?'

'*Oh, yes,*' the waif had nodded and they heard the sound of his laughter in their heads. '*They are already thinking of the welcome banquet they will give you when you return!*'

The three of them had travelled swiftly through the Nightwoods. For Nate, the journey was quite different from the one he had taken in the opposite direction. Then, every whisper he'd heard, every bloodshot eye he'd seen glinting from the shadows, had filled him with unease. With Eudoxia fit and well by his side, however, his spirits were buoyed up. What was more, the wild waifs in the depths of the Nightwoods all about them had seemed to notice, and left him and Eudoxia alone – giving Felderforth nothing to do but keep up as they strode on through the dark dank forest. By the time they got to the Thorn Tunnel, the waif guide was also in high spirits.

'*The Waif Trail shall flourish once again,*' said Felderforth. '*Now that that senile old tyrant, Golderayce One-Eye, has gone and the Riverrise spring is flowing freely once more.*' He smiled, the barbels at the corners of his mouth trembling with amusement. '*And how wonderful it is to hear real thoughts on the trail, instead of those false thoughts used to mask underthinking . . .*' He frowned, his huge black eyes growing larger as he stared along the path, then flapped a bony hand towards a faint patch of arched light, far ahead. '*There it is,*' he said, '*the Thorn Gate.*'

Eudoxia couldn't help herself. With her hands behind her, steadying the backpack on her shoulders, she broke into a run. Nate glanced round at Felderforth and shrugged.

'*Don't you worry about me, Nate,*' he said. '*I'll see you in Thorn*

Harbour. You go and catch up with the young mistress . . .' He chuckled. *'If you can!'*

Tightening the straps at his shoulder, Nate started after Eudoxia. He sprinted ahead over the springy ground, dodging and weaving through the lines of travellers, his eyes fixed on the flashes of gold ahead as Eudoxia's hair caught the light from the bobbing lampstaffs. He ran past a group of half a dozen lugtrolls, each one sandwiched between the wooden staves of heavily laden sumpwood sledges and, on the other side of them, the Thorn Gate opened up before him.

Eudoxia waited for Nate, seizing his hand when he caught up with her. She looked at him and flashed Nate a dazzling smile.

'I wanted us to go through the Thorn Gate together,' she said.

Hand in hand, they strode beneath the towering archway and out into the clearing beyond. The whole place was bustling. As well as all those arriving back from Riverrise, there were as many – if not more – about to set out on the Waif Trail. The two groups came together in a great swirling eddy, like two cloud banks converging.

Those returning from the City of Night looked weary, though happy, the sleds and limbers they were pulling piled high with boxes of salves, crates of ointments and tonics, and great earthenware pots sloshing with the priceless water from the Riverrise spring. In contrast, the expressions on the faces of those about to set off on the Waif Trail were a mixture of anticipation and anxiety. There were trogs, goblins, trolls and fourthlings, each with bulging backpacks and heavily laden sleds. Some of them had waif guides, some were still looking, and as Nate followed Eudoxia through the teeming crowds, his head filled with the voices of the waifs plying their trade.

It was, he thought, like being back in the Market Ledges of Riverrise.

Just up ahead, a party of waif custodians, no longer carried in curtained bowers but forced to walk, made their way through the hostile crowds. With them trudged a swarm of tiny red and black dwarves.

'Leaving the city?' Sneering voices from the waif guides sounded

in everyone's heads, triumphant that they could think freely at last. *'Well, good riddance to you and your slave drivers!'*

'Go lose yourselves in the daylight!'

'The waters of Riverrise, free to all in need!'

Not far off, a great gang of misshapen nameless ones stood surrounded by gabtroll matrons who, as Nate watched, bathed and tenderly dressed the creatures' many wounds.

'The City of Night can now become a truly great city.' A familiar voice sounded in Nate and Eudoxia's heads, and they turned to see Felderforth the waif staring up at them, his huge eyes glistening. *'Thank you, Nate Quarter, and travel well in the world of daylight.'*

Nate and Eudoxia both shook the waif's hand, before he slipped away into the teeming crowd.

'They're waiting for you,' his voice sounded in their heads as the guide disappeared from view.

Ahead of them were

the buildings of Thorn Harbour, silhouetted against the grey sky beyond. There were windowless warehouses and balconied rest cabins, slope-roofed weigh towers and rows of squat taverns and stores, each one with the bright globelamps crowning their ridge tiles and gable ends – lights that had looked so strange to Nate when he'd first arrived at the settlement but that now, after his time in the City of Night, looked absolutely normal.

He looked up at the bustling mooring platforms, black against the lampglow, brogtrolls and waifs busy loading and unloading the phraxbarges docked there. And as he looked, he found his gaze being drawn towards the jetty where the *Varis Lodd* had been tethered – half expecting to see the curious old-fashioned skyship still moored there, its even more curious old-fashioned captain making final adjustments to the spidersilk sails, the leadwood hull weights and sumpwood rudder . . .

But of course, Zelphyius Dax was not there. Nate had seen him departing with his own eyes. Yet the jutting berth, high up at the top of the mooring platform, was not empty. In place of the delicate-looking skycraft from the Second Age of Flight, with its tall masts and billowing white sails, was a vessel from the Third Age.

It was a magnificent phraxship that looked brand new, shiny varnish coating the curved bows and a burnished phraxchamber gleaming in the lamplight. A twisting ribbon of white steam streamed out from the top of the funnel. Up on board, staring out towards the Thorn Gate, was a tall figure in a short topcoat and crushed funnel hat, a telescope raised to one eye.

'Eudoxia,' Nate breathed, and pointed. 'Who does that look like?'

Eudoxia followed the line of his finger and let out a cry of delight.

'Professor!' she shouted and waved at him, both arms raised high above her head as she ran towards the broad staircase that led up onto the mooring platform. 'Professor! Professor!'

Whether it was the excited voice he heard, or the sight of the frantically waving figure cutting through the milling crowds, Nate wasn't sure. But all at once, the Professor looked round and, turning the eyeglass towards them, waved back.

The pair of them hurried on towards the mooring platforms. By the time they reached the bottom of the staircase, there were others standing at the Professor's shoulders – Squall Razortooth the sky pirate, wiping his hands on an oily rag, and Cirrus Gladehawk, a fine-looking black funnel hat of brushed quarmskin on his head. Nate and Eudoxia climbed the steps as quickly as they could, pushing against the stream of passengers disembarking from the host of other phraxships moored at the platforms.

'Nate!'

'Eudoxia!'

The excited voices rang out as they stepped onto the platform, and Nate looked up to see that his friends had left the phraxvessel to come and greet them.

'Here, let me take that for you,' said Cirrus Gladehawk, easing Eudoxia's backpack off her shoulders.

'It's so good to see you both,' said the Professor, hugging them each in turn.

'And looking so well!' said Squall, standing looking at them closely, his hands on his hips. 'From what that librarian scholar fellow was saying, we didn't know what to expect!'

'"Gravely ill," he said,' the Professor nodded, looking at Eudoxia. '"Not certain whether she'll make it to Riverrise," *he* said . . . Yet look at you!' He smiled and, spotting Eudoxia's grey topcoat, shook his head in joyful disbelief. 'Eudoxia,' he breathed, his eyes gleaming brightly. 'Nate. I thought I'd lost you both to the Hive Militia for ever . . .'

'Friend Nate!' The excited voice was coming from the far end of the wooden platform. 'Friend Nate! Mistress Eudoxia!'

Nate and Eudoxia turned to see Slip the grey goblin scuttler dashing towards them, a large bundle clasped to his chest, which he let drop to the ground as he drew close. He fell upon Nate and hugged him warmly.

'Slip *knew* he'd see friend Nate again! He knew it!' he exclaimed

565

delightedly. He pulled away. '*And* Mistress Eudoxia,' he said. 'Slip is so happy.'

He turned to Weelum the banderbear, who was shambling up behind him, his great body bowed beneath the weight of a dozen or more boxes, crates and packages tied up with string.

'Didn't Slip say we'd see them again?' the grey goblin demanded. 'Didn't he?'

'Wuh-wuh,' said Weelum. *A thousand times and more*, he confirmed, an indulgent smile on his huge face.

Nate laughed.

'Wuh-wuh wurra wuh!' said the banderbear, touching his claws gently to his chest, and extending his arm first to Nate, then to Eudoxia. *My heart is filled with joy at our reunion.*

'Yes, what he said,' laughed the Professor, and clapped a hand on Nate and Eudoxia's shoulder. 'Come on, the two of you, let's get you aboard the *Archemax*.'

'So this is the *Archemax*!' Nate exclaimed, turning towards the magnificent phraxship berthed at the platform. 'But the last I heard, the *Archemax* was a wreck, skewered at the top of an ironwood pine.'

'Not any more,' Cirrus Gladehawk told him proudly, tugging at his neatly pressed jacket and readjusting his funnel hat. 'Now she's the finest vessel ever to raise steam.'

'A lot has changed since the battle of the Midwood marshes,' the Professor said as they made their way back to the *Archemax*, Slip and Weelum carrying the provisions they'd bought from the well-stocked Thorn Harbour stalls below. 'When the militia returned, there was a revolution and Kulltuft Warhammer and his Clan Council cronies were overthrown. After Zelphyius brought us news of you, we left a very different Hive behind us, I can tell you.'

'And then, when we arrived here in Thorn Harbour,' Cirrus continued, 'the place was buzzing with tales of *your* exploits, Nate . . .'

'Toppling the Custodian General, opening the sluice gates at the

Riverrise spring!' Squall chuckled delightedly. 'We're all proud of you, Nate, lad.'

'We got here as quickly as we could,' Cirrus said, turning to Eudoxia, 'in view of your father's condition, so that he could see you one last time. Your waif guide sent word that you were coming . . .'

'See me one last time?' Eudoxia exclaimed. 'You mean he's here?'

The Professor looked up and nodded towards the *Archemax*, the phraxship swaying gently in the gathering breeze.

'Your father is dying, Eudoxia . . .' he began.

But Eudoxia had already turned and was running. Nate went with her. They pounded over the boards of the mooring platform towards the phraxship and leaped on board. Eudoxia looked round for a moment, before hurrying back over the new deck towards the aft cabin.

'Father!' she cried. 'Father!'

She seized the burnished handle of the freshly painted door to the master cabin, pulled it open, stepped inside – and stopped. The cabin was in semi-darkness, a single phraxlamp glowing dimly on the far side. Then, out of the stillness, Eudoxia heard a sound. It was the sound of breathing, low and rasping, though so faint that Eudoxia could have easily mistaken it for the wind outside sighing through the mooring rope – if it hadn't been for the coils of water vapour she saw twisting in the lamp glow.

'Father?' she said, her voice little more than a whisper.

'Eu . . . doxia . . .' a frail voice answered from the shadows.

Eudoxia stepped forward tentatively. And as she did so, she saw her father lying in a sumpwood cot, wrapped up in a thick quilted blanket, his head resting on a snowbird down pillow.

'Oh, Father,' Eudoxia breathed.

'I . . . saw you . . .' he gasped, the twists of vapour from his diseased lungs spilling out from between his thin blue-tinged lips. He turned his head slightly. 'From . . . out of the cabin . . . window. I . . . am so happy that . . .' His words gave out, and Galston Prade was suddenly seized by a fit of violent coughing. The cold wispy

567

mist filled the air above his head as his emaciated body was racked with wheezing convulsions, and his eyes, dark-ringed and sunken, stared imploringly at his daughter.

'Nate, Nate,' said Eudoxia desperately, reaching out towards him. 'The vial. Give me the vial . . .'

Nate fumbled with the buttons of his jacket and plunged a hand deep into the inside pocket. His trembling fingers closed round a glass vial, which he pulled out and passed to Eudoxia. The old man's coughing had stopped, but he was unable to speak, all his concentration devoted on the shallow rasping breaths he snatched at. Eudoxia pulled the cork from the bottle of glistening water and, stepping forward, placed a hand on her father's creased bony forehead. It was icy cold.

'Drink this, Father,' she whispered, tears filling her eyes. 'It comes from the Riverrise lake itself.'

Slowly she leaned towards him and, tilting the bottle, let a drop of water fall into his mouth between his parted lips. Then another. And another . . .

Behind Nate and Eudoxia, the others had crept through the open door and into the cabin. The Professor, Cirrus Gladehawk, Squall Razortooth, Weelum and Slip. They stared at Galston Prade, their breath held and eyes unblinking, while outside the gathering wind whistled round the moored vessel, tipping her from side to side.

The old man's eyes rolled in his head.

Eudoxia's green eyes were fixed on her father's face. At first, he looked just as ill as he had before, his grey skin taut and drawn, his papery eyelids closed. But then, even in the dim glow of the phraxlamp, she saw something.

'His lips,' she whispered. 'They're . . .'

Nate nodded. Almost imperceptibly, Galston Prade's thin lips were losing the metallic blue colour that had stained them and were suffused instead with a soft pink that, as Eudoxia watched, spread across her father's face. His hollow cheeks filled out, the dark rings around his eyes grew paler and faded away completely as the colour returned to his grey lifeless skin. Around his sagging jawline and

down his neck the flush of health spread. His jaw unclenched and the cable-like tendons in his neck were smoothed away. Inside the quilted blanket that swaddled his cadaverous body, his bony frame grew larger, broader, and his slumped posture became more upright. All at once, with a low grunt of effort, Galston Prade reached up and pulled the blanket away from him. His eyes slowly opened.

Eudoxia stared into them and, as she did so, she saw how the mist that had seemed to cloud them for so long was dissolving. And, by degrees, the eyes staring back at her began to fill with colour, turning from the pale phraxlung blue to a deep green, exactly the same shade as her own.

'Eudoxia,' he whispered, and when he spoke, the word was no longer accompanied by the deadly wisps of water vapour. Then Galston Prade climbed out of the sumpwood cot and straightened up.

'It feels wonderful, doesn't it?' Eudoxia said. 'It was the same for me, when Nate gave me the water of life.'

'Yes, Eudoxia,' said her father, grinning broadly. 'Yes, it does feel wonderful!'

Eudoxia fell into his arms. 'Oh, Father, Father,' she sobbed. 'I've missed you so much . . .'

Just then, a loud thud echoed through the *Archemax* as the wind caught her hull and sent the bow knocking hard into the mooring dock.

'The wind's picking up, by the sound of it,' said Cirrus Gladehawk. 'If we're going to leave on this expedition of yours, Professor, then it should be soon.'

The Professor nodded. 'Then let us set off,' he said.

Nate turned to him. 'Expedition?' he said. 'Expedition to where?'

· CHAPTER EIGHTY-TWO ·

Far below the *Archemax*, the phraxstorm had formed a great swirling wheel of cloud. Now it was whirling round and round above the Twilight Woods, drawn there by the phrax-laden air of the treacherous forest, the dark boiling clouds lit up by the golden glow of the woods beneath.

All at once, with a dazzling flash, a lightning bolt was disgorged by the storm and sent hurtling down into the woods.

'Did you see that!' said Eudoxia, pulling back and turning to her father, then to Nate, her eyes flashing with excitement as the air below resounded with deep rumbling thunder. 'We've just witnessed the creation of stormphrax!'

The three of them were standing on the mid deck of the phraxship. Behind them was the covered helm, where Cirrus Gladehawk was keeping a steely grip on the flight levers, with Weelum beside him, the gusty wind ruffling his thick fur. Above their heads, the great phraxchamber throbbed, Slip the grey goblin using a long metal spike to keep the cooling plates free of ice. Above him, at the very top, Squall Razortooth – his open tool pouch at his side – had removed a chamber panel and was realigning a twisted buoyancy rod. Eudoxia gripped the starboard bow tightly and leaned forward again, peering down over the side at the lightning storm below.

'That bolt of lightning will have solidified in the twilight air down there,' said Nate. 'Already it will be starting to bury itself in the earth as its tip becomes heavy in the darkness and drags the rest of the bolt down. It'll sink deeper and deeper, breaking into a million shards, until one day,' he said, turning towards Eudoxia, 'a phraxminer will find a piece of it far below ground. He'll break his back and risk his life digging it out . . .' He stared down at the glowing forest. 'Only

STERN

AFT CABINS

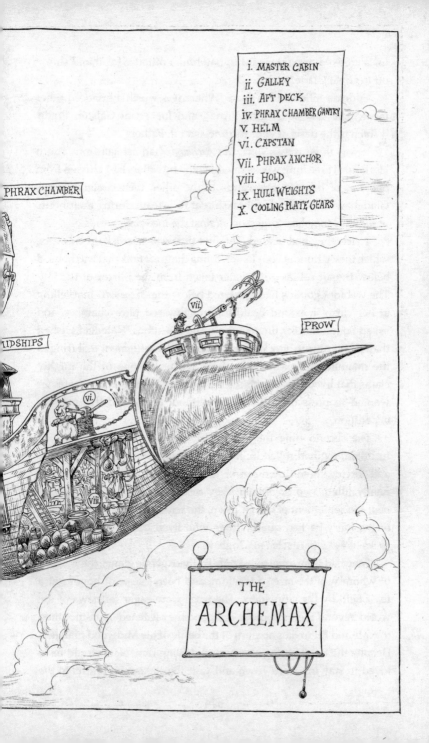

i. MASTER CABIN
ii. GALLEY
iii. AFT DECK
iv. PHRAX CHAMBER GANTRY
v. HELM
vi. CAPSTAN
vii. PHRAX ANCHOR
viii. HOLD
ix. HULL WEIGHTS
x. COOLING PLATE GEARS

PHRAX CHAMBER

MIDSHIPS

PROW

THE
ARCHEMAX

for a crooked mine sergeant to pay him a pittance for it and ship it off to Great Glade.'

Eudoxia followed his gaze. 'Where it is worth a hundred times more,' she said softly. She turned and looked at Galston Prade. 'Which is the basis of your fortune, isn't it, Father?'

It was three weeks since the *Archemax* had set sail from Thorn Harbour. Three long weeks in which the travellers had crossed from one end of the vast Edgelands to the other, their captain, Cirrus Gladehawk, keeping the phraxship at full steam during their hours of flight as they had forged on against the incoming winds.

Twice, they had landed. The first time was to stock up on water, which they'd done at Four Lakes, filling the great tank that was housed below the aft cabins with water taken from the Mirror of the Sky. The webfoot goblins had clustered below the *Archemax*, marvelling at her clean lines and beautifully engineered phraxchamber, and asked Squall the sky pirate a thousand questions. Nate had wished they'd had time to stay longer, to explore the settlement that fringed the magnificent lakes and perhaps even visit one of the mighty clams that lived in their depths. But they all knew that the Professor wanted to press on to the Edge without delay, and this was his expedition.

The second time they'd landed was when a broad front of turbulent fog had rolled in, making accurate navigation impossible and forcing them down out of the sky. It was only when the fog finally lifted, two days later, they discovered that they'd moored near the settlement of Gorge Town, the scree huts and rambleshacks of the hairy-backed quarry trogs who lived there, clinging to the rocks like sky barnacles to a logbait.

They had been greeted warmly by these gentle giants, the shortest of whom was the size of Weelum, and been guests of honour at a feast held by the city elders. The trogs were eager for news of the world beyond their remote gorges, and they listened open-mouthed to Nate and Eudoxia's account of the battle of the Midwood marshes. Despite the frequent fog storms and driving rain, Nate would have loved to stay in Gorge Town and visit the stalagmite forests in the dark caverns below the city. But once again, the Professor was anxious to forge ahead.

Now, the Deepwoods were behind them, and the *Archemax* was steaming towards the eastern tip of the Edgelands, where the mighty lip of rock jutted out into the sky beyond – and the mysterious cliff face plunged down into the darkness far below.

'I owe my fortune to stormphrax, it's true,' Galston Prade said, plucking at the sleeves of his quarm fur-trimmed topcoat. He turned the carved fromp-head cane thoughtfully in his hand. 'But it has also been the ruin of me,' he said, and sighed. 'And I don't mean phraxlung, though Sky knows that was bad enough.' He shook his head. 'I learned to adapt, without even thinking. I got used to pausing to catch my breath halfway up every staircase I took. And I pretended that I enjoyed the leisurely strolls around New Lake

that were forced upon me, telling myself that if I walked any faster, I'd miss the beautiful lake views. Though, of course, that option was never open to me . . .'

He reached out and took Eudoxia by both hands and looked deep into her eyes.

'No, stormphrax has dominated my life in other ways,' he said bleakly. 'I'm afraid I haven't been a very good father to you.'

'Oh, Father,' said Eudoxia. 'You did what you could. You were a wonderful father to me – and it can't have been easy for you when Mother died.'

'And you, my daughter, are as kind and beautiful as she was,' Galston said, gently squeezing Eudoxia's hands. 'But I allowed the Prade phraxmine to take over my life and the pursuit of stormphrax to poison my days, just as surely as the phraxdust ate away at my lungs. Now I must change.'

'But I love you just the way you are,' said Eudoxia, smiling through tears that she hadn't even noticed gathering in the corners of her eyes.

'Do you really, Eudoxia,' he said gently, and let go of her hands. 'I had a lot of time to think in the Gyle Palace in Hive. The closeness of death made me see everything differently. Felftis Brack, for instance . . .'

Eudoxia raised her eyebrows. 'Him!' she said, and snorted.

'He was a rogue, of course,' said Galston. 'I knew that when I hired him. I've used unscrupulous ambitious characters like Felftis to build up the profits in the mine for years, no questions asked. You see, I was always strong enough to control them. They were crooks and swindlers, but they were *my* crooks and swindlers! Then phraxlung took over and I became weak, and Felftis saw his chance.' He frowned, his face troubled. 'But was I truly any better than him? Would it have made any real difference to those hardworking miners at the phraxface if one phraxmine owner had been replaced by another?'

He turned to Nate, who was standing looking down awkwardly at the deck, his hands deep in his breeches' pockets.

'Young Nate here risked his life digging for phraxcrystals in my mine, only to be swindled out of a fair price.'

Hearing his name, Nate looked up, to see Eudoxia frowning at him.

'It . . . it wasn't your fault, sir,' he blustered, his cheeks flushing with colour. 'It was that mine sergeant, Grint Grayle . . .'

'Yes, Nate,' said Galston, kindly but firmly. 'But I appointed Felftis Brack, and he appointed Grint Grayle, who cheated and robbed you and the other miners. I could have done something to stop it – visited the mine, seen the conditions for myself. But I chose not to. Instead, I idled my time away in my mansion in New Lake, walking by the lake and organizing thousandsticks teams. It was easy for Felftis Brack to trick me into going to Hive, supposedly to recruit players. He knew I loved the game and how it took my mind off my other worries. I was a selfish short-sighted old fool . . .'

'But you were ill, Father,' Eudoxia protested.

'Maybe so,' Galston Prade said. 'But now, thanks to you both, I am well again, and things are going to change at the Prade mine. There will be no more flogging, no more withholding pay for petty offences – and no more phraxlung,' he said. 'No miner shall work at the phraxface for more than five, no four . . . for more than *three* years,' he announced, bringing the end of his cane down sharply on the deck, 'over which period of time, if paid a fair price for the crystals they mine,' he went on, warming to his theme, 'each miner will have earned enough to set himself up for a new life in Great Glade – a life which you and I, Nate, are in a position to offer him . . .'

'Me?' said Nate, surprised. 'I'm just a lamplighter.'

'A lamplighter who has inherited a phraxchamber works in Copperwood,' said Galston Prade, pushing his greying hair back from his forehead. 'It's a simple proposal. Since I own the phraxmine and you own the phraxchamber works . . .'

He paused when he saw the puzzled look on Nate and Eudoxia's faces.

'You mean you don't know about Friston Drew's will? But then, how stupid of me!' he exclaimed. 'How could you? We've all been so wrapped up in this expedition of the Professor's that this is the first time I've thought of our old lives back in Great Glade. You must forgive me,' said Galston. 'I knew Friston well,' he went on. 'We'd been near neighbours in New Lake for years, and I know how highly he valued you, Nate. I remember over dinner one evening, completely out of the blue, he turned to me and said, "How does Gremlop, Drew and Quarter sound to you?"'

Nate swallowed, remembering that fateful afternoon when Friston Drew had asked him the selfsame question.

'He told me that you were the son he never had,' said Galston.

'But he does have a son,' said Eudoxia. 'And I know Branxford. He's not going give up his inheritance without a fight.'

'But he already has, Eudoxia,' said Galston. 'When he sold his inheritance of the phraxchamber works to Felftis Brack, it wasn't even his to sell. Friston Drew had already named Nate in his will as the sole beneficiary in the event of his death. The will was found hidden among the papers in Felftis Brack's study when he was arrested. Besides,' he added gravely, 'according to my sources, Branxford Drew is in no position to fight for anything.'

'He isn't?' said Eudoxia.

Her father shook his head. 'Before the *Archemax* left Hive for Thorn Harbour, I received word that, at his trial, Felftis Brack named Branxford Drew as his accomplice in the explosion in the phraxchamber works – and the death of his poor dear father. That very day, Branxford tried to escape to the Western Woods in that phraxlighter of his and was shot out of the sky by a phraxmarine patrol ship. He went down in a blazing fireball.'

'Poor Branxford,' said Eudoxia. 'He was weak and spoilt, and caused so much harm, but he didn't deserve to die like that.'

For a moment, no one spoke. It was Galston who broke the silence at last.

'This is what I propose,' he said. 'When this voyage is over, we set up a phraxship yard. And not just any phraxship yard,' he said, his eyes twinkling with excitement. 'No, we'll establish the finest and most innovative shipbuilder's in the whole of Great Glade. Back in Hive I was ill, but even so, I saw how Cirrus and Squall worked to restore the *Archemax*.' He swept his arm round in a broad arc. 'Just look about you,' he said. 'There are more innovations in this one vessel than in the entire Great Glade fleet. With the Prade phraxmine and Gremlop, Drew and Quarter working alongside, the "Archemax Yard" could transform the nature of flight – and humble those haughty academics in the Cloud Quarter into the bargain. Never again will they be able to control the phraxship fleet, because we'll open up the skies to all! So, what do you say, Nate?'

'It . . . sounds very exciting,' said Nate, his head swimming.

'It will be,' said Galston, tapping his cane on the deck excitedly. 'Once the skies are open to all, the settlements will grow. Gorge Town, the Farrow Ridges, Four Lakes, the Northern Reaches, and hundreds of others will become great cities in their own right. Who knows,' he said with a smile as he gazed down at the glowing Twilight Woods, 'we might even be at the beginning of a *Fourth* Age of Flight!'

Galston put his arm round his daughter and gave her a hug.

'Let's leave young Nate to think it over, while we check on how Slip's getting along in the galley,' he said. 'Is it my imagination, or can I smell frying glimmeronions?'

Eudoxia laughed, and as the pair of them walked back along the deck, Nate turned his gaze to the ship's beaked prow. In the distance, he could see the edge of the Twilight Woods giving way to the verdant grasslands of the Mire beyond, which glowed a dazzling shade of lush green in the low sun. He was about to turn away and return to the aft cabin to go through his box of memories – Nate liked to go through its contents when there was thinking to be done – when something caught his attention.

It was the Professor.

The tall, slightly stooped figure was standing up at the prow of the phraxship, alone and staring out into the distance. The Professor turned and noticed Nate watching him.

'Ah, Nate,' he said, removing his wire-rimmed spectacles, breathing on the lenses and wiping them slowly up and down the lapel of his short topcoat. 'You find me lost in thoughts of what lies ahead.'

Nate approached the prow.

'The Edge cliff?' he said as he joined the Professor.

For a moment his friend said nothing. He put on his spectacles and resumed his steady gaze out across the glowing green landscape beyond. When he spoke, his voice was low, yet full of resolve.

'The Edge cliff. Yes, Nate,' he said, looking ahead. 'And unfinished business.'

'Your brother,' said Nate.

The Professor nodded. 'Ifflix was one of the finest scholars of his generation, and I want to find out what became of him,' he said. 'I owe him that much at least.' The low sun reflected in the panels of his spectacles as his mouth creased into a grim smile. 'You call me the Professor,' he said and laughed humourlessly. 'Yet I am nothing more than a sham.'

'But . . .' Nate started.

'It's true, Nate,' he said. 'Oh, I can tell you the names of all the Most High Academes who ruled ancient Sanctaphrax during the First Age. I could rattle off the names of the academies and minor schools. I could probably name a hundred of the trees that grow in the Deepwoods. But as for the true pursuit of knowledge, that's another thing entirely.' His face clouded over. 'I left that behind, many, many years ago.' He sighed. 'I was a good scholar,' he said. 'The best in my year – as my old professor, Cassix Lodestone, kindly reminded me a while ago. The mysteries of the Edge cliff have always fascinated me – just as they fascinated our archivist friends back in the Sumpwood Bridge Academy. What memories those two stirred up with their rock samples and light magnifiers and talk of glisters! Yet I gave it all up . . .'

He shook his head wearily.

'And I squandered my life gambling and brawling – and giving lectures to pampered fourthling matrons in the baskets of the skytaverns.' He smiled half-heartedly at Nate. 'A fine "professor" I turned out to be . . .' His face grew taut and his dark eyes narrowed as they stared through the lenses of his spectacles. 'But my brother, Ifflix, was different. He was prepared to risk everything in his attempt to discover the ultimate mystery, by descending into the darkness. Can you imagine it, Nate?' he said, his eyes glazed with wonder. 'Descending the Edge cliff itself, into the realm of myth and ancient superstition, to discover what truly lies beneath . . .'

He fell still. Nate looked away. Behind him, the yellow sun was sinking down towards the horizon over the Twilight Woods. Below the *Archemax*, with its funnel billowing a steady trail of steam, the swaying blades of thick grass rippled like water as a low breeze played over it.

'I'm grateful to you,' the Professor said. 'To all of you, for coming with me on this expedition to discover my brother's fate. I know I've seemed distant and distracted at times, Nate, wanting us to press on when you would have preferred to stay longer in the places we've visited, but that is because I have made a decision.'

'You have?' said Nate.

'Just like my brother, Ifflix,' said the Professor, 'I shall become a descender.'

· CHAPTER EIGHTY-THREE ·

'I'm taking her down!' Cirrus Gladehawk's voice sounded from the helm. 'This could be our last chance to take on water before the Edge.'

Eudoxia emerged from the aft cabins and hurried up to the prow to join Nate and the Professor.

'I don't want to miss this,' she said excitedly as the three of them looked down at the vast sea of grassland below them.

Squall Razortooth climbed down from the phraxchamber to the deck, where Slip the goblin met him, pulling off the stew-stained apron he was wearing and wiping his hands on it.

'Slip reckons supper can wait awhile, considering,' he smiled.

Behind him, Galston Prade, cane in hand, nodded in agreement. 'It's not every day you get to set foot in a desolate wilderness reborn,' he said.

'Weelum, to the anchor winch,' Cirrus commanded, sending the banderbear loping over to the ironwood capstan in the middle of the fore deck. 'Squall, prepare the phraxanchor if you please – the wide grapple, weighted for mud.'

'Aye aye, Captain,' the old sky pirate replied, joining Nate, Eudoxia and the Professor at the beaked brow.

Bending down, Squall lifted a hatch and stood back as a counterbalanced phraxcannon swung up into place. Hanging beneath it from the gun carriage was an array of anchors, from heavy-tipped barbs for rock anchorage and triple-pronged hooks for forest mooring, to the wide five-pronged grapple used when the ground was soft. As Nate and the others stepped back, Squall fitted the grapple with weights and threaded a thick chain through its shaft, before loading it into the muzzle of the phraxcannon.

Looking over the side, Nate saw what they were heading for: a circular pool of clear water, nestling in the lush swaying bladegrass of the Mire.

'Prepare to fire the anchor!' Cirrus bellowed. 'Stand by to winch us in.'

'Wuh-wuh!' Weelum called back, checking that the chain running from the capstan to the phraxanchor was free of obstructions and gripping the spokes of the capstan in his powerful claws.

Slowly, the *Archemax* descended. As it did so, a vast flock of red and blue birds rose out of the grass and fanned off across the sky in a tumult of flapping wings and loud indignant squawks. At the helm, with a loud *clank*, Cirrus shut off the thrust lever completely and began the delicate manoeuvre of bringing the phraxship into a low hover. He raised the hull weights, then delicately aligned the flight levers.

'Fire!' he commanded.

Taking careful aim, Squall fired the phraxcannon. In a cloud of billowing steam, the phraxanchor shot out from the *Archemax* in an arcing flight, trailing the heavy chain behind it.

It landed with a heavy squelching *thud*, and lodged itself in the thick matted vegetation beside the pool. A moment later, the *Archemax* came to a halt, hovering above the Mire as the chain stretched taut, the phraxchamber now humming softly and the faintest ribbon of white steam trailing from the top of the funnel.

'Winch us in, Weelum!' Cirrus called from the helm, and with a grunt of effort, the great banderbear began to turn the capstan.

As the chain was winched in, the *Archemax* descended towards the Mire, until it hovered no more than a few feet above the lush grasslands.

'Now let's fill up that water tank,' Cirrus called from the helm. He turned to the crew. 'Slip,' he said, 'help me with the water pipe. Weelum, to the pumps if you please – and Squall, keep an eye on the tank valve.'

As the grey goblin, banderbear and sky pirate set about their various tasks, Galston Prade and the Professor lowered a sumpwood ladder from the port bow.

'Don't stray too far,' called Cirrus as the two of them climbed down the ladder, followed by Nate and Eudoxia. 'The Mire can be a treacherous place.'

'That's it,' said Nate a moment later as he helped Eudoxia down the last rung and onto the ground.

He looked around, overwhelmed by the immensity of the endless grassland. Eudoxia took him by the hand and led him away from the phraxship and the pool, where Galston was now telling the Professor of his plans for a phraxship yard.

Nate and Eudoxia kept walking, going up and down as the ground rose and fell, for although it had looked flat from above, now that they were down below, they discovered that the grassy Mire was a series of low hills and shallow valleys. The ground beneath their feet was soft and springy and sometimes, when they put their boots down, it bubbled up with muddy water.

They passed by the ancient skeleton of a muglump, a fearsome creature that had inhabited the Mire when it was a world of bleached mud. The muglump's pitted carapace was set over barrelled ribs, with a sharp spike at the end of its whiplash tail and the bones of six stubby legs, each tipped with glinting rapier claws, splayed out and half buried in a grassy hillock. Nate and Eudoxia climbed to the top of the hillock, where they paused and looked back at the *Archemax* in the distance.

'I think we've gone far enough,' Eudoxia said, surveying the view.

Beside her, Nate turned slowly round. The grassland spread out in all directions, a seemingly unbroken expanse of green that, as the wind blew the long leaves this way and that, exposing first the dark tops of the blades then the pale green underside a moment later, looked almost luminous in the setting sun. And birds! There were so many birds that had made their home in this unpopulated corner of the Edge. The flock of red and blue birds they had disturbed was only one species among many.

As the sun sank down towards the horizon, thousands more emerged. Small yellow and brown chattering birds that gripped the spears of grass and pecked at the seeds clustered on their sides; purple birds with gold crests and lyre-like tail feathers that skimmed the surface of the grass, snapping at the mire midges and glowflies that clustered there; and long lines of tall flightless birds – with stubby wings, angular orange legs and thick, fur-like plumage in gaudy shades of turquoise and magenta – that strutted over the soft ground stabbing down into the earth with their long yellow bills, skewering sticklefish and marshsnails as they passed. And, with the sky slowly darkening, the air grew loud with a cacophony of chirrups, squawks, screeches and long keening cries that echoed across the grasslands.

'Eudoxia,' said Nate softly. 'Do you remember what I told you about the Riverrise spring?' he began.

'Yes, of course,' said Eudoxia, turning to Nate and noticing the strange troubled look on her friend's face. 'You said Golderayce tried to kill you, but that you pushed him and he fell to his death, and then you gathered the water of life and opened the sluice gates, so that all could benefit from the Riverrise Spring . . .'

'Well, that's not the whole truth,' said Nate hesitantly.

'It isn't?' said Eudoxia, searching his face for clues as to what he was thinking.

'No,' said Nate. 'I didn't say anything at first, because it was so incredible I could hardly believe it myself. I've been going over and over the events in the Garden of Life, trying to make sense of them in my head – but it all seems like a dream to me now.'

'What does, Nate?' said Eudoxia. 'What really happened up there?'

'If I tell you,' said Nate, 'do you promise not to laugh at me or think I'm mad?'

Eudoxia stared at Nate, her eyes flashing. 'I would never do that!' she exclaimed hotly. 'You are the best friend I've ever had, Nate Quarter, and I owe you my life. Whatever it is you tell me happened in the Gardens of Life, I'll believe you, I promise.'

'Golderayce didn't fall to his death,' said Nate. 'The truth is far stranger. A great caterbird swooped down out of the sky and deflected the dart that Golderayce had fired at me by flapping its wings and creating a back draft. The dart was turned back on Golderayce, and when it hit him, I saw him crumble to dust in front of my eyes. Then the caterbird flew away.' He shook his head. 'But that's not all . . .'

'Go on,' said Eudoxia intently.

'There were others up there besides Golderayce,' said Nate.

'Others?' asked Eudoxia.

'They called themselves "the Immortals",' Nate answered, a faraway look in his eyes. 'Two ancient figures from the First and Second Age. Golderayce had kept them imprisoned in the Garden of Life for centuries. One was the legendary sky pirate, Twig Verginix, who Squall sometimes talks about. The other was Rook Barkwater, the Freeglade Lancer the professor once mentioned. I saw them, Eudoxia, as plainly as I can see you now, and they talked to me. And then a great storm arrived at the Riverrise peak, and they rose up into it.'

'Rose up?' Eudoxia repeated, puzzled.

'I know it sounds incredible,' said Nate, 'but they began to glow, and then they rose up into a ball of light in the centre of the storm, and became young again . . . And they weren't alone. There was a third figure in the ball of light.'

'A third figure? Who was it?' asked Eudoxia.

Nate reached for the cord at his neck and pulled the portrait miniature from beneath his jacket.

'It was him,' he said, showing the portrait of Quintinius Verginix to his astonished friend.

'But this is the portrait your father gave you, for your memory box. Handed down through generations of your family, a portrait from the First Age,' said Eudoxia, 'which means . . .'

'I am related to Quintinius Verginix, knight academic,' said Nate, his eyes glistening. 'Unless, of course, I simply dreamed the whole thing.'

'If you say this is who you saw in the storm,' said Eudoxia, turning the portrait miniature over in her hand and letting it fall back on the cord around Nate's neck, 'then I believe you.'

'Have you seen him?'

A voice sounded from out of the sea of grass close by. Nate and Eudoxia spun round to see two figures emerging from the grass at the foot of the hillock and staring up at them.

They were a female and a young'un, both carrying packs on their backs, festooned with bales of cloth, cooking pots, water jars and utensils of various sorts. They were thin-faced and gangly, their dark blue-tinged hair sprouting in matted tufts from their heads and interlaced with clumps of fragrant wood lavender and white stormferns. They wore leather jerkins and breeches, and each had a high ribbed collar and cloak of woven moss that reached down to their feet.

It was to these that Nate and Eudoxia's eyes were drawn. They were thin and bird-like, with three long toes below a knobbly ankle that bent backwards, the shin rising to the knee like the hind leg of a tilder or gladebuck. As they approached, Nate could see how they both took quick springy strides on their curious legs. In addition to her other loads, the female carried a broad timber hand loom on her

587

back, complete with loom weights and weaving combs.

'Seen who?' replied Eudoxia, shielding her eyes against the setting sun.

'The guide,' said the female simply, springing up the low hillock, followed by the young'un at her heels. 'We're fettle-leggers from the Northern Reaches, simple weavers by trade, and he is guiding us to a new life in the fabled city on the edge of the world. I'm Wyver, and this is my daughter, Tentermist . . .' She reached out a bony long-fingered hand and touched the sleeve of Eudoxia's underjacket. 'Why, Sky bless you, miss, but you're wearing barkcloth woven by fettle-leggers just like us. Riverrise tailoring, by the cut of it – though I don't care for your topcoat. Very poor quality, if I might say so.'

'I wear it for sentimental reasons,' said Eudoxia, smoothing down the old Hive Militia topcoat. 'I'm afraid we haven't seen your guide, have we, Nate?'

Nate shook his head.

The fettle-legger young'un looked thin and exhausted. She was crouching at her mother's feet and staring up at them, a frightened imploring expression on her face.

Tears filled Wyver's eyes. 'There are over three hundred of us, from all of the fettle-legger villages around the Northern Reaches,' she said. 'Times are hard for poor weavers, what with the coming of the fog mills, with their mistwheels to power the looms. They can spin nightspider silk, bark cloth and mossweave by the phraxshipful in less than a tenth of the time it takes us. We were starving when the guide came and promised us a new life . . .'

She slumped to the ground, Tentermist clutching her by the shoulders and joining in her sobs.

'I couldn't leave my hand loom behind, even though we were going to the city of shining spires, where no one goes hungry – but it slowed Tentermist and me down, and now we're lost.'

'We're going to the Edge,' said Eudoxia, bending down and stroking the distraught fettle-legger's arm. 'You can travel with us, if you like.'

· CHAPTER EIGHTY-FOUR ·

A thick mist had risen up from the Mire during the night, and now swathed the grasslands in a dense white blanket. All around the *Archemax*, as the dawn broke, the strange cries of the birds echoed through the mist like waif whispers in the Nightwoods.

Nate shivered and did up the buttons of his green leather flight jacket, while beside him on the port deck, Eudoxia did the same to her grey topcoat. Their guests, the two fettle-leggers, crouched by the prow, surrounded by their belongings, their moss cloaks spread out from their high collars like small stiff tents. Despite the best efforts of Nate and the rest of the crew, they'd insisted on spending the night on the open deck.

'It's nothing more than a soft quilt of mist,' Wyver commented, glancing up and seeing Nate and Eudoxia. 'Not like the freezing fog storms of the Northern Reaches.'

'The guide spoke of a city of shining spires where it is always warm and sunny,' Tentermist chirped up. 'No need for stickle collars and moss cloaks there, he said.'

'This guide, did he tell you the name of the city you were travelling to?' asked Eudoxia, crinkling up her nose and thrusting her cold hands into her pockets.

Wyver shook her head, drops of dew from her hair sprinkling the high collar at her neck as she did so.

'Not exactly,' she replied with a smile. 'He just said that it was at the edge of world, and that poor folks such as us would be welcomed there, no matter where we'd come from.'

When Nate and Eudoxia had turned up the night before with the two fettle-leggers in tow, Cirrus Gladehawk had been as intrigued as all the others by their story.

'We wouldn't want to put you out, sir,' Wyver had said, 'only we're lost and have nowhere else to turn.'

'Not at all,' the captain had said. 'Please, you and the young'un, make yourselves comfortable. City of shining spires, you say?'

He shot the Professor a quizzical look. The Professor shook his head in reply.

'We'll be happy to take you with us to the Edge,' Cirrus had said. 'We'll raise steam at dawn. But as for this city of yours . . .'

Now, with the pale disc of the sun shining dimly through the thick mist, the phraxchamber of the *Archemax* began to hum and steam billowed out of its funnel. Slowly, as the phraxanchor at the prow was winched up, the phraxship rose in the air and set off towards the east.

As they continued across the sky, the fog brightened, then dulled, yet became no thinner. It was several hours later when Slip the grey goblin called out from the prow.

'Row of lights,' his voice echoed back along the phraxship. 'Starboard bow.'

Squall Razortooth, who was standing at the phraxchamber, tending to the cooling plates, looked across. Beside him, Weelum, a selection of tools ready and waiting to be passed to the sky pirate when he requested them, looked too.

'It must be the rest of your party,' said the Professor, his collar pulled up high against the cold damp air. 'Though in these conditions, it's hard to tell.'

Nate and Eudoxia looked down through the foggy air at the column of fuzzy yellow lights strung out in a line far below them. Tentermist giggled as they passed overhead, running round in excited circles on the fore deck, her strange feet tapping out a rhythmic dance on the planks.

'It *is* them!' she cried, her face beaming with delight. 'And we're going to get there first!'

A short while later, tall dark shapes began emerging out of the swirling fog below them – shapes which, as the *Archemax* came down lower in the sky, revealed themselves to be the remains of high walls and crumbling towers, all overgrown with lush vegetation, festooned with broad-fingered leaves and tangles of matted tendrils.

Standing beside the captain at the prow, the Professor gave a low rueful whistle through his teeth.

'So this is Old Undertown,' he said. 'Or leastways, what's left of it. So much for the shining spires . . .'

The *Archemax* steamed on over the strange mist-shrouded ruins with their sprouting ferns and towering clumps of vine, seemingly looking up towards them like the grey forms of giant nameless ones. As the mist thickened, Cirrus Gladehawk's hands danced over the flight levers, easing the propulsion duct shut and bringing the phraxship into a low hover. At the stern, Squall fired the twin anchor hooks. Their curved spikes caught on the vegetation below and Weelum winched them in. With a soft wheezing sigh, the *Archemax* came to a halt several feet above what had once been a city square.

Now, the fine buildings that lined it were little more than ivy-clad rubble, while the paving slabs were covered in a thick carpet of moss. Cirrus called for the sumpwood ladder to be lowered, and the crew of the *Archemax* climbed down into the eerie ruins, followed by the heavily laden fettle-leggers.

'The Stone Gardens and the Edgeriver waterfall lie to the east, beyond those mounds of scree,' said Cirrus, indicating a series of grey ridges which stretched away through the mist to their left. 'The Edgewater River itself flows somewhere beneath our feet, through what's left of the old sewers, as far as I can recollect . . .'

He continued looking around him.

'And we're standing in what was once a market square in the south of the city, not far from the palace of the old Undertown leagues.'

Nate looked around at the low weed-infested piles of fallen masonry and tried to imagine the bustling streets and crowded shops and stalls that must once have existed in this forlorn place on the edge of the world.

'Mother,' whispered Tentermist, shivering in her long moss cloak as she looked about her with wide frightened eyes. 'Where is the city of shining spires?'

Wyver bent down and hugged the young'un, her own eyes full of doubt and uncertainty. 'The guide knows,' she said. 'He'll be here soon, with Thegthern and Mollver and all the rest, and then he'll show us . . .'

Cirrus and the Professor exchanged glances, while Squall, Slip and Weelum shifted about uneasily on their feet.

'I for one would like to meet this so-called guide,' growled Squall, 'and ask him what he means by bringing humble working folk out here to this desolate place with the promise of a better life. Probably some lowdown Deepwoods swindler . . .'

'He's not!' protested Tentermist, leaping high on her strange legs and shaking her tiny fists at the old sky pirate. 'He's not! He had a wise face, and kind eyes. He understood and listened to us, all of us, even young'uns like me.'

'Perhaps, if you don't mind, Professor,' said Galston Prade, swinging his cane at a clump of broad-leafed weeds, 'might I suggest that we delay our expedition to the waterfall just until our friends here are reunited with their companions? Weelum can weave them a simple windbreak, Squall can make them a fire, and Slip and I shall brew some bristleweed tea.'

Cirrus nodded in agreement. 'The Stone Gardens are close by, and the party we passed will be here in an hour or so. I can run a few checks on the hull weights in the meantime. What do you say, Professor?'

'Very well,' said the Professor, noting by the looks on their faces that Nate and Eudoxia agreed with Galston's suggestion. 'Like Squall, I'd like to have a word with this guide of theirs too.' He removed his spectacles and wiped the mist from them, before putting them back on. 'While we wait, I intend to have a look around. My brother and his party might just have left some sign or other of having been here . . . Nate, Eudoxia, perhaps you'd like to join me?'

'Don't stray too far from the *Archemax*,' called Cirrus with his usual caution as they set off. 'Particularly in this fog.'

Eudoxia turned back and crouched down next to the troubled-looking young'un. 'Don't worry, Tentermist,' she said. 'My father and my friends will look after you until the other fettle-leggers get here, and then we can decide on the best thing to do.'

Tentermist nodded solemnly and pulled her moss cloak tightly around her. Eudoxia patted her on the shoulder, before straightening up and hurrying after Nate and the Professor, their bodies already indistinct in the fog.

She caught up with them a few moments later, and together the three of them continued into the eerie stillness of the abandoned city, the swirling mist laced with the fragrance of lush growth. The going was difficult. Beneath their feet, the mossy paving stones were slippery from the damp air and stuck out of the ground at all angles; gnarled knotted roots and stout woody stems thrusting up from below them. Some of the slabs had been smashed to pieces by huge lumps of masonry that had tumbled down from the surrounding buildings, forming an uneven jumble of rubble.

From every crack and crevice, vegetation sprouted – tall dense thorn bushes, tangles of tarrybriar suckers and black-stalked shrubs with broad flat leaves, their roots growing into the gaps between the stones where the mortar was crumbling; pale delicate ferns, clusters of tendrilled silverleafs, clumps of frondmoss and tall spiky bushes with dark mottled foliage . . . It was as though, just as the grassland had reseeded the polluted Mire, the lush vegetation had reclaimed the ruins of Undertown. The abandoned city had been transformed into a wild garden.

Through it all were the twisting finger-like swirls of fog, weaving in and out of the broken windows and tumbledown arches, between the crumbling pillars and round the cracked leaning towers, blurring the corners of the broken buildings and glazing each leaf, spike and tendril growing out of them with droplets of dew. And as the three travellers made their way deeper into the ruined city, heads down as they picked their way over the treacherous slabs and boulders, the foliage dripped on them like soft rain.

'It's so quiet,' said Eudoxia. 'And so eerie. Not so much a city as a ghost of a city . . .'

'It was abandoned long ago,' said Nate, 'sometime in the Second Age, I think.'

'That's right,' said the Professor, stepping up onto a great block of stone and looking round, his eyes glinting behind his spectacles. 'But what an incredible place it must once have been. Just imagine!' he said. 'Back in the First Age of Flight, this was the greatest city in all the Edge – or rather, one of the twin cities. For while here below was mighty Undertown, with its skyship yards, foundries and legendary sky pirate taverns, above there was the magnificent city of Sanctaphrax, built on the great floating rock and anchored by a massive chain . . .'

'A great floating rock,' said Eudoxia, a faraway look in her eyes. 'How I would love to have seen that!'

'The anchor chain was cut, isn't that right, Professor?' said Nate. 'And the whole city floated off into Open Sky.'

'A great tragedy,' said the Professor absentmindedly as he bent down and picked something up from beside his right boot. 'Then, in the Second Age,' he went on, 'Undertown itself was destroyed by a terrible storm. The black maelstrom, they called it. Though not before most of its inhabitants had escaped and journeyed to the Deepwoods, the legendary Rook Barkwater among them, to establish what became our own city of Great Glade.'

At the sound of Rook's name, Nate and Eudoxia exchanged looks, but the Professor didn't seem to notice. Instead, he had stepped down from the stone block and was staring intently at the object in his hand.

'It looks like a glader,' said Nate, peering down at the small gold coin nestling in the Professor's palm.

'It *is* a glader,' said the Professor. 'Someone from Great Glade has been here. And recently. Look how bright and shiny it is . . .'

'Your brother, do you think?' said Eudoxia. 'Or someone else from the descending party?'

'Maybe,' said the Professor thoughtfully.

He pocketed the coin and the three of them walked on through the ruins of the city, lost in thoughts of its extraordinary past. The dense foggy air whistled softly as it swirled through the cracks in the dilapidated buildings, like the haunted sighs and whispers of those who had once lived here, and whose ghostly presence remained, lurking in dark shadows.

They came to the crumbling remains of what must once have been a tall and elegant palace. Beneath their feet, the ground was littered with countless shards of shattered marble which, as they brushed away the thick lichen and moss that clung to its surface, revealed themselves to be carved fragments – fingers, ears; pieces of broken heads and undulating sections of stone-fashioned robes – of what must have been the hundreds of statues that once decorated its façade.

'Someone's had a fire here,' Nate said, kicking at the powdery ash and charred embers which nestled in the middle of a blackened circle of stones.

The Professor nodded. 'A woodtroll campfire by the look of it,' he observed, the toe of his boot prodding one of the charred embers, the unburned end of which looked almost like the head and shoulders of a hammelhorn. 'See how the stones are piled to prevent the burning logs from floating?'

Eudoxia spotted something in a clump of weeds close by and, stooping down, she picked it up.

'It's some kind of shoe,' she said.

Nate and the Professor looked at the ungainly-looking slipper in her hand, with its stubby heel, wooden sole and thick plaited leather uppers.

'It belonged to a cloddertrog matron,' said the Professor, taking it and turning it over in his hand. 'It's the sort of clog a simple cave-dweller might wear,' and added, 'It definitely doesn't belong to any of my brother's party . . .'

Just then, the sound of a steam klaxon boomed in the mist-filled air.

'That's the *Archemax*,' said Eudoxia. 'The fettle-leggers must have arrived!'

They turned and hurried back the way they'd come through the

597

eerie ruins. A short while later, with the fog beginning to thin, they emerged from the undergrowth to find the rubble-strewn square beneath the anchored *Archemax* crowded with newly arrived travellers.

Nate stared at the fettle-leggers around him. Like Wyver and Tentermist, they stood on bird-like feet, with scaly skin and three long clawed toes. They all had narrow chiselled faces and large browless eyes, with shocks of thick hair rising up above their head, herbs and fragrant dried tree ferns woven into the matted tangle. And while Wyver and Tentermist had been loaded down with what seemed to Nate to be heavy packs on their backs, these newcomers looked even more burdened.

Huge backpacks rested on the woven moss cloaks at their shoulders, each one bulging with a thousand items, with still more tied onto the outside; bedrolls and cooking pots, ropes, lanterns and phraxmuskets

– and, Nate noticed, the looms with which they wove the famous nightspider silk into fine lengths of shimmering cloth. It seemed that the fettle-leggers had bundled up their entire lives into these backpacks when they left the Northern Reaches, and had carried them all the way here to this desolate ruined city.

Nate's heart went out to them. What in Sky's name were they to do now? he wondered.

Spotting them, Galston Prade came striding over to Nate, Eudoxia and the Professor.

'They're good simple folk,' he said, 'who followed this guide of theirs all the way from the Northern Reaches. No sooner do they get to the outskirts of Undertown than this so-called guide vanishes into the mist, saying they're to wait here for his return. They're all talking about some sort of feast – a welcome perhaps, that the guide has promised them . . .'

The fettle-leggers were spread out across the square in exhausted-looking groups, while Squall, Weelum and Slip passed among them, pouring out steaming bristleweed tea from a brew kettle into the wooden bowls and flasks the travellers held out to them.

The Professor's hand went to the phraxpistol at his belt. 'I don't like it,' he said, his eyes narrowing as he scanned the ruins surrounding the square. 'This guide is probably no more than a brigand, with a gang of thieves lying in wait out there to ambush and rob these unfortunate weavers. Probably only holding off from attacking because they've spotted that we're here. I've seen some despicable scams in my time, but this tops the lot.'

The Professor paused. A fresh breeze had begun to blow, and with it the mist had finally cleared, sweeping away to the west to reveal the ruined city in all its leafy green confusion. A hush had fallen over the square, every head now turned to gaze up at the blue sky in the east and the astonishing sight it contained.

Through the crowds, Tentermist came cantering excitedly, her face flushed and eyes sparkling.

'Look! Look!' she exclaimed to Eudoxia, pointing to the sky. 'The city of shining spires!'

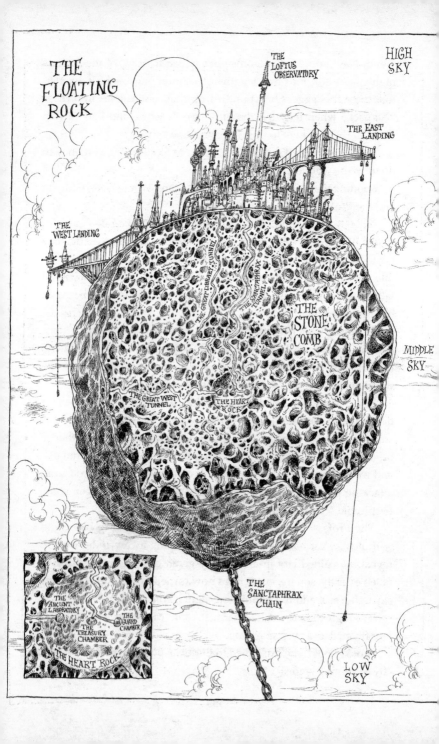

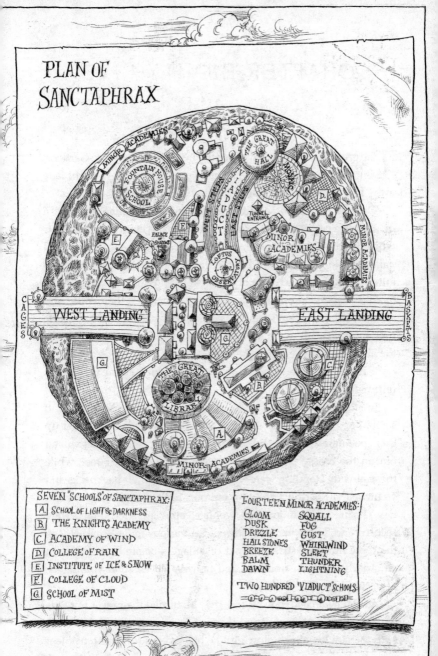

PLAN OF SANCTAPHRAX

MINOR ACADEMIES
FOUNTAIN HOUSE SCHOOL
THE GREAT HALL
MOSAIC
D
WEST SIDE VIADUCT EAST SIDE
TUNNEL ENTRANCE
PALACE OF SHADOWS
E
E
MINOR ACADEMIES
MINOR ACADEMIES
LOFTUS OBSERVATORY

CAGES
WEST LANDING
EAST LANDING
BASKETS

G
G
B
C
THE GREAT LIBRARY
B
A

MINOR ACADEMIES

SEVEN "SCHOOLS" OF SANCTAPHRAX:
A. SCHOOL OF LIGHT & DARKNESS
B. THE KNIGHTS ACADEMY
C. ACADEMY OF WIND
D. COLLEGE OF RAIN
E. INSTITUTE OF ICE & SNOW
F. COLLEGE OF CLOUD
G. SCHOOL OF MIST

FOURTEEN MINOR ACADEMIES:
GLOOM   SQUALL
DUSK   FOG
DRIZZLE   GUST
HAILSTONES   WHIRLWIND
BREEZE   SLEET
BALM   THUNDER
DAWN   LIGHTNING

TWO HUNDRED "VIADUCT" SCHOOLS

· CHAPTER EIGHTY-FIVE ·

The great floating rock hovered in the air above the Stone Gardens, immense and yet dream-like, as if at any moment it might fade away like the tendrils of thick mist that had cloaked it.

On top of the rock, glittering in the bright sunlight, was a magnificent city of elegant spires, castellated towers and tall minarets which reached up into the air at the top of gleaming academies and palaces, golden against the blue of the sky. Two immense platforms jutted out, one on each side of the great rock, with what looked like baskets suspended on ropes from heavy winches at their ends. And alongside the massive hanging weights that stabilized the gigantic rock from beneath was a long thick chain, which cut down through the air to the Stone Gardens beneath.

'Sanctaphrax,' breathed the Professor incredulously. 'It has returned.'

In the ruined square, all was movement; scurrying and scrabbling, bobbing and ducking as the fettle-leggers gathered up their belongings. Those who had been sitting on blankets spread out on the mossy paving stones were leaping to their feet, while those already standing were feverishly packing their backpacks and securing their bedrolls and cooking pots to the dangling straps and ties. The fire was extinguished, woollen capes and barkbonnets were secured and, to the insistent cries of the various fettle-legger elders, the three hundred strong crowd of villagers began to assemble in an orderly column – mothers and fathers, old'uns and young'uns, babes in arms.

As Nate watched, one by one, they all turned their faces towards the great floating city of Sanctaphrax, their eyes sparkling, their hair, with the sun behind it, glowing like haloes – and their strange feet tapping on the ground with excitement. At the back of the column, their faces wreathed in smiles, stood Wyver and Tentermist.

'Come,' said the Professor, as if stirring himself from a dream. 'We must get aboard the *Archemax* at once!'

They hurried across the square, only for Eudoxia to pause for a moment beside the fettle-legger young'un.

'The guide spoke the truth!' Tentermist said exultantly, her eyes fixed on the floating city. 'And we shall wait here for him to come for us, just as he promised!'

'Leave her, Eudoxia,' the Professor said gently. 'Whoever this guide is, my guess is that we'll find him up there.'

Reluctantly, Eudoxia bade farewell to the fetter-legger young'un and followed Nate and the Professor over to the hovering phraxship, its funnel already sending a thin plume of white steam snaking up into the air. Nate held the sumpwood ladder steady for Eudoxia to climb, then hurried up the shifting rungs himself.

'Wuh-wuh,' Weelum the banderbear greeted him happily as Nate dropped down onto the deck, and together they began winding in the twin anchor spikes at the stern.

At the helm, Cirrus Gladehawk, his eyes fixed straight ahead, pulled on the flight levers. First, at the funnel, the ribbon-like plume of steam thickened to a billowing cloud. Then the propulsion duct began to roar – causing some of those at the front of the crowd of fettle-leggers to cry out with surprise and shield their faces from the intense heat of the blast. The next moment, with a gentle lurch, the *Archemax* began to ascend.

Up at the phraxchamber, Squall Razortooth patted the humming metal sphere encouragingly. 'Steady as she goes,' he called down to Cirrus Gladehawk. 'We'll be up there in no time.'

The captain nodded as he pulled the central flight lever slowly back. Eudoxia hurried up to the prow of the phraxship to join her father, her gaze never straying for a moment from the great city in the sky ahead. A few moments later, Nate and the Professor joined them.

As the *Archemax* rose above the ruins of Undertown, Nate

glanced down and realized what a tiny area he and the other two had explored. The city below was vast and sprawling, spreading from one side of the point of the jutting Edge to the other.

Dilapidated factories and foundries fringed its western borders, where the Edgewater River disappeared, to flow through the fractured sewers beneath. To the north and south were crumbling towers and palaces, shrubs and saplings clinging to their broken walls and sprouting up out of their roofs; while looking to the east, Nate saw that Undertown must once have been twice as large for, as they flew over the ruins, the occasional pointed spire or jutting finger of brickwork showed that half a city more lay beneath the jumbled mass of vegetation and rubble.

As they approached the huge floating rock in the sky ahead, the rubble below gave way to the barren rocky pavement of the Stone Gardens, into which the Edgewater River bubbled up once more to resume its course to the lip of rock at the Edge itself.

Once, the Stone Gardens had been alive. Not with plants, but with the rocks themselves, which had sprouted from the ground, one upon the other, getting more and more buoyant as they'd grown. They'd formed great stacks that had risen ever taller, until the rock at the top had become so large and so buoyant it could be harvested and used in the sky galleons of the First Age of Flight. But then stone sickness had struck, turning the miraculous flight rocks to dust, and transforming the Stone Gardens into the barren pavement that Nate now looked down upon.

The *Archemax* came closer to the floating rock, and from the prow Nate and his companions could see clearly where the end of the mighty Sanctaphrax chain had now anchored itself. At the point where the waterfall thundered over the tip of the Edge cliff and fell into the abyss below, was a single jutting crag. This, the very tip of the Edge, round which the water flowed, had snagged the great iron ring at the end of the chain, like a stone finger through a gold band.

At the helm, Cirrus Gladehawk was battling with the flight levers as the *Archemax* was caught by turbulent winds. She pitched and juddered. Squall Razortooth ran a hasty check over the fragile cog lines and cotter pins connecting the controls to the phraxchamber, while Slip darted this way and that, battening down the open hatches and securing every loose item that threatened to be snatched away by the unpredictable gusts.

They rose slowly, the captain making constant readjustments to the flight levers and hull weights as they went. Before them was the face of the mighty floating rock. Its pitted surface glistened in the sunlight the *Archemax*'s shadow slid up over it. They passed a hanging basket which hung down from a minor jetty, then another. And looking up, they saw the jutting boards, rising stanchions and fluted pillars of the huge West Landing silhouetted against the sky above them.

'Ready with those tolley ropes, Weelum,' Cirrus Gladehawk called across from the helm. 'Squall to the fore deck. Slip to the stern.'

'Aye aye, Cap'n!' they both shouted back.

The *Archemax* ascended past the widest part of the rock. Nate held his breath. In the lea of the wind caused by the rock itself, the air fell abruptly still. The next moment as they rose steadily up above the level of the great wooden West Landing, Cirrus Gladehawk dextrously shut off the flight levers, one by one, and realigned the hull weights. The phraxship swung round, until its starboard bow was parallel to the jutting mooring platform.

'Now!' he bellowed.

At his command, Slip and Squall Razortooth jumped onto the landing. Weelum threw first one tolley rope across, then, hurrying back along the deck, the second, which they secured to the stanchion cleats of the West Landing. With a low sigh, the phraxchamber ceased its hum and the *Archemax* came to rest beside the broad landing.

'Just like putting in at the Midwood Decks,' said Cirrus nonchalantly, securing the rudder lock and stepping down from the helm.

But his crew were too preoccupied to notice their captain showing off. They had followed Slip and Squall over the side, and now stood on the polished planks of the great West Landing of Sanctaphrax, their faces glazed with disbelief.

Only Weelum the banderbear stayed on board the *Archemax*, refusing to budge from the helm, his eyes wide with fear, nostrils flared and small ears quivering.

'Wuh-wargh! Wuh-wargh!' he grunted, his paws flying in all directions.

'He says he won't set foot in the city,' said Nate to the others. 'He says it smells of death . . .'

'You lot go ahead,' said Squall. 'I'll stay here with my friend, Weelum. We'll be waiting for you on your return.'

'The city appears to be deserted,' said the Professor, drawing his phraxpistol and setting off along the landing, 'but I suggest we proceed with caution nonetheless.'

Following him, Nate, Eudoxia and Cirrus drew phraxpistols of their own, while Slip unhooked the hunting bow from his shoulder and inserted an arrow from the quiver at his belt. Behind them, Galston Prade twisted the carved fromp head of his cane and unsheathed the sword it encased.

At the end of the landing, they passed between two tall pitch-roofed buildings and, beneath their feet on the other side, the heavy boards abruptly gave way to a broad avenue set with red, white and black tiles laid out in complicated patterns. On either side of them, lining the great thoroughfare, were tall buildings, most of which were constructed from stone. Every one seemed more magnificent than the one before, the ornate decorations and intricate embellishments that adorned them sparkling in the sunlight.

'Look at that sundial,' said Eudoxia, pointing towards a huge circular disc, etched with lines and numbers, which had been mounted on the side of a lofty lattice-walled tower to her right. The elegant gnomon at its centre cast a long blade-like shadow that crossed midway between the numbers three and four.

'Beautiful,' Nate murmured.

To their right, was a circular building, its undulating roof rising to a point; far to their left, beyond a line of low towers, was a tall rotund building with a great bowl on its roof, from which water cascaded down.

'The Fountain House School,' said the Professor, marvelling at the sight. 'It's where the offspring of the academics began their education. Look at it! Perfectly preserved, after all this time . . .'

'And those?' asked Nate, pointing with his pistol to two vast spheres of wire at the top of impossibly tall and elegant twin towers.

Mist swirled round the curious spheres, seemingly weaving in and out of the twisted wires and giving out a soft tuneful humming.

'They're the towers of the mistsifters, one of the oldest academies in Sanctaphrax,' said the Professor, clearly enthralled by everything he saw about them.

There were so many wonderful buildings. Some had onion-shaped towers, some had needle-like spires; some were domed and inlaid with intricate mosaics of mirrors and semi precious stones. Some, like the tower Eudoxia had seen, were decorated with sundials, some with clocks, heavy weights hanging down the walls beneath their burnished faces, while others had campaniles, huge bronze bells dangling down between the sets of elegant white arches. One crenellated building had small round windows glazed with thousands of tiny panels; its grand neighbour had broader windows, with curling sills and huge single panes of glass that reflected the buildings opposite.

Nate knew that the academics back in the First Age had been obsessed with the weather – as obsessed as today's academics of Hive's Sumpwood Bridge were with sumpwood, and those in the Cloud Quarter of Great Glade with the properties of phrax – and that the individual architecture of the academies and schools around them must reflect a particular field of interest. Fog. Rain. Wind. Snow . . .

Arcane pieces of paraphernalia graced each wall and every rooftop. Propellor-shaped twists of burnished metal and arced nets made of fine silver mesh; forged plumb weights and calibrated dials, weathervanes and wind socks and, dangling down the side

of a tall round building from a jutting gantry, were a hundred or more blue bottles, attached one beneath the other to a length of plaited cable and jutting out at different angles.

As to which building went with which academic discipline though, Nate could only guess.

They continued through the deserted city. Vast walkways spanning the air soared over them; twisting flights of stairs and curved passageways led from one broad terrace to the next, and a lofty viaduct, fringed with steps, stretched off into the distance.

The Professor gazed up, his eyes gleaming with excitement through the lenses of his spectacles. He removed his crushed funnel hat with one hand and raked his hair with the other, before replacing the hat and shaking his head.

'This is incredible,' he said, slowly and earnestly. 'No sign of storm damage, no lightning strikes, hail-pitting or frost blight.' He swept his arm round in a wide arc. 'It's as magnificent as all the history scrolls I've read told me it was, and yet . . .' He shook his head. 'I don't know,' he said, for a moment uncharacteristically at a loss for words. 'How can this be?'

'The city has clearly been maintained to an astonishing degree,' agreed Galston Prade, 'though we have yet to encounter a single inhabitant.'

'This city is beautiful, to be sure,' said Slip softly from by Nate's side. 'But Slip doesn't like it . . .'

As they walked on, their footsteps echoed down the immaculately paved streets and across the broad open squares that opened up before them. And when they spoke, they kept their voices down, as though the city was somehow sleeping and not to be disturbed. Their hushed whispers faded into the deep shadows, or bounced back from the glittering walls – reinforcing the notion that, although perfectly preserved, the ancient floating city had apparently returned to the Edge without a single soul in it.

They walked across an airy square, a fountain at its centre. The water looked like liquid silver in the afternoon dazzle as it gushed up out of the embossed rose at the top of the fountain and streamed out through lateral spouts.

'How does it do that?' Nate wondered out loud. 'I mean, how does it flow? Up here, in the floating city . . .'

'The floating rock is porous, with reservoirs of water deep inside it,' the Professor told him. 'As the rock expands, it forces the water up into springs and wells all over the city.'

Nate nodded, his thoughts returning once again to Zelphyius Dax, who had yearned for the times before the power of phraxcrystals had ushered in the Third Age of Flight. Now, standing at the centre of this extraordinary city from the First Age, Nate considered that the old librarian scholar might have had a point. Yes, in recent times they had expanded far into the once seemingly endless Deepwoods, sailing their phraxvessels to the furthest corners of the Edge – but despite everything that had been gained, so much had clearly been lost . . .

Craning their necks as they passed a tall tower, Nate looked up at the pointed roof at its top and, set below it, the circle of windows with views off in all directions. It looked like some kind of observatory. A brace of white ravens perched on a jutting lightning rod, looking down at them askance and cawing malevolently. At the far side, the magnificent viaduct stretched out before them upon a series of towering arches, each one mounted with small towers, and with tall staircases set between them at the bottom.

Spotting something, Eudoxia suddenly broke away from the others and ran up the steps. Nate followed close on her heels a moment later, phraxpistol at the ready. He caught up with her at the top of the viaduct steps, to find Eudoxia staring down at the large quadrangle on the other side. The wide square was decorated with an intricate circular mosaic, with jagged bolts of lightning extending out from its centre, giving it the appearance of an intricately constructed cartwheel.

'I thought I saw someone,' she said, her face flushed.

They walked slowly down the steps to the quadrangle, which had low benches set out in rows all round it.

'Perhaps this is where the welcome feast takes place,' said Eudoxia. She turned to Nate. 'The one the guide told the fettle-leggers about.'

Behind them, the silhouetted figures of the others appeared at the top of the staircase and began to descend, their footsteps echoing round the quadrangle. Nate turned and his eyes fell on the huge building at the far end of the viaduct. It had narrow windows, high flying buttresses and was crowned with a vast dome. The footsteps grew louder as the Professor, followed closely by the others, approached.

'Well, well,' said the Professor, his fingertips playing absentmindedly with his side-whiskers. 'Someone is expecting visitors by the look of it.' He stared around the quadrangle. 'Yet the city is deserted.' He shook his head. 'The mystery deepens.' He raised his phraxpistol and fired it into the air. The sound of the shot was deafening, echoing through the bright deserted streets like a thunderclap.

Suddenly a low arched door with curlicue hinges and set into the wall of the domed building opened, and a tall robed figure stepped out. Bathed in shadow, he seemed almost to be glowing, his long flowing robes shimmering as he strode towards them.

He was tall and lean, with dark hair, a small beard and a thick black moustache, twisted into points. The ankle-length gown he was wearing was embroidered with pearls that gleamed like hailstones. Over it was a fur-lined cape with a curious interlocking spiral design stitched into the heavy cloth, and with a broad chequerboard collar resting on his shoulders. Various brass and copper instruments hung from his belt; some round, some perforated, and some with long calibrated shafts. Upon his head rested a tall four-cornered black and white hat, while in his hand he clutched a carved blackwood staff, its top set with a gold disc of the same design as the quadrangle mosaic.

'Put away your weapons, friends,' he said, a benevolent smile spreading across his handsome face as he approached. 'You'll find no need of them here in the city of shining spires.'

The Professor stepped back, holstering his pistol, a strange look of shock and disbelief on his face. Galston Prade stepped forward, sheathing his swordstick and holding out his hand.

'So you must be the guide we've heard so much about,' he said, smiling.

The academic nodded, but ignored Galston's outstretched hand. 'One of many,' he said simply.

Tearing his eyes away from the academic's radiant face, Nate suddenly realized that the quadrangle was fringed with other figures, dressed in robes of every colour and design.

There were academics from the School of Light and Darkness, their robes in numerous shades of grey, from slate-flecked white to storm-cloud black; cloudwatchers in white, red and brown, robed academics from the College of Rain and white and yellow hooded academics from the Academy of Squall; there were the deep orange robes of the Academy of Dawn, and the patterned cloaks of the Academies of Breeze, Hailstones and Gust, along with the bright

blue robes of the academics from the Viaduct Schools. The academics stood silently watching, smiles on their broad even-featured faces.

'We were awaiting the arrival of friends from the Northern Reaches,' the academic explained, 'but we are always happy to receive visitors to our beautiful city and share its wonders with them. What would you like to see? The Great Hall? The Palace of Shadows? Or the Knights Academy perhaps, where the great Quintinius Verginix studied in his youth?'

Nate gave a gasp of surprise at the mention of the name, and the academic smiled warmly at him.

'Ah, the Knights Academy it is, then. Please follow me.'

The academic turned and made his way across the quadrangle and up the viaduct steps. And as they followed, Nate was surprised to note that the watching academics had melted back into the shadows of the surrounding streets and doorways, as silently as they'd emerged.

As Eudoxia, Slip, Cirrus and Galston Prade climbed the steps behind the academic, Nate whispered to the Professor.

'There's something I've been meaning to tell you,' he said, 'about the Garden of Life. That academic mentioned Quintinius Verginix and—' Nate turned. 'Professor? Professor?'

But the Professor was gone.

· CHAPTER EIGHTY-SIX ·

The Professor emerged from the shadows of a tall pillar in the corner of the quadrangle and, glancing round him warily, headed back through the city. When the academics had stepped back into the shadows, he'd followed, only for them to disappear from view the moment they had turned the first corner. The Professor had retraced his steps, but hesitated when he saw the academic talking to Nate.

Knights Academy, he'd said, the Professor noted. Well, if he was quick, he could skirt round the Loftus Observatory and past the School of Mist, then cross by the West Landing and make it to the Knights Academy from the opposite direction before they got there.

But first, he had one stop to make.

He hurried along the side of the viaduct, past the observatory tower and, checking that the coast was clear, went round the back of the tall angular building with its perforated walls and two elegant sphere-crowned towers. Then, as he turned the corner at the far end, a strange building loomed up before him.

It was circular and, unlike so many of the other buildings, constructed from wood. The few windows it possessed were small and high up, while its fanned roof, rising up to a sharp point at the centre, resembled nothing so much as a huge umbrella. It was unmistakable. The Professor recognized it at once.

The Great Library of Sanctaphrax.

Hurrying up to the building, the Professor turned the handle, pushed the door and, having glanced round cautiously over his shoulders one last time, stepped inside. Instantly, the hallowed atmosphere of the cavernous library wrapped itself around him. It was cool and dry, smelled faintly of pinesap, and had an air of fusty bookishness about it that the passing centuries had done nothing to dispel.

Stepping across the hard-packed earthen floor, his footsteps echoing softly round the vaulted ceiling, the Professor's gaze fell upon the forest of square pillars. He took in the plaques at their base, words etched into them in an old-fashioned floral script; the climbing pegs, which jutted out from the sides of the wooden pillars; and the clusters of barkscrolls dangling in the shadow-filled air between the pulley ropes and hanging baskets far above his head like bunches of sapgrapes.

The Professor took a sharp intake of breath. Like everything else in the city, the Great Library was in pristine condition. There was not a trace of dust, no hint of damp; there were no fallen barkscrolls lying on the floor. It was, the Professor thought, his gaze fixed above his head as he wove in and out of the great pillars, almost too good to be true . . .

But he didn't have much time. Hurrying over to the circular walls, he ran his eyes over the ancient portraits of the Most High Academes hanging there. They were all present from down the centuries, their names inscribed below their portraits in ancient curling lettering: *Marborinus Quelt. Philbus Xant. Quelve Fundinix* . . . The names, like the stiff formal faces staring back at him, began to blur.

Suddenly, the Professor stopped, his eyes fixed on the portrait in front of him.

'*There* you are,' he murmured as he gazed at the likeness of the academic they had just met in the mosaic quadrangle, then read the inscription below. '*Linius Pallitax.* So it *is* you, just as I thought,' he mused to himself. 'Linius Pallitax, Most High Academe of Old Sanctaphrax who, if memory serves me right, died after a short illness following the fire that destroyed the Palace of Shadows . . .'

The next moment, from behind him, a hand shot out and closed round his mouth. He felt the chill of a cold blade as a dagger was pressed to his throat.

'So, you're real!' a hoarse croaking voice sounded in the Professor's ear.

· CHAPTER EIGHTY-SEVEN ·

'Ifflix,' gasped the Professor. 'Is it really you?' He reached up and seized his brother by both arms and pulled him closer.

'I was asking myself the very same question, Ambris,' said Ifflix. 'In this city of phantasmal visions, I've learned not to trust anything or anybody.'

He pulled away and, resheathing his knife at his belt, glanced around the deserted library suspiciously. The Professor looked his brother up and down, appraising the battered clothes of a descender that he wore – the thick double-breasted jacket, pitted and grazed by cliff rock, the padded breeches and heavy boots with their buttoned covers, now threadbare and scuffed. He smiled and reached forward, and ruffled his brother's long unkempt hair.

'I never thought I'd find you,' he said, shaking his head incredulously. 'Yet I had to try.'

'Thank Earth and Sky you did, brother,' Ifflix replied. 'Yet part of me wishes you'd stayed away.' He frowned, his face suddenly tense and serious. 'For this is a place of terrible danger . . .'

'Danger?' said the Professor. 'Is that why you jumped out at me like a mad cut-throat?'

'It's the only way,' came Ifflix's weary reply, 'to tell whether someone is real or not. If they bleed, they're real. If they slip through my fingers, they're not . . .'

The Professor frowned. 'You're speaking in riddles, Ifflix,' he said, and touched the scratch on the side of his neck. 'You've spent too long descending in the darkness.'

Ifflix smiled, but the Professor noticed the deep sadness in his brother's eyes.

'Perhaps so,' Ifflix said. 'There is much to tell you. But not here, Ambris. Follow me. There is something you must see for yourself . . .'

· CHAPTER EIGHTY-EIGHT ·

'This,' said the academic, smiling, 'is the Gate of Humility. It is the entrance into the Knights Academy. Follow me.' He bent double as he disappeared past a metal door and through the low opening in the towering west wall of the academy.

Stooping low, Eudoxia, Slip and Galston Prade followed the academic, intrigued by his relaxed air of authority and friendly demeanour. Nate was less sure. He bent forward and entered what he discovered was a low-ceilinged tunnel. Behind him, the metal door clanged shut; in front, Eudoxia and the others shuffled forward. As the ceiling came lower still, Nate was forced to crawl on all fours.

He emerged a moment later through a low opening, head bent and on his knees. Looking up, he found himself in a great open courtyard with the grandiose façade of the ancient Knights Academy in front of him.

'Tell me . . . *errm* . . .' Galston Prade said, hesitating.

'Linius Pallitax, Most High Academe,' the academic introduced himself, giving a small bow.

'Tell me, Linius,' Galston continued, brushing imaginary dust from the knees of his breeches, 'how this city of yours comes to be here, unchanged and perfectly preserved after all these centuries.'

'The Sanctaphrax rock was released from its anchor in Undertown many generations ago, it is true,' said the Most High Academe, crossing the courtyard towards the grand entrance hall of the academy. 'But a few academics refused to abandon the sacred rock. We remained with it on its extraordinary voyage into Open Sky, far beyond the Edgelands.'

Turning to them with a serene smile, the High Academe raised his eyes to the sky.

'In those uncharted regions, home to the great Mother Storm and much else besides, we encountered weather we could hitherto never have imagined – emotion storms, white maelstroms, glister squalls and swirling vortexes whose properties we have studied ever since. It is to these strange phenomena that we ascribe our long lives and extraordinary health.'

The High Academe opened the doors to the Knights Academy and stepped inside, followed by Eudoxia, Galston, Slip and Nate. Ahead of them was a magnificent staircase of carved blackwood winding up into the gloom.

'For centuries, we voyaged through the skies, our sacred rock providing for our every need. And we in turn, though few in number, lovingly took care of this city that nurtured us, as you can see.'

He indicated the carved staircase leading to the Upper Halls of the academy, and the high corridors which led off towards the Lower Halls.

'And then, Sky be blessed,' Linius Pallitax said, smiling benevolently, 'our sacred rock was blown back to its birth-place, and the Anchor Chain miraculously secured itself on the Edge cliff below. Now,' he said, with a sweep of his staff, 'we wish to repay our immense good fortune by opening up the city of shining spires to the poor, the oppressed and the downtrodden in this modern world of yours, and offer them sanctuary and peace here with us.'

'That's beautiful,' said Eudoxia, thinking of Tentermist the fettle-legger young'un in the ruins below.

'Yes,' said Nate, looking round the deserted academy. 'But where exactly *are* all these simple folk you have given sanctuary to?'

'All in good time,' the Most High Academe said simply.

With that he turned and, staff clacking on the marble floor, strode down the corridor. Slip the scuttler looked up as the academic passed him by and, as he did so, he saw the expression on the academic's face abruptly change. The smile disappeared. The eyes narrowed. And, for the briefest of moments, a long dark tongue darted out from between the Most High Academe's lips and flickered in the gloom.

Almost, Slip thought with a shudder, as though it was tasting the air.

· CHAPTER EIGHTY-NINE ·

'The expedition started well at first,' said Ifflix grimly, 'and we made an excellent descent down the great incline from the Edgeriver waterfall. But once we reached the phantasmal depths, the trouble began.' He turned and raised the flaming torch he was carrying, the flickering flames bathing his troubled face with golden light. 'The realm of Edge wraiths and half-formed creatures . . .'

The Professor raised his own torch and shone it up ahead, illuminating the porous walls of the long stone tunnel. 'Is it much further?' he asked.

Ifflix nodded. 'Still a way to go, Ambris,' he replied.

The two brothers were walking one behind the other through the honeycomb of stone tunnels inside the Sanctaphrax rock. Every now and then they would have to duck to avoid the low ceiling, or squeeze their way along a narrow stretch where the walls came in from both sides – only to broaden out a few strides further on, enabling them to walk side by side.

Entrance to the tunnel had been gained through a concealed trap door in the far corner of the library, now far above their heads. Ifflix had seized the sunken handle in the floor and tugged, and the Professor had looked down to see a dark tunnel snaking away beneath. Ifflix had unhooked the two torches from the wall and lit the black pitch at their ends, then handed one to his brother, and they'd set off. That had been almost an hour ago.

'We'd disembarked from the *Archemax* in the north of the Stone Gardens,' Ifflix continued. 'I'd had a long talk with the captain about the descent. We thought two weeks each way would be enough, though the captain had insisted that he would wait for six.'

The Professor nodded. It was just as Cirrus Gladehawk had

described, and he felt bad for ever having doubted him.

'But by the time we reached the depths, over a week had already passed,' said Ifflix. 'The four of us checked our equipment and supplies and continued the descent regardless. We'd gone too far to turn back then, though we hadn't yet even reached the fluted decline.' He shook his head. 'We took a gamble that we'd make a faster ascent if we had to.'

They had come to a fork where the tunnel split in two. One way was large and wide; the other, low and narrow. It was this second tunnel that Ifflix took.

'The winds down there in the depths were like nothing I've ever experienced, Ambris,' Ifflix told his brother breathlessly as they squeezed, side on, through a narrow gap. 'They roared and howled like the souls of the dead, swirling about us, ice cold and turbulent, setting our clothes flapping, snatching our hats from our heads and sending them tumbling down through the air.'

He glanced round at the Professor, who looked back at him, his eyes narrowed with sympathy.

'Worse than that,' Ifflix went on, 'they plucked at everything our fingers struggled to hold on to, as if with fingers of their own. The writhing ropes. The hook spikes we hammered into the cliff to hold them. The stone mallets themselves . . . Time and again, one or the other of us would let out a cry as something else – something utterly irreplaceable on that barren rockface – would be snatched from our grasp and disappear down into the swirl of black cloud far beneath us.' He shuddered. 'And each time *that* happened, the roaring and howling sounded almost like scornful laughter.'

'And yet you kept on,' said the Professor, a mixture of respect and disbelief in his voice.

'We kept on,' Ifflix agreed. 'We got into a routine. By day we would continue our descent, sometimes pausing for Lendil Spix to chip off a sample of rock, which Centix Thripp would record and log, noting the depth it was taken from. And when sunset came, Trapper Sluice would help us set up camp for the night – if camp is the right word for the curious rest places we created for ourselves on the vertical cliff face. Sometimes we would be lucky and find a ledge. More often than not, we would have to hammer our hook spikes directly into the rock to hang our hammocks from.' He turned to his brother. 'It's quite something sleeping in such a bed, Ambris, I can tell you. Rocked to and fro by the wild wind, while all that separates you from the abyss below is a thin layer of tilderhide.'

The Professor nodded earnestly. 'I can imagine,' he said, though, when he tried to think of the ships' hammocks he had slept in swinging from the cliff side, he found that he could not.

'On the eighteenth day of our descent, we lost the first member of our expedition,' said Ifflix, increasing his pace as he marched through a clear stretch of tunnel. 'Already behind in our schedule, we awoke to find Lendil Spix gone. He'd been careless, failing to hammer his hook spikes far enough into the rock, and they'd come loose . . .'

'He fell?'

Ifflix nodded bleakly. 'Of course, Trapper Sluice blamed himself, but it wasn't his fault.' He paused and his eyes glazed for a moment with memories. 'Hopefully, Spix never woke up . . .'

'And the rest of you still continued?' said the Professor.

'Having come so far, we weren't about to give up,' came the reply. 'We had reached the fluted decline at last, and it seemed to promise a clear descent into the blackest regions of all.'

The Professor waited as his brother navigated a particularly awkward section of the tunnel, where a large rock had fallen down, all but blocking their path. Scrambling up the pitted side, Ifflix turned and eased himself through the narrow gap beneath the ceiling. The Professor followed.

'Anyway,' said Ifflix, resuming his story as the tunnel widened and the Professor was once more able to join him at his side, 'down we went, painstakingly slowly, stride after treacherous stride, our bodies battered and buffeted by the ferocious winds.' He looked round at the Professor, and smiled at the expression on his face, so much more dour than he had remembered.

The Professor returned his gaze. 'And?' he said.

'And we continued down into the inky blackness,' Ifflix said simply, and trembled. 'Such a strange experience, Ambris. It was like being immersed in cold swirling water. It numbed our fingers and stoppered our ears; it filled our eyes, making it impossible to see the rock before us, despite the phraxlamps we wore around our necks . . .'

The Professor nodded thoughtfully.

'Trapper Sluice had hammered a hook spike into the rock at the top of the fluted decline and attached the longest rope we had to it. He was hoping that it might be long enough to take us right the way down the central flute . . .' He sighed. 'It wasn't. Nowhere near. Fumbling blindly, Trapper knocked in a second spike and set another rope hanging from it. Then, just as he was about to continue his descent, out of nowhere, there came an Edge wraith . . .'

'An Edge wraith?' the Professor repeated.

Ifflix nodded and swallowed hard. 'I saw it, Ambris, as if in slow motion.' His voice was low and tremulous. 'It was immense, with great bat-like wings and a wizened papery body. Its massive milk-white eyes stared out of a shrunken skull-like head – and its gaping jaws were lined with rows of needle teeth, the size of rapier blades.

'It zigzagged through the dense air impossibly slowly, luminescent and blurred. The odour of rotting flesh filled my nostrils. Then, with a *crack* and a *hiss*, the huge creature opened its cavernous jaws and sank its razor-sharp fangs into Trapper's body, ripping him away from the rockface, before flapping away into the depths on glowing wings. A moment later, we were plunged back into darkness.

'I never saw Trapper Sluice again – nor,' he added, 'the supplies he was carrying in his sumpwood backpack.'

The Professor took a sharp intake of breath.

'Thripp and I continued as best we could,' Ifflix went on. 'We did actually get to the bottom of the fluted decline. We left markers and rope rings every step of the way for others to follow after us,' he added, with a wry smile. 'The air was still there, but dark

– impenetrably dark. Too dark, certainly, for our paltry phraxlamps to see further than a dozen, maybe twenty strides, below us. It was a view which, no matter how far we descended, was never to change . . .'

'You didn't see the bottom of the Edge cliff then?' said the Professor, unable to keep the disappointment from his voice.

'Alas, no, Ambris,' said Ifflix. 'When the ropes we had ran out, there was no option for us but to start the long ascent back to the top once more. Despite our earlier optimism, it was to take us twice as long as the descent. Time and again we would have to stop, exhaustion making it impossible for us to continue, and all the while our supplies were running out. We were constantly hungry and thirsty. Our minds became addled. And not just through lack of sustenance, but – or so Centix claimed – because of the pernicious influence of the curious cliff face rock itself.' He paused. 'Perhaps it was that which made him do what he did,' he said softly.

The Professor turned to him, his brow furrowed.

His brother sighed. 'We were back above the depths by this time,' he said, 'but it was still dark, with the never-ending wind howling round us. "It's been an honour knowing you, Hentadile," Centix said, looking back at me, the strange smile on his face illuminated by our phraxlamps. The next thing I knew, he'd whipped his knife from his belt and, before I could stop him, he'd severed the rope and was plunging down into the abyss below.'

Ifflix turned to the Professor, his eyes sparkling.

'Suddenly I was alone, Ambris; alone on the cliff face. I don't know whether it was that fact that spurred me on, or realizing what might happen to me if I stayed any longer in the blackness, but I started climbing – and I kept climbing, pausing neither for breath nor water. I continued through the unchanging night, to the very top. There, pulling myself up the jutting rock with my last remaining ounce of strength, I crawled over the lip of the Edge – and collapsed . . .'

The tunnel had become narrower once again. The route the two brothers had taken had been slowly descending ever since they'd climbed down from the library. Now, for the first time, as Ifflix took a right-hand fork, the path became a gentle incline.

'The next thing I knew, a soft voice was asking me who I was,' said Ifflix. '"Your name?" it kept saying. "Your name?" "Your name . . . ?" I looked up to see a tall bearded figure smiling down at me. He was dressed in the clothes of an academic from the First Age; long robes, with pointed shoes on his feet and an elaborate four-pronged hat on his head.'

'The Most High Academe?' the Professor said.

Ifflix nodded grimly. 'Little did I know that, far from being rescued, I'd end up a fugitive in this terrible floating city, where every exit is guarded and I dare not show my face.' He shook his head. 'When I discovered the appalling truth, I escaped and hid.'

He raised his flaming torch. The light swooped along the tunnel ahead, gleaming on the rock – and on a low circular door set into it.

As they approached, the torchlight flickered on the stone door and the Professor saw that it had been carved with innumerable creatures. At their centre, he noticed the round symbol with its forks of lightning that he'd seen both on the mosaic quadrangle and at the top of the Most High Academe's staff. He turned to his brother.

'What is this place?' he asked.

'This, Ambris,' said Ifflix, his voice hushed and trembling, 'is the dark secret at the heart of the city of shining spires . . .'

· CHAPTER NINETY ·

The Knights Academy was one of the most extraordinary buildings Nate had ever entered. There were the four Lower Halls – the Hall of White Cloud, filled with furnaces and metalwork forges; the Hall of Storm Cloud, with its timber stores and woodworking benches; the magnificent Hall of High Cloud, with its great glass dome for cloudwatching and – Eudoxia's favourite – the Hall of Grey Cloud, with its prowlgrin roosts and stables, the air sweet with the smell of glade hay and meadow straw.

Then there were the Upper Halls, dark wood-panelled chambers at the top of the great spiral staircase. These were dominated by huge pulpits as big as Deepwoods' trees, ornately carved with designs of startling intricacy. Nate had counted at least twenty of these huge pulpits as they had wandered through the dimly lit central hall.

To think that this was only one of the seven great schools of Sanctaphrax! Nate thought. What other magnificent sights must they contain? It would take a lifetime to see them all. But then, by his own admission, the Most High Academe, Linius Pallitax, and his fellow academics had lived many lifetimes already in this extraordinary floating city of theirs.

Now, the kind-faced academic was standing up in one of the great blackwood pulpits talking to Galston, Cirrus and a wide-eyed nervous-looking Slip. Nate turned to Eudoxia, who was tracing an intricate carving of jumping tilder on the base of one of the pulpits with her finger.

'Don't you think it's odd, Eudoxia,' Nate said quietly, 'that this city is practically deserted, yet these guides have been bringing villagers here from all over the Deepwoods? Woodtrolls, clodder-trogs, even folk from Great Glade, if the evidence of what we found in the ruins is to be believed. So where are they?'

'You've seen how big this place is, Nate,' said Eudoxia, 'and this is just one academy of many. There are probably groups of Deepwooders living in other buildings in other parts of the city. I'm sure they'll all come to the welcome feast when the fettle-leggers arrive.'

'That's another thing,' said Nate hotly. 'You *want* to believe in this High Academe's story of sanctuary in the city of shining spires for Tentermist's sake, and the other fettle-leggers.'

'Of course I do,' said Eudoxia, her eyes glistening with passion, 'because I've seen the dark side of this modern world of ours. And so have you, Nate. The harshness of life in the phraxmines, the greed of Great Glade, the poverty of the downtrodden in Hive, and the cruelty of the waifs in Riverrise. And then there

was the battle . . . Have you forgotten the horror of the Midwood marshes?' She grasped Nate's hand. 'If Linius Pallitax and his academics are opening up this beautiful city of shining spires to the poor and ill-treated of our world like little Tentermist, then yes, Nate, I do want to believe that a kindness and generosity of spirit has returned to the Edge from another age.'

'But what if it's not true?' said Nate imploringly. 'There's something not quite right about this place, and I think we should warn the fettle-leggers before it's too late . . .'

Above them, in the pulpit, the sound of the High Academe's gentle voice had stopped and, looking up, Nate saw that Galston, Cirrus and Slip were climbing down the pulpit ladder towards them.

'Where did he go?' Nate called up to them.

'We were going to ask you the same thing,' said Galston, reaching the shiny tiled floor of the Central Hall, Slip and Cirrus following close behind.

'Slip looked down when we heard you and Mistress Eudoxia arguing, friend Nate,' said Slip, his eyes wide, 'and when Slip turned round, Linius Pallitax wasn't there.'

· CHAPTER NINETY-ONE ·

With a low grinding sound, the stone door swung open. Ifflix went through first, his flaming torch held high. The Professor followed, ducking down to avoid knocking his head. Straightening up, he raised his own torch – and gasped.

'Where *are* we?' he breathed, looking around.

He was standing at the edge of a vast dimly-lit cavern, which was filled with a gleaming array of glass apparatus. There were numerous flagons and glass spheres suspended from long thin tubes which crisscrossed the chamber and seemed to sprout from the curved upper walls and high domed ceiling like the tendrils of a plant. At the centre of the chamber, hovering in the air between a tripod of glass pipes, was a huge glistening globe, which looked as though it had been woven from light.

'Don't you recognize it, Ambris?' said Ifflix. 'From the barkscrolls and ancient histories we used to pore over back at the Great Glade Academy?'

Beside him, the Professor shook his head in disbelief. 'You don't mean . . . ?'

'Yes,' said Ifflix. 'This is the ancient laboratory of the First Scholars, lost for hundreds of years before being rediscovered by . . .'

'Linius Pallitax!' breathed the Professor, staring at the gleaming paraphernalia. 'You mean to say,' he said, turning to his brother, the colour draining from his face, 'that this is the very same laboratory in which the First Scholars attempted to create life?'

'And Linius Pallitax followed their insane folly centuries later,' nodded Ifflix, 'and created the demon we know to this day as the gloamglozer.'

'So the ancient tales are all true,' said the Professor, shaking his head in wonder.

'But that's not all,' said Ifflix. 'As you can see, the ancient laboratory is still in use.' He pointed to the phraxpistol at the Professor's belt. 'Only phraxfire can destroy the globe at the heart of this accursed apparatus. Sky knows, I've tried a hundred other ways. But now, with your help, brother,' Ifflix continued, holding out his hand, 'I can destroy it once and for all!'

The Professor handed Ifflix his phraxpistol and, taking it, his brother crossed the laboratory towards the glowing glass sphere. He pointed the phraxpistol directly at the globe, his hand shaking.

All at once, there was a cracking sound from high above.

'Ifflix!' shouted the Professor. 'Look out!'

Too late, Ifflix looked up to see that one of the thin tendrils of glass had detached itself from the domed ceiling above and was now hurtling down through the air towards the very spot on which he was standing. With a sickening crunch, the long thin shard of glass speared the descender through the chest and sent him crumpling to the ground.

'Ifflix! Ifflix!' cried the Professor, dashing to his brother's side.

He cradled his head in his arms as a dark pool of blood spread out across the laboratory floor.

'You can't die,' he pleaded. 'Not like this . . .'

Ifflix looked up into the Professor's eyes, which were misting with tears behind the wire-framed spectacles.

'Finish this . . .' he breathed, his eyes slowly closing. 'Finish this, for ever!'

From somewhere high up above, in the forest of curling glass tubes, there came the sound of soft low sniggering.

CHAPTER NINETY-TWO

'Leave the others and come with me,' the Professor whispered from the shadows.

Nate turned to see his friend, crushed funnel hat in hand and spectacles glinting, standing by an open door at the far side of the Central Hall. Eudoxia had been ignoring Nate since their little disagreement and was now, rather pointedly, showing Slip some carvings on a pulpit in the middle of the hall. Cirrus, arms folded and back arched, was examining the vaulted ceiling far above his head, with Galston standing by his side, tapping his fromp-headed cane absentmindedly on the polished wood tile floor.

'Where have you been, Professor?' asked Nate, hurrying over to his friend. 'And where are we going?'

The Professor smiled, before turning away and climbing the twisting flight of stairs that lay on the other side of the door, two at a time. His tongue flicked out from between his lips for the briefest of instants.

'You'll see,' he whispered over his shoulder.

Nate followed the Professor up the stairs and, emerging at last onto a wide gantry platform, found himself at the top of a tall wooden tower that rose up out of the gabled roof of the Upper Halls.

'This is the Gantry Tower,' said the Professor, turning to Nate and smiling broadly. 'It's where the knights academic of the First Age used to practise their stormchasing skills.'

He pointed to the ancient skyship moored at the top of the tower above their heads. Nate read the words carved into its prow in old-fashioned letters. *The Cloudslayer*.

'Just imagine it,' said the Professor, gazing up at the skyship with its spidersilk sails, curved lufwood hull and iron flight cage enclosing an ancient floating rock from the First Age of Flight. 'They trained in this academy to venture forth into the perilous Twilight Woods in pursuit of great storms aboard vessels such as this.'

He turned to Nate, his eyes bright with excitement.

'And there they'd enter the heart of the storm and wait for the lightning bolt to strike. Then those brave knights would descend into the Twilight Woods, clad in their magnificent armour and sitting astride their trusty prowlgrins, in order to grasp a shard of storm-phrax before it disappeared for ever into the earth beneath . . .'

'Not for ever,' said Nate softly.

'No, of course not,' smiled the Professor, eyeing Nate through his glinting spectacles. 'I'm forgetting that you're from the Third Age.'

'And so are you, Professor,' said Nate.

'Yes, so I am,' he replied with an easy laugh. 'So I am. Forgive me, I brought you up here so that you could enjoy with me this wonderful view of the city. That is where I've been, looking at the magnificent streets and walkways that surround us, and meeting their new inhabitants . . .'

'You've seen them?' said Nate excitedly. 'Deepwooders, here in Sanctaphrax?'

'But of course,' smiled the Professor. 'Woodtrolls, cloddertrogs, Hivers and Great Gladers, living side by side in simple harmony in the academies and schools.'

'Which ones, Professor?' asked Nate, scanning the deserted streets far below.

'Come here, to the edge of the gantry platform,' the Professor said, smiling, 'and I'll show you.'

· CHAPTER NINETY-THREE ·

The bells of Sanctaphrax were ringing out. From every campanile and belfry, gleaming in low sunlight, great brass bells were swinging to and fro, filling the air with sonorous peels. Loudest of all was the huge bell which tolled at the top of the distant great domed hall.

'It's wonderful!' Tentermist gasped as she broke away from her mother's hand and cantered round and round, her eyes closed and head thrown back.

'More wonderful than I could ever have imagined,' Wyver agreed.

The pair of them had been at the end of the long column of fettle-leggers waiting for the hanging baskets to take them up from the Stone Gardens to the great floating city. It had taken a couple of hours, but their turn had finally arrived. And now at last they were here. All round them, their fellow villagers were milling about on the East Landing, their feet tapping on the boards with eager anticipation.

'Welcome! Welcome!' purred the smiling professors who glided between them, their long robes sparkling in the golden twilight glow. 'Welcome to the city of shining spires!'

There were dozens of them – smiling benevolent figures, ushering their visitors across the landing and into the city itself. And as the chattering group continued up the broad, intricately tiled avenue and through the ornately decorated squares, more gowned academics appeared, emerging from the various buildings, from the humblest of minor schools to the grandest academy.

'This way,' they smiled. 'Follow us this way . . .'

As the fettle-leggers rounded the great curved viaduct, those at the front let out cries of delight as the mosaic quadrangle opened up before them.

'The welcome feast!' Tentermist exclaimed, squeezing Wyver's hand and dragging her forward. 'Here,' she said, and took a place at one of the benches. 'I'll sit here. You sit next to me.' Then, smoothing down her best embroidered spidersilk smock, she turned to her mother and smiled. 'And Mistress Eudoxia can sit here,' she said, patting the place beside her.

The benches filled quickly, the fettle-leggers eagerly taking their seats. Most were in their rest-day best clothes; many had garlands in their hair, newly fashioned from the weeds and wild flowers of the ruined city below. The air resounded with their excited voices as they surveyed the mosaic before them, with its strange intriguing design. All round the quadrangle, the academics gathered, beaming back happily at the faces that turned to look at them.

One of the fettle-leggers – a tall elderly male, his shock of hair as white as snow – turned to the others with a shrug of his shoulders. 'A welcome feast, the guide said, yet I see no food,' he complained loudly.

His companions grabbed his arm and urged him to sit down. An academic stepped forward in the flowing white robes of a professor from the School of Light and Darkness, a serene smile on his handsome face as he surveyed the expectant crowds staring back at him.

'It's the guide!' whispered Tentermist excitedly to her mother.

'You have journeyed far,' the professor said, his eyes sparkling a strange yellow in the twilight glow. 'Now, at last, you have entered the city of shining spires . . .'

A cheer went up – a cheer which drowned out the soft sound of slurping as a hundred or more tongues flicked out from a hundred or more mouths and tasted the air greedily. The academic's voice rang out.

'Let the welcome feast begin!'

· CHAPTER NINETY-FOUR ·

High up on the Gantry Tower of the Knights Academy, Nate listened to the sonorous chiming of the bells of Sanctaphrax. In the distance, the column of fettle-leggers were spilling out across the mosaic quadrangle and taking their places on the benches. From the academies and schools all over the city, brightly robed academics emerged in ones and twos and hurriedly made their way towards the square, like woodants sensing honey.

'We should warn them,' said Nate urgently, leaning as far as he dared over the gantry platform and gazing down at the mosaic quadrangle.

'Warn them?' said the Professor at his side. 'Warn them of what? There is nothing to fear . . .' he said, his voice low and quiet beside Nate's ear. 'Yet.'

· CHAPTER NINETY-FIVE ·

The Professor pushed open the trapdoor and emerged into the Great Library from the tunnel beneath. Far below him, at the centre of the heartrock, the ancient laboratory now lay smashed and ruined beyond repair.

The Professor's grief and his phraxpistol had destroyed the accursed place for good. Now it would serve as his brother Ifflix Hentadile's tomb. There would be time enough to honour his memory but now, the Professor told himself as he ran from the Great Library towards the Knights Academy, he had to warn the others.

All around him, the streets echoed to the sound of ringing bells, and in the distance the mosaic square seemed to be thronging with bright-robed academics. Skirting round the School of Mist, the Professor looked up at the tall Gantry Tower of the Knights Academy.

There, standing on the edge of a jutting platform, was Nate Quarter, staring back down at him, a look of bewildered confusion on his face. As the Professor ran towards the academy, he saw that his friend was not alone. There was another figure standing at his shoulder . . .

With a gasp of disbelief, the Professor stopped dead in his tracks as he gazed up at his own face looking back at him.

· CHAPTER NINETY-SIX ·

'Mother! Mother!' screamed Tentermist, leaping into Wyver's arms. 'What's happening?'

All around the square, the academics' smiling faces were dissolving in front of the fettle-leggers' eyes. From the red robes of the College of Rain, a bulbous head abruptly sprouted ridged horns, the features of the face below contorting into a snarling leering mask of evil. Beside it, a cloudwatcher became a grinning skulled demon with eyes of blazing red, while the ranks of the Academies of Breeze, Hailstones and Gust, threw back their hoods to reveal tentacled heads of rotting decay, pustules oozing grey slime and diseased-looking eyes popping from sockets on the ends of thin glistening strands.

The fettle-leggers threw back their heads and screamed with terror as the grisly apparitions closed in from three sides. As they did so, the creatures flicked out their long forked tongues, greedily lapping up the fear in the air.

In blind panic, the fettle-leggers stampeded across the square, leaping over upturned benches and discarded garlands as they did so, and ran down the broad avenue beside the College of Rain towards the East Landing. With raucous shrieks of delight, the monstrous apparitions swarmed after them, like woodwolves hunting tilder.

High up on the Gantry Tower, Nate turned to the Professor, only to find himself staring into the hideous face of a creature in swirling black robes, its body apparently hovering in mid-air above the boards of the gantry. Huge curling horns sprouted from either side of its misshapen head. Its features were disfigured by angry scars, the skin seemingly melted by fire or some noxious substance, leaving it puckered and scaly. Its mouth was a snarling mass of vicious fangs; its unblinking eyes, yellow. And at the tattered sleeves of the black robe were bony hands, the vicious talons that tipped them glinting in the twilight glow.

Nate recoiled in horror. He recognized the monstrous creature from descriptions in bedside stories and pictures in barkscrolls, as well as from innumerable old wives' tales. Never take its name in vain; and, if you should ever spill salt, then a pinch thrown over your shoulder was said to blind it. It was a shapeshifter, a deceiver, a tempter, gleefully luring its prey to its death with seductive promises, whispers and lies, and feeding off its victims' fear as it did so.

All at once, the creature drew back its lips in a twisted smile of triumph, and rasped:

'I am the Gloamglozer!'

· CHAPTER NINETY-SEVEN ·

'City of shining spires!' the gloamglozer spat, its sneering voice suddenly giving way to loud cackling laughter as it thrust its hideous face into Nate's. He smelled the stench of death in the creature's foul breath. 'City of nightmares, more like!' it hissed.

It pulled back and swept an arm round in a broad arc, chuckling malevolently.

'You've seen Sanctaphrax as I, the gloamglozer, wished you to see it,' it said, 'a beautiful illusion of the past. Now you shall see the city as it truly is!'

As if falling into shadow, the glistening towers and spires and elegant sweeping domes below them abruptly lost their sheen. They revealed themselves as shattered and tumbledown ruins, their stones chipped and broken, and mortar crumbling where a thousand turbulent storms had, little by little, attacked the once magnificent buildings down the centuries. Tiles were broken, castellations in pieces, while the whole eastern wing of the School of Light and Darkness was no more than a pile of rubble, destroyed long ago by a mighty lightning bolt that had left its fallen stones cracked and charred.

One by one, the other venerable schools and magnificent academies across the floating city revealed their true appearance as the glittering illusion melted away.

The plastered walls of the Institute of Ice and Snow were shattered; tiny fissures in the once mirror-adorned white plaster were now great jagged cracks where rain and ice and scorching sunlight had slowly but surely destroyed its façade, reducing the smooth surface to a shattered jigsaw puzzle of broken stone. The soaring towers of the School of Mist were pitted and leaning. One of the two great

spherical globes that had once crowned them was now a rusting tangle of twisted wires; the other lay crushed and crumpled on the broken courtyard slabs below.

And through it all, a warm fetid wind swept round the dilapidated buildings, sighing like the dying and carrying with it the rank odour of decay. Even the sky had changed, the bright blue giving way to a glowering curdled mass of yellow and grey, which stained the ruins below a sickly shade of shadow-filled ochre.

The great bowl at the top of the Fountain House School was in pieces, a steady *drip drip drip* of water falling from twists of black slime into the stagnant moat surrounding it. The magnificent Great Hall – seemingly so sturdy and solid only moments earlier – showed itself to be no more than a ruin, its walls crumbling and the gleaming dome now riven with a great zigzag crack that had split it in two.

Tall arches no longer spanned the streets, jagged stacks and strewn rubble marking where they'd tumbled centuries before. Windows were shattered, their decaying frames gaping like sightless eyes. The tiles that paved the streets were cracked or broken, and half the pieces of the coloured pottery and semi-precious stones that formed the vast complicated mosaics were missing. Fountains were dry, pillars stood at crazy angles, and bridges and walkways were broken. Stairways led nowhere . . .

In the Upper Halls of the Knights Academy, the blackwood pulpits revealed themselves to be rotting stumps with split timbers and blistered varnish, rotten and riddled with worms. Above, light streamed in through the broken roof to expose the decaying wood tiles of the great hall below.

Clocks had stopped, their cog and pulley mechanisms clogged with centuries of dust. Astrolabes and sextants, time gauges and weather meters no longer gleamed as if new, but now were caked in rust.

Outside, the intricate pieces of paraphernalia that had graced the buildings had suffered the same fate. From the propeller-shaped twists of burnished metal, the silver mesh nets, the forged plumb weights and calibrated dials, to the weather vanes and wind socks,

644

they had all rusted or disintegrated, and clung to the walls and rooftops like the empty skeletons of giant insects.

At the hail-pitted, frost-blighted wall of the College of Rain, an unravelling cable of rusting wires dangled down; beneath it, a heap of shattered blue glass.

And damage and decay was not all that had been laid bare. Like the ruins of its twin city, Undertown, which was overgrown with weeds and moss, tendrilled creepers and broad-leafed vines, so the floating city of Sanctaphrax was covered with growth. It was not, however, dense green vegetation which grew from its rocks and stones. Instead, during its long journey through the endless skies, the great floating rock and the city upon it had drawn the fungal growths and spectral creatures of the air to itself, like a vast logbait.

Tall jagged ruffs of yellow and orange fungus sprouted from the cracks and crevices. Clusters of suppurating toadstools, luminous air lichens and great tongue-like fronds grew out of the fissures in the broken stonework; while every cornice and shattered gable was festooned in diaphanous folds of lustrous threads that flapped in the groaning wind like tattered swathes of silk.

Clusters of transparent mist barnacles clung to the crumbling walls and roofs, their long hair-like tentacles swaying. Windsnappers with whiplash feelers and flat white shells clacked their curved claws. And oozing from every beam and joist and wooden tile were gelatinous skyworms with long slimy bodies that writhed and squirmed in great wriggling clumps, making the woodwork look like rotting flesh, riddled with ravenous maggots.

It wasn't only the ancient city that was a storm-blasted ruin, but also the mighty floating rock itself. The stone sickness that had afflicted the Stone Gardens centuries before, bringing the First Age of Flight to an abrupt end as it turned every flight rock to dust and destroyed the new Sanctaphrax rock, turned out also to have infected the great rock of old Sanctaphrax which had returned to the Edge. Its pitted surface no longer glistened in the sunlight. Instead, it was dull and rutted, pockmarked with great cavities that were eating into the stonecomb. Vast areas of the rock were drab grey and crumbling, while a thick dark liquid oozed from fissures and cracks and dripped down through the air like pus from gaping wounds.

From the ruined avenue that led from the mosaic quadrangle to the East Landing, the screams of the fettle-leggers filled the air as they fled the pursuing gloamglozers. Snapping at their heels, the cackling demons swooped and dived, their talons and fangs glinting as their tongues flicked in and out of their lipless mouths, gorging on the fettle-leggers' terror. With each gulp of fear-charged air, the demonic creatures seemed to grow larger and more terrifying.

A shrieking young'un, her eyes rolling in her head, broke away from the stampeding herd and made a dash for a shadow-filled alleyway – only to be driven back as a gnarled and leering face, its bloodshot eyeballs dangling on glistening stalks, loomed up before it . . .

On board the *Archemax*, Squall Razortooth gripped the helm.

'Wuh-wuh wurrgh!' Weelum the banderbear groaned, his delicate ears twitching as his eyes confirmed what his other senses had been telling him. This was indeed a dead city.

Beside him, Squall hurriedly fired up the phraxchamber and pulled two of the bone-handled flight levers back. The funnel billowed thick clouds of steam as the propulsion duct roared. He shoved the third flight lever forward, and the *Archemax* rose sharply, then listed to one side, its hull creaking. A moment later, there came the sound of cracking and splintering as the tolley ropes bit into the rotten wood of the bollards on the dilapidated West Landing, snapping first one, then the other, and the phraxship soared into the air.

Realigning the flight levers and hull weights with trembling fingers, Squall took the *Archemax* higher into the sky. With his hand gripping the rudder lever, he steered it round the diseased floating rock towards the sound of the terrified screams.

And then, in amongst the ravaged buildings, he saw them – the fettle-leggers, stampeding down the long central avenue towards the ruined remains of the great East Landing . . .

'Hold on tight, Weelum,' Squall said grimly. 'I'm taking her in!'

He pushed the three flight levers back in one smooth movement, and the *Archemax* swooped down through the sky in a steep dive.

Eudoxia froze, her green eyes wide with fear. She had reached the top of the stairs of the gantry tower when their polished treads and blackwood banister had seemingly melted away in front of her eyes. Now she saw that she was standing on a cracked wooden step, thin and worm-eaten, attached to the rotten timber walls of the leaning gantry tower.

Below, at the foot of the stairs, Slip, Cirrus and her father stared up at her helplessly, not daring to follow in case they caused the whole rotten staircase to collapse.

Eudoxia looked up. Through the crumbling doorway, at the end of a warped and splintered gantry platform, were two figures.

'Nate!'

At the sound of her voice, Nate's head jerked round, his eyes filled with terror, and as he did so, there was a soft cracking sound from beneath his feet and a piece of rotten wood tumbled down to the ground below – and Nate with it.

Instantly, the second figure lunged forward and seized him by the wrist. Then, with Nate wriggling helplessly as he dangled in mid-air, the figure slowly turned its face towards Eudoxia and fixed her with a malevolent gaze. Beneath its curling horns and blazing yellow eyes, its mouth opened and a black tongue flicked out and lapped at the air.

'Fear,' it breathed softly. 'Such delicious fear.'

Down below, alerted by Eudoxia's cry, the Professor drew his phraxpistol, kicking away a soft white tentacled tendril that was snaking over his left boot. Beside him, the crumbling wall of the Knights Academy was festooned with wriggling skyworms and mist barnacles. He gazed up at Nate and the gloamglozer at the top of the gantry tower and took aim.

'It's over!' the Professor shouted. 'The ancient laboratory is destroyed. You cannot create any more of your kind in that foul place . . .'

The gloamglozer's tongue flicked in and out as it turned its yellow eyes from Nate, to Eudoxia, then down to the Professor. An evil smile played on its lips as it leaned forward and whispered in Nate's ears.

'Fascinating,' it said, its voice low and rasping. It lapped greedily at the air. 'The taste of their fear for you is even sweeter than their fear for themselves . . .'

The gloamglozer raised its taloned fist until Nate's face was level with its own. Its yellow eyes flickered as they registered the terror in Nate's face, and then narrowed as they spotted the small lufwood portrait which hung from a cord round his neck.

'But what's this?' it hissed.

'Jump!' cried Squall Razortooth, his hands dancing over the flight levers as, battling against the turbulent wind, he brought the *Archemax* down as close as he dared to the East Landing.

The fettle-leggers had reached the landing's rotting boards and were stampeding over them towards the jagged timber edge.

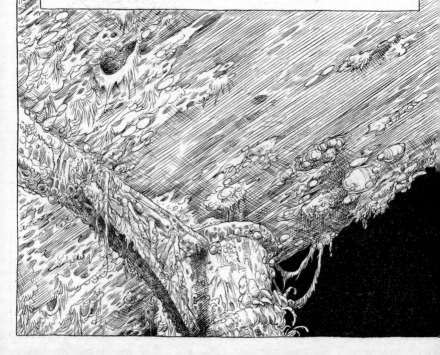

The leading fettle-legger didn't need telling twice. Flexing his legs and pushing off with his three-toed feet, he launched himself off the broken boards and soared out across the yawning abyss in a magnificent leap, landing with a loud *thud* a moment later on the middle of the fore deck of the phraxship.

He was followed a moment later by half a dozen more, who came down on the varnished boards at various points along the starboard deck. Soon the air was dark with leaping bodies as fettle-legger after terrified fettle-legger, young and old, sprang from the rotten platform towards the hovering phraxship in a great panic-stricken wave.

As they landed, the fettle-leggers clung on for dear life. Clambering over the top of the cabins and helm, they clutched hold of the beak-like prow and gripped the bows, their legs dangling down over the side.

At the helm, Squall pushed the central flight lever forward as far as it would go, causing the propulsion duct to roar and the great phraxchamber above his head to throb and pound.

'Wuh-wuh,' grunted the banderbear, fear in his eyes.

'I know, friend,' Squall murmured. 'But we're their only hope!'

Gripping hold of the shaking flight levers with jaw-clenched determination, Squall eased the *Archemax* away from the rock. The phraxship lurched unsteadily in the sky, the propulsion duct screeching in protest, while the throb and hum of the phraxchamber began to falter ominously under the heavy load.

'Come on, my beauty, you can do it,' Squall urged the juddering *Archemax*. 'We're depending on you.'

Suddenly, a terrified cry suddenly went up from the fettle-leggers. Squall glanced round to see that the gloamglozers had launched themselves from the East Landing in a mighty screeching flock and were now circling the *Archemax*, their ghastly leering faces rapt with delight as they plucked at the fingers that grasped so desperately to every inch of the struggling vessel.

'Let go!' they hissed, their tongues flicking in and out of their grotesque mouths. 'You have nothing to live for!'

* * *

Up at the top of the Gantry Tower, the gloamglozer's eyes narrowed.

'Can it really be?' it said softly, the curved talon tapping the portrait that hung from Nate's neck. 'Quintinius Verginix . . .'

'I . . . he . . . he's one of . . . of my ancestors,' Nate stammered, his voice low with terror as the creature's grip on his wrist increased.

The gloamglozer threw back its head and cackled with raucous laughter.

'Is he now? But this just gets better and better!' it exclaimed. It paused and, still gripping hold of Nate with one hand, reached up with the other and ran a long curved nail gently down its mutilated face. 'Long, long ago in this floating city, Quintinius Verginix did this to me,' it snarled. 'As I fled, I cursed him and his descendants for all time.' An evil smile spread across its features as it fixed Nate with a savage stare. 'Now I have returned – and who should come to my realm, but one of his descendants! This is sweet indeed . . .'

The gloamglozer's talons bit into the flesh of Nate's arm as its tongue flicked out into the air.

'Please, please,' Eudoxia sobbed helplessly.

'Release him!' the Professor shouted up from the street below.

'Release him?' purred the gloamglozer, glaring into Nate's face. 'Very well . . .'

And, opening its taloned hand, the smiling gloamglozer dropped Nate from the gantry tower.

· CHAPTER NINETY-EIGHT ·

As Nate fell in a flurry of stomach-churning movement, his arms and legs flailing in mid-air, faces flashed before his eyes, one after the other in a flickering blur.

His father, smiling back at him, his eyes full of love and concern. The simple features of his best friend, Rudd the cloddertrog. Friston Drew, staring at him, his kindly face lit by lamplight. Togtuft and Klug, the Sumpwood Bridge archivists, and Gomber and Gilmora, the gabtrolls who had welcomed him into their lamphouse. Rook and Twig, in the Garden of Life, and the young knight academic from the First Age, Quintinius Verginix . . .

All at once, the air was filled with the sound of large beating wings and Nate felt his shoulders being seized in a vice-like grip. The next moment he was no longer falling, but rising up into the air, soaring high over the broken towers and dilapidated buildings.

Nate looked down to see the nightmarish ruins grow small beneath his feet. Far below, the Professor was standing by the crumbling outer wall of the Knights Academy, looking up at him, his face a mask of astonishment behind his wire-framed spectacles.

Hovering near the East Landing, the *Archemax* – weighed down by hundreds of terrified fettle-leggers who were clinging to every deck, every spur, every railing and roof, even the mighty phraxchamber itself – struggled through the air. The trail of billowing steam was stark against the black abyss below as the blazing propulsion duct roared in fits and starts. All around it, the demonic gloamglozers swooped in and lunged at the cowering fettle-leggers, greedily savouring their terror.

At the top of the swaying gantry tower was Eudoxia, her face white with shock as she struggled to keep her balance on a single crumbling step. Below her, in the ruins of the tower, Galston Prade, Cirrus Gladehawk and Slip the scuttler were rooted to the spot as they gazed helplessly up at her.

And there, staring straight at him, its hideous face contorted into a grimace of hatred, Nate saw the gloamglozer hovering above the gantry platform.

Tearing his eyes away, Nate looked up to see that he was in the talons of the mighty caterbird. Its purple black plumage gleamed in the unearthly ochre light.

'You . . .' he gasped.

Swooping round in a broad circle, the caterbird glided down through the air towards the top of the Loftus Observatory. The small flock of what Nate had mistaken for white ravens perched there launched off, revealing themselves to be bloated white wreck wraiths, which screeched furiously as they flapped into the darkening sky. The caterbird hovered above the shattered roof of this, the tallest tower of Sanctaphrax and, opening its claws, carefully placed Nate on a patch of unbroken tiles near the summit, where a cluster of rusted wind funnels and rain gauges sprouted.

As Nate clung to the roof, the caterbird lowered its great curved beak and plucked the lufwood portrait from round his neck. Before Nate could stop it, the mighty bird flapped its powerful wings and soared up high into the curdled sky, taking Nate's medallion with it.

Shrieking with fury, the gloamglozer rose up from the gantry tower.

'Leave them!' it screeched at the gloamglozers still tormenting the petrified fettle-leggers aboard the juddering *Archemax*. 'I want the spawn of the knight academic!' It pointed a twisted claw at the roof of the Loftus Observatory.

In answer, the demonic creatures abruptly abandoned the phraxship and, in a flapping mass of gleaming horns, glinting fangs and black ragged robes, they soared up towards Nate.

With a cackle of laughter, the gloamglozer twisted round and swooped down towards where Eudoxia stood, frozen to the spot.

'Delicious!' it shrieked as it scraped her cheek with a razor-sharp talon, drawing an angry line, beaded with blood, as it hurtled past.

With a terrified scream, Eudoxia toppled backwards, managing – at the last moment – to grasp a length of rotten banister to prevent herself falling headlong down the tower. Below her, the staircase crumbled into worm-eaten splinters and dust. She was left hanging precariously from the jutting length of creaking blackwood nailed to the timber wall of the crumbling gantry tower, a thirty-stride drop to Squall, Cirrus and her father beneath.

Oblivious to her plight, the gloamglozer soared high into the air once more, only for the flash and crack of a phraxpistol shot to ring out from the street far below. The angry whine of a woodwasp cut through the fetid air as a leadwood bullet passed through the gloamglozer's body and disappeared into the slowly darkening sky beyond.

'Fool!' sneered the gloamglozer, glowering down at the figure of the Professor, steaming phraxpistol in hand. 'You cannot destroy me with your puny weapons. I am glister born, from Open Sky!'

It cackled raucously as it pressed its taloned hand gently against one of the thirteen tall, thin towers that surrounded the Knights Academy.

'Unlike you, I am immortal!'

With a low creaking sigh, the tower – once home to one of the academy's legendary stormchasing knights – swayed, then toppled forwards, collapsing into the street where the Professor stood, in a clatter of masonry and a billowing cloud of dust. Shrieking with triumph, the gloamglozer soared up towards the Loftus Observatory, its black tongue flicking greedily at the air.

'Hold on, Miss Eudoxia!' Slip's voice rang out from the shadows at the bottom of the gantry tower. 'Slip's coming to get you. Seen worse gallery collapses in the mine, Slip has. Just don't let go . . .'

High above the Loftus Observatory, the caterbird had disappeared into the ochre-coloured curdling clouds, which were now turning darker and beginning to swirl like a vast whirlpool. Nate scrambled up to the tower's pinnacle and clung to the rusting instruments clustered there. Around him, the nightmarish demons swooped and dived, their grotesque, half-rotted faces looming up at him through the gathering gloom, tongues lapping up his fear. With each passing dive, they raked the roof tiles with their talons, sending them crashing down into the ruins below, and increasing Nate's terror as the area of undamaged roof steadily diminished.

'Let go, spawn of Quintinius Verginix!' the gloamglozer taunted Nate as it hovered above him, its yellow eyes glowing. 'Your friends are dead! Why not follow them?'

Suddenly, far above the city, from within the swirling black vortex of cloud, there was a blinding flash of lightning and, as thunder cracked and rumbled, a beam of dazzling light cut through the air like a mighty lance. It hurtled down towards the great circular mosaic at the heart of Sanctaphrax

and struck the ground with a sound like shattering crystal.

And there it remained, a circular pool of white light at the very centre of the chipped and shattered mosaic of lightning bolts, like a searchlight shining down from the clouds. Grasping the rusting stump of a wind funnel, his feet slipping on the last few remaining roof tiles, Nate noticed instantly the effect it had on the cackling flock of gloamglozers around him.

As the pool of light fizzed and sparkled in the mosaic quadrangle below, the hideous creatures turned towards it, their eyes wide and their tongues flicking greedily out as they tasted the air. Above him, the gloamglozer quivered and trembled, its yellow eyes fixed on the quadrangle and its own tongue whipping in and out of its twisted mouth.

What was it, this new intriguing taste, it wondered as it salivated, so much more intense than even the mouthwatering fear of imminent death that it loved so much?

The gloamglozer shot out its tongue once more.

Delicious, this strange emotion, it thought, its eyes narrowing. Not sadness, regret, loss or suffering, but an intense infusion of all these feelings, marinaded for untold centuries, until now. It was irresistible . . .

The gloamglozer brushed past Nate without so much as a glance, and sped down through the air towards the intoxicating light, followed by its screeching cackling cohorts. As Nate watched from high up on the roof of the Loftus Observatory, the black-robed gloamglozers gathered round the mosaic quadrangle in a seething mass, their mouths gaping open in an ecstasy of greed.

Suddenly the light faded, like a mine lamp running out of darkelm oil, and there, at the centre of the ancient mosaic with its tiled lightning bolts spreading out like the intricate spokes of a wheel, stood three figures.

Nate gasped, almost letting go of the wind funnel as his heart missed a beat.

'The Immortals,' he murmured.

Standing there, looking at the writhing army of hideous

gloamglozers which surrounded them, were Quint, Twig and Rook – father, son and great grandson. They were not stooped and old, but in the first flush of youth, their faces shining.

Twig stood tall and proud, his dark hair plaited into the familiar tufts of the woodtrolls, hammelhornskin waistcoat bristling on his back. Standing shoulder to shoulder with him was the young Rook Barkwater, with his chequerboard collar and Freeglade Lancer tunic emblazoned with the red banderbear badge. And next to them, stepping forward, was the figure from Nate's lufwood portrait miniature, in ill-fitting knight academic's armour and oversized gauntlets.

It was Quintinius Verginix himself.

'I didn't imagine it,' Nate told himself. 'They *were* there in the Garden of Life . . .'

Hovering in front of Quint, unable to tear itself away, the gloamglozer gave a strange gurgling whimper, its yellow eyes transfixed by the sight of its ancient enemy. Holding the creature's gaze, the young knight academic thrust out a gauntleted hand and buried it deep within the folds of the gloamglozer's black robes.

The creature stared down at the arm embedded in its chest. Its yellow eyes rolled in their sockets and its horned head jerked back in a series of convulsive shudders.

Around it, the other gloamglozers shrank back, their hideous faces seemingly melting into grey featureless smudges with wide frightened eyes staring out from them.

Quint pulled back his hand to reveal a glowing red-tinged glister, no larger than a marsh gem. Slowly, he closed his gauntleted fist tight, and as he did so the gloamglozer shrivelled – horns, talons, black robes and all – and disintegrated into a pile of dry grey dust on the battered mosaic tiles.

With a wail of terror, the other gloamglozers launched themselves into the air – only for Twig and Rook to leap forwards, the fingers of their hands outstretched.

Nate watched open-mouthed from the top of the ruined tower as tendrils of lightning fizzed from their fingertips and skewered

the black flapping creatures in mid-flight. As if the ancient mosaic makers had created the mosaic as a prophecy, the pure white lightning shot out in all directions from the three Immortals standing at its centre.

All round, the gloam-glozers' faces contorted for the briefest of moments into spasms of shock, rage and pain, before exploding like hideous overripe seed heads. They disintegrated into spiralling showers of red glisters and grey dust, which blew away on the stiffening breeze. One after the other, the shrieking creatures, now increasingly tattered and bedraggled, were speared by the lightning bolts that spiralled out from the Immortals' fingers, and destroyed.

From far above him came the sound of the caterbird's mighty wings, and Nate felt himself being lifted once more by its powerful talons. The great bird swooped down to the mosaic quadrangle as the last gloamglozer exploded, its agonized cries dying on its lips. It set Nate down in front of the Immortals.

'You *are* real!' he breathed, his heart pounding as he gazed into their shining faces.

Quint lowered his hand and stepped towards him.

'We were once real,' he said quietly. 'As real as you, Nate Quarter.' He held the youth's gaze. 'Once, not far from this very spot, I sat for my portrait in one of the viaduct schools during the terrible winter of the cloudeater . . .'

He reached out and placed the portrait miniature back in Nate's hand.

'And I once voyaged aboard a sky pirate ship into Open Sky . . .' said Twig.

'While I,' said Rook, touching the banderbear badge on his tunic, 'once fought the goblin armies at the Battle of the Barley Fields . . .'

'All so long ago now,' Quint said. 'But none of us was granted a natural death. I faded into the white storm, while both Rook and Twig were kept alive at Riverrise. And so our stories had no end – until I returned in the storm to be united with them. What you see before you, Nate, is the memory of what we used to be. But behind these echoes of youth are the suffering, sadness and regrets of our long, long lives.

'It is what the gloamglozers found so irresistible.'

Quint smiled, and Nate recognized the expression on the knight academic's face from his beloved portrait miniature.

'Now it is time for us to fade into the past,' he said, gazing up at the dark clouds swirling overhead, 'for the story of our lives is finally at an end. For ever.'

Heavy raindrops began to fall, and as they increased, pattering on the mosaic tiles, so Quint, Twig and Rook began to fade away in front of Nate's eyes.

'While the story of *your* life, Nate Quarter,' Quint's voice sounded as the curtain of rain shrouded the Immortals from view, 'is just beginning.'

· CHAPTER NINETY-NINE ·

Far above Nate's head, from the vortex of dark swirling cloud, the torrential rain came pouring down. Lightning flickered from cloud to spiralling cloud, illuminating the air between and below and, as it did so, the rain sparkled. Inside each raindrop, the tiny fragments of chine that had been swept up from the shores of the Riverrise lake glittered like marsh gems in the dazzling white light.

The rain pelted down, cascading through the broken roofs and over the crumbling stairs of the towers and palaces; it filled the squares, splashing back on itself in the pools it had created. It formed streams and rivulets that sluiced down the streets and alleyways, coursed into the sewers and seeped through into the honeycomb of the mighty floating Sanctaphrax rock itself.

Filling the tunnels, and swirling ever deeper through the mighty rock, it penetrated to the very heartrock at the centre of the stonecomb. It sought out cracks and fissures in the dead rock, and trickled down into the laboratory deep at its heart. And, from the pile of shattered glass that lay across the floor, there came a tiny whimpered moan as the small shapeless body of the last gloamglozer hissed and fizzed, and died.

Stable, but moving slowly, the *Archemax* steamed past the rock, water now cascading from every crack and crevice. At the helm, Squall Razortooth craned his neck, looking over the heads of the multitude of fettle-leggers, at the surface of the floating rock itself.

It was changing, he realized.

The crumbling patches of dull grey were beginning to harden and glitter brightly in the darkness; the cavities and cracks lost their raw and wounded appearance, seeming almost to heal. And from deep within, there came a soft throbbing red glow as the heart of the mighty floating rock began once more to beat within it.

At the foot of the gantry tower, Slip emerged, carrying Eudoxia in his arms, and picked his way through the rubble, followed by Galston Prade and Cirrus Gladehawk. Around them, the air was thick with clouds of skyworms and mist barnacles, releasing their grip on the ruins and fleeing from the cleansing rain. As they stepped through a gaping hole in the east wall of the Knights Academy and made their way towards the mosaic quadrangle, they spotted a hand gripping a phraxpistol, sticking up from a pile of rubble and dust.

'Professor!' shouted Eudoxia, jumping out of Slip's arms and hobbling over.

'Careful, Miss Eudoxia,' Slip cautioned. 'Try not to put too much weight on that ankle.'

He joined her as she began to claw at the rubble, Cirrus and Galston pitching in beside them. A short while later, the Professor's head poked up out of the rubble, his spectacles coated in a thick layer of dust and his crushed funnel hat looking more battered than ever.

'Did I hit the hideous creature?' he asked with a bemused smile as the rain continued to fall, before taking off his hat and rubbing his head ruefully. 'It's strange,' he laughed. 'My head feels like a tower's just fallen on it!'

At that moment, from down the tiled street, there came the sound of cantering feet and a joyful cry rang out through the rain.

'Miss Eudoxia!' cried Tentermist the fettle-legger, rushing into her arms. 'Your friends, the sky pirate and the banderbear, saved us and the evil gloamglozers are all dead!' she spluttered, tripping over the words in her eagerness, before pausing, a look of concern on her face. 'But Miss Eudoxia, what happened to your face?'

Eudoxia raised a hand to her cheek, where the angry wound from the gloamglozer's talon stood out, red and bleeding.

'It's just a scratch,' she said uncertainly.

Rainwater fell into her upturned face, soaking her hair and running down her skin. The little fettle-legger gasped. As she watched, the wound on Eudoxia's cheek closed, became a thin red line, then

661

disappeared completely as the sparkling rain ran over it and dripped down from her chin.

'All better,' Tentermist smiled.

'Me too,' said the Professor, struggling to his feet, aided by Cirrus and Slip, as the *Archemax*'s steam klaxon sounded from the East Landing and more fettle-leggers appeared in the rain-soaked street. He looked round. 'Now where's Nate Quarter got to?'

· CHAPTER ONE HUNDRED ·

'At the dawn of time,' said the caterbird, fixing Nate with a dark purple eye, 'there were three ancient ones, of Sky, Earth and Water. I, the caterbird, am of the Sky. The mighty Sanctaphrax rock is of the Earth. And the Great Blueshell Clam is of the Water. We three are the oldest living things in the Edgelands, and were among the first seeds of life from Open Sky to be delivered to Riverrise by the Mother Storm.

'First, there came the Sanctaphrax rock. A tiny glister at Riverrise, it travelled down the Edgewater River and seeded itself in what was to become the Stone Gardens. In the second appearance of the Mother Storm, there came the Great Blueshell Clam, along with the seeds of life that were to grow into the mighty forests of the Deepwoods. It seeded itself in the lake known as the Mirror of the Sky.'

The creature nodded solemnly.

'I came down at the Riverrise spring when the Mother Storm visited for a third time. In my glister form, I found shelter in the lullabee groves. It was there that I wove the first of my many cocoons, and emerged as a creature of the Sky.'

The great caterbird shifted on the stone balustrade, its lustrous black feathers gleaming in the early evening light. It raised its head.

'The Mother Storm, on her endless progress through Open Sky, has visited the Riverrise spring countless times since, and on each occasion it has brought glisters to seed its sacred waters with new life. From Riverrise, that life has spread forth into the Edgelands and developed into the myriad different forms that inhabit this world . . .'

The caterbird ruffled its long black and white tail feathers in the light breeze.

'All life has come into being this way,' it said, turning its great curved beak towards Nate. 'All life, that is, except . . .'

'The gloamglozer,' breathed Nate.

'The gloamglozer,' confirmed the caterbird. 'It was created in the ancient laboratory, far from the sacred waters of the Riverrise spring. And with its creation came the disease known as stone sickness. When the gloamglozer escaped into the world, it spread the contagion to the Stone Gardens where slowly, unnoticed for years, stone sickness poisoned the floating rocks. Then came the fateful day when the Mother Storm returned and the great floating rock was released from its anchor chain. A new rock was born, but this only bloomed for a short while before the signs of disease became unmistakeable.'

The great bird shook its head.

'Those were dark times in the Edgelands,' it remembered. 'I, who have lived a thousand lifetimes – hatching, flying and then returning to glister form to weave a cocoon once more – had never known anything like them. I wished for nothing more than to return to the lullabee groves and begin my renewal. But I could not, for I was trapped . . .'

'Trapped?' echoed Nate.

'Twig had been at my hatching, and I had vowed to watch over him always,' the caterbird replied. 'I carried him, mortally wounded, to the Riverrise spring, where the waters revived him – only for Golderayce the waif to imprison him there. Drinking only of the water of life, Twig became an Immortal. And while *he* lived, so did I, bound to watch over him, but powerless to intervene unless his life was threatened, until after long long centuries of waiting, a storm like no other arrived at Riverrise. Twig, Rook and Quint had all been stormtouched. Now they were united, and their stories could come to an end. That left but one thing for me to do; follow Twig and the Immortals back here to the mighty Sanctaphrax rock and witness its healing . . .'

'So now you're free?' said Nate.

The caterbird turned its purple gaze back from the horizon and onto Nate.

'The story of Twig, Rook and Quint is over,' it said simply. 'They have returned to Open Sky as glisters, just as all things do one day. Even the ancient ones.'

The mighty bird spread its massive wings and launched itself off into the twilight sky.

'I gladly leave this age of phraxflight and great cities to you, Nate Quarter,' it called as it flew out into the immensity of Open Sky beyond the jutting lip of the Edge cliff. 'Farewell!'

· CHAPTER ONE HUNDRED AND ONE ·

'**B**ut why, Nate?' asked Eudoxia, her eyes filling with tears. 'Tell me why?'

The early-morning mist had cleared and bright sunshine now filled the Stone Gardens, their rocky pavement studded with tiny budding stones. At the jutting lip of the Edge cliff, which stood out against the blue sky like the figurehead of a mighty stone ship, the Edgewater River tumbled down into the abyss below.

A little way off, standing beside a great spike of metal, driven into the edge of the cliff, stood the Professor. He wore the heavy padded jacket and breeches of a descender, phraxlamps fitted to the side of his leather helmet. Strapped to his shoulders was a descender's backpack, bristling with crampons, rock picks and supplies, and with two gently steaming phraxglobes mounted at the top.

'It's hard to explain,' Nate began, taking her by the hand.

'Try, Nate,' Eudoxia said, her green eyes defiant, despite the tears. 'Explain to me in a way that I can understand . . .'

Nate gazed back at the beautiful mine owner's daughter standing before him. How could he explain? he wondered.

The others seemed so certain of where their futures lay. Weelum the banderbear and Squall the old sky pirate, inseparable for ever, saw theirs in the *Archemax* phraxship works in Great Glade, with Galston Prade and Cirrus Gladehawk masterminding the whole operation, determined to open up the skies to all. Then there was Slip the scuttler – dear Slip, who had shared Nate's many hardships ever since those dark days down in the mine. The grey goblin had decided that his future lay with Miss Eudoxia and the fettle-leggers, building a new life here in Sanctaphrax.

Already, Cirrus and Squall had anchored the chain in the middle of the ruins of old Undertown, and Galston had promised that the

Archemax would bring more settlers as soon as the phraxship works were up and running.

They all seemed to know exactly what they must do. Even the Professor, the former skytavern gambler and itinerant traveller, had discovered his true calling – which just left Nate.

The words Quintinius Verginix had spoken to him in the mosaic quadrangle had kept going round and round in his mind ever since.

'The story of *your* life, Nate Quarter, is just beginning.'

This wasn't the end, Nate now knew. His future didn't lie back in Great Glade, or any of the other cities or settlements of the Deepwoods, but in another direction entirely, he had decided.

'Why, Nate?' said Eudoxia. 'Why descend the Edge cliff into the unknown, when you could stay here with me?'

How *could* he explain? Nate thought.

'Because it's there, Eudoxia,' he said simply. 'Because it's there.'

Eudoxia threw herself into his arms and hugged him fiercely. 'Do what you have to do, Nate Quarter,' she whispered. 'But come back to me. Promise you'll come back to me . . .'

Nate ran his fingers through her golden hair, breathing in its fresh scent of gladegrass and wood lavender. Then, gently pulling away and stepping back, he picked up the descender's backpack at his feet and reached inside. Carefully, he took out his box of memories – with his birth parchment and silver naming spoon, his father's epaulettes, the Professor's splinters card and Squall Razortooth's sky crystals; the moustache of banderbear fur and the lufwood bullet which had so nearly taken his friend's life, and the vial of Riverrise water. He handed the box to Eudoxia and then, reaching inside his tunic, he took the portrait miniature and pulled the cord over his head. Stepping forward, he placed the portrait of Quint round Eudoxia's neck.

'I promise,' he said.

Pulling the backpack onto his shoulders, Nate turned and walked slowly over to where the Professor stood waiting for him. They attached their tether ropes to the great iron spike that the Professor's brother, Ifflix Hentadile, had driven into the rock two years earlier, and lowered themselves over the Edge.

High up in the cloudless blue sky, the bright morning sun shone down on the Edge – on the Deepwoods and the Twilight Woods, and the vast verdant Mire; on Undertown and Sanctaphrax, and on the Stone Gardens, where a golden-haired girl stood at the tip of rock looking down, her long shadow stretching back across the stone pavement behind her.

And far beneath, on the cliff face, it shone on two lone figures, slowly and painstakingly descending its glittering surface. They were heading for the top of the great fluted decline, their shadows already beginning to merge with the darkness.

Gradually, as the girl watched, the two descenders disappeared into the blackness below.

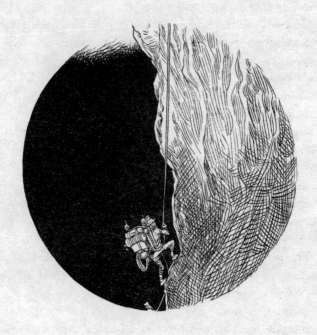

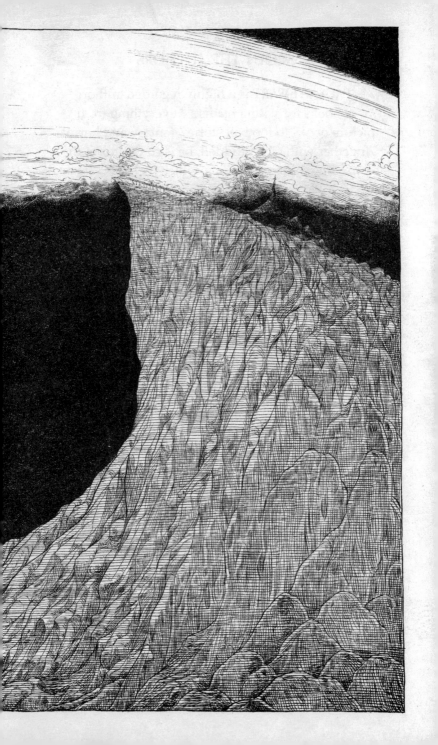

ABOUT THE AUTHORS

PAUL STEWART is a highly regarded author of books for young readers – everything from picture books to football stories, fantasy and horror. Together with Chris Riddell, he is co-creator of the *Far-Flung Adventures* series, which includes *Fergus Crane*, Gold Smarties Prize Winner, *Corby Flood* and *Hugo Pepper*, Silver Nestlé Prize Winners, and the *Barnaby Grimes* series. They are of course also co-creators of the bestselling *Edge Chronicles* series, which has sold over two million books and is now available in over thirty languages.

ABOUT THE AUTHORS

CHRIS RIDDELL is an accomplished graphic artist who has illustrated many acclaimed books for children, including *Pirate Diary* by Richard Platt, and *Gulliver*, which both won the Kate Greenaway Medal. His book *Ottoline and the Yellow Cat* was shortlisted for the Kate Greenaway Medal and won a Gold Nestle Prize. Together with Paul Stewart, he is co-creator of the *Far-Flung Adventures* series, which includes *Fergus Crane*, Gold Smarties Prize Winner, *Corby Flood* and *Hugo Pepper*, Silver Nestlé Prize Winners, and the *Barnaby Grimes* series. They are of course also co-creators of the bestselling *Edge Chronicles* series, which has sold over two million books and is now available in over thirty languages.

THE
EDGE CHRONICLES
FAN CLUB

Join the FREE Edge Chronicles Fan Club:
read Paul and Chris's diary and find out how they
work together, check out the awesome character
gallery, wonder at the interactive map and download
wallpaper. Plus loads of other stuff to see and do!

www.edgechronicles.co.uk

THE EDGE CHRONICLES

THE QUINT TRILOGY

Follow the adventures of Quint
in the first age of flight!

CURSE OF THE GLOAMGLOZER

Quint and Maris, daughter of the most
High Academe, are plunged into a terrifying
adventure which takes them deep into the rock
upon which Sanctaphrax is built. Here they
unwittingly invoke an ancient curse . . .

THE WINTER KNIGHTS

Quint is a new student at the Knights
Academy, struggling to survive the icy cold
of a never-ending winter, and the ancient
feuds that threaten Sanctaphrax.

CLASH OF THE SKY GALLEONS

Quint finds himself caught up in his father's
fight for revenge against the man who killed
his family. They are drawn into a deadly
pursuit, a pursuit that will ultimately lead
to the clash of the great sky galleons.

'The most amazing books ever'
Ellen, 10

'I hated reading . . .
now I'm a reading machine!'
Quinn, 15

THE EDGE CHRONICLES

THE TWIG TRILOGY

Follow the adventures of Twig
in the first age of flight!

BEYOND THE DEEPWOODS

Abandoned at birth in the perilous Deepwoods,
Twig does what he has always been warned
not to do, and strays from the path . . .

STORMCHASER

Twig, a young crew-member on the
Stormchaser sky ship, risks all to collect valuable
stormphrax from the heart of a Great Storm.

MIDNIGHT OVER SANCTAPHRAX

Far out in Open Sky, a ferocious storm is brewing.
In its path is the city of Sanctaphrax . . .

'Absolutely brilliant'
Lin-May, 13

*'Everything about the
Edge Chronicles is amazing'*
Cameron, 13

THE EDGE CHRONICLES

THE ROOK TRILOGY

Follow the adventures of Rook
in the second age of flight!

LAST OF THE SKY PIRATES

Rook dreams of becoming a librarian knight,
and sets out on a dangerous journey into the
Deepwoods and beyond. When he meets the last
sky pirate, he is thrust into a bold adventure . . .

VOX

Rook becomes involved in the evil scheming
of Vox Verlix – can he stop the Edgeworld
falling into total chaos?

FREEGLADER

Undertown is destroyed, and Rook and his
friends travel, with waifs and cloddertrogs,
to a new home in the Free Glades.

'They're the best!!'
Zaffie, 15

'Brilliant illustrations and magical storylines'
Tom, 14

BEYOND THE END . . .

Find out what happens beyond the end of THE IMMORTALS, in the incredible WEIRD NEW WORLDS blog.

www.**weird**new**worlds**.com

Hedgethorn Lammergyre and Forden Drew are now writing regular blogs from the Farrow Ridges, and posting drawings of the weird and wonderful landscapes, characters and creatures they encounter.